The Law of Douglas vanYssen

PAUL NEL

First published in South Africa in 2011 by
Scamp Fiction
an imprint of
Publishing Print Matters (Pty) Ltd
P O Box 640, Noordhoek 7979, Western Cape, South Africa
info@printmatters.co.za
www.printmatters.co.za

Copyright Text © 2011 Paul Nel

The moral right of the author has been asserted.

All rights reserved.
No part of this publication may be reproduced, stored in a retrieval system, or transmitted,
in any form or by any means, without the prior permission in writing of the publishers
or author, nor be otherwise circulated in any form of binding or cover other
than that in which it is published and without a similar condition,
including this condition being imposed on the subsequent purchaser.

A CIP catalogue record for this book is available at the
South African Library.

ISBN: 978-0-9802609-8-4

EDITOR
Robert Berold

BOOK DESIGN & PRODUCTION
Stuart-Clark & Associates cc, Cape Town

PROOF READING
Elisabeth Anderson

PRINTING & BINDING
Interpak Books, Pietermaritzburg

COVER PAINTING
Author's collection – artist unknown

ACKNOWLEDGEMENTS
Edwin Muir – Critical Essay on the Poetry of Robert Henryson, 1949

To my wife and my children.

Paul Nel was born in Oudtshoorn in 1939. He lived for many years in Cape Town, where in the early part of his career he worked in management of newspapers. In 1985 he moved to Johannesburg to head an Employee Benefit company. In 1999 he began an active retirement in Knysna, where he cycles, kayaks, plays golf, reads, and writes. Paul is married, with three children. He is now working on two more novels.

Chapter One

Oudtshoorn – 29 November 1926

ALBERT VAN YSSEN was a man of few words and many profound thoughts, a man washed in carbolic soap, a scholar and a stamp collector no less; tall and dignified. He in his tailor-made brown pin stripe suit and his dutiful wife dressed in her summer floral Crêpe de Chine frock waited in the shade of their veranda for Mr Fourie, the taxi driver to arrive. The toecaps of his shoes shone. He had polished them himself. His South African College old-boys tie smelled of mothballs and his shirt of lye and sunlight and ironing. Their suitcase, the hatbox and the wicker picnic basket stood next to them. He glanced at his watch. It was three fifteen in the afternoon. He proudly observed his wife. She smiled affectionately at him. They were on their way to Cape Town, to the graduation ceremony at the University of Cape Town, to witness the culmination of their son's academic career. The occasion would reward van Yssen for all the material sacrifices he had made. He sighed with satisfaction for he was to see his son Douglas receive his Masters Degree in History, *Cum Laude*.

He patted the large, intricately fashioned front door key in his pocket to reassure himself that he had locked the door, and remembered that he had not forgotten to turn off the main switch. He turned and tried the brass front door knob to make sure that the door was locked.

Fourie arrived early, as van Yssen always expected of him. He stopped opposite the gate in the picket fence. The scent of the pittosporum hedge was heavy.

Summer had become resident in the town of Oudtshoorn early in October. From the way it spread its haze in the early mornings and reduced the clear pastel colours of the sky and the dusty olive greens of the landscape to paler shades, it promised to be a relentless one.

At the station a porter transferred the luggage onto his barrow. Van Yssen paid Fourie, made sure that he knew when to fetch them from the station and said goodbye. While the porter stood discreetly behind them the van Yssens waited for the train to arrive.

Towards the east, where there had been only shimmering railway tracks trembling in the heat, a large black charging steam locomotive suddenly presented itself and immediately began to slow down.

The conductor stepped running from the moving train, his blue serge uniform worn shiny, his cap pushed back to reveal a tender white sweating forehead, to be confronted by van Yssen. "I am Mr van Yssen. My wife and I are on our way to Cape Town. I reserved a coupé by mail through Port Elizabeth...."

The conductor knew the type. He had already taken his passenger list from his inside pocket. He sighed, "Yes, Mr van Yssen, it is carriage 11094, compartment D. I wish you a pleasant journey." And with that he fled into the cafeteria, went around the back of the sweet counter past glass jars with angled throats filled with brightly coloured sweets, and dashed into the stationmaster's office.

Outside the heat was stifling. Water was let into the locomotives. A second locomotive had been coupled because of the mountain that lay ahead. Pepper trees stirred in the tepid movements of afternoon air. A heavily perspiring chef and his assistant, in grey check trousers, white tunics and chefs' hats, drooped their flaccid tattooed arms from the galley windows. Van Yssen led the way followed by his wife and the porter. The chef lifted his fat parboiled nicotine stained fingers, sucked on his cigarette, and turned to his assistant, "Funny old cunt to be dressed like that, and to keep his jacket and his waistcoat on, on a day like this."

Van Yssen courteously assisted his wife onto the train, and led the way to their compartment. He lifted the window off its catch and lowered it so that the porter could hand him the luggage. There was soot on the seat. Van Yssen found a two-shilling piece; a half-crown would have been too much. He pressed it into the porter's hand. The porter nodded without a word or a change in expression, turned his servile shoulders, and with a resigned stoop, pushed his barrow back through the heat towards the station entrance on the heels of his bad feet, wishing for the day to end.

 Van Yssen put their suitcase under the seat. The hatbox went onto the rack above the upper bunk, to be out of harm's way. The picnic basket was consigned to the floor under the hand basin, next to the heater. He had planned what he would do the night before. He sighed heavily and smiled contentedly at his wife. Another job well done. He took a large handkerchief from his trouser pocket, unfolded it and dusted the soot from the seat. They sat down, he on the outside next to the window, she next to him. He gently took her hand and held it in his large dry warm padded palm. The sound of Pinkerton's concerned baritone escaped from His Master's Voice and rose in his head, and a wave of emotion and excitement expanded in him.

 The conductor blew his rugby referee's whistle and the ice cream vendor moved away from the train disappointed. Holding on to a chromium-plated grab rail, the conductor leant from the steps of the guard's van with a frayed green flag in his free hand. The locomotive hooted and let out an enormous hiss of steam as the machine, in the Image of James Watt, exhaled to fill the clearing space of the locomotive's reciprocating cylinders with steam, first the one, and then the other, to drive the pistons out towards the wheels. Van Yssen's exhilaration cleared his mind, and he intoned to himself, as if in prayer, the words from his literature on steam locomotives, "The whole work done in the revolution, namely the integral force acting on the piston and the distance through which it moves, is represented by the enclosed area of the indicator diagram, a b c d" Only his lips moved. He should have been an engineer not a land surveyor. The coaches shuddered and squealed at their couplings as the locomotion stretched the train. The platform and the station building began to move. The people on the platform pivoted towards the moving train as it gathered speed. Where the railway line crossed George Road, the warning bell began to clang. Cars and animal-drawn carts stopped. An obstinate donkey was hard to control. The locomotive moved across the road, its wheels screeching as the rails curved southwards towards the red steel bridge that spanned the Olifants River.

Air began to move through the compartment as the train gathered more speed. Abruptly the metallic clatter of the wheels on the tracks became hollow while the machine was suspended high over the dry riverbed by the red steel bridge. There would be many more bridges on the way to Cape Town. On they went, through the cuttings hewed out of cochineal-coloured hills, past lucerne fields, ever upwards towards the Outeniqua Mountains.

With some satisfaction van Yssen reminded himself how much he loved trains and railways. He looked out of the window as the train rounded a bend, exuberant at the sight of the two Seven Class Garrett locomotives: in railwayman's parlance the train was double-headed. Each locomotive had a tender at the back and a tank in front. What pleasure that two such magnificent pieces of engineering would take care of the great mountain that lay ahead.

"It is nice to be on our way. You must be happy, my dear," Mrs van Yssen observed. "The locomotives looked so clean, where have they come from?"

"They would have been inspanned at Klipplaat, and will be changed at Voorbaai. The NCCR only operates between Mossel Bay and Worcester. They use the K Class Garretts from Mossel Bay." She was proud that he knew so much.

The dining car and the staff car had also been joined onto the train at Klipplaat. The staff car, a second-class coach, accommodated the catering staff as well as the conductor, and as many bags of coal as possible for the stoves in the galley of the dining car.

The conductor's master key rattled in the recessed metal handle of the sliding door. "Tickets please!"

The train moved rhythmically, in one piece; a great centipede. The steward arrived. The van Yssens ordered tea. Life was good. Van Yssen would have to find the bedding attendant before the tea arrived. "I should go and find the bedding attendant." His wife knew he would not rest until he had found the attendant.

When van Yssen returned the steward was lowering the hinged wooden table with his one hand while balancing the tray with their tea in his other hand. Mrs van Yssen sat timidly sideways, away from the possibility of a falling tray, with her stockinged legs pressed against the green leather upholstery to make room.

Mrs van Yssen poured tea from a well-worn silver-plated teapot into railway cups decorated with golden emblems of springbok heads. As the train moved further up the Outeniqua Mountains the landscape changed: the aridness of the Little Karroo gave way to temperate air. The breathless heavy heaving puffing sounds of the steam locomotives were amplified in the cuttings. The train moved cautiously along ledges above the precipitous slopes of the railway pass, through tunnels filled with smoke until it emerged at last high above the coastal plain, an endless vista of green velvet rolling hills, lush with indigenous vegetation. Monkey ropes and creepers draped from tall yellowwood trees.

From the upper reaches of the mountain the coastal light was softer. The air was cooler. The regularly recurring alternating sounds of the wheels clattering across the joints of the railway line were subdued and more rhythmic as the couplings between the coaches relaxed and the train descended towards the sea.

In the late afternoon the sweating humid station at George gave back all the heat and filth it had absorbed during the day. Groups of desultory coloured people sat like withered veld flowers, with dejected and forlorn faces, on their luggage of cardboard boxes held together with string, against the ochre-yellow distempered walls of the public toilets for non-whites.

A youth with a drawn face of pasty complexion studded with ripe pimples, a white shirt and a black bowtie and hair shorn quite short, walked up and down next to the train with a shabby wooden tray protruding horizontally from his waist and held around his thin straining neck by a wide stained leather strap. Displayed on the tray was a variety of brightly coloured sweets, combs, pink and blue hair clips, a cheap pipe and some packets of cigarettes in tens, twenties and fifties - Cavalla, CTC, Springbok, and matches.

The conductor's whistle blew. He signalled with his green flag to the driver who rested with his forearms on the railing of the cab, his black cap awry, sweating through his black shirt and braces. An energetic thick column of dark grey smoke gushed from the locomotive. The whistle blew a witty, cheeky tune. The driver winked at the two plump girls who had come to meet him and the stoker. They would give them something to remember when they got back later that evening from Mossel Bay. The ugly one in the floral dress realised what the driver's expression was saying and could feel her heart beating in more than one place.

With the light already fading, the journey to Mossel Bay began. From there they would travel westward into the night. The train gathered speed. The steward fetched the tea tray. It was attractive countryside, pity it was such a poor farming area, van Yssen reflected. The suurveld. The train slowed down and hooted when it passed the small station of Schimmelkranz. Three small children waved from next to the track, the eldest was barely twelve and held her baby sister on a cocked hip. Red and blue and yellow and white washing stirred on a line next to the stationmaster's house. On towards Great Brak River, parallel to the coastline, on a perfect, windless evening, the foaming milky surface of the sea made pink by the reflection of an orange firmament of cloud and the setting sun. Looking towards the setting sun, van Yssen observed the vast mists, released and set free from the sea, that swept ponderously over the land and up into the mountains. He could smell the organic elements of the ocean. His nose cleared. He turned to his wife. She had been looking intently at him. They looked into one another's eyes. There was no sound and no movement. She drew herself up against him. She put her left hand in under the flap of his jacket and into his warm trouser pocket, onto the intimacy of his athletic thigh and rested her head against his shoulder. And so they sat for a while.

While van Yssen mused and was lost in contemplation of the journey, and of Douglas' graduation, his wife's thoughts were assailed by the suggestions of the French Woman when she heard of their journey to Cape Town. She looked at the magnificent spectacle of the sea below them. "It is like an endless universe, like a great ocean, ever changing in its colours and its moods," Madame Jacquard had said.

Her first encounter with Madame Jacquard happened earlier in the year, in the late summer, in Church Street, opposite the sandstone Standard Bank on the shaded pavement under the veranda of Prince Vintcent Department Store. Mrs van Yssen had done her morning shopping. The French woman was ahead of her, walking in the same direction as she, her athletic legs and sturdy buttocks, emancipated from the constraints of a corset, moved in a loose kind of way. She carried a wickerwork basket containing a brown paper packet. Mrs van Yssen's instinct was to keep her distance. Since her inexplicable arrival in Oudtshoorn the year before, the French woman had been the subject of endless gossip. Mrs van Yssen had often encountered her, almost always on the same street corner, irrespective of the time of day, or the reason for going into town, as though they were destined to meet. She had seen the woman examining gloves in Bon Marche in her eccentric way. She was loud to a point of vulgarity, wore brightly coloured loose floral dresses, and invariably tied a silk scarf around her head. As she held up the gloves in the light coming through the shop window to see them better, she inhaled smoke from a thick cigarette with studious intensity and exhaled the smoke carelessly through her darkened nostrils. She saw her at the greengrocer as she disdainfully handled the cheese or the cuts of meat in the butcher shop. Better to keep even a greater distance. Mrs van Yssen took smaller steps and turned to look at the wares displayed in the shop window. She lent forward to open her umbrella before she left the shelter of the shop's veranda. When she looked up to resume her journey home, the French woman had turned and was approaching her. "I have the feeling that you are avoiding me." Mrs van Yssen was stunned. "I, I, I do not even know you," she stuttered and felt dizzy.

"The simple reason why you avoid me is because we are different. Or perhaps you just think I am different. Maybe we are more alike than you think. Come let us walk together, since we live in the same street, after all we are both going home. My name is Madame Jacquard. I know what your name is."

Mrs van Yssen was trapped. She felt the eyes of each critical inhabitant of Oudtshoorn. She had to flee from her heart's fluttering palpitations. She should not have had so much coffee that morning. She was so self-conscious that she could not feel her limbs. She trembled. "I still have to go to the bank."

"Then I shall come with you, and have a look at all those funny little men in there."

"Or perhaps we should rather go home."

"You are embarrassed by me, yes? I know that I am eccentric. Come let us go home then. Not all French persons are Catholic, you know."

They set off at a brisk pace in the direction of the suspension bridge. Although it was late summer the sun was still fierce. Mrs van Yssen resigned herself to her fate. The French Woman strode with self-assurance, her legs apart, her feet turned out like those of a ballet dancer. "You see, you are my first friend in all the time that I have been here. I have seen you in your garden. I have seen your son. It is a blessing to have a child. I had a child. You are the first friend I have in this place, but it is not all bad. My deprivation has inspired my work. It has made me more aware of what goes on inside my head, and for that matter, what happens in my heart. I did not know that there was so much inside me. It is like an endless universe, like a great ocean, ever changing in its colours and its moods, like a great canvas. I think you are a good person. You must come and have some tea with me tomorrow morning, we have much to talk about I am sure. I will expect you at exactly ten thirty tomorrow. You know where my house is."

"I thank you for your kind invitation."

Madame Jacquard had cast a spell over Mrs van Yssen.

Madame Jacquard's garden was overgrown, and neglected, perhaps Bohemian, Mrs van Yssen thought. She was nervous and relieved that her husband was away doing work in the Swellendam district. The house was set back from the road. The prospect that the French Woman could have forgotten about their arrangement, and gone out, brought a moment's hope of relief. Before Mrs van Yssen could knock, the door opened. Madame Jacquard stood at the entrance, holding out her arms, dressed in an artist's smock. "I am so utterly delighted that you have come. I have already made tea, and prepared some pastries for the two of us to have. We will take our tea in my studio."

The studio faced north to let in as much light as possible. It had two large sash windows. Mrs van Yssen had never been in an artist's studio before. There was an untidy red couch with a bright yellow throw over it, two easy chairs with a small round table between them upon which a teapot and cups had been arranged. A strong odour of oil paints and turpentine. Three easels stood together at odd angles like bored people at an exhibition. Several paintings were in various stages of completion – landscapes and still lifes, in bright striking colours. There were paintings on the floor resting against the walls of the studio. Mrs van Yssen looked around, stooping earnestly: she wanted to appear interested, but was too unsure of herself in the unfamiliar circumstances to make any comment.

"We will first have tea, and then I shall show you some of my work. Please do not be afraid of me. I am so glad that you have decided to come. Do please sit down." The two women drank their tea in silence. Each wanted to examine the other, and they took turns to do so. While Mrs van Yssen looked about the French Woman observed her, and while the French woman poured more tea Mrs van Yssen took her turn.

"You must have something to eat," Madame Jacquard said as she handed Mrs van Yssen a hand-painted plate with pastries. "I had to make them myself. You cannot purchase them in this town. It is a pity."

"How did you come to be here in Oudtshoorn?" Mrs van Yssen blurted out in an uncharacteristically tactless way.

"You have asked much sooner than the other people, which is good because you will then know the truth much sooner. If you mean this particular town, the answer is because I once had an ostrich feather boa. I wanted to see where the feathers came from. Do I have a husband? The answer is in the affirmative. Where is he? The answer is, you will never guess. He is in what we call the *Regiments Etrangers*, what you popularly refer to as the Foreign Legion. Yes – you may think I say it because it sounds romantic – it is perfectly true. He is out there," she made a sweeping gesture with an open palm and wide fingers, "somewhere, North Africa, Indochina, somewhere in one of the colonies. It was not of his or my choice that he is there. Perhaps I will tell you the full reason one day. For the same reason that he is there it was better for me not to stay in France, and as I said, I had an ostrich feather boa once. *Voilà*. Such is life. One day when he has served his term of duty, and becomes free again, we shall reunite."

"I myself have tried some watercolours, in a very modest way."

"Oh that is wonderful to hear, it is a very difficult medium indeed. You have to grasp the mood and the composition of the subject quickly and then reproduce it almost instantly. You have to be very quick. It looks so simple but it is not. You cannot hide your mistakes. It is like playing one of Mozart's early piano sonatas. Every hesitation, every tiniest mistake can be heard because the music is so pure in its simplicity. Perhaps you will show me what you have done?"

"I would be much too embarrassed, I am sure you are very accomplished."

"How did you come to be in Oudtshoorn?"

"My husband is a land surveyor. There was a great deal of work in the district."

"Your son? What does he do?"

"He is at the university, in Cape Town."

"Is he a teacher there? He looks so handsome."

"No, no, he is still a student."

"What does he study?"

"History."

"How charming, or should I say interesting. And what will he do when he is finished there?"

"He is going to teach at the Boys High School."

"Here, at this school here? When?"

"Yes, next year, we are so pleased that he will be at home again, after five years."

"He should live on his own by now. Does he have any attachment, a girl?"

"He has a friend, she is charming. He has several friends. What are you busy painting?"

"Most recently I have been working alternatively on a landscape and a still life; come let me show you." Madame Jacquard's hands and fingernails, stained with paint, turned an easel towards Mrs van Yssen – a scene of the lucerne fields that bordered the river, some houses with bright red roofs in the distance, a dusty gravel road, two dark green cypress trees like sentinels, and an anaemic sky drained of colour by the heat of the day. She moved the other easel around to face them. A blue glazed earthenware bowl containing ripe pomegranates stood on a piece of multicoloured printed cloth on a table near the window.

"So much colour! It is quite exciting."

"Those of us who were students of art in Europe in my time could not help but be influenced by the new movements, especially Impressionism, and Expressionism. More recently there have been the Fauves. If you like colour, you should see their colour. I am sure you have heard of them?"

"No, I am afraid not."

"When their work was first shown as part of a big exhibition in Paris, about twenty years ago, at the Grand Palais, the public was shocked. One woman critic even resorted to quoting Ruskin, and said, 'A pot of paint has been thrown over the public's head.' Why she bothered with poor old Ruskin one does not know; he was like a cross between a snarling dog and Don Quixote. The public was outraged at the work. But so it is with public opinion. The masses never understand a new language, especially when it is the language of the artist. And yet their work is accepted now. Oh! I hope I am not offending you with my ideas, they can be a bit avant-garde at times."

"No, not at all. How are the Impressionists different from the Expressionists?"

"It can be a very huge subject, and there can be many opinions about the subject. Expressionism comes from fantasy. We all have our fantasies, so we can understand where it comes from. Unfortunately it has a dark side – a contribution by the philosophers, miserable people like Nietzsche. As much as a fantasy can employ the imagination to distort things, the paintings of the Expressionists often contain distortions or exaggerations that are meant to demonstrate the artist's inner reaction to the reality around him. They have special ideas about colour. To them colour is more than colour, it has symbolic meaning. Remember what Goethe had to say about the meaning of colour? Now the Impressionists are very different. By the way, it was a painting by Monet that he called *Impression: Soleil Levant*, meaning Impression: Sunrise that started the use of the word. The people who were exhibiting with him at that time, as a result, became known as Impressionists. They painted outside, in nature, instead of in studios, but most important of all, it was how they began to understand the way in which light and colour worked, how even shadows are coloured, how nature revealed and presented itself to our perceptions, that was important. Their approach is very different from the academic tradition that went before. Their colours are gentle; light is broken up into its parts and assembled again in the form of tiny bits of paint on the canvas. There are things that I like in both movements, and as I said, I like the Fauves, but I especially like the Impressionists because they make no social comment. Their work is easy to like. There is no turbulence, or perhaps I should say disturbance, inside them. Your visit has inspired me so that I talk too much."

"What was Van Gogh?"

"I must compliment you on a very clever question. Perhaps you know more than you give yourself credit. Some say Expressionist, some say Post Impressionist. One wonders what he himself would have said. I think he just painted because he could not help himself."

Mrs van Yssen had crossed over into another world. She had dreamt of Europe; she had romanticised her Huguenot origins. Now here in her own street was a creature so different, so exotic, so intellectual, and at the same time so sensual and feminine, and accomplished, that she became intoxicated. "I must get going," she said.

"We must not try to resist what is planned for us," Madame Jacquard said.

Mrs van Yssen's departure was arrested for a moment by a feeling of discomfort. "I would like to visit you again. I have enjoyed meeting you, perhaps more than I am able to express now. Thank you very much for the tea, and the lovely pastries."

"If it is easier to come when your husband is away, I understand, or if you would like to say that I am giving you painting, or French, lessons."

Mrs van Yssen smiled demurely, and began the walk back to her house. She was uncomfortable: there had been too much intimacy.

"You are far away, what are you thinking about?" van Yssen asked.

"Ag, about all sorts of things."

When van Yssen went off on his next country visit three weeks later, Mrs van Yssen decided to pick a small bunch of white roses for the French woman.

She had not seen or heard of her since her first visit. It was ten in the morning and yet the house seemed asleep. There was no reply when she knocked. Perhaps she had knocked too gently. She would not knock a second time. She was being rescued from her indiscretion. It was fate that Madame Jacquard was out. As she turned to leave, the door opened. Madame Jacquard was in her dressing gown, she held a small handkerchief over her mouth, her eyes were red as though she had been crying, her cheeks were flushed, her greasy hair straggled over her head and her shoulders; where the silk scarf usually was, grey was visible. A string necklace of garlic cloves hung limp around her neck. "I have been very ill. First I thought it was just a summer cold then I realised it was the *grippe*. I have lost much weight. I could not even cook properly."

"I am so sorry to hear that you have not been well. I shall go home immediately and prepare some soup for you. As soon as it is ready I shall bring it to you. I picked these for you this morning." She pushed the bunch of roses towards Madame Jacquard who tried to smell them.

"That would be so kind of you. I cannot smell a thing, and I lose my breath so easily. It is quite strange. I must go and lie down again now, I feel a bit light-headed."

"Can I make you some tea before I go?"

"Yes but do not come too near me. You will get sick yourself."

The kitchen was in disarray. There was no clean crockery. Mrs van Yssen had to wash a cup and clean the teapot. An open tin of condensed milk stood on the window sill.

"Here is your tea," Mrs van Yssen said as she entered Madame Jacquard's bedroom. The air in the room was stale: odours of illness, urine, perfume, old food, rancid body, herbal infusions and the bed in which the woman had sweated. "I think we should open the window just a little. There is no bread. I shall bring some when I return. We must get your strength back. I will do some shopping for you. Betta can come and clean up. We cannot leave you here like this. I should have realised that something was wrong."

Madame Jacquard raised herself on her elbow, "Could I have a little more of the preserved milk, please? Thank you for your concern. I would like to protest and say that I can help myself, but this time I cannot refuse help. Thank you very much. I feel better, not so alone. A few nights ago I was delirious. I thought I was going to die. I saw my child."

Nursing Madame Jacquard back to health created a bond between the two women. When they had tea in the studio one sunny warm morning, Madame Jacquard had tears in her eyes. "I owe you a great debt," she said looking at Mrs van Yssen.

"I have told my husband about you. He would like to meet you. He has very high principles and a deep sense of right and wrong. My son says that he is like one of the old Roman jurists. He will not allow public opinion to sway him."

"Sometimes one's principles can be too rigid and lead to one's destruction, but I know what you mean."

"Why do you say that?"

"My husband is like that. But, we will not talk about that now. I would like to meet your husband. It will be nice to have a man in my house. I think you should come and have dinner with me one evening. I will make you real French food."

"I am looking forward to our meal tonight in the dining-car," van Yssen said and startled his wife.

"Strange that you should mention that now, I was just thinking about that first meal we had with Guillemette."

"What an experience that was," he reflected.

Madame Jacquard invited the van Yssens to dinner one evening in July. They walked the short distance to her house, white vapours swirled ahead of them as they exhaled. The distant Swartberg Mountains were covered in snow. The clear night sky was filled with stars. The Milky Way was so dense that it looked like a girdle of cloud. She had made a coal fire and laid the table for three. The crisp cold of the night was on their faces.

"Let me take your coats," she said. "It is good to have your company. Tonight I would like to show you my cooking. It was not easy to get all the things, the ingredients that I wanted, but I have tried. But first we must have a little bit of wine while we sit in front of the fire; it is very nice, I get it from the merchant in Cape Town; they bring it from Bordeaux. Everything is prepared so we can be comfortable.

Van Yssen sipped reluctantly at his wine. "I do not drink very much."

"It is not how much you drink, but rather how you drink. You must get your tongue around the wine. Caress it with your mouth, smell it with your nose right inside the glass. Look for its mystery and you will find more and more flavours, like solving a mystery. The wine is alive: as the evening goes on it will change its personality, like us it will become different. Come along Anneke, you must also try some. The wine is meant to clear the mouth and the palate between mouthfuls of food, so that the same food becomes a lot of new experiences. I believe that we should make the effort to develop our senses as much as we can; otherwise we go through life half asleep.

"First we are going to have soup: good traditional onion soup. The weather is perfect for nice hot soup. I hope you will enjoy it."

Madame Jacquard disappeared into the kitchen and returned with three soup plates on a tray. Van Yssen stared at the floating island in the middle of his plate. He hesitated, his spoon was poised.

"It must of course have cheese in it. I would have preferred to use my favourite, Fourme D'Ambert, it is so special, but I cannot obtain it here. I was able to get some Roquefort. It is a good substitute. Soup is one of the most favourite foods in France. In the past we even used to have soup for breakfast – my father often had soup for breakfast with some bread and wine and cheese."

A stew of meat and vegetables followed. Van Yssen was incredulous. "Without offending my good wife, I have never tasted anything like this, the variety of flavours. What magic have you performed?"

"You flatter me, but then, a French woman will always enjoy that! I am glad you have asked, because gastronomy should really be like a dialogue. We should discuss what we eat; we should describe what we experience. To me food must have excitement, how would you say, sensuality, and it must be made to give the guests their pleasure. It must contain surprises, like the theatre.

"I have used beef, some fresh vegetables – not easy to get in the winter – and if you look closely, I have put in some smoked sausages, a few cloves, and just a tiny bit of fresh garlic and red wine. I brought some garlic with me from France, and I have grown it here. It is the purple kind. I am able to make sure that the strength is just right."

"How do you do that?" Mrs van Yssen asked.

"My father showed me how. He was such a clever man. It depends on where you grow it and when. The season must be right. My father used to compare meals to the opera. He liked very much to cook."

"I would like to learn to cook some French food," Mrs van Yssen said with girlish enthusiasm.

"Then I will send to France for a copy of Escoffier's book as a gift for you, and teach you how to use it."

Madame Jacquard made to put some more coal onto the fire. Van Yssen intervened and did it for her. "You are so chivalrous, thank you, Albert." The wine and the food had created an atmosphere of conviviality. The new pieces of coal caught alight. The fire played on the walls of the room. Madame Jacquard and her two guests sat replete, and stared into the fire. Van Yssen said afterwards that he felt as though he was in some other country. When Mrs van Yssen went to thank Madame Jacquard the following week and told her how complimentary van Yssen had been and that he had said it was like being away in another land, Madame Jacquard replied, "When next you go away, you must make love properly to your husband. You must awaken the beast, the *fauve*, in him."

The van Yssens were woken from their reverie in front of the fire by Madame Jacquard's announcement, "And now for my *piece de resistance*!"

"Surely, we cannot eat any more," Mrs van Yssen sighed, with a hand on her stomach and her head apologetically to one side.

"The meal would not be complete without my *crème brulee*, my burnt cream. When I want to indulge myself I make one for myself. I even brought my own vanilla pods from home. They provide a more subtle taste than the essence. I have made each one of us a small one. It is so much more intimate."

Mrs van Yssen was pleased. Albert had a sweet tooth. The more the French woman impressed him the easier it would be for their relationship to flourish. She was pleased that she had discovered the French woman.

"She is an interesting person," van Yssen said on the way home while they walked arm in arm, close together, wrapped in their woollen coats, "And much more respectable than I had initially thought; quite worldly though, I would say, quite unusual."

Mrs van Yssen began to visit Madame Jacquard regularly.

One morning in the spring when the fruit trees filled the back garden with scented white and pink blossoms, the two women sat outside, having tea. Madame Jacquard looked up from under her large white straw hat, a red and green silk scarf tied around the bowl, "The coming of the summer months has aroused the trees. Are they not beautiful? They have so much love. Smell their thick perfume. They are so innocent, so unlike us. Our guilt steals away our innocence. We are so guilty about the most innocent things that we are prevented from living life fully."

"What do you mean?"

"I mean, consider physical love. It should be the most beautiful, natural thing in the world. It is how we make other people; how we make our own wonderful precious children, and yet the act of making love is considered an act of sin. Children are born in sin. How ridiculous! The trees and their blossoms do not think of that."

"Yes it is strange. But it depends on how we were brought up. My mother never explained anything to me. I was married when I was barely more than eighteen, and I had Douglas a year later. I am not sure how I managed that. It frightened me, but at least my husband is a gentle man. I am so clumsy. Even now we do not undress in front of each other. The only naked man I have seen is Douglas, as a boy."

Madame Jacquard sat back in her chair so that she could have a better look at Mrs van Yssen. "Oh my dear, how terrible, what a waste. But perhaps you are fortunate after all."

"How can I be?"

"You have a sense of transgression, and so does your husband."

Mrs van Yssen looked puzzled, "A sense of transgression?"

"The reason why you do not undress in front of one another is because you have a sense of transgression. When you consider your physical relationship with your husband, you perceive there to be certain barriers, barriers that you should not, or may not, cross. To do so would be wrong: a transgression. It is like the forbidden fruit. You may not pick it. You may not eat it. What is important to know is that it is not really forbidden, otherwise it would not have been created. We have in our own minds created the forbidden territory. It does not exist in an absolute sense. It is not part of a fundamental order of things; it belongs to the relative world. Now if you could bring yourself to go beyond what you regard as forbidden, the act of transgression would become an adventure in itself, and when you get to the other side of the barrier you will experience excitement and freedom of an entirely new dimension."

Mrs van Yssen sat silently.

"I know that what I am suggesting, it is not an easy thing to do. You must wait patiently for the right opportunity. The best time is when you go on holiday by yourselves. Or perhaps, when you go on your journey to Cape Town to see Douglas graduate. When you go to Cape Town it is to witness the climax of his studies. You will have to take the initiative, Albert won't. He fears passion because he thinks that he will lose it forever if he releases it. He does not understand that the more passion he releases the more it will grow. You must show yourself to him in the daylight. Let him see what he has touched but never seen. To men visual experiences are very strong, very important. Your courage must not fail you. Wear no underwear under your skirt."

Mrs van Yssen trembled. She blushed. "I do not know whether I will be able to do what I think you are suggesting."

"Oh you must, you must. Otherwise you would be committing a sin, and I would not have fulfilled my duty towards you. You must, otherwise it would be for me like having a great inspiration to paint my greatest work ever and to say to myself I do not know whether I will be able to, and then to do nothing; and what a sad tragic waste that would be."

Mrs van Yssen looked at her husband, his head turned, looking out of the window. The large ears with hair in them, the creases of his tanned neck from days in the sun, the straight nose, the intelligent blue eyes. He had become magnified by her emotions. She felt sorry for him. He toiled assiduously to sublimate his desire only to be defeated when his desire conquered his restraint and she surrendered to him dutifully and without movement and let him kiss her in the climax of his passion with a slack dry open mouth. Guillemette was right: if she did not seize the moment their relationship would remain fallow.

With one hand she turned his head towards her and kissed him on his temple. "It is good that we can be alone together. I want to be very close to you, Albert, closer than ever before."

He stammered, "How do you mean? Aren't we sitting right next to one another?"

"In a different way. Please don't think badly of me, I want to touch you and I want you to touch me. I want to kiss you now." His heart thumped. Blood surged into his head. She took her hand out of his pocket and wrapped both her arms tightly around his right arm. She let go of his arm, and pulled the skirt of her dress and petticoat up above her hips. In the soft rose coloured evening light he saw her suspenders and her smooth white thighs above her stockings. For a moment he was confused because he had expected to see her pants. Instead he saw what he had never seen before. He kissed her. Her face was flushed. He could feel himself caught in his pubic hairs leaking inside his loose underwear. He was nearly out of control.

A master key rattled in the unlocked door. His throat was dry. "No, wait, one moment I shall open it now," he squeaked. But it was too late. Even as Mrs van Yssen frantically rearranged her dress, the door slid open to reveal the steward who had come to take the dinner bookings. He got a sly look and winked at van Yssen, "I shall return later." He shut the door with a grin. "Well, well, well, what will the chef say when I tell him the old boy was trying to fuck the old lady!"

Van Yssen looked at his wife whose eyes filled with tears. Their first moment of real intimacy had been destroyed. She took his head in her hands and pulled it towards her face and kissed his eyes. He felt her tears on his forehead. She released herself from him, and sat down. He sat down next to her. She held his hand and in a girlish way leant her head against the rough cloth of his shoulder pad.

The train started to slow down to enter Great Brak River Station. The steward's key rattled in the door. "Come inside," called van Yssen.

"I have come to take your order for dinner, sir." He still wore his grin.

"We have decided to have dinner in the dining-saloon."

Mrs van Yssen looked at her husband. There was still all the food in the picnic basket. The steward left.

"I shall go and make the booking," van Yssen said, and left the compartment.

When the door shut behind him, Anneke van Yssen pushed her head back against the green leather of her seat. She shut her eyes, and let all her limbs loosen with satisfaction. She drew in her breath, full of sea air, and sighed with such power that her nostrils tingled. When the train was stationary in Great Brak River Station, van Yssen made his way past passengers in the corridor, past open compartment doors and other people's ways of travelling.

There was frantic activity in the galley of the dining-car. The overweight chef strode back and forth in the confined space, giving instructions to his staff. His sweating face had been made grey-white pastry by years in the steamy cauldron. Stubble grew like poisoned fungus. He was puffed up from tasting food and never ate a meal. He had a headache and was in a terrible mood because the chief steward had criticised him, and on top of that he had badly burnt the inside of his thumb with his cigarette when he fell asleep during his afternoon rest.

Van Yssen made a booking for two. Dinner would be at eight. They would be at Voorbaai then. It was a short haul to Mossel Bay. Van Yssen and his wife sat close together. Charles Nel had lent him a small blue-grey paperback volume entitled *The Battle of the Somme – Second Phase* by John Buchan, complete "With Official Illustrations and Maps." The word "Somme" was printed in large orange letters. The price: one shilling. Stamped on the cover were the words 'With the compliments of the Over-Seas Club, London W.C.' He wondered whether the old militarist had had an ulterior motive. In the back of the book was a foldout map. He briefly examined the map, and folded it again. Together they looked at the illustrations – photographs of battle scenes. The first showed a dark silhouetted, melancholy head of a horse peering from the left, an army truck and a horse and cart on a shiny muddy road against the setting sun under a cold threatening European sky. The caption read, 'Evening behind the line.' Other captions: 'A heavy gun in action', 'A German gun destroyed by our artillery', 'Final instructions before going into battle' showing an officer standing in front of perhaps a hundred soldiers in tin hats lying or sitting around him somewhere in an open field which had not so much as a leaf of vegetation. It went on, illustration after illustration of destruction and death, except for a photograph showing a Scottish pipe band led by a Pipe Major who followed a small white mongrel with black ears. The caption said, 'The victory of Martinpuich.'

And so they sat, intimately close together, he with his thoughts and she with hers, devoted, yet now excitingly unfamiliar. She was warm and soft. He was hard and tweed-rough. He thought of the bedding attendant. Almost imperceptibly, and then gradually louder, a melody from a six note hand-held xylophone came towards them, announcing dinner. The sound passed and faded away. Van Yssen's salivary glands gave little squirts. As they got up she put her arms under her husband's jacket. She kissed him with a warm moist mouth. The train stopped. They walked through the staff car, and past the galley. The chief steward welcomed them by name and showed them to their table. Dusk was approaching. To the left was the sea, darker now, slithering swirling silver. They saw their reflections in the windows of the dining-car.

"I am so looking forward to seeing Douglas tomorrow. The fellow has done so well. So bright," van Yssen mused.

"Just like his father."

"Come on now, my darling, a Masters degree *Cum Laude*, it is simply brilliant. Exceptional dedication. Our child who has become a man."

"He takes after you. He has your noble features: the broad forehead, the strong chin. The smile of his kind deep grey eyes. Our child."

"I have often wondered why he chose Roman history. Possibly his Latin?"

They had pea soup, and then fried fish. When the main dish of roast beef and vegetables arrived, the train began to move. For dessert they had red jelly with custard, followed by railway coffee, thick with milk and sugar.

They left the dining-car. As the train gathered speed rapidly they moved cautiously along the passages of the swaying coaches. The sound of the locomotives was different now. Darkness concealed the landscape, and all that was visible outside were patterns made by light from the windows. Inside were the reflected contents of the coaches: shiny wood panels, chromium plated fittings, and the panes of the windows that gave an additional dimension. They could smell the smoke from the locomotives, and the *boegoe* – the NCCR smell – unique to that trajectory.

When they reached their coupe the bedding attendant was leaving. The top bunk had been lowered and their beds made. Van Yssen found a shilling, "Thank you very much, we appreciate your attentiveness."

"Good night."

The van Yssens were alone in the sterilised odour of aseptic railway bedding. He shut the window, pulled up the shutter. There was soot on the bottom end of the navy blue blanket. The new conductor would be there soon.

"Shall we go to bed then?" Anneke asked.

"It is still early, let us read for a while. The new conductor has still to examine our tickets."

It was awkward to sit when the top bunk was down. The Battle of the Somme lay on the lid of the washbasin. The locomotives gathered speed and thrust themselves into the night with rhythmic determination. Van Yssen took the book. He put his head back and shut his eyes. How he loved his wife, and how he loved Douglas. He opened his eyes and looked at the photographs but saw nothing.

"Albert, when do you expect the conductor?"

"It won't be long, nevertheless before the bridge."

Van Yssen thought nervously about the bridge across the Gouritz River – about twenty-six miles from Mossel Bay. Although they had travelled across it many times he never said anything about it to his wife. It was originally designed for road traffic and the railway line was put across it some time after its completion. Traversing it by train was harrowing. The procedure was for the first of the two Garretts to be uncoupled and to make its way over the bridge by itself. Even the weight of one locomotive was enough to cause the bridge to sway. Before the second locomotive with the carriages could proceed, it had to wait for the oscillations of the bridge to stop. The passengers and railwaymen who knew the danger, waited in bated silence when the haul of the second locomotive began.

The van Yssens sat side by side and looked at the little pocket book. They listened for the conductor to appear from the metallic vibrations of the bogies. They were halfway to the bridge.

Van Yssen thought of his wife's passion, and wondered whether the moment could be recreated. He revived the image of the perfume-filled instant when her thighs were framed in suspenders and lace, and the division that was just visible through her pubic hairs. He bent over and kissed the nape of her neck. The conductor's key clattered in the door of the next compartment. When their door opened, van Yssen rose and took his wallet from his pocket. He handed their tickets to the conductor. The new conductor was stocky, ruddy round face, freshly dressed in the blue serge uniform of the NCCR, complete with a bushy orange moustache that looked as though it was part of his fancy dress.

"Good evening."

"The bridge is not too far now," van Yssen ventured.

"Not far," came the laconic reply. Humourless porcine fellow this, and diligent.

They were alone again. Van Yssen locked the door. The door was equipped with a catch that could be fastened from inside the compartment to prevent unwelcome entry. He hooked the arm of the catch into the bracket on the door while she watched. No one could enter now, except that the door could still be opened a few inches. At least the opening end was away from the bunks.

When van Yssen turned around, she was lying on the lower bunk. She held her arms out towards him. He sat down next to her, and leant over to kiss her. She was like a young girl. She lifted her hips and pulled up her dress. Where her stockings ended, the insides of her thighs were damp. He felt pressure in his head. He should have eaten less. He touched her. She made a delicate gasp. She began to undo his trousers. He was shaking. He took his jacket off. "Shall I turn the light off?" he asked.

"No, we must see everything."

He looked at her face, beautiful in her floral dress, her hair pinned back. She lay with her knees pulled up, her legs apart, her dress and petticoat around her waist. He looked down at the stockings, the suspenders, the thighs, and the place between her legs. He looked at her face to see her reaction. Her eyes were filled with tears.

"I love you so much, my dearest Albert."

He sat on the edge of the bunk and pushed his trousers down, together with his underwear. He forced his still-tied shoes off, socks and all, pushed his trousers off and left them on the floor. Except for his waistcoat, shirt and tie, he was naked.

"May I see, Albert?"

His mouth was dry; he had no reply, and leant back. She examined him lovingly. She pressed her face against him and held her arms around his buttocks.

"I love you so, Albert."

She lay back. He crawled heavily onto her. As she drew him in, he felt a quivering that quickened, first from the end of his spine, convulsing, pumping. She shuddered. He saw the subliminal pink sky beyond Great Brak River, and was carried along by the warm creamy froth of the surf. He heard the exquisite voice of Madame Butterfly, tragic with emotion.

They lay joined together until he became aware of his nakedness.

"I am so sorry," he said.

"I understand, my love. I am so very glad."

He took her head in his hands. He felt her amber earrings inside his palms; there was perspiration on the nape of her neck. He smelt the French perfume he had given her for her birthday. She kissed him. The Garretts were quieter. The train seemed to be free-wheeling. They were approaching the bridge.

"Let us put our pyjamas on," he said.

"Yes."

The train slowed rapidly. It stopped short of the bridge. After the front locomotive had been uncoupled, it proceeded in a cloud of steam across the vast gorge of the Gouritz River. The bridge swayed. Far below a thin shallow stream of water shimmered. The hissing second locomotive waited uneasily to deliver its string of appendages. While the train stood, they undressed. She took her dress off over her head, then her petticoat, while he watched. She removed her brassière, and stood only in her suspender belt and stockings, and the amber beads around her neck. She sat down next to him and unclipped her stockings, then undid her suspender belt from behind. Her clothing was on her pillow. She held her arms out to him. He took off his remaining clothes, and for the first time in their lives they were naked together in the light. They embraced and kissed. The train lurched and they nearly fell over. She giggled playfully. Van Yssen bent down and dragged their leather suitcase from under the bottom bunk. He put it onto the bunk, and opened it.

"No wait, Albert, you'll untidy the suitcase."

She had put his pyjamas and her nightdress as well as their dressing gowns on top of the other clothing. The train slowly made its perilous journey across the bridge. She put her nightdress on while he got into his pyjamas. She produced their cosmetic bag, washed her face in the basin filled with cold water, and dried herself with a towel she had brought along for the journey. With a bottle of tooth powder in one hand he brushed his teeth laboriously and thoroughly. The train seemed unsteady under them. She thought of finding her small Bible; she also had to go to the toilet. She valued her privacy, so it would not be easy. He also had to go. While she was brushing her teeth he put on his gown and his slippers, and said, "I need to go to the toilet, will be back now."

The bridge moved, like a heart beating irregularly. In the distance the first locomotive waited patiently while the driver and the stoker stood with their backs against the tender, watching the stealthily approaching train traversing the chasm. The moon was bright. A breeze moved from the land towards the sea. The grasses of the veld and the fynbos quivered. While the two locomotives were coupled, they got into her bunk, in between the stiff steam laundered railway sheets, clad in their nightclothes that smelt of Karoo sun and hot ironing in the kitchen at Oudtshoorn.

The train fled hastily from the bridge and raced across flat countryside. The moon had not yet come up.

"I wonder what Douglas is doing now?"

"He is bound to be with his friends," she replied.

"He is so intelligent. I am glad he chose teaching. It is a good career in these uncertain times."

"What do you mean by 'uncertain'? The war is over. Things have returned to normal."

Their sexual experience had altered Albert's mood; made him more serious, more formal. "After a slaughter of such proportions things will not be normal for a long time. There are large and deep wounds in Europe. They will take a long time to heal. Europe is the crucible of our civilisation. The political differences there come from the depths of the different psyches. There is an imbalance now. The world seeks equilibrium. There are problems in Russia; the socialistic experiment of a gang of thugs has become nothing less than a tyranny of the proletariat. Woodrow Wilson with his well-meant yet misplaced statesmanship is wandering among celestial bodies. The artificial way in which Europe was carved up at Versailles cannot endure."

She loved the intellectual Albert. The train gathered more speed. The tapping of the wheels had an easy cadence. Albert was satisfied. His head was clear. His body felt strong. He loved his wife. He was conscious of the clarity of his thought. She sensed the energy. She felt it in the tissues that were pressed against her and kissed him on his temple, then next to his ear and ran her lips across the soft smooth skin and the stubble of his beard that had grown since the morning. She felt secure. She pulled her nightdress up above her waist. He kissed her breasts through her nightdress. She felt the warmth of his body between the insides of her thighs. He removed his pyjama trousers.

They made love with such intensity that she was at last transported by her pleasure into a field of bright colours. He tasted her tears before he felt them. The train drove on into the night, through clouds of its own smoke. They heard the sounds of stations in the night, voices that lived in different places, picnic baskets that creaked, and felt the cold air of the night. When they reached Worcester in the early hours of the morning, van Yssen got onto the top bunk.

The steward brought coffee and fetched hot water so that van Yssen could shave. They kept a distance from each other until they had brushed their teeth, then washed and dressed. They sat close together before she said grace and in the silence of reflecting on the discovery of a new intimacy, began to eat the sandwiches and boiled eggs that she had prepared. She looked so familiar to him. The fair hair, bright green eyes, tiny freckles across her nose, the regular strong white teeth, the flowing feminine body in a tweed skirt and stockings. It was not long now before they would see their son. Down through the Du Toit's Kloof mountains, and on into the soft leafy green early summer vineyards of the Paarl Valley lying in the sun of the new day, until they reached the Woltemade Cemeteries to be reminded of their own mortality and the 1918 'flu.

The train moved stealthily through Woodstock and Salt River, and cautiously crept into Cape Town Station. Van Yssen opened the door of their coupé, and stepped into the passageway to lower a window. He looked out towards the front of the train, for Douglas and a porter. There were not many people on the platform. He saw Douglas standing with his back towards them; the strong body of the young man and his good bearing, the dark crew cut hair, and large ears. He was always so cheerful, relaxed, and full of buoyant good humour and energy, a fine confident man. Their eyes met. A surge of emotion brought tears to van Yssen's eyes.

Mrs van Yssen held her arms out to Douglas. He walked towards the window. He held his arms out to his mother as he approached and smiled enthusiastically. The chromium-plated window rail was in their way and the frame of the window covered in soot. He groped to embrace his mother. She kissed him on his forehead and tasted and smelled her son. She looked so beautiful. Her eyes were large from fulfilment. Van Yssen took Douglas' head in his hands and pressed his own head hard against his son's. They were indeed blessed.

"You do look beautiful, Ma!" he exclaimed.

Van Yssen gathered their things, and passed them to Douglas who handed them to the porter. Mrs van Yssen wore her tailored tweed suit and small hat, her brown leather handbag tucked under her arm.

"Great day tomorrow; second one, Douglas."

Douglas smiled and nodded.

"To stand again before the chancellor, and again *Cum Laude*?"

"What was your journey like, Ma?" Douglas asked.

"Lovely, I mean, wonderful, especially pleasant. Gosh, why am I muttering so. I love it so; I mean I'm so glad to be with you my child."

Douglas walked ahead of his parents

Anneke continued, "Do tell all, I can't wait."

Douglas did not reply. Van Yssen said, "Douglas?" Still there was no reply. In a louder voice, "Douglas?"

"Tell us all your news," she insisted.

"There's not much to tell. Things just continue. Recently my work has taken all my time. I don't even know what's happening in town. I must be utterly boring. What's happening in Oudtshoorn?"

"Garnett sends his best regards. He is working very hard. It is not easy to start a practice. He says he is so pleased that you are coming to Oudtshoorn. To think that you are going to be a teacher at your old school. He was saying that with your intellect you will be a great asset to the town."

◆

Chapter Two

THE VAN YSSENS' TAXI swept into the driveway of the Helmsley Hotel and stopped outside the entrance. "We'll be able to walk from here to the University Hall tomorrow morning," van Yssen said with satisfaction.

While the taxi driver carried their luggage into the foyer of the hotel, van Yssen signed the register and received their room keys from a nervous young clerk. "Oh, I nearly forgot!" The clerk said. "There is an envelope here for you, Mr van Yssen."

Van Yssen took the envelope of watermarked paper, and turned it over. There was a card inside.

"What is it, Albert?" Mrs van Yssen asked.

"It is an invitation. It is from the Judge and Mrs Rose. This is really a great honour. They are inviting us to have lunch with them tomorrow after the Graduation Ceremony, at the City Club. How marvellous. I will reply immediately to accept, and ask the taxi driver to deliver it, if you will give me the address, Douglas?"

"It is in Queen Victoria Street."

"No, not the Club, the Judge's address."

The taxi driver was dispatched to the Roses residence with a generous tip, and after the van Yssens had been shown to their room they went downstairs to the lounge where van Yssen ordered tea and scones with an air of celebration and *bonhomie*.

"Let us hear all your news, Douglas!" his mother said.

"Ag, there isn't much that is new, life goes on."

"Bearing in mind that we are going out to lunch, how long will the ceremony be tomorrow?" his father asked.

"I have brought the programme along."

"Go over it for me, I've left my glasses upstairs," his father said.

Douglas took the graduation programme from his inside pocket and unfolded it. "The Vice-Chancellor will constitute the Congregation; the National Anthem follows, and Reverend van Heerden will offer the Prayer. Professor Jolly, Dean of the Medical Faculty, will address the Congregation. The Award of Scholarships and Prizes will be announced. Then comes the presentation of the graduands to the Vice Chancellor, and after that some Honorary Degrees and the formal dissolution of the Congregation, and that's that."

"How many graduands are there this time?" his father asked.

"I knew you would ask." Douglas had written down the totals under the relevant sections of the list of names. "Twenty MAs, including me, then as usual the BAs make up the largest total, namely eighty, Science has only eight, Engineering ten, Law nine, Medicine sixteen, Commerce the least of all, namely two, and Education six. And then of course there are two Honorary Doctorates."

"Who are they?" his father asked.

"The Doctorate of Laws goes to President Reitz, and the one of Science to van der Sterr."

"It is astonishing how the numbers have grown. What does it make in total?"

"One hundred and fifty four."

"Our family knew the Reitzes quite well. He was a wonderful lawyer in his day. Studied at the Inner Temple in London. Comes from Swellendam, but then everybody north of the Orange River had to come from somewhere. He was the first president of the Union Senate, and he is still an active member of the University Council even at his age – must be over eighty now – not to mention his contribution to the *Akademie vir Taal*. Those who were so deeply divided and opposed so bitterly now sit side by side, yet I sometimes wonder whether there can ever be true reconciliation. Deep down the differences continue to smoulder. As for the old Dutchman van der Sterr, I must make a point of congratulating him. He thoroughly deserves his honour, a DSc is quite something and it is time that our profession received some recognition, even if his is for town planning."

"The programme does not mention it, but I gather that there will be a private ceremony prior to the constitution of the Congregation at which the Vice Chancellor will present Professor Jolly with an LLD gown and hood on behalf of the members of the Medical Faculty."

"So, if it starts at nine it should easily be over by noon. I wonder why there should be a private ceremony?"

"I think we should have a light lunch today, just some sandwiches at the Waldorf or somewhere, your mother would like to do some shopping. She does not often have the opportunity to be in the city. If there is anything you need?"

"I have everything. I just need to get some shoe polish. I have had my best shirt washed and ironed."

"We'll have dinner together here at the hotel tonight. And then if you would like to be here early tomorrow morning we could have a decent breakfast, before we go. I would like to get there early so that we can find good seats."

"I am so pleased to be with my son, my own Douglas," his mother said as she appraised him. "I know you sometimes find it boring but it would be so nice if you would come with me when I go shopping. Your father has already promised to come along, and I would like to show off my two men. Your father is so proud of you, and of what you have achieved. There is a great future ahead of you. I am a bit nervous about the lunch with the Roses tomorrow – they move in such elevated circles."

"They are just people, Ma, just flesh and bone, like us. Frances has no pretences, and neither has her mother. The Judge can be a bit stern at times, a bit crusty, but that's just his way," he laughed, "in case you have to appear in front of him later!"

Douglas woke early the next morning. The south-easterly wind had tugged at College House all night and howled across the chimney pots and that, together with the excitement generated by the anticipation of the next day and the invitation to lunch, had woken him several times during the night. By five o'clock he could no longer stay in bed. He shaved and had a hot bath. He still had to polish his shoes. He dressed with deliberation: a white shirt, his College House tie, his dark grey flannel suit, and black shoes, making sure that his socks were the same colour as his suit. He finally ran his towel over his brush-cut and was ready to leave for the hotel. He picked up his Graduation Programme, tucked it into his inside pocket, buttoned his jacket against the wind, pulled his door closed quietly, and headed for the Helmsley. He looked up at the mountain. When the tablecloth lay over it like that, the wind could blow for days. It was a pity for his parents. It would be howling in Orange Street.

Van Yssen too had slept fretfully. He had dreamt in distorted images of the train journey, of suddenly finding himself in a crowded swaying dining saloon just in his shirt, naked from the waist down with the wind thrashing through an open window blowing particles of soot against his tender extremities, of doors being forced open and twisted off their hinges and of their coach becoming uncoupled and falling down a gorge of infinite depth while steam hissed out of its roof while he sat astride his wife and calculated with a pencil and paper the rate at which they were falling. When he woke he did not know where he was. He looked around and saw his wife sleeping sweetly in the other bed.

He went to his wife's bed and crept in next to her warm soft body. He put his arm around her and lay there looking at her blond hair. She put her arm on his thigh.

"Douglas will be here any moment. I think I should rather go and bath," he said.

She pulled him closer. He kissed her in the nape of her neck and got out of bed.

The van Yssens found Douglas sitting in the lounge reading that morning's Cape Times.

"My goodness, you do look wonderful," he said to his mother. Mrs van Yssen had on a Prussian blue and white dress of figured crêpe that came to her ankles, with buttons down the entire front and a large white collar. She wore a white cloche hat with a plain band around it that matched the material of her dress.

"I am glad that you have put on that suit Douglas, it fits the occasion," his father said.

"I can remember you in your first suit, the one we got for your confirmation, how small you were then, just fourteen," his mother doted.

They finished their breakfast. Van Yssen looked at his watch. "We are making good time. I'll go and clean my teeth."

At ten minutes past eight the van Yssens ventured into Hof Street. When they reached Orange Street the blast of the roaring south-easter was so severe that Douglas and his father had to hold on to Mrs van Yssen to get her across the street while she held her hat down with one hand and her skirt with the other. In the shelter of Government Avenue things were better.

"One forgets how strong this wind can be," van Yssen gasped, once they were in the shelter of the Botanical Gardens. "Let us just stop and think for a moment, and plan the best route to the University Hall from here."

"We'll just go left at the top of Queen Victoria Street," Douglas said, "It's quite simple."

Van Yssen was surprised at the number of people who were already in the University Hall. He waited for his wife to return from the cloakroom, where she had gone to rearrange herself.

The graduands sat in their appointed seats. "I am afraid you will have to excuse me, please. Enjoy the proceedings," Douglas said. As he turned to go and join the other graduands, Frances Rose and her parents entered the auditorium. She waved cheerfully at him and he went to greet her.

"It's a pity about the wind, Douglas," the Judge said.

"Yes indeed it is. How are you Judge, Mrs Rose?" He smiled at Frances. "It is so nice to see you, Frances."

"Oh we are fine, thank you Douglas. It is quite an occasion, both of you graduating on the same day. We are looking forward to meeting your parents," Mrs Rose said warmly.

"They are just over there."

Van Yssen got up as Douglas and the Roses approached. Douglas introduced his parents. "Douglas has told us all about you. You must be very proud of him. We are looking forward to having you to lunch today," the Judge said.

"Yes we are indeed," Mrs Rose added.

Frances stood back, examining his parents, her head slightly to one side. Her eyes went up and down his father and then his mother. She was embarrassed when Douglas caught her eye.

"Douglas tells me that you have really distinguished yourself, Miss Rose."

"Do call her Frances, my good fellow," the Judge laughed. "Next thing you'll want me to call your son Mr van Yssen! I think we should get to our seats."

It was like being in church. Silence fell on the Congregation. His Excellency the Governor-General, the Earl of Athlone, appeared on the stage, followed by a procession: the Vice-Chancellor and Principal Sir Carruthers Beattie, the Chairman of the Council the Reverend Russell, the Deans of the eight faculties, and the Registrar.

Van Yssen shared his programme with his wife. The Vice-Chancellor stepped up to the lectern to constitute the Congregation. The Congregation rose as the organist played the introductory notes to the National Anthem. The graduands sang above the others, with the ebullience and relief of people who were at last seeing their destination after an arduous journey. After the Prayer, the Dean of the Medical Faculty, Professor Jolly, addressed the Congregation and made an impassioned plea for more research work.

The University Scholarships and Prizes were received. Parents were filled with pride and the recipients pleaded modesty.

It was the turn of those upon whom Master of Arts Degrees would be conferred: Anatomy, English, French (both with distinctions) amidst much hand-clapping, German, Hebrew. Douglas heard his name. He had butterflies in his solar plexus. "Henry Douglas van Yssen, Master of Arts in History, *Cum Laude*." He glanced at his parents. His father's eyes were filled with tears. His mother smiled. He looked at Frances. She was crying while her mother and the Judge were amused at her discomfort. There was thunderous applause when he was capped. His graceful movements were unaffected, elegant in his dark grey flannel suit, at ease in the illustrious company on the stage.

"He is an exceptional scholar," the Judge whispered to his wife.

"So is Frances."

"I know."

Frances was awarded her Bachelor of Arts Degree with distinctions in English and Latin. Douglas applauded enthusiastically with loud claps of his large energetic hands. It remained only for the two Honorary Doctorates to be awarded and the dissolution by the Vice Chancellor.

The orderly way in which the Congregation had sat in their rows became a bustle as the congregants alighted from their creaking wooden seats, releasing more fragrances of soap and perfume from their warm bodies. Parents went to embrace their offspring, started conversations, and generously congratulated others, hoping to receive even more congratulations in return. Frances went over to the van Yssens and gave Douglas a quick girlish hug.

"My congratulations to you Frances, two distinctions, my, how wonderful," van Yssen said as he shook her hand.

"And my heartiest congratulations Frances," Mrs van Yssen added.

"So what do you think of your son's achievement?" Frances asked

"We are so proud of him, thank you."

Van Yssen looked to see where the Roses were so that he could congratulate them. The Judge was in conversation with Athlone while Mrs Rose was exchanging pleasantries with Princess Alice. Athlone moved towards the entrance. They were approaching the van Yssens. The Judge moved to one side. "Let me introduce you – His Excellency the Governor-General, the Earl of Athlone, and Princess Alice, this is Mr and Mrs van Yssen." They shook hands with the Governor-General and his wife.

"How do you do," Athlone said, followed by Princess Alice.

"How do you do," the van Yssens replied.

"Your son has really distinguished himself, has he not?" Princess Alice smiled.

"Thank you," van Yssen said.

"The van Yssens are having lunch with us today," Judge Rose announced.

"That sounds like a capital idea to me," Athlone replied. "My heartiest congratulations to you," he said, shaking Douglas' hand. "You must have a fine career ahead of you."

Van Yssen felt a tap on his shoulder. It was the old President Reitz. "I thought I recognised you Albert, and you Anneke, and then when I heard your son's name, well, well, what a fine surprise. How marvellous to see you again after all these years." Turning to Athlone and the Judge he said, "Our families had close ties in the Free State, and now young Henry has done so very well; my congratulations to you, my boy."

"Thank you very much," Douglas said, "but we really ought to congratulate you, President Reitz."

"Ag, it is nothing, they just weren't sure how much longer I will be around, so they thought they would be kind to me before I finally depart! How long will you be staying Albert?"

"Only until tomorrow, President Reitz."

"More is the pity," Reitz said, "I would have liked to have you over. Do come and visit us when next you are in Cape Town." After Athlone and Princess Alice had shaken hands with Reitz, and the Roses had also congratulated him, Reitz slowly made his way to the entrance.

Athlone and his wife said their formal goodbyes and left with their entourage.

"I am feeling jolly hungry," the Judge announced. "We should get going now. We look forward to having you to lunch."

Frances waved a little goodbye.

Outside the wind was fiercer than ever as the van Yssens made their way back to the hotel. The taxi had been ordered for twelve thirty. Van Yssen and Douglas dashed to the men's cloakroom where they urinated heartily. Van Yssen combed his hair. "I must say to your credit, you have made really excellent friends, Douglas. It will do your career no end of good. Frances is a very attractive girl."

Douglas found it uncomfortable to speak about Frances in the cloakroom, and grinned.

The taxi dropped the van Yssens outside the City Club in Queen Victoria Street at five to one. Van Yssen looked up at the Mountain, and said, "van Donck and the devil are busy up there. The cloth lies heavily on the Mountain."

A concierge opened the door for them and escorted them into the lounge where the Roses were waiting. Judge Rose got up, "A hearty welcome to you on this special day for our young people. Do come and sit down. Mrs van Yssen, if you would like to sit with my wife. You and I can have a good chat, van Yssen, and we'll leave Douglas to entertain Frances. What will you have to drink? I am having a gin and my wife is having vermouth and soda."

A waiter stood ready.

"I would like to have some bottled ginger beer, please," van Yssen said to the Judge.

"And I will have some lemonade," Mrs van Yssen replied.

"Douglas tells us that you will be returning to Oudtshoorn tomorrow," Mrs Rose said to Mrs van Yssen. "You should have stayed a few more days. There is so much to do here, and to see. But, then I forget, you have probably done all that."

"We like coming here but Albert is so busy in his practice. He does not have any partners. The entire burden of his work is on his shoulders. And besides it is already December. The holidays have started and Christmas will be here before we know."

Frances and Douglas stood at the window. The Judge turned to van Yssen, "Colleagues of mine have been to Oudtshoorn for Circuit Court sittings, and I have been through the town on occasions. We will in fact be going quite close by there in a few days from now when we travel to Plettenberg Bay. How long have you been there?"

"If you mean in Oudtshoorn? I saw an opportunity there towards the end of the nineties. The town was beginning to boom, which meant that there was a strong demand for surveying work; there always is when places grow, when subdivisions are required, farm boundaries have to be determined, roads are built. Things were not that easy during the war, and the slump in 1921."

"Where did you study?"

"Oh here in Cape Town, like Douglas, here in the Gardens. It brings back so many memories. The old South African College, the Egyptian Building, the Lioness Gate. What fun we had, but I had to work hard."

"I have always had a healthy respect for mathematicians. I was reasonable at it but it never was my strongest suit. As it has turned out I have been better at lawsuits!" And he laughed.

"It intrigues me why some people are so much better at languages and related subjects while others are stronger in mathematics as though there is a kind of mutual exclusion. Why do you think that is?" van Yssen asked.

"Yes it is strange. I suppose it is like asking why the horse is different in appearance from the zebra. It is just one of those things."

"When will you be leaving for Plettenberg Bay?"

"Early on Friday morning. I will be driving myself. I quite enjoy the adventure. On Friday evening we shall stop with Elizabeth's cousin at Swellendam. On Saturday and Sunday we shall stay over in George, and do the final leg of the journey early on Monday morning."

"Interestingly enough," van Yssen commented, "Reitz was born in Swellendam."

"I know that you have mentioned it, but when will you be leaving for your holiday?" Douglas asked Frances.

"On Friday. We'll be there on Monday. I so wish you could have spent a few days with us at the seaside. It would have been frightfully nice to go for walks along the beach."

"Yes it would have been wonderful, but, I suppose I am going to be confined to Oudtshoorn until school starts."

Mrs Rose was in close conversation with Mrs van Yssen. "Oh, we have made the journey so many times that the preparation for it has become almost routine. I now even have a permanent reminder list so that nothing can be overlooked. Jeremy works very hard for most of the year and I have to ensure that he has no unnecessary burdens. I do so enjoy staying in the hotel at George,"

A waiter appeared. "Your table is ready, Sir," he said addressing the Judge.

"Well I suppose we had better go through," the Judge said.

"Have you managed to do some shopping?" Mrs Rose asked Mrs van Yssen.

"Yes, thank you, just a few little things. I wanted to get some Christmas things for Douglas and Albert, but I couldn't while they accompanied me. I shall have some time on my own this afternoon."

The Judge got up, and put his glass down on the small table next to him. "Shall I lead the way?"

The Judge had his own table at the Club. It stood strategically in a corner of the dining room where there was less traffic, and offered a good view of the Botanical Gardens.

There was a set menu: leek and onion soup to start with, followed by baked fish, roast beef and assorted vegetables, bread pudding, cheese and biscuits, toast with anchovies, and coffee.

"I have ordered some champagne, to celebrate the occasion," the Judge said once they were seated. "In the meantime have a look at the menu." He turned to the waiter, "I'll start with the soup."

Champagne glasses were brought to the table and the wine waiter presented a bottle of *Du Petit Caporal Grand Mousseux* to the Judge. He felt the temperature of the bottle and nodded. The waiter opened the bottle without allowing the cork to pop and poured some for the Judge. He tasted it, sucked his cheeks in and indicated with a patting of his hand on the table and a deep nod of his head that he was more than satisfied. When all the glasses had been charged the Judge raised his glass, "This is indeed an auspicious occasion. It is a great privilege for me to propose a toast to the academic success of Douglas and Frances, and to their graduation today."

"Hear, hear," van Yssen said and his wife smiled demurely.

"And my heartiest congratulations," Mrs Rose added.

The Judge took a good sip of his champagne, moved it about with his tongue and his cheeks, and swallowed it with pursed lips. "Hm, from Reims…" he said, and glanced approvingly at the little corporal standing dutifully on the label. "Good suggestion by that fellow. He considers himself a bit of a *sommelier*, and to judge by this, possibly with good reason."

The women decided not to have soup. The Judge sprinkled croûtons over his soup, and generously buttered a slice of Melba toast. Douglas followed suit, but his father declined both the croûtons and the toast. Van Yssen was careful with the champagne and Mrs van Yssen took chaste little sips, mindful of what the French woman had said about wine. Mrs Rose savoured the sensuous grassiness of the liquid and the mixture of acids and tannins that cleansed her mouth. She allowed the bubbles to tickle the sensitive areas inside her lips. "A week from now we will be dining at the seaside," she observed dreamily.

"From what Reitz said, you must be from the Free State?" the Judge asked van Yssen.

"Yes, near Fauresmith. My grandfather farmed in the district and my father was an attorney there."

"The Free State has produced some good jurists. Did you ever consider doing law?"

"From the time I started school I liked working with figures. I suppose engineering was the other discipline I could have followed. I like the precision of mathematics; the fact that it is as it is, and is not subject to different interpretations, unless of course you get into the more abstract or philosophical aspects of mathematics. At that level it is the language of ideas. At my level it is either right or wrong. I think Douglas would have made a good mathematician, but I fear that I might have turned his interest off by being too enthusiastic about it. I must confess, I do enjoy history; world affairs."

"How do you see the current state of the world?"

"I think it will take very many years for the effects of the war to disappear. Then there is Versailles, that at times seemed so reasonable, that continues to produce unintended consequences. What impact it will have on the Union remains to be seen. I sometimes worry about the Communists."

"The Germans needed to be taught a lesson, don't you think Douglas?" the Judge said somewhat challengingly.

Douglas had to avoid controversy. "Oh gosh, I was not really paying attention."

"Your father was talking about the consequences of the war."

"Let us have a happy day, dear," Mrs Rose suggested. "After all, we cannot undo the things of the past, and we cannot stop the consequences. We should go into the future with hope. In a few years from now all will be clear to us. It is like forecasting the weather. All we can hope for is good weather. And we are off on holiday soon."

"Let us hear what Douglas has to say, dear."

Douglas was compelled to respond. "I think Churchill was correct in his approach to avoid an Anglo-French Entente. It would only have antagonised the Germans more. It was the best solution for agreement to be reached among all three parties."

"Even though the Germans had not fulfilled all their obligations?" the Judge frowned.

"Yes, that is true," Douglas said, "but it was better for France and Germany to sort out their differences, and that is after all what Churchill told Doumerge. The Germans are still insecure about the territories that they lost in the east, it is like a large wound that is reluctant to heal. It was clever of Churchill to make sure that he always acted in keeping with the League Protocol. That way he had moral high ground. Everything had to be done to avoid another conflict."

"How do you see the agreement between the Germans and the Russians?" his father asked.

"In some ways it is worrying, especially if one is to believe the speculations in the press that the Russians are assisting the Germans in more sinister ways. And let us not discount, or perhaps I should say ignore, the tensions caused by anti-Americanism."

"That is the product of the politics of envy," the Judge said. "Europe does not like the prosperity that flourishes in America. Coolidge said as much in his Armistice Day speech. It was a carefully crafted and well-considered message, and I am afraid he was right. They might have lots of gangsters in America, but the distrust and suspicion that have spread their tentacles through Europe since the War are almost as nefarious."

Van Yssen was not sure where the discussion was heading, and it made him feel insecure. He wondered what the time was but dared not look at his watch. Frances smiled at him. "Are you looking forward to your holiday?" he asked.

"Oh, immensely!"

"How will you spend your time at Plettenberg Bay?" Mrs van Yssen asked.

"Well," Frances said with a warm smile and a sideways glance at Douglas, "I shall read, go for lots of walks along the beach, do some bathing. We'll play cards in the evening, listen to music – Daddy takes gramophone records along. I might even have the odd game of chess against my father. We sometimes spend the morning on the beach under umbrellas, and have tea there. It is lovely. I have some letters to write."

"It is quite astonishing how quickly time passes when one is on holiday," Mrs Rose observed. "As a child I spoilt many a good holiday by being concerned that it would end too soon. First there was my eager anticipation for the holiday to start, especially the holidays at the seaside. I sometimes had such nervous exhaustion the night before we were due to depart, that I woke up with such a blinding headache the next morning I hardly knew anything of the journey. We invariably got sunburnt at the beginning and spent a whole day or two indoors while we recovered. Then the counting of the remaining days began, like counting the number of sweets left in a packet. So the remaining days contained anticipation of regret, and were spoilt instead of being left to spend themselves generously."

The Judge laughed. "My wife's recollections of her childhood are charming as is the way she recounts her innocent times."

Van Yssen took his turn. "You remind me of the summer holidays we used to have as children. It was a great trek to the seaside, a great adventure. For some or other reason that was never clear to me, my father liked to go to Port Elizabeth, possibly because he liked playing golf there. We stayed in a hotel on the beachfront, which was wonderful for my mother, because she did not have to bother about cooking, or housekeeping. It was a treat to eat hotel food. My brother and I shared a room and my parents another room. There are some very good beaches for swimming, when the wind is not blowing."

"Do you play golf, van Yssen?" the Judge asked.

"My father tried to encourage me, but I have little natural aptitude."

"Albert is being modest. From all accounts he played quite well as a young man, but he is a perfectionist and if he is not going to be totally accomplished at something he would rather not do it at all."

"One is never totally accomplished at golf. That is the charm of the game. When last did you play?" the Judge asked.

"Oh, years and years ago. I cannot even remember what I did with my sticks."

"They're in the loft above the garage," his wife replied.

"Douglas tells me that you are a regular player, Judge," van Yssen said.

"I try to play once a week, usually on a Saturday afternoon."

"Daddy is a very competitive player," Frances said.

"That does not mean that I am very good. If the handicap is correct anyone can be competitive."

"I think we should teach Douglas to play," Frances suggested.

Douglas shook his head boyishly.

The meal was entering the torpid stage and there was still dessert and the cheese to come. Eagerness to converse gave way to languor. The Judge had doggedly eaten his way through the menu and washed his food down with the champagne that the others refused. He was already on leave, and the chauffeur would take him home to have an afternoon sleep.

"I think we should have our coffee in the lounge, it is more comfortable there," the Judge suggested. "Would you like a cigar, van Yssen? I know Douglas does not smoke."

"No thank you, Judge."

Shortly before three the Roses and the van Yssens prepared to leave the Club. The women made their way to the ladies retiring room on the first floor. Once they were all assembled, they said their goodbyes and wished each other merry Christmas.

"Elizabeth and I are so glad that you could have lunch with us," the Judge said, now quite red in the face, with the aroma of cigar smoke clinging to him.

"It was kind of you to invite us. We do appreciate it very much. We are pleased too that Frances has done so well. We hope to see more of you, Frances. We bid you a safe and uneventful journey to Plettenberg Bay, Judge, and wish you all a happy and restful holiday. Thank you again for your hospitality and for the excellent meal."

"Oh my dear fellow it was a great pleasure. I am sure you are more than pleased with your son's achievement. Travel well. And by the way, if you do have the chance, Douglas, do come and say hello while we are down there."

Frances and Douglas shook hands and she stood on one leg and gave him a small hug. While the Roses waved goodbye, the van Yssens went out into the wind to their waiting taxi.

◆

Chapter Three

Friday 3 December 1926

THE TRAIN DESCENDED from the Outeniqua Mountains into the Oudtshoorn basin. The cool air of the mountains gradually turned into dry afternoon summer heat and dust. Where the curved railway line made its way towards the station the leaves of sad dusty pepper trees stirred sullenly in a listless afternoon breeze. It was four o'clock in the afternoon.

Fourie was waiting on the platform. He took the luggage from the porter and fetched Douglas' trunk from the goods van. "His books will come by goods train," van Yssen said.

Douglas was again in his familiar surroundings, reminded of things he could not remember. It was different now. His career was about to begin. There was Frances. Her soft blond hair, little freckles across her nose, her bright green eyes. The journey had inspired his sentiments. He was inspired by the anticipation of his new career. At last he would be earning his own money, and be in a position to purchase a new bicycle – a Humber or a Rudge. He thought of Frances, of the end of term dance, of kissing her; the perfume of the flowers at night in the Botanical Gardens; her hair against his face, holding clammy hands and saying goodnight at midnight at her house, while her father's chauffeur waited, his back discreetly turned. She was so vulnerable. How would she cope on her own in Graaff Reinet?

"What are you thinking about, Douglas?" his mother asked.

He did not reply.

She leant forward and put her hand on his shoulder, "Did you hear me, Douglas?"

"Yes, I think so, what did you say, Ma?"

"It seems you are a long way away."

"Yes, I was just sitting and wondering."

"The Roses are fine people." van Yssen remarked. "I was very proud of you."

Douglas released himself from his preoccupations, and observed the passing houses. The asphalt surface of the road was blistered. People leant fecklessly over veranda railings and front walls of limestone houses. It was an afternoon of no teeth and braces and shirts without collars and yawning till eyes watered. Their white bare feet hurt when they went to see if the figs had started to ripen. Old women with hair on their chins filled their corsets and sweated with their legs apart while they fanned themselves with fly swatters and their chameleon eyes missed not a single thing that was worth pernicious gossip. It was an afternoon of sleep remembered and slops in pails that stood in darkening rooms next to untidy beds. To the west lay the river, a mere stream in summer; a long trail of mucous stretching from the mountains to the sea. Already shadows were growing longer and the vegetation on the banks of the river became darker green, as the first strains of cooler air drifted across the tasselled tops of the reeds.

"It is a long way for Judge Rose to travel to Plettenberg Bay, for their summer holiday," van Yssen thought aloud.

Betta made supper early. Van Yssen said grace rather longer than usual. He thanked the Lord that they were all together, that they had travelled safely, that they were all well. He asked God to bless the servants. They ate in the silence that follows a journey.

"So you said Garnett is doing well? I'd like to go and say hello to him this evening."

"I think he is doing very well, he is so popular. People like him. Besides he is caring. Always jolly, and likes a joke or two. He has a lot of sympathy for others." van Yssen observed. "Good bedside manner. Give him our best regards, tell him to come and visit."

Douglas went to his room to put on his walking shoes. His mind began to wander, and he stopped tying the laces. Sitting on his bed with his one leg across the knee of the other, his eyes fixed, he thought of Frances. He smelled the heavy jasmine scent of the night and imagined holding her head and her fragrant hair and perfume against him.

It was just more than a mile to the Nels' house. The western horizon was pink and orange-red. Overhead the blue of the sky was more intense. A large full moon was rising in the east. He would soon be able to see his shadow in the moonlight. How would he describe Frances to Garnett? What was she doing now? He felt the pleasant pulling of his leg muscles. He imagined her sitting in the setting sun on the veranda of their house at Plettenberg Bay reading her book. He had never been there. The Judge in his grey flannels and cream coloured shirt. It would be nice if he could visit her. He approached the river. The frogs were quiet. They used to be so noisy. He took his nose between his forefinger and his thumb and blew to clear his Eustachian tubes. His eardrums popped. An evening wind stirred the seed at the tops of the reeds. If he held his breath and listened closely he could hear them rustling, and the frogs.

He crossed the suspension bridge and went up Church Street hill. He turned left into Queen Street. Up past the Anglican Church and the public library. He was silent among his books, enclosed in his own intellectual world. *A (ab), absque, coram, de, palam, clam, cum, ex or e.* Twenty-three uses of the ablative. Further up along the street of churches where a reluctant unmusical child practised the piano. The dissonance of false notes irritated him. Bach's mathematical progression. Perhaps it is the way the universe was designed: concord, order and harmony. Woodrow Wilson, political economist, the remarkable clarity of his generalisation. Work and thought. He died in his sleep. Less than two years ago now, a delicate man. My legs feel good. Bismarck had thick ankles. He smelled the flowers of the frangipani tree at the gate to Gotland House before he saw it. He looked up at the synagogue constructed of sandstone, the English Schul. Rabbi Woolf from London out. High walls like a fortress to protect against undesirable influences. Eastern European architectural features set it apart from all the other places of worship. The sharp Gothic spires of the Dutch Reformed Church pointed upwards, always infinitely beseeching. The Shul stopped where its roof ended. The jail appeared on his right. Not much further now. In the distance the Swartberge loomed, dark foundry-grey against the night sky, a majestic, ancient dorsal fold in the earth's crust, the faithful source of innocent water.

The Nels were on their front veranda. Uncle Charlie the imperialist was holding forth about Versailles and Smuts. Old Louis was smoking a cigarette, half listening, and mostly thinking about Honiball's Ostrich Pills. It pays to advertise. Has been a few years now, since the boom. The ostrich business must come back, sometime. Louis searched for a point of contention. A legal mind must have a debate.

Louis and Uncle Charlie heard footsteps in the gravel. They peered into the dark.

"Good evening Uncle Louis, Uncle Charlie."

"Hello Douglas, gosh it's good to see you." Louis had been rescued from his monologue.

"Evening Douglas, welcome home." Uncle Charlie held out his hand.

"Is Garnett at home?"

"He's in the kitchen, with his mother. You know the way."

"Douglas! You rascal! How wonderful to see you!" Garnett exclaimed in his jolly way. They hugged each other.

"When did you arrive? I saw your father in town, before they left for Cape Town. He told me the wonderful news. *Cum Laude*. It's marvellous."

"I have to go to the surgery Douglas. Come along and tell me all your news." They left the house through the back door.

"Good night Mrs Nel. Nice to be back at home. See you soon. I had better go and say goodnight to your dad."

"Don't get caught up there."

Garnett waited for Douglas. "Do get in." The mudguards of Garnett's new Chevrolet gleamed in the moonlight.

"This is a lovely car, Garnie. When did you get it?"

"About a month ago. I do a great deal of driving in the district and my transport has to be reliable, especially for the visits to the farms."

Garnett parked his car outside the surgery. "Come inside Douglas, I don't have anything to do here, I just wanted to get away from all that squabbling at home." Douglas looked at the brass plate next to the entrance to the surgery. Dr Garnett Nel, BA MB ChB BAO.

"I'm going to make us some tea."

Garnett sipped his tea. "Tell me now Douglas, how are things going with that girl of yours? Have you at least managed to get her nice and hot and panting?"

"No, it's not like that. She's a very special person."

"You didn't say much when you were here in June."

"I wasn't sure whether she was really interested in me, but I must say that things have been a bit different recently."

"How are you going to manage to see her now that you're back here permanently?"

"They are holidaying at Plettenberg Bay."

"I would very much like to meet the woman. You will ultimately need my stamp of approval. Why don't we go and visit her, I need to run the car in properly. I must just see how soon I can get away. I'll speak to Lamprecht. I'm sure he won't mind. With the end of the year looming, the sooner we get back the better."

"You're pulling my leg, I know you."

"I'm darn serious. I need to get away. I'll do a spot of fishing. Hurter's house is bound to be free – it nearly always stands empty. I'll ring him tomorrow. We'll stop off to see the Leibners at Kaaimans. It will be fun, and besides, I want to have a look at that girl of yours. Has she got nice legs?"

"Please don't make fun of me. I'm smitten."

"Her old man is the Judge, isn't he?" The telephone rang. "It must be my mother. When? Why wasn't I told earlier? No, I never got any message. I'll be there right away." Garnett poured the rest of his tea into the washbasin. "They need me at the hospital. Perdepoot Schoeman's child is suffering from acute appendicitis. Lamprecht diagnosed it earlier. He wants me to operate immediately. Diemont is waiting to do the anaesthetic. Come, let's go. I'll give you a lift to the hospital."

"How long will it take Garnie?"

"The operation itself should not take more than about fifteen minutes. It's the preparation, and the time it will take for the boy to recover; it'll probably be about two hours in all. I'll 'phone you in the morning." The car went up the hill past the tennis club.

"Were you serious about going to Plettenberg Bay?"

"Of course I am! I know what it means to you. And I can't wait to see your girl. We'll talk about it in the morning. You've had a long day, and mine is about to start all over again."

"How will we let them know that we are coming?"

"The police at Plettenberg are bound to know that the Judge is there. We'll send a message via them."

"I can't believe that we're going to see Frances. I'm so damn grateful to you, Garnett."

"I'll 'phone Hurter in the morning about the house."

They entered the gate of the Royal South Cape Hospital and stopped at the front entrance. Garnett's face was serious. "See you tomorrow, Douglas? I must go now."

"I'll wait to hear from you in the morning. And good luck with the operation."

Garnett went into the subdued light of the solemn hospital corridor. The evening silence of the sick was palpable. He inhaled a blend of floor polish, surgical spirit, ether and illness and cooked food. He would make the first incision two to three inches long, probably less because it was a child, crossing McBurney's spot, or a little below it, parallel to the outer end of Poupart's ligament; fibres of the internal oblique and transversalis muscles divided together by a transverse incision. Avoid the motor nerves. First examine the child. Preliminary injection of morphia and atropine. Prefer ether. Cardiac stimulant. The open method, the child will be terrified of the mask.

Dr Diemont was already in the ward, sitting on the bed next to the boy, full of empathy, white haired, experienced, steady, taking his pulse. He glanced at Garnett over his spectacles and blinked a silent friendly welcome. It was a good thing that Diemont was there, he knew what he was doing. Garnett went to change in a room next to the operating theatre. He removed his outdoor clothes and donned an operating suit consisting of a soft white shirt, white drill trousers and a pair of clean shoes. He purified his hands and arms in a solution of bionide of mercury in methylated spirit, and then in a sublimate. He finally put on a sterilized operating gown reaching to his wrists, a sterilized cap and mask covering his whole face except his eyes, and sterilized thin rubber gloves reaching over the lower end of his sleeves. He preferred them to cotton gloves.

It was not necessary to shave the Schoeman child – he was only eleven. A theatre sister painted his lower abdominal region with a solution of iodine in rectified spirit.

The morphia and atropine were taking effect when the child was wheeled into the operating theatre. Dr Diemont employed a Schimmelbusch's mask covered with five layers of Turkey towelling. He placed a strip of gamgee tissue on the boy's face so that the metal portions of the mask rested in the tissue. A second piece with a hole cut out of the centre was placed on top of the mask. He dropped ether onto the mask at a sharp rate. "Breathe slowly and deeply, my child." With that he increased the rate of dropping gradually until there was virtually a constant stream of drops onto the mask. The child struggled, Garnett and the theatre sisters held him firmly. He began breathing deeply, his respirations became more regular, until automatic respiration indicated that he was under.

The area of the operation was surrounded by mackintoshes that in turn were covered with dry sterilised towels, fixed to the skin by means of towel clips. Garnett indicated where he was going to make the first incision, and more iodine solution was painted over that area. Diemont nodded that he was ready.

Once he was comfortable with the child's recovery, Garnett showered and changed. He went outside and hesitated before descending the front steps. He looked up into the night sky, at the stars and the yellow moon. How miraculous it was. He straightened his black and white striped silk tie. He patted the pocket of his coarsely woven white Eton styled jacket to find his car keys attached to a catenated copper chain and a cork.

The Nels' house was in darkness. Quarrelsomeness had given way to fitful snoring in hot stale night air. Louis lay with his back to his wife, as far away from her as possible. It was a lawyer's right to quarrel. Touching her could be construed as an approach, and an approach could be interpreted as an apology, an admission of guilt.

Garnett undressed. He carefully hung his clothes on two hangers, put shoe trees into his shoes, brushed his teeth, and got into bed. He thought of Douglas' girl. He imagined the road as it approached the Montagu Pass, the dark water of the Kaaimans River, the endless stretches of sand of the Wilderness beach and the sea and intestines with an angry red inflamed appendix protruding into an innocent small abdominal cavity held between bony hips. Blessed is the Lord who made the night stars. Sleep came over him like a shadow of cloud.

Chapter Four

Tuesday 7 December 1926

GARNETT FETCHED DOUGLAS shortly after five in the morning. An Indian cane fishing rod was tied to the passenger side of the car so that Douglas had to get in from the driver's side. Douglas wore a brightly coloured checked shirt, a bottle green hand-knitted pullover, a tweed jacket and brown gabardine trousers. Garnett had on his hunting jacket with leather patches on the elbows, a cream woollen shirt and grey flannel trousers. Douglas put his small leather suitcase next to Garnett's brown Gladstone bag.

Douglas had slept fitfully because of his excitement. His eyes felt as though they had grit in them. He was tired and nervous. He yawned. Garnett was in high spirits – he loved to motor. In front of them lay the George Road; beyond it the mountains and the coast. The flavours that came from the picnic basket told of tomato and meat sandwiches, of hard boiled eggs. The early morning air was cool.

The eastern sky was becoming lighter. The car crossed the red steel bridge over the Oliphants River, and passed Bakenskraal with its tall Cypress trees and green lucerne fields. A sand-coloured gravel road stretched out before them. It disappeared over the next hill, reappeared beyond it, and grew ever narrower over successive hills. The sides of the road had become built up into powdery ridges by graders that periodically scraped away the corrugations and resurfaced the road. Endless wire fences flanked the road, their runners, posts and wires and the vegetation beyond them covered in pale dust.

"Have you let the Judge know that we are coming, Douglas?" Garnett asked.

"I had to telephone the Plettenberg police and ask them to take a message to them. Hope they have done so, but then, they should be quite reliable I suppose."

"You could not have done more, and if they don't get the message, it will be a nice surprise for Frances."

"A surprise like that would hardly seem appropriate to the Roses. And what happens if there's some other fellow around? Could be embarrassing."

"Don't be stupid, Douglas, you would have known by now if there was anybody else."

"Things happen on holiday Garnie. We'll have to see."

"What have you been up to in the last few days?"

"Ag, reading, thinking about my work for next year. And talking about reading, my mother kept a review for me of Pauline Smith's latest book that was in the *Courant*."

"What is it called?"

"*The Beadle*."

"What is it about?"

"It's about a nicely disguised bit of scandal. According to the review, the Beadle in the book is an unmarried sharecropper who lives with two elderly sisters, Jacoba and Johanna and their small niece, Andrina. It seems as though it must have been somewhere up near Schoemanshoek. The niece is the Beadle's child. In his hypocritical way he hides it."

"My dad knew Dr Smith quite well. He considered him a real patrician – nice expression. He died in a London Hotel when he went to visit his wife and the two girls. She must have heard lots of stories from him. It was a great loss to the town when he died."

"My parents still speak of him. How he was the driving force behind the dramatic society, and the fun they had at his Gilbert and Sullivan productions. She will be arriving in Cape Town about the end of this month."

"Who?"

"Pauline Smith."

"My dad spoke of such a scandal. The old chap was a real dissembler. Pinched the cat in the dark, but God help you if you did what he did. People are bound to try and piece the real story together."

"Small town critics are always in awe of anyone who manages to have a book published. The review was pathetic: saying it would enrich the reputation of its author, that it has sympathetic and true to life touches and a plot that is mildly melodramatic. Shit. Scratching around for words as though he was trying to outdo the work he was reviewing. Bloody arse, he should rather have restrained himself." Douglas threw his head back and laughed heartily at his own dissonant humour. "I can't say that I really like her work. Quaint for Oudtshoorn, but not really up to world standards." His voice vibrated as the body of the car shivered furiously over corrugations. Garnett moved onto more even surfaces.

At the foot of the mountain the road turned east. The vegetation began to change. Karroo scrub turned into fine bush. Delicate early light illuminated the mountain. A stone cottage on the side of the road reminded Garnett of the tollhouse at the bottom of the pass, and his well-manicured fingers confirmed that he had put money into his fob pocket.

"We'll have breakfast at the bridge." Douglas was not listening.

They left George and headed for Kaaimans River. Douglas would have preferred not to visit the Leibners. He daydreamed of his images of affection with thickening passion: her shape in her soft foulard dress, her fair features, her green dreamy bright eyes, the pink mouth, strong white teeth in innocent clear saliva. The road was a pale chalky colour. The vegetation was alive, filled with the renewing green vigour of summer, drawing their sap from the earth. Small soft puffy clouds floated westwards over the undulating coastal hills. The day was growing warmer. Garnett glanced at Douglas. The crew cut, the clean look. Keen grey eyes full of wit. He was so brilliant, yet in some ways naively like a child, guileless, unpretentious.

Before the steep descent to the Kaaimans River, Garnett changed into second gear. The gearbox and differential whined. To their right Garnett caught his first glimpse of the black water of the Kaaimans River. He tapped Douglas on the shoulder and pointed to the water. A breeze drove shivers of silver reflections across the dark water, and stirred the reeds near the causeway. In the distance they could see the blue of the sea, the foaming white surf, and yellow sand at the mouth. They breathed in the soft air of the coast.

Garnett approached the narrow causeway warily. Its surface was barely a metre above the water. Once they were on the opposite bank of the river the Leibners' house became visible across the water. It stood against a hillside and was accessible only by boat. The morning light had reached it; its doors and windows wide open. Large colourful striped towels and bathing costumes were draped across wood and canvas deck-chairs that stood on the veranda that ran along the entire front of house, and around one side. When they were opposite the house Garnett stopped. There was no one in sight. Having breakfast. Or down at the beach. A clinker-built rowing dinghy was tethered to a small jetty in front of the house, its oars shipped. Douglas wished the Leibners were out so that they could proceed to Plettenberg. Garnett peered at the dark openings of the doors and windows. Pale white wood smoke drifted upwards from a chimney at the back of the house.

"Hallo!" Garnett called in a tenor voice.

Dr Leibner heard Garnett's call. He appeared at the front door, stuffing his shirt into his trousers. "Nice to see you," he called. "I'll bring the boat across."

As they waited Garnett and Douglas heard, across the silence of the estuary, the gurgling slapping of water against the hull of the boat, the creaking of rowlocks, and sucking sounds as the oars left the water. Leibner's broad back was towards them, clad in a cream coloured shirt, his sleeves rolled up. He pulled powerfully on the oars, enjoying the vigour of his effort, gauging with sideways glances the distance to the bank. Leibner beached the boat, shipped the oars, and jumped out. He had grown a moustache – a Prussian effort to complement his mensur scars. He looked a bit sheepish, waiting for an appropriate response. Douglas held out his hand.

"How are you Douglas? We've all heard about your success. Congratulations, and well done."

"Thank you Dr Leibner. It is nice to see you again."

Leibner turned to Garnett, "It is decent of you to come and visit us Garnett. We heard you were going to Plettenberg Bay."

"My goodness, but news does travel fast. Where did you hear it?" Garnett replied.

"I saw Hurter two days ago in George. He mentioned you were going into his house to stay for a few days. But come, let's go and have some breakfast. We hoped you would come by and you know how we enjoy having visitors. Get in, Garnett," Leibner said. Garnett and Douglas took off their shoes and rolled up their trouser legs. "Give us a strong shove Douglas, and jump in. Three Men in a Boat, Ja?"

Garnett looked out to sea. From the boat the agitated niveous surf seemed higher than they. He lifted his eyes up towards the house. A familiar large handsome woman, with strong athletic legs and a generous bust appeared. Fair hair sharp blue eyes. Garnett was confused. She looked as though she was astride the veranda, Kortenhoven, the lawyer's, step daughter: passionate, headstrong and self-willed to a point of intractable obstinacy. She watched her virile man returning in the dinghy. He had such energy.

"Is that Mrs Liebenfeld, Dr Leibner?" Asked Garnett.

"Oh yes she and her husband are visiting with us.

Garnett looked out to sea. The first small white horses were appearing on the surface. A pleasant sunny haze filled the coastal air. Leibner shipped the oars noisily and stepped splendidly from the centre seat onto the jetty. There were small beads of perspiration on his forehead. "Tie the boat up well. Do you know from a clove hitch, Douglas?"

"Hello boys! How are you?" hailed Mrs Liebenfeld heartily. "Breakfast is nearly ready. My husband is not feeling well; he has a problem with his leg and is resting in bed. Please excuse him."

Douglas walked up to Leibner and touched him on the arm to get his attention. "Dr Leibner, I need to go for a walk," he whispered in his ear.

"Behind the house, my good fellow"

When Douglas returned, he found Leibner and Garnett were seated on bentwood chairs at a large witels and stinkwood dining room table eating heartily. The meal was at the silent stage. They were concentrating on getting as much of the running fried egg yolks onto bits of bacon before resorting to bread. Percolated coffee was waiting. More bread and pampelmoes marmalade. Eventually Leibner rose from his seat, his cup of coffee in his hand. He burped gently, moved a small piece of bacon from between his teeth with his tongue and swallowed the taste. "Let's have the coffee outside on the veranda."

Chairs creaked, and moved noisily on the wooden floorboards, as everyone rose to follow Leibner outside.

"Who is the girl, Douglas?" Mrs Liebenfeld could not restrain her curiosity any longer.

"Well, I don't think I ought to be presumptuous, Mrs Liebenfeld. We studied together. She's really very nice. Frances Rose."

"Her father must be the Judge. But why are we all standing? Let us sit down and have a good talk," said Leibner enthusiastically. "We have the whole day before us. We have an historian and a doctor who studied overseas. We could have a good discussion about world events, ja, Douglas? How smart do you think now Versailles was, with the benefit of hindsight?"

It was nearly nine o'clock. Douglas began to wonder when they would ever leave. If they started on the consequences of the Treaty of Versailles, things could become drawn out. First there would be gentle sparring – to determine whether a previous quarrel had produced any persuasion. Each side would try to avoid striking the first hard political blow. Inevitably they would be drawn into the temptation of scratching at one another's feelings and then clawing at sensitivities. At the first sight of blood, reason and judgement would depart. The facts, such as they were, would become distorted and adapted to suit the argument. The six years since the last of the peace treaties were concluded had allowed perspectives to become obscured by national interests and the ambitions of individual politicians. The years of hope, that followed the war, had yielded a legacy of hatred. The irony of history: it is always recorded after the events; the facts are too numerous to process; the acceptable truth only emerges once some of the real truth is lost. He hoped they would avoid the subject.

"What is your specific history interest, Douglas?" Mrs Liebenfeld asked.

"I'm interested in modern history, but I like ancient history too."

"Then how do you think things will turn out in Europe, Douglas?" Leibner entreated.

"How was your visit overseas, Mrs Liebenfeld?" Douglas asked.

"The passage between Port Elizabeth and Cape Town was very rough. I did not think I would survive the Atlantic rollers off Agulhas. My husband has a constitution of iron. He spent every moment he could on deck. Up along the west coast it was better, and once we were past the bulge of Africa it was beautiful. Europe in the summer can be very hot. And you think Oudtshoorn can be hot!"

"Let us not hide behind the skirts of the women, Douglas. I value your opinion," Leibner persisted.

Douglas took a deep breath. "My own view is that we cannot ignore the past. The politics of self-interest, of nationalism, are very powerful. Go back a hundred years – a mere three, four generations. Or go back a little further – to before the Napoleonic wars – what is Germany today, then consisted of about eight or nine larger states and over three hundred smaller ones. It is a symptom..."

Leibner interrupted him, "But there were very powerful forces of local German patriotism at work already at that time."

"Yet there was very little German unity."

The sparring had begun. The spectators made themselves comfortable. Douglas continued, "I think one must expect, and concede for that matter, that there will always be some divergence of purpose. Some people wanted to see unity and others not. Remember it was also in the interest of Austria to keep the Confederation of German States weak. It was certainly a disappointment to those who had hoped for greater national unity. On top of it all, by granting constitutions, liberalism took root – and that definitely did not contribute to the unity cause."

Leibner was determined to stand his ground.

"And where did all the liberalism get them? All it got them were *burschenschaften*. My grandfather told us about the Wartburg Festival. Do you know about that, Douglas? The students were burning things – things of Prussian militarism. Things that looked too French – like the corsets the officers wore. Just imagine that. And pigtails worn by the infantry. All went up in smoke and flames. But Metternich took particular notice of that."

"He thought the Tsar was helping to fan the flames."

"But we are getting off the point. Forget about the past, let's look at the future," Leibner directed.

"All I'm saying is that the past must, at least to an extent, determine what will happen in the future," Douglas said. "If we were to look at a map of Europe when Germany was at the height of her power, and then what it looked like after the end of the peace treaties: you can't just redraw boundaries in the way it has been done, without any proper regard to all the old feelings of nationalism, without proper regard to financial and economic interests. That produces instability. And, there was, and still is, far too great an appetite for retribution. What a terrible tangled web of intrigue and confusion."

"Talking about retribution, they called Clemenceau a tiger. He was more like a damn hyena, tugging at a wounded Germany," said Leibner. "I can still see in front of my imagination the newspaper picture taken at the Paris Peace Conference: Wilson, Lloyd George and Clemenceau, all in their black top hats, like going happily to an execution. Presiding over the fate of Germany."

"I think we should at least set Wilson apart from the other two. He could distance himself, if you will forgive the pun, and he did promote the scheme for the League of Nations. I'm not saying it was perfect, but it was ironical that it was the USA who would refuse to ratify the Treaty of Versailles or have anything to do with the League. I think Bolshevism will also still give us a lot of trouble. Look at what has been happening in Russia." Douglas was prepared to throw anything at Leibner just to end the discussion and to get going.

"Smuts promoted the League. There has been so much despair and also outrage in Germany." Mrs Liebenfeld was pleased that she had contributed.

"The Facists will teach the Bolsheviks still a good lesson," Leibner continued. "In Italy they are in control. From all accounts Mussolini is doing a good job there. And after all he was elected. There is now order and discipline and also economically things are looking much better. To think that the Reparations Commission could have expected us to pay more than six billion British pounds. It is madness. Stresemann tried his best to be reasonable, but the damned persistence of the Allies made people mad, made people despair when all their savings evaporated; my cousin used million mark banknotes to paper the walls of his study – it was the cheapest thing. That fool Poincare did not help things either. After the Munich Putsch some people said that that new fellow Hitler is a crackpot. Maybe he is. But, he seems to have something to offer."

Douglas wanted to soften his counterpunch. "Last year's Locarno Pact must surely offer some hope. Briand seems reasonable enough. And with Germany joining the League…"

"Reasonable Frenchmen never last because they do not satisfy that peculiar appetite of the French."

Garnett was silent. Perhaps they should get ready to leave. They had still a long way to go. He thought of the problems in Ireland. Sinn Fein. The 'Irish troubles' they called them. The partitioning. Philip Gibbs was right: the Bolshevik cause was greatly assisted by the disillusionment that the war had produced.

"We really have enjoyed your hospitality, Mrs Liebenfeld," Garnett began.

"You are not already thinking of leaving, my dear fellow," Leibner replied. "We are just getting going and it is not that far to Plettenberg you know."

Garnett took the fob watch from his pocket. "It is getting on for nine thirty. Still a good two and a half hours and I think it would be good if we can get there before lunchtime. Hurter's maid is helping some people from Worcester. We need to find her and give her instructions before she becomes involved in serving lunch, and definitely before she goes off for the afternoon. I'm glad we stopped over."

"It looks to me your mind is made up, Garnett," Leibner sounded disappointed. "You can compensate by dropping in on the way back. We'll still be here for more than three weeks. Come for a whole day. Just drop in, we'll be expecting you when we see you." Mrs Liebenfeld moved forward to say goodbye. She patted Garnett on the shoulder. "It was so nice of the two of you to drop by. I hope you will have a lovely time at Plettenberg. And Douglas, we are all waiting to hear about the young lady."

Leibner had started towards the stone steps leading down to the dinghy. He was muttering to himself and shaking his head. He lifted his left hand and scratched the back of his head. His hair was cut quite short. At the boat he hesitated. He turned to Garnett and Douglas. "When did you say you are coming back?"

"We're not quite sure. But, it will be a few days," Garnett responded.

"Will you come and say hello?" Mrs Liebenfeld asked. She followed them down to the water.

"I'm sure we will," Garnett replied.

Leibner was already in the boat. "Come and get in, boys, let me take you across the water."

Douglas sat in the bow and Garnett at the stern. The wind had freshened. The chop on the water was higher and slapped noisily against the hull of the boat. Leibner was pensive. Douglas was not going to start any conversation. Garnett thought of his parents, of the family squabbles. Leibner avoided Garnett's eyes. He glanced sideways at the approaching shore. Garnett studied Leibner's movements. He was large and serious. His eyes were pale blue. His hair very dark grey. The mensur scars on his forehead. What courage. Leibner occupied much space. A powerful energy field like this would live a long time. It was difficult to get close to him. Perhaps even his passion was distant. He must be terrible if he ever lost his temper.

Douglas was relieved once they were on their way. He had never been to Plettenberg Bay. The name produced its own associations. Would Frances wear a bathing costume? What were her legs like? Would there be a gap at the top? Real love could cope with anything.

The tide had started to flow. Blue-green water from the sea was invading the Kaaimans River and diluting its dark brown water. At the end of the headland, the road turned left. Garnett hooted and slowed down to take the bend. As the bonnet of the car swept eastwards, they looked down at the cream coloured beaches bordered by olive green vegetation sprawled in bright sunlight, where the surf flowed onto the sand like lace continuously replicating itself, and beyond that, the sparkling blue of the sea. They smelled the sea and heard the pleading cries of gulls that soared in updrafts. In the distance lay the lakes, their water dark from the humic acids leached from beds of leaves that covered ancient forest floors.

The car travelled more easily down the hill towards Wilderness village. Garnett turned to Douglas, "I'm glad we avoided having too serious a discussion with Leibner. He's never been comfortable with Uncle Charlie's attitude and sees me as belonging to that camp. Did you hear what I said, Douglas?"

"Yes, I'm listening, but I don't know what to say. Instead of bringing order and peace and stability to Europe the 'war to end all wars' seems to have led to more instability these last five or six years than could ever have been imagined. I can understand Leibner's sensitivity, and his pride. He's a proud man. Getting involved with the Kortenhovens has not made things any simpler."

Chapter Five

GARNETT AND DOUGLAS drove into Plettenberg Bay at twenty to one in the afternoon. There were white horses on the sea. Not good fishing weather. They headed for the police station.

"Good afternoon Sergeant, I'm Doctor Nel from Oudtshoorn."

"Ah, good afternoon Doctor, you've come for Mr Hurter's keys. One moment, they're in the safe." The hefty sergeant with broad flat hips, his shiny blue serge tunic held securely in place by a polished Sam Brown, heaved his bandy legs around to change direction, his toes pointing inwards, and made his way over creaking floorboards towards the safe. He grunted as he knelt on one knee to open the safe door. "We got the message for Judge Rose. They are in the fourth house down from Hurter, further along to Robberg."

Hurter's house was situated on the dunes that overlooked the bay. It had a faded red corrugated iron roof, and walls of cast concrete imprinted with the grain of the wood used as shuttering. In places on the outer surfaces, pieces of seashell protruded. A veranda ran around the house. The walls had been washed with cream-coloured Murallo. A large white solitary seagull sat motionless on the chimney, his beak pointing into the wind. Douglas took it to be a good omen.

Garnett unlocked the front door. The house had not been used since the end of the previous summer, and had an odour of musty sea air and a hint of creosote. Sheets of yellow newspaper had been tacked onto the insides of the windows as protection against the sun. Cobwebs and dust abounded. The hinges of the doors and windows were covered in axle grease.

Garnett moved the car into the shade of a milkwood tree next to the house. It was time for lunch.

"You're rather quiet now, Douglas. Well, here we are, and there's no backing out now. I think we should send the maid over later this afternoon with a visiting card. I'm going to have a little snooze, if you'll wake me at about three thirty. Why don't you have a little rest yourself? A bit of beauty sleep?"

Douglas laughed nervously, "I'm not in the least bit sleepy or tired. Might just read a little, or go for a walk."

They cleared the lunch things. Garnett lay on his back on the *chaise longue* in the dining room. He folded his arms across his chest and closed his eyes. He saw the road ahead of him, the shining bonnet of the car, the forests, the sea. Life was so good. He was content. Leibner was a damn good dentist. What a clever fellow. No, brilliant. It must impress the Judge. His limbs felt heavy, he jerked, as though his foot had slipped from a step. He caught himself and fell asleep.

Douglas arranged a folding wood and canvas chair at the front of the house. He wanted to be conspicuous. Trophies of antelope horns were fixed to the walls of the veranda. The wind was disturbing. He had left his volume of Gibbon in his bag in the dining room. He let his mind wander. He looked out to sea. What an immense stretch of water. The tide was in. The bay was filled to its brim. He dozed off with his head to one side, breathing heavily through his mouth.

"Master ... Master?"

Douglas woke with a start and swallowed hard. The bright afternoon light made him blink. A short Hottentot woman in a pale blue uniform and a white apron stood in front of the veranda. Her face was heavily lined; she had a large bust and big buttocks; her white starched cap sat at an odd angle on several small pointed frizzy plaits. He was disorientated. "I am Master Hurter's maid. I am Sienna. I have come to help." She had small pleasant darting eyes. Her creased lisle stockings were too large. She wore a pair of felt bedroom slippers with a brown and yellow tartan pattern. She followed Douglas' eyes. "It is on account of the corns, Master," she said. "I think we should clean the house. It has been closed for quite a long time."

"Doctor is sleeping, as soon as he wakes."

"I will wait at the back, Sir." She walked to the back of the house through tall overgrown grass.

"Beware of the snakes."

She stopped and turned. "Master Hurter had to leave the cat here two years ago. He's become large and wild. He's been around here all the time. He keeps the creatures away."

Douglas' body was like lead from the short sleep. He imagined Frances in a white cotton dress with a lace pattern bodice, lying on her back, her left leg turned over the other one, her feet bare, her hair loosely around her head, her lips slightly apart as she slept on an iron bed in her room at the back of their house, the window open to the sound of the surf. He saw her father lying fully dressed asleep on his back next to his wife, a law journal across his stomach. His wife was on her side with her hands folded together under her cheek. She wore a hat. A large pin with an orange blob at the one end held the hat to her head to stop it from blowing off. He woke up again.

He eased himself stiffly from his chair and yawned till he had tears in his eyes. It was time to go for a walk. He took off his shoes and socks and neatly rolled his trousers up above his calves. He hung his pullover on the back of the chair, walked on tiptoe through the grass in front of the house to protect the tender undersides of his feet. When he reached the first dune he slid his feet into the sand and lifted his head to smell the sea air and the herbal scent of vegetation. He looked towards the Robberg. He put his hands into his trouser pockets and strode onto the beach. There was no one in sight. The sand above the high-water mark was soft. He walked down the steep part of the beach towards the foaming sheets of hissing surf driven up the beach. When the water receded he dug his toes into the wet sand and flicked patterns of slush.

He tried to see how far ahead he could flick the sand. At times he had to dash to avoid larger incoming waves. Was Garnett still asleep? He looked at his watch. It was only twenty to three. Oudtshoorn seemed distant now. He stopped to see which house the Roses were in. It was pleasant here. Never went to the beach much in Cape Town. What a business it was that time when they blocked Watermeyer's chimney at College House and filled his study with smoke. What a fun day that was. What a damn fuss they're all making of my studies. It was not as difficult as people imagine. Frances is impressed. She said as much. Her father always looks as though he's judging me. Must be bloody terrible always to be weighing this up against that, always attaching value, using this test or that. Assessing. Was a good advocate, coldly analytical. Not much emotion in the courtroom. Incisive and severe. Cut the prosecution to the quick. Should perhaps have done law. Dismantled them. Frances will be like a fragile flower in the dry Karroo. A railway station and a water tower, and a sandstone hotel and pepper trees and an occasional breeze. It is lovely here. Could stay here forever with her. The pleading gulls, the blue sky, the soft air, countless millions upon millions of bubbles rupturing in the surf to produce its whooshing sighing sounds, the cliffs, the yellow sand and the bush that comes down to the beach.

It was three. He continued on lazily towards the Robberg, far enough for it not to look as though he was parading in front of the Roses' house. The whole world seemed asleep. 'Dear God the very houses are asleep.' There must be many fishes down there in the sea, waiting for Garnett.

Was it possible to be aware without translating perceptions into words? He looked out to sea. For moments he could suspend his thoughts. It was like dreaming. One did not dream in words; like a silent film and yet it had meaning. He tried to see for how long he could suspend all thought until he thought about not thinking. He turned and looked back along the way he had come. Visible in the rays of the afternoon sun were large clouds of vapour drifting inland. There was a distant solitary figure on the beach. At first he could not tell whether it was coming towards him or moving away. Was Garnett already awake? Sienna would not be on the beach. Perhaps someone on holiday. It was time to go back for hot tea and ginger biscuits. He fixed his eyes on the sand in front of him. When the water withdrew, bubbles and air squirted from tiny holes.

When he looked up again the figure on the beach was closer. A giant seagull flapping its wings was a dress blowing in the wind. A white hat appeared. It was a woman. His heart leaped at the familiar movements. It was Frances. He ran towards her.

"Frances! How wonderful!" His words were carried away by the wind. He saw her mouth moving but heard no sound. She held out her arms.

"Frances! Dear Frances, how wonderful!"

"Dearest Douglas, I've been so excited ever since I heard you would be visiting. How nice of you to go to all this trouble. Where's your friend?" She put her arms around him and kissed him on his cheek. He hugged her.

"He's having a sleep. How has your holiday been?"

"Everybody is having a lovely rest. Daddy was very tired at the end of the session. He had some very trying cases. And you know Mother, she tends to worry about him. There aren't many people here – a bit too early for that. But it suits us. We've brought books, and it's nice to have Daddy with us all the time. His old sense of humour is returning. He really can be very funny once you get to know him, Douglas. He's not such an ogre as people imagine."

Douglas was embarrassed.

"Come and have some tea at our house while your friend sleeps. My mother got the cook to make lots and lots of all sorts of biscuits before we left."

Garnett had a sweet taste in his mouth when he woke. He needed to have a leak. He wondered when the maid would arrive. He walked to the back of the house. She was there.

"Good afternoon, Doctor, I am Sienna. I think we should clean the house. If Doctor would please open the back door, and unlock the pantry, everything is kept there."

"Do you cook, Sienna?"

"Not exactly everything. I can bake bread, and make breakfast. I can fry fish. I'll also be able to do the washing."

"I still have to go to the shop. Is there anything you need? " Garnett asked.

"We must make sure we have soap for the washing. Two bricks of blue soap should be enough. Also a block of blue. The salt might be hard. If Doctor is going to catch any fish we'll need flour and oil and eggs. How long will Doctor be staying?"

"We will leave on Friday morning."

"The other master came to look for Doctor. He is at the Judge's house. The people said Doctor must also go there. There's enough for me to do here, there's a lot of cleaning to do. I cannot find any matches."

Garnett heard Douglas' voice on the Roses' veranda. "Yes at four this morning," he was saying, his back to Garnett. "Garnett enjoys driving." Douglas stopped talking when Mrs Rose was distracted and saw Garnett.

"Let me introduce you to my friend, Garnett Nel. Garnett this is Judge Rose, Mrs Rose and Frances. Garnett shook Justice Rose's hand, "How do you do, Judge." He shook Mrs Rose's hand and smiled in his friendly, open way with his grey eyes and dark lashes. "How do you do, Frances. Douglas has told me so much about you."

"Do sit down," the Judge suggested. "What about some tea for you Doctor Nel? We're just about to have our second cups."

"That would be splendid, thank you."

Mrs Rose got up to pour the tea. "No, I'll do it Mother, please sit down," Frances jumped up enthusiastically. She was excited. Garnett observed her as closely as propriety would allow. Her cream-coloured cotton dress had a wide collar. She wore a large white straw hat with the brim turned up in front. Fair hair, striking green eyes, aquiline features, well-defined mouth, fairly tall, slim, good hips and legs.

"I believe you studied overseas, Doctor Nel?" the Judge asked.

"Yes, I was at Trinity College in Dublin. I've been back for just less than a year. A working man now."

"Did you join a practice in Oudtshoorn?" the Judge enquired.

"No, but I have a partner now. He joined me about three months ago. Lamprecht."

"So you squatted…"

"How are you finding things Doctor Nel?" Mrs Rose asked.

"I'm very glad to be able to say that my practice is doing well. I have been very busy indeed. My partner is also a qualified pharmacist. He was at Edinburgh. He'll take care of the dispensing side. I will take care of all the surgery. He's not very keen on that. It's really wonderful to be able to have a rest for a few days."

"How did you enjoy being overseas?" Frances asked.

"It was a great opportunity, even though I had to go cap in hand to an uncle of mine. I went cap in hand, and I mean that literally, and he drove a very hard bargain."

"Douglas mentioned to me that you, yourself, studied overseas, Justice Rose?"

"Yes, although I began my legal studies in Cape Town I completed my studies at Oxford. For a period I also practised as a barrister in London."

There was silence except for the sound of the surf and the cries of some gulls and Mrs Rose moving about in her chair.

"Is your family from Oudtshoorn?" the Judge asked.

"Well, yes, I was born there. My father is from the Somerset East district."

"Garnett's father practises as a Law Agent in Oudtshoorn," Douglas contributed.

The Judge smiled, "I have been through Oudtshoorn. Colleagues have been there for Circuit Court sittings. Damn hot there they say."

Frances handed her mother her tea. "How do you take your tea, Garnett?"

"With milk and sugar please, two sugars, please."

Frances offered Garnett the biscuit plate: almond macaroons, gingernuts and shortbread.

"My husband has a bit of a sweet tooth."

"So how will the two of you spend your time here, Douglas?" the Judge asked.

"Garnett's keen on angling. We've brought some fishing things. I, myself, have not had much experience of angling. I'll have to see how it goes. And I'll do some reading."

"I think it would be so nice to have some fresh fish," suggested Mrs Rose.

"We have to bring so much with us when we come on holiday, and it's not always easy to get really fresh food. Besides which, fish provides nourishment for the brain. Frances and her father both need that. And it is light and easy to digest. It was a pleasure to meet your parents, Douglas. Our Frances will soon be leaving home. She's taking up a teaching post at Graaff Reinet, Doctor Nel. What is your opinion of a daughter leaving home and taking up a profession? The world has changed so much."

Garnett looked at Frances. She was only nineteen or twenty. Perhaps twenty-one. She seemed so vulnerable, like a flower in bloom. Life was a wholesome, innocent, adventure without misfortune. Her breath must still be like a puppy's. She looked at Douglas and blushed. She was waiting for a reply. The Judge was going to measure him by his response.

"Well," Garnett began, "the world has certainly changed. We have been through one of the most unsettling periods, also the most rapidly changing times. We were talking about the effects of the war, when we visited our friend Doctor Leibner on the way here. Even though we have been somewhat isolated from events in Europe, they do affect us. Consider the speed with which news travels, how rapidly we transmit ideas. That makes the press a powerful social instrument. An ordinary example: consider how motor cars have developed. Scientists have made wonderful discoveries." He was desperately searching for ideas. The Judge was listening. Garnett's evidence was not coherent.

"What I am trying to say," Garnett started again. "What I am trying to say, is that a new social order is emerging." The afternoon sleep had made his mind dull. "There are so many new ideas that will influence our attitudes. Architects have gone off in new directions. Artists and writers are experimenting with all sorts of new forms. Some of it seems quite crazy! It is not so easy any more to believe that anything is permanent. If I think of my own field, how things have changed. It is a new world we are living in. I think Frances is doing a most adventurous thing, Mrs Rose. She is to be admired."

"It is a jolly long way to Graaff Reinet," Douglas said.

Garnett sipped his tea. He had spilt some of it in his saucer and the corner of his shortbread was soggy. He held the biscuit upside down to stop the soggy part from falling off. He looked up to see what the Judge's reaction was. The Judge was looking at him, without expression. Maybe Douglas would come to his rescue.

"Well, what you have said is interesting," Mrs Rose said, "but all that uncertainty gives me less comfort than I had hoped for. I suppose the sooner we get used to the idea of Frances being away the better. The die is cast. Her father seems to think it's a good idea."

The Judge rearranged himself in his chair. "I think you have made a good point Doctor Nel. While we are isolated here at the southern end of Africa, and thank heaven for some of that isolation, I am sure we are going to experience the effects of liberal developments. You are perfectly correct to assume that the events of the last two decades, will continue to change the world – change is inevitable. There will be good changes and there will be bad changes. My wife and I were in Europe a year ago. We have to preserve the good and resist that which is bad. But we have to have progress. I hope you will have success with your fishing. I would love some of your fresh fish."

Frances smiled enthusiastically. "Perhaps I could go along on one of your expeditions!"

"Do you know Mr Kuys, the Magistrate, Doctor Nel?" the Judge asked.

"Yes, we know him well. We play tennis at his house. He's a good player. He was outstanding when he was younger."

The shadows grew longer. The late afternoon chill made them appreciate their hot tea.

"It's so good to know that we have a doctor nearby," Mrs Rose said, "not that I am hoping for anyone to become ill, of course. How are you two young men going to cope with household things?"

"We are employing Mr Hurter's maid. She's already there, cleaning and getting things ready for our supper.

"Douglas, would you and Doctor Nel like to have lunch with us tomorrow?" Mrs Rose asked.

"We would be delighted," Garnett replied.

"When will you go fishing?" Frances wanted to know.

"It all depends on Garnett."

Douglas and Garnett moved towards the steps of the veranda. "I'll only be able to send word to the gillie this evening. If he is available we'll decide when to go. Depends on the weather and the tides. We also need to get some bait."

"Hope you have a pleasant evening, Frances, and thank you once again for your kind invitation, Mrs Rose," Douglas said.

Frances stood close to Douglas. "I am looking forward to the angling expedition. I have never been on one. That's if Daddy will let me go."

The Judge said nothing.

"I'm sure your father won't mind. He might even like to go himself. We look forward to seeing the two of you tomorrow. It was nice to meet you Doctor Nel."

Frances skipped onto the sand next to the house. They said more goodbyes and then their penultimate and then their ultimate goodbyes, and then waved while they separated.

"You were nice and quiet, hey Douglas? When the old chap started putting me to the test. I would have thought that you would come to my rescue. I couldn't get my thoughts straight. Must have been the long day, or the sleep this afternoon."

"I don't have to come to your rescue, Garnie. You are more than capable of dealing with him. He has that severe way about him. I'm not always sure of him. I never have full grasp of him. He's always distant."

"Maybe he is just protecting his daughter. Yet I must say I never really understand why people have to be like that, on guard or something. As though if he were to show any warmth he would be vulnerable. Perhaps it's just his nature, and has nothing to do with being a judge. Were you there the whole afternoon?"

"I fell asleep and woke when Sienna arrived. I decided to go for a walk along the beach, and when I was already on my way back to see how you were getting on, I met Frances strolling on the beach. So what do you think, Garnie?"

"What a find. She is absolutely wonderful. And the best of all is that she likes you."

"Do you really think so?"

"I have no doubt whatsoever."

The wind had begun to drop. The early evening was mild. In the distance there were three figures on the beach. Their elongated images and the clear colours of the evening sky were reflected in the shining sheets of water left behind by receding waves. A man and a woman and a small child were on the sands. The man chased the child in a playful manner, round and round the woman, and the child shrieked and hid his face in his mother's dress.

They made their way through the dunes to Hurter's house. A piece of a broom handle moved back and forth at the corner of the veranda.

"The house is nearly ready. If Doctor could just please help me to light the Primus."

Their bags had been arranged neatly along the one wall of the dining room and a cloth had been put over the table. Two oil lamps stood on the dark oak sideboard. Candles had been put into green and blue enamel candleholders and matches on the side of each holder. A picture, slightly buckled by the sea air, of Moses in the bulrushes adorned one wall.

"I think I'll take my things to the room," Douglas said. He picked up his suitcase and his loose things. He unpacked his clothes and hung his spare trousers and jacket in an unsteady cupboard with an oval mirror on the centre panel. He put his shaving things on the marble top washstand next to an enamel basin and large white porcelain jug. The frame of the cupboard was twisted which made the door difficult to open. He put his copy of Gibbon on the commode next to his bed and laid his pyjamas on his pillow.

They ate their supper at the big dining table by the light of the two oil lamps.

"What age is Frances, Douglas?"

"I'm sorry, what did you say?"

"I asked what age Frances is."

"She turned twenty in August."

"What a lovely girl. Let's have our coffee on the veranda."

Douglas fetched another outside chair.

"Garnie, I want to talk to you about the problem that I seem to be having with my hearing."

"Ag, we'll see to that when we get back to Oudtshoorn."

"What do you think it could be?"

"It is unlikely to be anything serious. There's not been any deafness in your family, or anything like that. Sometimes catarrhal conditions cause problems."

"I have not brought anything to read, not even a medical journal. Don't you find that Gibbon damn heavy going?"

"In the morning I find it exciting and at night it helps to put me to sleep! It is extraordinary to think what the man must have done to gather his material – huge volumes, and always material from original sources. It's fantastic how he organised the material. My father gave me the Bury edition when I completed my B.A. Must have cost him a pretty penny." Douglas was looking out to sea as he spoke. Garnett observed him closely from the side. The light of the lamp in the dining room fell on the side of his face. There was stubble on his strong jaw. His enthusiastic eyes were bright. "Gibbon had such an extraordinary grasp, and incredible literary judgement. He was capable of the most brilliant and delicate irony. He said of history 'Little more than the register of the crimes, follies and misfortunes of mankind.' Just think of that! Portly chap from all accounts. It is unique for one man to have had such a blend of skills and what endurance he must have had: some editions run into more than six volumes."

Douglas suddenly fell silent. They sipped their coffee. "Water boils at a higher temperature here at the coast," Garnett observed. "Gee, it is lovely here. I must build a holiday house one day."

Sienna could be heard washing the dishes. It was time to take her home. Douglas was still on the veranda when Garnett returned. "What about some tea? I'll go and boil the water."

"That's a nice idea."

They settled in their chairs and waited for the tea to draw. A folded newspaper lay on the floor.

"Where did this old *Courant* come from?" Douglas asked.

"I found it in the pantry."

Douglas turned over the front page. "The Judge mentioned Tielman Roos this afternoon..."

"I think it was I who mentioned him."

"Here's a bit about a visit to Oudtshoorn earlier in the year."

"What date is that?"

"Thursday August 19. The meeting was held at the Gaiety Theatre. Listen to this advertisement, 'Are you always ready for the Dance? Use Feluna Pills.' What on earth are the pills supposed to do, do you think?"

"It is to make you a bit randy or as the old people used to say *katools*. Hell, I must tell you what happened to Danie Roux and me in London once. We were over there for a fortnight for an end of term break. Giel de Villiers from Stellenbosch who was at St Bartholomew's put us up at his digs. One very foggy morning, you could hardly see your hand in front of your eyes, you had to navigate by the tramlines, we caught a tram to Piccadilly. While we were still on the landing, having just got on, you see, a lovely shapely girl made her way past us and up the stairs to the upper deck. She had on a fairly short dress and nice athletic legs. Both of us had a damn good look up her dress and I said to Danie in Afrikaans, 'Will she or won't she? And as quick as a flash she replied with a little smile, 'No she won't.' Boy, were we embarrassed! Imagine that happening in London. Imagine a coincidence like that. Hell! When we looked again she was gone. We never saw her again. I think she must have had a good sense of humour. She could have said nothing, after all. Taught us a good lesson. Probably wasn't as innocent as she pretended either."

Douglas laughed so that he spilt some of his tea. It was always rewarding to tell him a story because of the visible workings of his imagination and his endearing gaucheness as he snorted and laughed in anticipation of each new idea.

"How long have you known Frances, Douglas?" Garnett asked.

"Gee, let me think. I suppose for two and a half years or so."

"Has she had any attachments?"

"No, just the usual friends. She's led a very sheltered life."

"Why don't you ask her to marry you?"

"Steady on now Garnie …"

"It is quite apparent that she has strong feelings for you. You should strike while the iron is hot."

"The point is that I have nothing. I am going to live with my parents. I'll have the modest income, or call it a pittance, of a schoolteacher. On the one hand I'm scared of missing an opportunity, and on the other hand I am not ready to seize it. So I am afraid it will have to wait."

"There may be another way of looking at it. Frances knows your circumstances. She won't have excessive expectations, and neither will her parents. Within a year or two you'll be able to support her. It just means your engagement will have to be a bit longer. And what's so wrong with that? At least you'll have her on the hook."

"Ag, I don't know, Garnie. In their social circle there must be ever so many eligible bachelors. Besides, I don't think her old man is too keen on me. He intimated once that schoolteachers lack ambition. Ambition is everything to him. He's very hard."

Was Douglas soliciting encouragement or seeking despair? He seemed so incredibly ambitious and energetic about his intellectual enterprises. "Come Douglas, let's go and have a good night's rest. At least no patients will call me tonight. You take the lamp. I'll make do with a candle. See you in the morning, sleep well. Everything will turn out all right. Just have enough courage. We'll have a lovely day tomorrow. See you in the morning." Garnett patted Douglas on the shoulder, and with the candle to guide him, made his way to his bedroom. He undressed and put on his silk pyjamas. He brushed his teeth and spat the water into his chamber-pot. He got into bed and blew out the candle. The odour of the smoke from the wick mixed with the coastal night air. The moonlight shone through the window and cast the pattern of a veranda pillar and the lower part of the window frame on the bed and the floor. The sound of the sea was in the distance. The tide was coming in again. A small dog barked. Among the multitude of insect sounds there was a loud cricket. Tomorrow would be a windless sunny day. At low tide they would collect bait. He saw the early morning again and the road; the sugarbird, and blue lilies – they also call them Christmas candles – in the gardens at George, bastard saffron, Ericas, ivy leaved geraniums, the breakfast bridge, and the Kaaimans river. Leibner is not the cayman. The Judge is a shithouse. She's a lovely girl. Pity she belongs to Douglas. Nice legs. I'm a leg man. Good thing the fashions have changed. The movements of the journey began to repeat themselves in his body. He felt proud of the shining bonnet of his car and felt the vibrations of the steering wheel in his forearms. Never had a puncture. What a luck. Don't think about tomorrow. You'll become too excited to sleep. Don't become too excited about being excited. How could the fungus from the apricot jam cure an ulcerated sore? Strange to think of that. First the sound of the sea disappeared, and then he floated about in calm silent green water on a bright sunny day, his face turned happily upwards towards a bright blue sky, in which there was no sun.

Douglas put the lamp on the commode next to his bed. He ignored the Gibbon volume. They must have had a lot of time in those days. How could one man have accomplished so much? He sat on the edge of his bed, his right foot across his left knee, his shoe in both hands, ready to remove it. He put it down, and kicked it away gently. Might as well go to sleep with the other shoe on. What purpose is there after all? How can it work out? Withdraw. Shut yourself off. Let her take the initiative.

    He lay on his back, and gripped the cool iron bars behind his head. He looked at the wooden ceiling. In the patterns formed by the knots in the wood he saw the Judge's face. Beautiful Frances. To feel the shape of her body. To avoid a horn pull the bum back a little. He hated himself. Try and think of something else instead. Each time he tried to think of something, he thought of her and there was a contraction in his crotch that made him want to squeeze his buttocks together. He picked up his book and opened it at the bookmark. He put it down on his chest with the open side down, and looked at the flame of the lamp. Perhaps it would help to pray. Our Father who art in heaven. To be a father one would have to copulate. He shut the book and sat up and shook his head till it hurt inside. He took off his other shoe and began to undress. A honeymoon: if they could be naked together in a bed. He got into bed and took his book, opened it and began to read with the same intense concentration that had brought academic distinction, until he heard only the clashing of Roman armour in battle and the sound of wheels running over the stones of the Via Appia and saw dusty Roman vineyards in the late summer afternoon.

He blew out the flame of the lamp and held the pillow in his arms. He kissed the part that formed Frances' cheek and went to sleep.

A light brown mare with a flaxen mane galloped along a water's edge. The water covered a hill like a shroud of footmarks in the sand. It shouldn't flow uphill. The mare threw her head back. He wanted to kiss her under her ear that turned into a ripe burst fig. She was pregnant. Strong pulsating arteries, under a fell coat of sweat, converged on the womb where the eternal woman's child sat entombed in bright light. Grass full of ample seed waved and nodded sagely in the wind on the slopes of the Sermon on the Mount that became a universe with many swirling centres. In the distant sky a city emitted orange-pink light into the clouds like the setting sun, and the first drops of rain plopped into the dust next to an old mimosa tree and turned into semen.

◆

Chapter Six

Wednesday 8 December 1926

GARNETT WAS THE FIRST TO WAKE. He heard Sienna in the kitchen. It was a grey overcast day. A fishy sea mist was in the house. It began to drizzle. They would still be able to get bait. It would be good to have a swim. Always warmer when it rains. He got up and put on his dressing gown. He looked at his fob watch. Twelve minutes past seven. He yawned and wandered along the passage to the kitchen. He heard the Primus before he reached the kitchen door, and the sound of the saucepan lid heaving and falling above the boiling water.

"Good morning, Sienna. You're early."

"Good morning Doctor. The weather is not good." She had not got wet. It was warm in the kitchen. "I will make the tea now. Martiens is waiting at the back."

"Thank you very much. Please make sure he has something to eat and drink. Tell him I will be there soon."

"The young missus was already walking on the beach early this morning. She was alone," Sienna remarked.

Garnett found Martiens sitting on the back steps.

"Môre Martiens."

Martiens got up. "Môre Dokter." He was a tall coloured man of fairly light complexion. His dark hair was wavy, and he held his hat upside down in both hands. His features were unmistakably European and his eyes were green. "My father was a German."

"I am glad you could come. We'll be here only for a few days. I would like to do some fishing. The weather could have been better."

"It is not bad weather for fishing. The water must not be too bright. When the tide goes out I make the bait. There's no other work."

"Sienna will give you something to eat."

Garnett found Douglas in the passage, toothbrush in hand. "Did you sleep well? Sienna says Frances was out on the beach early this morning. Come, we're going for a swim."

They stood in the dining room in their full-length woollen bathing costumes, straps over the shoulders, and large openings under the armpits; Garnett in dark green and Douglas in maroon. On the veranda they stood there in an early morning misty sea air, savouring their tea. The surface of the sea was flat and the foam that lay heavily upon it dragged itself slowly around in circles. The air was dense.

"I had a wonderful sleep," Garnett said with a tone of satisfaction."

Oudtshoorn is a lot higher above sea level. It's easier to breathe down here, one sleeps better."

"If we are still going to get the bait, will we be in time for lunch, Garnie?"

"It's only at noon and you don't want to be sitting at their door when it opens. Don't appear too keen. They know why you've come to visit."

"Hell, isn't it a bit cold to swim?"

"Once you're in it won't be so bad, and afterwards you'll be glad you did."

Garnett and Douglas made their way down through the partly overgrown footpath to the beach, swaying on their white tender feet across bits of broken twigs and other vegetation in the sand, their towels wrapped around their shoulders. With their arms clasped across their chests, they waded into the water and jumped up, as the waves approached, to protect their testicles from the cold. Then almost in unison they plunged under an approaching wave. They surfaced and whisked their heads, as was fashionable, to flick water from their faces and swam and dived in under the frothy fresh salty sea. The Judge watched them through his field glasses. Van Yssen is energetic. May the water cool his balls. There may not be enough water in the ocean to do that.

Eventually Garnett ran from the surf. He hopped first on one foot then on the other with his head held sideways to get rid of water in his ears. While Douglas waded from the surf, Garnett dashed around in circles leaning sharply in towards the centre of the circle and making the circle ever smaller until he was nearly dizzy.

"Still the old *Victor Ludorum* hey, Garnic!"

"I'm a bit too fat. Could do with less lard. Must say I'm hungry though. Wonder what Sienna has cooked up?"

Hunched up and with their towels around their shoulders, elbows tucked in against their ribs, teeth chattering, they made their way back to the house. Water drained from their costumes and ran uncomfortably down the insides of their thighs. In front of the veranda Sienna stood ready with a jug of water so that they could wash the sand from their feet.

They ate, snug in the old clothes that they had brought along for fishing. Garnett's Boys High rugby jersey smelt of mothballs. The tide was still ebbing. The cloudiness and mist were becoming lighter. The surf was almost soundless below the abandoned beach.

Garnett went to the back of the house to fetch Martiens. He was busy preparing an Indian cane gaff, fixing a piece of red rubber motor car inner tube, cut into strips, onto the straight part of the gaff's hook. Nodding towards his handiwork he said, "This is to get the octopus out from under the rocks. Still the best bait for cob."

Garnett and Douglas set off along the beach in the direction of the whaling station. Martiens followed, with the gaff, an empty sugar pocket and a khaki army surplus bag containing knives and a rusty tyre lever. It was nearly twenty to nine.

"Martiens?" Garnett asked.

"Ja Dokter?"

"Which are the best spots?"

"Skurveband of Bosluiskop. Over the Robberg, in the direction of Knysna. Will require a bit of walking and carrying, but it will be worth the trouble. It is easier to get to Bosluiskop than Skurvebank."

"If we could just catch a good octopus, Martiens."

"Let me have the gaff, Doctor. It will be one two three. They think the inner tube is another octopus and then they run away. And then I'll have him."

Martiens had hold of the gaff. He inspected smaller rock pools for overhangs under which octopuses were likely to shelter. He put the hook with the decoy into the water and swept it in under the dark inner edges of the pool. One pool followed another. "They are hiding." He tried yet another pool without success.

"Martiens, ek think we should rather leave the octopus,"

"Just a little more time Doctor."

Martiens moved to another pool, about three feet deep. Douglas had lost interest. He stared out to sea. As Martiens put the gaff into the water a huge octopus darted towards the decoy, squirting dark ink. Martiens held the end of the gaff still. As the octopus enveloped the red rubber with his tentacles, Martiens jerked the hook into its head and pulled it out of the water. The creature writhed and twisted. Black ink oozed from it. Some of its tentacles flayed the air seeking a purchase. Martiens flung it off the gaff and smashed it against the rocks. The moment that the octopus was stunned Martiens grabbed it. He got a hold of the head and turned it inside out. Some of the tentacles wrapped themselves around his arm. He flung the octopus onto the rocks, retrieved the gaff and put the hook through the octopus. "All that is left is to get a few crabs." Martiens was pleased with himself.

There were hardly any people on the beach. Near the hotel four children ran along the edge of the water. An elderly couple walked hand in hand towards them. The woman's hat was tied down under her chin with a peach-coloured chiffon scarf. They exchanged cordial greetings. When they had passed, Garnett glanced back, and found the woman staring at them.

The Roses' house was approaching. Douglas looked up. It would be wonderful to live like this forever. The judge and his two women were having tea on the veranda. Thin smoke rose from the kitchen chimney. Frances saw them first. She jumped up to wave and ran towards them. The judge followed her onto the beach. He was in a hearty mood. "Good morning Douglas, good morning, Doctor Nel. I trust you've had a successful morning. I might come along on your excursion, that is if you don't mind having me along."

"We would be flattered." Douglas dreaded the idea.

"We're so looking forward to having you over." Frances was excited.

"Well," said Garnett, "I suppose we had better get along if we are going to be punctual."

"I'll walk with you," Frances said. "It's such a lovely day."

"Your mother might need some help, Frances," the Judge suggested.

"Oh, now really Daddy, everything has been prepared. I'll be back presently. It's so nice to have some of my own company."

"We'll see you in a short while then, Douglas." The Judge turned towards his house.

Frances skipped ahead of them, now sideways and then backwards. Her dress blew against her legs, and her fair hair over her face. Douglas and Frances waited on the veranda while Garnett and Martiens saw to their bait. She moved close enough to him for the material of their clothes to touch. Douglas did not know what to do. He thought how he had kissed her after the Leavers' Dance and put his arm around her waist. She responded by putting her arm around him.

Sienna was busy in the kitchen. She had put a large pot of water on the stove for Garnett's bath and put a galvanised tin bath ready in his room.

Douglas and Frances heard Garnett's footsteps in the passage and let go of each other. "I am so pleased that you are more positive about teaching next year, Douglas," Frances said.

"Yes, I have been thinking more about it. At least I know Dr Archer and some of the other teachers. Archer has a will of his own. Wants things to be done only his way. The fellow before me evidently had problems with that."

Through the bedroom window at the far side they heard the sounds of Garnett bathing, above it a little Irish tune he was humming. A jug filled with warm water stood on the floor next to the bath. He soaped his hair and worked it into a thick white lather. With one eye shut he glanced at the jug and gripped the handle. It slipped in his hand. Soap crept perilously close to his left eye. He splashed some of the water from the jug onto the handle and with a new squeaky grip poured water over his head. The sensation of the lukewarm water flowing over his head and his body almost gave him goose-pimples.

Douglas again put his arm around Frances. She moved closer to him and let their sides touch. He smelt her hair and a subtle touch of perfume. He felt the warmth of her thigh. He heard his own heartbeat and the rushing noise of the surf. Garnett was still splashing. The washing on the clothes-line flapped in the wind. "If you will excuse me for a moment, Frances, I think I should go and put on some longs, and change my shoes." She gave him an approving squeeze before she disentangled herself.

Garnett appeared. "You're looking very smart, Garnett," Frances said admiringly.

He smiled his easy smile. Dimples formed in his cheeks.

"Douglas won't be long."

"Do you always catch fish every time you go?"

"Not always but most of the time. It is important to know exactly where to go. And I dare say it would be nice to catch something decent."

Douglas had washed his hands and his face. There was still moisture around his hairline.

"Carry on, I'll be with you in a moment, have to give some instructions to Sienna," Garnett said.

Chapter Seven

WHEN GARNETT, Douglas and Frances arrived at the Roses' house, they found the Judge and Mrs Rose on deck chairs in the shade of their veranda.

"Well it really is nice to have you over Doctor Nel, Douglas," Mrs Rose said as she held her hand out to greet them. The Judge nodded and touched his white panama hat to acknowledge their arrival. And then as an afterthought, "Do sit down. Pull up a chair." He closed his law journal and put it on his lap.

Frances went to the dining room to fetch ginger beer. A bottle and some glasses stood ready on a tray on an ornately carved dark wooden sideboard. A solitary colourful print of Capri, as seen from an elevated garden with small pink climbing roses, by an obscure English artist, adorned the wall above the sideboard. The glasses clinked as she carried the tray. The cork of the ginger beer bottle was held down with string, to keep the fizz in. Garnett got up. "Let me help you with that, Frances. If you hold it, I'll undo the cork. Hold it away from your face." He pulled aside the ends of the bow but the cork stayed in the bottle. He took the bottle and pulled out the cork. Mrs Rose watched apprehensively. The ginger beer was flat.

"Oh my! Do go and get another bottle please, Frances dear. It must just have been a poor cork. My mother's recipe never fails."

The cork of the next bottle sat at a desperate angle, precariously held in by the string. Garnett pushed the string to one side and the cork shot out with a loud pop and bounced against the roof of the veranda. A wisp of gas curled from the bottle.

"This beer has more than enough fizz, add some from the other bottle. Turn the bottle to stir the ginger sediment, Frances."

"So how are things in Oudtshoorn these days, Doctor Nel?" the Judge asked when they were seated.

"Fine I suppose. The farmers are not having an easy time. Many relied too heavily on the ostriches. Even the ones who have survived now have uncomfortable burdens of interest. The banks own more of their farms than they do. It was amazing to see the evaporation of so much wealth. It was there one moment and gone the next. Some people literally walked out of their houses and left their farms with doors and windows standing open. I suppose to begin with the boom was an illusion. The survivors turned to mixed farming. The economy of the town relies on farming."

"Several of Garnett's patients are farmers," Douglas contributed.

"With few exceptions farmers are an improvident lot," the Judge observed.

His wife looked sternly at him, "There are some really scenic parts around Oudtshoorn,"

"Having grown up there I suppose I am used to it, but visitors seem to find certain places attractive," Garnett said.

"I would love to see those places. We should really make a plan to do some sightseeing, dear."

"All in good time. I would rather spend more time in Europe."

"I would love to visit Russia," Mrs Rose said wistfully. "But that's out of the question now that the poor Tsar has gone."

"The ginger beer is really very good, Mrs Rose," Douglas observed. He burped gently with his fist against his mouth and let the ginger flavour go up his nose.

"I endorse that," added Garnett.

"And you, young man," said the Judge with uncharacteristic familiarity, turning to Douglas, "I trust you are looking forward to next year?" Before Douglas could respond he added, "Douglas is very highly thought of at our University, Doctor Nel, or so my friends in the Senate tell me."

Frances smiled.

"We are all aware of Douglas' achievements, Judge, and proud of them."

"Now that the doors of the school are looming it has occurred to me I might actually have enjoyed journalism," Douglas ventured.

"And been the editor before long," Frances bubbled.

"It takes many a long year to reach such a position, Frances dear," warned Mrs Rose.

"I know Mother."

"And think of all those odd hours Mr Wainwright has to work," Mrs Rose continued. "Never a decent holiday. Those poor children. If his political masters were not so demanding..."

"I don't think we should indulge ourselves," the Judge interrupted. "Arthur Wainwright is committed to his cause. There is no need for, or question of, the publishers dictating or prescribing to him."

The conversation would have to find another direction.

"Garnett says they are definitely going fishing tomorrow," Frances said.

"Let's talk about it over lunch," Mrs Rose suggested.

The Judge's chair creaked so much when he got up that Garnett hoped that it would break.

There were eight stinkwood chairs around the dining room table. Raffia place mats had been put underneath a white damask tablecloth. Glass and silver salt and pepper pots, bone napkin rings, a small arrangement of flowers. Sheffield cutlery with bone handles, including a large carving knife and fork. The Judge took command at the head of the table. Mrs Rose and Frances took up their positions on either side of him. "Douglas, if you would like to sit next to Frances; Doctor Nel, if you would please sit next to my wife. It makes the passing easier."

Mrs Rose picked up a small silver bell and shook it sharply. A coloured maid arrived with a tray containing white porcelain dishes and plates. She put the tray down at the bottom of the table and placed the plates in front of the Judge. She fetched the roast leg of lamb. The Judge carved and dished up meat. They helped themselves to vegetables.

"I hope you eat everything."

Garnett and Douglas were starving.

Yellow pumpkin with cinnamon sprinkled over it, mashed potatoes, finely chopped green beans. The maid returned with a gravy boat and spoon. "I nearly forget the gravy."

"Shall we say grace?" The Judge closed his eyes. "For what we are about to receive may the Lord make us truly grateful. Amen." He began to eat, and they followed.

"The food is delicious," Douglas ventured.

"I am so glad you are enjoying it," Mrs Rose replied.

"Yes, really very nice, thank you. Lovely mutton," Garnett added.

"So you're planning to go fishing in the morning, Doctor Nel?" the Judge asked.

"More than likely. I'll speak to my gillie this afternoon."

"If you do decide to go, at what time will you start?" Frances asked.

"To give ourselves the best chance, we should leave quite early, to get a line in the water before first light."

"Before first light!" Mrs Rose exclaimed, "my husband is a night owl, you'll never get him up early enough to go along."

"You know Daddy better than that Mother; if he puts his mind to something."

"I'll simply go to bed early. Frances is keen to go along. It will be an interesting outing for her, and I dare say, I could do with a little exercise."

"I understand dear that you have a need for masculine activities, but I find it quite astonishing that women of Frances' generation should be so infatuated with adventure. University education for women! Dresses so short they are just below the knees. What next! What would my mother have said?"

"It is high time that women became more emancipated. They have a contribution to make to society," the Judge said rather awkwardly with his mouth full.

"Aren't you being a little patronising, dear, a man pleading our case!"

"Not in the least." The Judge emptied his mouth and cleared his throat. "It may interest you to know, and indeed introduces an element of irony into this conversation, that Emmeline Pankhurst, no less, was married to a barrister, who himself was a powerful advocate of women's suffrage. I am not holding her out as the best example and I must declare that I cannot agree with her methods – after all she's been in and out of jail – and the bomb affair at Lloyd George's house. She was fortunate to receive only three years penal servitude for that. However, I seem to have strayed from the point. Must be the sea air."

"I think the events she created ran ahead of her at times," Frances said.

"What do you mean by that, Frances?" her father asked.

"I concede that her militancy did her cause a lot of harm. I also have a problem with the way in which she involved her daughters, and continues to do so. But the Pankhursts aside, there often were intense discussions at university about the role of women. Douglas and I have had our discussions. I think women should be allowed to reach their full potential; they should be given all the opportunities they deserve. But they should remain women in all respects. After all, our femininity is special, it has its own peculiar strengths and virtues; it is uniquely unselfish."

"Now, now, don't become too serious child, it might spoil the appetites of your guests." Mrs Rose turned to Garnett. "Frances is her father's child, she should have become a barrister. From the moment she began to talk she made it plain that she was exercising her mind. I am sure as a doctor you will agree that too much thinking is not good for one's health. I therefore simply refuse to think too much. It can give me the most dreadful headache. I suppose I have to be thankful for small blessings: that Frances has chosen to remain a woman."

The last remark brought a smile of discomfort to the Judge's face. He caught Garnett's observant glance and moved about in his chair. "My wife is a very good tennis player. Do you play tennis, Doctor Nel?"

"Yes indeed I do, and I enjoy it very much."

The claws of the Roses' stiff-legged fox terrier made scratching sounds on the wooden floorboards as he trotted in. He flopped down under the table, sighed heavily, and resumed his midday sleep.

The meal was beginning to dull the senses, and made the mood around the table torpid. The tide was in. The energetic sound of the sea at high tide came through the open dining room windows. Garnett and Mrs Rose faced the sea. The window frames were painted green. The corners of the panes had not been cleaned properly. The bay was filled to the brim. Its leaden surface heaved about awkwardly. Waves flung themselves down and crashed desperately onto the sand. The maroon and olive green brocade curtains had been brought from Cape Town.

"My Uncle Charles tells a lovely story about a Christmas dinner when he was a boy," Garnett began. "It was evidently their tradition to have very elaborate Christmas dinners. Ham, turkey, other meats – a real feast. They had put two tables together in the dining room; outside on the stoep a smaller table for the younger children. There were Christmas hats, decorations of greenery on the table, mistletoe. There was a great deal of anticipation, because it was the tradition, to put a gold sovereign into the Christmas pudding." Garnett suppressed a little laugh. "Anyway," he continued, "because the Christmas pudding was always very large, especially the younger members of the family, and younger guests, those with the larger appetites, decided that they would hold back so that they would have enough room for the Christmas pudding to give themselves the best chance of eating their way to the sovereign. The turkey and the goose were delicious but they ate modestly. By the time the cook carried in the pudding – steaming hot, spicy – many around the table were still hungry and the cook wondered why so little of his food had been eaten. Brandy was poured over the pudding and ceremoniously set alight. The brandy was a little overpowering for the younger ones, and not enough for the older ones." Garnett stopped to have another mouth-full of food. He speared a block of mutton and put a little of each of the vegetables on top of his fork for a mixture of flavours.

Frances was enjoying the story. Mrs Rose had stopped eating. "Do carry on. Who got the sovereign?" Douglas smiled at the Judge but got no reaction.

Garnett chuckled. "I'm coming to that." He swallowed. "Anyway, they ate and ate and ate. They could not eat too fast for fear of swallowing the coin. They took little bites and chewed until the pudding was liquid. The little ones' tummies burnt from the brandy. The pudding shrank but there was no sign of the sovereign. One of the young ones outside exclaimed excitedly when he bit into a walnut shell. Eventually there was one helping of pudding left. My grandfather knew the coin had to be in there. He dished it up for himself with a naughty smile as everyone watched. The little ones hung onto the windowsills and stood around the table. Bit by bit he ate the last helping, smiling as he went. There was one spoonful left. He took a deep breath and put the spoon in his mouth. He chewed while feeling with his tongue. There was nothing. Someone must have swallowed the coin. And thoughts turned to ways of retrieving it."

The Judge was amused.

"Oh my! Oh my! What happened?" Mrs Rose clapped her hands.

"My grandfather thought one of the kids had swallowed the sovereign. He was quite mean in some ways and resented the thought of losing a sovereign. There was a long unhappy anticlimax. Finally the cook appeared in the doorway. He was pale. He held up his hand, the sovereign between his forefinger and his thumb, 'I forgot to put the money into the pudding.' My grandfather called the cook a damn fool but at least he was honest. He took the coin and put it in his waistcoat pocket, 'Well that's that, perhaps we'll have two sovereigns in next year's pudding.' Turning to the little ones he said, 'and don't be so greedy the next time.'"

At first it sounded as if the fox terrier under the table had sighed but as soon as the stinking odour diffused they realised the dog had farted. Mrs Rose gave it a kick and the creature ran yelping from the room with a limp. He looked back resentfully from the veranda and shook himself.

"Confounded dog," Mrs Rose exclaimed.

Garnett wondered what they had fed the animal.

Frances was embarrassed. She blushed so that even her arms were puce.

Mrs Rose would have offered the guests more food. Instead she rang the bell.

"Yes Madam?"

"I would be glad if you would please clear the table, Martha. You may take the plates."

Garnett and Douglas could have done with another helping. No doubt the old man would have cold mutton for supper.

"Well," said Mrs Rose when the maid had left the dining room, "I don't have a hot pudding, but we have preserved peaches. Frances made custard and we'll have some tea."

"I do hope you and Frances will come along tomorrow, Judge Rose," Garnett said. "I hope we have not overstayed our welcome. I'm sure you would like to rest."

"I seldom sleep in the afternoon," Frances replied.

"Thank you very much for a delicious meal, Mrs Rose," Garnett said.

Douglas said his thanks. Frances put her arm through his. Garnett was looking forward to his afternoon sleep. The sea air had got to him.

Once they were out of earshot, Garnett said, "Just when the old lady was about to offer us more food the damned dog farted. And such a stink. I wonder what they feed the damn thing!"

Douglas laughed.

"I think I'll have forty winks if you don't mind Douglas, especially if we are going to get up early in the morning. I'll see what Sam thinks and then we can let the Roses know."

When Garnett woke he realised that the sun had caught his face and forearms and also the back of his legs. The skin of his nose was tender to the touch. He felt heavy. Should have brushed his teeth. His calf muscles were stiff. He looked at his alarm clock. It was after four. The mood of the day had changed. Large soft low drifting clouds cast shadows that darkened the room at times. He thought of Douglas and Frances. Schoolteacher Frances stood in front of the class. Those lovely legs, hips. Douglas' mother in the floral dress. Pepper trees and donkeys. Images of the sea at low tide and the rock pools kept on returning. He listened for the surf. In his dreamlike state he could transport himself anywhere. He floated above the bed.

In the Roses' house the Judge and his wife slept on their brass double bed. He was on his back in his cream coloured pyjamas, his feet partly covered with a fat faded green eiderdown. Mrs Rose lay on her side with her back to him in her underwear and dressing gown. Her mouth was open and her tongue lay in the bottom corner of her mouth. Her eyelids flickered. She jerked as Frances' train lurched from Cape Town Station, on its way to Graaff Reinet. Too clever for her own good is Frances. She woke, swallowed, and closed her eyes again. Must think of supper. She yawned a drawn out yawn and saliva came into her mouth. She turned on her back and looked at her husband. Oblivious to the world as always. Law, law and more law. Clever fellow her father had said, ambitious too. Runs in families her mother had said. Merchants are born. Men are made to think. Their brains are different. Frances is very taken with van Yssen. His father is a land surveyor. All very romantic and exciting.

When Mrs Rose sat up her husband woke. She had her back to him.

Good strong body. Sporting girl. He stroked her back. Her face was full of sleep. She stroked his forearm with both her hands. "I am going to make some tea, would you like some, dear?"

"That would be nice thank you," he said intimately. "I'll get dressed."

Garnett went outside. The tide was ebbing rapidly. He saw Douglas and Frances in the distance, walking along the beach. How had they had managed to rendezvous? Nature has its way. Douglas walked deliberately, his head forward. Frances frolicked and zigzagged, moving alternatively closer to and further from Douglas.

Garnett went down to the beach to meet them. Frances reached him first. "Did you have a good sleep then?"

"I had a wonderful rest, thank you. I needed it. I've been very busy at work.

"We strolled towards Seal Point," Douglas explained.

"Frances, I've thought about tomorrow. If you and your dad would like to come along you would be most welcome. If we could meet at four thirty?"

She clapped her hands excitedly. "What should we bring along?"

"You'll need good walking shoes and thick socks, and a hat."

"Which way will we go?" asked Frances.

"Probably to Bosluiskop. It is about an hour's walk from here. I hope it is not too far for you. Will your dad manage?"

"Oh yes, he's as strong as a horse."

"There are quite steep climbs. But I am sure it will all go well."

"At least we'll have a doctor with us!"

They passed the Roses' house.

"van Yssen does not waste much time," the Judge muttered to his wife.

"They are only here for a few days dear. And he did come here to see Frances. We know that." Recurring images of his wife's hips on their afternoon bed restrained the Judge, and made him less reluctant about his daughter's romance. And besides, van Yssen was a fine young man with an exceptional mind.

"They saw a lot of each other at university. He's upset at the prospect of their separation. That is why he has come here. It is quite natural. And I don't think their romance is of a passing nature. They have too much in common," Mrs Rose mused.

The Judge followed his wife's mouth as she spoke. What she had been denied in intellectual gifts she had been compensated for with a strong back, good breasts, handsome enthusiastic hips, striking legs, lots of intuition, and common sense.

The sun was still high even though it was nearly five. From the back of the house through the milkwood trees Sienna had seen Garnett and Douglas and Frances approaching and went to the kitchen to boil water. She fetched a plate from the sideboard in the dining room and biscuits from the pantry.

Douglas carried chairs onto the grass in front of the house.

"Douglas told me how much you enjoy your work, Garnett. It must give you great satisfaction."

"Douglas is flattering me. I'm not nearly as good at my work as he is at his. I enjoy helping people. It is rewarding to repair people. The body does most of it itself, of course, even in the case of surgical intervention."

"Have you done many operations?" Frances asked.

"I probably enjoy surgery most."

"Look at his hands Frances – perfect instruments."

Garnett was self-conscious. He thought of his dirty nails. That swine Woodburne had humiliated him in front of the whole class in his final year.

"How often do you operate?" Frances asked.

"Oh, sometimes there are emergencies. For example, to remove an appendix, an obstruction, or lesser things like tonsils, adenoids."

"Do you ever deliver babies?"

Douglas was embarrassed. Images of bloody fluids, cords, tubes, distended tissues, gore and the flimsy sack that had enclosed the calf that was squeezed out of a dilated passage on his uncle's farm. It was messy and happened at the worst extremities of the anatomy.

"Babies are wonderful. They are quite eager to come into the world. Every time one is delivered I marvel. Drenched in emotion, the midwife, the beauty of the mother's reaction. It is really wonderful. Most rewarding I must say."

They heard cups clinking above Sienna's footsteps in the passage. "Middag Master, middag Madam." And she put the tray down.

"Dankie, Sienna," Douglas said.

"I'll pour the tea," Frances offered.

"Perhaps we should let it draw a little," Garnett suggested. Sienna had covered the teapot with a red, green and brown hand knitted cosy.

"Where were we?" Douglas asked somewhat absent-mindedly.

"Garnett was telling us about babies."

"And I was thinking about horses."

" I'm looking forward to tomorrow. Daddy's a bit difficult at times. It is his manner: he knows exactly what he wants. I think that makes him impatient, even with my mother. The cookies are very nice. Who made them?"

"My mother," Garnett replied.

"How many of you are there in your family, Garnett?" Frances asked.

"I have four sisters and four brothers. I am the eldest."

"It must be nice to be part of such a big family. I'm an only child."

"We have lots of fun, but lots of quarrels too, eh, Douglas?"

◆

Chapter Eight

Thursday 9 December 1926

THE DRUMMER RATTLED and played on the shiny dented surface of his tin drum while his Westclox alarm danced about and made faces at Garnett. He took the clock from the cake tin where he had put it to make sure it would wake him, and turned off the alarm. It was quarter to four. He lay back in his bed. His head rested against the iron headrest. Would be nice to have just a little snooze. What would the Judge think of him if he were late? He sat up. And lay down again, on his side. His bladder felt uncomfortable. He got out of bed. It was dark. He went outside. An unnaturally warm offshore breeze swept through the coastal vegetation.

The Roses' maid, Martha, had started the fire in the wood stove early. The lid of a black kettle rattled uncomfortably. The missus preferred tea. Let the water just start to boil, pour some of it into the pot to warm the pot, empty the pot, one heaped teaspoon for each cup, add boiling water. These people are full of shit. But work is scarce.

The Judge lay against his wife's back , his arm around her, a breast cupped in his learned hand. He smelt his own breath. There must be a little mutton stuck in his teeth. The back of his wife's neck was rancid. The trousers of his pyjamas had become uncomfortably twisted. His back was stiff. Something he had eaten the night before had given him flatulence.

Frances had woken early. She sat on the chair in her room tying her shoelaces while she imagined holding Douglas' face in her hands. She touched his warm mouth with her thumb. She stroked the short hair at the back of his neck. Her father came into her room, "I will be ready in a short while, those two won't be too punctual. I think we're ahead of them."

The Judge dressed quickly. Martha took his tea to the dining room. On his way to the privy the Judge saw light in Hurter's house, and figures moving about.

Martiens folded his blankets neatly and put them to one side before he carried his mattress from the kitchen to the back veranda. He was hungry. Sienna had made some sandwiches for him the night before. He sat down on the back steps. He chewed his bread slowly, mixed it with his saliva and savoured the apricot jam, his eyes still in his head.

Douglas stood over the washbasin in his room, and splashed cold water into his face. He had not slept well. The sound of the sea was full of despair. Night was ending here and starting somewhere else.

The Judge and Frances were outside when Garnett and Douglas arrived. Frances had tied a floral scarf under her chin. She wore a tweed skirt, stockings, lace-up brown walking shoes, a white blouse with long sleeves and a home knitted cream jersey drawn in around her waist with a threaded ribbon. She held a wide brimmed straw hat in one hand. The Judge was in a hunting jacket, plus fours and brown walking boots. He carried a small knapsack over his shoulder and his pith helmet in one hand.

The sea was calm. The tide had started to flow. They would have to take the higher route. Douglas was pensive. Garnett did not know what to say. On their left small early morning waves flopped onto the beach and hissed softly as they spread onto the sand. At times the procession moved higher up on the beach to avoid rising water and then as it receded, went back onto the easier, harder sand. The lower edges of the Robberg were shrouded in a silent skirt of fret.

Frances took Douglas' hand.

Douglas thought of something worthwhile to say.

"Do we have to go right across the Robberg, Martiens?" Frances asked.

"Yes Missus, to the other side. That where we want to go."

"How wide is the Robberg?" She continued

"I don't know how wide, or how fat it is, but it's far."

Gentle early morning wind blew from the land. The first sea gulls shrieked forlornly. Garnett gradually increased his pace. He could hear the Judge's breathing. He felt the sea air in his nose. He popped his ears. Good to expand the Eustachian tubes. Equalises pressure. "How are the two of you doing back there?" He called to Frances and Douglas.

"We have never ever been across the Robberg in all the time that we have come here on holiday," Frances remarked.

"How long does it take you to travel here from Cape Town, Judge?" Garnett asked.

"I like driving," the Judge replied. "The idea of a long journey produces some kind of exuberance in me. My wife enjoys it too. She is quite adventurous in her own way. We spread the journey over three days. Which means we sleep over twice. My wife has a cousin who is a merchant in Swellendam. From Swellendam we go to George. We take rooms in the Hawthorndene Hotel. And then it's just a short distance here. The holiday starts when we leave home."

They walked in silence for some time. The Robberg grew larger. The wind shifted onshore. When the mist began to lift they reached the end of the beach.

"Martiens should go ahead now to show the way," Garnett said.

The going was more difficult, through soft dry sand. Frances got sand into her shoes and Douglas helped her along by holding her arm. It was a relief when they reached a grass-covered path through the fynbos. "I must get the sand out of my shoes," Frances said. "Do carry on, Douglas will help me."

She sat down on the path, her legs to one side. Her skirt was slightly above one knee. Douglas knelt down next to her. She put her hand on her ankle and drew her foot nearer to remove her shoe. Her legs parted and her skirt slid up over her petticoat. She looked up at him. He was too afraid to look down. The Judge, Garnett and Martiens were about forty paces ahead. Frances pulled at the one end of her shoelace. Douglas held her ankle and removed her shoe. As he looked down, he saw the inside of her thigh. The image dissolved in his grey eyes. The place where her silk stocking ended and soft flesh began; the colour of her skin, the hem of her stocking, the straining suspender strap, the slippery textures and subtle shades of her underwear. He looked up. She blushed and twisted her hips to bring her legs together.

Douglas held her shoe upside down by its shank and knocked the cuff on the ground. He put his fingers inside the shoe to loosen the remaining sand. Frances handed him the other shoe. She put her shoes on again and Douglas helped her to her feet. She looked to see where her father was. He and Garnett and Martiens had stopped, and were looking out to sea. She stood on her toes and kissed Douglas on his temple. "I'm fine now," she squeezed his hand. "Let's go."

The hike up the Robberg was heavy going and they had to wait several times to let the Judge catch his breath. Once they were on the ridge of the promontory the endless plaintive sounds of the ocean, spilling itself forever onto the land, vanished and they were in an atmosphere of silence until they heard the reverberations of their own feet on the path and the swishing rustling of vegetation against their clothing and their shoes. A breeze detached itself from the rest of the air and drifted through the fynbos. A sparrow chirped. The east grew luminous and the radiance of the day expanded to meet them, as if they were walking into approaching time. The ineluctable movements of planets and stars, the machinery that would bring the light, became the effect of perceptions – for each one the dawn approached at a different rate. The sea lay below them, white silver, pink mother of pearl, stirring.

Douglas and Frances were losing ground. Walking behind her Douglas enjoyed the movements of her hips. The image prompted fantasies: sensuous stocking hems, suspender ends and infinite flesh, and that which he did not dare imagine. He wanted to touch her, to smell her. He had a sensation of walking next to himself. He felt threatened by the salacious proportions of his thoughts and tried to distract himself. But his will was impotent. He could not rescue himself.

They walked on in silence. Martiens thought of the money he was going to earn, and what he would be able to buy the two little ones. The one had a bad cold. Snot running into his mouth. A few pennies' worth of sweets wrapped in newspaper. A little tin of snuff for Dora; chewing tobacco for the old chap, and food. Who knows, perhaps some fish to take home. That even a Hottentot could be so fortunate.

The Judge thought of his wife. She was playful when on holiday. He looked back to see where Frances and Douglas were. He stopped and let Garnett pass. "Douglas," he called, did you do much Catullus?"

Douglas and Frances caught up with him.

"I beg your pardon, Judge?"

"I said did you do much Catullus?"

Douglas blushed. "A fair amount."

Frances was silent.

"Did you enjoy him?"

Damned if you answer, damned if you don't.

The Judge was no Latin scholar but wanted to show Douglas what he knew. "Rome's greatest lyric poet. Born in Verona of a patrician family. Did you know that his father was host to Caesar himself?"

"I am aware that he knew Cicero," Douglas responded.

"He once referred to 'a purse full of cobwebs'. Could have meant 'muisneste'; you know what I mean, Douglas?"

Douglas was self-conscious.

"It is commonly thought that the most important influence in his life was Clodia. Remember her? Just think of it: a Villa at Tibur, a retreat on Lake Garda, even a yacht. Clodia was some woman. Glad I did not have to sit in judgement on her. There's nothing new, is there? Poor Catullus, he was a babe in the woods with that woman."

Frances felt uneasy about her father's mood. He had the same scabrous tone as the time when she overheard him and his brother talking about the incident at Oxford. An erotic photograph of a man and a woman that some fellow had sent to his brother from Port Said. Caused quite a rumpus at Oxford. Her uncle was nearly sent down. "Daddy, Catullus was a sensitive man. His work showed a great tenderness. I like sensitive men."

"A good jurist must have a grasp of all facets of life," came the Judge's defence. "But I suppose you can do worse than to rely on Gibbon, hey Douglas? Remember the sedition of Antioch? When the statues were destroyed? Theodosius was emperor then. My friend Malcolm Searle likes to quote him: 'if the exercise of justice is the most important duty, the indulgence of mercy is the most exquisite pleasure of a sovereign.' Dear old Malcolm. He is so forgiving."

Douglas was back on familiar ground. They were still on the level part of the promontory.

Gericke se Bank was a wide rocky shelf that sloped gradually into the sea from the lowest part of the promontory. Its surface was coarse and comfortable to walk on. The sea was calm. The surge was gentle.

The Judge took off his knapsack. He put his stick above it so that it would not roll away. Frances stretched and yawned with her arms held up in the air. Garnett and Martiens prepared the tackle.

"How far out should I cast, Martiens?"

"Give it a good distance, the musselcracker likes deeper waters, Doctor."

Garnett took a long sweeping back-swing and flung the lead out to sea. The reel whirred and spun to release the fishing line. His fingers were firmly on the running line and the wooden edge of the reel to avoid an overrun. It was a good cast. The sinker and the hook with its luckless crab splashed into the sea about eighty yards away. He let line out as he retreated.

"I would not have thought it possible to get it out that far," the Judge said.

"All we have to do now is to wait for the fish to take the bait and swallow it," Frances said enthusiastically. "But first I think it is time for some hot coffee and something to eat."

There was a faint stirring of Garnett's line. Then a slight tugging. He held his breath. Must be very patient now and not strike too early. Or was it just small fish playing with the crab, or the movement of the water? The ratchet of the reel screamed. The end of the rod was plucked downwards. He staggered to his feet and almost lost his balance. He let the line run so that he could compose himself. He used his hand as a brake. He jerked the rod sharply backwards to ensure that the hook would be well embedded in the fish, and took up the slack in the line.

"Bring him in quickly, doctor," Martiens shouted. "Don't give him a chance to crawl in under the ledges. See how he moves this way and that way, back and forth. He wants to shear the line. Bring him to the surface as quickly as possible, the line is more than strong enough. Garnett was pleased to have a coach. It was difficult to resist taking up some of the slack in the line. He kept his eyes on the place where the line entered the sea. Swells of transparent blue-green water surged and ebbed. He felt a breeze on his neck. Reflections of sunlight on the water.

The line moved to his left. "As I expected," Martiens said. "Doctor must remain patient. The hook is well into him. As long as he does not fray the line." The line moved out to sea. "Leave him now, but not for too long. He's searching for deeper water."

Garnett let the fish move away. "I am going to start lifting him now, Martiens."

"Just be careful, Doctor."

The Judge turned to speak to Douglas. "Nel seems to be making some progress." But Douglas was looking at Frances' face and seeing her suspenders.

"I beg your pardon, Judge, you were saying?"

The Judge imagined what young Catullus might have done on holiday.

"I said that Nel seems to be making some progress."

The critical moment was approaching. It would have been better not to have the fish on the line. Then there would have been nothing to lose. Better to have failed altogether than to almost succeed now. He would have to rely on Martiens' skill with the gaff. The fish was at the water's edge, struggling desperately. Martiens lunged at it with the gaff and caught it under the gills. As the fish made a last vigorous attempt to free itself Martiens slipped and fell. He clung to the gaff. Douglas rushed to help. He grabbed Martiens by the collar of his shirt to prevent him from sliding into the sea. He handed the gaff to Douglas, "Take the gaff Master, I am all right. Pull the fish up." He grabbed the gaff and dragged the fish up the slope as it thrashed about and gasped for air. Blood flowed from Martiens' left ankle. Frances clasped her hands together. The Judge chuckled at the commotion.

Garnett hit the fish over the head with a tyre lever. Its movements slowed. He took a knife, pushed it through the lower part of the gills, slit the sinews below the gills and pushed the head of the fish back until its spinal cord snapped. The fish had become a meal.

Garnett sat down and helped himself to a sandwich and coffee. He smelt the coffee in the kitchen of their house in Oudtshoorn. He was fourteen again, barefoot, in shorts, in the late afternoon. Ripe syringa berries had got stuck between his toes. The glow of the rekindled wood stove warmed his front. Unseasonable rain had brought a chill to the air and the scent of the first raindrops plopping into the dust. Although he had scrubbed his hands, they still had black grease ingrained from Uncle Charlie's bicycle shop. "You are not doing enough schoolwork, Garnie," his mother called as she approached from the passage.

"Uncle Charlie wants me to work for him in the shop."

"You are capable of greater things."

"You've done jolly well, Doctor Nel," the Judge said. "It's a frightfully large fish, I dare say. How much would you say it weighs?"

"I have a spring balance in my bag. We'll have a look in a moment. I think we should get going. It's going to be a quite a job getting this fish back."

"Forty seven pounds!" the Judge exclaimed.

"That must be a record." Frances clapped her hands.

Garnett smiled. "All credit to Martiens."

Martiens slit the fish's underside and took its innards out. Overhead seagulls shrieked.

"We'll have to tie it onto the gaff and two of us will carry it between us," Garnett suggested.

It was eight o'clock. It was becoming warmer. They began their climb and left the sea below them. The growing heat released aromatic fragrances from the vegetation. The sound of the sea came and went. The fish swayed between the two bearers.

Frances admired Douglas' legs. She remembered the last University House rugby match. It had rained the night before. Douglas was tall, full of mud, with steam coming off him in the August chill. He was so willing. He knelt down to tie his boot lace and looked up at her with a boyish smile. She saw his white scalp beneath his dark hair, his forehead washed clean by his sweat. And the intelligent smiling grey-blue eyes. He was clean-shaven when he fetched her for the House Dance that night, purified by his exertion. There was a hint of victorious beer on his breath and the odour of cigar smoke clung to the lapels of his dinner jacket. Like a warrior returning. He had kissed her for the first time that evening under a palm tree outside the women's residence and she had gasped when she felt the ticklish excitement inside her lower lip – delicate as the first traces of jasmine in the early spring.

The Robberg had woken up. Its colours were clear, its back a dusty olive green and its russet-brown grim folded walls stood in an agitated sea, utterly motionless, defiant of the movement of the water.

The Judge anticipated delicate fresh firm white fish flesh on his plate. Nothing could be better. He would suggest that the fish be prepared at their house. What they did not consume could be curried and shared with Nel to take back to Oudtshoorn. "I would like to make a proposition, Doctor Nel," the Judge suggested, "which I hope you will find entertaining. If you would arrange for your man to clean the fish properly, and bring it over to our house, at your convenience of course, we could all have supper together this evening, especially since you will be leaving tomorrow; a sort of farewell celebration, you know. Martha has a special gift for frying fish. We could fry some and the rest could be pickled for you to take back home."

"I would like to give Martiens some of the fish as his share."

"It's a delicacy, my good man. I'm told they like the head. It makes good soup. Once heard of a case in which a coloured fellow assaulted another, and damn nearly killed him, over a bowl of fish soup. They were both drunk. The accused pleaded leniency because, or so he said, the one eye of the fish head kept staring at him, and he thought it was the plaintiff mocking him. One wonders what they could have been drinking. I'm sure he would enjoy the head. It has been a hard slog up and down those hills."

Garnett said nothing for a while. The scaly silver brown body of the fish swung haplessly from the shaft of the gaff, its head bent back, its eyes dull. The flaps of its gaping belly slapped against each other. The body was not yet cold and they were already apportioning their inheritance.

"We'll clean the fish, and I'll send it over to your house. We would very much like to have supper with you this evening, thank you. I'm sure Douglas is pleased." Garnett was feeling reckless. There was a hint of asperity in his voice. "Frances must also be pleased."

Frances had fallen behind. Garnett was relieved that she did not hear the remark. She was drawing patterns with her toe in the wet sand. A simple daisy shape, a rectangle onto which she put a roof and chimney, the round face onto a stick figure of a child.

Douglas looked round to see where she was. The man and the woman with their child were on the beach again. The three of them could walk along the beach this evening after dinner. Get Garnie to suggest it. Her parents would regard him as the chaperone. Like putting the fox into the henhouse to look after the chickens. He chuckled. The mischief of his idea animated memories of his cousin, as they had done so many times. The images waited to be released from constraints of puritanical guilt. His fantasies, the actors in his bawdy music hall, were ready to perform. Should he let the curtain of petticoats and lace underwear rise? He had the free will to let it stay down. Does one really have free will? Since he saw Frances' thighs his desire had invaded his whole body. He measured how far they still were from the Roses' house. He could not look at Frances. He would pretend to be lost in contemplation.

The curtain rose. He was lying next to his eldest girl cousin on a patch of grass among the reeds next to the river. She was on her back. He was fourteen. She was seventeen. They watched clouds scudding overhead as the sky seemed to fall over. It was Sunday afternoon and the rest of the world was smothered in a sleep of carnal dreams.

"Do you know where babies come from, Douglas?" she asked.

"I have some idea."

"I have watched the horses do it on the farm. Mummy always made sure we were distracted when the mares had to be serviced. They even brought a special stallion there once. The men did not shut the gate of the paddock properly. Chrissie and I were on the swing under the walnut tree while mummy and daddy slept that afternoon, and the stallion got to one of the mares. It was wonderful. He put his front legs around the mare while she made playful movements with her head. He bit her sides gently till her tail went up to one side. We could see his thingy. It had become as large as the policemen's truncheon. He jabbed about until it was in the mare. He then wriggled and threw his head back with a triumphant sound, and then just stood still for a while on his hind legs, with the mare under him. After he slid off they stood side by side and rubbed their heads together. It was so romantic. Why do people say such horrid things about the way babies are made? Do you want to touch me there?"

Douglas was not sure whether he had heard correctly. "What do you mean?"

"Put your hand into my knickers, silly."

He turned towards her. She took his hand and put it inside her pants. His disbelief of what was happening was so great that he could hardly comprehend what he was feeling and his incomprehension was made greater by the unfamiliarity of what he was touching. She was warm and slightly moist. "Press harder, you silly, a bit more. Now stop immediately, or I shall have to tell mummy."

She sat bolt upright, slightly flushed. "Do want to feel once more?"

He put his hand back. This time for a bit longer, not knowing what to do. "Stop, or I'll have to tell mummy."

He avoided her blue eyes that Sunday night at supper, whenever they smiled dreamily at him across the innocent white tablecloth.

They were close to the house now. Frances had caught up to them. She ran past the others until she was opposite Douglas. "We could go for a walk this afternoon. Just like we did yesterday, that is if you are not too tired? Let those who want to sleep, sleep. It is too wonderful a day to waste, isn't it?"

Sienna arrived at the back door of the Roses' house. The top half of the stable door was open. Martha turned around when Sienna's shadow darkened the room. "I have brought the fish."

"I will call my madam."

Sienna heard footsteps approaching. Mrs Rose appeared, followed by the Judge. "Thank you so much." Martha returned to the kitchen and stood to one side. Sienna handed the dish to Martha.

"My goodness, your arms must be tired," Mrs Rose said in her patronising colonial voice. Sienna smiled uneasily. "Please thank Doctor Nel. I am sure we are going to enjoy the fish."

"Thanks Medim," Sienna said and left for the Hurters' house.

Mrs Rose took the cloth off the fish.

"He's kept the tail," the Judge said.

"And why shouldn't he my dear, after all, he caught the fish."

"It's the best part. That's why he kept it. I would have thought we could all have had a bit. That's all I meant. Let's drop the subject. I suppose we'll still have to pickle some for them to take home."

Garnett and Douglas sat in the sombre dining room, in the company of dark remaindered furniture, consigned to the holiday home, to be made sticky by the sea air. They ate fresh brown bread and butter and the freshly fried tail of the mussel cracker.

"What are you thinking about, Garnie?"

"That it was a good thing that my mother forced me to repeat matric. I would have been in Uncle Charlie's bicycle shop, or the garage, now. Fixing the Judge's car."

"You've been very quiet, Douglas."

Douglas was embarrassed.

"I can see how you feel about Frances."

"Ag Garnie."

"The two of you will make a wonderful couple. Her parents like you. It's all most fortunate. As though it were destined to happen. But you must seize the moment. You cannot let indecision get the better of you. Take her for a walk along the beach later on. I'm going to have forty winks. We won't leave too early tomorrow."

Chapter Nine

DOUGLAS WANDERED down to the beach as soon as Garnett went to have his nap. Frances saw him approaching and went outside, putting on her hat.

"My mother and father are going to have a sleep. We have the whole world to ourselves," she said enthusiastically.

The afternoon wind had come up.

"If there were people at the furthest end of the beach, do you think we would be able to see them, Frances?"

Frances put her head forward and narrowed her eyes to peer into the distance. "No, I don't think so."

"So even if we were to be nearly there no one would be able to see us."

"Why do you say that?"

"It would be exciting to be completely alone with you."

"Do you dream much, Douglas?" Frances asked this suddenly as if she had prepared the question for a special reason.

"Why do you ask?"

"My cousin, Fiona Chisholm, whom you must meet the next time she comes over from England, was telling me, in her last letter, about the new prominent Swiss psychologist Carl Jung and his dream theory. He and Freud have discovered a part of the mind known as the unconscious. I think we have spoken about this before. It is like a world of its own that connects everything and controls all that we do. Fiona's interested because her father is a clinical neurologist who studied under a man called Breuer in Vienna. Breuer, she says, has cured hysteria by means of hypnosis. Dr Chisholm believes that we will soon be able to explain virtually all human behaviour, and perhaps even understand how life originated. But, let me not digress, I was asking you about your dreams."

"I don't really know. I don't dream that often. I dreamt the first night we were here. It must have been something I ate, I think. I sometimes dream when I have had a lot of meat in the evening."

"What did you dream?"

"It was all confused. About a horse." Douglas thought about his cousin.

"Was it a pleasant dream?"

"It was not unpleasant. It was very clear. The colours I saw were very bright."

"Are you not going to ask me about my dreams?"

"How inconsiderate of me. Do tell me about your dreams."

"I had a most wonderful dream last night. You and I were having the most flirtatious amours. We were together on a ship, steaming towards Europe, on our way to Paris. We were sitting on the scrubbed wooden deck on the most perfectly warm sun-filled day, at a table covered with a brilliantly white cloth, having tea and a small plate of Petit Beurres. It was frightfully nice. The crunchy butter taste. The fragrance of the Indian tea. We were alone on the ship. It was sailing by itself under a cobalt blue sky. The whole thing to ourselves. It was your ship. My destiny. I was your inamorata."

Douglas looked back to see how far they had walked. He held her delicate hand. It was cool from the excitement of her description and a little moist. Her shoulder touched his arm.

"So, what do you make of my dream?"

"Your description has a lovely poetic quality."

"Do you think dreams have predictive meaning?"

"I haven't really thought about it."

"I hope they do. It has been so wonderful to have you here in this lovely place by the sea. At the end of our holiday we will return to Cape Town and you will be in Oudtshoorn. I will go away to Graaff Reinet and you will remain behind. You will begin your career, and I will start teaching." Frances took off her hat. "The grips in my hair are hurting my scalp." She adjusted the grips and put her hat back on.

They walked along in silence. Douglas searched for something to say. A small sandpiper darted along the wet sand, and stopped to look at them, its head askance.

"Isn't it sweet," Frances said. "It is so vulnerable, so fragile, and yet it needs no looking after." She looked up. "The European swifts have returned. Imagine the journey they have to make all the way from the northern hemisphere and then back each year. Daddy says they even return to the same nests of the year before. Have you seen how they feed their young?"

"We have some nests under the eave of the outbuilding at the Hurters' house."

"I thought more about what you said about teaching."

"Oh I suppose it will be all right. I don't have any misgivings about the subject matter. In a way I am looking forward to it I suppose. I was silly about journalism yesterday. I don't know what came over me. At least I will be earning some money of my own. I am looking forward to that. Garnett is doing jolly well for himself."

"You should perhaps have thought about a lectureship at the university. There are so many opportunities if one considers how fast it is growing. Just the other day Daddy was saying that the number of professorships has nearly doubled since the end of the war. There are almost fifty now and the number of students has almost quadrupled. The plans to move to Groote Schuur are well advanced. It is such a pity that you could not come with us when the Earl of Athlone laid the foundation stone of the Wernher and Beit Laboratories last year. To be part of all that history. Mummy was ill when the Prince of Wales laid the foundation stone of the Men's Residence. Daddy was there alone. He says the Prince is a bit of a rake. He drank a lot with some young libertines at Kelvin Grove, and kept some very doubtful female company. I would have thought that he would set an example, what with being the Chancellor of the University and all that. Do you also sometimes expect people in elevated positions to have superior morality?"

Douglas saw an opportunity to redeem his own temptations, "Some of the greatest individuals have also had great weaknesses. Take Shaw as an example, Nobel Prize and all. They say he is pretty coarse. Your father mentioned Catullus this morning. Those who are capable of the greatest good also seem to be capable of some of the worst things."

"It will be my first time away from my parents, ever. In some ways it will be nice to be independent. I try to think of it as an adventure. Going into the unknown. Just think of our ancestors who left the countries of their birth to come to Africa. All I am going to do is to travel a few hundred miles to the northeast, really. What I like about teaching Latin is that everything is so well defined. It is compact and neat. And there will not be much marking to do, unlike history.

"I am a bit nervous about the accommodation: Marshall's Boarding House. That's where most of the teachers stay. I am relieved that I won't have to share with anyone. Anyway, it's not for ever. When you were Chairman of the Students' Council, did you ever have to attend Professor du Toit's Spreekklub?"

"Yes, why do you ask?"

"Daddy says he is part of the Nationalist movement."

"That is interesting, I felt that he was really more interested in promoting Dutch literature and language and Dutch ideas than Afrikaans."

"I wish you would tell Daddy that."

"Did you ever meet du Toit's daughter? She was in Mill Hope."

"She was pointed out to me once but we were never introduced."

"She is quite a pretty girl. Loved the mountain walks. Was athletic."

"Do you like athletic girls Douglas?"

"I didn't mean it like that."

"I don't mind." She squeezed his hand and put her head against his shoulder, the brim of her straw hat bent against her cheek.

He contemplated the feeling of holding Frances' hand. He flattened his palm to get more intimate contact. Their palms sucked together. He let go of her hand and put his arm around her waist. He felt her hip and her ribs and smelt her fragrance. She put her arm around him. It was awkward to walk like that. She was below him on the slope of the beach. Silence produced the intimacy that they had hoped their conversation would bring.

Sea gulls screeched in their distant sky. The Robberg never seemed to get closer. The vaporous sea breath that had promised to provide them with privacy never appeared. They would have to rely on distance to compress the clouds into a veil.

The Judge and his wife lay on their brass bed. The maid had gone to her room. Frances had gone for a walk with Douglas. Mrs Rose had suggested over lunch to Frances that she and Douglas should go for a walk. The Judge admired the calculating way in which her unfailing instinct could create a whisper of suggestion – enough to provoke arousal.

He was in his silk pyjamas, Mrs Rose in her petticoat. She still had her stockings on. He lay on his back with his hands behind his head. She rolled onto her side and pressed herself against him. He put his hand on her thigh where her stocking became flesh. They lay like that, each waiting for a reaction. The afternoon wind moved the curtains.

"I think I should close the windows so that the curtains will stay in place," he said and got up from the bed with exaggerated clumsiness to ensure that his back remained towards her.

While he was busy securing the windows and adjusting the curtains she got up and locked the bedroom door. She pushed down her pants and drew the large white porcelain chamber pot from under the bed and in under her. She squatted and urinated as silently as she could while she stared at the polished wooden floorboards. When she had finished she took off her pants, wiped herself with a small towel from the washstand and rubbed perfume between her thighs while he pretended not to see. She lay down next to him, and pulled her petticoat up above her hips. He saw the copper colour of the protruding hair below her suspender belt.

"Now remember, we are on holiday dear," she said in an affectedly coquettish voice, "there is nothing waiting for you, so let's not be in any hurry now."

The lack of cross ventilation made them sweat. She delighted herself and her husband with her strong athletic tennis-playing frame and felt him convulse with pleasure. When they had spent themselves, the Judge sighed and gave her a little perfunctory kiss on the cheek to show his appreciation for a job well done and fell asleep with his mouth open. She sat patiently over the chamber pot and relieved herself of her husband's seed. When the tickling stopped she went quietly to the washstand, poured water onto a face cloth and wiped first her flushed face, her neck, arms, then her sensitive nether regions. She put on a brightly coloured floral print silk dressing gown, unlocked the bedroom door and went to the kitchen to make herself tea which she sipped standing, with her legs slightly apart, at the window of the dining room, looking dreamily out to sea.

Douglas and Frances let go of each other. Frances skipped towards the water's edge and turned to look back in the direction from which they had come. "I imagine the whole village must be asleep by now, including Mummy and Daddy. They sleep a lot while they're on holiday. You've never really been one to sleep during the day, have you?"

"It seems a bit of a waste of time to me."

"Do you remember those endless debates last year about evolution when the Scopes trial was on?"

"Yes, why do you ask about that now?"

"I have been meaning to ask Garnett what his views are, I mean, as a medical doctor and a scientist."

"The whole issue of evolution is so controversial. I mean no one really knows. It remains a theory, and always will. No matter how much evidence is collected, and no matter how good the evidence, nobody can produce the kind of proof that normal scientific experimentation demands. The concept is too large."

"You don't have to prove everything. Even if it can be shown that just one species has evolved, the inference is there. Surely?"

"I have no strong feelings. I think that it all comes down to a religious issue rather than a scientific one, a battle between fundamentalists and people of more liberal persuasions. What the fundamentalists cannot accept is the fact the Darwin has removed, or at the very least severely questioned, the notion of a mysterious invisible governing or guiding force in nature."

"Why can we not believe that God created evolution? That it is His way of working?"

"Yes indeed!"

"Why do you refuse to be drawn?"

"I'm quite happy to discuss it."

He put his arm around her again. She moved away, turned, and stood in front of him. She put her arms around his neck, lifted herself onto her bare toes and kissed him. The sand tickled the sensitive areas between her toes. When she had finished kissing him he hugged her. The way in which she yielded to him aroused him. They walked on towards the Robberg. The houses they had left behind were invisible.

"When Mummy and Daddy went to England last year, they also spent some time in Paris. Daddy thinks the artists and the writers there have gone quite mad. He attributes it to the war. Also a reaction to Victorian values, not that they were much prevalent there."

"We are living in exciting times."

Garnett woke shortly after three thirty. His earlier anticipation of pleasant events, that had brought happy associations and feelings of inner equilibrium, had deserted him. His awareness now had heavy definition and a dark edge from which he could not escape. The high-pitched bark of a dog that he would not otherwise have heard, irritated him. The sound of the surf was too loud. He felt disconnected and uncomfortable. He resented the fact that they were in a rented house while the Roses owned theirs, and that the Judge had been to Oxford where he had acquired his superior attitude and aloofness. The way he had raised his eyebrows when Dublin was mentioned. There was sweat in his hair and a bitter taste in his mouth. The solution would be to go for a swim. But he did not like the thought of getting wet. Why does the sea have to be wet? What is wetness really? In an absolute sense? Wet. The more you say the word the stranger it sounds. Wet.

Chapter Ten

GARNETT AND DOUGLAS arrived at the Roses' house shortly after seven. It was still quite light.

The wind had dropped. The pink evening sky was silent except for the sounds of the waves. The Judge was on the veranda, looking out to sea. "Ah! Here you are. Welcome, come aboard!"

"Grab a chair Doctor Nel. Make yourself at home. What a wonderful evening."

"I was just contemplating the evening. I was reminded of a visit two years ago to Newport, Rhode Island. Had some wonderful sailing there with friends. They have a yawl, a jolly boat. Have you done much sailing Doctor Nel?"

"No, none at all. But I often admired the sailing vessels off the coast of Ireland and England."

"A yawl is a fore-and-aft rigged sail-boat that carries a mainsail and one or several jibs, with a mizzenmast far aft. The one we were on was about sixty-five feet long. Built in the Netherlands and sailed to Newport across the Atlantic. It could sleep twelve and had the most marvellous facilities. We never slept on it though. Only did day sailing. Do take a chair, and sit down."

The outside table was covered with a brightly coloured cloth. A small table had been brought out from the front room. On it stood a His Master's Voice gramophone, five or six records, and a tin of needles. The gramophone had a base of cherry wood, its trumpet a giant fluted St Joseph's lily, brass on the outside and vermilion red on the inside.

"I thought we should have some music tonight. And eat outside as we used to do in Italy. The weather has been kind to us. We are pleased to have you over. We won't be too late since you presumably want to travel before the heat of the day. We'll wait for the sun to go down some more. I wonder where the women are? What about a drink? I am having a gin, and there is some beer."

"Beer would be very nice, thank you," Garnett replied.

"Yes, that would be nice," Douglas said.

"The beer is on the sideboard in the dining room, if you would be so good, please, Douglas."

Garnett and Douglas stood on the veranda, pewter beer mugs in hand, in the light of the setting sun. The Judge was in his wicker chair. Garnett lifted his beer mug in a student-like gesture of proposing a toast, and tasted the bitterness of the hops through the head of the beer. Mrs Rose and Frances arrived.

"Good evening Doctor Nel, hello Douglas!" Mrs Rose was in a happy mood.

"Hello Garnett," Frances said.

"It was kind of you to have us here again, thank you."

"Good evening Mrs Rose, hello Frances," Douglas replied.

"It was the least we could do, after all, when you supplied our supper. It was frightfully nice of you."

"What would you like to drink, my dear?"

"I'll have some vermouth and soda, please."

"A bit of ginger beer for you, Frances?"

"Yes, thank you Daddy."

Douglas helped the Judge get the drinks.

The Judge waited till they were settled on the veranda. "Let's have some music! I have brought along a few gramophone recordings. There's some Verdi – Rigoletto, the Girl of the Golden West by Puccini, Leoncavallo's Pagliacci, and more inside. All performed by Caruso. Who has a request?"

"Garnett has a jolly good voice," Douglas remarked.

"So then, it is you Doctor Nel who will have first choice."

Garnett examined the records. *La donna e mobile. Bella figlia dell'amore.* "Rigoletto I think."

The Judge removed the record from its brown paper sleeve and placed it on the turntable. He wound the gramophone, started the turntable moving and placed the stylus in the outermost groove. At first there was only a scratching sound of the needle finding its way into the groove. They waited in anticipation: the waltz time introduction by the orchestra, the pause. A voice of seductive beauty and great power surged from the trumpet of the gramophone into the heavy atmosphere of the seaside evening. "*La don-na e mo-bi-le, Qual piu-ma al ven-to ...*"

Next was the aria "No! *Pagliacco non son.*"

It ended as it had begun, with the careless scratching of the wandering needle. They sat in silence for a while. The Judge got up reverently and removed the stylus from the record. He stopped the gramophone with the quiet care of one who did not want to disturb the precious atmosphere that he had created, raised his glass higher than he might have done ordinarily, and moved to the edge of the veranda. He stood there facing the sea. "How wonderful! Those magnificent, vigorous, dramatic outbursts. To think that we are able to hear his voice, here in this remote end of Africa, five years after his death. Science has made him immortal. Is it not remarkable? What do you say Douglas? Such sound! Captured forever!"

"Did you enjoy that Doctor Nel?"

"Yes I did, very much. His range of vocal effects makes me feel humble. The ease with which he captures the verisimo style of Leoncavallo, the way he enriches his baritone with smouldering colours and timbre, the way he phrases the music; it is really amazing."

"It is such a lovely evening," the Judge said. "I think we should have another drink before supper." He poured himself another gin. "There's more beer

Douglas, help yourselves." The Judge handed his wife a glass of vermouth and soda and settled into his chair. He breathed in deeply and sighed contentedly.

"Douglas and I were talking about evolution this afternoon. I said I would ask you what your views are, Garnett."

"I don't think we should hark back to that awfully silly trial in Chappatooga." Mrs Rose would much have preferred a lighter subject.

"The name is Chattanooga, dear, the place in Rhea county Tennessee, and as I mentioned to you before, the trial was held in the town of Dayton."

"You yourself said it was called Monkeyville, Jeremy."

Garnett was sympathetic. "I also think it was a rather silly trial, Mrs Rose, but to be fair, it focused a lot of attention on the issue of evolution versus fundamentalism, and from that perspective was probably a good thing."

"Why do you say it is a good thing?" the Judge asked.

"After all it was the fundamentalists who challenged Scopes. Fundamentalism has its roots in religious prejudice. To the fundamentalists it was just too much to accept the idea that 'man is descended from lower animals' or even to contemplate the possibility. However, perhaps both Scopes and the fundamentalists got it wrong because as I understand it, Darwin never said that man was descended from lower animals. He merely postulated that there is 'some process of transformation,' and went in search of evidence. The emotional way in which the Scopes issue was handled from both sides was in sharp contrast to the painstaking way in which Darwin set about his task. What he produced was overwhelming evidence, and it is unlikely that one can account for the facts that he exposed by any other hypothesis than the one he put forward. To his great credit, he was a true scientist – far more scientific than the fundamentalists, and for that matter, far more honest. It is said of him that he was at all times prepared to abandon every hypothesis and every fixed idea when new or different evidence presented itself. He was the personification of the truly objective observer. He would give up any hypothesis if the facts opposed it. Sadly, some of the misperceptions that the fundamentalists have stem from the understanding of the concept of 'species'."

"How do you mean?" Frances asked.

"A man called Ray conceived of the idea of 'species' for the purposes of creating a system of biological classification which became known as the binomial system. In terms of Ray's system a species came to be regarded as a unit, or category, of creation. Once people thought in terms of units of creation, and the units became well defined, it was quite easy to imagine that there could be no transition between the units. So, what was meant to be quite simply and purely a practical classification was transformed into a rigid doctrine. The next step was to worship the doctrine. On the other side are those who worship the scriptures. They forget that the scriptures are made for man, and not man for the scriptures. What the fundamentalists especially did not like was Darwin's dismissal of the notion of mysterious forces governing nature."

"You make it all sound so simple, and so clear, Doctor Nel, Frances and my husband are sometimes so impatient with me."

"Surely, for there to be selection of any kind there must be variation to begin with, otherwise there would be no differences from which to select," Frances responded.

Douglas wanted to make a contribution. "That is exactly right, Frances, and remember, Darwin also defined other factors, apart from variation, that in his opinion contribute to the process of evolution: heredity, and the struggle for survival or what one might call the struggle for existence."

"Perhaps we should not see evolution as being in conflict with the religious idea of the Creation. Perhaps it is just part of the way in which the creation expresses itself," Frances said.

"I don't have a problem with that approach," Garnett replied. "After all, Darwin himself was part of the creation. He could not stand apart from it. He probably just presented aspects of reality as he understood them."

"I think Frances made an interesting point," the Judge observed, "when she mentioned variation. Selection per se can only take place between existing forms and variations of those forms. However, the question remains in which direction the selection will occur. Why should what we regard as the strongest or the best be selected in preference to what we see as the inferior or the lesser. I say this because I would argue that selection cannot be prophetic. What John Stuart Mill said springs to mind: he described nature as a 'wasteful bungler.'"

"I have a problem with the kind of thinking that suggests that things happen at random." Garnett said. "It is rather difficult for me to explain. It seems to me that everything has a reason, or happens for a reason. What I have at times experienced in my work goes beyond what science can explain. People who should die recover and live. And the opposite also happens. There seems to be so much more than we can explain rationally. Some of the things I have seen suggest to me that we are just very small players on a very large stage. It is presumptuous to think that we as minor players can explain the greater reality."

Martha appeared in the front doorway. "The supper is ready Madam."

"We are nearly ready, thank you, Martha, I will ring the bell."

"I find your approach interesting, Doctor Nel," the Judge said. "We'll continue the discussion while we have supper. I would also like to hear what Douglas has to say. He's been conspicuously quiet for a man of his learning. Hey, Douglas?"

"While Garnett was expressing his views I could not help but be reminded of Huxley's attitude towards Darwin," Douglas said.

"You never said anything about that this afternoon," Frances said.

"To be honest, I never thought about it this afternoon."

"What Douglas is really saying is that he was thinking about you my dear, and not about nature's charms," Mrs Rose suggested.

"Come, come now, it seems as if I will have to call the lot of you to order," the Judge bellowed, "Let's adjourn for supper, and put Douglas on trial later. But before we start, let's light the lamps."

Mrs Rose rang the bell. "Shall we sit as we did yesterday?"

The Judge said grace.

Martha had baked a loaf of brown bread earlier that afternoon. The Judge passed the breadboard to Douglas. "Won't you cut the bread for us, Douglas? Always make sure the upper crust of the bread is pointing towards you when you cut bread, especially when it is fresh. The slices will turn out perfectly that way. I've never been able to work out why, but that was a lesson my grandfather taught whenever he had the opportunity. We'll start with some soup."

Martha brought a white porcelain soup tureen, and placed it in front of the Judge. A silver ladle waited. In the moving flame of the lamp the tureen cast a shadow on the Judge's front. He removed the lid. Blended flavours of thick vegetable soup enriched with the leftovers of the previous day's mutton escaped in a vaporous column.

The beer had stimulated Garnett's appetite.

When the Judge had dispensed the soup and offered slices of bread, butter was passed around. Mrs Rose cut her bread into small squares and put her butter on the edge of her side plate. She buttered a square, took a small bite, and while she chewed examined the marks her teeth had left in the butter. She swallowed her bread and let a spoon of hot soup dissolve the butter left in her mouth.

"I dare say I really enjoyed our expedition this morning. Being out in the sun, the marvellous exercise. The spoils of our efforts are waiting in the kitchen," the Judge enthused.

"It is a pity that you have to return so soon. We will still be here for more than a week," Mrs Rose mused. "Frances will miss the company."

The prospect of going back to Oudtshoorn made Douglas pensive.

"Douglas, tell us where you see yourself in this matter of evolution? And since you mentioned Huxley, I am intrigued to know why you regard his role as relevant," the Judge said with a tone of encouragement.

"I mentioned Huxley because he was probably the most authoritative commentator on Darwin's work. One could even say that his evaluation of Darwin bestowed special recognition on Darwin's work. But let me go back a little. If we look back over the last seventy odd years there is no gainsaying the fact that the publication of the *Origin of the Species* must be regarded as a most prominent landmark in the history of modern science. I say this because Darwin's method eventually penetrated virtually all regions of scientific enquiry. Now, taking into account Huxley's background and his thinking, Darwin's publication was to Huxley like finding a missing link – I'm sorry for the pun – in the form of a practical working premise. What is more, and this is very important, Huxley also found Darwin's objective and utterly honest approach, which Garnett referred to earlier, to be compatible with his own thinking and his own method of scientific research. Like Darwin he was prepared to follow the answer wherever the question took him; even, and this is important, even if it would actually have meant refuting Darwin's theory. Credit for Huxley's attitude must go to Carlyle who influenced him to sacrifice all pretence, right to the point that he was even prepared to disapprove of Carlyle's refusal to accept Darwin's hypothesis!

"What is interesting about Huxley is that he saw the theory of evolution not so much as speculation, but rather as a description of certain realities. To me such a departure point is attractive because it is consistent with a deductive approach, which is the approach I believe a scientist ought to have. The critics have all along had an inductive approach, and that is why the protagonists and the antagonists are missing each other. Quite simply, their premises, their departure points, are entirely different and in conflict with each other."

"Are you then saying that we are descended from apes?" Mrs Rose asked.

"Please do let Douglas finish dear," came the exasperated tone from the Judge.

"Douglas is not saying that, Mummy."

"I am so sorry Mrs Rose, perhaps we should change the subject." Douglas feared a confrontation.

"Please carry on Douglas." the Judge was enthralled.

Douglas felt constrained to join the threads that had unravelled in Mrs Rose's mind. "I am not entirely sure of my own position. If we say that we are descended from apes, why are we different from the apes that are left? If we argue that we descended from certain types of apes, then it still means that the apes from which we descended were different from the apes that remained apes. Which in a sense brings us back to Huxley. Remember, he was never prepared to accept Darwin's theories without qualification. While Darwin seems to suggest that an organism may gradually change or adapt to its environment by a process of transition, Huxley thought that transmutation was possible. There was his famous utterance, 'nobody can presume to say what the order of nature must be.' What it comes down to is that there is no evidence, in the scientific sense, of the kinds of universal structures that the fundamentalists presume to exist. To him their clinging to beliefs in structures that they presume to exist is in conflict with the notion of total surrender to the will of God. In the sense that he was prepared to surrender himself to the will of Science he came closer to the essential truth than the so-called believers. I also think he understood more than Darwin."

"Your soup is getting cold, Douglas," Mrs Rose observed.

"Man cannot live by bread alone, Mummy."

The beer had gone to Douglas' head. It was an excuse for him to eat. He felt like an actor eating on stage, with all eyes on him. As he leant over his plate to have his first mouthful of soup, his elevated awareness seemed to tilt his body upwards.

"What do you make of his 'law and morals' lecture?" the Judge asked.

"Let poor Douglas eat, dear."

The bread was good but lacked salt. Douglas glanced at the other plates. He was far behind. He would soon catch up. He had more soup, and then some more. He felt perspiration on the top of his head.

"I think I'll have a little more. What about you, Doctor Nel, some more soup?" the Judge suggested.

"That would be very nice thank you."

To Garnett's relief Mrs Rose offered him some more bread. "And some butter."

Douglas formulated his response to the Judge's question. He had his own views of the law, and they were somewhat cynical. He nodded his head in appreciation as he sipped his soup. It pleased Mrs Rose.

"I must say it is a frightfully stimulating discussion," Frances exclaimed. "I'm glad we left it for this evening, like leaving the best for last."

"I was hoping for something cheerful and light, like a French soufflé with a hint of vanilla," Mrs Rose said enthusiastically.

The Judge smiled at his wife. "We'll put some more music on when we've had our meal. Would you like some more soup Douglas?"

"No thank you, Judge, I have done quite well."

"What about you, Frances?"

"No thank you, Daddy."

"You may ring for Martha, dear."

The fish was carried in on a large porcelain platter. It had been filleted and pan-fried to a golden perfection in a batter so light that its silver skin showed through in places. The Judge had been tempted to propose a toast to 'absent friends' meaning the tail of the fish, but deference for Douglas' scholarly eloquence held him in check. What a companion he would make for Frances. To introduce even the smallest element of controversy or discord now might blemish the spell that had been cast to produce the exquisite occasion. What children they would have. Frances was flushed. It pleased him to see how much Douglas' discourse had animated Frances – it seemed to transcend even her physical attraction to him.

"This fish," the Judge mumbled with a hot piece in his mouth, "is the finest food that you could find anywhere on this earth. And the magical way in which Martha fried it makes it even better. We are indeed most fortunate. And what gives eating it a further dimension is the fact that we saw how it was caught."

"Are we not becoming a bit sentimental, dear?" Mrs Rose smiled.

The Judge was embarrassed. Just as he could not sing in tune, he lacked poetic sense. He would have given a great deal to be able to sing in tune. But it was never to be. Ironically it made his admiration of Caruso's artistry so much greater. "Well, you all know what I mean," he laughed bashfully. "Anyway, to say the least, the fish is frightfully good. But, as I asked earlier, Douglas, what do you make of Huxley's 'law and morals' lecture?"

"I dare say it has puzzled me. I'm not sure that I quite understand what

Huxley meant. I have an impression that he himself was not altogether certain of his position. It was as though he had some sort of conflict within himself. He speaks of the intuitive and suggests that our aesthetic sense may be compared to our moral sense, or the other way around, I am not sure. At any rate, his proposition is that our moral sense is intuitive. It is interesting to me that he employs such an abstract or metaphysical premise from which to proceed to reason that 'law and morals' are 'restraints upon the struggle for existence between men in society.' So what it suggests to me is that, although he proposes that man's moral sense is intuitive in origin, it ultimately evolved into something that was purely utilitarian. I suspect there is a contradiction. According to him the cosmic process has no bearing on moral ends. He claims to have been unable to find any trace of a moral purpose in nature and concludes that moral purpose is purely an instrument of 'human manufacture.' We would do well to remind ourselves that the lecture was delivered a year before his death. It was in a sense a final formal declaration. I am not sure." Douglas fell into thought. There was silence at the table.

"Your whole life has been devoted to the law, dear, how do you see it?" Mrs Rose ventured, in the hope that she could make amends for her earlier remarks.

"Well now, let me see." He paused to have some more fish. "About Huxley's greatness there can be no doubt. I tend to agree with Douglas: his philosophical perspective is not clear to me. I have not read the lecture myself, or the essay in which it is contained. To me man's morality is a given. The law as we inherited it from the Romans is certainly a unique creation. It is, as Huxley says of morality, 'of exclusive human manufacture.' It forms the fabric of our society. It matters very little what its origins are, as long as its purpose is clear. The fact is that it is there and it can never be removed from society as we know it, for without it society cannot exist."

"If I may just add, Judge," Douglas interrupted, "He was of the opinion that the ethical progress of society did not depend on trying to imitate the cosmic process, or trying to escape from it, but in taking a stance against it."

"You are so quiet, Garnett," Frances observed. "What do you make of all of this?"

Garnett was not familiar with Huxley's work.

The Judge was irritated that he had made a poor start with his argument and that he was not permitted to develop a theme. He should not have ventured into unknown territory against a heavyweight.

"If Douglas admits to being confused," Garnett said, "who am I to throw light on the subject?" There was no response, and he took it to mean that they were waiting for him to continue. "The problem that I have with what has been said is that we seem to see the intellect as supreme; reason has to provide all the answers. We seem to assume that Nature has been constructed or fashioned in a mechanical kind of way. To discover the ultimate truth, all we have to do is to identify all the bits and pieces of which reality is made up. Like taking a jigsaw puzzle apart and understanding more of the picture it forms by looking at the pieces. And in this regard we cannot ignore what has happened to the scientific world since the time of Darwin. Consider the impact of Einstein's work. His views have turned the world upside down and shaken the foundations of the scientific establishment. Einstein has shown that what seemed to be absolute is not so. I must confess that I don't understand all he says – and there has been a tendency to give his ideas a sensational and popular quality – but the way in which he has shown up the limitations of Newtonian physics has been a bitter pill to swallow for the intellectuals and philosophers who relied on the certainty, or apparent certainty, that the establishment of the last century owned. It is uncomfortable to imagine that there is no such thing as absolute length or absolute time."

"At what time will you be leaving tomorrow morning, Doctor Nel?" Mrs Rose asked.

"Oh gosh, I haven't really thought of that. I like to leave as early as possible, to beat the heat, so to speak. Oudtshoorn can be jolly hot at this time of the year. But there is no reason to leave too early. We don't have that far to travel."

"Why have we changed the subject?" Frances asked.

Mrs Rose was determined to alter the mood. "I had hoped that we would have a happy light evening. We don't want our dear guests to be subjected to discussions and interrogations about all the frightfully tedious things that are happening in our mad world. We shouldn't have all our happy and familiar notions destroyed. It makes one feel uncomfortable. Next, you will again be discussing the ideas of that man Freud, and believe the strange things that they say happen in our minds. It is all very unsettling to say the least. It was all so romantic with the music and the drinks. Cheer us up Doctor Nel. You never told us what happened to the cook who forgot to put the gold sovereign into the Christmas pudding."

"To be truthful, I have no idea at all what happened to him. I feel sure my grandfather rather enjoyed the whole episode. He dined out on that story for the rest of his life. I think the cook remained with them until he retired. Probably as some kind of reward for giving the story to my grandfather."

Douglas wanted to please Frances. "You are perfectly right, Frances, when you say that we are living at a strange time in history. I often wonder how later generations will judge us. By the way, thinking about Huxley's Romanes lecture also made me think of Asquith's Romanes lecture and the reference he made in that to Lytton Strachey's *Eminent Victorians*. I only read the whole quartet recently. Strachey was of course very critical of the war effort. But I am digressing horribly, I do apologise."

The Judge interrupted, "And many of my generation are still very critical of Strachey and his set. He is a spoilt brat who has started or joined all kinds of secret groups. What disturbs me is the insidious influence that he and his cohorts have had, and still have. He was quite subversive during the war, not to mention the remarks he made under cross-examination during his trial. A great many sacrificed their lives for a just cause while he and his ilk lay about and refused to defend the very society which gave them liberal protection. It was quite unconscionable, quite unconscionable, to say the least. Cambridge was always just that much different from Oxford."

Douglas was taken aback. "I am not saying that I in any way support or even agree with his views. I am only concerned about what is happening now, in this post war period, in England, and in Europe. One cannot but wonder how this period will eventually be viewed. History by definition is a chronological record of events and their causes; it is always looking back. But we look back from a limited viewpoint. History is never as we see it now; it is always as somebody else will see it in the future. We are never sure how objective we are. And, then, when you come to think of it, we who study it really only ever study other peoples' points of view."

Frances moved about apprehensively in her chair. "I think we are still in a period of change. The war has had a profound effect on the combatant societies. If you come to think of it, there was bound to be a dramatic reaction. Think also of the way in which the post-war issues have been settled. What were meant to be solutions produced unintended consequences."

"There are certainly enough problems." Mrs Rose exclaimed. "Just think of those terrible fascists in Italy. Caruso made me think of that earlier, but I did not want to say so."

"And the communists that are emerging everywhere, like mushrooms in a dark cellar – in Europe, here in the Union, in America, in China. The old social order is dying. It is a great pity," the Judge added.

"I find the names of those Italians so delightfully romantic," Mrs Rose said enthusiastically. "What did you say Mussolini's troops are called, dear?"

"I don't quite see the relevance, dear, but they are known as the *Fasci de Combattimento*, we simply refer to them as Blackshirts which is as close to blackguards as you can get. Strange fellow Mussolini: he employs Lenin's ideas and yet derides the communists. His thugs sweep all opposition before them. His endeavours are socialistic yet he engineered the murder of Matteotti. The rest of the world stands by and does little more than utter weak protestations. He is a real showman, larger than life, like the ringmaster in a circus. Makes me think of Kaiser Wilhelm sitting on a damn military saddle at his desk during the war. What are those German friends of yours called, the ones you visited on your way here, Doctor Nel?"

"Leibner, but he came here before the turn of the century, and was very discreet during the war."

Garnett had little food left. He tried to eat as slowly as possible. Mrs Rose had finished her food. The Judge and Douglas still had quite a bit to eat. Frances picked at her fish.

"You mentioned Einstein, Doctor Nel," the Judge continued, "did you know that he was a pacifist? Did not support the German war effort."

"It seems to me, my dear, that you are quite taken with the idea of Einstein being a pacifist, as long as he is on the other side, but you find the same attitude deplorable when it comes to Strachey and his friends," Mrs Rose remarked.

The Judge glowered at her. His afternoon sleep had left in him a residue of irritability that reacted with the gin, and was made worse because of his wife's flippancy. His hopes that a happy evening would act as an antidote to his mood were transformed into heavy resentment. The spell that never existed now lay in pieces.

For an uncomfortable time there was silence.

"Do you ever go to Knysna, Doctor Nel?" Mrs Rose enquired sweetly.

"I have a friend there, a colleague really, a fellow who started medicine with me in Cape Town. He has a good practice in Knysna. I have been to visit him once or twice. His house is near the hotel at the Heads. Cairncross is his name. Bertie Cairncross."

"Pretty opinionated lot the Knysna gentry, lots of hubris," the Judge remarked. "A friend of ours sent me a cutting from the Herald earlier this year. A lovely article by a fellow called Stent who made a tour of what he called the 'garden route'. He said most of the aristocracy of Knysna boast of royal blood in their veins. They are like Southern Gentlemen. Their fortunes are failing because the forests are giving out. Lived long in splendour on the sale of timber. My view is that they simply plundered and raped the area. It's a disgrace. If they were indeed so noble where was the oblige?"

"If I recall, he also spoke about the beauty of their houses – houses which he said grew naturally, as it were, as though they had not been built from the very beginning as a set plan." Mrs Rose's instinct never failed her.

Garnett wanted the evening to end happily. "There is a private hotel near the Heads. Owned by a Scottish family called Brown. Bertie stayed there for some time while his house was being built. It is a tidy establishment, well run by Mrs Brown who was a nursing sister. We had lots of fun there. They provided small iron canoes for the children. We, and the other grown-ups, took headers and dived off boats. Some of the locals surf in boats, standing in the stern on the incoming tide. Once at night we went out by boat and used a lantern in the boat to lure springers."

"In some parts of the world using a light in that way is forbidden," the Judge observed.

"And I can see the reason for that, and would tend to agree that it is a practice not to be encouraged." Garnett responded.

"We have been to the Heads," Frances said. "I thought they were rather grim bluffs. We watched the warships of the Cape Squadron coming in through the Heads. Strandlopers and Hottentots lived in the caves and fissures."

"Talking about the Hottentots and the Strandlopers, what do you make of General Hertzog's policy of native segregation, Douglas?" The Judge asked.

Political discussions, his father had warned Douglas, had the potential to do irreparable harm to relationships. "It has the potential to create a great deal of controversy. It has many facets. Recently someone said in parliament that he thought that the ultimate fate of the African Continent might depend on the wisdom of the decision that is reached. The statement was perhaps a bit dramatic, and we cannot know what the consequences will be, but there is no doubt that the Colour Bar Bill will put the natives outside the pale of civilisation. As such it is in conflict with the League of Nations' idea that social progress and development of backward peoples is a sacred responsibility of the civilised nations."

"You make your quotations most precisely, Douglas. I must compliment you on that," the Judge said, "but the League can hardly be expected to understand our circumstances."

"What about a little more food for you Doctor Nel?" Mrs Rose enquired.

"Yes, thank you."

"A bit of everything?"

"Yes, thank you, that would be very nice thank you."

Garnett handed Mrs Rose his plate. The Judge served Garnett more fish. "Please help yourself to the rest Doctor Nel."

Mrs Rose turned to Douglas, "Something more for you, Douglas?"

"No, thank you Mrs Rose, I have done very well."

"There is no point in offering Frances any," the Judge said, "she has the appetite of a bird."

"We are having preserved pear halves and fresh cream for dessert," Mrs Rose announced," and then we shall adjourn to the veranda. Perhaps we ought to listen to some more music and end the evening in a happy way. Our dear guests have to have an early night, considering how early we all got up this morning."

Dessert was served and the table cleared. Martha smiled coyly at the shower of compliments about the fish she had fried. The Judge alighted slowly from his chair, stiff from the morning walk. The night air had become heavier and carried the sounds of the sea more distinctly into the silence of the night.

"I think we should have a bit of Madama Butterfly," the Judge suggested.

"It is interesting to me how the Europeans have been flirting with Japanese ideas," Frances said.

"Why is it strange to you, dear girl?" Mrs Rose asked.

"Their culture is so different, Mummy."

"Is that not precisely why the Europeans are so intrigued?" Mrs Rose responded.

"Japan has been quite shut off from the rest of the world until quite recently," the Judge interrupted. "Remember they are island people – easy to become insular. Being surrounded by sea made it easy for them to develop a homogeneous culture. There was not much chance of cross-pollination of ideas as is the case when you are part of a large continent. Such circumstances must give rise to the development of a strong culture. But I must say, from all accounts they are a strange lot. Their politics are dominated by lawless bands of thugs that murder and assassinate all that they find disagreeable. And like in Weimar, hardly any punishment is ever handed out."

"Not unlike the Italians and the Russians," Douglas added.

Frances was still preoccupied. "It is the influence of War that has sanctioned thuggery. What we consider a civilised society formally carried out the methodical slaughter of millions of people in the most brutal and barbaric way. What an example, if not an inspiration, it must have been to the wrong people."

"So Douglas, tell me," Mrs Rose asked, "how do you feel about your teaching post next year?"

"Frances and I spoke about it this afternoon. I feel quite comfortable about it in some ways. The subject matter itself should not present any difficulties. I am not sure that I will make a good teacher. But that remains to be seen. I have had a look at the syllabuses for next year. As I said to Frances, it is the beginning of my career. There may still be other opportunities."

"Douglas will make a wonderful teacher," Garnett said. "He has a great sense of humour that the boys will like. His approach is likely to be refreshing because he knows his subject so well. The boys will respect that. The worst teachers are the ones who have to pretend. Children find them out very quickly."

"I think Garnett is quite right, and you jolly well know that he is, Douglas," Frances applauded.

The Judge took a gramophone record from its brown paper sleeve. He placed it on the turntable and wound the gramophone. He turned to his audience with an air of expectation. "Are you ready for some more music?" He asked. "I have chosen a piece from Puccini's Madama Butterfly. We spoke about Japan earlier. The part in which Lieutenant Pinkerton and the US Consul Sharpless have drinks while they wait for Butterfly to arrive for the wedding ceremony."

The voice, which had waited patiently in the Bakelite grooves of the record while the Roses and their guests ate, and held their discourses, was given life. The atmosphere that now received Caruso's voice had become deprived of the romantic anticipation that inspired it earlier that evening. The voice that had been so rich was now thin. The night air was chilly. The music came to an end.

"I think we should all walk down to the water's edge," Mrs Rose proposed. "It is such a wonderful night."

"The wind has come up a bit," the Judge replied.

"We can hardly call it wind, my dear. A breeze if anything. As my Uncle Alastair would have said, 'a mere zephyr.' If I may just get my shawl."

The Judge stepped down stiffly onto the sand. Garnett, Douglas and Frances followed. They waited for Mrs Rose.

"You three go ahead, I'll wait for my wife."

Mrs Rose took her husband's arm. Frances had taken Douglas' arm, aware that her parents were observing them. In an effort to be more demonstrative as the time of their separation approached, she put her arm around Douglas. He was self-conscious and reluctant to respond, but felt compelled to support her initiative, and put his arm around her. She tilted her head towards his shoulder. Mrs Rose squeezed her husband's arm.

When they reached the edge of the water they stood in silence, looking out to sea. The waves, swollen with white phosphorescence, moved rhythmically. Breezes came from the land, transporting pockets of warm air.

Garnett stood on his own; to one side. The dissonant associations of the Rigoletto and his daughter came upon him as he observed the Judge and Frances. He tried in vain to repel the ghost-like thoughts that invaded his better self but they clung to him. The whore presented herself with lascivious movements. The assassin enjoyed Garnett's discomfort. Time was dislocated at the shoulder – the worst kind of dislocation.

"Elizabeth and I will go back to the house now." It was the first time that the Judge had used his wife's name in front of Douglas. "Do stay for a while. I think we should say our goodbyes now. It was good to see you Douglas. Good luck for next year. I know you will be a great success. And do stay in touch with us. Doctor Nel, it was really good to meet you. Douglas told us about you. I wish you well in your career. I hope you will have an uneventful journey back to Oudtshoorn tomorrow. And thank you for the lovely fish. My legs are a bit weary now."

Mrs Rose took Garnett's hand. "It was so jolly decent of you to bring Douglas to see us, Doctor Nel. I am sure Frances is pleased. May I wish you a most pleasant journey. And may you have a good night's rest. Goodbye." She made a stylish gesture with her hand.

"I won't be long Mummy." Frances called after her parents.

When the Roses reached their house, the Judge's spirit had lifted. He began to put away the gramophone records and carried the gramophone inside. The night air had revived his desire for his wife, but they would have to wait until Frances was asleep. He would pretend to read for a while, and encourage her to keep him company. It would complete the day.

"I think I will go and get ready for bed," Mrs Rose announced.

"I will read for a while. Why don't you come and keep me company, my dear. It would be nice if you could sit with me."

"There is not much point if you are not going to talk to me. I will wait for you to come to bed."

"It was really kind of you to bring Douglas to see us, Garnett," Frances said. "I shall miss him a great deal next term. We saw each other quite often at university. Being here with him has meant much to me. Thank you." She kissed Garnett on his cheek.

"Thank you Frances. It was lovely to meet you. Douglas is very fortunate to have you as a friend." It did not sound quite right. "I will go up to the house now." He shook Frances' hand. "See you when I see you Douglas."

Garnett looked up into the cloudless sky. Near Hurters' house he was inspired to stop and observe the sky more intently. He stood without thought. The dense benevolence of the milky way reached him. He understood why the de Bruin boy survived.

Douglas and Frances walked arm in arm back to the Roses' house.

"You must write me Douglas, soon, please?" Frances asked.

"Of course I shall."

"And I will write to you. I shall miss you."

"I will miss you too."

Both Frances and Douglas expected that her parents would have gone to bed. When they reached the veranda they saw the Judge sitting at the dining table, his book in the circle of light produced by a lamp. He leant back in his chair, his hands behind his head. His eyes were closed. Douglas wanted to retreat. "Is that you Frances?" The Judge called.

"Yes Daddy, we're home."

"That was a short walk. Well Douglas," the Judge said, "I suppose all good things come to an end. We've said our goodbyes. Do come and visit us in Cape Town. You will be most welcome."

"Goodnight Douglas," Frances said with a lump in her throat, and fighting back her tears.

"Goodnight Frances." He shook her hand clumsily.

She laughed through her tears and hugged him, to her father's amusement.

Douglas walked home slowly. Garnett looked out into the night; sipped his sweet creamy tea. The familiar teapot, a tin of condensed milk and a spare cup were waiting.

"Well, that was an interesting evening" Garnett said. "It looks as though the old chap has some life in him. But intellect and pride dominate. There's no doubt about that. When we arrived here Mrs Rose seemed two dimensional, like a cut-out paper doll. Now she seems to have so much more warmth than I had imagined. And I must say, I like your Frances very much. Well, I'm glad we came. It's just a pity that it has been for such a short time."

"Yes, they are interesting people. The old chap is held in high regard in legal circles." Fatigue, and his preoccupation with the impending separation from Frances had caught up with Douglas. "Gee, I must say, it's been a long, long day. But it's been a good day."

"Perhaps we should turn in soon. You were at your brilliant best tonight. What a mind you have, and old Rose knows it."

They sat in silence, staring into the dark blue night. In the distance the waves made silver white foaming lines. Garnett had another half a cup of tea. His heart was beating irregularly.

"Let's go to bed. Leave the front door open. It will allow air to circulate.

"When do you want to leave, Garnie?"

"I'll set the alarm for seven. We'll have a good swim, a good breakfast, tidy up and be on the road before nine."

Garnett lay in his bed listening to the sounds of the surf. He contemplated the transition from consciousness to sleep. He floated in the waves. He walked in the hills above the sea and brought in the mussel cracker.

He heard Douglas' words at the Roses' dining table and saw Frances' adoring green eyes as he constructed his arguments and fetched knowledge from a seemingly inexhaustible intuitive source.

Outside, Douglas had fallen asleep in his chair. His legs were crossed and his arms folded across his body. His head was to one side. A thin thread of tea-stained saliva stretched from the corner of his mouth onto the collar of his shirt.

Garnett slipped on the rocks of Gericke se Bank. The jolt woke him. He turned on his side.

Douglas felt Frances' cold hand against his own. He woke to find a small dog licking his hand. It was late. His neck was sore from being at an odd angle. He staggered to bed, undressed quietly, so that he would not wake up too much, and put his head down on his cool pillow.

◆

Chapter Eleven

Friday 10 December 1926

VAN YSSEN WAS READING his newspaper when Garnett and Douglas arrived. He rose awkwardly and called to his wife, "They're back!"

Mrs van Yssen had been writing letters. She blinked in the bright sunlight. She held her hands out and kissed Douglas' forehead. "Hello Garnett. I hope you had a happy stay. How are the Roses? I dare not ask Douglas! You know what it's like!"

"Oh come on Ma. Don't start that again. The Judge and Mrs Rose are just fine, and before you ask, Frances sends her best regards."

"We received an early Christmas card from the Roses."

"I must get going," Garnett said. "I must get to the surgery." He helped Douglas carry his things from the car.

"Thank you for everything Garnett," van Yssen said. "I hope we'll see you soon. Give my regards to your parents."

"Yes, thank you very much Garnett, " Mrs van Yssen added. "We must make an opportunity to get together."

"Sounds like a lovely idea. I must be off. Cheerio."

The three van Yssens held hands as van Yssen said grace and used the opportunity granted to him by the merciful Lord to thank Him for letting them be together again as a family, and for Douglas and his achievements. Such was the intensity of emotion aroused in van Yssen by the poignancy of the occasion, that he also took the opportunity to give the Lord a silent but solemn undertaking not to indulge himself again in extravagant intimacy with his wife, for he still feared that he would be punished for the passionate lust that had got the better of him on the train.

Mrs van Yssen's curiosity got the better of her. "So tell us about your visit, Douglas. I would love to go to Plettenberg Bay at some stage, if only your father would consent. I have never been there. I tried to imagine the house you were in, and what the beach was like. And what the Roses' house is like. Frances is such a sweet girl and so accomplished. You are already nearly twenty five."

Van Yssen cleared his throat and put his knife down rather heavily on his plate. "Douglas has his to career consider. That should be a priority. There is some hard work ahead next year. Archer is a demanding man from all accounts. Teaching posts are not easy to come by in Oudtshoorn."

"Oh, Albert they are young only once."

The skin on Douglas' back felt tight from the salt water. He looked forward to a warm bath.

"Did Garnett catch any fish?" Mrs van Yssen asked.

"We went yesterday morning, early. The Judge and Frances came along. We went to a place called Gericke se Bank, on the other side of the Robberg. The Judge offered to have the fish prepared at their house and invited us to eat with them. He had a gramophone there. He played some opera music. It was a lovely evening. He was quite jolly and not as stern as he usually is."

"Luscombe knows the family. Both Judge Rose and his brother went to Oxford. There was a bit of a scandal there involving his brother. I gather there are people at the bar who feel his appointment was a political one. They say he's quite tough."

"I thought you said he was a good advocate and a formidable adversary?" Douglas said.

"Oh he was a good advocate, but as a Judge he is uncompromising, especially towards the coloureds."

"To begin with he was not all that friendly towards Garnett. He probed his background. He was a bit disparaging about Trinity College. But in the end he warmed to him. Mrs Rose acted as a foil and compensated graciously. Frances of course adored Garnett's charm."

"When does your first term start?" van Yssen asked Douglas.

"On Monday the tenth. Dad, if you don't mind I would very much like to buy Frances something for Christmas."

"Have you not left it a little bit late?" His father asked.

"Christmas is two weeks from tomorrow."

"What do you have in mind?" His mother asked.

"I thought of getting her a copy of Elizabeth Gaskell's *Life of Charlotte Bronte*. If we could get in touch with Maskew Miller, to see if they have it, although I am jolly sure I saw it there when we were browsing; there are two volumes. They could have it delivered. The Roses will only be leaving for Cape Town on Monday. Next Friday is Christmas. We could telegraph the details and have it put on our account."

"I will accompany you to the post office later, when it is cooler," she said. Douglas sat on the edge of his bed. He lay back. His legs dangled over the edge of the bed. He looked up at the patterns on the pressed steel ceiling and searched for a sign. He felt the vibrations of the car under him as it went over the corrugations of the road. He put his hands behind his head and lifted his leg onto the bed. Images of the green shining bonnet sprinkled with dust; the cone shaped silver back ends of the headlights over which distorted forms of the passing landscape flowed and scattered in confused directions, the whipping movements of the tips of the Indian cane fishing rods, the scent of the brown leather seats and hot engine oil and petrol fumes.

A feeling of despair enveloped him. Its form emerged from the emptiness left by departing expectations. The reality of returning to the circumstances that would trap him, now that he was home, had driven away all romantic anticipation. He would use his reason against the threatening presence. He analysed the origins of his mood. It was a function not so much of something that was present, but rather of something that had disappeared. The hopes of events to come were gone. He re-lived the anticipation of escaping to the seaside, that had inflated his feelings of affection, visions of a perfect sparkling blue sea, yellow sand and faded sun bleached colours that made his spirit lighter, ascend, and flutter on the washing line.

Things were so simple to Garnett. He was so jolly. He was full of fun. He just did things. He was popular: a prophet who had returned to his own country and been welcomed there by the simple folk of the village who were more than willing to pay him for curing them of all their ills, imagined or otherwise. It would be the more difficult for the new schoolmaster to succeed. He would be watched, he would be judged. The Judge would judge him. His doubt was made worse by his lack of resolution. If only Frances would have given him a clearer signal. He would write to her. It would be easier to write to her. Putting it down on paper would signify a greater commitment. It was perhaps better that he had left it until it could be put in writing. He was good at doing that. Garnett had probably just scraped through matric. He felt the car under him. He saw the river mouth at Kaaimans, where tea coloured water met the sea; the clear mountain water under the bridge in the Montagu pass on whose surface dry leaves, made yellow and brown by their circumstances, hardly suspended, turned lazily and floated. He thought of his cousin and the truncheon. The pale green reeds on the banks of the muddy brown river swayed in the lazy Sunday afternoon breeze and transported him without his knowledge into an afternoon dream of brightly coloured fields over which fleecy white clouds drifted across a great windswept beach visited by people he did not know. In thought, and in a green dress flapping around her legs, the woman with a child next to her walked into the wind on the beach. Her hands behind her back; her head tilted forward in contemplation.

"I thought I should wake you if you still want to make arrangements to send Frances a gift for Christmas," his mother said with her delicate hand on his shoulder. "I have brought you some coffee." He looked into her green eyes. The same colour as Frances' eyes. He loved her. "Have your coffee, my son. I will go with you to the post office. They close at four."

"I didn't want to tell dad, but I have been having trouble with my ears, particularly the right ear. The other one sings now and again. Garnett also noticed it when we were away. He said he would have a look at them."

"Oh, I'm sure it is nothing. You are strong and healthy. It can't be anything. Probably just wax. Garnett will remove it and everything will be just fine. Have your coffee, I'll close the back door and then we can go."

--------♦--------

Chapter Twelve

Friday 25 December 1926

AN UNSEASONABLE COLD FRONT had reached Cape Town in the early hours of Christmas day, promising to bring rain showers. When the Roses made their way to St Georges Cathedral for the Christmas service, Lion's Head was obscured by cloud; the north-westerly wind was freshening and it was becoming heavily overcast. Frances sat between her mother and father in the back seat of their chauffeur driven Armstrong Siddeley car. The Judge enjoyed the perfume of his two women in the back of the car. The threatening weather made him feel snug. He looked down at Frances' slender hands resting on her thighs that were elegantly wrapped in a floral crepe de Chine dress. She began putting on her cream coloured buckskin gloves. The skill with which she fastened the small buttons on the inside of the gloves intrigued him. That someone so deft could be so innocent. His sense of her innocence made him uncomfortable. He knew how to deal with guilt, but not with innocence. He had dominion over the guilty, but no power over the innocent. They were beyond his reach. Innocence once lost can never be retrieved. He broke out in light sweat. It must have been like that in paradise, a defining moment from which there was no turning back. A horrible twisted image of Lot and his wife appeared before him. His daughter belonged to one world. He had crossed over into another.

At the church, Doyle opened the car door. The Judge led the way into the church, nodding and smiling, from one side to the other, at friends and acquaintances, while Mrs Rose imitated him. It was meant to be a joyous occasion after all. Seeing the congregants before her, Frances imagined herself walking into the classroom on the first day of term. She thought of Douglas. She had opened his gift very early that morning. She had put on her dressing gown and gone discreetly to her parents' room to show them Douglas' gift. Her father had amplified her pleasure when he put his generous stamp of approval on Douglas' choice, and had quite lavishly praised the good taste it displayed. When she returned to her room to dress for church, the first thing she did was to pick up her pale green cloche hat. She undid the flirtatious shape of the cream bow on the side of the hat, used as a love symbol, and tied it in an arrow-like shape to signify that she had given her promise of love. When the family got into the car to leave for church Mrs Rose noticed the alteration. It was creased: evidence of a sudden decision. It was a pity that Frances could not have asked for the ribbon to be ironed. She had had plenty of time. But, that was Frances, all the studying and over-use of her brain had made her vague.

Once the Roses were seated Frances indulged herself in a daydream about Douglas: his handsome face, his strong legs when he walked on the beach in his bathing suit, his jolly smile, the way wrinkles formed at the sides of his eyes when he laughed. How solid he was when she leant against him. She resolved to sit and love him the whole time she was in church and do it with such intensity that he was bound to sense her passion.

There was a murmur among the congregants near the entrance: the Governor General, the Earl of Athlone and his wife, Princess Alice and their entourage had arrived. The sight of Athlone reminded the Judge of the dashing Prince of Wales in his knickerbockers and his brightly knitted Fair Isle pullover at Royal Cape. Now there was a fellow who gave the lie to innocence. Carousing and whoring with the Kelvin Grove set. If the news had reached his discreet ears, more people knew about it than the world was prepared to admit.

The service of lessons and carols was conducted by the Dean of the Cathedral.

Frances was woken from her daydreaming when the organ sounded the first notes of the opening hymn, *Once in Royal David's City*. She started thinking of Douglas during the bidding prayers and how he might have selected her book. She was so moved when the first carol, *Still the Night, Holy the Night*, was sung that she got goose pimples on her forearms. When the first lesson was read in which God promises Abraham that in his Seed shall all the nations of the Earth be blessed, she thought of Abraham's seed. A tableau vivant had been created just in front of the sanctuary. As the reading of the scripture progressed more figures were added to the scene. The prophecies of Isaiah and Micah were heard, as was the visit of the Angel Gabriel to the Virgin Mary. The Archbishop, William Marlborough Carter, had asked the Earl of Athlone to read the fifth lesson in which Luke told about the birth of Jesus. The shepherds went to the manger followed by the Wise Men. Athlone looked at the bible in front of him. He lifted his eyes and waited for the murmurs, the coughs, and the creaking of pews to stop, and then began reading in a high-pitched voice. The Archbishop himself read the lesson in which John unfolded the Mystery of the Incarnation. And finally, there were the closing prayers and blessing, followed by the final carol, *O Come All ye Faithful*.

Outside the wind swirled and gusted, loosening dust, cobwebs and old leaves from crannies and corners of buildings. It was not a day to stand around after church. The Judge dithered. He decided to wait for Athlone and his party to be sent off by the Archbishop, before he hailed the driver. Not a good idea to get caught up in the pomp and other social niceties outside the church today. On the other hand, it might be construed that he was deliberately avoiding the Governor General, so he led his wife and his daughter down the aisle, but when they emerged from the church, Athlone was already getting into his car.

The Roses lived in a large double-storey Victorian house in the Gardens. The elaborately moulded front door with equally elaborate brass fittings, had upper half panes of colourful stained glass. Cast iron work from MacFarlane's Glasgow Foundries adorned the veranda.

The drawing room contained a collection of disparate things. An easy chair with buttoned upholstery, a cabinet veneered with ebony and a panel of Japanese lacquer, an armchair in Hepplewhite style made of satin wood, a Louis XIV overmantle mirror, a Regency model roll-top desk. In addition there were many framed portraits, some paintings and a William Morris Madonna and Child. There was also a library sofa of carved walnut with buttoned upholstery, and a tripod table. Gilded bookbinding's on inset bookshelves made golden reflections of the light from the sash windows. The two fireplaces had marble surrounds and cast iron grates bordered with Minton tiles that depicted stylised flowers.

Promptly at noon the first guests arrived. They were two of Frances' friends: Florence Cairncross and her handsome fiancé, Christopher Borcherds. They were shown into the drawing room by a maid.

Frances heard their arrival and hurried to the drawing room. "My dears," she exclaimed with theatrical exuberance, "merry Christmas, how nice of you to come! I hope we will have a wonderfully festive day together. I am so very thrilled to see you," and embraced Florence and Christopher in turn. "Let us get you something to drink. I think the weather is turning bad. Here," as she stepped towards a small table on which a large bowl of punch had been placed together with a variety of other beverages, "I confess that I have had ever such a small private tasting of the punch, and even if I must say so myself, it really is worth trying, to start with."

"You seem so happy, Frances, so extremely happily excited, dear girl," Florence said. "Is there something we should know?"

"Oh! I am just so pleased so see you, the two of you together, I mean. Christopher is looking so dashing, don't you think, Florrie?"

Christopher smiled bashfully.

"Who all are going to be here today?" Florence asked.

"Well … there will be the three of us," Frances giggled, and then putting on a serious and gruff voice, "the old judge president and his dear wife, my mother and father, and my aunt and uncle."

The Judge President, Sir Malcolm Searle, and his wife were next to arrive. Justice Rose welcomed them. "How nice of you to come Malcolm, hello Margaret, merry Christmas, you know Florence Cairncross and her young man Christopher Borcherds?"

"Florence we know of course, and we have indeed had the pleasure of meeting Mr Borcherds, and it is so nice to see you again," Mrs Searle replied.

Mrs Rose entered the room with her hands cupped together in front of her, the right hand above the left, as lieder singers hold their hands. She wore an Egyptian green overblouse and matching skirt made of Silk Tiflis. The front panel, lower parts of the sleeves and cuffs were embroidered in hieroglyphic patterns. The neck of the overblouse was cut square and its waistline rested on her hips

"Merry Christmas Margaret. My, how elegant you look," Mrs Searle complimented.

"I have only just put it on for the first time. Jeremy saw it at Cleghorn and Harris. The change in the weather has given me a good reason to wear it."

"Your mother is really a thoroughly modern woman, Frances. She has such a marvellous fashion sense," Mrs Searle continued.

A maid entered. She waited for the conversation between Mrs Rose and Mrs Searle to end before she stepped closer to Mrs Rose, "Mr Sterling and Mrs Sterling have arrived, Madam."

"Please do show them in, Gladys"

"Mr Sterling would like to have a private word with you Madam."

"Please excuse me for a few moments."

The Judge had taken charge of the guests in the drawing room, "We'll have drinks first, make yourselves comfortable. Will you have your usual Malcolm?"

"Thank you, yes."

The Judge placed a large Waterford glass containing equal quantities of malt whisky and water on a small tray held by one of the maids who in turn offered it to Sir Malcolm Searle. He immediately sipped the whisky, sucked his cheeks in, rolled the whisky around in his mouth so that his large grey walrus moustache tilted from side to side, and swallowed it with a good smack of his large pink lips. "Damn good stuff this that you have here," he said holding up the glass to have another look at the colour. "Damn good indeed. I bet those bootleggers in America would like to get their hands on some of this. Ha! Ha!"

Searle joined the three young people. "I think it is better to be with people of my own age than with the old fogies," he said when he reached them, quite unaware that he had interrupted their conversation.

"It is very generous of you to side with us, Sir Malcolm," Frances flirted.

"Now the real reason why I wanted to come and speak to you," Sir Malcolm said with a naughty glint in the eye, "is because I saw you in church this morning my dear Frances. It seems as though the Roses did not notice that the Searles were there too. Your father was preoccupied, and as for you, well, what could it have been that you had on your sweet young mind?"

The colour rose in Frances' cheeks. Florence was ready to come to her rescue, but found the presence of the Judge President too formidable.

"And do you know why I know that you are preoccupied? The bow in your hat gave it away. It is as simple as that."

Frances was crimson.

Mrs Rose entered the drawing room followed by her brother and sister-in-law. Ethel Sterling's nose was red and streaming. She had the most dreadful summer cold.

"Poor Ethel has a terrible cold. I think we should fix Ethel something with ground ginger in it. Can you think of anything suitable, my dear?" Mrs Rose enquired from her husband.

"Hello Sir Malcolm, hello Margaret. A very merry Christmas to you." James Sterling said, shaking hands with the Searles.

When all their guests had drinks, the judge proposed a toast, and formally wished all a merry Christmas. While there were convenient distractions, the Judge President leant over towards Frances, "I really did not mean to embarrass you my dear, I do apologise for what has turned out to be an indiscretion on my part, when I really meant what I said with interested affection. Do forgive me."

Frances looked into Searle's kind face, put her hand through his arm, and squeezed it as she pressed her head against his shoulder. "You are one of my most favourite men, and you will be the first one to know all when the time is right." With a large warm puffy hand Searle gently and reassuringly patted the hand that Frances had put through his arm.

"So, James," the Judge said turning to his brother-in-law, and asked more as a condescending formality than out of interest, "how are things on the farm?"

"Oh well, I suppose we muddle along, You know what farming is like, we are victims of the weather, of the soil; we are at the mercy of all sorts of things, but we'll get by, I'm sure. The young plum trees that we put in during the early spring are growing well. I have also put in some more vines. I am sure there must be a future for good wine."

"Always experimenting, old boy," Searle said, stepping closer, "nothing wrong with that, I say. A capital thing, experimentation. Where would we be without it? There would be no progress, would there? I heard you say that you have put in more vines. What variety have you planted?"

"The fellow at Stellenbosch University, a man called Perold, has produced an entirely new grape. He has crossed Pinot Noir stock with Hermitage, to make something that is quite unique. I am trying some of his plants. In three years' time we will know how they bear."

"That's quite an adventurous step," Rose commented.

"My dear brother is an adventurous man, and is to be admired for that, Jeremy," Mrs Rose said, coming to her brother's aid.

"I do not think we should stay too late today. Ethel has such a terrible cold, and it looks as though we are going to have some much needed rain later on."

"We have not really got started and you are already thinking of leaving," Rose remonstrated.

"I would have expected your children here today, James. After all, it is Christmas. My two chaps are both away overseas, alas," Searle said.

"They are spending their Christmas holidays with Ethel's mother and father."

"And where is that?" Searle asked.

"Ethel's parents have a cottage at Bokbaai, up along the West Coast. The children have a wonderful time there. They fish, they swim, eat plenty of good food. It is a marvellous place: the cottage is built on a shelf of rock that rises from the sea, almost within the reach of the spray at spring tide. They've named the property 'Seaspray.' Ethel's old father has all the patience and kindness a grandfather should have, and so has her mother. The children enjoy being with them. Quaintly enough they have two kitchens up there. The place is quite windy, so depending on which way the wind is blowing they decide which kitchen to use. They catch crayfish and boil them in a forty-four gallon drum. They make bread in a pot."

"Sounds like a lot of jolly good fun to me, but I am not quite sure where the place is," Searle said.

"It is about half way up to Yzerfontein, probably about twenty miles from here. It is a lovely secluded spot; there is an old gabled homestead there that is quite a landmark."

"When you say 'gabled' what do you mean?" Searle asked.

"It is an old Dutch style building. They say it was built well over a hundred years ago. It now belongs to a Basson family. We collect milk from them, they also supply us with meat when we are there."

"The sea is very cold up along that coast, it can't be that nice to swim," Rose said.

"Cold never bothers the young ones," Searle commented.

Mrs Searle went over to Frances. "Come, let us sit down, and tell me all your news, Frances. I am told that your friend, young van Yssen did exceptionally well…"

Searle had heard his wife. "Come along then James, let's go and sit with my wife."

When they were seated Searle continued, "van Yssen has indeed done very well. On one count he obtained his masters degree *Cum Laude*. Do you realise what that involves, my dear?" He gave Frances a tiny wink. "You have to get a first or better in every single exam from the beginning to the end, and for every dissertation. If you falter just once, there's no *Cum Laude*. Quite remarkable, quite remarkable." He decided not to mention the other count on which van Yssen had done well.

"I have just been informed by the cook that the turkey is ready, and I think, if we are going to let it remain succulent, we should go to the dining room, if you please," Mrs Rose announced.

A large mahogany table, inlaid with rosewood and sycamore, with matching upholstered balloon-back chairs stood in the centre of the dining room. A pet sideboard made of oak with carved boxwood panels looked out of place against the left hand wall. The walls of the dining room had richly textured flocked wallpaper, and the ceilings were highly ornate. A large Adam fireplace had been built into the inner wall. Various porcelain ornaments stood on the mantelpiece.

Nine places had been set. Solid silver cutlery images were reflected in the polished mahogany tabletop. Gleaming cut glass wine glasses and fragile champagne glasses had been positioned with care. In the centre of the table there were holly and mistletoe decorations. Mrs Rose had produced, by hand, small menu cards, each inscribed with a jolly greeting, and a special quotation for each member of the company.

Mrs Rose showed the guests to their seats.

"Christopher, before you sit down," the Judge said, addressing Borcherds, "would you be so good as to open the champagne for us? When you've done, Gladys will do the necessary and pour for us. I hope it is cold enough."

"Certainly Judge." Christopher received the bottle from the maid and examined the label. De Rochegre from Epernay. An escutcheon on the label displayed the vintage date as 1921.

All eyes were on Christopher, waiting for the cork to pop. He was a bit nervous. He prised the cork out cautiously, and pushed it back into the bottle just as it about to pop, so that there was a disappointing hiss instead of a festive sound. The Judge felt let down. Hope he does better with that young woman of his. The maid ceremoniously poured the champagne. "Let us raise our glasses and drink to health and happiness in the future, and my very best wishes to all of you. It is so good of you to be with us today," the Judge said.

Searle put his stamp of approval on the beverage, "Really very fine champagne this, Jeremy, French quality at its best!" He took another sip and savoured it. "Delicately fruity, light and so very smooth. Lovely, really lovely." He was in a festive mood. "Let us see what my little menu says." He started reading his quotation out loud,

'The Law is the true embodiment
Of everything that's excellent.
It has no kind of fault or flaw,
And I, my lords embody the Law.
Sir W.S. Gilbert.'

Rather a bit extravagant, dear Elizabeth. But thank you very much! Let's see what the others have."

"Read yours, Florence," Frances urged.

Florence had already looked at her menu and was self-conscious. She hesitated.

"Go on Florrie," Frances said.

Florence held her card up,

"'Oh, thou art fairer than the evening air
Clad in the beauty of a thousand stars.'" She giggled. Christopher smiled at her.

"Who wrote that?" Searle asked.

"Shakespeare's old rival, Marlowe," James Sterling blurted.

The Judge was irritated because he did not know the answer. "It is your turn James, let's hear what your quotation is."

Sterling had glanced at his card, he shifted his shoulders awkwardly, "'Thou speakest wiser than thou art ware of.' From *As You Like it* by Shakespeare."

"Well, well, well," Searle exclaimed, and how appropriate, what astonishing timing."

There was enthusiastic laughter.

"It is Christopher's next," the Judge announced.

"'*Sic itur ad astra.* – Thus shall you go to the stars.' Vergil," Borcherds read, and looked up to see what the reaction would be. Mrs. Searle clapped her hands gently in muted applause and smiled sweetly at Borcherds. "We all know that you will go very far in your civil engineering career."

"Now it is Margaret's turn to amuse us."

" 'A woman whose dresses are made in Paris and whose marriage has been made in Heaven might be equally biased for and against free imports.' Saki (H.H. Munro)."

"Where on earth did you find all these wonderfully apt quotations, Elizabeth?" Sterling asked.

"Elizabeth usually spends an awfully long time searching for them, and not even I or Frances are permitted to know what she is doing," the Judge said proudly. "I wonder what she has chosen for herself?"

Mrs Rose read her own card, "'*Nunc scio quid sit amour.* – At last I know what Love really is like.' Virgil."

"Bravo! Bravo!" Searle exclaimed. "How elegant; she chose a quotation to compliment you Jeremy, you old rascal."

The Judge squirmed at Searle's familiarity. There are some who say that the reason why he is such a good jurist is because he is so human, so natural, a man of the world.

"And now it is my turn, 'A man hath no better thing under the sun than to eat, and to drink, and to be merry.' Ecclesiastes."

"Ethel has not had her chance, Jeremy," Mrs Rose interjected before there could be any response to the Judge's quotation.

"Oh, it does not really matter, I can hardly speak," Ethel said in a voice choking with phlegm.

While the quotations were read the maid carried in the turkey and placed it on a side table. The Judge got up and sharpened the knife with large movements and the warlike sound of metal on metal. He carved clumsily, but was surprisingly efficient.

The Judge had obtained Beaujolais wine from the merchants Ellwood and Chase in Long Street. Searle eyed it with relish. He had decided to enjoy himself, and was determined to ensure that the rest of the company would be happy, and merry, on Christmas Day.

"May we have another toast," Searle said raising his glass, "To Elizabeth and Jeremy and their guests. Thank you for entertaining us so royally today. To Elizabeth and Jeremy."

Glasses were raised, glances and nods were exchanged, and the individuals around the table became silent as they ate their food, until all that could be heard were the sounds of masticating mouths and the sounds of the table.

Frances caught her Aunt Ethel's eye, "You have been unusually quiet today, Ethel, even bearing in mind that you are not feeling well, is there anything we can do for you, or get for you?"

"It is better for me just to endure my condition quietly, thank you, Frances. It will just have to run its course. I'll go to bed early tonight and tuck myself in. In a few days I will be much better."

"We have not had occasion to ask you about your holiday. Tell us all about it Elizabeth." Mrs Searle asked.

"It was quite, quite wonderful, we had good weather, Jeremy was able to relax and rest." Mrs Rose glanced at her husband. "We also had a visit from two delightful young men, a Doctor Nel from Oudtshoorn, and Douglas van Yssen. Such nice young people."

"Young van Yssen did very well, I gather," Mrs Searle picked up the thread of her earlier remark.

Judge Rose moved his shoulders impatiently. He was eager to respond, "What a remarkable intellect, and as you all well know, I do not easily hand out praise. Quite remarkable. He is a good foil for Frances' sharp mind, and she is a good match for his."

Frances smiled embarrassedly.

"Well, well, well," Searle uttered, as he looked around from under his bushy eyebrows.

"What is van Yssen going to do now that he has completed his studies?" Mrs Searle asked.

Frances moved her shoulders. "Like me, Douglas is going to teach. He has a post at the Boys High School in Oudtshoorn where he will teach history as his first subject and Latin as his second."

"The man's Latin is almost fluent," Judge Rose boasted.

"A rare experience for you Jeremy, hey!" Searle teased.

"Yes, rare indeed. We went on a fishing outing at Plettenberg Bay and I tempted him with a reference to Catullus. It was immediately clear that he knew not only his Roman history, but that he was thoroughly familiar, and I dare say in a scholarly sort of way, with the subtleties and intricacies of Catullus' Latin."

Frances was pleased at her father's rather creative adaptation. She would let it remain their little conspiracy.

"While you people have been doing all the talking, I have been doing all the eating," Searle said good-humouredly. "The turkey is so damned good I think I shall have some more." He patted his lips with his napkin. "When are we going to have some golf, Jeremy?"

"I think some time next week, if you like."

"Do you play, James?" Searle asked Sterling.

"I used to play a bit, before farming took up all my time."

"Rum thing that," Searle responded. "All work and no play, you know. And what about you Christopher?"

"Christopher is jolly good," Florence said enthusiastically. "He has even taken me to the course and made me play some shots."

"Florence is really the one with the best potential of the two of us," Jeremy replied.

"Women and golf! Bah! They will surely never be able to compete with men, besides golf clubs were conceived as refuges from women!" Searle's intention was to bait Frances. "Aren't you going to say something Frances?"

"Not if you want me to."

"I'll tell you what, I will take you to golf, even before you leave for Graaff Reinet, and I'll show you the ropes," was his peace offering.

"I shall take you up on that, Sir Malcolm, I surely shall, and I shall hold you to account if you fail to carry out your promise."

"A chap called Nel who is a doctor in Oudtshoorn whom we met at Plettenberg Bay, happened to mention a Cairncross of Knysna, a medical man evidently. Is he by any chance related to you Florence?" Mrs Rose asked.

"Yes indeed he is, Bertie is a cousin."

"You have never mentioned him before," Mrs Rose replied.

"Oh, there was no particular reason why I should not have mentioned him. He studied at Edinburgh, and was away for so many years, and besides I was only sixteen when he left. We lost some contact. He is a delightful man and most capable too."

"I think it is time for dessert. I have taken Sir Malcolm's sweet tooth into account," Mrs Rose announced.

Frances looked at Florence. "You promised to tell me about the party you and Christopher went to in London. I am sure we would all like to hear about it."

"Well it was all rather wild, perhaps it would be indiscreet to tell you now." Florence had had a little too much wine. She was trying to restrain herself but was finding it difficult. She chuckled.

Judge Rose feared the worst. Mrs Searle was uneasy.

"Come on, don't be a stick in the mud, let us hear about the party," Searle encouraged.

"Don't listen to my husband, if you would prefer not to Florence," Mrs Searle advised.

"Well, I think I shall tell you all about it after all. It wasn't that bad, really." Christopher took her hand and squeezed it. "Where shall I begin? Now, as you all are no doubt aware, there is Tutmania all over London. The place is infested with Egyptian things and ideas. It is so utterly fashionable. Mrs Rose could have walked right out of the pages of a fashion magazine."

"What did the women wear?" Frances asked.

"You mean to the party?"

"Yes, to the party."

"Hand printed silks, loosely cut, some decorated with glass beads, Cleo earrings and scarab shaped jewellery. The colours were lovely: Coptic blue, sakkara, carnelian. There were women who had bathed in iodine to give their skins a reddish colour. One girl who had done that had some magnificent pearls that were beautifully offset against the reddish colour of her skin. The bright rich colours of the clothes were striking, except for the men of course – they just wore their drab evening dress. One woman even wore a headdress that looked like Cleopatra's, or perhaps a cross between an Art Deco sunburst and Cleopatra's headdress. Wow! That was stunning, and oh, she had used lashings of Kohl to give herself Egyptian eyes."

"And the dances, the dances my dear Frances. The Black Bottom and the Charleston, and how those people could dance! With little or no inhibitions, until the sweat poured off them, although it was already jolly cold in November. Glass beads on some of the dresses dazzling brilliantly under electric lights. It was such fun, wasn't it, Chris?"

While Florence told her story, the plates were cleared and a traditional Christmas pudding was served, with a rich brandy sauce. Thereafter the Roses and their guests had coffee and Christmas cake in the drawing room. The men sipped brandy. Searle and James Sterling smoked cigars. Gradually torpor set in, yawns were stifled, and conversation evaporated.

Searle put his left index finger into his waistcoat pocket and dug out his fob watch. "Good Lord, look at the time. How the day has flown. It is nearly three thirty. I don't think we should overstay our welcome, dear." He stubbed out his half smoked cigar, and grunted as he levered himself out of his chair with his elbow. "Margaret and I would like to thank you Jeremy, and especially you, Elizabeth, for your excellent food and good company. I think we should be on our way." Searle stepped over to Frances and gave her a hug. Goodbyes were said to the others as he shook their hands. He wished Christopher well with his career, and encouraged Ethel Sterling to have a speedy recovery.

It was raining, and the Searles' chauffeur, who had spent his time in the kitchen eating enthusiastically and embarrassing the maids and the cook with bawdy stories, brought the car around and assisted the Searles while he held an umbrella for them.

The Roses stood in their doorway smiling and waving goodbye; Mrs Rose said under her breath, "That was rather abrupt."

"He is like that, like a puppy who is suddenly overcome with fatigue. He's gone off home to have a 'catnap', as he would say. He is known to have fallen asleep on the bench. It is not good to have him on the bench after lunch. But a better jurist is hard to find."

When the Roses returned to the drawing room the other guests were getting ready to leave.

Searle was nearly asleep in the back of their car when his wife asked him, "The Sterlings, they always seem to be struggling?"

"He is a nice enough chap, a bit lacking in ambition, I think he irritates Jeremy. I would not be surprised if he is a remittance man. He turned up here from England. And I don't think he pleased anyone when he married his Ethel. It is a pity that Jeremy wears his heart on his sleeve. It must hurt Elizabeth, I am sure, but she never says anything, puts on a brave face."

"Ethel seems like a perfectly nice person to me."

"Jeremy is a snob. It shows in his judgements. It makes him hard and it causes him to be inflexible, to lack compassion, which is really a great pity, because he has a good mind. He attaches too much importance to appearance, to conspicuous success. What the French call 'eclat.' In law we speak of substance over form. With him it is often, and I mean this in the social sense, form over substance!" Searle yawned audibly. The rain beat down on the car. The chauffeur could hardly see. A good nap under the eiderdown would be very special in such weather.

Chapter Thirteen

Wednesday 5 January 1927

DOUGLAS WAS PREPARING his first history lessons at the veranda table, and having morning tea, when the postman arrived. He went to the gate to receive the mail. His mother had heard the gate opening and came to see who it was. He removed the envelope with the familiar handwriting.

"I'll see to things in the kitchen while you read your letter, dear."

He opened the letter. There was a high-pitched ringing sound in his right ear.

> Invermark Road
> Gardens
> Cape Town.
>
> December 26, 1926
>
> Dearest Douglas
> You cannot begin to imagine how much pleasure your gift brought me. Thank you so very, very much. I feel quite mean that I did not send you anything, but I shall make it up to you.
>
> I have started reading the first volume. It is lovely. When I went to my parents' bedroom yesterday morning to show them what you had sent me, Daddy was most impressed and made a special point of complimenting you on your good taste. He was quite taken. As you well know, he is not generous with praise, and when we had our friends over yesterday, including the Searles, he spoke very highly of you. It makes me feel good to know that he likes and respects you so much. The presentation of the Brontes is so vividly real, but we shall discuss that some other time. What a pity that they had such tragic lives.
>
> I am sure you would like to know what we did for Christmas. Well, as I said, we had friends over, but perhaps I should begin at the beginning. We went to the service in the Cathedral where I thought a lot about you. The wind was howling outside and rattling the corrugated iron sheets used to shut off the part where the building is going on. After church we had tea and waited for our guests to arrive. My mother had her brother and aunt Ethel over. Florrie and Christopher were here – you can see that Christopher likes her awfully much – and then of course the Searles. Sir Malcolm was in great form and very amusing. He was jovial, and teased me a little, without being too beastly, but I cannot tell you now what he teased me about. It will have to wait. He has promised to take me to Royal Cape to try my hand at golf. Can you imagine me playing golf? Alas, he

probably won't even remember. Next week would be a good time for golf because it is so quiet here: everyone seems to have gone somewhere for the Christmas holidays. Daddy doesn't like the idea of women playing golf. He says golf clubs are refuges from women! Or was it Sir Malcolm who said it? I am certain that it is just that they fear competition from us, that it will show them up.

Talking about things being quiet, I was saying to my father that it reminds me of Saturnalia. His dry response was "sub sole nihil novi!" How witty! Remember how you and I were once amused about the similarities between Roman times and our times. How they closed the schools and the law courts at this time of the year. I still find the account of dear old Cicero writing to a friend back home and telling him how a minor tribe had given him a gift by surrendering to him – desperately amusing. I am reminded of the discussion you and Daddy had about Catullus when we went fishing and how much Catullus loved parties and festivities. I recall how he described the festival as representing the best of days. For me it would be the best of days if you were here. The prospect of not seeing you for months on end does not bear thinking. After all, we did see one another almost every day, and now that has come to an end. In the past the holidays never separated us for long. Your absence was made tolerable by the knowledge that you would return to me. It means much to me that you are so constant in your ways and so reliable.

My mother produced lovely menu cards with amusing quotations for each of us. Most of them were read out loud, but somehow we missed mine, and Aunt Ethel's. Considering her views about women studying, she at least had the good grace to choose something for me from Tennyson that was kind. It seems as though your patience with her has paid dividends. My quotation read, "Wearing all that weight of learning lightly like a flower." Rather sweet, don't you think?

Please do write to me, dearest man. By the time you receive my letter New Year will have come and gone. We are not planning anything special. I think we are going to have drinks with the Searles. Daddy likes to go to bed early on New Year's Eve and to wake up in the New Year.

Mummy and Daddy have gone to bed. I am alone in my room, and am beginning to feel weary after a long day that was filled with much excitement. I will write again when I get to Graaff Reinet. Please write soon and let me know all.

With my affection,
Frances.

P.S. I forgot to mention Garnett. Please give him my best regards and tell him that we discovered that Florrie is indeed a cousin of his friend Bertie Cairncross at Knysna.

Douglas to Frances Thursday 6 January 1927

Dear Frances,

Thank you so much for your letter. I am glad that you like your books. I am sure we will have some interesting discussions when next we have the opportunity. The thought that you are leaving Cape Town, with which we are both so familiar, gives me the perception that you are going very far away. It is strange how we perceive things, how the mind will distort the geographical reality when our emotions influence it sufficiently. Also, the prospect of not seeing you for a long time, that makes it seem as if you will be really far away. It distresses me to think that you will be all on your own. It worries me a great deal. It is not that I believe that you are incapable of looking after yourself, I know you are, it is because young women seem so fragile and vulnerable to me.

It certainly seems as though your high days and holidays were festive. Ours were more modest. We went to the Kuys' for our Christmas dinner. At this time of the year most people are at the seaside. Apart from the Kuyses and our family, the only guest was a Mr Pienaar. He is an amusing fellow. His wife could not accompany him because she is a chronic hypochondriac. My mother says she feels sorry for her because she is so miserable. She evidently spends most of her time in bed imagining that she has some dreadful malady. As soon as she becomes bored with one condition, she selects another, which says a great deal for her ingenuity. It must be wretched to live with a person like that, yet Pienaar seems to accept his lot with forbearance, and is always hale and hearty. He regaled us to some colourful cricketing stories about a recent match between a Michaelhouse Old Boys Eleven and a local George Eleven. My father held forth about one of his pet subjects: the effects on the Union of the activities of the Labour movement in Britain.

Oudtshoorn is so plain and uncomplicated and lacking in sophistication compared to Cape Town, and so dry and unbelievably hot. I am sure Graaff Reinet will not be much different.

As the time approaches for school to start I am growing apprehensive. I have better moments, when I feel that I will be able to face the prospect more easily, and moments when I am anxious. As the fateful day draws closer the time intervals between doubt and confidence become ever shorter, like oscillations that are becoming more rapid.

I am astonished that I am able to make these revelations about myself to you, that I am able to disclose my innermost feelings. I take comfort from the candour of our friendship and the trust that we have in each other. At the same time I feel that I should not burden you with trivial apprehensions. It is sometimes easier to say things in a letter even though committing oneself to writing gives permanence.

At times I have doubts about coming back here to teach. I wonder whether I should have stayed in Cape Town and furthered my studies, or done journalism, or perhaps thought of a lectureship. But the die is cast for now, and besides it means a lot to my father to have me here. He has been looking forward to it so much my mother tells me. Alas, we can never have clarity about the future. If only there could be a sign of some kind. When I go for our evening walks with my father I examine the clouds, I search for patterns in the leaves of the trees, I count curb stones for signs, but it is almost as though there is a conspiracy to prevent any clarity from appearing. I feel as irresolute as Hamlet. I feel incomplete, and the only rational conclusion that I am able to reach is that I fell more in love with you than ever when we were at Plettenberg Bay. I feel helpless. I read the same page again and again, and nothing enters my head. It is like having an illness for which there is only one cure. It feels to me that only you can make me complete again, to have the confidence that I need to forge my new life.

I am rambling. I am incoherent and my letter lacks composition and form. Forgive me. What makes me feel even worse is that I should have told you exactly how I feel about you when we were at Plettenberg Bay. You are so direct and open about everything, and I am not. I envy you.

I am missing you so much. I must make plans to come and visit you in Graaff Reinet.

Love,
Douglas.

Frances to Douglas Friday January 7, 1927
Dearest Douglas,
I arrived in Graaff Reinet this morning. It is terribly hot. My journey was uneventful except that it was filled with sentiment – the kind of sentiment that travelling seems to evoke. On the one hand one feels sadness and a sense of loss when you leave loved ones and a familiar place, and on the other hand there is a sense of pleading anticipation of one's destination.

I tried to imagine what it would be like here, and as always, things were different from what I expected. The station was on the right hand side of the railway tracks, and not on the left as I had thought. I imagined Miss Price to be short and round. She is tall and flat; carries herself well; a handsome woman, if a bit school-marmish. She and some of the other teachers have board and lodgings at Marshall's Boarding House. Others have houses in the town.

I have been asked to have tea with the Putticks tomorrow morning. Evidently this is an honour not accorded everyone, and I suspect that it is because I am the only new teacher. Mr Puttick has been here since 1922 when the school changed from being a church school to a government school. We are currently in the Graaff Reinet College building, which is in Bourke Street, while the new school is being built.

My room overlooks the back garden of the boarding house. A small lawn, beds with dahlias, roses and stocks and pansies. A fig tree. Granadilla creeper over a pig wire fence, and some melancholy pepper trees just outside the property. There seem to be lots of coloured people about. They travel, as they do elsewhere, on makeshift donkey carts. The animals always seem so resigned to their fate and their toil. At the back corners of the boarding house there are two large corrugated water tanks in which rainwater is collected. The irrigation sluits that run along the one side of the property are bone dry.

I miss you very much. You are so far away. While on the train I tried to imagine what you could be doing at the different times of the day. It is strange to think that we both start teaching for the very first time on Monday morning. Just tomorrow and Sunday to go. I must admit that I am a bit nervous. I don't know which of my subjects I am going to prefer. At times I expect it could be Latin. The pupils are from surrounding farms as well as from the town itself. Teaching Latin from standard six all the way through to matric level will at least give me the opportunity to get to know all the pupils.

I am writing at a small table in my room. A porcelain vase is filled with sweet peas that have a delicious scent.

Eight weeks of term seem very long, especially after an extended holiday. I really enjoyed your visit to Plettenberg Bay so much. Daddy said so too. Mummy said she wished that you could have stayed longer. I like your friend Garnett. He is so jolly, and fortunate to like his work so much.

I hear the gong going for dinner. It is not unlike the gong that they play on the train to announce dinner. Mother instructed the cook to make lots of sandwiches for the journey, some boiled eggs, and she packed some fruit: yellow cling peaches and grapes and a pear. I ordered tea for breakfast and some pea soup for lunch, and had my evening meal in the dining saloon. Daddy gave the bedding attendant a generous tip before we left Cape Town so he made my bed before he attended to any of the other passengers. He was very helpful and decent. There were only two of us in our compartment and that made the journey very comfortable. My travelling companion, an elderly Miss du Toit from Stellenbosch, was on her way to East London to visit her brother who is the Town Clerk there. Before her retirement she was attached to the theological faculty of the University in some sort of secretarial capacity. She had quite a sweet nature and prayed a lot. She knelt at her bunk and read her bible before retiring. She asked me to which denomination I belonged and did not seem to be pleased when I said Anglican, although she was probably relieved that I was not a Catholic.

I am back in my room. We have had quite a nice dinner. I liked the vegetable soup and the roast beef with gravy. All of us sat at one big table. I sat next to Joan Peacock who is also from Cape Town. She has pale blue eyes, flaxen hair, which she wears in a large bun, and is rather masculine.

One of the teachers, a Miss Bremer, became engaged during the December holidays. With her head held coyly to one side Miss Price, who is the most senior, made a little toast to her with a glass of water and wished her well. To which Miss Peacock responded by looking at Miss Dempsey the hockey coach and saying that she cannot stand the idea of having a man near her. She tried to pass it off as a bit of a joke but the remark was hardly relevant. It must be really dreadful to become a spinster. One wonders what goes wrong in people's lives that they end up all alone and have to make compromises with members of their own gender.

I cannot wait for you to let me know how your teaching is going. We are expected to attend church on Sunday mornings. There is a large Dutch Reformed church here in the town. It is a very good example of Gothic architecture and is built of sandstone and has an elegant, tall spire that rises up into the pale summer air. The church serves the farming community, and as you told me about Oudtshoorn, no doubt also becomes filled to capacity for communion services. We Anglicans have the much more modest St James Church. It is small, but at least has the distinction of being one of the oldest. Our services are conducted by the Reverend Basil Southey, and I gather there are sometimes visits by the Bishop of Kimberley.

I hope that you will be able to visit us in Cape Town during the holidays. Mummy said that she would be very disappointed if you did not come. Before I left I went to the library to read more about Elizabeth Gaskell: how she met Wordsworth at Ambleside, and how she was encouraged in her work by Dickens; of course she was also influenced by him. Daddy said that you must write something in the front of each volume. Please will you do so when you next come to visit us? When I mentioned Dickens, Daddy said that it was a coincidence that I was going to Graaff Reinet because Dickens had obtained a Supreme Court order that stopped the newspaper in Graaff Reinet from publishing *Great Expectations*. He thinks it was the first time that protection of copyright was sought in the Cape Colony.

I plan to have a lovely lengthy lazy bath now, during which I shall contemplate a great deal, and then I shall retire to bed to resume my reading, and to have affectionate thoughts as I hold your book in my hands. I am still on the first volume, so there is a lot left to savour.

With all my affection,
Frances.

Douglas to Frances, Saturday 15 January 1927
Dear Frances,
The first week of my career as a schoolteacher has ended, and I am still alive. And on top of that it was not as bad as I expected it to be, but what a shock it is to think that I too passed through the rigours of school. One

forgets what it is like when you have been at University for as long as I was. The rigid approach, the confined space in which one has to move. I am not referring to the building itself. It is much more than adequate. In fact it is quite imposing, perhaps even grand. It is a large sandstone building with a tall iron-domed tower. It was designed about seventeen years ago by a pair of architects, a Mr Bullock and a Mr Vixseboxse, who did quite a lot of work in Oudtshoorn and surrounding areas, and is the pride of Dr Archer our headmaster. (They possibly also did work further afield and it would be interesting to know if they did anything in Graaff Reinet?) You would swear Archer himself had had a hand in the design of the school. He took me by the arm on Monday afternoon after school, and tugging intermittently at the sleeve of my jacket, gave me a guided tour of the building. First we had to go outside onto the pavement, and when that did not give us an adequate perspective, we had to go across the street, and stood there with our backs against a scented privet hedge and admired the building. He half jokingly said that I should pay close attention to what he had to say, because it was expected of all staff members to know the history of the school, and to impart it to the boys so that they would constantly be reminded of their privilege. Teachers were sometimes asked to accompany important visitors and School Inspectors around the building. He said in a confiding way that the architectural presence of the school was such that it is known to have intimidated an Inspector or two to the point of persuading them to comment more favourably on the standard of academic work!

Although I looked as hard as I could, while Archer lectured, I could not find a trace of what he called the 'exuberant quality' that Bullock was meant to have contributed to the appearance of the building or the 'Republican influence' of the other fellow. I suppose I am being a bit heartless, or perhaps insensitive. You know me: my needs are simple to the point of being Spartan.

The staff room is a very serious place, and there is a well-established pecking order among staff members. As the newcomer I am the last to be served my tea. The headmaster's secretary serves the tea, and hands around the biscuits. Archer sits upright and keen at the head of the staff table, and no matter how hot it is here, we are not permitted to remove our jackets. Strangely enough, I am the only 'local boy' on the staff, and it is either that, or my qualifications, that seem to have made some of the staff members rather distant; or perhaps it is the natural resentment that all newcomers encounter. The more I have tried to be relaxed and natural and to use my sense of humour as best I can, the more awkward I feel. When Archer makes a fuss of me it makes things worse.

We have thirteen on the staff including the secretary. Four are women all of whom are old maids. They do a fine job by all accounts and their presence contributes a certain quality of propriety to the staff room atmosphere. What would we do without women! Each day they sit together at the staff room table, old fashioned and united in their cause. By the way, each member of staff has his or her own chair, and heaven help you if you sit on the wrong chair, as I did on the first day. Miss Naude seems to have been here longest and teaches the standard three and four classes. She shares a house with Miss Olivier who looks after the standard ones and twos. These two vestals seem particularly close, as though they are involved in a conspiracy to be good and pure! They are somewhat inscrutable and it is not easy to engage them in conversation. I have tried, but apart from being polite, they speak mostly to one another. Of the men Bertie Hurford, who teaches English to standards nine and ten, has been the most friendly. He qualified at Leeds and I yet have to learn what brought him to the shores of the Grobbelaars River. No doubt time will reveal all. I shall tell you about the other members of staff as I get to know them better. I shall do so in instalments.

The staff room reminds me how strong the divide over the language issue remains: it moves about like a silent ghost. The awareness of language differences seems to be strongest on the part of the Afrikaans speakers who behave as though they are threatened. It is they more than the English speakers who want to know your allegiance. There is little room for neutrality. I find it awkward. My father has done everything he can to have a neutral position in order to be seen as behaving with professional correctness. Yet even in his case he is regarded with suspicion. It would probably have been better for him to take a stance: friend and foe would have respected more. You try to please everybody and you end up not pleasing anyone. No wonder we ended up going to the Presbyterian Church.

The boys in my classes are much what I would have expected. There are the ones who want to impress, the indifferent ones, the plodders who beaver away, the ones who are lazy and bored, the rebellious ones at the back of the class who want to challenge me as baboons challenge the dominant male. They will soon find themselves engrossed in history and in the front of the class. I have anything between twelve and seventeen boys in a class, so it is quite manageable, and I am able to get to know the individuals quite well.

I am most interested and eager to hear from you about your adventures in Graaff Reinet. I was never at a co-educational school and for that matter neither were you, and it is difficult to imagine what it must be like to have boys and girls in the same class. Do write and tell all.

I still have a problem with the hearing in my right ear. My mother thinks it is nothing serious, but it has persisted for too long now. I am planning to go and see Garnett about it tomorrow morning to have it sorted out.

I have spent a great deal of my time since Christmas reading, mostly The Decline and Fall. *Some days I feel as though I have bitten off much* more than I want to chew. But then, when I again and again return to the realisation how much easier it is to read the work than it must have been for Gibbon to write it, I am humbled, and simply continue to grind away. Of course the literature in itself is so beautiful, although the style can be a bit tangled at times. What I find inspiring is that he was able to create a theme and then weave it through the historical events, and to maintain it for as long as it transported the meaning he wished to convey. He must have had a lot of energy. Earlier today I was reading about Constantine's legal reforms. Whereas he had so many fine attributes, the way in which he dealt with the practice of the ancients to kill their newborn, and the cruelty with which he punished the crime of rape are chilling and disturbing and surely makes his emotional stability questionable. Really strong people are compassionate.

I spent most of the week before the start of school preparing lessons, and went to visit the Nels on Tuesday evening. It is a walk of about a mile and a half. When I left it was growing dark, and the full moon was rising above the eastern hills. It lifted itself, large and yellow, and caused the trees to cast stygian shadows on the surface of the street. The reeds near the river stirred. I saw two elderly people walking their dog. When I arrived at the Nels' house they were talking about the new telephone link across the Atlantic. Just imagine someone sitting in London and speaking to a friend or business associate in New York. I wonder how long it takes for the sound to travel over that distance. Once they had done with the telephone link they debated the way in which fascism is gaining strength in Europe. Garnett's Uncle Charles reckoned that the rise of communism is largely to blame for the popularity of fascism, the latter being a reaction to the former. All quite interesting.

On the way back, at about ten o'clock, I felt quite sad I missed you so much. When I crossed the causeway and saw the wind on the water I thought fond thoughts of you. I cannot begin to tell you how much I am missing you.

Love
Douglas.

When Douglas had finished his letter to Frances he left for Garnett's surgery. There were five people in the waiting room when Douglas arrived. He sat down on the only remaining chair and looked for something to read. There was nothing. He should have brought a book. Garnett's door opened, and Sister de Wet escorted a young woman from the rooms to the dispensary. Garnett caught a glimpse of Douglas through his open door and waved to him. The next patient was shown in. It would be a long wait.

When at last it was Douglas' turn, there were no other patients left. Only the ones who really had to see the doctor did so on a Saturday morning.

"Hello Douglas, let's have a look at your ears. Do sit down. Tell me how it started."

"I think it has been going on for about a year, when I noticed, sometimes, that my right ear was not functioning too well; ringing in the ear, sometimes. And I noticed that when I was a passenger in a car, I could not hear the driver's words so clearly. Recently it has been a bit worse."

"Come let us have a look," Garnett said. He inspected the aural speculum for the presence of wax or suppuration. It was clear. The position of the handle of the malleus seemed normal. The opacity of the membrane was within limits.

He produced his fob watch and held it to Douglas' right ear. "Can you hear the watch?"

"Yes."

Garnett held the watch to Douglas' left ear.

"Yes."

"Was the sound equally strong?"

"No, the left ear was clearer."

Garnett again held the watch next to Douglas' right ear.

"I will now gradually move the watch further away. Tell me when you stop hearing it."

As soon as the watch was taken away from the ear Douglas said, "It's gone." Garnett did it again, each time with the same result. He picked up a tuning fork. "This is a deep toned tuning fork." He struck the tuning fork on the edge of his table and held the stem against the mastoid process of the right ear. "How did that sound? I will do it several times, and I want you to tell me for how long you can hear the sound.

"I am going to use a special little instrument, just really a little whistle, to test your hearing of notes of high pitch. It was designed by a chap called Galton. It is amazing how clever and yet obviously simple some of these things are."

The hearing in the right ear was worse than in the left ear, which indicated that the left ear had begun to compensate for the loss of hearing. Garnett looked at the whites of Douglas' eyes. They had a bluish tinge. "I am not sure," he said in a vague sort of way.

"Sure of what?"

"Sure of what your problem is. When are you likely to be in Cape Town next?"

"Why?"

"Don't be nervous. It is not something to be too excited about, but I think you should perhaps get another opinion – that of a specialist. I would in the meantime do an inflation of the middle ear. Not today, we need some time for that."

"What is that?"

"A simple procedure. I will use a Eustachian catheter to get access to your middle ear to make sure that the air can get in there. We will compare your hearing before and after the catheter has been put in."

"My mother was expecting you only to syringe my ears."

"Let's not draw any conclusions until I have completed my tests. I have to go to the hospital. I'll give you a lift home, if you like."

Mrs van Yssen was in the garden cutting chrysanthemums when Garnett's car stopped outside. She put her basket down and went to the gate to welcome them. "How good your timing is Garnett, the kettle has just boiled. So? Have you fixed my son's ears?"

"There was nothing that I could fix, for now, Mrs van Yssen."

"Garnett thinks I should obtain a second opinion, possibly in Cape Town."

"Whatever for? There cannot be anything wrong with a strong young man of his age, surely?"

"There is nothing to be alarmed about. I have a bit of time to spare before I have to be at the hospital. We'll discuss it over tea," Garnett suggested.

When they were seated Mrs van Yssen looked thoughtfully at Garnett, "Why have you mentioned a second opinion?"

Garnett laughed, "You know doctors, Mrs van Yssen, they always like to have help, and particularly in the case of friends who are patients. And I want to stress the latter, it is better to be safe and have a second opinion. I have no other motive. I have asked Douglas to come to the surgery next week and to let me do an inflation of his middle ear. It is quite harmless and a quite painless procedure and will tell us whether or not he has an infection of the middle ear. Nice tea this. I have been busy all morning and have not had a chance to drink anything."

"Please forgive me for questioning your approach, Garnett. I suppose Douglas could go to Cape Town during the next school holidays."

"Perhaps he'll find a better reason for going! Thing is, I love ear nose and throat work. I think I will specialise in it at some time. My friend Danie Roux and I have talked about it. Douglas, did I ever tell you about the congress that we as final year students were asked to attend in Vienna? Danie Roux and I, and some chap from India, were on our way to Vienna by train. When we left the three of us found ourselves together in a compartment with a very quiet serious looking man whose head was all but buried in a book. Danie was reading from the programme. One of the papers to be delivered was on the treatment of asthma. Danie's mother is asthmatic, so the subject interested him. The paper promised to deal with findings of the role of foreign proteins in the development of asthma. Implicating foreign proteins is quite a controversial subject, and so the three of us from Trinity College had a right royal debate, and came to the conclusion that the idea of linking asthma to allergies was clearly nonsensical, and we speculated how the paper would be received at the congress. When we had finished quarrelling we asked the man behind the book where he was going. To the same congress as we he said. Where was he from we asked? From Guy's Hospital. What did he do there and what was the purpose of his visit to the congress? To deliver a paper he said. On which subject? Asthma! He was Professor Poulton who was in fact Physician to Guy's Hospital and a man most highly respected in his field. His work has gained much ground recently. And of course he was right about the link between asthma and allergies. Such is the impetuosity of youth. Hell, it was embarrassing. We made such fools of ourselves. The foundations of our arguments were without any substance. Gosh, what a business." He threw his head back and had a good infectious laugh. Douglas guffawed.

"Do you think Douglas has an allergy?"

"No, mother," Douglas replied. "Garnett is just trying to produce a diversion. I know his little tricks."

"I must be going soon." Garnett felt his cup. "As soon as my cup is cold."

While Douglas and Mrs van Yssen were saying goodbye, van Yssen arrived. Garnett got out of his car to greet van Yssen.

"I hope you have cleaned Douglas' ears well, Garnett. He must be able to hear everything that goes on in class," van Yssen said.

"His ears are perfectly clean, Mr van Yssen. We need to have another look at them. But I must be on my way now. They are waiting for me at the hospital and Dr Diemont does not like to be kept waiting. Hope to see you soon Douglas," Garnett unwittingly raised his voice.

"Thank you for your help," van Yssen said. "We will no doubt see you in the near future."

Diemont was waiting for Garnett. He was pacing up and down in the corridor outside the operating theatre. "I am so sorry that I am late. A patient delayed me unexpectedly. I'll scrub as quickly as I can." While Garnett scrubbed his hands and his forearms Diemont strolled into the washroom. "I really am so sorry to have inconvenienced you, Dr Diemont."

"These thing happen. And it won't be the last time. Besides, a D and C can always wait. A Saturday is a good time to do it. She can have a good rest on the Sabbath."

"May I ask you something Dr Diemont, before we proceed?"

"Certainly."

"The question is purely hypothetical at this stage."

"You know I would never break a confidence."

"Yes I know that Dr Diemont, but let us suppose that I examined a patient, a young man in his early to mid twenties this morning. He is perfectly strong and healthy. He has come to me because of a gradual loss of hearing in one ear. He speaks of some occasional ringing in that ear and also in the other one. My initial examination shows nothing abnormal. I intend to do an inflation of the middle ear next week. What would you look for, someone with your experience?"

"Is there a family history of deafness?"

"I am not sure."

"What do the whites of his eyes show?"

"It is interesting that you should ask that. If anything they were slightly blue."

"That may not be a good sign."

"I thought so too. What does it suggest to you?"

"Otosclerosis is the first thing that comes to mind. And that explains why you were late. His maternal grandfather went deaf at an early age. Always look into the family history. There is more to inheritance than we suppose."

"We can't be sure."

"Of course we can't be sure."

"Come let us get on with our work, Garnett. There is nothing you can do until you have done further tests. For what it is worth there is a chap called Yearsley, at St. James' Hospital, an aural surgeon who claims to have had success in treating otosclerosis using the electrophonoid method. He started early last year and already claims remarkable success. So even if things turn out for the worst, help may be at hand. Come along now."

"How did you know it was Douglas?" Garnett asked as they walked into the operating theatre.

"I saw him getting into your car as I left my house."

After lunch van Yssen and his wife went to have their Saturday afternoon rest. He got into his pyjamas. She took her dress off and put her dressing gown on over her petticoat. They said nothing for a while. He was restless. He took the *Oudtshoorn Courant* from the table next to the bed. "What was the cause of your father's deafness?"

"He never talked about it. He felt it was a disgrace to suffer from a defect."

"When did his trouble start?"

"Quite early on. But he was already an adult."

"Let us see what Garnett has to say next week. If necessary we'll get a second opinion, as he has suggested. I am sure Douglas won't mind going to Cape Town."

Anneke van Yssen let out a shuddering sigh.

Van Yssen turned his head sideways to look at her, "I think the best is not to say anything or give the impression that we are concerned. It will serve no purpose."

She fell asleep before he did and was woken by his gasping snoring. She got up carefully, not to disturb him, and went into the drawing room. She sat on her favourite couch covered in brightly coloured flower pattern Sanderson linen and stared through the window at the shiny dark green leaves of the Kakamas Peach tree. The peaches were ripening, turning yellow. Not a leaf stirred. She should have closed the shutters to keep the heat out. She looked to the left at the walnut tree that she and Albert had planted when she was pregnant with Douglas. Its trunk was gnarled, the joints of the branches almost arthritic, its small beryline leaves suffocating in the heat, and yet it was bearing fruit, the walnuts that she had sent to Douglas through the post.

In his bed, his mouth open, and his eyes flickering fitfully under their heavy lids, van Yssen dreamed restlessly of Anneke's father. He with his big ears, and spiky hair like Douglas, standing at the edge of a dusty field while oxen drew a plough through furrows of fertility. His large hand scattered seed while he intoned, "The sins of the fathers shall be carried forth in their seed."

Van Yssen was startled from his unpleasant sleep by the unnatural images and the hollowness of the voice of the man in his dream. He was bathed in sweat. His heart was pounding. He had a headache. He swung his legs over the edge of the bed and sat up. There was a grave darkness in him.

When Douglas returned from school on Monday January 17, there were two place settings at the dining table. His mother had waited to have lunch with him. She enjoyed hearing about his day's activities. When she heard the front door opening she went to greet him. "Hello my son, there is a surprise for you. I put it on the table." She smiled. Frances' letter was next to his place setting. "I will ask Betta to bring our food."

Douglas unfolded his napkin. The envelope was thick. The familiar handwriting was striking.

"Why is Dad not here for lunch?" Douglas asked when he heard his mother's footsteps.

"He has gone to Uniondale to do the survey."

"Oh yes, I completely forgot. I am so preoccupied. I could hardly concentrate in class today. I should have remembered when there were only two places at the table. When did he say he would be back?"

"He will be gone for three nights, so on Thursday."

"I have to go and see Garnett again on Thursday."

"I am sure everything will turn out well. Tell me all about school today."

"I must say that I am getting into it. I'm not nervous any more. There was a jolly lively discussion in the staff room today between Rivett and Saunders about the way in which batting should be coached. The first eleven have not been doing as well as they did in the recent past. Saunders took over the coaching job at the start of this season, and is quite touchy about the performance of the team. From what I can gather, it was when they lost to George last year, just before the start of the holidays, that some of the parents made certain comments. It all seems so small minded. Van Selm has been getting very good results with the juniors, but, as you can imagine, there is a lot of pride involved, as well as some professional jealousy."

"Are you not going to open Frances' letter?"

"All in good time, Mother, all in good time. I might have forty winks after lunch. I'll read it when I go to lie down."

"I love these frikadels in the cabbage leaves," Douglas commented.

"I know you do." She watched as he finished his frikadels, and soaked up their juices, speckled with tiny globules of fat, with a piece of bread, and how he relished the aftertaste.

Douglas settled himself on his bed. He took a small tin of butterscotch from the drawer of the table next to his bed. As he opened it saliva squirted into his mouth. He popped the fattest sweet he could find into his mouth. He made himself comfortable and opened Frances' letter. He sniffed the pages. There was only the scent of writing paper and Croxley ink. He pressed the pages against his forehead. He was embarrassed about the blandness of his letter to her. He put his shoes on. He arranged his writing paper, took the cap off his fountain pen, and began to search for appropriate words. She said she was going to have a bath. She was telling him that she was going to be naked. He put another butterscotch into his mouth. Perhaps it would be better to read her letter again.

His thoughts wandered. He saw the fruit trees outside his window, and they had no meaning. He saw the grass sprouting tall from the damp places bordering the water furrow. His bedroom was plain. The wardrobe with his few clothes, the small red Chinese carpet, the boxes of books that he would unpack when Stander delivered the bookshelf; the well-worn surface of his yellowwood table; the drawer in which there were still some of his cast-iron toy cars and farm machinery. He could not remember why he had put the fat piece of string in there. The radiating patterns on the ceiling yielded no inspiration. The house was asleep. He made his way to the kitchen as silently as possible so that the wooden floors wouldn't creak, treading wherever possible on the parts where the nails were visible to put his weight on the joists. A blue and white dishcloth draped over the edge of the sink was becoming stiff. The freshly scrubbed kitchen table smelled of blue soap. He carried the tea tray to the living room to find his mother reading the newspaper.

"How is Frances? How is she finding Graaff Reinet?"

"I think she is probably still wondering about that herself. She wrote before school actually started. She tells about her journey and her accommodation and some of the teachers. She has invited me to visit her in Cape Town during the holidays. I think I would like to go if you and Dad agree. I'll use my own money."

"Of course it will be all right for you to go. Douglas, now that we are alone together, there are some things that I feel I should say to you. We all too often leave things that we should say unsaid. It is easier for me to say these things when we are alone. Not that I want you to think that I would keep anything from your father, it is just that it is easier to have intimate moments with you when we are alone. Just as we used to play at the bottom of the garden when you were small, making our rivers and dams, or reading to you on early winter evenings in front of the fire before you went to bed in your flannel pyjamas.

"Mothers find it very difficult to share their sons, especially their only sons. But this girl, this Frances, she is so beautiful in every way, she is so wholesome, I am not sure how to put this: I become so overwhelmed with affection for her, that I can imagine what you must feel, how you must love her. I once had a certain very special moment with your father, when my excitement was so intense that it was almost unbearable. My soul soared like a pure white expanse, like a piece of great music." She had tears in her eyes.

He took her hand, "Come on now Ma."

"No, don't say anything. I must tell you how I feel now that I have crossed a threshold that I never thought I could cross. We may never again have a moment like this. The two of you were meant for each other. She loves you so much. Women sense these things. I noticed how she looked at you when we were in Cape Town. You must go to Cape Town during the holidays. What was it that Horace said? *Carpe diem*. I know it is still some way off, but at least it is something to look forward to, for both of you. Write to her and tell her that you will go. Make your bookings as soon as possible and let her know that you have done so. You must have decent accommodation. Stay at the Helmsley. You need new clothes. Go and see Jack Pienaar.

"Frances is so beautiful. Her fair hair, her features, her eyes, her elegant feminine hands and the innocent figure that is still angular. You are so fortunate."

The emotion that Frances' letter had aroused was encouraged by his mother's intimacy and became so intense that he felt as though their souls wanted to touch. He wanted to become one with his mother. There would be no going back unless he stopped now at the edge of the void. But it was too late for their spirits had already touched. The tea made him sweat a little. The caffeine heightened his awareness. He waited until he was back in his familiar reality, woken from a dream.

"Did you say anything?" he asked.

"No nothing."

Douglas needed to urinate and went outside. It was easier to go in behind the coal shed and to pee on the nettles. Damn things sting you so they deserve to be pissed on. While he buttoned his fly he looked up to see Miss Rubenstein from next-door sitting on a wooden crate under the palm tree that grew in her chicken coop, peering at him from under the large brim of her straw hat, and wagging her finger in disapproval. He shrugged and turned his back to her.

He went to his table and read Frances' letter again. It had occurred to him, while he was having his second cup of tea, that there was no reference to his letter. Perhaps he had been too impetuous with his declaration of love. An impulse like that once recorded can never be retrieved. It would be better to be somewhat restrained in future. She was waiting for his first letter. He looked at the calendar on the wall. It took anything between six and ten days for mail to reach Cape Town. So at best it would have been delivered in Cape Town on the day she got to Graaff Reinet. What an ass he was.

Monday January 17, 1927 Douglas to Frances
Dear Frances
I received your lovely letter of the 7th when I returned from school this afternoon. It is a relief to know that you are safe. I did write to you on the 6th but it seems as though my letter could have arrived in Cape Town after you left. I trust that it has been forwarded to you. You must have thought badly of me for not replying, and yet you have written. I also wrote to you on Friday, so it would seem as though we have missives hurtling back and

forth between us. It would be good to get a dialogue going, just as we used to do in Cape Town. To be successful we will have to synchronise our correspondence. I will telephone you this evening to see whether you approve.

I liked your description of the feelings that travelling evokes.

I know exactly what you mean. I have experienced such feelings and sentiments many times as I travelled back and forth between Cape Town and Oudtshoorn. Boarding the train and setting off for some distant destination seems to change one. I have often wondered whether this is not because of something that is deeply rooted in the human psyche: as though we are really meant to be perpetual travellers in a vast universe. Think of the old Vikings. How they had the courage to set off into the unknown. Think of Homer. (Hell of a funny name for a fellow who was never at home!)

Your Miss du Toits of this world are in a way like Protestant Nuns. The irony is that much as they may dislike the Catholic faith and all that goes with it, they in their own way do mimic the Catholics by artificially separating themselves from perfectly natural aspects of Creation. One might call them adherents of the Natural Order of Artificial Women. And yet I suppose that they too are a part of Creation, and have a right to live as they choose. It just seems like such a waste. I liked your descriptions of the women staff members. There are far too many spinsters, and as for being attracted to your own kind, well!

Mr Puttick has a reputation of being a very good headmaster.

My father was saying that he has heard that he appears to be a bit distant at times. Could just be his English manner. It would be interesting to hear what you think of him.

I imagine you in your room, at your table with your small vase of sweet peas, and the scene outside. It is remarkable how similar our towns are.

As I mentioned in my letter of Saturday, I was more apprehensive about teaching than I cared to say, but the worst is over now. The boys are quite decent. The difficult ones are probably just seeking attention. If you make the work interesting for them they are likely to enjoy themselves. My hope is to inspire them, especially if I think how much my studies meant to me and how enriching my academic work has been. I find it difficult to understand that people do not want to study, that they do not want to read.

You speak of the eight weeks that lie ahead. Happily it is now no longer eight weeks to the end of term, only seven. How the first week has flown. Tempus fugit. When you receive this, another week will have passed and then there will be only six weeks left – just one and a half months. I would very much like to accept your kind invitation to visit you in Cape Town, and will make my train bookings and accommodation arrangements in the next day or so. It would be very nice if we could travel on the same train. Would you please let me know when your return booking is for. I will ask you this evening. I have been to see Garnett about my ear, and although he is going to have another look at it on Thursday, he thinks that it may be wise to obtain a second opinion from a specialist in Cape Town. If he still feels that way on Thursday, I will go when I visit you.

We too, have an excellent example of Gothic architecture. Hopefully when you visit us one day I will show it to you. Astonishingly our Dutch Reformed Church has stained glass windows and sculptures of angels that hold the pulpit aloft in their hands. The point you make of the way people feel about belonging to a particular denomination is interesting. It never ceases to intrigue me how divisive religion can be.

I still think quite often of our walks on the beach, especially when I go to bed at night. I see the clear green swells and hear the waves crashing and hissing as they exhale the air from their white foam.

It was extremely interesting what you said about Dickens and Graaff Reinet. Who would have thought that he of all people would have made legal history there? How was the matter ultimately resolved? I am pleased that you are enjoying Gaskell.

I wonder what she would have said if she had known about Charlotte's letters to her teacher. Fortunately you are a liberated woman. You have your parents to thank for that. Your mother is so natural and unaffected. I remarked to Garnett, how modern she is in her ways, especially considering that her formative years were in the last century. Clearly your father admires his smart daughter, and has given you the opportunity and freedom, as well as his encouragement, to give expression to your ambitions. The repression and sublimation of natural instincts during the last century must have done terrible harm to people – no wonder that the new psychotherapy has found fertile ground trying to repair the damage. There can be no doubt that the war has been the major contributor to the profound changes in our social attitudes. It was sufficiently cataclysmic to bring down the old order so that the killing fields could produce a fresh crop of ideas. It is a pity that we have to destroy in order to renew, but that seems to be the way of things.

I am most excited about seeing you soon. It will be wonderful to be on the train together, to share that unique experience of which we spoke earlier, of travelling together, of being alone together. The prospect of only another six weeks will now be easier to endure, or more difficult. You are such a great inspiration to me. You make me feel that I want to do something special with my life, and I must thank you for that.

With all my love
Douglas.

Douglas and his mother enjoyed their supper – fish cakes that Betta had made. "I wonder whether Dad would mind very much if I made a telephone call to

Frances this evening? I looked up the number of Marshall's Boarding House when I was at the Post Office."

"I am sure he would not mind. He does not like to make trunk calls because of the cost. I thought you wrote to her today?"

"Our letters are crossing in the mail, and it is becoming very confusing."

"I think that is a good idea, but ring after eight, if you don't mind."

The day was coming to a satisfactory conclusion. He would immerse himself in history preparation, and go to sleep.

At five minutes past eight Douglas went to the end of the passage, where the telephone stood on a small shelf fixed to the wall. He turned the handle, lifted the handset, and asked the exchange for the number of Marshall's Boarding House. He felt his heartbeat.

"Marshall's!" An irritable woman's voice answered.

"Good evening. This is Douglas van Yssen. I am telephoning from Oudtshoorn." The line crackled menacingly. "Could I speak to Miss Rose, please?"

"It's a bit late. Hold on. I'll see if she is there."

Douglas heard the handset being put down, a door squeaking and fading footsteps. After what seemed like an age the footsteps returned. "She is either not in her room or she is asleep. Would you like to leave a message for her?"

"Who am I speaking to please?"

"You are speaking to Mrs Marshall."

"I would be most grateful if you could please let her know that I telephoned."

"Hold on, she has just come in."

Douglas heard Mrs Marshall's voice. "There is a telephone call for you Miss Rose," she said politely.

"Is that you Daddy?" Frances asked.

"No, it is I, it's Douglas."

"Douglas! What a surprise, how unexpected, how wonderful."

"It is so nice to hear your voice. I am missing you," he heard himself saying. "I am telephoning to let you know that I will be able to go to Cape Town at the end of the term, and I thought that it would be an idea if we could be on the same train. I am sure you have already made your return booking, so if you could let me know when you plan to leave, I will make my booking accordingly."

"Oh, that is so wonderful, so exciting. I cannot remember the exact date, but I will look at my ticket and mail the information to you tomorrow. Oh, I cannot contain myself, it is so, I do not know what words to use, it is so exquisite to hear your voice. Tell me all, tell me what you have been doing what you have been thinking."

"Well, I miss you a great deal, and our conversations. It is as though my best friend has gone away."

"I feel that way too."

"Frances, it would seem that our letters are crossing in the post, and I was thinking that it would be an idea to time our writing so that we could have a proper dialogue?"

There was a crackling sound on the line.

"Hello, Hello?" Douglas said.

"As long as this is not a ruse to write to me less often than you ought to," she teased.

"Well I wrote to you today, and mailed the letter this afternoon. So if you would wait until you get it before you write."

"How long will you be staying in Cape Town?"

"I think for about a week."

"How smashing! I shall be so excited tonight that I will not be able to sleep. Mummy gave me some camomile with instructions to use it to buoy up my spirits – she must have anticipated how much I would miss you – but it evidently also has a calming effect, so I shall have some before retiring. I have an audience so I cannot say all that I would want to say, please understand."

"Are you still there, Frances?" Douglas asked.

"Yes, she's gone, so let me say, before she returns, how much I am missing you. I think of you all day and the worst is when I go to bed at night. How I would love to be with you all and every minute of every day."

"I, I also think of you all the time."

"All my love," Frances said quickly. "I look forward to your letter. Sweet dreams."

"I cannot wait to see you, lots of love."

"Goodbye now," she said.

"Bye Frances."

18 January 1927 Frances to Douglas

Dearest Douglas

Even though I agreed to wait for your letter of the 17th before I wrote again, I received your letter of the 6th today and thought it would be better if I replied immediately to let you know as soon as possible when I will be travelling to Cape Town. School closes on Friday March 11, and I will be leaving here the following day. It is so exciting to think that we will be on the same train. I shall write to my parents. Where do you plan to stay? Doyle can fetch us from the station.

Turning to your letter, I too feel that we are now so much further apart, even though we are closer. I agree with you, it is made worse by the knowledge that we will not see one another for such an awfully long time, but then the prospect of travelling with you, and having you to myself in Cape Town will make our separation bearable. And how could you ever have imagined that I would be anything but thrilled with your gift.

As far as the gatherings at Christmas are concerned, it is the joy of being with friends, much more than the grandness of the occasion that I really like. Knowing how stimulating you find other people you are sure to find interesting things to talk about in any company. As for the simple ways of Oudtshoorn, I am sure Graaff Reinet is quite similar, and yet I am beginning to sense that it will be easier to make friends here than in the city – I like the sincerity and directness of the people here. Your friend Mr Pienaar sounds like a real salt of the earth character. What a life he must lead with a woman who imagines herself to be ill all the time. Poor man! He must be having a thin time of it.

It means more to me than mere words can express that you feel you want to share your feelings with me. At times I feel so much love for you that I want to bare my entire soul to you, to be inside your thoughts, to be elevated to such a level that we are able to communicate without words. I think you were right to have made the choice to start teaching – it is good experience – although I am sure that either journalism or a lectureship would have suited you equally well. Your father is very proud of you and it must mean a lot to him to have you at home. I noticed how he doted when he looked at you.

I am not sure why you of all people should search for signs.

You are so strong, and so accomplished. You alone should decide on your destiny. (By the way, your suggestion that our letters should be in the form of a dialogue, I realise now, is an excellent one because of the way I am responding to your letter.) Above all, don't compare yourself to Hamlet. You are much more resolute, and if your affection for me has made you feel helpless, you flatter me greatly by conceding that I at least have some power over you.

If your first week of school has been anything like mine it will not have been so bad. I am getting to know my colleagues and my pupils. Mr Puttick has been awfully nice to me. As I told you, I was invited to tea at their house. He has one of those tidy small faces and wears round-rimmed spectacles. He is from England but I did not want to pry too much. Like you he is an M.A., I think from Leeds, and his subject is English literature – we had lots to discuss, but more about that some other time. It is difficult to tell his age because he has such a marvellously good complexion. He has two sons who are still at school in England.

To my surprise I find standing in front of the class quite exhilarating. It is exciting to try and stimulate the minds of the pupils, to take them on a journey into a world of ideas.

The children of the platteland are so much more receptive and unquestioning than those in the city. They are much less spoilt and better disciplined, and I have no difficulty managing the classes. Each teacher has his or her own classroom and the pupils move about between periods. It makes sense if you come to think about it, because you can hardly move the science laboratory or the biology room about!

Sport is quite important at the school, especially rugby and cricket. The first cricket match of this year (against Grey in Bloemfontein) will be played in a fortnight's time. By the way the rugby field is named the Puttick Field.

At this stage I have quite a lot of preparation to do each evening for the lessons of the following day. No doubt the burden will become less as time progresses.

Daddy gave me a box camera before I left with instructions to take lots of photographs. I have begun to do that and will bring them along for you to see. Perhaps you could do the same for me so that I will be able to see where my dear Douglas lives, and teaches and everything to do with Oudtshoorn.

Loads of love
Frances.

Chapter Fourteen

Thursday 20 January 1927

VAN YSSEN RETURNED from Uniondale just after six in the evening. His car was covered in dust. Drifts of brown dust lay between the tyres and the rims of the wheels, and on the ledge where the windscreen joined its frame. There was dust inside the car. He had been on the road for most of the afternoon and had travelled with the windows open because of the heat. There was dust on the sleeves of his white overcoat.

On his way to Uniondale he had thought much about Douglas' hearing. The sentiment of departure enlarged the issue until it assumed harmful proportions. He could not contain the resentment he felt towards his wife's father and he began to feel resentment towards her for passing her father's deafness on to his son. As the days passed he felt remorse and then the feeling of remorse grew so strong that he resolved that he would be forgiving. Yet the thought that his son could have such a blemish as deafness kept on intruding upon his resolution, and supplied his resentment with the energy to restrain forgiveness.

Mrs van Yssen went to greet him as he approached the house. When she embraced him he stood stiffly and held on to his bag. She kissed him on his cheek and put her arm through his.

When they had had supper Douglas announced that he was going to visit Garnett. He fetched a pullover from his room, said goodnight to his parents, and disappeared down the garden path into the moonless night.

"Let us have our tea outside," van Yssen suggested.

"What a lovely evening," Mrs van Yssen said.

"There is no moon," he replied.

"I find the dark night quite romantic, Albert, listening to the sounds of the insects and the frogs." A dog barked in the distance and the penetrating sound of a train whistle travelled across the river. The stars were unusually clear.

"Did you ever mention your father's deafness to Douglas?"

"I might have said something in passing, not that I can remember. Why do you ask?"

"I have been thinking while I was away that it might be a good thing if we did not mention it."

"Why is that?"

"I think we should wait to see what Garnett says."

"Why should my father's deafness matter?"

"In case it is hereditary."

"Oh Albert, I know you so well, I know how easily you become troubled, and how easily certain things can disturb your equilibrium, but are we not seeing spectres? Why don't we do exactly as you have suggested, and wait to see what Garnett says on Saturday?"

"Where did the figs and the peaches come from?"

"From Jack Pienaar. I telephoned to thank him. We had such a wonderful time, meeting the Roses in Cape Town, an introduction to the Governor General, being with our friends at Christmas time. I love you so very much. You have been so good to me. Let us have faith. Douglas' problem could just be a minor one that Garnett will sort out, or someone in Cape Town. Besides, Douglas would grasp at any excuse to go to Cape Town to see Frances. If their friendship takes its natural course we will be blessed to have her as our daughter-in-law. I gave Douglas permission to telephone her on Monday night. I saw his look afterwards. He is stricken."

"The fellow has much to do. He can't afford to be distracted now."

"Oh Albert, it does not have to be a distraction, it could be an inspiration. Just think of the circles in which he will be moving."

"There is hardly anything wrong with the circles in which we move."

"Yes I know that, but it will create wonderful opportunities for Douglas."

She poured more for him. She remained standing next to him with her hand on his shoulder. He had after all been away for a few days. His shoulder was hard and motionless. "I think I will go and prepare for bed."

"I'll sit for a while and plan my work for tomorrow." Van Yssen sat and looked into the night while he sipped his tea. The fragrance of the roses that Anneke had planted when she was pregnant with Douglas drifted towards him. He saw her on her hands and knees pushing down the soil around the stems of the young plants, her hair hanging loose on the one side of her head, her face flushed, and he wanted to forgive her for her father's deafness but his resentment was too strong. When he went to their bedroom she was already asleep.

Saturday 22 January 1927

Douglas woke early, shaved, had a bath, made sure he washed his ears very well, dried himself vigorously and cleaned his ear passages with the twirled corner of his towel. The weather had become cooler two days earlier as a cold front swept over the South Western Districts. He put on a light pullover. The second week of school was over. After next week only five would remain.

When he arrived at Garnett's rooms there were two people waiting. Sister de Wet appeared. "Good morning Mr van Yssen, Doctor will be here presently. He was delayed at the hospital."

Douglas had hardly picked up a copy of the Saturday Evening Post when Garnett rushed in. "Come inside, Douglas, I am so sorry that I am late. I was delayed at the hospital." He closed the door of his consulting room, and squeezed his legs together, "I have to go and see a man about a horse; I had too much liquid this morning." He ran out through the back door.

Garnett returned and washed his hands. "What I would like to do to start with, is to check your hearing again with the watch, before I inflate your middle ear."

"Hell, I'm a bit scared, you're not going to hurt me, are you?"

"Heavens, no. It won't even be uncomfortable. It's quite simple really. All I'm going to do is to insert a small catheter, a little rubber tube, from the back of your throat into the canal that goes to your middle ear, the Eustachian tube. It might tickle a little. Then I am going to use an auscultation tube to listen for the sound of the air that I will be pumping gently into your middle ear. Once I am certain that your middle ear has been inflated we will once again test your hearing, to see how much difference there is. And that's that. But first let us check your hearing distances with the watch."

He took out his fob watch and held it next to Douglas' right ear. "You said last time that you could hear the watch?"

"Yes I can hear it now."

Garnett moved the watch away about three inches, "And now?"

"Only faintly."

Garnett moved it a few inches further away, "And now?"

"No, nothing."

Garnett seated Douglas on a chair opposite himself. "I want you to open your mouth nice and wide now." He began to insert the catheter. "Are you all right, Douglas?"

He nodded.

"How are things going at school?" Garnett asked.

Douglas could not answer, but gave him the thumbs-up with his left hand.

"There, close your mouth gently now, but please keep still while I pump air in." Garnett put the one end of the auscultation tube in the external meatus of Douglas' right ear and the other end in his own ear, and gently squeezed the red rubber bulb at the end of the catheter. He pumped a bit more. "There, there, I can hear the air now. That's fine, I'm sure it is fully inflated." He removed the auscultation tube. "We must now let you listen to the watch again."

He repeated the earlier procedure with the watch. The result was the same.

"What do you think?" Douglas mumbled, the catheter still in his mouth.

Garnett was silent, his hand over his mouth, staring at the floor. "Let me remove the catheter."

"What does it mean?" Douglas asked.

"I'm not sure. How is the other ear?"

"It's fine, really fine."

"Let's see what the watch tells us."

Garnett did a distance test with the watch. The left ear seemed fine.

"Are you aware of any hearing impairment in your family?"

"Not that I can think of, except that my mother did mention her father, my grandfather. He died when I was three or four so I didn't really know him.

My grandmother spoke of the old man's deafness. I'll have to ask my mother. Why do you ask? What could it have to do with my hearing?"

"It is better to have a full history." Garnett made notes in Douglas' file.

"When did you first notice the problem with your hearing?"

"I'm not sure, it could be a year or maybe two years ago. It seems to have happened so gradually, really slowly."

"Did you ever receive a blow on the ear? Rugby or something like that?"

"Not that I am aware of, no."

"I think we have done enough for today. I would like to discuss it with Dr Diemont if you don't mind. He has a lot of experience. Would you have any objection?"

"No not at all."

"I enjoyed your visit on Monday night. It would be nice if we could go down to Herold's Bay for a weekend. I would still like to get you interested in fishing. Just imagine all the fun we could have and the trips we could go on."

"I don't think I was cut out for that, but I would nevertheless like to go along. What do you think is wrong with my ear?"

"I am not sure. One would normally find this type of thing in older people, but you are so young, and healthy, that's why I would like to get Diemont's opinion. And as I mentioned before, if you go to Cape Town in the school holidays we can get a second opinion from a specialist. In the meantime I would not make too much of it. You definitely do not have any infection; there is no evidence of catarrh or anything like that."

"Do you think that it might just be a passing thing that will come right by itself?"

"Possibly, but let's wait and see."

"You seem preoccupied?"

"No, not at all, nothing, I'm just a bit lost. I want to be thorough, and certain of all my facts. Don't look so worried," Garnett said with kindly smiling eyes.

Douglas thanked Garnett, promised to visit him soon and went out into the bright mid-morning sunlight. He blinked. Something in Garnett's manner made him uneasy, something like the shadow of a dove flying between him and the sun that scattered foreboding. The sky dulled and he looked up to see whether there was a cloud. There was none. Doubt had absorbed clarity. Or had his eyes adapted to the light? He sighed, shrugged his shoulders, shook his head and began to make his way across the street. Garnett is inexperienced. Someone in Cape Town will sort it out.

Mr and Mrs van Yssen waited for Douglas to return. Van Yssen was reading the newspaper and she was writing a letter to her aunt in Malmesbury. The wheat fields there would be golden stubble now, and the bluegum trees swaying in the summer wind. She looked up when she heard the hinges of the garden gate. She searched Douglas' face, to see how the examination had gone. He smiled a somewhat wan smile.

"What did Garnett find?" His father asked.

"Nothing."

"Isn't that wonderful news!" His mother exclaimed.

"He seemed uncertain, and wants to discuss it with Dr Diemont."

"I'm not keen to have our private affairs aired in town, and we should tell Garnett that in no uncertain terms," his father objected.

"Dad, Garnett asked me whether I would have any objection. It was I who said no."

"You should have been more circumspect."

"I am sure there will be no breach of any confidentiality. Dr Diemont is most discreet and correct," his mother appeased.

"Why does he need Diemont to give an opinion?"

"He said he was not sure what the nature of the problem is. He was most thorough. He did what he called an inflation of the middle ear, and tested my hearing. The left ear seems to be quite normal, but my hearing in my right ear is not that good. He asked whether there has been any deafness in our family."

"What did you tell him?" His father asked.

"I said I thought Ma had mentioned her father's deafness, but that I was not sure."

"I need to see to something in the kitchen," Mrs van Yssen said.

"What was the problem with my grandfather's hearing?" Douglas asked.

"He was deaf, but it does not necessarily mean anything," van Yssen replied.

"Why did he become deaf?"

"I don't really know. When I met your mother he was deaf."

"Was he already old then?"

"Ja, we were engaged for a while, about three years, before we married. I met him a while before we became engaged. Perhaps three years before that. You were born two years after we were married, and he died when you were four. He was well over sixty then."

Mrs van Yssen returned rubbing cream into her hands.

"Anneke what was the cause of your father's deafness?"

"I don't know. It seemed as though he was always deaf."

"Was there any specific episode associated with it?" Douglas asked.

"How do you mean?" His mother asked.

"Like a bang on the head, or a particular illness, or something like that?"

"Not that I am aware of."

"Did Garnett make any definite diagnosis?" van Yssen asked.

"He did say that there was no evidence of any infection. He also said that he thought that I should go and see a good ear nose and throat specialist when I go to Cape Town in the holidays."

"When did you decide to go to Cape Town?" His father was put out.

"Albert, you were in Uniondale. Douglas and I simply discussed the possibility. Nothing has been finalised. Douglas is a grown man. You were already married at his age."

"As long as I am consulted, after all we live under one roof. I thought we could do something together in the school holidays. But, if Douglas wants to go to Cape Town, then so it must be. It is a good idea to see a specialist. Garnett qualified only recently. At least he is taking a cautious approach. When is he going to speak to Diemont?"

"I have no idea."

"Are you still going to play tennis this afternoon?"

"Yes, I am looking forward to it. I took the opportunity when I was in town to pop in to Hepworths to look at some clothes. They are having a sale soon. I'll wait for that. Jack Pienaar says business has been slow so they have lots of stock and there will be lots of bargains. It is quite strange to think that I will be getting my first cheque at the end of next week even though I have only been teaching for two weeks.

"Dad, I asked Frances, when I telephoned her to let me know when she will be travelling to Cape Town so that I can be on the same train. It would be rather nice if we could travel together."

"I am sure you will enjoy it."

Garnett was on his way to the hospital early the following morning when he saw Diemont's car ahead of him. At the hospital Diemont waited for him.

"Good morning Dr Diemont."

"Morning young man. Lovely morning. At least some of the heat has gone."

"I wonder whether I could please ask you something, Dr Diemont."

"Certainly, what is troubling you?"

"If you would prefer, I would be more than happy to come to your rooms."

"Is it that serious?"

"I am not sure. It is about Douglas van Yssen."

"What we talked about the other day?"

"Yes."

"You said you were going to do a more detailed examination?"

"Yes, I did so yesterday. There is no infection, and the inflation did not produce any improvement in his hearing."

"Did you ask him about his family history?"

"Yes."

"And?"

"He said that his mother may have mentioned that his grandfather had been deaf."

"I know he was deaf; as deaf as a doorpost. You mentioned the other day that the whites of his eyes had a bluish tinge?"

"I specifically looked for that yesterday, and I am afraid to say it is quite pronounced."

"That together with what you found yesterday suggests the possibility of otosclerosis."

"I know. What would you do if you were in my position?"

"I would send him to a specialist. Let someone else make the final diagnosis. You are too close to him and the van Yssens. His father will not easily forgive the messenger who bears ill tidings."

Diemont took Garnett's elbow and began to walk towards the hospital entrance.

"If our suspicions are correct, Garnett, and I hope they are not, it will be a great tragedy but there is nothing anybody can do to change the course of that particular disease." Garnett opened his mouth to reply. Diemont held up his hand. "Yes I know I told you about Yearsley and his electro-therapy. I did some more reading and it has made me sceptical. Everything depends on the progress of the disease, and even then it seems to bring only temporary relief. I am not sure we should give false hope. It can only be done in England, and it could be a waste of time and money."

"The left ear seems to be fine. In your opinion are both ears always affected, or can it be confined to one ear?"

"If it is otosclerosis, the left ear will follow the right ear as the left foot follows the right. It will just be a matter of time."

"How long?"

"Two, three, four or five years."

They reached the front entrance of the hospital.

"I will recommend that he sees a specialist."

Garnett did his hospital round, saw that all was well at his surgery and went home. His family had gone to church. Only the maid was there. He found a copy of the *Oudtshoorn Courant* lying on the dining room table, and sat down. He tried to read the paper. He lowered the paper onto his lap, and removed it when he realised that the ink would come off on his linen trousers. He clasped his hands behind his head, and shut his eyes. He felt helpless. Tears came to his eyes. What a cad he had been to tease Douglas about Frances. He was startled when the maid put a tray down on the table. "Is master all right?" He was embarrassed. "Ja,ja." He dried his eyes, blew his nose in his handkerchief, and sniffed a bit. He felt better. He would wait a few days and then telephone Douglas about seeing a specialist.

◆

Chapter Fifteen

Wednesday 26 January 1927

"THERE IS A LETTER for you from Frances. I have put it in your room," Mrs van Yssen said when Douglas returned home from school.

His mother sat with him while he had lunch.

"At what time will Dad be back this afternoon?'

"He won't be late. Have you had a successful day at the school?"

"Yes, things are becoming easier. Latin is a cakewalk. The classes are small. Probably because some boys chose to do Greek."

"Perhaps they intend doing theology?"

"Could be, I never thought of that. Frances said she would let me know when she will be travelling to Cape Town."

"Perhaps it is in her letter."

"Yes I expect so. Garnett has arranged for me so see Dr Roux on the Wednesday morning – the sixteenth. I'll be back on the nineteenth."

Douglas carried his plate and the dishes to the kitchen, thanked his mother for lunch and went to his room. He sat down at his desk and opened Frances' letter. He looked at the dates she gave. He read certain phrases. 'Make our separation more bearable.' 'More than mere words can express that you feel…' 'I want to bare my entire soul to you.' 'To be inside your thoughts.' 'You are so strong and so accomplished.' 'Your affection for me.' 'You are more resolute.' 'Pleased that we will, I cannot tell you how pleased that we will travel together.' He was tempted to respond immediately. That would contradict his proposals. The best laid schemes o' mice an' men/ Gang aft a-gley. He read the letter again.

His mother was in her favourite place in the living room.

"I always enjoy being alone with you."

"I forgot to mention, I spoke to Madame Jacquard on the way back from school yesterday. She is quite interesting, as you said."

His mother looked at the patterns of the Chinese carpet.

"She said that she would like to have us over."

"Who?"

"Madame Jacquard."

"She is quite Bohemian."

"I realise that. It makes her interesting. She mentioned that she spent Christmas on her own. It must have been quite difficult for her."

"We should have asked her over."

"She said she might soon be going to Mossel Bay for a week. She says she craves sea air and she wants to paint some beach scenes. She said the light is particularly good at this time of the year – like that of southern Europe. She is certainly very different. It must be nice to travel."

"Yes it must be really nice to travel. I have had to create fantasies all my life, through books and magazines, and more recently the bioscope has shown me other places."

"The Roses have travelled a lot. Garnett was fortunate. He spent some of his holidays in England and Scotland and Wales, and also on the Continent. He has some lovely stories to tell. The Judge sometimes took Frances out of school when she was younger, for their overseas visits. He said travelling was more educational. It will be difficult for her to get away now that she is teaching."

Frances to Douglas. Thursday 27 January
Dearest Douglas
Since I received your letter of the 17th yesterday. I hope that you will wait until you get this letter before you reply! Admirable as your discipline and restraint are, it is I who should be the one to restrain myself since it is more in the nature and education of women to be so. Yet, my absence from you has impaired somewhat my natural restraint and I must confess that I cannot wait to see you.

You speak of the effect of travelling – it is quite extraordinary. It is no more pronounced than when one sets off for a very distant destination. It seems the further away the destination, the greater the effect. I am sure it has to do with a heightened sense of anticipation; in other words the stronger the anticipation, the greater the effect. Your idea of something rooted in the human psyche, that makes us perpetual travellers, is quite fascinating. Could it be – in this regard I am reminded of our discussion about evolution and what goes with it – that we have a need to migrate in order to ensure that our genetic material can be distributed as widely as possible? (By the way, I like your witty reference to Homer. Daddy will love it. He thinks you have a great dry sense of humour.)

I also like your comment about the Protestant Nuns, and the other nuns for that matter. It is indeed a waste, and from a Darwinian perspective one wonders what nature's intention could be for such creatures. Could it be that it is nature's way of eliminating certain individuals from the process of natural selection?

The more I see of Mr Puttick the more I like him. He is even-handed and absolutely constant in his behaviour. He is scrupulously fair, which is a quality that earns respect, and I would not say that he is at all aloof. It is his English reserve, and nothing more than that. His academic achievements are quite outstanding, and as a consequence he expects a great deal from others, yet he sets the pace himself, as behoves any true leader.

I like him.

I often think of the lovely time we had together at the seaside, even though it was for such a brief period, and I fervently hope that you will be able to persuade your father to take a house at Plettenberg Bay at the end of the year so that we will be able to be together in the wonderful atmosphere of your poetic description of the green swells and the foam of the waves – it so transported my thoughts that I could feel the sands under my bare feet as I read your words. (You should consider writing some poetry.) Do urge your father to consider taking a house, please.

I cannot begin to tell you how thrilled I feel about travelling to Cape Town with you. I have already written to my parents to tell them that you will be visiting, and I am sure they are as pleased as I am.

Coming back to what you said about the nuns. At times I find the notion of sublimation and repression of natural instincts rather confusing. In a sense it is our noble forms of restraint as human beings that set us apart from the animal kingdom and make us civilised. Yet often the kind of restraint that we practise reduces us; that kind of restraint seems to demand that we deprive ourselves of and deny ourselves aspects of our existence that are quite natural. In doing so we take parts of ourselves away, and we thus become incomplete. As incomplete beings we surely cannot function fully. And without the latter society cannot be normal. We can only create sustainable moral order by functioning as complete beings, not by taking away parts of our essential being. One does indeed wonder what Elizabeth Gaskell would have thought of Charlotte's letters, and can only hope that she would have had sympathetic understanding. As I have told you before, I have a great deal of sympathy for Charlotte, and would choose to look for beauty in her physical relationship. The sublimation and repression that you mention, because it is so unnatural, create dark dank corners in the mind where all kinds of demons are hatched. I am not sure how I feel about the future of psychotherapy. It seems to me that those who advocate it and who practise it want to rearrange things in people's minds. But how do you find, let alone rearrange, the hidden bits that have been pushed into the dark corners?

I can only pray that I will be able to lead a full and well-rounded life as a woman. Sometimes when I daydream I find myself sitting outside on a veranda of a house overlooking the sea. It is my house. It is a calm day with only tiny little breezes brushing against my hair and my face. The sea sparkles and dazzles but all the other colours are faded, even the colour of the sand. The Prussian blue and magenta red and lemon yellow of fishing boats that have been pulled up onto the beach are faded. Even the olive greens of the coastal vegetation seem subdued in the haze that shrouds the hills. And I imagine how happy I could be with you there always beside me. I would like to visit you in Oudtshoorn one day, but not in the summer. The heat here is quite beastly.

I still have some preparation to do before I go to bed. There is an awful noise outside at the moment. It sounds as if a coloured and his wife are having the most ghastly quarrel, and has quite unnerved me and driven away my delicate thoughts. I shall make myself some tea and hope that they will have moved on by the time I return to my work.

I know you will write as soon as you receive this letter, dear Douglas. Time will pass, and then suddenly, when my train steams into your station, we shall be together again.

Lots and heaps of love
Frances.

Douglas to Frances 6 March 1927
Dearest Frances
Thank you for your letter. My parents have gone to church.

We have had a spell of cooler weather and it is pleasant out of doors. My parents and I were having our breakfast on the veranda yesterday morning when the postman arrived. It is always exciting to see your handwriting on the envelope. Your letters seem to have so much more substance than mine so I have resolved to spend the entire morning fashioning a reply worthy of your considerable efforts.

I trust that you will be pleased to know that I have made my reservations. I have to see a Specialist, Dr Roux, about my ear in the afternoon of Wednesday the 16th and have made my return booking for the 19th – the Friday. I have written to the Helmsley Hotel and made my booking there. I only trust and hope that they will be able to accommodate me.

Life at school has become more of a routine now, and even at this early stage of the year we are slightly ahead with the syllabus. That will leave more time for revision, and as we all know, one can never have too much of that.

A few days ago my father, quite unsolicited, spoke about going to Plettenberg Bay at the end of the year. My mother responded with great enthusiasm and urged him to make the necessary arrangements at the earliest. I tried to conceal my enthusiasm, but the cunning old fox watched for my reaction from under his bushy eyebrows. I will leave it to my mother to prod him, but I know him well and I think we might as well assume that it is a fait accompli.

It is you who should consider writing poetry. Your description of your daydream is so vivid and rich in imagery that it makes me realise how ordinary my descriptive attempts are. You have a great gift for language and such a wonderful literary sense that it would be a wanton waste not to employ your talent fully. I find it hard to go beyond the boundaries set by my inhibitions, and that is probably also the reason for my choice of subjects. It is easy to be dispassionate about the facts of history or the structure of Latin syntax and since neither challenges my inhibited state they produce no discomfort. Speaking about inhibitions reminds me of your observations about the function of restraint in human society. I find your observations most interesting, and I agree with most of what you have so logically set out, but I fear that it is very difficult to deal with all the elements within us that inhibit or restrain us. There is a very thin line between the restraint that generates our morality and makes us civilised, and the inhibitions that our upbringing and our environment bestow on us. Although they have the same source, the former is a virtue and the latter a bit of a villain that takes some of our fullness from us. I suppose in the end we should try to get away from the absolutes of right and wrong and consider ways of leading, as you have pointed out, well-rounded lives. If we look back in history – even to biblical times – we find in all societies episodes of moral conflict. Times of decadent permissiveness are followed by periods of narrow moral rectitude. As though there are over-corrections in both directions.

I think that both extremes are undesirable. Fate determines in which cycle we find ourselves. Ours is to have emerged from a century of repression and I dare say a great deal of hypocrisy, into a new world of rapid change, hopefully for the better. We should be grateful that we have behind us the war to end all wars.

My mother has made an interesting new friend. She is a French woman who has come to live in Oudtshoorn, not far from us, in the same street. She simply appeared here one day, about a year ago, lived in a local hotel until she found a house to buy. Her husband was evidently involved in a 'matter of honour' as a consequence of which he was compelled to join the Foreign Legion. She is an artist and rather eccentric, one could even say a trifle Bohemian. As is so typical of the mentality of small town people she was virtually ostracised, and for no apparent reason, other than local prejudice because she was so different. My parents have had dinner with her and she has been to our house. She is outspoken, to the point of being provocative, and it is astonishing how my father, whom I see as exceedingly conservative, has warmed to her. When she visits he sits and grins with sparkling eyes when he listens to her outrageous tales of Paris. Although he is reserved, and certainly appears to be exceedingly so, I have always suspected that there is something contrary in him, a strange subdued smouldering kind of rebelliousness. It is so difficult to know what happens in the minds of others, even one's own parents!

I visited the Nels a few days ago. Garnett's father and his Uncle Charles, as usual, held forth on world affairs. Old Charles is a bachelor, who according to the French woman, her name is Madame Jacquard, is quite a sly ladies-man. The imagination boggles. I wonder how she knows. Anyway, the theme of the conversation last Wednesday evening was Communism. Uncle Charlie was strongly of the opinion that one of the greatest evils of Communism is the way in which it has encouraged Anti-Communism to become a force that has allowed Fascism to gain power and to assemble political allies. It is an interesting point of view. He cautions that we ought to be wary of 'that new fellow' in Russia, meaning Stalin. I cannot see why he should prejudge the man – perhaps the upheaval that he has brought about in the Communist Party will do Russia a great deal of good. On the other hand, I must concede, according to some press reports, refugees from Russia speak of endless arrests and summary executions, and of how scared people are to talk openly. Just think how lucky we are to live here in the Union.

A subject that the Nels currently cannot resist is the Flag issue. Especially now that the Provincial Elections are looming the issue has become especially prominent. As staunch SAP supporters both Louis and Charles Nel have taken similar positions, and what frustrates Louis most is that the two of them are in agreement. They are united in brotherly fashion, rejoicing about the fact that Labour fared so badly last year and lost so much support, and they chortle at the prospect of the Flag issue tearing Labour apart. But then Labour is its own worst enemy – imagine members getting up at the conference in Port Elizabeth and suggesting that the Government should be told that if they did not get the Red Flag, they would not support the Flag issue at all.

It is fascinating, especially from the historical perspective, how something as abstract, as symbolic, as a flag, can extract so much sentiment, and reveal so much about the political sentiments in this country. Instead of seeing the matter as a problem, as they seem to do, politicians should employ the energy that the debate is generating as a thrust towards clearer direction.

Garnett's father can be quarrelsome at times, and has a rather crushing attitude towards his sons. He rants and always has to be right and pretends to know everything and constantly reminds his audience that he does not suffer fools gladly, and that he is a Latin scholar. He has a great liking for Cicero and quotes little bits that he has memorised from Pro Archia. I asked him what he likes best about the work and to his credit he said he likes it especially because it probably contains the very words that Cicero spoke, and is not an edited version. Poor Garnett, he does not like confrontation and has such a kind and sympathetic nature, as becomes a good doctor, and yet his father seems to taunt him in order to draw him into nightly debates. Garnett frequently escapes by visiting his surgery after supper or doing late hospital rounds. Fortunately Charlie stands up to Louis and manages to defuse some of the tense situations.

It will be strange to be in Cape Town now that I have finished my studies. I would like to visit the University, and my father would like me to go and say hello to President Reitz.

I want to tell you again how much I am looking forward to seeing you. My parents would very much like to see you and will take me to the station. I do hope that the trouble that I am having with my ear is of a passing nature. It is so irritating to have a constant dullness in the one side of my head and sometimes a nagging ringing in my ear – it will be a great relief when it is fixed.

I think of you when I go to sleep at night and when I open my eyes in the morning.

With all my love and affection.
Douglas.

Frances received Douglas' letter on February 17 and replied on Saturday February 19.

Dearest Douglas

Your letter was waiting for me at the reception desk on Thursday evening, and was handed to me by the unprepossessing Mrs Marshall, with a slight tremor of her hand. She opened her mouth to say something but must have thought better of it, and just smiled at me in an awkwardly intimate way as though we shared something special. Shudder! Letters are usually delivered here in the morning, and I wondered why she did not give it to me at lunchtime. At dinner that evening I mentioned what had happened to Jessica Price and she told me in whispered tones that there was a suspicion that Mrs Marshall had at times in the past opened some of the mail. When I went back to my room, I examined the envelope for evidence that it had been tampered with, but could find none.

If the post continues to be as slow as it has been recently – I shall be able to post this letter only on Monday – there will not be time for a reply from you to reach me before I leave, so I suggest that we wait to resume our correspondence after the school holidays. That way no letter will lie here to tempt Mrs Marshall. (Just in case the suspicions have any grounds.) I hate the insecurity that my suspicion breeds.

I cannot believe how rapidly time has rushed by. My classes are going well and I now actually look forward with anticipation to each day's teaching. At the same time I am making considerable progress with my book, and I am looking forward to discussing it with you, rather than to comment on it now. At times it has evoked such intense feelings in me, bordering on emotional congestion, that it would be much more appropriate to sit closely next to you and to hold your hand while we discuss it. And talking about sitting next to you, the holidays are so short that it would make perfect sense if we could also travel back together. I could come back a bit earlier or you a bit, just a day or two, later? Please consider it dearest?

I am concerned about your ear but I am sure your Dr Roux will find a suitable treatment. You have always been so very healthy and strong and I shouldn't wonder that it is only a little trivial thing.

I have had a strong feeling, like a premonition, that you would be going to Plettenberg Bay at the end of the year. As I have mentioned to you before, I sometimes have the weirdest sensation of absolute certainty about things to come. It seems as though all my wishes are being fulfilled, and as if everything is coming together as planned. I am so happy. I see the hand of destiny arranging our lives, like planets being aligned.

I think you are flattering in what you say about my literary talents, and as for poetry, the great poets have been people with exceptional raw talent and in most instances their lives have been influenced by the kinds of experiences – usually tragic – that have heightened their awareness and amplified their spirituality. I am afraid my life has been much too conventional to awaken in me the sensibility that is necessary to produce poetry of value. It is interesting what you say about inhibitions. In this context I think we should also consider the extent to which our behaviour is the product of conditioning. Sometimes it seems to me that we are people moving about in near-hypnotic states, as if directed by others, without our own will. When we are small and still able to see things in new and innocent ways, adults want us to see things differently so that we may conform. Instead of fostering the virtues of new perspectives offered by the newcomers to our world we destroy what they have to offer us so that we may remain comfortable in our traditional ways, and protect our vested interests. I see each and every day in class young minds bursting with enthusiasm and ideas. The really outstanding teachers (and we know how extremely rare they are) will encourage enquiring minds to develop, and the poor ones (of whom there are many), because what they have to offer is so limited, will put down every attempt made by the pupils who want to go beyond the ordinary, and drive things towards a lowest common denominator. It is almost as if we are trapped in a world of conventions and rules – it is from this that I would like to be liberated. It seems as though Madame Jacquard is indeed unconventional and liberated, and that is exactly why she was ostracised. I am not saying that we should not have formal social structures; we do indeed need to have them, but we need structures that encourage progressive change, and allow us enough freedom to reach our full potential. Perhaps that is why we have wars: to break the old order down. But it should not be necessary to destroy in order to build.

Enough of my strange ideas – which I am not articulating very well – my reasoning is disturbed by my angry thoughts at the possibility of having your letter opened. I hate myself for having such dark suspicions. Possibly the woman is completely innocent. I did not sleep very well last night. It would seem as though it is cat-mating season and there was the most awful primeval growling and pleading wails all night long right outside my window. My, what a noisy lot of infernal blighters! They must have rested all day while I had to go to work!

The Nels seem to have loads of fun. I like your description of Garnett's father and his uncle and have built up pictures of them in my mind. Poor Garnett, it is rather rummy that he has to escape from the quarrels. I could see that he absolutely does not like confrontation.

As you well know, Daddy is strongly opposed to Fascism, even though he has great respect for the Romans. I am not so sure that he would not help to tie bundles of sticks together. He likes the essential substance of order but not the form of Fascism. It is sometimes difficult to gauge what Daddy is thinking for the simple reason that he feels that his position requires him to conceal all his personal political feelings. He does not even say anything to my mother, possibly because he fears what she may say. I think it is an interesting point of view that Communism has encouraged Fascism. Even in the Flag issue there are the clear footprints of the Reds. The issue is such a flawless mirror of the politics of this country, and I don't think it is going to be easy to resolve, or for that matter resolved quickly. Is it not astonishing, how similar the politics today are to those of Roman times? How personal quarrels, and dark political intrigues can bedevil some of the best intentions? Imagine if Pompeius and Lucullus instead of opposing each other could have worked together? I am sure that some of the personal political differences that we witness today had their origin in the Boer War, when Botha, Smuts and Hertzog were all comrades.

Like you and Garnett I find it hideously irritating when the adults adopt their patronising attitudes about things that they imagine us to be totally ignorant of. They carry with them the baggage of the last century while we can at least claim to have been borne in a more enlightened time.

You may be amused to know that last week I received flowers from a young farmer in the district, a certain Freddie Urquhart, with a charming little note to say that he would like to meet me. Evidently he is a member of one of he more prominent families in the district. Joan Peacock seems to have a hand in this affair since she once mentioned Urquhart's name to me and asked me whether we knew the family. I said no and added that I did not wish to compromise any existing relationships. She looked me up and down as though to imply that I was a stick in the mud, or that she did not want to believe me. Yet my response does not seem to have deterred either Mr Urquhart or Miss Peacock and I shall have to make it even more plain to them, without being utterly rude! I have as yet made no effort to respond to the note, and the breezy confidence with which Joan Peacock first approached the matter seems to have given way to a more subdued attitude on her part.

I am feeling a bit weary, possibly just some nervous exhaustion because all has been so new and strange, and I am so desperately glad the end of the term is now in sight. It will be easier to resume next term now that I have my bearings. Still, there will be a lot of preparation to be done.

I so wish you were here so that I could show you off to all, my dearest most handsome man.

Lots and heaps and heaps of love
Frances.

Tuesday 2 March 1927

Douglas was in a pensive mood when he rode home from school. The bright greens of summer were beginning to fade. Near the river a warm breeze swept through a string of ash trees bordering lucerne fields. Their leaves rustled, deprived of the sap that had made them soft in the spring.

His mother was at the front door. "Why is Dad here?" he asked.

"He has a terrible summer cold. He went as far as De Rust. He said he was so dizzy that he felt he would be a hazard to others and himself if he continued. I put him to bed, and Betta brewed some wild wormwood for him. He is asleep. There is a letter from Frances for you."

Van Yssen lay asleep in his bed, bathed in pale sweat. His feverish eyes flickered unevenly under heavy greasy lids. He dreamt of his deaf dead doornail father-in-law. They stood together in a dark brown ploughed field that tilted so precipitously that it threatened to let them fall into the silver mist of a ravine at the bottom of which his father-in-law beckoned. Van Yssen tried to get his trigonometry calculations right but the man in the ravine could not understand him. He shouted louder and louder but could not make a sound. The rain fell on his face and he began to slide down the muddy slope. He woke and found himself clinging to the bed. He was drenched.

His wife found him on the edge of the bed. "I'll fetch you some fresh pyjamas."

When she had seen to her husband Mrs van Yssen went to the kitchen with his pyjamas. Douglas was warming milk. "Frances would like me to travel back from Cape Town with her. It will mean coming back a day or two later."

"I would not discuss it with your father until he is better. You know how he dislikes the unexpected. Why are you so preoccupied?"

"Oh, it's nothing. Have you ever heard of Urquharts at Graaff Reinet?"

"No, your father knows so many more people, perhaps you should ask him. Why do you ask?"

"Oh, it's really nothing, just some chap called Freddie Urquhart who evidently sent Frances flowers and begged for an introduction. One of her colleagues seems to have had a hand in it."

"I am sure that your father will have no objection to your staying an extra few days."

Saturday 11 March 1927

As usual the van Yssens arrived at the station too early. "Make certain that you have your tickets Douglas," his father advised. Douglas took out his wallet and displayed his train and bedding tickets. Mrs van Yssen looked young in a pale blue pure linen dress and white wide rimmed straw hat that lit up her face and gave her green eyes a dreamy look. She glanced at Douglas and smiled.

"Perhaps a glass of ginger beer or lemonade might be an idea," Mrs van Yssen suggested. "Except that I am not really keen to sit down here in this dress."

Douglas walked to the end of the platform. He looked along the tracks in the direction from which the train was expected and glanced at his watch. It was ten minutes to four. The platform was busier. When he looked up again the train had stopped about two hundred yards from the station. "What is he waiting for?" he asked his father.

"They may not enter the station before the scheduled time. So he must wait until four."

Frances saw the van Yssen s before they saw her. She hurried to the end of her coach and jumped onto the platform. She flung her arms around Douglas and pressed the side of her head against his chest. "Oh, how lovely it is to see you," she exclaimed. Douglas patted her back. She held Douglas. "Let me have a good look at you, dearest man. It is so wonderful to see familiar people."

"I am glad to see you," he said sheepishly.

She shook hands with the van Yssens. "It is so good to see you again."

"We would not have missed the opportunity of seeing you, Frances." van Yssen had a satisfied smile. "I think Douglas should put his luggage into his compartment."

Mrs van Yssen regarded Frances closely. She was even more beautiful than she remembered.

"Joan Peacock is travelling to Cape Town with me. She's just gone to get something from the shop."

When the time came for the train to leave the van Yssen s shook Frances' hand and Douglas' mother gave him a kiss on the cheek. They stood on the platform and waited until the train was gone. "They're a handsome couple," Mrs van Yssen remarked.

The train made its way towards the mountain. Douglas and Frances sat to one side. Joan Peacock studied Douglas when he and Frances were not looking. She was sure she had seen him before, somewhere.

"I think I will go to the dining saloon and have some tea," she announced, "You are welcome to join me."

"We shall be there presently. Douglas still has to see to his things."

When Joan Peacock had left Douglas sat opposite Frances and held her hands. The movements and sounds of the train vanished. He looked into her eyes, the tiny freckles on the bridge of her nose. She smiled innocently and revealed her regular white teeth. He looked at her hair and the condensate of microscopic blond hairs on her temples, illuminated and turned into gold by the late afternoon sun. She was more alive than he remembered. She had so many more dimensions than he had come to imagine. He fell in love with her again.

Frances felt the pulses in his hands. Tears filled her eyes. "I love you so much," she said. His mouth was dry. "I love you too," he said.

She took his big head in her hands and pressed it against her body.

When Douglas and Frances reached the dining saloon Joan Peacock was ready to leave.

"Anyway, I shall leave the two of you to your own devices. It was nice to meet you."

"Yes, it was good to meet you," Douglas smiled.

"She does not seem to like me very much," Douglas observed.

"She's awkward with men, poor thing. She was actually quite restrained today. She's wary of you because she suspects that I may have told you about her matchmaking efforts with Freddie Urquhart."

"It never occurred to me."

"My dearest Douglas, always seeing the good in others, never a suspicious mind. I love you for that."

A steward brought more boiling water. "The saloon will close in half an hour so that we can prepare for dinner."

"Thank you," Douglas said. "We would like to make a booking for dinner please."

"For how many, sir?"

"Just the two us, please."

"I am sure Joan is having a rest, let's go to your compartment," Frances suggested.

The train was in the mountain now. The gasps of the engines quickened. The bedding attendant was preparing beds for an elderly couple at the far end of Douglas' coach.

"Now that I know where you are, I think I should be getting back so that I can change for dinner."

"It is still quite early, and I will be going as I am."

"I have been in these clothes all day, since early this morning."

"At least wait until the bedding attendant comes."

She sat down. "Come and sit next to me then."

Outside clouds and mist swirled. Pinkish-yellow late afternoon sunlight darted intermittently into the compartment and played on the surfaces, alternatively expanding and shrinking the interior space. They sat holding hands and Frances rested her head on his shoulder. They looked at the green expanses of the coastal plain, vivid where the sun shone and tinged with pale blue early autumn hues in the shady places. "The air is so much softer here," Frances observed. "Especially after the Karoo. The light is different. It is like this in the south of France. You would really enjoy it overseas. All this movement makes me think of what you said in your letters about travelling, about being… "

The bedding attendant arrived. "I'll take you back to your compartment."

The train had gathered speed on its way down the mountain and they walked unsteadily along the rocking corridors, holding onto side rails. Douglas remembered hitting his head against one of the doorframes when he was small. Frances was cautious of the landings where footplates slid from side to side and couplings tugged against blurred speeding tracks that rushed past underneath. Wind rushed through her hair and blew her dress against curves and protuberances of her body. They passed through the saloon where the tables were being laid.

At the door of her compartment he kissed her on her temple. "I will be here at seven, I'm jolly hungry now." She knocked gently and opened the door. Joan Peacock was asleep on her bunk, with her back towards them. Frances waved her fingers at him as she disappeared.

He sat at the window of his compartment and looked at the landscape below. They would soon be in George. He sniffed Frances' perfume on his jacket. He saw her dress against her body and the insides of her thighs on the Robberg. He had fleeting memories of conversations at Plettenberg Bay, and the Leibners. He had never travelled to Cape Town at this time of the year. George station was quiet. He strolled towards the engines. It was cool in the late afternoon. Frances would have put up the shutters while she changed. The engine driver touched his cap and nodded to Douglas. "Good afternoon," Douglas said. The driver lifted his hand in acknowledgment.

Frances opened the door of her compartment as he arrived. She smiled her winsome smile.

The Chief Steward showed them to their table. Reflections of the lights sparkled in silver-plated cutlery and glasses. The atmosphere was convivial. The sky was overcast. The sun had set. When they looked out they saw their own images in the windows of the dining car, superimposed on the sombre rushing landscape that was preparing for the night. They looked at each another. Her young blue-green eyes were radiant, her delicious pure mouth, her soft lips; her white clean teeth smiled her shy smile. He lost all sense of time and no longer perceived her only with his senses. Their awareness fused. Tears came to her eyes when she grasped the significance. They sat in silence for a while, like lovers, unconcerned that they were naked. The train's movements returned, then the rhythmic clattering of the wheels over the gaps in the tracks. When they again became conscious they were different.

The train travelled above the dunes past Great Brak River. In the distance silver reflections floated on a windless sea. He took her hand. The steward stood next to them. The family at the table opposite stared. "May I offer you the menu sir?"

Frances took the menu with her free hand. "Thank you."

"Shall I wait?"

"Do give us a few minutes, please," she said.

"I have never seen you in that blouse," Douglas said. "It suits you so well."

"Thank you. We went shopping before I left Cape Town. This is the first time that I have worn it. I kept it for you. My skirt is new too, and my shoes. In fact every piece of clothing that I am wearing is entirely new. Your clothes are also new, I have noticed. I like them. You look so fashionable. How is your ear?"

"It is not bothering me too much at present, but my hearing is not as good as in the other ear."

Douglas ordered a small bottle of white wine, "as a toast to the journey." Frances skipped the soup and had a small portion of fish and the main course of fried chicken.

"How is Garnett?" she enquired.

"He's fine, always jolly. It must be nice to be like that. I tend to brood a bit every now and again."

"Oh, my darling man, what nonsense, I've never known you to brood. You're perhaps a trifle serious at times, a hint of gravitas, perhaps, but certainly not brooding, not at all." She smiled sympathetically and shook her head. "I like your father. Considering how self-assured my father is, it is quite amusing how much in awe he is of mathematicians. After you left us at Plettenberg Bay he spoke of a case that involved a dispute over the position of a beacon. A land surveyor gave expert evidence, and he said he had difficulty following the evidence. He said he should have discussed some of the principles involved with your father. He can be quite dogged."

"As I have said before, I think my father would have liked me to have done something more scientific or mathematical. I sometimes sense that there is a nagging disappointment. He considers history too subjective and vague, imprecise. We have had our discussions. He has been careful not to discourage me, for which I thank him, but the innuendo is there nevertheless."

"Your father is very proud of you."

"I accept that, but I think he would have been more proud if I had studied one of the sciences. We always want to please our parents. As for history, much has been said about its virtues and its shortcomings. I have to concede that it is a bit like looking out of the back window when travelling by car. Things only become clear when they are about to disappear in the distance. I don't think human nature has changed much over the last few thousand years. Emotionally, and possibly even spiritually, we are the same as we always were. That is why history repeats itself. Scientific and economic developments have changed the way we live, and let's hope it is for the better, but inside the wrapping the contents remain the same. Then of course there is the question of the effect that history has on history. But, it is getting too serious."

"I love you best when you are so intense."

The stewards were glad to bid them goodnight. There was not a soul about as they headed for Frances' compartment. The interior of the train was quieter: as though darkness had absorbed some of the sound and movement. Frances stopped before she reached the door of her compartment. Her cheeks were flushed from the wine.

"We have not had much chance to talk. The people next to us inhibited me. I imagined we would have so much more time together," he said.

"We'll have lots of time to talk in Cape Town. I would come to your compartment, but Joan is a gossip. She already made a little snide remark about this afternoon. But if you would like to kiss me?"

He took her in his arms. She pressed her whole body against him and lifted her face. He could taste the coffee in her mouth; his teeth touched hers. She stroked the back of his head and made a small whimpering noise when the short bristles of his hair tickled the inside of her hand. A shiver ran down his spine. He breathed heavily. He stopped kissing her and just held her tightly, her head against his chest. He smelt her hair. She looked up at him, "I love you."

"I love you too."

"I don't want us to be separate, any more."

"What shall we do?"

"I suppose we could elope, for a start."

"I have no money."

"That is not important. We could go and live, well somewhere, the house at Plettenberg Bay. You could start a newspaper, I could teach, or give lessons. Just think how romantic it could be, just think. Shall I come to your compartment?"

"What about Joan?"

"If we are considering eloping, it would mean nothing really. She could report to all our startled colleagues in Graaff Reinet that she was there when it happened!"

"Come now Frances, we are not really considering that. What would your father say?" Douglas was amused.

She held her head coquettishly to one side, "He would be a trifle annoyed at first, and then hopefully he would see the amusing side. My mother would consider it awfully, awfully romantic, and then insist that we get married properly so that she could give a grand reception. Kiss me again, very slowly."

The train reduced speed for its perilous crossing of the Gouritz River. Frances heard the rattling of the conductor's key on the railing further along, and drew away from Douglas. They assumed a casual pose. "*Goeie naand*, good evening. Perhaps I should just get your tickets now. We will be crossing the bridge shortly. Afterwards most people will want to go to bed to sleep. Word is that it is raining in Cape Town. I remember that you are Miss Rose, in here with Miss Peacock, and you are mister?"

"van Yssen ."

"I remember your father, Mr van Yssen."

When the conductor had left Joan Peacock looked at Frances in a quizzical way, "Well are you coming in or staying out?"

"I think we would like to chat for a while," Frances suggested. Her cheeks had a slight rash from Douglas' beard.

"You are welcome to chat here, I shall read my book. Or, why don't you go to Douglas' compartment. You were there this afternoon so you must know the way."

Frances blushed. She felt her anger rising. "It was broad daylight this afternoon," she stammered.

"So what does it matter whether it is light or dark if the door is shut?"

There was awkward silence.

"Oh, don't be so serious Frances, I am only teasing, and you are taking every bit of bait. Or perhaps I'm just a teeny bit jealous of your handsome clever man."

"I think it would be best if I turned in," Douglas said. He held Frances' hand. "I'll see you tomorrow morning." He kissed her on her cheek. "Goodnight Joan, sleep well."

Frances followed him into the passage. She was visibly upset. Her hand trembled as she waved him a little goodbye.

Douglas sat down on his bunk. The train gathered speed rapidly. There was no turning back now. He would propose to Frances, and they could become privately engaged. In the June holidays there could be a formal engagement. He pulled his suitcase from under the seat, and started to unpack his things for the night. She liked his clothes. She looked so beautiful herself. He had a slight erection. Could not go to the washroom like that. Imagine walking down the aisle, I mean passage, like that in my dressing gown. Think of something else: like standing in front of the class, or talking to Archer. That would have helped if he were not led into temptation by the images of the reeds at the side of the river always swaying in the same Sunday afternoon breeze, and palpable fantasies of his girl cousin that emerged from their slippery recesses. How well he knew his temptations, created in his own image. Like close relatives they were gifted in deception because they understood him so well. Like old retainers they assumed illusive subtlety when his thoughts were elevated; when his mind was coarse they feigned a bolder form and, like drinking companions, conspired with him to be unworthy. Would it not be better to yield to his temptations, and by doing so destroy them?

He began to undress. He made sure that the door was locked. He got into his pyjamas, put on his scarlet dressing gown, gathered his towel and toiletry bag and made his way to the washroom at the end of the coach. The open door was banging from the movements of the train. There was a wretched stench inside. It took his breath away, and he decided to go to the other end of the coach.

When he got into bed the stench still clung to his pyjamas. He got out of bed and lowered both windows a fraction, and used the opportunity to hang his clothes wider apart. All notions of romance had been driven away. He lay down, and got up again, to get his copy of *Carry on Jeeves* from his suitcase. Just a bit of light relief. No harm in that. He lay and chuckled to himself as he read. He wondered what Frances was doing. This was good wholesome stuff, bloody funny in parts. It would put him into a good humour for the morning. Have happy thoughts before you go to sleep. Joan Peacock is a bitch. She bullies Frances, should be taught a lesson, except it would make things worse. He loved Frances. He ran his tongue along the inside of his lips and thought how he had kissed her. Her mouth was succulent. He wondered how she would be lying. They both had bottom bunks.

He listened to the sounds of the train. When he put his left ear on the pillow the sound reduced. Miss Krige did smack him on the right ear in class once when he was little. It was sore for days afterwards. Perhaps it was just from that. He never thought to tell Garnett. He felt better. He sighed with satisfaction. Surely a good omen: what was virtually a proposal on Frances' part, and now the fortuitous reminder of Miss Krige's assault. Frances must be asleep by now, limp with innocence, her flaxen hair on her pillow, perspiration in the folds of her neck. Where would her hands be? Back to Bertie Wooster. 'No, sir. I do not. Soft silk shirts with evening costume are not worn, sir.' Jeeves at his most stern. Ordering shirtings from Peabody and Simms. He saw the drawers in which the hosiery was kept at Hepworths and read what he saw, until what he saw was what he read, and the words became floating images. The book fell from his hand. Why would Wodehouse write about Pienaar? He saw the sea at Mossel Bay. When he woke the light was still on. He turned it off, and made himself comfortable on his side, sighed with great satisfaction and went to sleep.

◆

Chapter Sixteen

Sunday 12 March 1927

A NORTH-WESTERLY WIND blustered against the glass panels of the Victorian station roof and swept in through entrances and openings, onto the platforms. It bustled and tugged agitatedly, at skirts and hats. Judge Rose waited in a long grey cashmere double breasted overcoat and fedora speckled with a few drops of rain, umbrella in hand, looking into the distance. Mrs Rose wore a sap-green slouch hat and matching overcoat.

Frances waved and caught her mother's eye.

"There they are!" Mrs Rose exclaimed.

The train jerked to a halt. Frances ran to the end of the coach, hurried onto the platform and embraced her father, then her mother. She turned to see where Douglas was. He followed at a discreet distance, tall and elegant, smiling at Frances' delight. The Judge smiled warmly at Frances. Some of the innocent girlishness had gone. What he had remembered more and more as her absence lengthened was a younger Frances. He remembered best his most affectionate moments when she was first becoming a woman. There were traces of lines around her eyes.

Mrs Rose shook Douglas' hand. "A warm welcome, Douglas. I am so glad that you could accompany Frances."

"It is good to be here, thank you Mrs Rose."

"Ah, Douglas," the Judge exclaimed, "how are you, my good man?"

"I am very well, thank you Judge. I trust that you are well?"

"In rude health my dear man, rude health. I think we should get a porter. Rather awkward weather."

"My dear, dear daughter, how exquisite to see you. I have missed you so very, very much." Mrs Rose and Frances embraced one another. "When you were small, I was able to say, 'how you have grown,' after an absence. I was almost tempted to do that now."

"Oh mother you are so sweet!"

The car trundled through the rain, tyres swishing, engine sounds muffled by the damp air, windscreen wipers dashing about with little effect. Inside the car the windows were beginning to mist over. Doyle wiped the condensation from the windscreen with the back of his glove, and drove more slowly. Frances enthusiastically peered out of the side windows and even out of the back window, curious to see where they were. The houses were still asleep. Dripping oak trees were silent, their bark darkened by the rain, touches of autumn colours in their leaves. An intrepid stroller in a raincoat with an umbrella and large rimmed hat was taking a recalcitrant white bull terrier, made pink by the rain, for a walk.

Frances smelt the familiar friendly odour of home. Douglas was reminded of his early visits to the house.

"You know where the guest cloakroom is Douglas. We will be in the drawing room. Tea will be ready presently," the Judge suggested.

"Thank you Judge."

Douglas sniffed his hands as he walked to the drawing room. Pears soap had absolved odours of nether places. They should have soap like that at home. A coal fire burnt vermilion red in the drawing room. Small blue flames swayed over the glowing coals, their thin reflections animating the green art deco nasturtium leaves inside the glaze of the tile surround of the fireplace.

The Judge folded his newspaper. "Mother and daughter will join us presently. I trust you had a good journey?"

"Yes indeed, thank you. It was uneventful."

The Judge frowned, and glanced mischievously from under his eyebrows at Douglas, "Uneventful, you say? When you're travelling with my daughter? Uneventful!"

"It was indeed a privilege to accompany Frances, I simply meant that nothing untoward happened, that it went well."

The Judge enjoyed Douglas' discomfort. "Honest people often make clumsy witnesses, Douglas. They tie themselves up in knots – Shakespeare speaks about the guilt of the innocent. I like your candour, my good fellow. I like it very much. But, I hear the ladies approaching."

Frances skipped into the drawing room and put her arm through Douglas' arm. "Shall I ask for the tea to be brought in, Mummy, I would like to say hello to Gladys and Hope?"

"Gladys is away for the weekend, dear, only Hope is on duty today."

Frances went to the kitchen and returned with Hope carrying the tea tray.

"Good morning Mr van Yssen."

"Good morning, Hope, it is good to be in Cape Town again."

Hope clasped her hands self-consciously, "I nearly forgot the flapjacks – they're in the warming drawer."

"I know how much you like our flapjacks, Douglas, and I thought we would give you a welcoming treat," Mrs Rose announced.

"They never make anything special for me," the Judge complained.

"Oh come now dear, that is not so, you have lots of other treats. You've just become spoilt, and besides, you are embarrassing Douglas. He'll soon be thinking that it is he who has deprived you so terribly!"

Frances squeezed Douglas' arm.

"Douglas, Frances has told us a little about your first term in her letters, but we would like to hear more. Tell us how your parents are; tell us about your colleagues, the pupils, in fact, tell us everything," Mrs Rose asked.

"I think it is safe to say that things have gone better than I feared. We have a marvellous school building – sandstone, imposing tower."

"I'm so envious! Our new building is still being built – judging by the gables it is going to be in the Dutch style," Frances interjected.

"Education is a big issue in Oudtshoorn," Douglas said.

"It's a big issue in the whole of the Union, and so it should be. It means you're investing in the future. These flapjacks are delicious. Do you think you could spare a bit of that honey that James sent us, Elizabeth?" The Judge asked.

"Certainly dear, I'm glad you like it so much."

"Coming back to education: it is essential if society is going to make progress. The Romans recognised that. They caught Greeks and made them slaves so they could teach their children. But you know that Douglas. Would you like to try some of this honey?"

"Yes, thank you very much, Judge."

"Frances tells us that you have a problem with your ear, and that you are seeing a doctor on Wednesday?" the Judge asked.

"Yes, hopefully something trivial. One of my teachers once smacked me on the ear when I was little. It hurt for quite a few days afterwards. It could possibly have something to do with that. I went to Garnett Nel, and he did some tests. So far he has reserved his diagnosis. He is cautious, and has recommended that I see an ear nose and throat specialist here this week."

"You never mentioned that you'd been smacked on the ear," Frances said.

"To be truthful, I only remembered it last night when I was in bed. I never mentioned it to Garnett either. I had forgotten all about it. It was quite a relief when it occurred to me. Who knows, perhaps I need not even see the specialist. I will telephone Garnett this evening."

"I told you that I have a good feeling about this," Frances said.

"I must confess that I have had a few anxious moments, but when I remembered, I think she was called Miss Krige, when I remembered her handiwork, I was relieved."

"All is well that ends well." Mrs Rose sipped her tea.

The Judge cleared his throat. "I don't think we should detain Douglas much longer. I heard the car arriving. Let him go and do what is necessary, Doyle will wait for him, and bring him back so that we may have an early lunch."

Douglas got up.

"Don't rush poor Douglas, dear, he has not even had a second cup."

"I think Judge Rose is quite correct, I should get to the hotel."

"Frances will you please ask Hope to summon Doyle," Mrs Rose asked.

"It is the Helmsley, is it Sir?" It was raining heavily.

"Yes thank you, Doyle."

The sky was dark. Lions Head was invisible – a sign of more rain to come. Douglas shivered in the back of the car. There were yellow grass cuttings in the wet welts of his shoes. It was damn pleasant next to the fire. Rainwater rushed along stone gutters on the sides of the road, away from the mountain and down to the sea. He could hear the water splashing against the tyres and the running boards as they turned in to the hotel grounds.

"Let me give you a hand Sir."

"No, no it's quite fine thank you, I'll manage. I don't want you to get any more wet."

"I'm used to that Sir."

"Doyle, I hope you won't take offence, but I have brought along food my mother packed for me, and that I have not eaten. Do you have any suggestion what we could do with it?"

"I would dearly like to take it home for my sister's children, Sir. She would be most grateful to you for your generosity. Times are quite hard. It is the circumstances she finds herself in."

"Take the basket to the kitchen when we get back, inconspicuously if you please, and let Hope unpack the food, except the biltong, and let me have the basket back, please."

"What does inconspicuously mean, Sir?"

"It means without attracting undue attention, if you know what I mean."

"I comprehend, Sir."

"Thank you very much Doyle. I won't be long."

Douglas rang the bell at the reception desk. The owner, Mr Eyers himself, emerged, dressed in his Sunday best.

"I'm Douglas van Yssen, I made a booking."

Eyers put on his spectacles and with his head down rummaged for the hotel register. "We were expecting you. I see it is becoming a family tradition for the van Yssens to stay at the Helmsley. Please give your parents my best wishes. We have given you a north facing room, near the bathroom. I trust that it is not really necessary to say it but I will say it nevertheless: this is a residential establishment and no liquor is allowed on the premises. For what it is worth, my sentiments are with the Americans. I trust you will have a pleasant stay."

Francis heard the wheels of the car grinding in the driveway. She opened the door for Douglas. Hope took his umbrella and his raincoat. Frances put her arm through his as they walked towards the drawing room. "I am so glad that your ear is going to be fine. Lunch will be ready in a while. Daddy has gone to his study to see to some work. Mummy is writing to her mother." She held him back by his sleeve. "We could have gone for a brisk walk before lunch, but for the weather. Let's go to the front reception room, it is brighter there. It is so splendid to have you here, and it is so good to be home."

They heard the Judge stirring in his study, and the sound of papers being shuffled. His chair groaned. He strolled into the reception room with his thumbs in the pockets of his waistcoat. "I am jolly hungry. Must be the weather. Would you like a drink Douglas?"

"No thank you Judge."

"What about you Frances?"

"I'll wait until lunch is served, thank you, Daddy."

The Judge's stomach rumbled loudly. He patted it. "Let's go and find your mother."

The Judge said grace once the soup had been served, and was so keen to start eating that he scalded his tongue. "Damnation," he exclaimed, "to think that I am still so foolish at my age." He drank some cold water. "It's an awful feeling. It takes the sense of taste away." He carved the roast beef. "The new butcher seems to have excellent meat. Hope he keeps it up. They always start off well. How hungry are you Douglas?"

"How can you ask him that Jeremy? You can hardly expect him to say how hungry he is."

"We had tea very late. I am asking out of consideration, dear."

Frances smiled uneasily at Douglas. The Judge put an extra slice of beef onto Douglas' plate. Once he had served himself most generously he sat down clumsily on the one side of his chair. "Gosh," he said, "my coordination is dashed poor today. Good thing I am not playing golf. Please start – the food is becoming cold. I nearly forgot to propose a toast." He raised his wineglass, "To your return home, dear Frances and your visit to Cape Town, Douglas."

"It has been so good to have home food again, Mummy, the meal was delicious."

"I'm so glad you're home my dear."

"I have asked Doyle to be at your disposal. If you and Frances would like to go for a drive," the Judge announced.

"That's a frightfully splendid idea, don't you think? All snug in the back of the car, seeing all the familiar sights." Frances looked enthusiastically at Douglas

"It's a wonderful idea, thank you very much, and thank you for the splendid meal, Mrs Rose, Judge."

The Judge took his napkin from his lap, and placed it unfolded on the table. He watched to see what Douglas would do with his napkin as he got up heavily from his chair. His one knee made a loud cracking noise. Douglas started folding his napkin to put it back into the napkin ring. "Well, I'll be off to have forty winks then. The food was excellent Elizabeth, as always. Are you coming to have a rest, dear?"

"I think I'll rather read, thank you, dear."

Mrs Rose stayed with Frances and Douglas and had coffee.

"Are you not going to have your rest, Mummy?"

"It is so comfortable here by the fire; the view of the mountain framed by the window, the autumn leaves, like an impressionist painting. I shall stay here and read."

"What are you reading?" Frances asked.

Mrs Rose reached for an olive green book with gold lettering on the cover, on the floor next to her, and put it onto her lap. She patted it. *The Forsyte*

Saga: I am so enjoying it – even more the second time. And it just goes on and on, I become so involved with the characters, Swithin, Soames the solicitor and connoisseur, young Jolyon the underwriter and artist. I am sure Doyle has had his lunch, so why don't the two of you go for your drive, now?"

The air was clear and crisp after the rain. Water trickled in the gutters. The mountain towered above its grim wet grey rock faces. In one place a small waterfall gushed. Confused vaporous white and grey clouds with flossy curls drifted across the face of the mountain. Doyle opened the car door for them. At the suggestion of her mother Frances took along a tartan rug in the reds and greens of the Stuart plaid. She covered their knees and sat close to Douglas.

"Where would you like to go Miss Frances?" Doyle enquired.

"Let's go to the sea! After all the drought and heat we have endured. It should be stormy and rough after the rain. Sea Point will be just fine." Frances enjoyed being in charge. Douglas was amused. "What are you laughing at?" she asked.

"You."

"And what have I done, may I ask?"

"You remind me of a woman who has got hold of the reins of a spider or a landau, and takes pleasure from being in control of the horses."

Frances puffed herself up and moved away from him. She squared her shoulders and flounced with mock annoyance and pretence of hurt feelings, finding it difficult to conceal the good humour in her eyes. "I simply enjoy being at home," she said pertly. She moved closer to him so that their thighs touched. She removed the glove from her left hand. "Feel my hand – it is frozen." He enclosed her hand in his large soft warm hand. She lent her head against his shoulder and moved their hands in under the rug. Doyle looked in the rear view mirror to see why they had stopped talking so abruptly. It doesn't matter what their class, we're all the same, maybe even worse.

Adderley Street was quiet. A family was doing window-shopping, and had stopped to see what was on display at Cleghorn and Harris. They had a Dalmatian on a leash and a small child with a pale pink pixie cap in a pushcart. Near the turn into Strand Street three French sailors stood about desultorily while the wind tugged at their uniforms and blew their white collars against the backs of their heads. "I suppose this must seem like good weather to them," Douglas said.

"I think we should go to Mouille Point and past the light house at Green Point please, Doyle," Frances suggested. "And then perhaps on to Camps Bay?"

"That is a splendid suggestion Miss Frances."

Doyle took the road towards the Victoria Basin. They rounded the bend at the hospital and a gust of wind shook the car as the angry sea in Granger Bay greeted them. The level of the ocean seemed even higher than they. At Green Point and Three Anchor Bay the waves pounded the shore with huge and relentless thuds as they destroyed themselves on the rocks and exploded into white foaming spray. Froth sprinkled with cinnamon heaved and surged in the gullies. Dark brown tubes of kelp and green seaweed, hapless victims of the storm, lay scattered limp and lifeless on the sand. Frances opened the window slightly, "Oh smell the sea!" Douglas smelled her perfume as he inhaled a mixture of salt, iodine and faint fishiness. He wanted to kiss her neck. The sky was becoming lighter in places.

"I would like to walk on the beach, so let's hurry on to Camps Bay," Frances rubbed her hands enthusiastically. "It will be like our walks at Plettenberg Bay, darling man."

Douglas smiled at her. "I hope you are dressed warmly enough."

"Don't be so unromantic. Even if it should prove a bit cold, you can always make me warm afterwards. You know how devious I am."

On Green Point Common an elderly couple took an afternoon walk. The man, with a ruddy face and large frame in a Harris Tweed jacket and matching hat, stopped and began to do elaborate arm exercises with a pair of Indian clubs while his wife stood with her back to him. "Aren't they dear?" Frances said. "It could be us in fifty years time! Is this as fast as you can go Doyle?"

"It would not be wise to go much faster, Miss Frances. People know this car, they could say something to the Judge and it would be hard to explain. Besides it is dangerous to drive too fast."

"I suppose you're right. There's a good tearoom at Camps Bay. I think we should go there afterwards. I have brought some money along and it will be my treat Douglas." He opened his mouth. She put her index finger over his lips. "None of this. You have been more than generous to me, in fact you spoilt me on the train, and now it is my turn. After all, I am a working woman now – strange how that sounds. Daddy still refers to the working classes, as though it is a shame to work. I hope you will join us for tea Doyle?"

"I don't think I should Miss Frances, the Judge would not approve, and after all I am employed by him, Miss. He is very strict about what he refers to as protocol. I am not always quite sure what that means, but I get a feeling that it has something to do with people keeping their correct distance. Also, I have only just finished my lunch, and it is not yet teatime for me. I keep odd hours."

"Very well then, but I shall have some scones packed for you to take home to your family."

Although it was windy at Camps Bay Frances insisted on a walk on the beach. Douglas stopped to absorb as much as possible of the atmosphere. He listened to the crashing surf; he looked up at the towering mountains, and across the beach. They were the only people. In the distance Doyle was leaning against the mudguard of the car, his one leg crossed over the other, his small frame dapper in his grey uniform, his cap held in front of him with both hands, his stiff flannel breeches, his forehead white beneath his wavy dark hair, his brown knee-high leather boots gleaming in the silver afternoon light.

Frances put her arm through his. She was getting sand into her shoes. "Gee, this is so different," he said. "To think that I was in Oudtshoorn yesterday morning, and now I am walking on the beach in Cape Town. It is incredible how rapidly we are able to travel these days."

She gripped his arm tightly. "I want you to kiss me."

"Here on the beach?"

"Yes here in the open, in the wind, next to the great big ocean. The openness we have always shared is how I want our relationship to be, always. I want the whole world to see how much you mean to me. Why conceal how wholesome our love is? Cast your Calvinistic inhibitions to the wind and kiss me."

Douglas smelt her perfume again and held the back of her head in his hand. Her cheek was cold against his nose. Her mouth was warm. He put his other arm around her waist and pressed her against him. He could feel her underclothes. She took her mouth away from his and looked up into his eyes, "I love you Douglas, do it again." She was trembling.

"I shall always remember this." Her bottom lip quivered.

Douglas could taste her mouth as they walked along silently with their arms around each other. "I have thought about what you said yesterday, about eloping."

She let go of him and turned to face him, "And?" Her face was full of expectation.

"I really do love you very much Frances, more than you can imagine. It is just that I find it so difficult to express myself."

"I know you do, that's why I have ventured to say the things I said, to help you."

"I realise that and I am grateful to you. I feel clumsy, oh I am talking nonsense. Let me start again. I have never loved anyone else, and I would like to marry you, and I don't know what you must think of me for being so reticent, it is just my circumstances."

"My darling man, your circumstances, as you refer to them, are not as much of an obstacle as you may imagine. We could become engaged now, privately if you like. You could speak to Daddy. It is an ideal opportunity, you know. Then in the June holidays we could have a formal engagement here in Cape Town. It would be wonderful. This is so thrilling. I shall never forget this place. Do ask me properly to marry you."

"Dearest Frances, will you please marry me?"

"Yes, yes, yes! I will marry you." She clapped her hands together and jumped up and down like a child who had received a present. She flung her arms around him and hugged him. "Oh how wonderful, thank you, thank you."

Douglas was as happy as he was amused. He smiled at her. "I think you should get out of the wind now. Let us go and have our tea." Holding hands they made their way up the loose sand with stumbling difficulty. From his distance Doyle watched. He could see from Frances' radiance that something had happened. She gave him an embarrassed little wave and a shy satisfied smile as they passed the car and stamped their feet to get rid of the sand. A bell above the door of the tearoom announced their arrival. The floorboards creaked as they entered. Two couples were having tea at tables near a window. There were also a mother and father with two noisy small overdressed children in their Sunday best. The owner welcomed them. "A table for two?" He enquired in a thick Dutch accent and a theatrical grimace as he glanced through the window for inspiration of how much the people from such a car were likely to spend.

Francis ordered tea and chocolate éclairs. "I wonder whether you would please be so good," she asked the owner, "as to let our man have some hot tea, and if you could please arrange for him to have six scones with plenty of cream and strawberry jam to take home to his family."

Douglas studied her as he had done so often before, her eyes, her soft pink symmetrical mouth, perfect teeth. Her ears were perfect. Her golden hair generated its own light. She looked into his grey eyes, at his large forehead.

Their realisation of their commitment expanded. Although it was still formless, it gave certainty. They looked at one another and saw nothing else. They did not hear the shrieks of the children or the murmurs of the other people in the tearoom or the sound of crockery and cutlery, or the rushing sounds of the waves. The deliberately clumsy arrival of the tea and éclairs startled them from their reverie. They smiled at one another. He saw finely quivering tissue on the underside of her upper lip that he had not seen before, and discovered a greater complexity of greens in her eyes. She looked at his relaxed hands, fingers interlocked, on the table in front of him. How well his nails were manicured. Traces of ink were ingrained in the skin of his middle finger and thumb. The letters he wrote to her. She stroked his hands.

The owner poured their tea. They helped themselves to milk. Frances cut a small piece off the éclair with her cake fork and savoured it with closed eyes. A bit of cream stuck to the corner of her mouth. A prehensile pink tongue drew it into her mouth. She grinned at him. "Have yours, it is delicious."

"I think I am more in love with you than I have ever been. I first want to look at you before I indulge in lesser things," he whispered.

"I feel exactly the same, silly, except that I can't wait to embrace you. Everything seems different. I feel as though I have been dreaming until now. Now everything is clear. What do you want me to say to Daddy?"

"Gee, the prospect of speaking to your father disconcerts me. What if he turns me down?"

"How could you ever, ever think that! Both Daddy and Mummy admire you. We have all known you for years, if you come to think of it – for years. Never in all this time has there been anything but enthusiasm for our friendship. On the way back from Plettenberg Bay, in the car, they were speaking most complimentarily about you. In fact they were more than complimentary. I won't tell you everything that was said because it will make you swollen headed. Daddy thinks you have a marvellous brain. And as you know yourself it is quite something for him to acknowledge that in others. After our graduation, on the way to luncheon, he said, 'van Yssen is most fortunate to have a son like Douglas.' We won't say anything when we get home. I shall speak to Mummy this evening, and tell her what we have decided. I will swear her to secrecy and then inform Daddy tomorrow that you wish to make an appointment to see him. He is sure to know what that implies."

Douglas had images of the Judge in his study, leaning back at his desk with his thumbs in his waistcoat pockets, while he himself stood dutifully erect in his tweed jacket and well polished shoes, with his hands behind his back, waiting for the verdict. His father had once said, that when confronted by an overbearing person in authority, imagine him in nothing but his underwear, it brings him down to size.

"What are you thinking about?"

He caught himself. "I am thinking of asking your father. I hope he will not think it is indecently sudden."

"He has always encouraged me to be modern in my ways. Daddy likes adventure, like when he went on our fishing expedition. So he might even like the idea of something a bit impulsive."

"What if he interrogates me about my financial means?"

"He knows your position, and he won't do that, besides we're not going to get married tomorrow or next week, or something outrageous like that. Furthermore, as a good tactician he is sure to bear in mind that the way he has brought me up makes me quite capable of eloping. He will want to follow the conventional course. It will temper his thinking. Mummy is such a romantic, and such a matchmaker – her father bred horses." She giggled. "Your tea is getting cold."

Doyle walked up and down on the pavement on the opposite side of the road, rubbing his hands. The sky had darkened. Perhaps more rain was coming. They finished their éclairs and tea. She proudly took some coins from her handbag, and proceeded to pay the bill. The owner opened the door for them and carried the scones for Doyle in a large brown paper bag.

They drove back to the Gardens the way they had come. In the city rain began to fall. "I would like to thank your parents for their most generous hospitality today, and then I should get back to the Helmsley. I did think of visiting the Watermeyers, but I shall give it a miss. I ought to telephone my parents to tell them our news. My mother will be thrilled. My father does not like surprises, and he is sure to express his concern about the financial implications. He could even be more stern than your father."

She snuggled up against him. The oak trees had begun to drip again. They could hear the rain on the roof of the car.

"I had thought of walking down to the hotel."

"It is too wet for that. Doyle will take you."

At the Roses' house Douglas and Frances scampered out of the car and dashed through the rain to the front door. She opened the door, "We're back, hello?"

Some water ran down between Douglas' collar and his neck. He waited in the entrance hall for Frances to find her parents and to announce their arrival and his departure. Her mother had fallen asleep in front of the fire, her book across her lap. The Judge was in his study, humming to himself in his tone-deaf way. A lilting piece of legal prose had dislodged a melodic phrase from Rigoletto and it had got stuck in his head. He could not remember which part of the opera it was from. He kept on hearing it again and again. It was irritating him. Something like that could go on for blooming hours.

Frances gently put her hand on her mother's shoulder. Mrs Rose woke with a start, "Jeremy!"

"No, it is I, Mother. Douglas and I have just returned."

Mrs Rose was confused. "Is your father here?"

"We have only just arrived. Daddy is probably still sleeping."

"No, no he was awake. Oh my what a mess I am."

"Douglas would just like to say goodbye."

"I won't be more that a few minutes, bring him in, bring him in." She got up stiffly and yawned. "My, what a funny expression you have Frances? Like a cat that has eaten cream."

While Mrs Rose was in her room, Frances took Douglas to the drawing room and went in search of her father. He was in his study. "Douglas would like to say goodbye, Daddy."

"I trust you enjoyed yourselves?"

"Yes, thank you. We went all the way to Camps Bay, and had a scrumptious tea there. And we managed to have a walk along the beach during a gap in the weather. It was so thrilling. It is raining again, so do you think that Doyle could take Douglas to his hotel, please."

"Of course, of course, your wish is my command." He got up, and they went to the drawing room where Douglas was warming himself next to the fire.

"I would like to thank you most sincerely Judge Rose for you kind hospitality, and for the most delicious lunch."

"It is really nothing, my good man. You are most welcome at any time."

Mrs Rose reappeared.

"I would like thank you for a lovely day, Mrs Rose, and particularly for the delicious Christmas pudding. It is so pleasant to be in Cape Town again."

"My dear Douglas, it has been our pleasure to have you over. Doyle is going to take Douglas to his hotel, dear."

"Something is going on with those two," Mrs Rose said when Frances took Douglas to the door. The Judge tilted his head enquiringly to one side and looked at his wife from under his tidy bushy eyebrows.

"I am not surprised. They have known one another for a long time."

Frances skipped into the room. "What are you two talking about?"

"Oh, just this and that, husband and wife talk." Her mother stared at the fire. The Judge put his hands into his pockets and rocked back and forth.

"Did you have a pleasant afternoon, dear?" Her mother asked.

While the Judge worked in his study Frances and her mother sat down at the fireside.

"We had an amazing time. We went all the way to Camps Bay, and had tea there, and éclairs."

"It is good to have you all to myself."

"It is so nice to be home. I am so excited."

"So it would seem."

"I have something that I want to discuss with you in the greatest confidence, Mummy. Please give me your word that you will not divulge a word, not to anyone, not even Daddy."

"It must be quite serious. I am not comfortable about keeping things from your father."

"Please, please just promise, just for once?"

"Very well then, I promise."

Frances' colour rose. She opened her mouth as if to speak and took a deep breath.

"Well, you see, what happened on the beach at Camps Bay this afternoon while you were sitting here reading your book, and daddy was snoring on his Sunday afternoon bed, was…"

"Come now Frances, what happened?"

"Well, you see, what happened," she wrung her hands.

"Oh for heaven's sake, Frances, what is the matter that you can't get to the point!"

"Well you see what happened, was that Douglas proposed to me!"

Her mother clapped her hands together. "How utterly exciting, but why not tell daddy?"

"Douglas is a little bit apprehensive about asking daddy. He is a bit intimidated by daddy."

"It is quite natural, most people are. Even I am at times. You're the only one who is not. He is your greatest admirer. I have been expecting something like this for a while, and I suspect so has your father. I am sure he considers Douglas more than acceptable. I am so excited for you my dear and you know I absolutely adore Douglas. He is so handsome and so bright. It is just perfect."

"Douglas is concerned that he does not yet have the means to support me. I told him it is of no consequence if we are so much in love."

"You discussed it previously then?"

"Well, in a manner of speaking. But it was the result of a rather flippant remark I made about eloping."

"Eloping will never do, Frances, don't you ever consider that. I want you to have the most thoroughly beautiful wedding imaginable. I have waited for the day ever since you were born."

"We think that we should become privately engaged now, if everyone agrees, and become formally engaged in the June holidays.

"That is a splendid idea; an elegant way of doing things. You may tell

Douglas that you discussed it with me and, without making it sound as though I am improperly enthusiastic, tell him of my support. That will make it easier for him. It all reminds me of your father having to pluck up the courage to ask my father for my hand in marriage. If I could let you into a secret, my father did not much like your father. He considered him a somewhat opinionated, swaggering young toff. My father liked things to be plain, but he swallowed his pride for my sake, and things turned out well. He does not make many demands of me, which I am not sure is the way I would always like things to be. But I am indulging myself. Over time my father came to respect daddy's abilities, and his reliable way. I think he gave daddy quite a hard time when he asked for my hand. I hope he remembers that and treats Douglas kindly. Now what would you like me to do to assist?"

"I am not sure."

Mrs Rose enjoyed the event that was unfolding. Her eyes were fixed in her head as she stared at the flames in the hearth. "I have a plan. Tonight when we go to bed I will tell him that I suspect that something is afoot with the two of you, and ask him playfully what his reaction would be if Douglas were to propose to you." She paused to reflect. "On the other hand that may not be such a good idea, because if it then were to happen over the next few days he would suspect me of being part of a conspiracy, and that could anger him. No, I think the best thing to do would be to keep matters straightforward and simple and to simply tell him, I mean you should tell him that Douglas would like to make an appointment to see him. He will know what that means. If you are direct it will make it easier for everybody, especially Douglas. Your father prefers the direct frontal assault as he calls it."

"When shall I approach him?"

"Go to him now – seize the moment; employ the enthusiasm of your excitement."

"You mean right, right now?"

"Yes, don't think, just go."

"Gosh, golly gosh!"

Frances straightened her hair, cast her mother a beseeching look, and marched to her father's study. He was perusing a document. She stood at the door. He began to turn towards her while his eyes still remained on the page. He put his finger on the document and looked over his spectacles, "Yes my dear?"

"Douglas would like to make an appointment to see you in private."

He smiled. "Now why on earth would he need to make an appointment when he visits us regularly? And he could have spoken to me at any time today? Surely he knows that I am quite accessible. Pray tell him that he is free to speak to me at any time. Why an appointment, it sounds so formal? He is not in any difficulty, is he?"

Frances was pale.

"So when does he have in mind?"

"Whenever it suits you. Apart from his appointment on Wednesday his week is quite free."

"Tell him to come tomorrow evening. Do you have any idea why he wants to see me, my dear?"

Frances was close to tears. Her bottom lip was beginning to curl and quiver like the day she fell off her tricycle in the back garden. He had gone too far. He got up from his desk. "Give your old father a good hug. I know why he wants to see me, and it's fine, more than fine."

She sobbed. "I am so happy, so very happy."

"Let us go and tell your mother." He looked at the shape of his fair daughter as she walked along the passage to the drawing room. He put his hand on the lapel of his jacket where her face had been. It was wet with her tears.

Chapter Seventeen

DOYLE DROVE DOUGLAS to the Hotel. "Thank you very much for all your help today Doyle. I appreciate it very much. It has been quite a long day."

"It has been my pleasure sir. Thank you for the food. It has been an honour to be with you and Miss Frances on this day." He looked Douglas in the eye and lifted the peak of his cap in a form of salute. The rain had stopped. He drove off in his modest way to a modest part of Woodstock, where the grindingly poor houses were damp with misery and children coughed all night.

Douglas had hardly unpacked his things when the dinner gong sounded. It was already half past six. He washed his hands and splashed cold water onto his face. He dried his face with the laundry scented hotel towel, and went to seek comfort in Sunday evening hotel food.

On his way past the reception desk he remembered to telephone his parents. He was the first guest in the dining room. His feet echoed in the empty room as he waded through the starched white tablecloths and silver plated cutlery. A waiter appeared. "You must be Mr van Yssen, Mr Eyers told us to expect you. Your table is ready." Douglas examined the menu. "I'll start with the soup, please, and then I will have the fish kedgeree." Good Scottish thrift.

Douglas' soup arrived: murky French onion soup on which a raft of rigid bright yellow cheese drifted among droplets of fat. He stirred the soup to let it cool. The waiter had not bothered to give the two at the other table the menu: they were clearly going to make their way through whatever there was to eat. Permanent guests. The fellow had his napkin tucked into his shirt collar; he held his spoon clumsily in his fist. He slurped his soup. He then had two helpings of fish kedgeree and a generous helping of bread pudding.

"Tea and coffee and biscuits will be served in the guest lounge, Sir."

Mr Eyers was at the reception desk, making sure that everything was in order, ready for the start of the week. Sundays purified his spirit, a cathartic distillation he called it. "Good evening my good fellow. I trust you have had a satisfactory day?"

"Good evening Mr Eyers. Yes, thank you, I wonder if you could please be of assistance to me?"

Eyers lowered his head to see over his spectacles. "Let's see what it is that you require."

"I need to make a telephone call to my parents in Oudtshoorn. I promised them."

"You've left it quite late, but I am sure we can make a plan provided you do not speak too long. It's a costly business, trunk calls. The telephone is on the wall next to my office, just ring the exchange and ask for your number. Then go and have some coffee. I will call you when the call comes through."

Eyers called Douglas before he could reach the lounge.

"Hello Ma, it's Douglas."

"We were so worried, we thought you would ring this morning. I am glad you're safe. How is Frances?"

"Yes I am fine, thanks. I am talking in the passage next to Mr Eyers' office. How is Dad?"

"He is standing next to me, all ears. He was saying how quiet the house is without you."

"Ma, I have some special news, very special news, if you get the drift, very special."

"Can it be what I think it is? Oh Albert!"

"What do you think it could be Ma?"

"To do with Frances?"

"Yes, it has."

Her voice dropped. "Is it good news?"

"Very good news, it happened on the beach at Camps Bay this afternoon."

She shrieked. "Oh Albert, Douglas can't talk, he is in the passage of the hotel, but he has proposed to Frances."

"In the passage of the hotel?"

"No, on the beach at Camps Bay, this afternoon."

He faintly heard his father muttering something about rather sudden.

"Oh my dearest son, I am so happy. I am thrilled. It is such a blessing. Say hello to your father."

"Hello Dad, it's Douglas here."

"Who else could make your romantic mother so happy. It is a pity that you cannot speak more freely. Go to the post office early in the morning and telephone from there, and give us all the details."

"I have not spoken to the Judge yet."

"Never mind that it is always just a formality."

"I don't think it will be so in his case."

"We're all human, Douglas. He wants his daughter to be happy. Besides, he greatly respects you. He'll welcome your proposal."

"You are always so reassuring, Dad."

"Proceed boldly Douglas, here is your mother again, she is just drying her eyes, she is so overcome. Here she is."

"Goodnight Dad."

"Hello Ma. I will telephone early tomorrow morning. I am relieved that you approve."

"You know that we approve. God bless you my child."

"Goodnight Ma, sleep tight."

"Goodnight my dear boy."

Douglas put the telephone onto its hook and rang off.

Douglas went outside. The rain had stopped. Even a few stars were visible. He nevertheless fetched his raincoat and started in the direction of Orange Street. He would go past Hidding Hall, and then into the City. He passed a butcher shop in which empty steel hooks waited for luckless carcasses. He passed a shoemaker's shop. We eat them and we wear them. Should damn well have realised that it was the smack on his ear, and should have told Garnett that. Some drops of rain began to fall. He looked at the sky. There were no stars. He sought shelter under the roof of an antique dealer's shop. At the first lull he beat a hasty retreat. He stamped his feet to rid his shoes of excess water as he ascended the red polished steps at the entrance of the hotel.

Eyers was at reception. "Ah Mr van Yssen, there is a message for you from Miss Rose. She would like you to telephone her. She left the number. She said to telephone any time before nine thirty. You may use the telephone in the passage."

"Thank you."

Douglas' looked at the handwritten message and asked the exchange for the number.

"Hello, this is Frances!"

"Hello Frances, Douglas here. You left a message. Is everything all right?"

"Yes indeed, dearest man. I wanted to let you know that I have spoken to my parents and Daddy has suggested that you have a word with him tomorrow evening. Mummy proposed that you should have a sundowner with us. Isn't that wonderful? Aren't you pleased?"

"Gosh, I got such a start when I received your message. But yes, it is good news, very good news. Are you well?"

"I am so happy, I cannot tell you how happy, my love."

"At what time tomorrow?"

"Half past six would be perfect. Mummy has invited us to have tea tomorrow morning, at Cartwrights. She is thrilled – you know how romantic she is. We could meet at eleven, the three of us. Would that suit you?"

"How did your father react?"

"He did at first pretend, in a mischievous way, that he couldn't imagine why you wanted to see him. He teased until he nearly drove me to tears, but he knew from the outset why you want to see him, so much so that he had to console me, when I eventually did cry. Mummy says her father gave him a pretty hard time, but that will not happen to you. He feels remorse for having been insensitive."

"Gee, it's a relief. I am speaking in the hotel passage, and there is not much privacy. I wish I could be with you now, but tomorrow will have to do. Please forgive my low reaction, but I know you will understand – as you always do."

"Thank you so much for telephoning. Love you."

"I love you too, dear heart, sweet dreams, until tomorrow."

Douglas was exuberant with relief. He nearly fell when the toe of his shoe missed a step as he skipped up the stairs to his room. He paused on the balcony. The lights of the city twinkled below. He drew the cold damp night air in through his nose and thought of the clear night skies of Oudtshoorn in which the Milky Way had the density of white cloud.

He took his *The Rummy Affair Of Old Biffy*. One wonders where he got all his ideas. It would be nice to travel. Madame Jacquard could be their guide. He liked her. Frances would like her. Too Bohemian? His father liked her. His wrist itched. When he scratched it with his teeth he smelt Frances' perfume. He put his book down and turned on his side and imagined that she was lying next to him – her golden hair spread across the pillow. They would lie close together in cold weather like this. His feet were beginning to warm. Do people ever get tired of having intercourse? They must surely? His parents must have stopped by now – impossible to imagine otherwise. The Judge could still be active though – strong bugger. He started reading again. When he woke the light was still on. He turned the light off and hopped back into bed and fell asleep almost immediately.

In the early hours of the morning when the sky was already grey he found himself strolling along on the polished parquet flooring of a large art gallery. He looked down and saw his own reflection far below him. It was strange that there were no paintings, only sculptures. He could look through them because they were made of thought. Although they were silent and made no movement they uttered inaudible colourless sounds of ideas. The walls and the ceiling had no colour and the floor had no colour. He nodded to the sculptures as though they were friends. They were silent and yet they spoke to him in whispers. Why was there a knock on the ornate doors of the gallery? Why could he hear in that silence? The knock was there again. It was the waiter with his tea. He looked at his watch. It was six thirty. Breakfast would be from seven to nine.

He arrived at Cartwrights at a quarter to eleven, and took a seat in the waiting area of the tearoom, on the first floor. The maitre d' appeared, "A table Sir?"

"I am expecting some guests."

"How many guests Sir?"

"Two guests."

"I have a very nice table for you, at the window, in the sun. Let me show you to your table. I will receive your guests, your name is?"

"Douglas van Yssen ."

"Thank you Sir, please follow me."

The maitre d' pulled out a chair for Douglas and handed him a napkin. Douglas unfolded his newspaper and read the leader. It railed against the legacy of distrust that the Nationalists had helped to create for Labour. His mind wandered. He looked up to clear his thoughts and saw Frances and her mother arriving. Frances waved her special little wave. She did not wait to be shown to the table or for her mother, and made straight for Douglas. She was radiantly confident in her cloche hat – its bow tied in the shape of an arrow. At Christmas time it had been tied in hope, now it signified an accomplishment. She embraced him, and kissed him on his mouth, flushed with happiness.

"Hello Douglas, how good to see you." Mrs Rose kissed him on his cheek.

He could feel the warmth of her body." Good morning Mrs Rose."

A waiter hovered.

"Let us sit down, the whole world is watching," Frances pleaded.

"Now listen to me Douglas," Mrs Rose commanded, "this is a very special occasion for me, and our tea this morning will be my treat. And besides I have already made the necessary arrangements with the maitre d', we have an account here."

"But Mrs Rose…"

Mrs Rose directed herself at Douglas. "I feel that I should tell you, if it will put you at ease, Douglas, that I am so pleased, about the news. I have admired you from the first times we met, and you came to our house. Recently I came across some snapshots of you and Frances when we went for the first walk along a bleak Muizenberg Beach – the day my hat blew off and you ran after it so gallantly – you were so boyish then. I have always wanted a son. I am so pleased."

Frances glowed.

"Have you let your parents know? Mrs Rose asked.

"Yes I telephoned them last night."

"And?"

"If I may reply rather indirectly. My mother and I had tea on our own one afternoon during term – my father was somewhere in the district. She spoke about Frances. She was quite emotional. I am embarrassing myself now."

Frances looked at him expectantly.

"I am not sure which one of us, whether I am, or my mother is, most in love with Frances! She said how special Frances is. It was wonderful because in the past no one that I may even have glanced at, however nice, was ever good enough. In the end the two of us just sat there in silence until our tea was cold. So she is very pleased. My father too."

The waiter had returned. "You will have tea, Douglas? Or would you prefer something else?"

"Tea, thank you."

"We'll have tea for three and if you could please let us see what is on the cake trolley."

"You mentioned that you and Douglas had chocolate éclairs yesterday afternoon, Francis, I think I shall have one – as a kind of celebration – if you know what I mean."

"I had a jolly big breakfast," Douglas said.

"Come on now, do have something, it is a special occasion."

"A meringue would be nice, thank you."

"How did you guess? I shall have the same." Frances was in a happy mood. She held his hand and smiled at him and glanced at her mother for approval.

"It seems as though I am surrounding myself with intellectuals. I sometimes wonder whether I will be able to cope. I am not even sure all the thinking that people do these days is good for the brain. It is so tiring. I am sure people lived much longer when they did not have to think so much."

"Oh come now mother, you are much smarter than you give yourself credit. You have much more common sense than either Daddy or I, you are more practical, and your instincts are flawless. In fact I have often thought that you are the compass of our family. Not to mention your business acumen. You ride well; you play good tennis."

"My, my, you are in a flattering mood. Now Douglas, I gather we are going to have the pleasure of seeing you this evening. About six. We'll have sundowners. My husband is quite comfortable with the developments, so there is no need to feel that you are going to be intimidated."

"Doyle will come and fetch you, if you like." Frances said.

"Oh, I'll walk. It will do me good."

"You are more than welcome to use Doyle." Mrs Rose looked at the clock on the wall. "Gosh it is nearly twelve. I told Doyle to fetch us at a quarter past. I have a luncheon appointment with my brother. He has come into town to discuss a family matter. He'll be delighted about the news. Frances has not seen him since Christmas so she will accompany me." She signalled to the waiter. She had left half of her chocolate éclair and began to get up from her chair. She extended her hand. "Oh what am I doing?" He stood up. She kissed him on his cheek. "We'll see you this evening then."

Frances gave Douglas a tempting kiss and skipped off after her mother with a sideways glance of affection. Douglas gathered his newspaper. It would be a good idea to go and find Dr Roux's rooms. He took the piece of paper from his wallet. 'Room 315, third floor Cartwright's Building, Adderley Street.' Sitting all morning two floors below the good Doctor. He decided to go to the hotel for lunch.

At five o'clock Douglas left for the Roses' house. He enjoyed the walk. At the front door he ran his hand over his short hair and his face and straightened his jacket. He tapped the brass knocker on the front door. Hope opened the door with a knowing look, showed him into the reception room, and left to announce his arrival. Frances appeared holding her arms out to him. Her hair was fresh. Her warm neck released the fragrance of her perfume. The rustle of Mrs Rose's dress interrupted their kiss. "Good evening Douglas."

The Judge entered the room unheard. "Goodness gracious, what have we here? A gathering of admirers? Let us go through to the drawing room and have a drink."

A silver tray stood ready on the tripod table near the window. On it was a large and a small cocktail shaker, a soda siphon, a bucket of ice and a collection of bottles. Hope was hovering. "I'll see to the drinks, thank you Hope," the Judge announced. "Well now, let's see. I am not going to have my usual. I have decided that we should have cocktails tonight. Where is our little recipe book Elizabeth? We got into the habit of having cocktails in America, before the prohibition of course, wouldn't do anything criminal, like drinking alcohol there, Douglas."

"What a fibber you are Jeremy. My husband is just having you on Douglas. When we were there the first time, just after the armistice, cocktails were all the rage, and the last time we went he had his usual drink in the evening on the flimsy pretext that prohibition did not apply to him as a foreign citizen. I dare say, for all practical purposes alcohol was quite freely available. The recipe book is behind you on the bookshelf, dear."

"I think people actually drink more because of it than they might do otherwise. Forbidden fruit and all that." The Judge peered through his reading spectacles and paged through a small book. "A Bobby Burns sounds like the right thing. I think I shall make a large one, and then we can all have some. If you find that you don't like it feel free to have something else." The Judge placed iced cubes into the shaker, followed by measures of Scotch whisky with equal quantities of sweet vermouth, and added liberal dashes of Benedictine liqueur. "I get the best results if I let it stand for a while. Elizabeth, if you and Frances would be so good as to entertain yourselves for a while I could go off with Douglas to hear what he wants to see me about. That is if you still want to see me Douglas?"

"Yes I rather do, Judge." Douglas' hands were clammy.

The Judge went down the passage to his study. Douglas looked back anxiously at Frances. The Judge was already seated when Douglas entered his study. "Pull up a pew Douglas, there's one over there." The Judge sat back in his swivel chair, interlocked his fingers and put his thumbs against his chin. "Very well then, what do we have on the agenda?" he asked jovially.

"Judge if I may come to the point directly, please. I have proposed to Frances, and I would now formally like to ask you for her hand in marriage, please."

"I take it she has consented?" He was sterner now.

Douglas did not expect that. He felt his face grow hot and his hands trembled as he stared at the Judge. 'Imagine that he has no clothes on.' He could not hold the Judge's gaze, and looked down at the floor. He moved about till his chair creaked. "Yes she has," he let out a hoarse squeak.

"I know damn well that she has, dear boy!" he laughed. "I didn't mean to unsettle you. I have been aware for a long time of Frances' affection for you. Women are strange but wonderful creatures Douglas: I don't think that we can ever understand exactly how they feel about us, how utterly unconditional their affection is. And that requires that we act with great responsibility lest we devalue their love. All I ask of you is never to hurt my daughter. I am not going to ask you about your means, for both of us know that you have just started earning. However, a man with your intellect and academic achievements has the potential to become very successful, and it is in your potential that I am placing my trust. Yes, you may have my daughter's hand in marriage."

"Thank you very much Judge. I do hope that I will not disappoint you or Frances. I have never loved anyone else, and I admire and respect her a great deal. If I may just say, please, bearing in mind my utterly modest means, that our engagement may of necessity be somewhat protracted. Also, we had thought that if it would be acceptable to you and to Mrs Rose to make a formal announcement only in the June holidays?"

"That sounds like excellent planning. It would give us time to arrange everything. We could have an engagement party here; it would give your parents time to make suitable plans to come to Cape Town; you could invite some friends. Yes, that sounds like a very good idea, a well measured beginning." He got up. "Let us go and find our women. It is time for us to have a celebration."

The women were surprised to hear the footsteps returning so soon. Mrs Rose smiled at Frances. "It seems as though your father has behaved as he promised he would," she whispered, and Frances gripped her arm excitedly. Mother and daughter tried to be expressionless as the Judge entered the room, followed by a sheepish looking Douglas.

"My dear, Douglas has asked me for Frances' hand in marriage and I have happily agreed. It is time to propose a toast to the young people and their future."

"Oh how wonderful, how wonderful," Mrs Rose clasped her hands and pressed them to her breast. She was at the same time excited and relieved. She walked over to Douglas and kissed his cheek. "You may now kiss Frances, Douglas." To Mrs Rose's delight Douglas gave Frances a kiss of familiar succulence, and she observed how the soft rosy inside of Frances' bottom lip clung to Douglas mouth as they disengaged. "Oh Jeremy, how romantic. This is indeed a happy day. When shall we make the announcement?"

Frances looked at Douglas for a cue. "Mummy, what Douglas and I considered was that we should have a formal announcement only during the June holidays."

"I think that is a capital idea, Elizabeth, Douglas mentioned it. It will give us time to make proper arrangements. We could have an engagement party at the Club."

"No doubt we will think of the finer details nearer the time."

Condensation ran down the sides of the shaker. The Judge wrapped a napkin around it and shook it vigorously. "You need to get a sort of rhythm going. It has to be shaken well." He shook it some more before he unscrewed the lid. He looked inside the shaker. He poured foaming liquid into glasses. "We need a bit of orange peel. There we are." He raised his glass of pale orange liquid, "Let me see how it has turned out." He took a sip and moved the fluid about with his tongue and his cheeks, while the others watched. He rolled his eyes about as he searched for the response of his senses. "Yum, delicious, even better than before, delicious. Here my dear, Frances, Douglas." He handed the glasses around, and lifted his glass, "To your future dear Frances, and Douglas and a tribute to Mr Burns himself."

"To Douglas and Frances." Mrs Rose raised her glass before she took a ceremonial sip. She shuddered at the unfamiliar aroma of the drink.

Frances watched her mother and remembered her father's early cocktail experiments. She took her first sip cautiously. She tried to swallow. The potent mixture caught her throat. She coughed and spluttered uncomfortably. "Wow, this is worse than paraffin. I'd rather have champagne, if you don't mind Daddy." She glanced to see how Douglas was doing. After Frances' reaction Douglas did not want to offend the Judge's enthusiasm. "It is most unusual, most interesting." He took another sip.

"I wonder who thought of all these strange concoctions," Mrs Rose said huskily, "but here's to the two of you. May you have a wonderfully happy future!"

"I think this is splendid stuff, sorry to have wasted it on philistines. You should have more perseverance Frances. It grows on you." The Judge peered into the shaker to see how much was left. "One thing we may be certain of and that is that the four of us will always remember this drink. To be sure we will tell our children and grandchildren of the night when I introduced you to the Scottish poet. Something else Douglas, Elizabeth?"

"I am more than fine thank you Judge." Douglas was willing to test the effect of the cocktail.

"I think I'll join Frances and have some champagne please dear. Why don't we sit down? I am suddenly weary now. It must be nervous exhaustion I think. Frances won't you please ring for Hope? We have prepared some snacks, a light supper really. I trust you had some lunch today, Douglas."

"Oh yes I did indeed, Mrs Rose, thank you." He wanted to make a good impression. He was experiencing such relief that he feared that he was not going to behave entirely rationally. It would be better to leave early and return when he was in control of all his faculties, and his Judgement. The alcohol was beginning to have an effect. It would be better to eat something. While he was in that abstraction Hope arrived with delicious hot angels on horseback, small chipolata sausages, prunes wrapped in pink bacon. Plates, small knives and forks and napkins arrived.

"Gosh, I'm suddenly quite hungry," the Judge muttered. "May I offer you anything, dear?"

At the Judge's insistence Frances and Douglas helped themselves next. The food settled Douglas' mind. The atmosphere grew more and more convivial. The fire crackled. Frances and Douglas held hands. Mrs Rose's cheeks glowed.

"I'll yet have to get you to play golf Douglas – great refuge from women!"

"That won't do Jeremy, you are doing your best to corrupt my future son-in-law. My husband is just teasing you Douglas, let's talk about the rest of the week. I have been thinking and would very much like you to have dinner with us on Friday evening, we are having the Searles over, and maybe one or two other friends. You have met Sir Malcolm."

Eventually it was time for Douglas to leave. Happy goodbyes were said and the Judge became quite familiar. Douglas and Frances went outside together. It was a mild evening. Where the sun had set the sky was still pale. In the east it was a brilliant blue. The evening star was visible. She pointed at it. "Venus has come to greet us to seal our pact."

---◆---

Chapter Eighteen

DOUGLAS STOOD for a while outside the Helmsley Hotel. There was a hint of southeaster. He smelt the scent of damp decaying oak leaves and roses behind a white garden wall, releasing their last perfume before autumn reduced their petals at the end of their short summer life. A car rushed past. Bloody weird stuff he had drunk, like an anaesthetic. Keats' hemlock. It was not like beer that rushed in and departed quickly. He thought of Garnett, and looked at his watch. It was nearly nine. He was close to the top end of Adderley Street. He smelt flowers in the Avenue. What a thing it is to touch a woman. The first woman he ever touched was his mother. He tried to remember what she had felt like then. He recalled putting his arms around her waist and holding her buttocks and pressing his head into her tummy above her mound; slipping his hand in under her clothing when she lay in bed next to him at night to read to him, to feel her breast. First her one nipple grew hard between his thumb and forefinger. Then he would feel the other titty until that nipple grew hard, and go back to the first one. He always enjoyed remembering how he had touched his cousin. To heighten the experience he magnified small details: the texture of the curliness of her copper coloured pubic hair against his palm, the slippery mucous that seeped onto his fingers. He avoided washing his fingers that night so that he could continue to sniff and savour their sour leavening as he lay in bed, in the unfamiliar surroundings and linseed oil odours of the spare room on his cousin's farm.

Frances returned to the drawing room after saying goodbye to Douglas. Her mother smiled affectionately.

"Come and sit with us, my dear child." Her father patted his thigh, "I know how happy you are."

"It all happened so suddenly."

"Or perhaps spontaneously; sometimes that is the best way," her mother said.

"We realise how much Douglas means to you Frances. The van Yssens are fine people, and Douglas, quite apart from his marvellous intellect, is a solid fellow." The judge had started on the other half of his cocktail, resolute to the point of being reckless.

"It's a jolly long drink you're having dear," his wife commented.

"Except for what Douglas had, no one would help me, so I'll just have to persevere on my own. I am in such a jolly mood. I think I will just have another bite of something."

"Douglas was quite nervous when he went to speak to you."

"It was to be expected Mummy. Daddy often appears rather severe."

"What I liked about the fellow was that he came straight to the point." Bobby Burns was seeping further into his tissues. He went to help himself to some more food. He munched a large black prune wrapped in pink bacon, and dislodged a piece of chipolata from the side of one of his molars with his tongue. His eye fell on the brightly illustrated dustcover of the cocktail book, on whose cover a line drawing of a young woman, shapely legs, glass in hand and a fetchingly naughty derriere swayed suggestively in the surface of his cocktail. He looked at his wife. "We've all had a long day Elizabeth, and I think we should go to bed early. I have another long day ahead of me tomorrow."

"There's no point in going to sleep too early, or I will only lie awake in the early hours." She looked at Frances. Douglas is as strong as a lion. More is the pity that so much carnal pleasure should be squandered on the innocent.

The judge put his head back and poured the last of his drink down his throat. He smacked his lips with satisfaction. "I have a few things to get ready for the morrow." He made a silly little clowning double step. His wife glared disapprovingly.

"Is poor Hope still here Mummy? What's wrong with Daddy?"

"I think he is slightly bedewed," she whispered. "We should let her go, if you would be so good as to ring for her, please."

When Hope had cleared the cocktail things, and said goodnight, Frances and her mother sat for a while. The Judge could be heard shuffling papers and moving about on his chair. The grandfather clock in the corner ticked loudly and made troublesome sounds before it struck nine. Frances giggled softly.

"What are you laughing about?"

"Daddy – he was quite funny. I wonder what Douglas would be like when he's tipsy."

"I think he would just become more and more amiable, and amusing; witty too, I suppose. Quote a bit of Latin or something, tell a Scottish joke, I suppose."

"He is exactly like that! I think I shall go to bed now and read my book, if you don't mind. Thank you so much for everything." Frances got up and kissed her mother on her head. "I love you Mother."

Mrs Rose held onto Frances' hand and felt the small sentimental bones that reminded her how delicate Frances was when she was small. "Goodnight my child. May God bless you."

Frances washed herself, brushed her teeth and put on her nightdress. She sat in front of her mirror and brushed her hair. Her scalp hurt a little where her hat had pushed her hair in the wrong direction. She got in between cold percale sheets with the *Life of Charlotte Bronte* in her hand. A few pages remained. She struggled to concentrate. Her mind was on the events of the last two days. Douglas' charming smile dominated. Fine wrinkles had begun to form around his eyes from all his laughing. His beard was gunmetal coloured steel brush in the late afternoon. She touched it with the palm of her hand and felt the rocking movements of the train. The book slipped from her hand and she was not sure whether she had fallen asleep. When she woke her light was still on and she got up to switch it off. Her bed was warm now and she turned her pillow over so that it would be cool against her face. She inhaled night air through her nose and felt it in the cavities around her eyes. With a trembling sigh she surrendered herself to the formless happiness of her love.

Tuesday 14 March 1927

Douglas was woken during the early hours of the morning by a throbbing at the back of his head, and a thirst so severe that it almost made him panic. His bladder was throbbing. He pulled the chamber pot from under the bed. He missed the edge of the pot and urinated down the inside of his thigh before he could redirect his stream. Not a good start to the day. He took his wet pyjama pants off. His headache had invaded his entire cranium or else a very large landrace must have shat in his head. He snorted at his own humour, drank as much water as possible and lay down.

There was a knock on his door. "There's a telephone call for you Mr van Yssen, a Dr Nel, it's a trunk call from Oudtshoorn."

"I'll telephone him as soon as I am dressed, thank you."

Douglas bathed and dressed hurriedly.

"Hello Garnie!"

"You sound cheerful, what's news? How are you?"

"Hell, do I have some news! I got completely carried away on Sunday, what with travelling to Cape Town, and then going for a walk on the beach at Camps Bay with Frances and proposed to her."

"What are you saying!"

"I asked her old man last night, and the old fellow was quite amenable."

"Well I never. Is that why you 'phoned last night?"

"That was part of the reason. I wanted to mention something about my ear."

"What is it?"

"I was lying in bed on the train and something made me remember that bloody Miss Krige, in standard four. She smacked me a hell of a shot on the ear. You may even remember it. I could hardly hear for days in that ear. What a bitch she was. Do you think that it could explain my problem? Because then I could cancel the appointment with Dr Roux?"

"You are in Cape Town now, right there on Roux's doorstep. Rather let him have a thorough look. Then we can be certain."

"Certain of what?"

"That it was the smack on the ear. You know what I'm like, I like certainty. Just go and see Roux. I will feel more comfortable if we get a second opinion. It is difficult to carry all the responsibility myself. Go for my sake, please."

"If you insist. I have already been to make sure that I know where his rooms are."

"Gee I am so pleased for you. Frances is a lovely girl. You are very lucky. I take it that it is public knowledge?"

"It will be a private engagement for now and we'll make a formal announcement in June. Her dad spoke about an engagement party. I would like you to come to Cape Town then if you can see your way clear. Anyway let me stop all this jabbering, I'll see you at the end of the week. We'll be leaving on Saturday, and arriving on Sunday. In the meantime please just keep it under your hat."

"I haven't been to Cape Town for donkey's years. I am already looking forward to it. Let me know what Roux says. And please give Frances my very best regards. I might even come to the station to meet the two of you on Sunday morning. I'll see you then."

The wheels of the Judge's Armstrong Siddeley crunched the gravel surface of the hotel driveway. Frances waved and bounced up and down with enthusiasm in the back seat. Douglas did not wait for Doyle to open the door. He jumped in beside Frances and kissed her. She gripped the inside of his arm and gave a little gasp when she felt his mouth against hers. Doyle's eye watched in the rear view mirror.

"Good afternoon Doyle, I trust you are well?"

"Good afternoon Sir, yes I am well thank you." Douglas held Frances' warm hand. "I hope your family is well, Doyle."

"It is always better when the weather improves, Sir."

"We're going to the museum Doyle. Douglas, I thought it might be an idea for us to go to the top of Adderley Street, and to walk through the gardens."

"That sounds splendid."

"That's what it will be then Doyle. If you could fetch us, I think at the top of Queen Victoria Street at about a quarter past five, if that suits you Douglas?"

"Sounds excellent." There were new dimensions in Frances' voice and mannerisms. Her green eyes shone, the small blood vessels of her alabaster skin were alive, and when she gesticulated the flesh of her hands was translucent against the light from the side windows. The original energy that had inspired the first woman in anticipation of fulfilment had found its way into Frances. She tilted the side of her head onto his tweed shoulder to beguile him.

She put her arm through his as they started up the Avenue. There were some familiar faces from their student days.

"Florrie was quite nosy when I asked to change our arrangements. I think she could tell from my voice that something was afoot, she pressed me a trifle and I had to let out just a little to appease her. I have sworn her to secrecy so please don't think that I have broken a confidence."

"I have always liked her. She's plucky, considering all she's been through, and I must confess that I have told Garnett. He too has been sworn to secrecy and I know I can trust him."

"You're always so complimentary about everybody, it's a sign of your strength."

"You flatter me. You don't know my dark side."

"You don't have a dark side. I know that – a woman's intuition never errs. You might have a mischievous or naughty side, but not a dark side, never."

"You are so sweet, and so dear, and so supporting, and I love you for that."

"Now don't be patronising, Douglas, you know how I dislike that."

They did not have to wait long for their tea to arrive. Douglas smiled at her while he stretched his legs and sat back with his hands behind his head. He looked up at the blue afternoon sky that seemed to tilt as wispy cotton wool clouds drifted across it from the southeast. "I am so happy to be here with you, Frances. So much has happened since we left Oudtshoorn that it feels as though I have been away for a month."

"Do tell me what happened between you and daddy when you went to ask him for my hand in marriage, Douglas. Mummy and I are dying to know, and we dare not ask him."

"Well it was really a matter between men," he taunted with a grin. "I'm not sure it would be good form to disclose any details."

"You are being awfully rummy and behaving like a chauvinist, like one of those coves at daddy's golf club, and I know you're not really like that. Just tell me, was he pleasant to you?"

"Oh yes, more than pleasant."

"What else?"

"Do you want me to kiss you?"

Frances blushed. "Of course I do you silly man."

Douglas got up and kissed her on her forehead. As he turned to sit down again he lost his balance and knocked his tea over.

"That comes from being silly," she laughed.

A waiter hurried to clean the mess and brought a fresh cup and more tea. When they were settled again, he continued. "Your father was really very accommodating and understanding. I didn't know where to begin, and of course he knew that I was nervous, it's not something one does every day of one's life, you know. I had rehearsed some things to say but when the time came I just got straight to the point. What did unsettle me a bit, after I told him that I had asked you to marry me, he enquired whether you had consented."

"What a hideous thing to do!"

"No it was not like that, he was just being full of mischief. For a few moments I thought I was really up against it, and then he laughed and said quite sympathetically that he did not want to unsettle me. That broke the ice. I felt constrained to remind him of my very modest means – as though he was not already aware of that – and he said that he quite understood my position, for which I am grateful. I said that the engagement might have to be a bit extended, and asked him if a formal announcement could be made in June. He seemed to like that idea. And then we came to join you and your mother."

"I think we'll have to give Joan Peacock a lift to the station on Saturday."

"What made you think of her?"

"Her misplaced attempt to get me to go out with Freddie Urquhart. Do you feel any different now?"

"How do you mean?"

"Now that we are engaged." She put her hand on his.

"Oh yes, very different, indeed. I am sure it has not quite sunk in. I am still a little bit stunned – in a nice way. What thrills me the most is that we have so much in common, and you have been such a marvellous friend to me, and you are so romantic. It is wonderful to love a friend as much as I love you."

"What a lovely thing to say."

"It is difficult to convey exactly what I mean, especially when I am as emotionally charged as I have been in the last two days, the words never come out right."

"I wish we could go away together," she whispered.

"Gee that would be something." Douglas rocked forward on his chair.

Frances leant intimately towards him so that she could not be overheard. "It occurred to me when I woke this morning and was lying in bed that we will be living together not long from now. It was such an extraordinary thing to contemplate that it gave me quite a start. All my life I have slept in my own bed, alone, and now there is the prospect of actually lying in bed with another person, of the opposite sex. It is so extraordinary to think of that: to prepare to go to sleep together, to wake up together, never to be apart, it is amazing, just truly amazing I must say. It went around and around in my head. Do you know what I mean?"

"I think I do. I have not contemplated anything particular. I just have a sort of general feeling, an all-encompassing, unconditional kind of feeling that makes me want to enclose you. I have become congested with emotion."

"I suppose I too am a bit confused."

"At least we can share our confusion. Let us just agree to enjoy our present condition. Although I had so hoped to marry you one day, I hardly imagined that I would have the courage to ask you so soon. I am glad I did. I'm very glad. I almost can't believe that you have consented."

"I belong to you Douglas. I think I have always belonged to you."

"I have sometimes just a little difficulty with the concept of destiny."

"What difficulty?"

"Well, I suppose it pre-supposes a hidden entity that determines what will happen in the future. As though there is some kind of controlling hand shaping really very small events, and I have to ask myself why that would be so. I think things are much more random than we sometimes imagine. In our search for meaning we pre-suppose order and we are not comfortable with reality as a random affair."

"Golly gosh! We are back with Darwin, aren't we? 'Nobody can presume what the order of nature should be.'"

Douglas laughed. "I did not think of that now, but bear in mind that I spoke of discomfort. Life does indeed have spontaneous meaning for me. Connecting meaning and order is problematical, finding a rational explanation for the shaping hand, is what I find difficult. When we used to go to the Dutch Reformed Church I had immense problems with the Doctrine of Predestination, and reconciling it with the concept of Free Will. And I don't know what the answer is. Sometimes I see it one way, and at other times I see it another way. What does destiny mean to you?"

"I think there is purpose in everything. I sometimes look at a beautiful flower or a painting, and there is something in the object that resounds in me. There is what the French call 'correspondence', a kind of resonance."

"There probably is a simple scientific explanation for that."

"What I am talking about goes beyond science. It has to do with being part of something greater."

"But surely unless something is scientifically verifiable it has no validity?"

"I remain convinced that there is more to it than that. But let's not quibble, dearest man. What I do know is that I love you very much, even though it cannot be scientifically verified." Frances looked about. The last of the other patrons had left in the lengthening pale blue shadows of the late early autumn afternoon. She could talk less allusively now. "Have you ever thought of having children?"

Douglas bridled humorously. "I find the idea quite strange in some ways."

"Strange in what way?"

"Well just think of it: two people are stranded on a desert island, a man and a woman. There are no other human beings on the island. From the two of them other human beings can be created. Don't you think that is quite extraordinary?"

"Possibly from a man's point of view but not from a woman's point of view."

"Why should there be a difference?"

"Because we are so different. It is natural for me to consider bearing children; that they will come out of me. So your example of the island doesn't sound strange at all. Men are not so intimately involved; you don't hatch out babies. I would like to have lots of children, like lovely puppies, and I would like to lie with them at night and read to them – none of the Victorian nonsense of sending children away. I would love to have them as friends. Daddy would have liked a son. So he doted on me instead. Intellectually we have a lot in common. In some respects he is clinical and cold. I am aware that the legal fraternity, and for that matter the press, consider Daddy to be quite a harsh judge. I am not sure why that should be so. He seems so fair to me. Mummy, in a rare moment of intimacy – remember what you told me about the conversation you had with your mother – Mummy has let on that she thinks he fears his peers will think he is weak. She hinted at feelings of insecurity and alluded to Sir Malcolm's sense of compassion, a compassion that elevates him and gives him the stature of a man of great strength. It endows him with a mantle of respect. There's a sweet irony in that. When I was much younger I once listened to a discussion between Daddy and Sir Malcolm. Sir Malcolm was saying that he suspected that the old original lawmakers, he was referring to the Romans, had a unique innate sense of justice, a pure sense of what was right and wrong, and especially of what was fair, and it was in such soil that the first roots of the law took hold. Then, as people are wont to do in other ways, and especially with religion, the original message gradually became corrupted until much of the original meaning was lost. The law became an object of intellectual abstraction and an arena for gladiatorial contests between the representatives of litigants, sometimes with scant concern for the litigants or the accused. The contrast in Daddy's and Sir Malcolm's views was shrill. The impression has never left me. I remember being disappointed."

"How did the discussion end?"

"Oh, it was a civilised affair. Daddy either could not or did not want to see the telling point that Sir Malcolm was making, and proceeded to produce an argument that I certainly did not understand at the time, but which I realised later, was jurisprudentially so convoluted that it did none other than to prove Sir Malcolm right. Sir Malcolm's reasoning came from the heart, and Daddy's from the head. In the end they had to agree to disagree."

Douglas waited for some of the fresh tea to be poured.

Frances looked lovingly at him. "Did your mother read much to you when you were small?"

"Yes, why do you ask?"

"I am looking forward to reading to my children. Some of my best memories are of being bathed, put into my pyjamas and fed, sitting snugly on my mother's lap in front of the fire and listening while she read to me; fighting off sleep until I woke the next morning with the winter sun streaming in through the sash window, unsure of what had been read to me or whether I had dreamt. My imagination became reality."

"What did she read to you?"

"My early staple diet was fairy tales: The Princess Nobody: a story of Fairyland after the drawings of Richard Doyle. Then there were the Fables – Aesop and De La Fontaine. My, those were salad days. I suppose my best was Alice's Adventures, and oh, Andrew Lang's books. I carried his Blue Fairy Book around the house and sat with it on my lap at meal times. I could not be separated from it any more than I could from my blanket. Did you have a blanket?"

"My mother still has it in her chest of drawers."

"There were also the brothers Grimm. Their stories frightened me and my mother put them away. When I was a bit older, making 'houses' with sheets and blankets under pieces of furniture, I would tempt myself into taking the ominously Grimm book from behind the sliding glass of the bookshelf in Mummy's sewing room and carry it surreptitiously into one of my shelters there to look at the illustrations until I was too frightened to leave the seclusion of my hiding place."

"I found them dark, almost sinister. I remember my father saying that they did not create the stories, they merely compiled an anthology. They were fine scholars."

"I find it abhorrent to frighten children."

"I agree." Douglas looked at his watch. "I don't want to rush you, but I think we should start thinking about leaving if we are not going to keep Doyle waiting too long."

Wednesday 16 March 1927

Douglas arrived at Dr Roux's consulting rooms a few minutes early. A large overbearing antiseptic nursing sister waited for him. She stared at him severely. "Are you van Yssen from Oudtshoorn?"

Douglas looked her straight in eye and waited until she moved about uncomfortably.

"Yes."

"Doctor has another patient."

"Do you mean that he has only one other patient?"

She glared at him, puffed herself up and let out her air with a slap of the elbows to her ribs.

"I have come a long way, so I'll just wait," he said.

"Don't play with me young man."

"I would never dream of doing that," he said with a twinkle in his eyes and picked up the morning newspaper. He looked around the reception room, at the ball and claw furniture, the patchwork wall-hanging and matching cushions, pot plants, anthuriums, hen and chickens with variegated leaves and maidenhair ferns, lace sun-filter curtaining, and on the wall opposite a miserable colourless religious tract clinging to its faith, no doubt placed there to appease the sensibilities of a devout receptionist.

Douglas scanned the headlines and opened the newspaper at the leader page. Halfway through the main leader, Roux's door opened. A handsome young woman in a cream linen suit and wide rimmed pink hat decorated with bright yellow silk roses smiled at Douglas with a sway of her hips and waved a coquettish little goodbye to the disapproval of the nursing sister.

Dr Roux appeared in the doorway. He was a small man in his late forties with slicked back dark hair, a small sallow round podgy face and little piercing dark eyes. He wore a white tunic that was buttoned all the way up to his neck. He nodded at Douglas, "Do come inside Mr van Yssen. Come and sit down, and tell me all about your problem." When they were seated opposite each other at his desk, he took a pencil and a notepad.

"Tell me all about yourself."

"Has Garnett Nel not told you?"

"Yes, he has written to me, but I would like you to tell me yourself what you have been experiencing. Tell me everything. Begin at the beginning, but first let me have some personal details. Your date of birth, your occupation, where you grew up, family history and so on."

"Gosh, let me see. I was born on January 17, 1903. I grew up in Oudtshoorn, went to university here until the end of last year. I am now teaching in Oudtshoorn. My hearing has always been good, until about two years ago, when I noticed that I sometimes had difficulty with my right ear."

"Is there any family history of deafness?"

"I gather my grandfather had a bit of a problem."

"Maternal or paternal?"

"Maternal."

"Do carry on, and don't worry about me, I write slowly."

"I forgot to tell Garnett Nel, when he examined me, that one of my junior school teachers, I think it was in standard three or four, gave me quite a severe smack on the ear. I could not hear properly with that ear for days afterwards. I only remembered it on the way here. I feel that it is perhaps a bit of a sham to come and see you, perhaps a waste of your time, if there is such a simple explanation for my problem."

"How old is your grandfather now?"

"He died years ago when I was quite small."

"How severe was his deafness?"

"My mother has never said much about it. She was a bit embarrassed about it, so I don't know much about his condition."

"What subject do you teach?"

"History."

"My father loved history," Roux remarked as he wrote. "Have you had any childhood diseases, or any other diseases?"

"Just the usual things – mumps, chicken pox, measles."

"Normal measles, or German measles?"

"I suppose normal measles."

"Any operations?"

"No, not at all."

"Any injuries?"

"No."

"You look very healthy. Nel wrote to me to tell me of his examination. He seems like a capable fellow. What I am going to do is not going to be much different from what he did. Would you please be so kind as to take your shirt off, and your trousers. Leave your underpants on and take your vest off, please."

Roux began with his sinuses, examined the glands in his neck, and under his arms and his groin. He took his blood pressure, listened to his heart and his breathing, and examined the inside of his hands. He examined his nasal passages and looked into his ears and his eyes. "I am going to do an inflation of the middle ear."

"Garnett has already done that."

"Yes he told me, and as I said, he seems quite competent, but each of us has his own way of doing it and a second opinion won't hurt. You may put your clothes back on now, please." The procedure was almost identical to Garnett's but more repetitive. Roux made notes as he went.

"You certainly have no ear infection," he said frowning and scratching the top of his head. "Please come and stand at the window. I want to have another look at your eyes. How hard did the woman hit you on the ear?"

"Oh, it was quite a smack. She was large and strong, like sister outside. She had a furious temper: thought I was talking when all the time it was the chap next to me. I had little hearing in that ear for days afterwards."

"Well that's quite interesting. I think we have done for the day. When are you going back to Oudtshoorn?"

"On Saturday."

"I'll telephone Nel in the next day or two and let him know what I think."

"So there's nothing wrong apart from the effect of the smack."

"That is possible."

"Thank you so much, thank you very much, it's such a relief. Gee."

Roux took Douglas by the elbow and guided him towards the door; he opened it for him and shook Douglas' hand. "I will telephone Nel this afternoon."

Douglas gave the receptionist a smug flirtatious smile and to his delight provoked a hiss and a sneer. He fairly skipped out of the door on a sensation of relief. Outside on the pavement he felt the sun on his face. He could not decide what to do next. He waited for ideas to form. The warm feeling of the sun pressed on his shoulders. What a relief. His father would be thrilled. Poor old Garnie, he would be pleased, he is always so concerned about others. What a time he was having. Excitement went though him and made his scalp itch. Engaged to the most beautiful and smartest girl in the whole world; the weather was good; his ears were fine. And he was earning money. The chalk-coloured road to Plettenberg Bay appeared before him and he began to wander along a similar road through one of Madame Jacquard's paintings whose images inspired a fantasy of bright green fields, in which leafy oak trees stood and red and pink poppies grew against a pale horizon that was indistinguishable from the blue grey of the sea beyond it.

Hope announced that Douglas was on the telephone. "Douglas, I have been so worried, I have left message after message at the Helmsley. Where have you been, what did Dr Roux say?"

"All is well dear girl. All is well. I told Roux about the smack I had on the ear in junior school and from all accounts it seems as though that could be the cause of the trouble. He is going to telephone Garnett to put his mind to rest. I had the feeling that Garnett was overly concerned after he examined me in Oudtshoorn. Everyone can stop fretting now."

"I am so very, very glad. I am so relieved, but then I knew all along that all would be well. I am missing you. The weather is so perfect. Mummy suggested that we should get Doyle to take the two us down to the pier for a stroll. Now don't protest. *Carpe diem*. We will pick you up at three. Love you lots. Bye now."

Louis Nel, Uncle Charlie and Garnett were sitting on the veranda in the fading pink light of an early autumn evening, each thinking his own after-supper thoughts. Uncle Charlie's digestive juices rumbled. Garnett flicked a piece of cobweb from the turn-up of his baggy cream trousers.

"Garnett," his mother called, in a voice altered to impress the caller, "there's another doctor, a Dr Roux on the telephone from Cape Town."

"Excuse me please."

"Dr Nel this is Roux here. Do you speak English or Afrikaans?"

"It does not matter."

"Your friend saw me today. I examined him thoroughly. I told him that I would telephone you. There is no obvious pathology, which instead of giving me comfort gives me concern. Evidently his grandfather was deaf. I don't want to cause unnecessary alarm, but clinically everything suggests incipient otosclerosis. He seems like such a fine fellow with a good future ahead of him that I have been quite disturbed at the prospect that he could be afflicted with what I can at best describe as the *bete noire* of otology so I took the trouble to examine again this afternoon some of the literature on the subject. The classical condition, as Denker described it, and I don't want to sound as though I am lecturing you, has a triad of symptoms – I am looking at the book as I speak – deafness, tinnitus and paracusis Willisii. All these conditions are present as well as the salmon-pink reflex showing through the drum-membranes from the inner tympanic wall. There is of course also the colour of the eyes, which you no doubt noticed. It is quite marked. The hearing in the right ear is worse than in the other ear. That happens sometimes. Deafness does not necessarily progress at the same rate in the two ears. I was unable to determine whether he suffers from intestinal intoxication, perhaps you could do that."

Garnett broke out in a sweat.

"Are you there?"

Garnett could hardly speak.

"Damn telephone, are you there?"

"Yes," Garnett said hoarsely.

"You will have to break the news to him, and the sooner the better so that he can seek treatment."

"What treatment do you have in mind?"

"From recent accounts it would seem as though a man in England has had some quite remarkable success with electrophonoid treatment. The prospect of treatment should modify the shock of my diagnosis. I wish I could have had better news, but there it is."

"I did discuss my initial examination with an older colleague of mine here in Oudtshoorn."

"Who was that?"

"Dr Diemont."

"I know Diemont."

"Interestingly enough his first reaction was that we are looking at otosclerosis. He knows van Yssen's family history. I have a special interest in ear nose and throat work. Who is the otologist you were referring to?"

"A chap called Yearsley, at St James Hospital. I know it is not easy to bring bad tidings, but such is life. At least Yearsley offers some hope. He'll have to travel to England for the treatment. Is there anything else?"

"No, no it's fine. I'll manage. I must thank you for your help and your candour."

"If there is anything else please let me know. If van Yssen wants me to refer him, I will write to Yearsley."

Garnett returned to the veranda where his father and Uncle Charlie were talking in hushed tones and stopped when they heard his footsteps. They looked at him expectantly.

"What's the matter Garnett?" his father asked.

"Just a medical matter."

"Anything you can share with us?"

"You know what it's like Dad, like in your profession."

"Anyone we know?" Uncle Charlie asked.

"I doubt it. I think I should go down to the surgery and then to the hospital for the evening round. Goodnight Uncle Charlie, Dad."

"That boy has changed since he has been away. He is damn conscientious."

"That's correct, but I want him to help the others now with their studies. He must be making money."

"Have a heart Louis, he's just started, and nobody helped him, he had to go cap in hand to that heartless bastard who's charging him four percent. With hindsight it seems reasonable but it was usurious at the time. Damn iniquity. He's got to pay him back before he can help anybody else."

"He's the eldest and must help the others. I've done enough."

Still enchanted by the happy events of the day Douglas went down to dinner at half past seven. He examined the menu and found that he was pleasantly hungry. Saliva squirted from the glands in his cheeks. Images of the day softened the edges of his perception: Frances in a thistle-green knitted frock that brought out the colour of her eyes and clung to her contours, the smell of the sea beneath the pier, and its intense blue movement. His vegetable soup arrived. 'I am so pleased about the outcome this morning, Douglas,' she said with her arm through his, trying, skipping, to walk in step with him. 'Tell me about Dr Roux. You must let your parents know as soon as possible, and Garnett.' 'Roux will telephone Garnett this evening to confirm that it was only that incident when I was small. Gee, I feel so good. You know how one always worries and expects the worst. Why expect the worst?' 'It is a protective mechanism. To be on one's guard. Mummy is so glad. Deafness is a terrible thing.' She squeezed his arm. The sea was calm. In the distance a mixture of air and cold Atlantic sea water made an opaque pale green wave. 'What was Dr Roux like?' 'I liked him. He has a real battleaxe of a Sister. Hates men. I pretended to flirt with her.' 'Douglas, you scoundrel! I turn my back and you jolly well get up to all sorts of things.' "I'll have the fish thank you." A couple with four teenage children, three girls and a boy entered the dining room. The eldest girl's pace slackened. She gave Douglas a lingering look.

◆

Chapter Nineteen

Saturday 19 March 1927

IT WAS TWO THIRTY. Departure was approaching. He waited at the entrance of the hotel. A grey haze lay over the city. The car entered the driveway. The Judge and Mrs Rose were in a sombre mood. The journey to the station was punctuated by heavy sighs and sniffs from a tearful Mrs Rose.

"Come now dear, we cannot be seen crying in public," the Judge said.

The train stood ready. People milled about and talked in tones that preserved the equanimity improvised to soften the final moments of separation. Luggage was handed through the train windows; porters hurriedly manoeuvred their barrows through the growing bustle. Douglas received Frances' luggage from Doyle and stowed it in her compartment. There was no sign of Joan Peacock. He attended to his own things and went back onto the platform.

"It has been a lovely visit," Mrs Rose observed. She took Douglas' hand. "I am pleased that all has turned out well. I am looking forward to your visit in June. May God speed you Douglas." Her bottom lip curled and she blinked as she fought her tears. "You are strong Frances, like your father. I hope you will have a good term. You should be more settled now. Do write and let us know your progress."

The Judge took Frances' hand. "My but you are radiant!"

The conductor's whistle screamed shrilly. It was time to board.

The hot, saturated stuffy odours of warm leather, sun-baked varnish and cleaning materials that had accumulated while the train waited, departed on wafting Atlantic sea air.

"The saloon should be open by now. Let's go and have something, and make a dinner booking for this evening," Douglas proposed.

"I need to go to the washroom first, if you don't mind waiting for a few moments please." She hesitated "I am so pleased she's not here. We can be alone."

He watched her body moving along the narrow corridor, her hair bobbing, her shoulders turned sideways. The train gathered more speed. He remained in the corridor, his thoughts lost in a featureless moving landscape. Douglas and Frances went to his compartment after tea. At times in the years that followed when Douglas thought of Frances, he recalled that part of their journey, and remembered the conversation they had, sitting close together in his coupé, holding hands while the train made its way through the tall grim Elandskloof and Witsen Mountains; how they discussed their future, their enthusiasm encouraged by the beauty of the passing vineyards in autumn mixtures of oxide red, ochre yellow and burnt sienna against a pale blue sky illuminated by the last fading light of the day. They were inspired by the certainty of their new relationship. The excitement of being driven along by the train expanded their awareness of each other as if propelling them to a common purpose.

"I don't think that I could ever marry anybody else," she said.

"You flatter me. I am sure you could."

"It hurts me that you could think that I would ever consider anybody else. What I am saying has nothing to do with flattery but has everything to do with sincerity. We were meant for each other. Even when I am not with you I am constantly aware of your presence. Kiss me." He turned sideways to get a better purchase of her. He looked at her mouth before he started kissing her. She shuddered with pleasure. She withdrew to catch her breath. She swallowed and put her head on his shoulder. "Please take your jacket off so that I can get closer to you." He obliged and released a mixture of carbolic soap and faint perspiration. She took a bottle of perfume from her handbag and dabbed small amounts behind her ears and on her neck. She leant against him and put her arm through his. "I feel secure because you are so reliable. I trust you. There is nothing about you that ever irritates me. Every movement and gesture you make pleases me, the way you walk, the way you eat and chew your food, your colouring, the clothes you wear. Your humour is so subtle and delicate, and dry. Everything. Do you feel the same about me?"

"When I am with you, everything is clouded by my passion. When I am away from you the definition returns, the small details. Recalling the details gives me pleasure."

"Is there anything that irritates you about me? Be honest."

"Yes."

She bit her lip. "What."

"That we are not already married."

They kissed again, becoming more adept and intimate. "I know that I have said it before, but it is so important to me that Daddy admires you so much. Mummy loved you from the beginning. I think she is attracted to you. I can see it in the way she sometimes looks at you. She has learnt to restrain herself, but the original thrill when she sees you, like the other morning at Cartwrights, is still there."

"I love your mother."

"Daddy does not easily take to other people. He is especially critical of young men. He seems to think that they are mostly indolent, lacking in ambition, or just plain cads. He was very proud of you at our graduation. I heard him tell Sir Malcolm how he enjoyed introducing you to Athlone."

"It frightens me that he expects so much of me. After all I am just a novice school teacher."

She put her finger across his lips and shook her head. "You are a very smart man, Douglas. This is only the beginning of your career. Who knows what heights you will ascend. There is not a thing that you are not capable of,

I am sure of that. And I shall help you and support you in every endeavour. I want to bear your children; I want to see you in your carpet slippers studiously reading to our son in front of a fire in the hearth. I do so frightfully want us to be happy. We could have dinner parties and have interesting friends over, and go on holidays to the seaside, or travel overseas. I wonder what we should call our first born if it is a boy. What names do you like?"

"I would have liked to be called Andrew. I have always liked that name."

"I like that."

"I am so relieved about my visit to Dr Roux. At times I had some really bad feelings, like dark shadows, coming over me. That's all gone now. My relief has inspired me. I even thought, as you spoke about the future, that I might consider doing a doctorate. I could enjoy lecturing."

"Oh how wonderful! I could teach to support us. I am sure Daddy will help. You could be one of the youngest history professors ever. Wouldn't that be something!"

Douglas hugged her. "It is going to be very difficult to be separated from you for a whole term. I don't know how I am going to endure it."

"Let us not squander our remaining moments anticipating separation. In a little more than eight weeks we'll be back in Cape Town. Joan has been so meddlesome, I think I shall tell her in great confidence, and swear her to great secrecy, about our engagement and watch with amusement how the news spreads."

"Would that be wise?"

"I don't wish to be wise. Considering how she has behaved towards me, and how nosy she is. Don't you see how elegant my plan is? She won't be able to keep the news to herself and she'll have to suffer the consequences of breaking the confidence and telling the others. I shall witness the change in the way they'll look at me, and how they will whisper in the corridors. Oh it will be lovely! It will also get rid of that Freddie Urquhart notion for once and for all."

Douglas chuckled.

The light was fading when they descended into the Hex River Valley. Outside the landscape of streams, rivers, orchards and towering mountains raced past: the future was becoming the past. Flashes of colourful light darted through the compartment windows and flickered on interior surfaces. Frances' perfume, her soft warm body against him stirring with the movements of the train aroused Douglas and he recalled the flesh of her thigh above her stocking when he took the sand out of her shoe. He kissed the side of her head.

"I am so very, very happy Douglas my love." The dinner gong sounded. "I must go and change, dearest." She smiled and held his gaze to discourage his peripheral vision from seeing the intimate way in which she ran her hands across the places of her body to straighten her dress and pull her petticoat into its correct position.

The excited ecstasy that Douglas experienced that evening imprinted images and sensations in his memory. When in later years he recalled their dinner that evening he could remember what they ate. He would forever be able to taste the texture of thick salty pea soup, the crumbed sole that refused to release its spine, slices of roast beef that reflected colours of mother of pearl before thick brown steaming gravy was ladled over it by the steward, and a soufflé containing ground orange peel that had gone a bit flat. He remembered his feverish passion, how radiant Frances' skin was, or was it the rash from his beard? Her green eyes were made more intense by the combustion of her feelings. How soft her expression was. They kissed goodnight outside her compartment, awkwardly pressing as much as possible of their bodies together. When she became aware of his tumescence she pressed even harder against him.

Sunday 20 March 1927

When the train left George station it was becoming light. Douglas was shaving when there was a knock on his door. He put his razor down, held a towel to his neck and opened the door. He would have expected Frances to retreat. Instead she said, "I'll stay and watch you shave. Carry on, don't be embarrassed. I often used to watch Daddy shave. Lather your face again so that I can see. I like the scent of your shaving soap. I like it when you raise your muscular bare arm and turn your head to the side."

"We're being reckless, Frances. Anyone who arrives now will think that you spent the night here."

"I didn't, and that is all that matters. I'll watch you shave when we are married. Will we bath together?"

"I don't think that my parents have ever undressed in front of one another."

"Mummy and Daddy are quite natural. They're often naked together in their room or in the bathroom. I like that. I used to get into the bath with them when I was small. We were like three wet slippery seals in a tub!"

"I would have to get used to the idea. I think I would be shy."

The train clattered across the red steel bridge that spanned the Olifant's River, slowed before the last bend and crawled towards the station, past the clanging bells that warned the George Road traffic of its arrival. The van Yssens waited beside the sad pepper trees next to the platform. He was a statue cast in grey tweed speckled with grey-green moss, she a dutiful foot or two behind him, eager to see her son and his fiancée.

Frances and Douglas were at the landing when the train stopped. He helped her onto the platform. "My dear Frances," Mrs van Yssen said, "We are so very pleased to see you. You seem so well." Frances kissed Mrs van Yssen.

"Good morning Mr van Yssen." He shook her hand clumsily for fear of being too familiar.

"Good morning Frances, how are you?"

"I'm fine thank you Mr van Yssen, very well in fact." She smiled at Douglas.

"I wish you could have spent a few days with us Frances. But there will be other times, I am sure," van Yssen said. "In these circumstances it is customary to wish the woman well and to congratulate the man. I think Douglas is an extremely fortunate young man. We really could not have wished for him to have anyone more fetching than you."

Douglas put his arm around Frances' shoulder.

"I feel we should offer you something, Frances, perhaps some tea?"

"Golly, we have just had breakfast, perhaps we should just stretch our legs. There is not much time left before the train leaves. I have always had an irrational fear of being left behind."

The conductor came past. "Please board now, the train is leaving. We have some time to make up."

Frances hurriedly said goodbye to the van Yssens and Douglas helped her onto the train. He followed her onto the landing and kissed her goodbye. The train started moving and he had to jump onto the platform. Frances waved with a small white handkerchief and waved and waved it until it became a flickering white butterfly that accompanied the train and danced in its swirling pale grey steam until it disappeared.

The station was silent except for the squeaking wheel of the consumptive porter's barrow. The car's transmission whined and the engine hummed while they tried to find something appropriate to say. "It is so good to have you back at home," his mother said. "I nearly forgot to mention, Garnett telephoned, he wants you to ring him. We'll have some tea and some chocolate cake I made yesterday, and then I want to hear all your news."

Church bells rang in the distance and the autumn poplar trees near the river swayed in the wind that announced a change in weather.

"I'll give him a tinkle this evening."

◆

Chapter Twenty

Sunday 20 March 1927

A WESTERLY BREEZE drifted through the van Yssens' house as they sat in fading light having their Sunday evening supper. The telephone rang.

"It must be Frances," Douglas said enthusiastically, "I'll get it."

"This is Douglas speaking."

"You've got a special voice, hey?" Garnett said, "When you think it's your fiancée."

"Garnie! I was going to give you a ring! How are you? I must come and see you, and tell you about it, and also my visit to Dr Roux."

"When shall we get together?"

"I'll come and see you tomorrow evening if it suits you."

"I would rather come over to you, if that's alright? It's a bit crowded here at home; my aunt and her two children have arrived out of the blue. Let's say about half past seven?"

"That was dear old Garnie."

"He is a good friend to you," his father said.

"I am sure Roux would have phoned him by now. He wants to hear all my news. He's coming over tomorrow evening."

"The way you young people use the telephone! You'll soon stop writing letters at this rate," his father commented.

They had tea on the veranda in the scent of flowers mixed with the smells of astringent tannins of drying peach and walnut leaves and a faint fermenting odour of fruit that had fallen from the trees and vine trellis. Van Yssen looked at Douglas' profile, his shining eyes, the stubble that had formed on his face. How strong he had become. He would soon enjoy a woman of his own. He looked up at the heavens, dense with stars. A dog barked in the distance. The leaves of the trees rustled as a puff of warm air moved through the garden. A shooting star streaked across the sky and he made a wish: that their good fortune would continue, and that he might celebrate Douglas' homecoming with his wife, if it was not too much of an imposition.

The telephone rang. Douglas went to answer it.

"That was quick," his father said.

"It is for ma, it's Mrs Hops."

It was nearly eight thirty before Frances called. It had been very hot in the Karroo, she said. The telephone had been in constant use. She was feeling nervous about classes tomorrow. He listened to her beautiful voice, told her what a pleasant evening it was and how pleased his parents were to have him back at home. Garnett was coming to see him tomorrow evening. He could see that his mother was desperate to ask him everything. It would have to wait until after school tomorrow when the two of them were alone – his father was going to the Swellendam district for a few days. He told her how much he loved her. The thought that she was alone had occupied his thoughts all day and his concern for her made him realise how much his love for her was growing.

Monday 21 March 1927

Van Yssen left very early for Swellendam. He was happy and relaxed. He headed south, for the distant blue-grey mountains. He smelt the intimate sour smell of his wife on his hairy hands. He had slept well against her soft body. He had had a happy dream of Madame Jacquard's buttocks moving about in her floral dress. Two nights away is a long time. Anneke gave herself to him, almost as though she enjoyed it. They had sinned on the train and although he expected to be punished for that, nothing had happened. Perhaps because he had been so repentant afterwards. He was very grateful. Yet it would be imprudent to become too complacent and think that he had been let off the hook completely because no one knew how or when God's punishment would be delivered. Rather than to tempt fate he pushed his adulterous images of Madame Jacquard from his mind. He stopped short of saying a prayer. Stoffel was in the back seat of the car. It was always a problem to find him a place to stay.

Douglas and his mother were outside when Garnett arrived. He had completed his evening hospital round. He walked up the garden path in unnatural orange evening light that made his cream linen suit luminous, and blackened his navy blue silk tie with white polka dots. He had rehearsed what to say. Now that the time had arrived, his nerve threatened to fail. He was desperate to put it off, but he dared not. It would have been better for Roux to break the news.

"You look strained and tired, Garnett." Mrs van Yssen frowned. "What can I get you? Some tea? Something to eat? My husband is away."

"Tea would be nice thank you, Mrs van Yssen, I have had supper." Garnett observed her as she walked down the passage to the kitchen. She must have been very attractive when she was young. He turned to Douglas. "I must talk to you alone."

"Yes, I understand, it would be better if we could… I'll suggest that we go for a stroll."

Douglas carried the tea tray to the veranda. "When we've had our tea, Ma I think I'll take Garnett for a walk. He'll sleep better after that. One does not sleep well when one is over-tired."

Mrs van Yssen watched her son and his friend as they walked down the garden path to the front gate in the pittosporum hedge. The Teacher and the Doctor. She saw them again as small boys, barefoot in their khaki shorts, feet full of mud from playing in the river, exhausted and hungry. Douglas was taller and quiet. Garnett was always so jolly – sporting and active, not given to schoolwork. Douglas was bookish. Afternoons spent on the oil-stained wooden floorboards of Uncle Charlie's bicycle shop. Now they were men. Their bones had become robust, their tissues hard.

"Garnie, I must tell you about my engagement. It just suddenly happened, there on Camps Bay beach. I hadn't planned it. And now, all of a sudden things feel settled, the future has meaning and clarity, I have purpose. Frances and I discussed the possibility of doing my Doctorate, and perhaps getting a position at the university. The Judge was more than decent when I asked him for Frances' hand. In fact, he was quite warm towards me, if you can credit that. We had a wonderful dinner at Frances' house on Friday evening. Sir Malcolm Searle was there, and so were Florrie Cairncross and Chris Borcherds, Florrie's fiancé. Our formal engagement will be in Cape Town during the June holidays. I imagine it will be quite an affair, and as I said, I would be so glad if you could see your way clear to be there. It would mean a lot to me."

"She's a remarkable catch."

"We had a lovely journey from Cape Town. We sat and just talked and talked about all sorts of things, about the future, about having children, if you can believe that, even what we would call our son. To think how scared I was of proposing to her. You must have been aware of my cowardly misgivings when we were at Plettenberg Bay. My lack of resolution at that time. I must have been insufferable. Now everything is different. And to crown matters Dr Roux indicated that my hearing is not going to be a problem. I don't mind admitting to you that I was a little worried at times, especially when I started having a slight ringing in the other ear, which I did not mention to him. I am glad I did not bother with that now that we know what the cause was."

"Roux telephoned me on Wednesday evening."

"You dog! So he has already confirmed everything, and you did not say anything?"

"What exactly did he say to you?" Garnett asked.

"I can't remember. I was so relieved. He did pretty much what you did, except that he performed more hearing tests, and made notes. Why do you ask?"

"Well, he seems a bit concerned."

"Concerned? Concerned about what? I told him exactly what had happened when I got smacked."

"Roux is very experienced. That's why I suggested that you should go and see him."

"I respect that, but what is there to be concerned about?"

"He is concerned about your family history."

"My parents are fine."

"Yes but evidently your maternal grandfather had a problem. Douglas, I want to be direct with you. After I saw you I learnt that your maternal grandfather suffered from a severe form of deafness. That's why I suggested a second opinion." Garnett stopped and faced Douglas. He could barely see Douglas' features. "Roux is of the opinion that you may be suffering from the same condition as your grandfather. Otosclerosis. All the clinical symptoms are present."

Douglas' one knee began to tremble and he broke out in a sweat. Garnett put his hand on Douglas' sleeve. "In the past there would have been no cure, and complete loss of hearing would have followed, but fortunately, because of the wonderful progress of modern medicine, I am able to hold out the prospect of a cure, and if not a cure then hopefully a way of arresting the progress of the disease."

"What do I do now? I'll have to tell my parents. I'll have to tell Frances." His voice was breaking. "What did you say it is called?"

"Otosclerosis."

"How does it work? I mean what is it?"

"For reasons we do not fully understand, the little bones in the middle ear, the hammer, anvil and stirrup fuse; become joined together, or calcify. When that happens, instead of sound vibrations being transmitted from the eardrum along the little bones to the fenestra rotunda, the round window, and from there to the inner ear and ultimately to the audio nerve and to the brain, the vibrations are blocked. As a result nothing reaches the inner ear."

"How can he be sure that it is otosclerosis? Shouldn't we have another opinion? Perhaps I could just have a mild form."

"He has had many years of clinical experience – he would not have made such a diagnosis, especially such an important one, unless he was absolutely sure of himself."

Douglas staggered. He held his head and took out his handkerchief and mopped his forehead.

Garnett took his arm. "Let's go back."

"What should I say to my mother? I feel so sorry for her. She'll take it badly and my father is away."

"If you like, I'll speak to her."

"I would appreciate that."

Mrs van Yssen was still on the veranda next to the cold cups and empty teapot. "You're back so soon, it could not have been much more than a stroll.

"We have a problem, Ma," Douglas announced. "Garnett would like to speak to you."

"I am really very sorry to have to tell you this Mrs van Yssen, but there is a problem with Douglas' hearing."

"But we were told that all is fine!"

"Douglas may have formed an incorrect conclusion."

"A wrong conclusion? How on earth is that possible?"

"Dr Roux did not inform Douglas of his diagnosis, and that, coupled with Douglas' explanation of the smack that he had on his ear when he was in junior school may have created an impression that Dr Roux took that as the reason for his hearing problem. It is possible that Douglas suffers from the same condition as your father did."

"Oh my goodness! Oh my goodness, dear Lord. How do you know about my father? You never even knew him!"

"Douglas mentioned to Dr Roux that his grandfather had a hearing problem."

"My father was completely deaf, completely. You could fire a rifle next to his head and he would not hear a thing."

"I was very concerned after I examined Douglas, Mrs van Yssen, and sought the opinion of an older colleague. He was somewhat familiar with the family history."

"Diemont. We had better not mention that to my husband, he could regard it as a breach of confidentiality. He is very correct and sensitive about such things. Oh my goodness."

She began to sob quietly. "Just when I believed that everything was going so well, and he is engaged to be married. What shall we do? What will become of us?"

Douglas put his arm around her heaving shoulders. "All is not lost Ma. Garnett says there is now a cure for my kind of problem."

"A cure?" She asked as she sniffed, and dabbed her eyes with a small handkerchief that had tiny blue and pink flowers embroidered on it.

"Dr Roux mentioned to me, and I had seen reports in the medical literature, that a Dr Yearsley in England has had considerable success in treating people with otosclerosis – that's what we call the condition that Douglas has – by using special electrical apparatus. Yearsley has been treating such cases since 1925 and from all accounts he has had quite remarkable results. The only problem is that Douglas will have to go to England for the treatment; it is not available here."

"So you see Ma, all is well that ends well."

"Praise the Lord." She embraced Garnett. "Thank you for being such a good friend and taking such excellent care of Douglas. Albert will be back on Wednesday afternoon. I would be glad if you could explain everything to him. We will tell him when he gets back, but if you could please, please, have supper with us on Wednesday, just to reassure him. And if there are any questions, he has a very analytical mind, you could reassure him. He will be very upset."

"I shall most certainly have supper with you on Wednesday, but I think I should get going now. I have a long day ahead of me tomorrow, starting with an operation early to morrow morning."

"I'll come with you to the car," Douglas suggested.

"Stay with your mother, I'll be fine. Let's have hope, at least there is the prospect of relief. Goodnight Mrs van Yssen." He patted Douglas' shoulder. "Try to get some rest. You'll be fine again one of these days, Douglas."

They watched Garnett shut the garden gate. The lights of his car came on. Douglas put the teacups onto the tray and carried it to the kitchen. When he returned to the veranda his mother was still there. A hopeless shudder ran through her as she sighed. Together they looked out into the darkness. She turned and embraced him and pressed herself against him. "I still have some things to prepare for tomorrow, Ma. I have locked the back door. You go to bed now. I will lock the front door." She took his head in her hands and drew it towards her to kiss him on the forehead. He followed her into the house. She seemed to have shrunk and tried to conceal her eyes from him to spare him her grief.

Mrs van Yssen sat on the edge of her bed with her head in her hands. After some time she unbuttoned the front of her dress. She got up as if in a trance and undressed herself. How would she break the news to Albert? The thought of him made her avert her eyes from her body while she put on her nightdress. She washed her face in the basin on the washstand and applied night cream to her face. When she saw her red eyes in the mirror contrasted against the white cream she started crying again. She made sure the bedroom door was properly shut. She wet a facecloth and wiped her nether regions. She was still tender from the night before. Earlier while she sat on the veranda, before she heard the news, her sensitive pubis had reminded her with affection of Albert's vigorous pleasure. She had feared that Douglas might hear them, and the thought that she could have wished that he would not hear startled her and filled her with revulsion of any intimacy. As she knelt to pray at the side of her bed, her right knee came to rest painfully on a small pebble, presumably carried in by a shoe. Instead of removing it she decided, for the sake of penance, to suffer as much exquisite pain as possible and pressed her knee down harder. Dear Lord, please hear the prayer of your most humble servant. Please be with Douglas. Please heal him. Forgive my sins and what I have done to deserve this punishment. I know you are a forgiving Father who understands the love and concern of a mother better than anyone. Please help my son so that he will not suffer as my father did. He has inherited his affliction through me. Please be with Albert in the difficult days that lie ahead, and give him wisdom that will bring peace and understanding. I am prepared to make any sacrifice that you may ask and to serve you in any way possible, and I will do so without condition. May you be blessed dear God. Please bless Frances and her parents. Amen. Had she said enough to God? He was distant. Had He forsaken her? Her clarity of perception was gone. Uncertainty assailed her. That which had been precious, the porcelain in their living room, the Tinus de Jongh painting in the passage, her new shoes that had received a scuff mark the first day she wore them, all of that now had no value.

When she got up from her prayer there was blood on her nightdress where her knee had been. She lifted her dress and washed the blood off with cold water from her art deco porcelain jug. She looked at the St Joseph's lilies on her chest of drawers, which Madame Jacquard had grown from bulbs brought from Paris. In the bright light of that afternoon they had flaunted their delicate beauty; their shining fleshy apple green stigmas, their cadmium yellow powdered stamens trembled exquisitely inside pale jade sanctuaries formed by their fluted trumpets. The intricate features of the flowers that had inspired her then, and lifted her thoughts as she contemplated the future, now had no meaning.

She picked up her Bible. The brown leather bookmark, which Albert had made for her, protruded from the gilded edges of the pages. She opened it at the bookmark. Psalm One Hundred and Twenty One. 'I will lift up mine eyes unto the hills, from whence cometh my help.'

Douglas lay on his bed, still fully clothed, condemned to deafness. He put his index fingers into his ears and pressed them inwards until the passages hurt. He could hear and feel only the movements of his fingers in his ears. That is what it would be like, only worse because he would then not be able to hear even the movements of his fingers. He would not be able to hear Frances' voice again, nor the sound of the rustling reeds and the dry leaves of the autumn trees near the river. Mouths would mock him without sound. He looked at the papers on his desk. What point is there in preparing? At least there was hope. He got up and sat down at his table. He paged through his history textbook, picked up his *Algemeene Geschiedenis door* J W Pik and began to make notes. *De Tijd van Napoleon*; *de Roemrijke Tijd der Napoleontische Heerschappij 1799 – 1807*. The glorious period of Napoleonic Rule. Napoleon's coup d'etat, the Constitution of Sieyes, the System of Notabilites, *het Rijksbestuur*. Good stuff. Thank goodness for the miracles of modern medicine.

Anneke turned off her light and opened her bedroom door to permit air to circulate. Light still showed under Douglas' door. She clasped her hands and sobbed quietly.

She slept fitfully. She was visited frequently during the night by sensations of dreadful despair. At three o'clock, the hour when people ebb away from this world, she felt as though her soul was being crushed. Why could she not bring herself to believe that the treatment would be successful? What had happened to her faith? She felt as though she was being pressed into a dark place, assailed by evil writhing forms, sinking into hopelessness. Why could she not, as she had done as a child, kneeling at her bed with her fair plaits resting on her small shoulders, simply pray and ask God to heal her son? She had no doubt then. The unlapsed innocence that she had brought with her when she arrived in this world, the formless innocence that had connected her to God, had turned into worldliness. She wept bitterly in the shadow of a gigantic image of Albert. She needed to relieve herself, and squatted over her porcelain chamber pot. When she heard her urine ringing musically against the side of the pot the sound enchanted her, and brought back meaning. The sky was becoming lighter.

She went to the kitchen to boil water for the morning coffee; unlocked the back door for Betta. While the coffee percolated she watched as hot water sputtered into the bath. She lay and watched the vapour rising from the surface. She observed her body without remorse.

Douglas bounced into the dining room. She was having her coffee, contemplating how to respond to him. "Hello Ma!" He walked over to her and kissed her on her forehead. "You look terribly tired. When is dad coming back?"

"He'll be here tomorrow afternoon."

"I'd better eat, and get going. There is a special staff meeting this morning. Wonder what Dr Archer has in mind."

Douglas ate enthusiastically. "Don't fret Ma. I have a good feeling about things. Thank goodness for modern medicine. I'll save every penny of my salary to help to pay for the treatment. Perhaps my ears will clear up of their own accord. I'll write to Frances this afternoon. It's premature to don the sackcloth and ashes. Strange as it may sound, in a sense it is a relief to me to know what I am up against. If I know what the problem is I can fight it." He munched his marmalade toast happily and sipped coffee in between mouthfuls. "I am sorry to leave you on your own. I can see that you are upset, but I am going to have to trot."

"Take care of yourself. I love you very much, my boy."

He kissed her on the side of her head, collected his books and papers and fetched his bicycle at the back of the house.

When she had had her breakfast Mrs van Yssen took a broad rimmed straw hat from the hat stand in the passage, collected a basket from the pantry and picked some of the last remaining roses. She was standing in contemplation, trying to recapture the sense of comfort that she had got from the flowers in her room, searching for a sign, when she was distracted by a reflection in the glass of the living room window. Why was the postman so early? Madame Jacquard stood at the garden gate with a small bunch of violets in her hand.

"Last night I could not sleep and thought of you, Anneke. I was troubled, for some reason, and now I find you here with eyes that tell me why. I think we should sit down and have some coffee. Here, I have brought these for you." Mrs van Yssen smelt the purple scent of the violets and started sobbing softly. Madame Jacquard took her by the arm and walked with her to the veranda. "You sit here Anneke, I will tell Betta to make fresh coffee."

"I must go and get a handkerchief, so I'll arrange for the coffee. You stay here. I am pleased that you have come to see me. Thank you so much for the violets Guillemette, I shall put them in water."

Mrs van Yssen poured their coffee.

"Please tell me why you are so sad?" Madame Jacquard asked.

"It is my son. Douglas has a problem with his hearing, his ears."

"But surely that will pass?"

"He is suffering from the same condition as my father. I think I have passed my father's deafness on to my son."

"Why do you think that it is the same thing?"

"He went to see Garnett Nel, who sent him to see a specialist in Cape Town. The specialist has confirmed the worst fears that we could possibly have had."

"Was your father's deafness a bad one?"

"The worst you could possibly imagine. He was as deaf as a doornail."

"As deaf as what?"

"Oh it is just an expression that we have. A doornail. We have an expression that says that when you are completely deaf you can hear as little as a doornail can hear. Yes he was completely deaf. And now it has come to this. Garnett Nel visited us last night and broke the news to us. It was terrible. Douglas was white with shock, and trembling. In confidence I must tell you that he has just become privately engaged to the most lovely girl imaginable – the daughter of an eminent judge in Cape Town. I mentioned her to you. She and Douglas were at university together. She is teaching at Graaff Reinet." Anneke started crying again. She sobbed softly. "Albert is not here, he has gone to Swellendam. I cannot imagine what his reaction will be when he hears the news. He always scorned my father's deafness – he regarded it as a flaw; like a character flaw, as though my father was a cripple. And now his son, whom he worships, has inherited my father's deafness." She dabbed her eyes with her handkerchief, and loudly blew her streaming nose. "Oh my goodness, oh my goodness. We are being punished. God is punishing us."

"When will Albert be back?"

"Tomorrow afternoon. I will have to tell him. Garnett will come and speak to Albert."

"Is there no cure? No treatment?"

"Garnett told us that that there is a Doctor in London who is able to treat Douglas."

"But that is good news. You should have courage from that. The cloud has a silver lining."

"Oh I hope so, I hope so. But he will have to go to England for the treatment."

"Then send the girl along with him. Let them get married now."

"We could not do that."

"Why not?"

"It would seem improper. They are only privately engaged now. It would be the wrong reason to get married so suddenly. I think Douglas will only go for treatment next year."

"Why wait so long?"

"It all has to be planned. He cannot resign from his teaching post just like that. Arrangements have to be made. His passage will have to be booked, and accommodation arranged in London."

"How long does the treatment take?"

"I have no idea. Poor Douglas, he even said this morning before he left for school that he would save his pennies to pay for the treatment." Anneke started crying again. "Albert was in such a good humour when he left yesterday morning. There he is in Swellendam, completely unaware of our plight. I am so glad that you have come to see me, Guillemette. I cannot imagine what Albert's reaction is going to be. It is sometimes so difficult for me to understand what he is thinking. He has such a great mind; I am not his equal. He does not show emotion. Things are either right or wrong; there is no in-between. Everything must be perfect. He does not tolerate blemishes very well: a dent in the furniture, or a scratch, or a damaged page in a book. If something is damaged he wants to get rid of it. He will say God is punishing us. I think he feels guilty because of what we did on the train. He thinks we sinned; I can tell from the way he has behaved since that time."

"When did Douglas' problem start?"

"He has complained of his one ear for more that a year."

"Then how could this be punishment for what you did if the deafness started before?"

"How do we know how God works? He could have anticipated that we would sin."

"I think you are punishing yourself, no one else is punishing you."

"I have prayed and prayed for forgiveness, but the strange thing is that I do not really feel guilty for what we did. I feel guilty because I do not feel guilty. And when I remember how close we were, how much I loved Albert at that moment. It was more beautiful than I could ever describe. That beauty takes away the feeling of guilt that I try to have."

"Do you say this thing because you are trying to be nice to me because I told you what to do on the train? So that I would not regret what I suggested?"

"No, no not at all. You gave me good advice. I shall never forget the moment when our love was consummated. Instead of perverting my feelings it has improved them and made me see the beauty of God's creation more clearly. Albert now appears to me – and I love him very much believe me – at times more attractive, and at the same time he appears more formidable. He is a Calvinist at heart, for all his protestations that he holds liberal ideas about religious doctrine."

"Superstitions are hard to abandon."

"How do you mean?"

"People mix up superstition with religion. If they have enough superstitions they think they are religious. Also, I do not know why we have to mix up what is perfectly natural with religion. Religion has perverted, to use your word, what is natural and beautiful into something that people feel guilty about. We let the intellect get too much in the way of these things. The priests make the rules for other people while they themselves do not participate. You will have to be strong Anneke. You and Albert should not become divided. All three of you should together seek a solution. Albert will look around for something to blame, or someone to blame. Perhaps, who knows, there is no one to blame. Human beings find it hard to accept life for what it is. I know because I have had very difficult times. We think too much of cause and effect. It is convenient to think like that when things are going well. It is easy to think when things are going well that we are being rewarded for being good children, but the real test comes when things go wrong. The test is how well we can deal with adversity. And coming back to the idea of being punished, if God is our Father, and we are his children, think of your own son, how badly must your own son sin against you for you as his parent to make one of his children deaf? If you cannot bring yourself to do that, do you think that the God who has made everything could do that to his children? There must be a better explanation. To blame yourself now will not help."

"Albert did not like my father very much. He will blame him, and see me as the one who passed on the illness." She started crying again. "Poor Douglas and he is so brilliant."

"That is indeed a blessing. He could get a wonderful research job, or work as a critic or an editor. He could write history books. But we are being too pessimistic. We must put first things first. First all our energy must be concentrated on the treatment. For all we know it will be a great success and in months from now we will laugh cheerfully about how miserable we were. Albert will be happy and a normal man again. Viola! My best advice to you, when you tell Albert what has happened, is to concentrate on the solution and not on the problem. Tell him how fortunate you are that the problem has occurred at a time when there have been great scientific advances. Emphasise that there is a solution. Emphasise that there is hope and through science God has provided a solution. If you have the correct attitude Douglas will also benefit. If he believes he can be healed it will make it more possible."

Anneke smiled through her tears. "God has answered my prayers. He has sent you to me. Bless you Guillemette, thank you so much. I must go and get another handkerchief, and wash my face. I feel better already."

"Put some cold water on your eyes, and do it many times today so that Albert will not see your condition. It will give your emotions away. I should go home now. I am busy with a painting that I am enjoying very much. I must finish it before I go to Mossel Bay."

They walked to the garden gate. Madame Jacquard put her hand on Anneke's arm. "Come and visit me whenever you feel the need. And have courage."

Anneke sat with the *Oudtshoorn Courant* in her hands, not reading, contemplating what to say to Albert, when she heard Douglas' bicycle in the driveway.

"Hello my boy. Have you had a successful day?"

"Yes, I have been fine, thank you. The staff meeting was quite interesting.

I'll tell you about it later, but right now I am famished." He smiled through his sadness.

"Put your things away, I will get your lunch from the oven."

"Thanks Ma."

She watched him eat. The bobotie was hot and when he put the first fork-full into his mouth he had to hold his mouth open and breath in and out quickly to cool the food.

"Wow! I nearly burnt my mouth. It's very good. I like the pickle. Yellow peaches are always the best," he said in between mouthfuls. "Have you had a nice day? You seemed pretty upset when I left this morning."

"Yes, I am fine. Madame Jacquard came to visit me."

"You did not mention that she was coming."

"It was unexpected. She is like that. Besides she had no one to send with a visiting card. She avoids convention. She brought me some lovely violets. We had coffee together."

"What is her news? I did mention to you the other day that I saw her and she told me that she was going to Mossel Bay?"

"She said so. She did not have much news. She is intuitive. She lives in her world of ideas. She is not given to gossip. I have been thinking about your hearing. I thought about it most of the night. I am beginning to see things in better perspective. You yourself said this morning that it is not a time for sackcloth and ashes, and I agree with you. We are fortunate that your problem has occurred at a time when it is possible to treat your condition. All our energy should now be concentrated on sending you to London, the sooner the better. We should go ahead with your engagement, as planned, in June and you should leave soon afterwards directly from Cape Town. It is always better to treat medical conditions as soon as possible. Dr Roux's diagnosis will come as a shock to your father, as indeed it was to you, and I fear that his reaction will be severe. You know him as well as I do. He does not handle bad news well, so I think what we should do is to emphasise the good news, the treatment, and that the doctor in London has had considerable success."

"I said I would write to Frances this afternoon. I agree that we should remain optimistic. I sometimes have dark thoughts, but then I suppose we all do. It must be terrible to be deaf. You have never spoken much about grandfather. When did he become deaf?"

"By the time that he was thirty he could no longer hear."

"How deaf was he."

"Completely."

"And his father?"

"He was fine."

"And other family members before him?"

"I think there was some hearing trouble, but it was quite common in those days. They could not treat deafness as they can today."

"Do you think I could have inherited my condition?"

"I am not qualified to say. We should ask Garnett, or Dr Roux."

"Roux asked me at some length about my family history. I wonder whether he suspected something."

"I think doctors do that as a matter of routine."

"I might stroll over to see Garnett this evening. It was such a shock to me last night that I did not hear half of what he was saying. It would be better to know more before Dad gets home."

Tuesday 22 March 1927

Dearly Beloved Frances

Let me begin by saying, as I said on the telephone on Sunday evening, that I am missing you more than words can ever express. My thoughts were with you from the moment that I saw your beautiful face framed in the window of the train drawing away from me as your pale arm gracefully waved goodbye. I cannot wait for the time when we will be together constantly.

I received quite a shock last evening when Garnett visited me and my mother – my father is away at Swellendam doing a survey. Contrary to the happy conclusion that I had drawn that my problem with my ear was merely the result of the unfortunate incident with the teacher when I was small, Garnett informed me that Dr Roux had telephoned him from Cape Town to tell him that I am suffering from a potentially more serious condition. Nevertheless the good news is that the condition is treatable.

A doctor in London has had considerable success using special equipment to treat the condition. The treatment is not available in the Union, so I shall have to go to London. My mother feels that I should go there sooner rather than later, possibly in the second half of the year. How Dr Archer will respond I cannot tell. We will just have to find a way. Garnett is coming over tomorrow evening to have supper with us and to discuss the way forward. I am afraid my mother has taken the news rather badly and I fear that my father will be most upset when he discovers what has transpired. No doubt my mother's reaction has been inflated by the fact that her father suffered from a similar condition and I sense that she feels she may have passed a flaw on to me. It is all very sad to say the least but I refuse to feel sorry for myself. My first concern is for those who are dear to me. You now come first.

It disturbs me that my problem should bring unhappiness to others. I cannot imagine what my father will say when we break the news to him. I expect that my mother will do that.

I am most hopeful that my condition will be treated successfully and would like to suggest that the arrangements for our engagement should go ahead as planned. I shall make enquiries to determine when passages will be available from Cape Town so that I could leave for England directly afterwards. I have asked Garnett to come to our engagement and he has agreed. He likes you very much. Of course everything rests on the assumption that Dr Yearsley will see his way clear to treat me.

I feel as though the comfort and certainty that I had begun to enjoy as a result of our relationship have received a severe jolt, and I have to confess that I feel quite unsettled. Travelling overseas on my own will be like staggering blindfolded into the unknown.

No doubt my uncertainty stems from the reason for going. If the reason had been different – like going on holiday with you – I would not experience such a cheerless oppression of spirit, and disheartenment. All around me is clothed in dull grey worsted foreboding.

You are the only true meaning I have. You give me hope that I shall survive this disappointment. I shall write to you again in the next day or two, hopefully in a better frame of mind.

With all my everlasting love,
Douglas.

Wednesday 23 March 1927

Mrs van Yssen was splashing cold water on her eyes when she heard her husband's car arriving. She listened for the sounds that would predict his frame of mind. He whistled cheerfully as he approached the house while Stoffel unpacked the land surveying equipment and took the luggage from the car. She heard the hinges of the fly screen at the back door squealing as he entered the kitchen. She went to meet him.

"You're back early," She said wringing her hands. "It is good to have you back." She kissed him on his cheek.

"Goodness wife, you could do better than that!" He kissed her on her mouth. "I finished my work sooner than anticipated. Some coffee would be welcome. Where's Douglas? His bicycle is not here."

"He's gone to Bowles to buy writing paper. He wrote to Frances yesterday."

"I'll wash my hands. Put a cup ready for Douglas so that we can all have coffee together. And talking about dining, I thought, on the way back, that we should go and have dinner at the Queens Hotel this evening to celebrate Douglas' engagement."

"I have asked Garnett to have supper with us this evening."

"Then he could come with us to the Queens."

"I have already prepared food."

"We can have that tomorrow evening."

"Albert there is something that I must discuss with you."

"Nothing can be so important that it cannot wait. I have been gone since Monday and I want us to have a special occasion."

"There is a reason why Garnett is coming here this evening."

"What reason?"

"Dr Roux telephoned Garnett and has recommended that Douglas should have – as a precaution – treatment for his hearing."

He frowned and searched her eyes for meaning. "Treatment? What kind of treatment, for what?"

"It is just something that we have to be practical about, my dear. While you wash your hands I will get your coffee ready and Douglas should be home any minute. Let us all sit down and discuss what has to be discussed."

Douglas found his father's car in the garage when he returned. He stood his bicycle against the wall of the house and went through the front door. The bathroom door was closed and he proceeded to the kitchen.

"Hello Douglas," his mother said with a brave smile. "Your father has just got back. I have not really had a chance to speak to him. I just mentioned that Dr Roux has recommended treatment. I stressed the precautionary aspect. Dad suggested that we have dinner at the Queens Hotel this evening to celebrate your engagement, before I could mention Dr Roux. We are going to have coffee together in the dining room."

"So my boy, how are you?" Douglas heard his father's loud voice behind him. "What's this I hear?"

"Here Mother, let me take the tray. How was your visit to Swellendam Dad?"

"It was unbearably hot. You think Oudtshoorn can get hot. But there you also have humidity. Being out in the sun did not help. How did you come to speak to Garnett?"

"I wanted to go and visit him on Monday evening, and he said he would rather come here. They have visitors."

"This coffee is nice. What did he say?"

"He said it would be better if he visited me after his hospital round."

"No, I mean about your hearing?"

Douglas looked at his mother to see whether she wished to speak.

"Well, which one of you is going to tell me what is going on?"

"What he said Dad, is that Dr Roux had telephoned to say that I am suffering from a condition known as otosclerosis. In the past this could eventually have led to permanent deafness, but it is now possible to treat the condition successfully."

Van Yssen stared at the reflection of the ceiling that floated on the surface of his black coffee. The clock ticked loudly in the corner. Anneke could hear her husband's breathing. Douglas' chair creaked. The roof made contracting sounds. Rose petals lay in their own images on the gleaming surface of the table. The mechanism of the clock whirred as it prepared itself to strike the half hour. Outer edges of a small whirlwind scattered early autumn leaves in the garden.

"Treatment. What kind of treatment?"

"Garnett only told us on Monday evening Dad. We don't know yet. That's why we suggested that Garnett should come over and discuss it with all three of us."

"I trust that you are not keeping anything from me."

"Why would we do such a thing Albert, at this time?"

"Perhaps to spare my feelings. Has it anything to do with the blow on your ear?"

"Not as far as I can gather."

"Garnett will be here at seven," Mrs van Yssen said. "Let us wait for him to tell us more."

"Well, well, what can I say? In the circumstances it will be better to stay at home."

"Would you like some more coffee Albert?"

"No thank you." Van Yssen looked up at the ceiling. His hands were numb. It must be from handling the theodolite, or the corrugations through the steering wheel. He was still disorientated. His anticipation of a celebratory occasion had made his expectations so powerful that it was difficult to receive other ideas. "When did you say Garnett would be here?"

"Seven o'clock."

"I'm sure I'll be all right Dad."

Van Yssen looked at his wife.

"I asked Betta to stay. I had better go and see to the supper."

Douglas observed the falling leaves outside. His father looked at his profile, the chiselled aquiline nose, intelligent eyes, afternoon stubble, his white scalp showing through the brush-cut hair. Douglas turned his head towards his father. Van Yssen looked the other way. "It is getting cooler now, I think I'll go for a walk, and then have a bath before Garnett arrives. Would you like to come along Douglas?"

"The matrics are writing a test tomorrow and I still have some preparation to do, if you don't mind, Dad."

"As you wish."

"I do have to carry on with my work, Dad."

Van Yssen gathered his hat and walking stick and strode into the late afternoon not knowing quite in which direction to go. Go down to the river. He had walked past the weeping willow trees next to the river, with his father, the day after his baby sister died. His father's eyes were red with grief, staring straight ahead. He walked proudly erect, his hands behind his back. We must be strong Albert, for your mother's sake. He put his hand on Albert's bony little shoulder. From the open doorway, in his knickerbockers and brown boots, his cap in his hand, peering past a screen, he had observed his father and mother sitting next to his sister's bed where she lay pale. The Doctor in his dark suit sat resigned at the foot of her bed. Open the curtains please, she had said in a voice unnaturally mature, it is getting darker in here. His father looked out of the window across the brightly sunlit garden of their stone farmhouse and at the tiny hands folded on her tummy. She sighed and stopped breathing. His father's head dropped. Albert's eyes filled with tears as they had done many times. It was becoming darker now near the river. The next day they put on her favourite smocked dress before they buried her. He pushed the images away so that he could go home to his people.

"Hello Albert!"

He started. It was Denis Kuys. "Hello Denis, you're a long way from home."

"I saw you leaving your house. It was not easy to catch up with you. How are you?"

"I'm fine thank you, I have just returned from Swellendam – division of land in terms of a will. And how are you doing?"

"Fine, fine, we should play tennis sometime."

"That would be nice."

"You don't seem yourself Albert?"

"Oh, I've just had a tiring trip."

"I'll walk back with you."

Van Yssen lay in his bath. In the same insidious way that blight had crept into his father's best wheat crop, doubt crept into his mind and began to corrupt the certainty and hope that he had felt earlier. He tried to drive away the apprehension that threatened him. He washed his hair. He reminded himself again of his father's strength in the presence of his mother's dignified grief. At least Douglas was alive, and there was hope that his condition could be treated. He submerged his head to get the soap out of his hair.

Douglas was still in his room when Garnett arrived. Garnett was dressed casually in grey flannels, cream viyella shirt and a Trinity College blue blazer. His mother had picked chrysanthemums for Mrs van Yssen. He knocked. Van Yssen's tall figure appeared in the passage. "I think I should put a light on, eh Garnett? Good evening. What on earth do you have there?"

"Good evening Mr van Yssen. Flowers for Mrs van Yssen, from my mother."

"Flowers, how good of her. Let us sit outside. I'll get my wife to put the flowers in some water. Please thank your mother. Douglas will be with us presently."

A cricket started to chirp. Garnett listened for other sounds. In the distance frogs were beginning to croak and cluck. The members of the symphony orchestra were tuning their instruments. He heard footsteps on the passage floor, and a knock on what was presumably Douglas's door.

Mrs van Yssen came towards him and shook his hand. "Thank you so much for the flowers, and thank your dear mother."

"The food will be ready in a trifle," Mrs van Yssen announced.

"We'll chat while we wait. Do sit down Garnett. I hope you are hungry," van Yssen suggested.

"Hello Garnie, it was nice of you to come."

Van Yssen cleared his throat. "So what is this that I hear about Douglas' hearing, Garnett?"

"Dr Roux telephoned me from Cape Town. He is of the opinion that Douglas may be suffering from a condition known as otosclerosis."

"May be suffering, or is suffering?"

"Some conditions are difficult to diagnose, Mr van Yssen, and otosclerosis is one of those. We have to rely on clinical symptoms and family history. I questioned Roux rather closely. He is certain of his diagnosis. He is a very experienced capable man, with a huge reputation. He is unlikely to pronounce without being confident that his diagnosis is correct – especially in a case like this."

"Why do you say 'in a case like this'?"

"Well I mean otosclerosis is a serious matter, and to treat it will require going to London, so he'll make sure that he is right."

"Let us go back to the beginning. Explain to us precisely what otosclerosis is."

"Supper is ready," Mrs van Yssen announced. "We can continue to talk at table. I would also like to hear what Garnett has to say."

"You sit here, Garnett, next to me," van Yssen said. "Shall we say grace?" They shut their eyes and bowed their heads. "For what we are about to receive, Lord may we be truly thankful. Please be with our family and our friend, and please bestow your loving mercy on Douglas. Amen."

"I have prepared some onion soup from a recipe that Madame Jacquard gave me, I hope you will enjoy it, it is something different." Mrs van Yssen rang the bell. Garnett unfolded his napkin."

"Evening Doctor," Betta said as she carried in the soup tureen.

"Good evening Betta, I hope you are well?" Garnett replied.

"Very well thank you, Doctor." She put the tray down on a side table and placed the tureen in front of van Yssen.

"Anneke, Garnett was just beginning to explain to us the nature of Douglas' problem and the implications."

Garnett was careful with the hot grated cheese on the surface of the soup.

"I had some French onion soup at the Helmsley," Douglas said.

"You should have told me, son," his mother said.

"This is so much better. It is excellent."

"Douglas is always so complimentary about my food Garnett, it is so rewarding to cook for him."

"I had some onion soup once in Paris, and this beats it hands down Mrs van Yssen. I was quite interested to learn that the traditional French breakfast used to be soup, and still is in large parts of France, especially among the working classes."

"They're an odd lot," van Yssen said. "Tell my wife what you said about Dr Roux's diagnosis.

"I mentioned that otosclerosis is one of the more difficult things to diagnose, Mrs van Yssen, and I ventured to suggest that Dr Roux would not have expressed a firm opinion unless he was certain of his diagnosis."

"I asked Garnett to explain to us exactly what the condition is," van Yssen said.

"It would be best to draw a diagram." Garnett patted his pockets for a piece of paper and produced a Heynes Mathew invoice. He turned it over, stroked it with the back of his hand to get the creases out, took a pencil from his pocket and started drawing. He commented as he drew, "the pinna, or auricle, outer ear canal, the ear drum, the hammer or malleus, the incus or anvil and then the stirrup or stapes, which by the way, is the smallest bone in the human body and which links to the cochlea from where nerve impulses are transmitted to the brain." Following the parts of his drawing with the tip of his pencil he explained, "What happens is that sound vibrations are received by the eardrum and the vibrating eardrum causes the hammer to vibrate. From there the vibrations are sent along to the other two little bones until they reach the cochlea. In the case of otosclerosis the three bones become fused together, for reasons we do not understand, and because they can then no longer vibrate and send the sound signals to the cochlea impulses cannot reach the brain. What Dr Yearsley's electrophonoid treatment does, and he has had a great deal of success with it, is to gently shake loose the little bones so that they can resume transmission. In some cases the stapes can become attached to the membrane of the fenestra rotunda, which is where it interfaces with the cochlea, and since this is potentially disastrous, it is especially important to loosen the stapes from that membrane. So in some respects it is all rather simple, but effective."

"Eat your soup, Garnett, it is getting cold," van Yssen said. "You explain it well. I grasp the mechanical principles. So what is the next step?"

"Douglas will have to go to London for treatment," Garnett replied.

"Why can it not be done here?" van Yssen asked.

"There is no suitable equipment in the Union."

"Then he'll have to go to London," van Yssen said. "The sooner the better. How will we get in touch with Yearsley?"

"Dr Roux will do that. I will speak to him tomorrow, if you wish."

"I would appreciate that." van Yssen turned to Douglas. "I shall make an appointment to go and see Dr Archer as soon as possible, Son, and inform him of your circumstances.

We are near the end of March now. We have barely two months to make arrangements, and there is your engagement. You could leave from Cape Town. We'll have to see what passages are available, accommodation over there, and all the rest."

"I can't imagine that Dr Archer will be happy to let me go so soon after starting."

"We are giving him nearly a whole term's notice, and then on top of that there are compelling medical reasons. Leave it to me, my boy," van Yssen said. "I think we are all ready for our fish now. Will you ring for Betta, my dear? How much do you know about the treatment, Garnett, the success rate and so forth?"

"Dr Roux tells me that Yearsley has had remarkable success. He has treated a large number of individuals who have suffered from various kinds of deafness; among those were thirteen individuals with otosclerosis, and of those thirteen, ten were treated successfully, two partially successfully and in only one case did the treatment not have an effect. That is pretty good by any measure, I am sure you will agree."

"You are very quiet, Son," van Yssen said.

"You all seem to be going to so much trouble on my behalf, and it is all going to be so expensive. I have hardly started earning."

"Don't be silly Douglas, you're a fine young man with exceptional talent, we need to make sure that you reach your full potential. We cannot permit any setback to get in our way. I have a little nest egg – for emergencies – and I am sure we will manage. It is time for dessert. I must thank you for being so thorough Garnett."

"And I must add my thanks Garnett," Mrs van Yssen said. "The disappointment of hearing of Dr Roux's diagnosis was a great shock to me." She started to cry. "I am so relieved. I was so happy before all this happened."

"Come now Mother, everything will turn out all right. How long will the treatment take Garnie?"

"I am not sure, but I think you should allow yourself about a month in England. If you're going all that way you should give yourself enough time over there." Garnett replied. "It will be a three month trip, three weeks on the ship, a month there and then three weeks passage back – as good as three months. That will take you into the fourth term, so the best that we can hope for is that you will able to start teaching again at the start of next year."

Van Yssen caught his wife's eye while she served dessert of cling peaches and cream. He smiled at her.

Douglas accompanied Garnett to his car.

"I hope you're not hiding anything from me Garnie, or dressing things up to make them look better than they are?"

"I would not do that. Otosclerosis is a serious problem. It is a real blessing that someone has found a way of treating it. That is the good news. He is a man of considerable standing internationally, and he has published his results in the most prestigious journals. That is the best information that is currently available, and we have to pin our hopes on it. That is all that we can do."

"What happens if I am one of the odd cases that does not respond?"

"Give yourself the chance of being treated successfully. We cannot plan for disaster. We dare not lie down now. Have faith my friend. It will turn out well. Have a good night's rest. And by the way, good luck with the history test tomorrow. Your dad will sort Archer out."

The van Yssens performed their ritual ablutions and took turns to undress in the bathroom. They sat on their separate beds, back-to-back, silent, not knowing what to say. She picked up her bible and began to read. She heard his bed creaking as he lay down and arranged himself. "I think I'll turn in. It has been a long day," he said with an exaggerated sigh, his hands behind his head.

He glanced at her. "Oh I do apologise for interrupting. I understand how you feel. It has also been a great blow to me."

"I know that, I knew it would be. I was so concerned about you. It was terrible to be here on my own. And it made me so sad when poor Douglas tried to comfort me."

"I wonder what the Roses will say. We are being punished, it is some kind of reckoning. There will always be some kind of reckoning."

"I am not sure that it is helpful to think like that."

"If it is so we have to face it."

"Yes, if it is so. But, if we look on the bright side, God may have blessed us by providing a cure."

"That is so. Whatever lies ahead we have to face with fortitude, and above all with dignity. I thought of my father, earlier, when I went for my walk, and of the way he accepted the death of my little sister, how he remained a pillar of strength, the *pater familias*, when there was a sea of grief around him. His unwavering strength held us all together and made us stronger. Yet inside him he must have suffered terrible torment."

"It may be my father's deafness that is being visited upon Douglas. And I have passed it on to him."

"There was no cure in his day. Come and lie next to me."

"I cannot. I cannot bring myself to…"

"I do not mean like that."

"I am too sad for physical contact."

"I too am sad."

"I think we should get some rest. The days ahead will be difficult. What are you going to say to Archer?"

"I have not thought much about that. I don't want the word to spread. News travels fast, especially bad news. I know that Garnett will maintain professional confidentiality. The dilemma is that I have to tell Archer as soon as possible, and the term has already started. Douglas must leave as soon as possible. The engagement must go ahead exactly as planned otherwise it will create the wrong impression with the Roses, and we can't afford that." He turned off the light next to his bed, lifted his sheet and blankets and got into bed.

"I mentioned to you that Douglas went to get some writing paper. I am sure he told her about his condition. I don't think he could bring himself to tell her over the telephone." Anneke walked around the bottom end of van Yssen's bed and kissed him on his temple.

His large body convulsed and he moaned as he uttered muffled dry sobs. She knelt next to his bed and put her head against his shoulder while she prayed and stroked his hair. When he was calm she kissed him again. She lay awake until his breathing was regular.

Friday 25 March 1927

Douglas arrived home from school.

"There is a letter for you in your room, from Frances," his mother said.

"Thank you. Where is Dad?"

"He's having lunch at the Queens Hotel with Dr Archer."

"That was a clever thing to do. Archer loves food."

"I think the idea was to get him away from the school premises, onto neutral ground as it were. He also had to go to the bank."

"Are you playing tennis tomorrow?"

"Yes we are, Garnett arranged it."

"Who all are playing?"

"Just four of us, Bertie Hurford and David Rivett will make up the other two."

"That sounds like a nice group."

"Yes they're good chaps. Nice players too. Good competition."

When they had had their lunch Douglas went to his room and opened Frances' letter.

Sunday 20 March 1927 – 9.20

Dear beloved Douglas,

Even though I spoke to you earlier this evening, I nevertheless feel that I should write to you. I had such intensely romantic feelings towards you that I could not sleep without conveying to you what I feel. I was quite miserable earlier on at being back here and away from my loved ones but I am better now, on account of taking some camomile tea that has buoyed up my spirit.

(I obtained some boiling water from the kitchen, and used my little teapot.)

It is quite wonderful to think that we will be back together in Cape Town in a little more than eight weeks, and the thought of our formal engagement – to announce to the whole world that we are betrothed – is practically more than I can imagine, and makes me quite dizzy. Oh how I love you dear Douglas. As soon as we are apart, the intensity of my affection seems to grow. There is after all some truth in the silly little saying that absence makes the heart grow fonder. Isn't it strange that it should be so? It is a new experience for me to be so much in love and a trifle confusing. Just more than eight weeks, so if we knuckle down and concentrate on the schoolwork, time will no doubt pass quickly.

As the train rumbled on towards Graaff Reinet I thought of our conversations on the way here. Like the movements of the carriages that are still in my body, parts of our conversation keep repeating themselves in my thoughts, and the atmosphere that was generated by the intimacy of discussing having a son is still almost tangible. It was so wonderful! I could weep it is so wonderful.

I am utterly pleased with your positive attitude about furthering your career. You have such a gigantic intellect, you must make the most of it, and I will do all I can to encourage you to rise to great heights, and I promise that I shall support you in all your endeavours. Although it is quite obvious to most how talented you are, I believe that I more than anyone else know what your true potential is. You have been created to have a great mind, and I have been put alongside you to make you realise what a gift you have – sometimes very talented people are not fully aware of their talents and they need others to help them unlock all their potential.

When I think of you I sometimes recall the first time I saw you.

It was outside the library in the early spring. I still wore my overcoat to lectures because of the chill. You had your Harris Tweed jacket on with its leather patches on the elbows and a College House woollen scarf. And you wore a hat set at a jolly angle. You were in earnest conversation with someone and had two books under your arm, the one threatening to fall so that I wanted to push it into position. Already then you appeared larger than the other men, not in a physical sense, but in the sense of having stature. You stood out. My, what a day that was. I went home and told Mummy, and she said very little for fear of my disappointment if I did not see you again. And then I think of the first time you kissed me, after the dance in the night that was saturated with the scent of jasmine. I can still feel your bearded face against mine. Do you remember?

I have such great hope for the future, our future, and I cannot wait until we are together again. Sleep well dearest.

With all my fondest love,
Frances.

Douglas read the letter again. There was a knock at his door. It was his mother. "What did Frances say?"

"Just a bit about the rest of the journey to Graaff Reinet. She's all on her own and just wanted to say a few things before she went to bed. You know how it is."

"I ought to go and have a short sleep, why don't you have some rest yourself? Your father is unlikely to be back before four. I forgot to mention to you, we have been asked to have some oysters from Mossel Bay at the Elleys this evening, and to play cards. The Cloetes and the Gordons will be there, and perhaps the Baileys and Pococks. They said they would appreciate it if you would come along."

"Gee, I have so much reading to do, and besides I thought of going to see Garnett to ask him about Dr Yearsley and find out whether he has been in touch with Dr Roux."

"The Elleys will be disappointed I am sure, but I understand. You seem distracted, are you sure that you are alright?"

"Ja, I'm just fine thanks."

While a blustery dry wind swept through the branches of the ash trees outside the hospital and made dust and dried leaves swirl, Garnett was removing the adenoids of a fourteen-year-old girl. Dr Diemont sat at the head end of the operating table. He had finished administering the anaesthetic. "I am looking forward to a quiet weekend," he said. "I need some rest. I had a difficult and protracted delivery last night. We should have brought the woman to the hospital. I need some sleep."

Diemont led the way to the washroom. They disrobed themselves and washed their hands and faces. "How is young van Yssen getting on?" Diemont asked.

"You were right Dr Diemont. I sent him to see Dr Anton Roux in Cape Town, in fact Douglas saw him only last week, and Roux's diagnosis confirms your suspicions that it is otosclerosis."

"I wish I could have been wrong."

"Roux has recommended that Douglas go to see a Dr Yearsley in London to have electrophonoid treatment. From all accounts Yearsley has had phenomenal success with patients who suffer from the condition."

"I am aware of some of the claims."

"You don't sound too enthusiastic?"

"It may be that I am tired right now, but I sincerely hope that it will benefit the young man. Otosclerosis is a terrible thing. From what I can gather, the electrophonoid treatment, if it is given at the right time, can possibly shake loose the calcifying bones, especially the stapes, and restore or improve hearing, but it cannot repair damage to the nerves. There is no remedy for that. I don't want to dampen your enthusiasm, and it is right to go for treatment. Considering the ghastliness of the prognosis, anything is worth trying. I think you should be aware of possible disappointment. If hopes are raised, and then dashed, it can be very painful, not to mention the expense. Yet, if you have already held out hope you cannot now retreat." Diemont looked Garnett in the eye. "I would have done exactly what you have done, if it is any consolation."

"Thank you, Dr Diemont."

They dressed themselves and combed their wet hair. When they reached Diemont's car Diemont patted Garnett on the shoulder. "You are a fine Doctor, Garnett."

◆

Chapter Twenty-one

Tuesday 5 April 1927

THE POSTMAN handed Frances' letter to Mrs van Yssen at the garden gate. It was the only mail that day. She put the letter into the pocket of the apron she wore for gardening. When she had finished painting sulphur solution onto the stems of her roses, she washed her hands, took off her apron and put on a hat. She told Betta that she would be out for a while and crossed the road to be on the shaded part of the sidewalk and headed for Madame Jacquard's house.

While she waited for her knock to be answered she thought of the time of Madame Jacquard's illness. Today was different. It was a bright end-of-summer day. Soon there would be the days when it was cold in the shade and hot in the sun. The fruit trees in Madame Jacquard's orchard were preparing for the winter. She heard footsteps. "Anneke! I knew you would come. I have made some coffee. Come and tell me what is happening. Let me look at you. You look much better. That is a good thing. Where would you like us to sit down?"

"I like your studio."

"It is better and the coffee is already there. So Anneke, tell me, how is Albert?"

"I am not sure."

"Not sure?"

"I feared the worst when he received the news. But he remained calm, almost unnaturally calm. He went to bed quite early and he was up early the next morning to work in his study. He went to see Dr Archer; they had lunch together, and he told him of Douglas' problem and that he has to go to London. Archer was uncomfortable about letting Douglas go at the end of this term but when he realised how serious the position is, was quite sympathetic, and said that Douglas could start again at the beginning of next year, or even in the fourth term, if he returns in time. Douglas wrote to Frances and told her of the diagnosis. I hope everything will be all right. We have decided that the engagement should go ahead as planned, and immediately afterwards Douglas will sail for England."

"You have done a lot. I admire you. Sometimes when men do not react strongly it is because they are sad. Your men do not cry. French men will sometimes cry, but it is not weakness. Fathers love their sons in a way women do not understand. Albert's reaction could be so little because of shock to him or he could still be denying to himself what has happened. After a while things could come to the surface. The first sign will be his temper. If that does happen you must be patient because in time it will pass on. Also, he will look for something to give blame to. Whatever can irritate him he will blame. At times of problems we sometimes say things we should not say, and saying the wrong things can cause wounds that do not want to heal. I am struggling with my English today. But more important, how is Douglas? We speak of Albert but we do not speak of Douglas. Imagine how he must feel. Becoming engaged is by itself difficult enough for the emotions, and now to have this also on his mind. And concern of what the girl and her parents may think of his prospects. He must be suffering."

"He has remained quite cheerful."

"He is hiding his grief from you, to protect you. He is carrying the heavy burden of threatening deafness and he is smiling so that you will think he cannot feel what he is carrying. Make your attention to him available. Don't say anything, or ask anything, just let him know that you are available to him all the time. That way he will want to talk to you."

"We are all hoping that the treatment will be successful."

"If the great doctor in London has had so many successes, why should there be doubt?"

"One always fears that there may be exceptions."

"If you have doubt Douglas will feel it. You must not have doubt. Think every minute of every day that the treatment will be good and your son will be normal. Do not allow any other thought to come into your head. That way you will make an atmosphere inside your house that will heal the spirit."

"You are so wise Guillemette, you have given me such good counsel."

"You flatter me. You see the way I deal with things is really quite simple. It is like when I paint. When my mind is balanced I know what is right: when the proportions are right, when the colour is right, when the shapes and the textures are right. At the time when you know things are right there is no process of reason. It is like music. If you think about what you are listening to, you no longer hear the music. It would have been much more helpful if Descartes had said, 'I do not think therefore I am.' You have to follow your intuition."

Mrs van Yssen moved about in her chair.

"I am sorry if I have upset you, or confused you Anneke. I apologise for talking too much today. People think I am strange, and so I am. It is because my reference point is different. Let me explain. When I was a little girl we lived in the country. I lived my whole life in the country before I went to study in Paris. I sat one sunny day in our garden with its grey stone wall at a time when the apple trees were in blossom. That day I found much more in the blossoms than before. They had a beauty that was so intense, the focus of their detail was so sharp, their subtle colours were so pure, and I was suddenly not anymore separate from them. At that moment the blossoms trembled but there was no wind. From that moment I was different because I went for an instant into another world. I tried to explain to my parents, and later to others, what I had experienced but they looked at me as if I was disturbed. I can now see their world more clearly, but they cannot see mine. My father muttered that he thought I had eaten bread with mould on it. What I saw was so pure and so normal that it became the measure by which I judge all things."

"I saw something very special in my St Joseph's lilies the other day that inspired me, and gave me such a positive feeling. They were so beautiful."

"But that is wonderful, my dear."

"Or it could have been that I saw something special because I was happy because things seemed to be going so well."

"These things have great subtlety."

"I should be getting home. I do apologise for just arriving as I did."

"I am so glad that you came. Do you remember the first day we met?"

"I shall never forget that. How is your painting going?"

"At times better than at other times. You know how it is. Every day is different. Take some pastries for Albert's sweet tooth."

"No I cannot."

"Yes you can." Madame Jacquard strode to her pantry, unearthed a crumpled brown paper packet, opened it and put the remaining pastries into it. "Give it to him with his tea this afternoon."

"Thank you so much. And thank you for listening to me and being such a good friend."

"Come whenever you feel you want to."

"Goodbye."

Madame Jacquard held Anneke's hands. "Goodbye my dear."

Douglas found his mother asleep in her easy chair in the drawing room. He was about to leave when she woke.

"Hello Ma."

She straightened her dress and began to get up stiffly. "There's a letter for you from Frances. I've put it on the dining table. Have you had a good day?"

"Not bad for a Tuesday. It is becoming more routine. I am enjoying it so much I sometimes can't believe that they are actually paying me for what I do. I talk about what I like best and other people give me money for it. Apart from setting and marking tests, and I imagine exams, it is really not like work. Dr Archer called me to his office today after the staff meeting."

"What did he say."

"He was more than sympathetic. So much so that I wonder what Dad must have said to him. He said he fully understood my situation, and that I could have leave of absence from the end of this term. He has co-opted his wife who previously taught history, but said he was a bit concerned about the matrics."

"I am relieved to hear that everything is sorted out. Go and have your food now, you must be starving."

27 March 1927

My most dearly beloved man,

I can understand that you must have been utterly devastated to be told about Dr Roux's opinion. I regret that I could not have been at your side, since you are now my responsibility. It is such good news that suitable treatment is available, and the further good news is that you will be going to London to receive it. I agree too that it would be best if you could go as soon as possible so that we can get the treatment behind us and continue with out lives. London is such an exciting place, and the journey by sea! I wish we could have gone together. My earlier thought of eloping crossed my mind. We could find a little place to stay in London and go and see all the wonderful things. You will enjoy the British Museum, to stand within inches of magnificent antiquities! I can understand your apprehension about travelling but I wish to reassure you that the anticipation will be the worst. As soon as your journey begins – the atmosphere on the ship will be intoxicating – and you arrive in the wonderful new bustling environment with its red trams you will begin to enjoy your adventure.

I have no doubt that the treatment will be successful. I have always sensed, since we first met, that our lives would be inextricably bound, and that our relationship would grow and flourish endlessly. Yet even in the unlikely event that the treatment turns out not to be successful, and if the problem with your hearing were to become worse, it shall not make one iota of difference to my love and support for you. My love for you is unconditional and no external events, or what may happen in the future, can alter that. What you must appreciate, my love, as I have reassured you before, your intellectual gifts make you unassailable and will dwarf anything that may afflict you.

You are greatly blessed. In lesser individuals afflictions sometimes turn into hopeless handicaps, while great individuals often stand astride their disabilities. Just think of the great Beethoven. From the time of his fifth symphony he never heard a note he composed, except when he clenched a stick between his teeth and put it on the soundboard of the piano to pick up some of the vibrations, and yet some of his greatest and most spiritual music was produced later, after he had gone completely deaf. And the bitterest irony of all was that he wrote music, music for others to listen to that he himself could not hear. I want to weep when I think of that. Nowhere in the world of artistic achievement, and possibly any achievement, can we find a greater triumph of the mind over adversity.

You are so fortunate: no matter what happens to your hearing, you will still be able to work. You could do research, you could write, you could be the modern day Gibbon. The possibilities are endless. Therefore I have no fear of the future. None whatsoever. We shall cross each bridge as we come to it, and make each step of our journey count. Daddy told me once about a farmer in the Karroo who lost the lower part of his leg when a tractor fell on him. When he had recovered sufficiently they fitted him with a wooden leg and when he was strong enough he climbed the highest mountain on his farm. He said afterwards that if he had not lost his leg he would never have climbed the mountain.

I appreciate your concern for your parents' reaction, and no doubt they are concerned about the way that the news has affected you but there is no point in feeling sorry for ourselves. We must act, and our engagement must go ahead as anticipated. I shall not make a fuss of what has transpired to my parents. When I write my next weekly letter to them I shall mention that you will be going to England to have your ear fixed, and I am sure that the prospect of your visit to London will please them, since they themselves so much enjoy travelling abroad. The engagement party will become a happy send-off. I am thrilled that Garnett will be there. Tell him that I will never forgive him if he lets us down.

Before I forget, we should fix some dates as soon as possible. I shall ask my parents to suggest some dates.

I love you more each day, such is the miracle of love that it is endless and has no boundaries and can expand infinitely. Is that not utterly remarkable?

I cannot wait to see my handsome man again.

All my fondest love and affections,
Frances.

Mrs van Yssen listened for Douglas' sounds. She heard his chair creaking. She no longer heard the cutlery on his plate. He sighed as he got up. She heard him approach. He had the letter in his hand. "Although I find it somewhat embarrassing, I would like you to read the letter, Ma. I'll take my things to the kitchen in the meantime."

When he returned she smiled at him through fluttering tears. "It is a beautiful letter. Thank you so very much for sharing it with me. I will always keep it in my heart. A woman's love is very powerful. I love her as if she is my own child. You are very fortunate."

Douglas took the letter and went to his room, too emotional to say anything.

5 April 1927

Dearest Frances

I want to write to you now while I am still so inspired by what you have said. Thank you so much. I want you to know that I love you more and more, my dearest love, as each day passes.

I am thoroughly conscious of my many shortcomings and they make me self-critical to the point that I often doubt myself. On top of that I am aware how uniquely precious and special you are that I am often quite nervous that I might disappoint you, as though I am handling a priceless porcelain figurine that I fear I might drop, so to receive your wonderfully reassuring and uplifting letter has cheered me more than you could possibly imagine. Your support means everything to me. Each new facet of our relationship nourishes my love for you. If only I could embrace you, and feel your warmth against me.

Now to more mundane things: everything has been sorted out at school, and Dr Archer has agreed to let me go at the end of this term. He has indicated that he will allow me to return at the end of next term, should I return in time, or at worst, at the beginning of next year. (I cannot wait for our holiday at the end of the year.) We have set in motion preparations for my visit to London. As far as the dates for the engagement are concerned, my parents indicated to me already some time ago that they have absolutely nothing planned for that time of the year, and that any dates that may suit your parents will be acceptable to them. We realise just how busy your father's schedule is. My father has indicated that he would like to travel to Cape Town by car, so that he has his own transport there. Garnett will accompany them and share the driving. I could not endure the thought of us going by car while you travel on your own by train, so I will join you on the train. I will also have quite a bit of luggage so the arrangement will make perfect sense, provided you are agreeable. School closes on Friday the third of June, It would be splendid if we could depart on a day that would mean avoiding Joan's company.

Each day I try to imagine what you could be doing. Do write and tell me. Tell me of the most mundane and ordinary things. Tell me about your colleagues, the pupils, what you are wearing, what the weather is like, everything. You have such marvellous descriptions, such an ability to see meaning in detail; such powers of observation that let you grasp essential meaning. It means a great deal to me that we are able to share so much. What is remarkable about this is that I would have presumed, before I was smitten, that if two individuals had coinciding views it would be a bit like putting two identical photographs together and have mere duplication. But the miracle is that it is not so. The one image actually enhances the other. It is also quite strange to me that a relationship, which requires no contest, can give me such a sense of achievement.

My father is more introverted than usual. He spends a lot of his time in his study or at his office in town. He seems reluctant to accept social engagements, and I fear that it may be because of my condition. Yet he shows remarkable strength and has gone about making the arrangements with Dr Archer and my trip to London in his usual methodical way. He has written to a friend at the Embassy in London and asked him to arrange accommodation for me. I fear that my mother is suffering because of my father's distant behaviour, and I hope that all will soon return to normal. School is going fine and I have some excellent colleagues. Two fellows, Bertie Hurford and David Rivett are particularly decent. Bertie teaches English to the nines and tens and David science to the sevens and eights. David should really be doing the nines and tens, and I expect he will be promoted next year at the expense of the incumbent who is pretty useless. Garnett and I played tennis with them a while ago, at the Magistrate's Residency, and we had a marvellous time. The contest was fierce, and the last set, in which Garnett and I played against the two of them, was finally won with the score at thirteen eleven. (Garnett and I won!) The evening before we went to some friends by the name of Elley to have oysters from Mossel Bay – there was some other food too, thank goodness – and we played cards. The Elleys invited mutual friends, the Cloetes, Gordons and the Pococks. Initially I did not want to go but my mother was so insistent that I relented. I prefer bridge, but rummy was the chosen option, and in the end we had a rather jolly time.

There is evidently a major scandal in town. The women spoke insinuatingly and in hushed tones about it. It involves the dentist whom Garnett and I visited on the way to see you at Plettenberg Bay and the stepdaughter of a prominent citizen, who together with her husband was staying with the dentist when we stopped at Kaaimans River. Cloete and Pocock debated international affairs. They spoke about the ascendancy of Stalin and the resulting upheavals in the Communist Party. Cloete considers the proleteriat a shaggy lot that cannot be trusted; he reckons that like the Roman proleteriat they are the lowest of the low. He said it must be dreadful to live in Russia considering the ongoing arrests and the fear that people have of speaking their minds. Curiously the tourist trade to Russia is booming. I cannot imagine why tourists still want to go there and that there could be demand for air services, of all things, to take people there. Elley is the silent type, he has a permanent benevolent grin – he breeds racehorses. They asked him what he thought of developments in Russia and he said unless it had to do with horses he would not know. He added that he preferred to listen than to express views. I am sure that you will find Oudtshoorn amusing what with all its swirling social currents. Nothing was mentioned about my condition or my intended visit to London.

It would have been so nice if you could have been here so that I could show you off.

I love you very much.

With all my deepest affection and love,
Douglas.

Chapter Twenty-two

Sunday 5 June 1927

THE VAN YSSENS were already on the station platform when the Roses arrived.

"How excellent to see you again my dear van Yssen, Mrs van Yssen," the Judge said jovially.

Mrs Rose shook van Yssen's hand and greeted Mrs van Yssen. "I think it is time for me to call you Anneke," she said. "Please call me Elizabeth." Turning to van Yssen she said, "And I shall call you Albert."

"We are informed that the train is on time," the Judge said. He put his hands behind his back and straightened his shoulders.

"What a beautiful dress," Mrs Rose said, admiring Mrs van Yssen's shift frock. Mrs van Yssen self-consciously stroked the deep burgundy silk chiffon on which cream acorns and abstract flowers moved as she touched them. "It's an Escher print, if I am not mistaken? And I do so like the cap sleeves and the matching jacket."

"Albert has spoilt me."

"You have fine taste Anneke."

"I trust that you had a pleasant journey, and that your accommodation is comfortable?" the Judge enquired.

"We gather that Doctor Nel has accompanied you. I hope that you will bring him along for tea," Mrs Rose said.

"We met Nel at Plettenberg Bay at the end of last year. He caught an enormous fish. We ate it except that he kept the best bit for himself."

"Oh Jeremy, it was his fish after all, and he generously gave most of it to us. He is an interesting young man."

"Garnett and Douglas have known each other all their lives. I'm glad Garnett could come along," van Yssen said.

"Douglas has a great adventure ahead of him, has he not, going to London?" Mrs Rose sad.

"He'll enjoy his visit overseas," the Judge said. "Where will he be staying?"

"He will be staying in Lancaster Gate, near Hyde Park." van Yssen said.

"A good area." The Judge nodded his approval. "How did you manage to arrange accommodation there?"

"I have a friend at South Africa House, he helped us," van Yssen replied. "I hear the train."

The towering front end of the steam engine approached. Anticipation was palpable. Arms waved. Emotions gathered. Faces appeared at windows. People moved forward to get to friends and relatives and children. Frances and

Douglas smiled happily. Douglas helped her from the train and she ran towards her parents. She kissed her mother and father and shook hands with Mr and Mrs van Yssen. "It is so wonderful to be home! How are you all?" She alternately clasped her hands and held them animatedly to the sides of her face.

Douglas greeted the Judge and Mrs Rose and said an informal hello to his parents. He shook Doyle's hand.

"It is good to see you again Sir," Doyle said.

"My daughter is looking radiant, thanks to you, Douglas."

"Thank you Judge, it is good to be back. I still have to get the luggage." Mrs Rose put her hand on Douglas' sleeve, "I have invited your parents and Garnett Nel to have tea with us this morning, at about eleven. We have so much to discuss."

Frances gave Douglas a peck on the cheek before she got into her father's car.

The van Yssens and Garnett arrived at the Rose's residence shortly before eleven.

"This is a rather nice house," Garnett said.

Mrs van Yssen straightened her dress self-consciously. It had taken on a special significance since Mrs Rose's compliment.

"We'll have tea in the drawing room," Mrs Rose announced. "You know the way Douglas. My husband will join us presently. He had an unexpected telephone call. Telephones can be a beastly nuisance don't you think? Come and sit here with me Anneke." Mrs Rose disposed the cushions to create as much comfort as possible. "Frances will be along in a moment, Douglas. Please make yourself at home Doctor Nel. Albert, if you would like to sit over there, tea will be here in a few short moments. It is so very charming to have you all here; our celebrations have begun. I just adore special occasions."

The Judge entered the drawing room. Garnett got up to greet him.

"Please sit my good man." Garnett shook his hand. "So much has happened since we last met, eh Nel? It seems like many, many moons ago that you caught that fish. I gather that you decided to send your friend off to London to have his ear fixed?"

"It was not really my decision, Judge, we are merely following the specialist's recommendation."

"So what are they going to do to him there?"

"There is a form of treatment available there, known as electrophonoid treatment, which was developed by a man called Adolphe Zund-Burguet, and is now routinely used by a Doctor Yearsley to treat people who suffer from certain conditions."

"What is Douglas' 'condition' as you put it?"

"In some individuals the little bones in the middle ear sometimes fuse together with a resultant loss of hearing."

"You don't have to simplify things for me my dear fellow, I quite frequently have to interpret the evidence of expert witnesses. What do you medical people call the condition?"

"Otosclerosis."

"And I gather from what Frances has told us in her letters, that the condition is eminently treatable?"

"The advances, in recent times, in the field of medicine are so remarkable that it is at times difficult to keep abreast of things. To judge by the literature that has been published about Yearsley's results – he has had a cure rate of close to ninety percent – the prospects of having Douglas' ear fixed are excellent."

"What causes otosclerosis?" The Judge persisted.

Mrs Rose looked out of the window. "What a lovely Sunday morning. How kind the weather has been to us." Mrs van Yssen looked at her husband. He pretended to be interested in the elephant pattern of a blue-grey Persian carpet.

"We don't know," Garnett replied.

"The miracle of modern medicine: that we can cure conditions without knowing their causes, quite remarkable, a miracle indeed." The Judge raised his eyebrows sceptically.

"That is not as strange as it may seem," Garnett replied. "We take aspirin when we have a headache, but often we do not know what causes the headache or exactly how the aspirin works. Recently I had a woman patient with an ulcerated sore on her shin, which, despite all my efforts, would not heal. She asked me whether she could use an old farmer's remedy and applied mould grown on apricot jam to her shin. Within a matter of about ten days the wound had healed. I don't know how that worked, and we probably never will. She used nothing else, so it must have been the mould. There have been astonishing developments in medicine, and if a treatment is efficacious we must use it. If we were to wait until we understand everything we will make no progress and end up understanding nothing. I would humbly suggest Judge Rose that in your field too things are not always cut and dried. I have on occasions read my father's law reports. What is intriguing is that I read an argument in a case and find it plausible. Then I read the reply and I am persuaded that it is better, and when I read the Judgement, which sometimes agrees with neither argument, I find it the most plausible. Then to crown matters, when the case goes on appeal the ruling is overturned. So it appears that it is in the nature of things to have uncertainty."

The Judge cleared his throat, "Yes, well."

Frances entered the room. Van Yssen got up from his chair. "Why is it so quiet in here?" She said.

"We have been thoroughly reassured by Doctor Nel that Douglas' treatment is going to be successful," her mother said.

"Hello Garnett!" Frances shook his hand firmly. "I hope Douglas has told you how thrilled and glad I am that you have come to Cape Town for our engagement. I knew I could count on you."

Hope arrived with the tea, and freshly baked scones, strawberry jam and cream. "Shall we sit at the table?" Mrs Rose suggested.

"You have indicated to me Anneke, that you will have nine guests, including Dr Nel. You would be most welcome to invite more guests, but we understand that most of your friends are in Oudtshoorn."

Van Yssen squared himself as though for an announcement. "Our friends Denis and Alice Kuyses will be arriving tomorrow. I will fetch them from the station. They will be staying at the Helmsley with us. William Richie, Douglas' professor, and his wife, and the Malans from Stellenbosch have confirmed that they will be coming. I was keen to see President Reitz and when I told him about the occasion, he said he would like to see Douglas. He was quite taken with him at the graduation. He and his wife will be there. We have had a long family association."

"It will be an honour to have President Reitz," Mrs Rose said.

The Judge took a piece of paper from his pocket. "Let us consider our programme for Wednesday."

"Before you proceed, dear, I would just like to thank Anneke for her letter of welcome. It was warm and moving. Jeremy thought so too. Thank you very much," Mrs Rose said.

"Judge, I would like to confirm our invitation for lunch on Tuesday," van Yssen said.

"Yes, yes of course, we are indeed looking forward to that, thank you, but now to back to Wednesday. In consideration of our discussion Albert, we have invited only our closest friends. We have reserved a room at the City Club. As you know the dress is formal. The time is six thirty for seven. It will be a light supper." He folded his paper over and put it on the table. "Here is a list of our guests."

"Please read out the names dear."

"Very well then, Sir Malcolm Searle and Margaret, the Sterlings, Elizabeth's brother and his wife Ethel, the other engaged couple, Florrie Cairncross and her young man Christopher Borcherds. Elizabeth has invited Florrie's and Christopher's parents, as well as the Wainwrights. I have asked two colleagues of long standing who are also regular golfing partners, Judge Halliday and Judge Vincent and their wives. We'll have sixteen in all."

Mrs Rose waited for a reaction. "It is such a pity that you could not have invited more of your friends. We would love to meet them, but I am sure we shall have the opportunity in due course."

"It is going to be a splendid occasion! I am so thrilled," Frances said enthusiastically.

When the teacups were sufficiently cold, van Yssen got up from his chair. "I am sure you have much to discuss with Frances. Thank you for the tea and the lovely scones. We have thoroughly enjoyed coming to your attractive home."

While the Roses and the van Yssens exchanged pleasantries Douglas manoeuvred Frances to one side. "I will fetch you tomorrow at about ten thirty to look at rings, if that is all right with you?"

"Of course it will be dearest, but please don't be extravagant for my sake." She squeezed his hand affectionately. "Isn't it wonderful that we all get on so well, like one big family." Garnett kept a discreet distance. Frances put her arm through his. "You have no idea, Garnett, just how jolly much I appreciate that you have taken the trouble to come to Cape Town. Thank you too for what you have done for Douglas. I shall always remember it gratefully."

The Judge and Mrs Rose and Frances went inside. "Quite an interesting lot those people from Oudtshoorn."

Douglas and his father arrived at Murdoch's Jewellers as their doors opened at nine o'clock. A middle-aged man in striped trousers and a morning coat stepped forward. "Mr van Yssen I take it?"

"Yes and you must be Mr Murdoch. How do you do. This is my son Douglas."

"Everything is ready. The birthstone for a young lady born in May is emerald. The only reservation that I might have about choosing an emerald is if the young lady's hand is too conspicuously white, which I trust is not the case. If it were, a diamond might have been a better choice, or an emerald set in little diamonds. If you would like to sit down over here with me." An assistant carried in a padded tray with five rings. "These vary very little in price but we can always see what we can do."

"They look wonderful," Douglas said.

"I fancy they are the finest," Mr Murdoch replied. "When will the young lady make her choice?"

"Douglas and his fiancée will be here at ten thirty."

"I trust that you are satisfied Mr van Yssen?"

"Yes I am. We shall make payment when my son collects the ring."

Garnett and Douglas left the hotel in van Yssen's car just after ten o'clock to fetch Frances. Frances had actually been ready quite early but was advised by her mother to practise restraint lest she seemed too keen. "Douglas understands my enthusiasm, Mother, I don't have to pretend with him."

"It is not only Douglas that you have to deal with, Frances, it is also Garnett Nel. Things must be done correctly. You young people have such a flagrant disregard for etiquette."

"It is the way of the future, mother and a better way at that. We cannot turn the clock back, and besides uncle James has told me what a rebel you were."

"I trust you are both well this fine morning? Seems as if summer has had a reprieve – almost an Indian summer. How do you find Cape Town, Doctor Nel?" She stepped close to Douglas and put her arm through his. "And how are you my dear boy?"

"It is most agreeable, thank you, Mrs Rose. I know it reasonably well. I studied here for a year before I went to Ireland," Garnett replied.

"I am a bit nervous, I must confess, Mrs Rose."

Frances arrived. She had on a pretty pink summer dress and held her chin up for approval. It was softly styled with an adjustable drawstring neckline below which wide gauge silk mesh was embroidered with silk floss to produce a pattern of blue morning glories against bright green foliage. Long sleeves closed at her wrists with delicate mop buttons. Garnett looked at her shapely legs in pale pink hose and her attractive feet in white kid shoes.

Douglas stepped forward, "My goodness Frances, you grow more beautiful each day."

"What a sweet thing to say Douglas," Mrs Rose said.

Frances pecked Douglas on the cheek. "You make me more beautiful. Now shall we go?"

They said goodbye and motored to Adderley Street.

Mr Murdoch was waiting for them when they entered his shop just after half past ten.

"May I introduce my fiancée Mr Murdoch, Miss Rose. Frances this is Mr Murdoch."

Murdoch could hardly contain his pleasure. "You must be Justice Rose's daughter."

Frances blushed.

"Come, come, let us then have a look at the exquisite rings your young man has selected for you. We were informed that you favour a birth stone." The tray with the rings arrived, covered with a piece of chamois leather. "I have been informed that your birth stone is the emerald." He drew the chamois aside. "The finest emeralds you will find anywhere. They are from India."

"They are so beautiful, so very beautiful," Frances clasped her hands together. "Oh my word, oh my word." She looked at Douglas who seemed embarrassed.

"They are there for you to choose from, Miss Rose."

Frances pointed at two of the rings. "I particularly like those." She paused. "But I think I prefer this one. Yes, this one." Murdoch extended his arms and pulled up his sleeves as a conjurer would. He moved forward theatrically, took the ring Frances had selected and slowly and sensuously slipped it over her wedding finger. The stone was cut square and bevelled along the sides and corners, and set in an understated way in eighteen-carat gold. Frances held her hand away from her and extended her fingers.

"I love this so much that there is no need to try on the others," she said. "Do I have to take it off again?"

"We must make sure the size is right," Murdoch insisted.

"The size is perfect, everything about it is perfect, thank you so much dear Douglas." She embraced him.

"Let me measure your finger please, Miss Rose." Murdoch removed the ring, measured its inside diameter, then measured Frances' finger. "Well, well, it is the right size. Invariably we have to alter the size. It is like a good omen. Mr van Yssen you indicated that you would collect it in the morning. I can see no reason why you should not take it with you now." Douglas opened his mouth to protest. "I quite understand, Sir, take it now and I shall still expect you in the morning. I shall have it packaged."

"What exquisite taste you have Douglas, it is exactly what I have always dreamt of. Oh how marvellous, I am so happy, my love." She leant forward gently to smell the roses in a small crystal vase and then took his hand and smiled at him.

They were examining some of the other things in the shop when Murdoch returned. "May I use this opportunity to extend my heartiest and most sincere congratulations to you Mr van Yssen and I wish you great deal of happiness for the future, Miss Rose."

"That was quick," Garnett said when they were back in the car.

"Douglas is so very clever, he knew exactly what to get. The ring is beautiful, Garnett, but I am afraid you," she said playfully, "and everybody else, will just have to wait until Wednesday to see it."

Wednesday 8 June 1927

Douglas and Frances arranged to meet at her house for morning tea so that he could formally present her with her ring. Douglas was shown into the drawing room by Gladys, and stood looking out of the window into the early autumn garden, when Mrs Rose arrived. "We are all so excited about this evening. Frances will be with you presently. I am going to leave the two of you alone since I have some shopping to do. Are you looking forward to this evening?"

"I am always a bit apprehensive about special events."

"That is a good thing, to have a butterfly or two, it sharpens one's wits. Jeremy likes to quote Doctor Johnson, 'Depend upon it, Sir, when a man knows he is going to be hanged in a fortnight, it concentrates his mind wonderfully.'"

"That is an utterly objectionable comment Mother, you are upsetting my dear man, as though something awful is awaiting him." Frances kissed Douglas on his cheek and coyly put her arm through his.

"You look lovely Frances, and you Mrs Rose."

Mrs Rose chuckled. "Thank you Douglas. I suppose I had better get going. I will see you later my dears."

Frances took Douglas' hands and looked into his eyes. "Come and sit down next to me. Daddy said how pleasant the luncheon was yesterday. He regrets that he could not stay longer – pressures of work. I really like your parents. I can see what you mean when you say that your father is really soft hearted, even though he appears brusque. Perhaps brusque is not the right word, perhaps I should have said, oh I don't know how to describe it, at first I was a bit frightened of him, I think. He has such intellectual resources. Besides, people of few words can be quite intimidating at times."

Frances heard her mother leaving.

Douglas was aroused by his anticipation of the intimacy of putting the ring onto Frances' finger. He had dreamt in the night of the way the golden band had been pushed along her willing wedding finger by Mr Murdoch while he looked on; the colour of her flesh and the pattern of her skin magnified in the polished gold, and the green emerald in her ring made brighter by her eyes.

In her eagerness to reach the moment when their engagement would be consummated she nearly scalded her tongue with the hot tea. They looked at one another while they drank their tea. He wondered when to take the ring from his pocket. She considered how to react. When he put his cup down his hand was shaking. He patted his jacket pocket, felt the bulge made by the box. Frances watched as he opened the box, and saw her ring again. She put her left hand on his thigh. He took her hand and slid the ring onto her wedding finger. They tried to kiss but it was awkward to kiss her from her left so he got up and sat on her right, as they had done on the train. She became limp as she surrendered herself to him and he put his hand on her breast.

Douglas and Garnett had last looks at themselves in the bevelled mirror, put final touches to their hair, pulled down the fronts of their tailcoats to straighten them and went downstairs to the lounge to meet the van Yssens and the Kuyses.

"It is nearly six thirty," van Yssen said, "we should get going. Can't let our guests be the first to arrive."

"The men look so dashing, if only I were young again!" Alice Kuys said sweetly.

The car was filled with a mixture of perfume, talcum powder, starched shirts, and freshly pressed woollen eveningwear and shoe polish. Outside the City Club an attendant showed them into a reserved parking place. They were met at the door by the manager and shown upstairs. The Judge and his wife were at the door to welcome them.

"Hello Albert," the Judge said loudly, "and Anneke, do come inside, we are pleased to have you."

"Thank you, Judge, these are our friends Denis Kuys and his wife Alice."

"For heaven's sake, please call me Jeremy. How do you do Mr Kuys, Mrs Kuys. Your old friend Reitz is already here. He's over there, talking to Sir Malcolm. Come inside. And thank you for coming to Cape Town for the occasion," he said turning to the Kuyses.

Van Yssen introduced Mrs Rose and they proceeded to the far end of the room where President Reitz and Sir Malcolm Searle were in animated and jovial conversation. A pianist took sheet music from a well-worn brown satchel and prepared himself to play. Frances was talking to Florrie Cairncross and Christopher Borcherds. Frances wore a sophisticated black silk velvet and lace slipover gown with classic deco seaming. A dark self tie at the neckline accentuated the lines of her slender neck and blond hair. Appliquéd velvet cuffs mimicked her gestures. Florrie took Frances' hand again and admired her ring. Douglas looked to see where Frances was. When he saw her he fell in love with her as though he had just seen her for the first time.

"Come Garnett, let me introduce you to Frances' friend Florrie Cairncross and her fiancé."

Douglas was next to Frances when she saw him. She held her arms out to him affectionately. "Douglas! You look so handsome!"

"And you look so beautiful, that I have fallen in love again." He kissed her on her temple, and she put her arm through his.

"You know Florrie, Douglas. Garnett, let me introduce you to my dearest, dearest friend Florrie Cairncross, and her fiancé Christopher Borcherds."

"How do you do," Garnett said. "I think I know your cousin Bertie. Frances mentioned you when we were at Plettenberg Bay."

More guests arrived. The Judge and Mrs Rose circulated and made introductions. Drinks were served. The pianist struck the first chords of Scott Joplin's *Maple Leaf Rag*. Conversations grew louder; there was happy laughter. The air became thick with the scent of women, wisps of cigar smoke, merriment and good cheer. At the one end of the room tables had been laid. *Maple Leaf Rag* ended and there was enthusiastic applause. Cries of 'more' and Scott Joplin continued.

"So, how is your farming going, James? Damn good Christmas luncheon we had. Pity you had to leave early. It seems as though there is bad weather coming."

"We are likely to have the first snow."

The Judge walked over to Douglas and Frances, "I think the two of you should circulate, give all the guests some attention."

"That must be Reitz over there? Corking good chap he is. Wonder how the devil he came to be here?"

Arm in arm they began to move about. The women admired Frances' ring and congratulated Douglas.

"It's a fine thing to have Athlone as president of the club, don't you think?"

"My wife wants to know where the ladies' retiring rooms are, Jeremy. Can we get someone to show her please?"

"Amalgamation with the Civil Service Club is a thoroughly sticky issue if you ask me, my dear Vincent. I don't like the idea at all."

"I have known Frances all her life and she has never looked more radiant."

"Is it not an utterly romantic occasion?"

The pianist played *I'll Be With You In Apple Blossom Time*.

"What a dashed divine sentiment, 'I'll be with you to change your name to mine.'"

The pianist got into his stride. It was time for a waltz. He played *Three O'clock In The Morning* and *Deep In My Heart*.

One of the waiters put more coal on the fire.

Mrs Rose walked over to her husband. "Why don't we propose the toast now, Jeremy? The atmosphere is just perfect."

"I think it is a good idea." He walked over to the pianist and nodded to him. The music faded away. The room was silent. The Judge stood ready with his glass in his hand. "The time has arrived for me to propose the toast. May I ask you all to charge your glasses." He looked about the room and smiled at Frances and Douglas. He waited. Douglas' heart missed a beat. Garnett watched his nervous friend. The Judge lifted his glass. "I propose we drink to the health of our beloved daughter Frances and the remarkable young man that she has decided to add permanently to our family, Douglas van Yssen."

"Hear, hear," Sir Malcolm cheered.

"To Frances and Douglas."

"To Frances and Douglas. Speech!"

When the tall handsome figure of Douglas stepped forward the guests were spellbound. He put his fist to his mouth and gently cleared his throat. "Frances and I would like to thank you all most sincerely for your good wishes." He paused and turned to Frances who looked up into his face. "I don't have to tell you just how lucky I am that Frances has agreed to marry me. I am conscious of the responsibility that I now bear to prove that Frances has made the right choice. I am tremendously proud of Frances and I love and respect her more than any of you could ever imagine. I would like to thank Judge Rose and Mrs Rose for hosting us this evening and for all their generous kindness towards my family and me. A special word of thanks must go to our dear friends who have travelled here from Oudtshoorn to be with us this evening. Thank you."

There was enthusiastic applause. The Judge smiled at his wife with satisfaction. He went over to the van Yssens. "What a marvellous reply, eh Albert? You must be proud of your son, Anneke?"

The pianist resumed playing.

"Thank you, Jeremy," Albert replied.

"I gather the young people will be going out to dinner tomorrow evening, to the Mount Nelson," Mrs Rose said.

"I think it is appropriate, Doyle will see to them." the Judge added. "And we'll all be at the docks to see Douglas off on Friday afternoon."

"I can't bear to think how Frances will feel. She is so attached to Douglas, if only she could have gone along. She knows London well," Mrs Rose said.

"Well, the die is cast, and we can only hope and pray that all will go well with Douglas," his mother said.

"According to young Nel, the man in London has had a great deal of success. On such a night as this we must believe that everything will turn out well," the Judge said. "Supper will be served presently. I take it the seating arrangements meet with your approval, Albert?"

"Yes, yes indeed."

"I simply adore Frances' ring, Anneke, it is exquisite, just look at her, she cannot keep her eyes off it, she's enthralled," Mrs Rose said.

The head waiter went up to the Judge and whispered in his ear. The pianist played softly. "Ladies and gentlemen, I would be pleased if you would take your seats, as supper will now be served," the Judge announced.

The first course was liver pate and Melba toast. It was followed by chicken consommé that contained delicate amounts of small noodles in the shape of letters of the alphabet. Pan-seared Atlantic salmon escalope was next accompanied by mesclun salad. Champagne was served. Conversations grew more animated. The mood became increasingly festive when the pianist started to play melodies from *The Merry Widow* by Franz Lehar.

"Garnett went to a performance of *The Merry Widow* in Vienna," Mrs van Yssen said to Mrs Rose. "He has such a marvellous tenor voice. He sang the loveliest songs in the car on the way here."

"I like *The Merry Widow*," the Judge enthused, "do you think he would consider singing us a song?"

"He has a really very good voice," Mrs van Yssen insisted.

"He might be a bit embarrassed, he's not prepared for something like this," Douglas said.

"We'll corner him when we have had dessert," the Judge laughed.

"He has often entertained us at home," Kuys ventured. "If you can get him to sing you'll see how good he is."

"When we have our coffee, Douglas, I suggest you go and ask him to sing, it will be like a soiree. I would enjoy that very much. Ask him to do me a special favour," the Judge prompted.

When Douglas got up to go and ask Garnett to sing, the conspirators' eyes followed him. They saw Garnett shaking his head, and Douglas turning his head sideways to plead. Douglas put his hands together. Garnett shook his head again. Douglas whispered into his ear. Garnett was reconsidering. They saw him hold up his index finger. It meant, 'yes but just one.'

"He has consented but would like to sing a song of his choice. He needs to discuss it with the pianist before an announcement is made," Douglas said.

"What is he going to sing?" The Judge asked.

"He would not tell me. I said you had requested something from *The Merry Widow*, and he said he would consider that."

After supper the torpor that follows food and drink spread itself. Cigars were offered. The Judge got up from his seat. "I am pleased to announce that as a special concession to our happy couple, Douglas' friend, Doctor Garnett Nel from Oudtshoorn, has agreed to sing for us. Since this was not planned, I cannot tell you what he has decided to sing, but I am sure that we will all enjoy it very much. I present to you Doctor Garnett Nel." There was applause.

Garnett went over to the grand piano and stood with one hand on the edge of the open sound box. The pianist played the introduction of the Maytime song *Sweetheart, Sweetheart, Sweetheart*.

"How utterly romantic," Mrs Rose whispered.

The pianist nodded with his head and his shoulders. The audience was tense with expectation. Garnett's rich tenor voice filled the room with such romantic ardour that it brought sentimental tears to some. Each measured phrase, each clear syllable displayed his musicality. The pianist smiled and played beyond himself. When the song ended there was first stunned silence, then thunderous applause. Cries of 'bravo,' 'encore.' Garnett bowed and walked back to his seat, nodding from side to side to acknowledge the applause.

The Judge stood up and applauded. He waited for the volume of the complimentary remarks to decrease. "I would like to thank Garnett Nel for his wonderfully professional performance, and the artistic way in which he rendered what has become such a favourite. How appropriate for the occasion. Thank you very much. Utterly marvellous."

Reitz was first to leave, as though protocol demanded it. The manager brought his overcoat to the door when he saw Reitz saying goodnight to Douglas and Frances. Reitz and his wife thanked the Judge and Mrs Rose, and van Yssen accompanied them to the door where his chauffeur took his arm and helped him down the stairs.

Sir Malcolm Searle and his two colleagues were next to go.

When the pianist stopped playing, only the Roses, the van Yssens, the Kuyses and Douglas and Frances and Garnett remained. The fire grew colder. The sound of the wind outside could be heard.

"We have had a wonderful evening Jeremy, thank you for a most memorable occasion," van Yssen said, as he stifled a yawn. He was suddenly wearier than anticipated.

"I too am pleased about the way things went, Albert. It was a worthy occasion. Shall we go home? I could do with a good night's rest."

"Thank you so much Judge," Douglas said. "And thank you very much Mrs Rose."

"It was a great pleasure, my boy."

Frances put her head on Douglas' shoulder and yawned widely without putting her hand over her mouth.

"Dashed fine voice you have Garnett," the Judge said. "I shall make arrangements to do Circuit Court duty in Oudtshoorn, and we shall no doubt see more of you and Mrs Kuys. Thank you for coming to the announcement."

Douglas and Frances followed the others to the door so that they could have some privacy to kiss. They stayed behind on the upper landing of the stairs. Frances put her arms in under the sides of his tailcoat and felt the warmth of his sides and his back muscles and he kissed her soft mouth as she pressed her body against him.

Chapter Twenty-three

Friday 10 June 1927

THE *TRAFFORD HALL*, its flags flying, resplendent in the colours of the Ellerman and Bucknall Line, was moored at the A Berth of the Docks. The ship trembled in a cold brisk grey north westerly wind that sent shifting shivers across the water, and unravelled smoke from its funnels. Stewards and other crew members hurried about in anticipation of departure while last minute supplies of fresh fruit, vegetables, meats and dairy products were loaded, and passengers were shown to their quarters.

The Kuyses stayed in the car on the pretext of the inclement weather while Garnett accompanied Douglas and his parents aboard the ship. They went first to the purser and then saw to it that Douglas' luggage, which consisted of a strapped brown leather suitcase and a holdall, was safely stowed in his cabin. Mrs van Yssen had never been on a ship before and was curious to see her son's cabin. She gazed about at the fitted carpets into which Ellerman and Bucknall emblems were woven, the grand staircase that gave access to the different levels of the ship. Garnett showed her the dining room, the various decks, the swimming pool where Neptune would perform his duties when they crossed the equator. The ship had a scent of its own: mixtures of freshly applied varnish, scrubbed wooden decks, faint coal smoke blended with fishy odours of the sea, and wax polish on the linoleum surfaces of the passages.

"I think we should go back ashore," Douglas said, "Frances and her parents should be arriving any time now."

As they headed for the stairs a large genial man in an officer's uniform with a deep bass voice of authority, held out his hand to greet them. "Welcome aboard, I am Captain Lloyd."

"How do you do," van Yssen responded, shaking Lloyd's hand. "Only one of us, my son Douglas, here, will be sailing with you. My wife and I, and our friend Dr Nel have come to see Douglas off."

Lloyd turned to Douglas, "Have you sailed much before, Mr van Yssen?"

"No, no, never before."

"Then you're in for a pleasant time, I can assure you. There are bound to be some lovely young ladies on board," he laughed loudly.

"Thank you very much, Captain Lloyd, I am sure that you will look well after my son. I think we should get going. We are expecting friends."

"Jolly good, jolly good," Lloyd laughed merrily.

When the Roses arrived at the quayside, Garnett, Douglas and his parents were descending the gangplank. Frances fought back her tears when she saw Douglas. Her mother patted her hand. Her father cast himself in the role of a brave leader and decided that it would be appropriate to wear an earnest expression to keep emotions in check. Mr and Mrs Kuys got out of van Yssens' car when they saw the Judge arriving, and walked over to say good afternoon.

"Ah, there you are, what's happened to the van Yssens?" the Judge said.

Kuys pointed towards the ship and before he could say anything the Judge had spotted them. "Jolly good voice that chap has."

"I must say that Alice and I had a wonderful evening, Judge. We would like to thank you for your hospitality. It was a rather special occasion."

"Oh good, you've met my wife, I am sure."

"Of course dear, Mr and Mrs Kuys were at our table with us." Mrs Rose smiled in a welcoming way.

"Yes indeed, indeed. I think we should give the young people a chance to be alone together," the Judge suggested. "Douglas could take Frances on board and show her his cabin."

The van Yssens joined the Roses and the Kuyses and Douglas hugged Frances. She was sniffing.

"Why don't you go and show Frances your cabin Douglas, we still have more than half and hour before the gangplank goes up," the Judge suggested.

"Come on Douglas," Frances took his hand.

Mrs Rose watched them climb the gangplank. "It is not easy for Frances."

"Douglas has been quite miserable too," Mrs van Yssen said.

"These things are bound to happen," the Judge rejoined.

Douglas and Frances were hand in hand. "It would seem as though there are not too many passengers," Douglas said.

Captain Lloyd was talking to the purser at the entrance to the tourist class deck. He looked up and saw Frances. For a moment he could not place Douglas. "Mr van Yssen, you are back. What a charming companion you have!"

"May I introduce my fiancée, Miss Rose to you, Captain Lloyd. Frances this is Captain Lloyd."

"How do you do Miss Rose."

"How do you do, Captain Lloyd."

"What a pity that you are not accompanying us. The weather is bound to improve. A day's good sailing along the west coast and the sun will be out. We hope to leave on time. There is no reason not to. If you will excuse me?"

Douglas showed Frances his cabin. "I would normally have been sharing with someone but as it has turned out I will be on my own." They wandered out onto the deck, away from the quayside, into the teeth of the wind.

"Let's go back to your cabin for a while," she suggested as she rearranged her hat. "I want you to kiss me in a very special way so that I will dream of it while you are abroad."

They stood and kissed and pressed their bodies together, and listened to one another's breathing. She looked into his eyes and put his hand on her breast. "You may do that whenever you wish now that we are engaged." They kissed until her face was red from his beard.

"I love you Frances. I think we should get going,"

"I love you too, so much."

She looked at herself in the mirror, quickly powdered her face and straightened her hat. When they reached the gangplank crew were preparing to lift it. "I will be back right now," Douglas called to them and ran onto the quayside with Frances to the amusement of onlookers. He quickly bade the Roses goodbye, then his parents and the Kuyses and Garnett. Garnett gave him a hug and patted him on the back as he turned to give Frances a final kiss, and a lingering embrace, before running up the gangplank and onto the deck. He stood there while the ship's horn gave an organic moo that drowned out the sound of the band, playing with irresistible rhythm John Philip Souza's march, *Hands Across The Sea*. Stevedores removed the mooring ropes from the bollards. He patted the side pockets of his jacket to find the streamers that his mother had bought, looked to see what the other passengers were doing, and as the tugboat began to push the ship from the quay he threw the rolled end of the streamer towards the waiting friends, which Frances managed to catch despite the wind.

"It's good luck," her mother cried, and blew kisses to Douglas.

Mrs van Yssen followed Mrs Rose's example and the others waved, their hands like flags in the wind. Streamers snapped and as the ship drew away whirlpools swirled in the oily water at its bow and stern. Frances rolled her end of the streamer round her hand, and put it into the pocket of her coat. Darker smoke came from the ship's funnels as she hesitated in the middle of the Victoria Basin, before being shepherded to the harbour mouth by two tugboats. The van Yssens and their friends waved until their arms were sore and the ship began heading in the direction of Greenpoint and out towards the open sea.

Monday 13 June 1927.

Dearest Frances

I thought it would be best if I wrote to you as soon as possible.

I miss you more than I am able to describe. I keep on thinking of how we said goodbye in my cabin, and I imagine that I am still able to smell your perfume on the lapels of my jacket. I have kept myself busy by reading as much as I can. I am onto my fourth volume of Gibbon. Some of the passages are so striking and have such remarkable literary quality that I read them again and again.

The weather has improved greatly, and yesterday morning the sea was almost like a millpond. The predictions of the crew are that it will stay like this for several days. It is quite warm and deck games are in full swing; a real holiday spirit prevails. Captain Lloyd is a genial host and has the capacity to make his guests feel at home. He has an especially nice way with young children, and if little ones disappear they are sure to be on the upper bridge deck; they even found a very small one, after the most desperate search, for fear that he may have gone overboard, sleeping in the Captain's bunk! All is well that ends well, and the relief of the child's parents was beyond comprehension. The infant had evidently slipped upstairs while his nanny averted her eyes for a moment. The poor woman was even more distraught than the parents and had to be given sugar water by one of the stewards. Lloyd handled the situation very calmly. He is a great charmer and at our first formal dinner on Friday night the gallant Captain presented the women with sprigs of white heather, and afterwards danced with most of them.

I am not much good at the deck games but I am trying, and managed to help my partner, a Doctor Louw from Pretoria, win the tennis quoits competition. He and his wife are on honeymoon, and plan to spend some time travelling on the Continent. He has a son of about ten who is travelling with them. From what I can gather his first wife died in the 'flu epidemic. His new wife is so kind to the boy, it is touching to see, and it is amazing to see how much he loves his new mother.

It would have been wonderful to have you with me now, and I think we should, when we get married, go overseas for our honeymoon. It is so romantic on board ship – I suppose until I become seasick.

Monday 20 June 1927

Yesterday we saw land at last, Cape Verde. When I saw the bright green trees I actually experienced a considerable sense of relief.

We passed within a quarter mile of land and the houses with their predominantly red roofs and although it was a bit hazy the houses were clearly visible. There is a lighthouse perched on top of the cliffs and another on some rocks in the sea. Wrecks, which lie about like carcases of animals, are a grim reminder of the treacherous waters. We saw boats sailing offshore with really queer sails.

As land began to disappear, the weather changed and we came to the end of what from all accounts was a record run. The speed with which the weather altered was quite unsettling. As the wind became stronger and the sea grew choppy, passengers disappeared from the decks. As I write the boat is pitching and yawing. What was a glorious bright blue sea only hours ago, is now ominously dark and threatening. To give you an idea of how severe the wind is, we were scheduled to reach Teneriffe at four this afternoon, but the headwind is now such that we will only arrive there tomorrow morning.

Tuesday 21 June 1927

Captain Lloyd yesterday promised to have me called to see the peak of Teneriffe at first light. There it was, all of sixty-five miles away, faintly outlined against the grey early morning sky. The prospect of going ashore, onto firm ground was inviting and the place which had seemed so glamorous from afar, and made more glorious by my anticipation, turned out to be a disappointment. The cobbled streets were filthy and narrow and the houses squalid. However I did see houses with tiled roofs and caught glimpses of cool pleasant inner courts, with palms and other tropical plants, some of which had marbled surfaces. Would-be guides flocked around to the point of being a nuisance. One took us to a wonderful old church. Enormous amounts of fresh fruit and vegetables were available and the ship has taken on supplies. The shops display silks and linens, ivory ornaments and beads. There were boys diving for money from a boat near the ship.

The water is very clear, like Reckitt's Blue, and they were able to go after the coins as they slowly sank.

Wednesday 22 June 1927
We sailed from Teneriffe this morning into dank mist and clammy cold and passed cruel grey rocks.

Sunday 26 June 1927
We saw so many lights and ships near Plymouth, and there was great excitement when we encountered the first English lighthouse. Eventually the lights of Plymouth itself, gleaming in the dark, were visible. Breakfast was served at the unearthly hour of four in the morning. Some wag remarked that we could well have been on a hospital ship! Then as the first light arrived, you know how it suddenly bursts upon one, and the first rays of sunlight appeared, we saw beautiful England on a bright summer's day. The town itself is grey, the buildings are grey and beyond it were hills of bright green velvet. A porter took my luggage to the boat train. He looked so foreign: red cheeks and a very large nose decorated with hundreds of little purple veins, no doubt bestowed on him by many years of beer drinking. He muttered so in his local dialect that I could hardly understand what he was saying.

The boat train departed punctually at nine. I obtained a window seat from which I was able to observe the countryside. Even the Cape and Stellenbosch appear dry by comparison to the green fields that I saw. As the train sped along, and it did go much faster than our local ones, we passed charming country lanes flanked by beautiful hedges, foxgloves in full bloom, bright red sad poppies, cheerful daisies and buttercups. I know how you love flowers. There were stately trees and placid brown rivers. Everything seems so benign compared to the savage beauty of our country. At one o'clock we steamed into Paddington Station. Gosh, what a crush that was.

The Louw's bade me farewell as did the others with whom I became friendly during the passage here, and about whom I shall tell you more in due course, and I took a taxi to Lancaster Gate. There was some soot in the cab, and when I started dusting the seat with my handkerchief the driver, who from appearances was an irritable fellow became quite indignant, brought the car to an abrupt halt and turning to me, asked me whether I would prefer to get a better cab. It was a bit disconcerting to say the least and I tried to be as polite as possible, not that I had uttered a sound, mind you. I said no and he continued on his way, muttering the whole time.

My attention to this unpleasant affair was distracted by the charming ivy-clad church with a tall spire in the centre of the square in Lancaster Gate. I paid the cab driver, who would not help me with my luggage, and found myself standing in the street outside my accommodation. Just across the street is the eight-mile long Hyde Park. But I suppose this is all old hat to you.

Monday 27 June 1927

My accommodation is more than comfortable, and I have a window that gives me a view of Hyde Park. I cannot get used to the intense greenery. There are endless plane trees and the grass is a soft green with a hint of blue, to give it a colour such as we do not see at home. The weather is balmy, at times quite hot. It seems weird as I always imagine the places in the northern hemisphere to be cold.

I miss you terribly. My desire to see you and to touch you has been made more intense by the distance of our separation, and my emotions towards you have become amplified in proportion to that distance. The further I have travelled from my familiar surroundings the more sharply I perceive what I have left behind, like stepping away from a painting to see it more clearly. I can see every little detail of your beautiful face, the shining strands of your fair hair, your eyes, all those things, as I have never seen them even when I was with you. So too it is with my recollections of my home. I see the garden, the inside of my room, my parents, the school, and the pupils, with greater definition. As my senses have become heightened I have been awakened to the new circumstances in which I find myself.

My first appointment with Dr Yearsley is at ten tomorrow. Thanks to all the trouble that Garnett took to get information through Dr Roux, I have some idea of what to expect, and as I have mentioned to you the sittings are going to be of short duration, just five to eight minutes each. It is such a pity that I could not have had the treatment in the Union, for then it would not have been necessary for us to be separated for so long.

It is so hot outside, that I cannot quite believe it. I went this morning into the city. From the top of a bus I could see what appeared like a seething mass of humanity. Except for the odd big political gathering or sporting event we never see so many people together at home, and yet it is *a daily occurrence here. In Oxford Street there was an endless stream of traffic, and I wondered where they are all going. How different the policemen are: they are polite and knowledgeable. One very tall one, who had what sounded like a Yorkshire accent, directed me to Cook's Office where I transacted my money transfer. I then took a leisurely stroll along Oxford Street, and visited some of the marvellous shops, Marshall & Snelgrove, John Lewis, Jays. They are truly astounding. On top of one of the shops, I can't remember which, the most important news of the day flashes out in letters. I caught a bus from Oxford Street to South Africa House. From Oxford Street the bus turned into Regent Street, and I saw the Liberty Building. We went around the curved street into Piccadilly Circus and from there to Trafalgar Square and South Africa House to see my father's friend, Mr Sauer, who kindly arranged my accommodation, so that I could thank him personally. My dad said that I had met him when I was small, but I could not for the life of me remember him. He turned out to be a stocky amiable man with a short neck and a permanent smile. We had tea and delicious shortbread biscuits that he wolfed down in his large wood-panelled office overlooking Trafalgar Square. On the one wall was a Beukes painting of a valley below the Swartberg Pass. We spoke Afrikaans and I must say it was nice to hear Sauer's Boland accent with its rolling r's – that lovely remnant of the pronunciation brought to us by the Huguenots. His English is grammatically impeccable. I will be having dinner with him and his wife next week.*

From Trafalgar Square I went to Northumberland Avenue to the South African branch of the Standard Bank to collect my savings book. On the way I caught glimpses of the Thames, and on the opposite side is Scotland Yard.

Wednesday 29 June 1927

I went for my appointment with Dr Yearsley yesterday, and it was quite interesting. The good news is that he has suggested, because my condition is still in its early stages, that treatment could be more concentrated, and as a consequence the whole process will take less time. Instead of having one sitting a day, I will have two. I still have to have a total of fifty. The series will be split into one session of thirty sittings and another of twenty. The two sessions will be separated by a two-week period. So all in all the treatment will take seven weeks, and depending on the availability of a berth home I could be leaving as soon as eight weeks from now.

Yearsley went to great lengths to explain how the treatment is done. He is a bit of a philosopher and quoted the 'illustrious Trousseau' (whoever he may be) as saying that chronic infections require chronic treatments. He added that Trousseau had spoken with wisdom and justice and those, whether doctors or patients, who cannot realise the truth of this saying are to be pitied. He spoke in old-fashioned tones, looking me straight in the eye as though he was delivering a sermon. He said, as I imagine a priest would talk to a condemned man, that 'the deaf are easily subject to alternations of hope and dejection.' He said it was necessary for him as a doctor to understand the art of instilling into the deaf, moderation in both directions.

He said 'it was unwise to give rise to excessive hopes,' but that it was equally necessary to encourage and to reassure me 'when I am the prey of a crisis of impatience and despair.' He further said that it may happen, during patterns of changing weather, that I could get a cold in the head, or some other indisposition, which could cause the loss in a few hours of the good effect of treatment pursued for several weeks. He said that I was not to be alarmed if that happened because it has been proved that 'the auditory gains realised would reappear when the local irritation goes.'

I think it would be best for you to send my mail care of South Africa House, as we discussed.

I love you with all my heart, my dearest Frances, and I hope to see you in two months time.

Please send my best regards to your parents when you write to them, and tell them that all is well.

All my love
Douglas

Thursday 30 June 1927
Dear Frances
I had my first sitting in Dr Yearsley's rooms earlier today. His assistant, who operates the electrophonoid apparatus, Mr Walton, in his long white overcoat, who is of indeterminate age and who has his dark hair slicked back over his head, and a pencil-thin moustache, informed me, whispering between his teeth, that he prefers to be called Mr Yearsley, in the tradition of Harley Street specialists. So I shall call him Mr Yearsley from now on. I suspect he endured being called 'Doctor' because he saw me as some rube from the outer reaches of one of the far-flung colonies. And that was precisely the point! His attitude did soften a bit when he asked me what I did for a living and I told him, and he asked me about my qualifications.

Yearsley himself does not administer any of the treatment although he did do the preliminary hearing tests, and did supervise the setting up of the equipment and the start of the treatment. The effect is almost like listening to a musical instrument. He explained that the sound current on the one hand, (making appropriate gestures with his hands) and the dynamic phenomenon which produces the tactile sensation in the ears on the other hand, 'must be suited to my auditory sensibility.' The result of this is that greater intensity of sound is given to my right ear than to my left. Since it is not possible for me as the patient to communicate verbally with the operator, we had to arrange in advance hand signals to indicate whether the optimum point of sound had been reached or passed.

I was seated quite comfortably in an armchair placed to one side of the apparatus, and had in each hand one of the transmitters, of which the handle is lengthened or shortened according to need. Mr Walton then ensured that the transmitters were placed so that the circular opening of each one corresponded to the opening of each ear. There is a thing called the accumulator that connects to the apparatus. Once the transmitters are properly in position an electric current is established, and when the connection is made, sound is heard. I have to communicate with the operator to inform him if the sound that I hear and the resulting sensation, is weak, medium, or strong. This is done for each ear until the sensations in the two ears are the same. Once there is equal sensation the sitting properly begins and the first of four exercises is carried out. The exercises do not last more than about half a minute each, and essentially involve altering the scale of the sound according to various patterns. During the process I experienced tickling sensations that changed in length and intensity. I was quite sensitive to the high notes produced by one of the registers of the apparatus, and at one stage felt a little giddy. The four exercises are repeated in different registers. At the end of the sitting I experienced a slight sensation of oppression in my right ear. I informed Mr Walton of this and he performed a light suction massage on both ears by means of a small aspiration pump. The feeling soon passed and gave place to a most agreeable feeling of freedom in my head.

I was asked to see Mr Yearsley when I had finished. He was at his desk in his grey three-piece suit, complete with golden fob watch chain, two of his well-manicured pale white fingers in the small pocket of his waistcoat. He has short grey hair and a bristly grey moustache, and round steel rimmed well-polished spectacles behind which his small brown eyes seem to dart about zealously. He emphasised that it was essential for me to be interested in what was being done, and I assured him that I had found the whole procedure quite fascinating. As though he was not completely convinced of my sincerity he insisted that my attention must be kept unflagging, as if I myself were performing the manipulation of the apparatus. He stressed again that I was not to expect a rapid or miraculous cure, and that there was no actual known treatment capable of curing a chronic or progressive deafness. Such candour gives me heart, strange as it may seem, for it speaks of forthright honesty. He said an improvement of greater or lesser importance alone is possible and the electrophonoid method remains the one and only treatment from which really satisfactory and often remarkable results are possible, provided always that it is applied with intelligent patience.

Well, that is that. The plan is for me to have my treatment at the same time each day, and since it is summer time, I will have it at nine in the morning, to give me time to get to Harley Street, and to allow me to have as much free time as possible.

My landlady is a large woman with a jolly disposition. She has a good sense of humour and laughs a lot. She is a widow – lost her husband in the trenches. She has a son who is in the civil service and is currently stationed in India. She speaks fondly of her son, and also has a daughter who is married to a sheep farmer in Australia. She seems to think that South Africa is similar to Australia and was quite pleased to learn that both my grandfathers were of farming stock. I cannot think of anything worse than farming, but I suppose it is a way of making a living, if you have to. I nearly forgot to mention her name: Mrs Berryl Foxcroft. I think she is quite pleased to have company and rather spoils me. She makes me the most generous breakfasts, and is particular about making tea. We have high tea together, and find lots to talk about. I have found a good route to Harley Street and when I have been stuffed full of food, Mrs Foxcroft sends me off for my treatment.

I will be having dinner with the Sauer's a week from tomorrow, and will write to tell you all about it. Time has gone quite rapidly, and I have not seen or done very much, but I do feel as though I am settling in. When I feel as if I am adrift I comfort myself by thinking about you. How I would have loved to have you here. Whenever I think about you I consider ways of expressing my feelings for you, and how I could describe them to you. Ironically the intensity of my feelings somehow always seems to overwhelm the thought processes required. The more passionately I feel the less I am able to say. Is that not strange that we should be so?

So all that I can say in the simplest terms is that I am so much in love with you, and the experiences that I am having here are sharpening my wits so that I shall return to you much enriched, and with a greater capacity to love and understand you.

I send you all my affections.
Douglas.

When Douglas went to mail his letter he had an impulse to go to South Africa House to enquire whether there was any mail for him. There were letters from his parents, from Garnett, and from Frances. What a feast. He found a tearoom near the Hay Market where he ordered scones and tea while he opened his letters. Frances' letter was on top, then Garnett's, and then the letter from his parents, written mostly by his mother with a lengthy tailpiece by his father. He imagined that he could hear the crackling of the paper better with his right ear. It was a good start.

Saturday 11 June 1927
Dearest beloved Douglas,
It was truly heartbreaking to see your ship sailing past the breakwater and turning away towards the open sea, the dark smoke from the funnels

signalling its intention to embark on a long journey. When only the stern was visible I sobbed and received a severe glance from my father. He does not like Mummy and me to show any emotion in public, and says that it is undignified to do that, and compromises his position. What made it worse was that I cried in front of the Kuyses and Garnett. It would have been fine if it had been only your parents because we are practically one family now, and Daddy would have understood that. Mummy consoled me in the car on the way home and I noticed that Doyle was staring at my red eyes in the rear view mirror, so much so that Daddy told him to keep his eyes on the road.

Last night the atmosphere around our dinner table was so oppressed that Hope enquired whether there was anything wrong with the food. I think your departure has even affected Daddy more than he is prepared to admit. He was so thrilled with the way the engagement party went and with the dignified way in which you replied to his speech. Appearances have always been paramount to him. Mummy has not said very much but I can see that she is taking strain. She wiped away a tear or two in the car on the way home, and I fear that her sadness at your departure is made greater by her concern for me. I have told you many times how much she likes you, and I think it is more than that, and who can blame any woman for feeling that way. I love her warmth.

I miss you, how I miss you. The thought that we will be separated for months does not bear thinking of. But it is all in a good cause, and I know you shall return to me, repaired and well. We must agree that we will never again be separated like this. Being away from you during term was bad enough, but at least then I knew that we were less than a day apart. Now it is different – we are weeks apart. Time is the significance of distance. I am so excited about the adventure that you are having in London. Please use every opportunity to absorb as much as possible. One day we will visit London together and we will go together to all the interesting places.

Please let me know at the earliest about your treatment. Do not spare any detail when you write for every word that I receive from you ties us together.

I could not even read properly last night. I kept on seeing the interior of your cabin, and feeling your body against me, and I jealously wanted to preserve how you felt, and the scent of your shaving soap, for as long as possible. I turned off my light and folded my arms across my body as I imagined I was embracing you until I floated off into sleep. And then I had an unusual dream. It was almost the same as the one I had at Plettenberg Bay, of us together on a ship steaming towards Europe. Only this time we were married. The ship was the same as before, the same scrubbed decks, the absence of passengers and crew, the blue sky, only this time there was a child, I think a little boy, smiling sweetly and peering at us from behind one of the life boats.

I played peek-a-boo with him while you looked on with amusement. He did not seem to be our child, and I was puzzled how he came to be aboard the ship. I was so concerned about him that I could not get back to sleep. When I finally did manage to sleep I dreamt again, this time of us walking along the beach, on a lovely summer's day. We laughed and we smiled and we whispered to one another without words and understood why we loved each other so much.

I still have nearly three weeks before school starts. I intend spending some time with Florrie, and Mummy has arranged for us to spend a few days on the farm with the Sterlings. It will be cold there at this time of the year but the farm is so beautiful in winter: the leafless bleak oak trees wet and black against the light blue sky after the rain, wood smoke coming from the chimney; inside the living room a crackling fire, in the kitchen, thick with smoke from the woodstove, the servants making sausage for our breakfasts to have with fresh bread and butter. I am starting to salivate. And I almost forgot, freshly ground coffee, and bitter marmalade. At night we will have wonderful conversations around the fire or just sit and read before wading through cold air to our beds with hot water bottles and puffy eiderdowns. There will be walks through the dormant pruned vineyards with their sour scent of decaying leaves.

I have decided to bury myself in my work next term. It will make time pass more quickly, and then soon after, you will be back, dearest heart of mine. I love my ring so much, and still cannot keep my eyes off it. Thank you for spoiling me. It gives expression to our promise. It symbolises the bond that there is now between us. It is so wonderful. I love you.

Lots of kisses and hugs.
Frances.

Tuesday 19 July 1927
Dearly beloved Frances,
On Thursday I shall be having the last of my first thirty sittings.

I cannot believe that time has flown so rapidly. I have had an interesting time since I wrote to you last week. Needless to say I miss you terribly, and have begun to count the days. You will be glad to know that I have managed, now that my programme of treatment is so clearly defined, to make a booking for my return journey, and believe it or not, it is on the Trafford Hall, with my good friend Captain Lloyd. My treatment will be completed on the 18th of August and we are due to leave Plymouth two days later.

I am pleased to be going back on the same ship and Lloyd is such a likeable man. So, all things being well, I shall arrive in Cape Town on about the 8th of September. It is hard to believe that I will have been gone for nearly three months.

I have a distinct impression that the treatment that I am having is benefiting me, and imagine that the hearing in my ear is better. Yearsley says that he prefers not to do hearing tests at this stage and intends doing the first such test at the start of my second series of sittings.

The Sauer's have been unbelievably kind and generous. They have invited me to go to Scotland with them for a week. They have been to Scotland several times, and say they would like to go again soon because they like it so much, but I have a feeling that they have specially arranged this visit for my benefit. I have used my spare time, of which I have plenty, to visit as many places of interest as possible. The Sauer's motored me through Hyde Park last Sunday, then to Park Lane, past the Duke of York's residence, Buckingham Palace, and along the Embankment. We eventually reached Bow Bells where the Cockneys are born, and saw the Coster King in a donkey cart complete with a jacket plastered with hundreds of buttons. We finally motored over the Serpentine where the scenery had a quality of unreality, like a painting or a photograph, people in pleasure boats on tranquil water that reflected the colours of objects around it and darting flocks of sparrows.

Mrs Sauer is a large happy woman. She has blond hair and pale blue eyes. She is Dutch. Mr Sauer met her when he spent a year studying law at Leyden University. She speaks English with a broad Dutch accent, and has an earthy sense of humour that almost borders on being vulgar. He giggles embarrassedly when she is in full cry, and makes pacifying gestures with his hand, as though he is patting the air, to calm her down. My dad and Mr Sauer were together at Cape Town. He says my dad was extremely hard-working, but quite mischievous one year during hospital rag. He would not elaborate.

The plan is for us to travel to Scotland by train, and I am looking forward to it.

There is so much that I want to share with you. I am almost embarrassed that I am only discovering the wonderful things of this city now, at this time of my life, when you have been here several times. Gosh what I have missed, travelling only between Oudtshoorn and Cape Town! How different my perspectives would have been if I had come here before. I am self-conscious about telling you what I am experiencing when you have no doubt seen all of it, but at least you are in a position to grasp my utter delight. I have been to the art galleries, St Paul's Cathedral, Westminster Abbey, the Houses of Parliament, the Royal Exchange, and I must admit even Madame Tussaud's where there are figures of Generals Botha, de Wet and Smuts.

The British Museum is glorious.

I visited Hampton Court with its magnificent park and graceful deer. For someone with my interest in history it was eerie to stroll about the corridors and halls where kings and queens wandered, and to see the beds in which they slept. On my visit to Windsor Castle I was able to see the Indian treasures, although I had an uncomfortable feeling that they belonged elsewhere – that they were pillaged. The tapestries are exceptional. Seeing the Queen's dolls' house made me realise how much all small children are the same.

The Sauer's took me to the Royal Theatre in Drury Lane to see *Bitter Sweet* by Noel Coward, and we are due to see *Journey's End* which is about the horrors of war, when we return from Scotland.

It is strange how things mostly turn out for the best. If I had not had the problem with my ear, it would probably have been years before I got to London. And I realise that I have only scratched the surface. I know the weather can be pretty miserable, Garnett told me about the ghastly black fog in winter when you cannot see your hands in front of your face, and have to find your way about by following the overhead cables of the trams, but I dare say that I could easily come and live here. The visit has awakened a huge desire to go to Europe, to see at first hand the old cities and ancient places and their treasures. May we be so fortunate as to do that when we are married. I cannot imagine anyone with whom I would like to share such experiences more, than you, my dearest love. I am so inspired.

I realise that you are back at school now. Please let me know how things are, as I said before, all the little details. Talking about school, I have just realised to my utter delight, after looking at my calendar that this is the longest term of the year, and it ends on the 9th of September, the day after my arrival. I would very much like to see you, and if my father is agreeable, I could stay in Cape Town for a few, say three or four, days. I will have to get back to Oudtshoorn as soon as possible so that I can resume teaching at the beginning of next term, and I will have a great deal of catching up and preparation to do, and I need the money.

I am so excited that I will find it hard to go to sleep. I'll have to scrounge some Horlicks from Mrs Foxcroft.

I love you dearest Frances.
Douglas.

P.S. I'm so glad you like your ring.

Monday 1 August 1927
Dear Frances
I returned from Scotland yesterday. My treatment resumes on Thursday and in a little more than two weeks I shall sail home. We had a really interesting time in Scotland, but first I want to tell you how much I miss you and how much I love you. I think of you all the time. At different times of the day I imagine what you are doing, how you are dressed, what the weather is like, what you are looking like while you are standing in front

of the class. It is incredible that I will be able to see you in little more than five weeks. I am glad to report that my ear seems to be a lot better. That and the prospect of being with you have made my spirits soar.

I cannot remember whether you ever mentioned going to Scotland? I made some notes as we went so that I could give you my account. I have come to enjoy writing to you about my experiences.

Our train literally flew northwards. The countryside changed dramatically as we went. There were black smoky towns with hideous mine-dumps and enormous mounds of rusty scrap-iron. The places were engulfed in palls of dark smoke that seemed incapable of lifting and once we managed to steam from under the murky blankets it was a relief. Thereafter we saw pleasing regular green fields and grey stonewalls around lush paddocks. North of Leeds we observed Melrose with its ruined abbey – the surroundings that made a poet of Scott.

On the evening of our arrival in Edinburgh a young family friend of the Sauers, Charles Morgan, who is studying medicine in Edinburgh, came to dinner with us. He is from Worcester (in the Union) and we chatted about everything. He was desperate to have first hand news from home and to have contact with South Africans because he will be over here for several years. Before we knew it was midnight because it stays light for so long.

On the way to Edinburgh Castle on top of Castle Rock we saw the flower-clock by the side of Princes Street. Edinburgh Castle is brimful of historic interest. Mr Sauer took me to see the Scots-American War Memorial. There are carvings on the walls, arrays of flags, and swords of various regiments. Charles Nel would have enjoyed seeing it all. There is a palpable atmosphere in the hall of the Memorial of sorrow and tears.

On a previous visit to Scotland the Sauer's got to know a Mr W G Burn Murdoch who is a well-known Scottish artist and historian. He and I immediately struck a chord when he learnt of my interest in history, although his interest is limited almost exclusively to Scottish history. He called for us and after motoring us through the streets of Edinburgh took us to see Holyrood Palace at the foot of Arthur's Seat close to the slums of Edinburgh, once inhabited by Scotland's nobles.

From the top of Arthur's Seat there is a splendid view of what Mr Burn Murdoch described as this Athens of the North, the grand old city with its blue-grey buildings and hills. We motored across the Forth Bridge that is a marvel of modern engineering – it is nearly one and a half miles long.

In the evening Mr Burn Murdoch, who seems to have endless energy to match his enthusiasm for all things Scottish, took us to see the Argyle Sword Dance danced by four young men at Arthur Lodge. Chinese lanterns illuminated the twilight. Swords in the form of a large cross lay in the centre of the soft green grass of the lawn over which the kilted dancers danced to the skirling music of a piper who marched to and fro.

Mr Burn Murdoch arranged a wonderful luncheon outing for us on the Sunday. He had invited Lady Margaret Sackville, a Captain Russel who is the great grandson of Sir Peregrine Maitland, who, you will recall, was one of former governors at the Cape. From all this it would seem as though the Sauers are really well connected, and it accounts for their eagerness to visit Scotland. The motor drive was a circular one and was the best part of 100 miles there and back. One of the guests was a Mr Spencer-Thomson, and on the way back we went to his house. We saw Melrose Abbey whose beauty was portrayed by Scott in The Lay of the Last Minstrel, and to my great fascination, the Roman Camp of Newstead. Mrs Spencer-Thomson is from South Africa and still speaks jolly good Afrikaans to the amusement of her husband who stood about shaking his head. He said the only Afrikaans he knew was 'kirk.'

We took a train to Glasgow and from there went to the Highlands for two days. The weather was poor and we encountered the thickest mist one can imagine in Drumochter Pass in the Grampian Mountains. The lochs are breathtakingly beautiful. When there was the odd shaft of sunlight they gleamed and glittered. The mountains have a rugged wild beauty and the rivers flash silver as they plunge over blue-grey boulders. From the Drumochter Pass we went south and over the Killiecranckie Pass to the Taymouth Castle. There were some magnificent pieces of armoury on the top of the main staircase. Queen Victoria and Prince Albert once occupied some of the apartments, which have now been turned into a library.

Mrs Foxcroft was very pleased to see me on my return, and gave me a big hug. She said that she has become used to having a man in the house again, and was sad at the prospect of my departure. She must have married young for despite the fact that she has two grown-up children she is still in her forties. I will miss her and promised that when we visit England one day we would visit her.

My time here is running out. After next week there will be no point in writing because I will reach you before my mail does. My ear is definitely better.

I look forward to seeing you.
Heaps and heaps of love.
Douglas

Monday 8 August 1927
Dearest beloved Frances
I now have just one more week of treatment left. Mr Yearsley did a hearing test last Thursday before my sitting resumed, and I am pleased to report that there is about a fifty percent improvement. He says that he is most pleased with my progress and was confident the second session will continue to bring about further improvement. Isn't that good news?
I will have only one free day between the last of my sittings and my

departure. I have bought you a small gift but cannot tell you what it is. Wouldn't you say that is beastly of me? Just teasing, it is a book! Or perhaps it is not.

My thoughts are now focused more on leaving and seeing you than on things here, and some of the days are dragging. I shall say goodbye to the Sauers over the weekend and take them out to dinner. I have some money left and since they have been so kind to me, they paid for our entire visit to Scotland, I bought Mrs Sauer an art nouveau glass vase. It is a sort of smoky colour, elaborately decorated and is very heavy. It comes from France and is made by a man called Lalique. There are lots of his things about so they are not too expensive.

We have had some rainy weather. I don't suppose we could have summer forever.

I dreamt such a happy dream about you the night before last. We were strolling along the beach at Camps Bay, just like the day I asked you to marry me. It was so vivid. The waves were crashing, and the wind was blowing violently, but you did not have a hair out of place and your clothes did not move. It was as though you were being carried along in a vacuum, pure and unassailable, and I, the elements tugged and tore at me until I entered the bubble that surrounded you and I too was protected and warm, and smelled your body and your perfume. As a consequence yesterday was a happy day.

I was thinking about you on the farm. The way you described it aroused memories of the Boland. Soon it will be summer there and buds and blossoms will begin to form to herald the spring. That is when I will see you again, to begin a new chapter in our lives, like the start of a new season.

I love you with all my heart.
Douglas.

Chapter Twenty-Four

Wednesday 10 August 1927

DOUGLAS' TRAIN was due to depart from Paddington Station at nine in the morning. Mrs Foxcroft accompanied him in a cab and waited with him until the train was ready to leave. She had tears in her eyes and was so overwhelmed by the realisation that she would not see him again that she submitted to impulse, took his head between her hands and kissed him on his forehead. Mr Sauer had been called to an urgent meeting at the Department of Home Affairs and was unable to get to the station. As the train started moving Mrs Sauer ran bewildered and out of breath onto the platform clutching a packet. She could not reach Douglas' outstretched hand in time. "He was my lodger," Mrs Foxcroft said and blew her nose loudly into a perfumed handkerchief.

Mrs Sauer looked her up and down, "He spoke very well of you." She took a deep breath. "I brought him some snapshots I took on our visit to Scotland."

When Douglas had gone the two women walked to the station entrance.

"I hope they have cured his deafness, it is such a ghastly affliction. It is better to be blind." Mrs Foxcroft dabbed her eyes.

"Every night I have prayed for him."

They shook hands and went their separate ways.

Drenching rain subdued activities around the *Trafford Hall* where she lay at her moorings, faithfully waiting to commence yet another journey. Those who manned her had lost count of the number of times she had plied between South Africa and England. There was a new purser and Douglas did not see Captain Lloyd until dinner that evening when they were already well on their way.

"Welcome Mr van Yssen, we meet once again. It must be some months? How was your visit to England?"

"I had a most interesting and edifying time, thank you Captain Lloyd, but I am looking forward to going home now."

He drew Douglas' sleeve to one side, "You mentioned to me on the outward bound journey that you were going to England for medical reasons?"

"Your memory serves you well, yes, I had a little problem with my hearing. Treatment was lengthy but my condition seems to have improved considerably."

"Jolly good, now if you will excuse me." Lloyd bowed slightly, and walked towards the Captain's table with his hands behind his back and his head held forward.

The band played a Strauss waltz. The murky sea was calm and the ship steady.

Her engines throbbed reassuringly, sparkles of light danced in the facets of the cut glasses on the dinner tables; conversations released the romantic excitement of making new acquaintances and anticipation of the journey. Douglas observed the other passengers. They were preparing nervously to audition for the parts they would play during the journey. The older thespians, stiff and awkward like penguins in their evening dress, relied on acquired techniques to compensate for a lack of talent, and reduced themselves to caricatures that expelled only mirthless laughter. He longed for the sincerity of the honest vegetation of the Cape coast, the simplicity of poor people on a donkey cart. He would soon be home and eat his mother's frikadels wrapped in cabbage leaves.

The Captain stood ready at his table. The band stopped playing. "Ladies and gentlemen." Conversations evaporated. "Ladies and gentlemen, could I have your attention please. Please be seated. There is no seating plan on our first night at sea. Please make yourselves at home. From tomorrow night our guests will be seated according to a plan to encourage you to circulate and to make new acquaintances."

There were two other couples at the table with Douglas. A mining engineer from Johannesburg, Mr Glatthaar, his wife, and friends of theirs, Mr Osborne, a stockbroker, and his wife. Douglas introduced himself. The band continued with its Viennese theme. Mrs Osborne's upper body swayed to the rhythm of the music. Her husband patted her hand and shook his head. She stopped. "The music is so nice," she said.

"Yes dear, I know."

"Are you from the Cape, Mr van Yssen?" Mrs Glatthaar asked.

"From Oudtshoorn."

"The ostrich feather place," Osborne exclaimed. "People lost a lot of money there, it was a bubble waiting to pop. Anything to do with fashion is precarious, and animals. When war was declared the feathers became worthless. Better to be in something solid, like gold. Ask Glatthaar."

"It is such a mild evening, I think we should go for a stroll on deck, and have an early night. I need a good rest, after all the travelling and sleeping in strange beds," Osborne observed.

Sunday 28 August 1927

The journey had been uneventful and the ship was making good time in fair weather and was approaching the bulge of Africa.

Douglas had lunch on his own. Afterwards he sauntered onto the starboard deck. He looked at the clear sky, the deserted turquoise-green sea. There were few passengers about. There would be deck games later. He sat down on a deck chair, and pulled the front of his panama hat down to shield his eyes from the sun. He could smell the sea. A piercing blast from the ship's siren was followed by a child's cry: "Mummy, Mummy, the ship's on fire!" He sat up. Dense black smoke poured from an open hatch. He jumped to his feet.

Captain Lloyd ran onto the deck, pulling on his jacket. Crew scrambled to get to fire hoses. The Chief Officer arrived out of breath. "Get water down the hatch!" Lloyd ordered. "Get the smoke masks and equipment. Hurry! We'll need lengths of rope. Keep the passengers away."

An elderly gaunt grey man in a deerstalker was standing next to Douglas. "Dear God, we are four hundred miles from anywhere." Douglas looked across the endless sea. Lloyd and the Chief Officer made bowman's knots around their waists. Crew joined lengths of rope together. Smoke masks were held ready. Others began to crank the handle of the air pump and testing the outlet to determine whether it was operating properly. Once Lloyd and the Chief Officer had donned their masks, the ends of two air hoses from the pump were attached to their masks, and they were lowered through the hatch from which the smoke came. Crew and passengers pumped air into the masks. "May we please have volunteers to take over the pump when those who are now working can no longer manage," the Second Officer shouted. The ship was turned around to lessen the chance of the wind fanning the flames.

Most passengers were out on deck. They stood solemnly awaiting their fate. The elderly grey man in the deerstalker was shaking his head: "How can this happen, in this day and age! It is a disgrace, there is nothing but sea for hundreds of miles."

"Shut up you fool," an elderly woman said in a loud voice, "you are making things worse, pull yourself together. You are frightening the children, and the rest of us. We need to be calm; we need to show some character. Instead of standing about making silly remarks you could go and help with the hoses and the pump."

It seemed like an eternity before Lloyd was hoisted back onto the deck. His white uniform was black with soot. He limped badly. "Falling cargo," he said to the Second Officer as he pointed to his leg. "I think Bernie's hand is trapped under some of the cargo. Take someone with you. It's the damned synthetic wool. Dangerous stuff. We must hurry; it is flaming down there. Keep the hoses going. We'll need some passenger volunteers. I would suggest we get life boats checked. He was white with pain now and nearly fell as the ship's doctor rushed to his aid. "We will keep you posted."

EXTRACTS FROM THE SHIP'S LOG
28 August 1927
Second Officer and a junior officer descended into the inferno to rescue the First Officer. Water continued to be pumped into the hold. First Officer was lifted onto deck with his right hand and forearm severely injured, carried to the sickbay. Ship's doctor operated immediately, to try and prevent loss of hand.

During afternoon, and into the night, teams of two continued to descend into the hold to direct the fire hoses.

29 August 1927

By noon estimated eight hundred and forty tons of water pumped into hold. No further sign of smoke. Large amount of water in hold caused ship to list to starboard, which added to the anxiety and discomfort of passengers. At two o'clock in the afternoon because of further violent lurch to starboard, two elderly passengers hurt, one a knee and the other an ankle. Immediate investigation revealed that some of the cargo had shifted due to movement of water in hold, and indications are that water will have to be pumped from hold. The Captain is reluctant to pump the water out too soon for fear that the fire will start again.

30 August 1927.

Due to extreme discomfort of passengers order has been given for the water to be pumped out of hold, and for the cargo to be rearranged as much as is practically possible. Once ship righted Captain carried out an inspection and confirmed that the fire was indeed out. Confirmation that synthetic wool was responsible for fire possibly as result of spontaneous combustion.

Watchmen posted in hold as precaution.

Wednesday 31 August 1927.

The injured ship was eventually ready to resume its journey. An acrid odour of burning clung to every surface. During the three days of fighting the fire there had been no progress with the journey, and it became clear to Douglas that their arrival in Cape Town would be delayed, both because of the time already lost, and the fact that the rest of the journey would be slow. There might still be enough time to see Frances before she left for Graaff Reinet.

When Captain Lloyd limped into the dining saloon that evening, his face seared by the extreme heat, and a bandaged hand, there was thunderous applause. The passengers rose from their chairs and continued to applaud until he sat down. Once the passengers were seated again he got to his feet with some difficulty. "A few housekeeping matters. Needless to say, we have telegraphed our office in Cape Town to let them know that everything is now under control. We have kept a watchful eye on the cargo and as things now stand there is no sign of fire. We are patrolling the hold twenty-four hours a day. However, you must please understand that the fire means that we will have a considerable delay. At best we will arrive in Cape Town four days later than scheduled. We have decided to allow passengers the opportunity to use our wireless facilities to send messages to family and friends so that any fears that they may have may be allayed. News of the fire is likely to spread faster than the fire itself and the story is no doubt all over the newspapers. To prevent a stampede to the Marconi Room we have drawn names and numbers from a hat, and access to the Marconi Room will be according to numbers, naturally from low to high. The names and numbers have been pinned to a temporary notice board, which you will find outside the door. Furthermore, messages will be limited to thirty words, excluding addresses. My suggestion is that you write out your messages before going to the wireless room and hand them to the operators. If it is not done in that way, you will forfeit your turn. I hope you have a pleasant evening. And, oh, by the way, I will not be able to start the first dance this evening!"

There was more applause as the band resumed playing.

Lloyd got up again and the band stopped playing. "To my shame I forgot to mention that the First Officer's hand has been saved. He will take some time to recover, but recover he will, thanks to the doctor's skills, and our medical facilities."

Thursday 1 September 1927

Douglas wired Frances as follows.
> FIRE AT SEA NOW EXTINGUISHED *STOP* ALL WELL *STOP* FOUR DAY DELAY *STOP* SCHEDULED TO ARRIVE THIRTEEN SEPTEMBER *STOP* PLEASE LET PARENTS KNOW *STOP* ALL MY LOVE DOUGLAS.

A slender youth of about fourteen, with a fair complexion, ruddy cheeks and an upturned nose with large nostrils, in a dull sap-green uniform with red piping, his telegraph cap set at an important angle, dismounted from his bicycle outside the Roses' house. He straightened his uniform and knocked on the front door. Hope signed for the telegram. She gave the boy a sixpence, thanked him.

"What is it?" Mrs Rose called.

"A wire, for Miss Frances, Madam."

"Give it to me, Hope. I will call Frances."

Mrs Rose went to Frances' room, knocked on the door, went in and found Frances dozing in her chair, an upturned open book about to slip from her lap. She touched Frances' shoulder. "I have a wire for you, dear."

"Oh my goodness, I never receive telegrams," she said as she began to open the orange envelope. "It's from Douglas, from the ship. They've had a fire at sea."

"Oh Lord!"

"No, no all is well. His arrival will be delayed, but he is still likely to get here before I have to leave."

After the fire the mood on the ship was different. Her progress seemed slower now that she had been hurt. The water pumps were left standing on the deck. The air pump and smoke masks, covered by a tarpaulin, stood ready. The journey that some had wished would never end could now not be completed soon enough. Deck games became a dispirited duty. When couples danced in the evening their bodies were stiff and their movements no longer as rhythmic.

Sunday 11 September 1927

The prospect of not getting to Cape Town before Frances left for Graaff Reinet was a great disappointment to Douglas, and when he next had the opportunity to speak to Captain Lloyd he explained his position and asked if he could wire Frances.

Frances was alone at home when the wire arrived. When her mother returned from bridge late in the afternoon she handed her the wire. "They are having one spell of bad luck after the other on board the *Trafford Hall*, Mummy. As though the fire was not enough, there was trouble with the ship's engines on Thursday, and they have to sail at reduced speed. It appears as though Douglas may now only arrive after I will have departed."

Mrs Rose had had a glass of sherry after bridge, and a second one. Her cheeks were flushed. "How utterly rummy for you Frances. I was so looking forward to seeing your Douglas."

Sunday 18 September 1927

As though the misfortunes that she had suffered were not enough, the *Trafford Hall* sailed into a north-westerly gale when she approached the Cape of Good Hope. The wind had greatly agitated the surface of the sea, changing it into ominous cold greys and lifeless blues. Squalls of rain drenched the ship's superstructure and washed over its deserted decks. Swells of more than twenty feet thwarted her passage as she pitched into gloomy troughs and smashed through crests of breathless foam while she doggedly made her way to Table Bay.

Douglas tossed and turned restlessly all night in his bunk and imagined the worst as the ship shuddered and trembled and her engines raced when her propellers came out of the water. Just after midnight, the weather still heavy, the ship entered Table Bay and anchored in the roadstead. Frustrated that the ship had not yielded, the disgruntled seas in the shallow bay continued to pound and flog her mercilessly. On the bridge weary officers waited for dawn. Below, in vapours of hot oil and steamy metal surfaces of the engine room, weary men had visions of their women while they kept the steam up in case the ship dragged her anchors. At dawn the wind began to abate. Towards the east, openings in the clouds revealed cold sunlight. Although squalls continued intermittently, the sea was calmer and the prospect of docking became real. At ten o'clock the engines began to move the ship forward so that the anchors could be hoisted. Two tugboats waited for her at the entrance to the harbour and assisted her to her berth.

Douglas saw the Roses arriving. Doyle opened the car door. The Judge buttoned his coat and adjusted his hat. "I think you should stay in the car, dear, it is quite windy." He looked up at the ship. Douglas appeared at the head of the gangplank. "There he is, Doyle, he'll need some help with his things."

The Judge held out his hand. "Our traveller returns. Welcome home. I gather your visit to England has been a great success."

Mrs Rose embraced Douglas. "How well you look, dear boy! We have missed you. Poor Frances, she left yesterday. She was so miserable. She had so hoped to see you. Poor dear. She loved your letters. She read them again and again. We will go straight home and have tea. We cannot wait to hear all your news, especially about the dreadful fire. We had sleepless nights when the newspapers carried the story, and had to keep it from Frances for fear of upsetting her, until your wire arrived. The weather has been foul."

"I think you should telephone your parents Douglas," the Judge suggested. "I spoke to your father this morning. He asked for you to leave as soon as possible for Oudtshoorn. We have been in touch with the station and there are seats available. Your headmaster is evidently worried about the preparation of the matrics and is keen to have you back as soon as possible."

Mrs Rose patted Douglas' shoulder. "You are to have lunch with us, and we'll take you to the station. We had hoped that you would be able to stay with us, at least for one night, but regrettably that seems impossible now."

The top of Table Mountain was shrouded in swirling mist and cloud. The wet windswept streets of the city were deserted. Oak trees in the Gardens had their delicate fresh new green leaves. There were blossoms on fruit trees. It was strange to be here without Frances. Doyle carried Douglas' bags into the hallway. "It is good to see you again Mr Douglas."

"It is good to see you too Doyle."

Douglas washed his hands in the cloakroom, and went to the living room where the Judge was reading his newspaper in front of the fire. He put the paper down. "Thought we had had the last fire of the winter and then this weather descended upon us. Elizabeth will be with us presently. The fire on board your ship must have been quite a thing? And then there was engine trouble I believe?"

"There was near pandemonium."

"How did the treatment for your hearing go?"

"It was a surprisingly pleasant experience, no discomfort to speak of."

"Any improvement?"

"Oh yes, indeed. All kinds of sounds have returned."

"I am glad to hear that. How did you like London?"

"As I said to Frances in one of my letters, I think I could quite easily live there."

"Live there! Bah! My, oh my! You should spend a winter there, then you would have second thoughts."

"I liked the sense of history, the sense of tradition, the civilised countryside, the museums and art galleries, the libraries, the courtesy of the people. And being just across the channel from Europe."

"You will have your chance. You could go there for your honeymoon."

Mrs Rose entered the living room. "What did you say about honeymoon, dear?"

"Douglas was talking about Europe, and I said he and Frances should go there for their honeymoon."

"What a splendid idea, dear."

"Douglas was going to tell me about the fire on the ship."

"It must have been awfully harrowing, Douglas?"

"Yes, it was. We were literally hundreds of miles from the nearest ships. The Captain and the crew were heroic. It did cross my mind that the ship was going to sink it was listing so badly."

"How thoroughly awful, that doesn't bear thinking of." Mrs Rose was visibly upset.

"You look tired, Douglas, you should catch a few winks after lunch."

"I do apologise for that. The sea was very rough the last few days and became worse as we approached the Cape. I'll have a good sleep on the train tonight. I already feel more settled, being back. How is Frances?"

"As Elizabeth said, very sad that she missed you. But well otherwise."

"How is she getting on at school?"

"From all accounts enjoying her work. It might be an idea for you to take your father's car and visit her one weekend," the Judge said.

"What a capital idea, Jeremy!" Mrs Rose enthused. "Douglas, before I attend to the kitchen staff, I would like to mention that Jeremy has bought you a little homecoming gift."

The Judge smiled magnanimously. Mrs Rose fetched a parcel wrapped in red paper and tied with a blue ribbon. Douglas got up from his chair. "Here you are my dear boy, with all our affection," and she kissed him on his cheek.

"Go on, open it," the Judge said.

Douglas put the parcel down on the tea table, and took the wrapping off. The books toppled sideways: *A History of Greece* by George Grote, in Ten Volumes, bound in leather, with the emblem of Bristol Grammar School embossed in gold on the covers. He picked up one of the volumes and held it to his face, and smelled it. "These are priceless. Oh my goodness, oh my goodness. Thank you very much. Thank you Judge, thank you Mrs Rose. I am overwhelmed."

"I saw the books at the antique dealer in Long Street, and knew that you would like them. Frances was hoping to be here when we gave them to you. You know her, she would have jumped for joy. She so enjoys giving. Telephone her tomorrow when you get back to Oudtshoorn," the Judge said.

"Thank you so much, these will be the prize books on my bookshelves when we have our own home."

———— ◆ ————

Chapter Twenty-Five

Monday 19 September 1927

IT WAS A COOL MORNING, underneath a thin fleece of lime washed clouds that made the sunlight pale. Mr and Mrs van Yssen waited on the platform of Oudtshoorn station for Douglas' train. They avoided one another's glances. The train, that had so many times entered the station in different guises and varying moods, was shorter, and swayed and clattered emptily because it carried only a reluctant few.

When they saw Douglas he was leaning from the window his right arm extended triumphantly. His broad smile dispelled their last vestiges of anxiety. They were together again. His mother hugged and kissed him on his temples as she wept with joy. "We missed you so much. You look so well!"

His father shook his hand vigorously. "It is wonderful to have you back." His voice was breaking.

"I missed you too. It was a long time to be away. "

"Come, let us get your luggage to the car," van Yssen said.

Everything looked embarrassingly small to Douglas; so ordinary, so drab. The houses that lined the road were disappointing. To think that one could live in a place like this forever.

"We gather that Dr Archer is desperate to have you back. I said you would start tomorrow. I think it would be a good idea to drop in to see him later in the morning, to discuss resumption of your duties. He would appreciate it very much. Tell us about your treatment."

"It has made quite a noticeable difference, but I think its real value is that it will stop deterioration of my hearing. He did hearing tests and there was a good improvement. He said he would write to Dr Roux, who will no doubt pass the report on to Garnett."

Douglas carried his bags into his room. He observed the prosaic interior. The room was generous in size compared to his London accommodation. They had polished the floor and freshly made his bed. The things on his table had been rearranged. The books he had left were piled up high in an illiterate way in the left-hand corner.

"We're going to have tea on the veranda, Douglas," his mother called.

"I'll be there now, Ma."

Van Yssen made himself comfortable in the large cane chair on the veranda. Only his feet were in the sun. He looked at his watch. His wife handed him his tea and offered him a rusk. The fruit trees were in blossom, bright blue irises on top of their crisp matt grey-green stems, and some cobalt blue lavender flowers. Two wagtails drank water from the hollowed-out sandstone beneath the dripping tap under the fig tree. Small flying insects hovered and darted about in the spring air. He drew the heavy scents of the garden into his nose.

"The garden is beautiful, Ma. I must really thank you for the opportunity you gave me, Dad. From the moment that I arrived in Plymouth, all the way to Paddington Station, the first sight of the City, the overwhelming impression I had was of a cultured world, steeped in tradition on a scale that I would never have imagined. My most overwhelming impression of London is its size, and the grand scale of its buildings. It is impossible to comprehend how much energy must have been expended to build a place like that. It is astonishing what man's imagination and ingenuity are capable of. Curiously no one seems to be aware of it. The British have an extraordinary sense of tradition. It is hell of a strange to me to see white people digging in the streets, and how white servants behaved. I felt awkward when Mrs Foxcroft's charwoman came in to do the house. She was middle aged, and called me 'Sir.' Although she was white there was a social barrier that separated her. Yet she was quite comfortable with her lot, and not in the least self-conscious. My impulse was to do things for her, help her, because she was an older woman. What was even stranger was to see two Indian men eating in a restaurant, and people of all colours travelling together on the same buses, and trains.

"And speaking of tradition, gosh, I went to take a look at Harrow school, and also Eton. Well, well, I could hardly believe it. I mean our Boys' High has a fine building, but the size of those two schools, Harrow is virtually the size of a town. I walked along the streets there, Grove Hill Road, Peterborough Road. The only single story building I remember is the Chapel. There's a building called Newlands, like in Cape Town. Eton was founded in the early fourteen hundreds, just think of that, about five hundred years ago. What a tradition! Lupton's Tower, a huge façade of reddish brick, was built four hundred years ago by the same man, whose name escapes me for the moment, who worked on Hampton Court. There are about a thousand boys and well over a hundred masters, as well as part-time staff."

"Drink your tea, my boy, it is getting cold," his mother said.

"I dare say you seem inspired, and I am glad that you've had the exposure," van Yssen said. "It is difficult for me to comprehend what it must be like over there. The only impressions I have are from what I have read. You wrote that the Sauers were very generous."

"That is an understatement. They were extraordinarily generous and kind to me. The visit to Scotland, gee-whiz! They like going there. They have made friends there. The Highlands are beautiful, but then so are our mountain areas. I was awake early this morning when we crossed the Outeniqua Mountains. But I had better go and see Dr Archer. My bicycle wheels will no doubt need some air."

"I hope the pump is there, I saw Jafta with it in his hand the other day," his father said.

"I think I'll have a little more tea before I go. Your tea is the best Ma."

Douglas went to his room to collect his jacket, and to the garage to find his bicycle. Both wheels had been pumped hard, and the pump was back in its place on the shelf. He put his bicycle clips onto his trouser legs. Most of the ash trees that bordered the road had fresh green leaves. Near the river the scent of freshly cut lucerne rushed through his hair. He was glad to be back in his familiar surroundings. He could hear the rushing sounds of his tyres on the road.

Douglas parked his bicycle next to one of the junior classrooms and heard the seven times table being recited. He entered the building. Desks creaked, and the odd teacher's voice could be heard through open doorways. A pencil clattered onto wooden floorboards. As he passed the standard four classroom he caught a glimpse of Ester Naude, her large corseted buttocks protruding towards him, with a short cane in her hand, about to beat the palms of a flinching blond boy with tears in his eyes. He waved to the boys in the class. Miss Naude turned abruptly to see what the distraction was. She put the cane behind her back and smiled sheepishly at him. He nodded and continued to Dr Archer's office. His steps sounded loud on the floor of the passage.

"Mr van Yssen! What a pleasure to see you. You look well."

"Good morning, Dr Archer, yes it is good to be back." When Douglas entered Archer's officc it felt as though he had to leave part of himself outside. Only the old Douglas was permitted to enter. What he had accumulated overseas had to remain outside. He was once again subservient to the Headmaster.

"Draw up a chair, my good fellow. We're about to have first break. Please join us for tea in the staff room. Your colleagues I am sure would like to see you. Your history periods are only after the lunch break, you could start straight away, I would appreciate that. We do not have much time before the final examinations. I am not worried about Latin."

"I have done no preparation for today."

"I thoroughly appreciate that, what with all the travails on board ship and the unexpected delay. Rest assured, I thoroughly understand. But there is no time like the present, and you could simply assess where the boys are with their work, and then you will be better prepared for tomorrow. Have some tea, go home, collect what you think you might need and come back in time to do the last two periods. By the way, your father tells me that your treatment was successful. Praise be to the Almighty for His great mercy." Archer got up, put his hand on Douglas' sleeve and tilted his head towards him. "With your ability, now that the obstacle of your deafness is out of the way, there is of course nothing to stop you from taking my place one day, Douglas."

The history periods passed more quickly than Douglas had anticipated, and he was relieved to find that Mrs Archer had diligently covered everything in the syllabus. He went to see Dr Archer.

"I wondered how you were getting on Mr van Yssen? How did the classes go?"

"Mrs Archer has done a marvellous job, Dr Archer. If we obtain good results this year, which I am sure we will, all the tribute must go to her."

"That's what she said about you when she started with your classes. But then we have a strong matric class this year."

"We will do some revision in the weeks ahead, and set some tests, but I am sure everything will be all right, Dr Archer."

Douglas telephoned Frances after supper. Mrs Marshall answered and insisted on knowing who it was that wanted to talk to Miss Rose. Douglas gave his name.

"You must be the fiancé?"

"Thank you."

He listened to the sounds on the telephone. It must be near the kitchen, or the dining room judging by the clatter of cutlery and crockery. It was a while before she got to the telephone. She was breathless. "Douglas, my dearest man, you are back! How simply wonderful."

"I am so sorry that I could not see you in Cape Town."

"You poor dear, it must have been awfully wretched on board that beastly ship."

"It was rather nerve wracking, but how are you? It is so wonderful to hear your voice."

"I am well. I hear that your treatment went well."

"It has made a considerable difference. I hear sounds that I have not heard in ages. Your voice sounds so wonderful."

"As usual I have company, and I cannot express myself as fully as I would like to, dearest."

"I understand, and expected as much. I will write to you tonight, but I wanted to telephone you to say that my father has agreed to let me have the use of his car so that I can come to Graaff Reinet to see you. In about four weeks' time."

She squealed with delight and made little jumps up and down. "I cannot wait, how wonderful, I cannot wait!"

"I thought of asking Garnett to accompany me."

"If you could let me know exactly when you will be able to come, I will make a booking at the hotel. How long will you be staying?"

"The idea is to leave on Friday afternoon, immediately after school, and return after lunch on the Sunday."

"I am so excited, do write to me tonight and tell me all. It is a bit awkward here."

"I love you Frances. I cannot wait to see you."

"I love you too," she whispered. "Goodbye for now. I am so pleased you are safely back."

"Bye, sweet dreams."

Douglas next telephoned Garnett. Mrs Nel answered.

"Douglas! We heard all the news, about the fire on the ship and all the trouble with the engine. Your father told Mr Kaplan and he told my husband. What a terrible ordeal."

Douglas chuckled. "Could I please speak to Garnett?"

"I am afraid he is not here. There has been some emergency, at the hospital. I will ask him to give you a ring."

"Thank you Mrs Nel. Please give him my best regards and tell him that I am looking forward to seeing him."

"Goodnight now." She put the telephone down.

Friday 23 September 1927

Garnett returned to his surgery shortly after ten in the morning having completed his hospital rounds. He had had an awful nightmare during the early hours. He could not remember what he had dreamt. The sense of being threatened remained. Even a good breakfast and strong coffee failed to drive it away. The child who had miraculously survived severe pneumonia, failed to bring cheer. His father saw him arrive, from his office next to the surgery, and strode out onto the veranda with an envelope in his hand. "This was meant for you, the postman made a mistake."

It was from Dr Roux in Cape Town. He looked at the date stamp. September 10.

"How long has this been here, Dad?"

"Just a couple of days."

"I wish you had given it to me earlier."

"Don't be cheeky young man. I have done my best."

Garnett did not look up. "Thanks Dad." He opened the letter. He turned on the pretext of being absorbed in the contents, and went into his surgery. He scanned the letter. 'Quite good progress according to Yearsley.' He looked at the report. 'Thirty percent improvement in hearing of the right ear. Twenty percent in the left ear.' A greater improvement would have been more reassuring, as lesser improvements in some cases point to incipient nerve damage.' Garnett sat down and began to read the covering letter and report more thoroughly. Reality overtook prescience. He sat at his desk with his head in his hands. He was not in a state of mind to see patients.

On his evening round Garnett encountered Dr Diemont in the main passage of the hospital.

"I see your friend van Yssen is back," Diemont said. "How did he get on?"

"His hearing has improved quite a lot."

"That's good to hear, really good. That fellow in London must have discovered something really special."

"Yearsley appears to be a cautious man, careful not to create unrealistic expectations. I received his report today." Garnett's head dropped slightly and he looked down at the floor.

"It's like that is it?"

"Yearsley said he had hoped for a greater improvement, and if one reads between the lines, he hints that there is already some nerve damage."

Diemont put his hand on Garnett's shoulder. Garnett could not look at him. "You have done the right thing Garnett. I would have done exactly what you did. We'll just have to wait and see how things turn out. You'll have to do your best to control your emotions so that you do not take any hope away. It will not be easy. Hope is a powerful force."

"Why does it have to happen to a person like that?"

"Nobody knows. You will drive yourself mad if you insist on an answer."

Garnett sighed. He had tears in his eyes when he looked up at Diemont.

Friday 14 October 1927

Douglas arrived home from school just after half past one in the afternoon. His bag was already in his father's car. His mother had put sandwiches and a thermos flask into a basket.

"I put petrol into the car this morning Douglas," his father announced.

"Thanks Dad. Bye Ma." He kissed her and shook his father's hand. "Garnett must be waiting, I'd better hurry. It still gets dark quite early."

Van Yssen winced as the car nearly touched the gatepost on the way out.

"He'll be fine with a bit of practice," his mother said. "Garnett is a good instructor."

"Yes I know. It is only a piece of tin."

Douglas was in a buoyant mood. He drove cautiously towards the Nels' house. He cast glances at the shining bonnet of the car. Streaming reflections of trees flitted across it. As he got to the intersection with St Saviour Street, Garnett arrived at the stop street. Military precision.

"I'm sorry I am late," Garnett apologised. "Just want to get out of this suit, won't be more than a few ticks. See you now."

"My mother has packed some food for the journey."

"I've also got some." Garnett ran into the house.

Douglas headed east, past the cemetery towards De Rust. The condition of the road was good. "One easily forgets how much more comfortable a big car is," Garnett observed. "Vary the distance of your view, it is less tiring. And try not to listen to the radio, it is a distraction, besides reception here is usually very poor during the day." He tapped the dashboard lightly with his fingers, "This is a good purchase your father made."

"He got it just before the new model arrived." Douglas looked at the passing farms. There were peach and apricot orchards, a few vines, the odd sheep grazing in wheat stubble fields, striking terra cotta coloured hills partly covered in brilliant green succulent vegetation. "I sometimes wonder how these people make a living," he remarked. "When do you think Yearsley's report will arrive, Garnie?"

"Oh, I have received it."

"And you said nothing?"

"It is technical. He's pleased with your progress, but you already knew that, it's really just a crossing of the T's and dotting of the I's."

"So its all good news then?"

"It's good news alright."

"I would have thought you'd be more excited."

"You know me Douglas, I am the eternal optimist, always the optimist, I even believe in miracles, much to the amusement of my colleagues – the doubting Thomases of my profession. It is just that I have found that it makes sense to be as restrained in victory as I would be in defeat. I am very pleased with your progress. It is a comfort to me that there has been a significant improvement in your hearing, I thank God for that, and I pray that your hearing will continue to improve."

"You are such a good friend to me."

"Where did you say we will be staying?"

"At Bunton's Hotel. Frances inspected the rooms; besides, her father stayed there once, and that's a good recommendation."

"I feel as though I am on holiday, but I can see you'll only be able to relax once you get to Graaff Reinet," Garnett said. "Once we are through Perdepoort and past Volstruisleegte it's a pretty straight road. We're making good time. We should still be there a little after half past six."

"This must be Perderpoort."

The car swerved violently. "Careful!" Garnett shouted. "Turn the wheel in the other direction. Brake carefully."

Douglas brought the car to a halt. Garnett got out. "Not too serious, we have a flat wheel. Left front. Let me move the car a bit back to a level spot for the jack."

"Damn it," Douglas muttered.

"It's not serious, we'll be going in a jiffy. Get the jack and the wheel spanner."

It took the better part of an hour to repair the flat tyre and more time for them to clean their hands using black tea from Garnett's flask.

"We're going to be pretty late, poor Frances," Douglas said with concern.

"It cannot be helped. There's no point in rushing now."

When Douglas and Garnett finally arrived at Marshall's Boarding house, Frances was sitting at the window in the dim yellow light of the lounge. They saw her, upright on the edge of her chair, her chin resting on the knuckles of her clasped hands. She had tied her hair back. She had been startled so many times by movements and sounds in the street expecting each time that it was

Douglas' arrival that she did not respond to the sound of the car. Only when the car doors slammed shut did her head turn. For a moment she did not know whether she was imagining that they had arrived. Then she saw the familiar figure of her man and burst into tears as she ran outside towards him. She sobbed as she kissed him and clung to him.

"I was so very worried," she cried. "Hello Garnett, you brought him here safely." And she hugged him. "I tried to make myself look pretty," she started crying again, "and look at me now; my eyes are all red and swollen."

An elderly couple strolled past. The man shook his head disapprovingly. "Young women of today are so rash."

"What happened that you are so late?" Frances asked.

"We had a flat wheel," Douglas said.

"What shall we do now?" Frances asked and dabbed her eyes with her handkerchief. She blew her nose, and smiled. "I suppose you two must be starving? And so am I."

"They said they would keep dinner for us at our Hotel, come and have dinner with us," Garnett suggested."

"I'll get my coat. I'll be two ticks." She ran into the boarding house.

A young woman came down the stairs, saw the two men, hesitated and hurried back upstairs. She went to Frances' room and knocked on the door before opening it. Frances was doing her face. "He's the tall one, tell me he's the tall dark one, golly gosh Frances, what a dish! You lucky thing, oh, you are so lucky. You'll be the envy of every eligible woman in town."

"It's sweet of you Jessica," Frances smiled. "I was so worried when they were late, and then I cried when they arrived.

"Who is the other one?"

"Douglas' friend, Garnett Nel."

"He's nice too."

"Very nice man."

"Where are you going?"

"I thought they would be here much earlier. We're all going to have dinner at Brunton's."

"That should be lovely. Come, let me straighten your collar, Frances."

The dining room was empty except for an elderly waiter, an Irishman, whose florid face was evidence that he had had a few drinks in his time. The menu had been removed, and without asking he plonked plates of thick pea soup, with smoked sausage cut into it, down in front of each of them.

"I cannot wait for you to tell me everything, Douglas," Frances said. "Garnett, we are all so grateful for what you have done for Douglas. It is simply marvellous that he has been cured. Bless you for that." She put her hand endearingly on Garnett's sleeve. "I missed Douglas so. I felt worse knowing that he was far away. He wrote marvellous letters. And now you are here, dearest. What are we going to do tomorrow?"

"The two of you should go somewhere, a picnic," Garnett suggested.

"It would not do for us to go unchaperoned, and besides it wouldn't bear thinking to leave you on your own, Garnett."

"I'll be fine, I have some reading to do."

"We'll all go on a picnic. The most favourite spot is the Van Ryneveldpas Dam. It is just a few miles away and is quite a spectacle to behold. That is what we will do. There will be no arguments. We could ask the hotel to prepare a basket for us?"

When they had finished their meal Garnett smiled at Frances. "We have had a long day, and I think I will turn in. You walk Frances back, Douglas. Surely the old sourpusses could not object to that. Even if two people who are formally engaged were to hold hands! And besides the vicar is probably pinching the cat in the dark right now."

"Garnett, you scoundrel!" Frances laughed and laughed till she had tears in her eyes.

Douglas and Frances left the hotel. He put his arm around her shoulder. Their thighs and their hips touched. They synchronised their steps. She shuddered.

"Are you cold?"

"No not at all, it's the thrill of being with you, of us being together again, touching one another. I noticed at dinner how much better your hearing is. I watched you and you did not strain or watch our mouths as much as you used to."

"I was not aware that I did that."

"Garnett must be pleased with your progress."

"Yes he is. He said so, and from all accounts Mr Yearsley's report is also positive."

"What is it like being back at school?"

"Good, very good. I can't believe that I am really here. It is amazing. This morning I was teaching in Oudtshoorn, and this evening I am having dinner here in Graaff Reinet with you. Growing up as I have, and possibly because I have travelled so little, I seem to have a peculiar sense of place, and distance. I don't recall having been here before. We never went anywhere when I was small. It was a huge experience for me to go to England. It was so different from anything I could have imagined."

"Oh, my dear love, you are so serious! Let your mind take leave of you, and employ your heart." She affectionately put her head against his shoulder.

Douglas felt his pulses racing. He hugged her shoulder. She had such beautiful ankles. Her brogues fitted well. He put his hand around her waist and felt the movements of her hips. Her back was strong. He looked at her face in the light of a passing house. There was no moon. Ahead of them on the opposite side of the street there was a row of tall cypress trees, black against the white walls of a church hall. "Let's cross," he said.

They went into the shadows of the trees. She stood on her toes while he kissed her. They pressed themselves together. He opened her coat and put his hands around her. He felt the texture of her dress and the folds and ridges of her underwear, and the movements of her back muscles.

She leant with her back against the wall so that he could push harder against her. "Oh my love, my love, I missed you so much," she said. "We must get married soon." He did not know what to do about his swollen groin and moved his hips away from her. "No, no don't," she said, "its fine, it's how it should be. It's natural."

"I love you Frances."

"And I love you too, Douglas."

He was trembling when they crossed the road to continue to the Boarding House.

Saturday 15 October 1927

They arrived at Marshall's Boarding House shortly before half past ten. Frances was not ready. Douglas walked around the car and examined the tyres. Garnett sauntered about lost in thought. Frances finally arrived. She wore a green and light brown speckled tweed skirt that came to her knees. She had a brown leather handbag under her arm, and a blue and green woollen tartan rug in her other hand. Her calves were shapelier than Garnett remembered. Her eyes were radiant. Her blond hair was tied back. Her mouth was fresh when she smiled. He had forgotten how beautiful she was.

"Good morning Douglas." She kissed him on his cheek. Garnett saw the curtains of one of the upstairs rooms move. Garnett stared at the window, and the curtain was abruptly drawn. "Hello Garnett. Shall we go then, before the whole of the establishment has to be introduced?"

"You can't blame them Frances. They only want to see the knight that has managed to conquer such a fair maiden as you," Garnett said.

Douglas blushed.

"You're a fine old flatterer, Garnett Nel," she said while Douglas opened the passenger door for her. "When I was quite young my mother warned me about men like you, and to think that you are meant to be our chaperone!" She teased. "You must have had lots of girlfriends in Ireland."

"The Irish girls are beautiful, but I never saw anyone as fetching as you, Frances, not in all the years I was there. But the best is that you are such a nice person."

Douglas listened to the puckish banter and smiled to himself. It was setting the tone for a happy day. "You'd better direct me, Frances, if you can tear yourself away from Garnett."

"Look at that water!" Garnett exclaimed. "Amazing, as far as the eye can see. Huge project this. I always marvel that there are people with the foresight to plan and construct something on this scale."

They stopped in the parking area that overlooked the dam. Frances was the first to get out of the car. "I once asked my father why people wanted to settle here in Graaff Reinet. He looked at me as though the answer should have been plainly obvious, and he said, 'It was because of the availability of water. As simple as that.' The dam has tamed the waters of the river, so that the farmers can have reliable irrigation. You certainly cannot rely only on the rainfall here."

"The wall is huge," Douglas said.

"It is well over a thousand feet long."

"My goodness," Garnett said. "Shall we walk along the wall?"

"Wait, let me get my camera," Frances said.

They strolled along the wall. To their left was a vast shining surface of muddy-brown windless water reflecting the images of the banks of the dam so clearly that it was impossible to tell where the land ended and the water began. On the opposite side two jets of water spouted from sluice gates and fell away into the riverbed below.

"The wall is wider than I imagined," Douglas said.

Garnett caught up with them. "Those must be the remains of the coffer dams, down below there."

"What are coffer dams?" Frances asked.

"When they build a large dam like this they first build walls around the areas where they are going to put the wall, to keep the water out of the construction area. The walled areas within which they work are known as coffer dams."

"You are so practical, Garnett, you know everything," she exclaimed. "Here, let me take a picture of the two of you." Douglas and Garnett posed self consciously as Frances looked into the viewfinder of her box camera. "Say 'cheese'," she said. They smiled as the shutter clicked.

"I think I'll get back to the car. I have a medical journal to read. I'll also get the picnic things ready."

Neither Frances nor Douglas protested. "I'll see you later then."

Garnett made himself comfortable in the back of the car with a copy of The Lancet. He looked to see where Douglas and Frances were. They were two small figures at the other end of the wall. Her arm was through his, her head affectionately on his shoulder.

"Please don't think badly of me for last night, Douglas."

"How do you mean?"

"When I pressed myself against you. I had such an intense desire for us to have physical intimacy. I could feel your body stirring." She gripped his arm more tightly. "I cannot wait to be married. I lay awake in bed for ages last night. I was so excited that I could not get to sleep. You must not be embarrassed when your body responds as it did. I find it quite flattering that I am able to excite you." Douglas took his pullover off. "I am looking forward to being at the seaside at the end of the year, to swim in the sea with you. It is not very long to go now," she continued. "Everything will be different now that we are engaged. Tell me about London."

"It was quite wonderful." He was still preoccupied.

"Describe everything to me."

"You've been there so many times."

"I want to know what you felt."

"The scale of London and the sense of tradition."

"It did all develop over many, many years of course."

"Yes, that is true, but still, to have had the imagination to design the buildings, the churches, the streets. Everything here, even in Cape Town seems so small and ordinary now. Coming from Oudtshoorn, I was so proud to be in a city like Cape Town. You must have sensed my extravagant pride at times, and must have marvelled at my innocence, at my simplicity. And dear person that you are, you were kind enough never to embarrass me."

"I love you Douglas. Many people travel the world and see very little. You are different. What is inside you will awake when you are exposed to the great achievements of civilisation."

"I am so inspired Frances, so inspired. I am fortunate that we caught the problem with my ear so early. It is as if a huge stone has been lifted from my chest. The dark foreboding, that was like a shadow at times, has gone. I want to make a success of my life. I want us to get married soon. When I went to see Dr Archer, he spoke of me taking over from him some day. Going overseas has somehow altered me."

"I knew it, I knew it. I knew you would be ambitious. It is so good to hear you speak like this. Oh it is so exciting. You have brought me a gift." She threw her head back and laughed with spontaneous pleasure.

He put his arm around her shoulders. They stood a while and looked at the water.

"Poor Garnett, he's on his own. Let's go and find him." She suggested. "What are we going to do tomorrow?"

"We'll have to leave by about eleven thirty. I would like us to have dinner this evening, at the hotel. I have already made the arrangement with Mr Brunton, if that suits you."

"That would be fine, in fact it would be lovely, thank you, and thank you for coming all this way to see me. I am so happy, Douglas. Now tell me more about the places you visited."

"One of the first places I made a bee-line for, was the British Museum. I knew it would be something special, but it was more than that: to find myself standing inches away from things made thousands of years ago was incredible."

"Like what?"

"Well, let me see. I started with some of the older things. Egyptian faience and glazed pottery, lotus cups in blue glaze, a throw-stick from the tomb of King Ikhnaton going back to the eighteenth dynasty, cartonnages and woodcarvings, tools and weapons – mainly bronze, but some iron; figure sculptures going right back to the first dynasty, about 3200 B.C."

"I haven't asked you about the fire on your ship. How insensitive of me, it must have been terribly scary?"

"It was no joke!" He laughed.

They reached the car, and she peeped inside. "I think Garnett is asleep."

"No, just dozing a little," Garnett said pushing himself up.

"I'm starving!" Frances exclaimed.

"So am I," Garnett said.

"Douglas was telling me about his visits to the British Museum."

"I can imagine how you must have enjoyed that, Douglas."

"It was terrific. I was telling Frances about some of the amazing treasures I saw. In the end what enthralled me most were Greek artefacts."

Garnett got out of the car with the picnic basket, and Frances spread her rug in the shade of the tree. "Carry on Douglas, I am listening," she said. "I know when you're in full cry."

Douglas stood with his hands in his trouser pockets and rocked back and forth on his feet. "There were pieces from the east pediment of the Parthenon. Some of the head and arms were missing but even without those parts the figures still had energy and movement. One part depicts the birth of Athena; there was a figure of Victory. What I found incredible was the way in which the marble was sculpted to give garments the appearance of soft cloth that enhanced the forms of the bodies they clothed. There I stood and I saw the same things that Plato and Socrates saw. That was unbelievable. There was a head of young Alexander from Cyrene with its aquiline features. The art contains such pure forms: only the gods themselves could have inspired such perfection. And as I contemplated perfection my thoughts inevitably turned to the wonder of the Parthenon: the mathematically calculated curvilinear aspects, the enlargement of the corner columns, because they receive more light, so that they appear to be the same size as the other columns, the swellings in the shafts of the outer columns to make the marble seem more alive – where did those people come from? How could a civilisation with such unrivalled abilities disappear?"

"I think we should make some of the food disappear," Garnett suggested.

"What have we got?" Frances asked.

Garnett unpacked the picnic basket. "Some Lemos to drink, and some ginger beer. A chicken pie that looks delicious, fresh bread, butter, preserves, apples and oranges, cheese and a flask of coffee. Wow!"

"Shall we just help ourselves?"

"We'll help ourselves, thank you," Douglas said.

"Did it not bother you that those blooming Parthenon Marbles were looted?"

"Gee, I suppose there are different points of view. Who knows, if Elgin did not take them to England someone else, the French, or perhaps the Germans might have taken them. The Turks didn't care. They gave permission for the Marbles to go to England, and they were after all the rulers at the time."

Garnett lay on his side, propped up on one elbow and sipped his coffee. Frances came up the hill towards them. "What was that you said about marbles?"

"We're talking about the Parthenon Marbles," Douglas said.

"Fine mess that was."

"They were bought, quite legally from the Turks, and saved from destruction," Douglas said.

"Dearest man of mine, are you being serious or are you just being otherwise? Is sawing some of the sculptures in half and mutilating them so that they could be transported more easily, saving them from destruction? And the way they were allowed to deteriorate in the damp of London. I saw some of the blackened figures myself. The man was prepared to steal that which even the barbarians had considered sacred. Elgin was a shameless thief. The Greek porters who carried the crates with the figures down to Piraeus heard moaning and weeping coming from the crates. I shudder."

"Dearest Frances, I was not examining Elgin's motives or justifying the way in which he behaved. Whatever his motives were, they should be separated from the consequences of his actions – possibly unintended consequences. Over the centuries the whole of the Acropolis was the scene of conflict and siege and looting. Morosini plundered the place and smashed some of the sculptures while trying to remove them. Considering what had happened before, Elgin's motives might even have been nobler than we give him credit.

But what I really wanted to say, when I consider only what I saw, and detach myself from such issues as Elgin, the effect that those pieces had on me was profound. The purity, the clarity, the harmony and the grace of the lines and the forms touched something very deep. It made me sad, and unsettled me, to think that such a civilisation could disappear, so much so, that for some time I found it quite difficult to reconcile myself to the transient nature of things."

"Who was Morosoni?" Garnett asked.

"Morosini. The Venetian general who laid siege there in the sixteen eighties."

Only the thin piercing metallic droning of cicadas could be heard. "Some coffee Frances?"

"Yes, thank you Garnett."

"It is my turn to go for a walk now," Douglas said.

Garnett watched him walking down the slope towards the dam. "What a talent he is."

"I know. I am very fortunate." She looked at her ring. "I am going to have green fig preserve with my cheese. I am glad to have a few moments alone with you, because I want to thank you for what you have done for Douglas. I cannot tell you how thrilled I am, and how utterly relieved I am that his deafness has been cured. It would have been terrible; I cannot bear to think of it. I could see in Cape Town, when his parents were there for our engagement, how much strain there was in their faces. Now all of our worst fears have been allayed. I noticed yesterday evening, when we spoke, that his eyes no longer followed our lips as before. Purpose has returned. I prayed so much for him, and my prayers have been answered. Thank you so very much. You are a wonderful friend to both of us."

Garnett smiled at her. Her keen green eyes searched his face for reassurance. "I have done very little. I was not sure what was wrong, and suggested that he should go and see Dr Roux. It is not easy to have a close childhood friend as a patient. I am pleased that there has been progress, and I am glad that Douglas has had the opportunity to go overseas. That has transformed him if anything has. I know how being overseas expanded my horizons. The two of you should try to spend more time on your own. Go for a drive or something, on your own."

"That would never do in a town like this. The bigots would have a field day. And besides, it is nice to be with you. I am sure we will have enough privacy when we go to Plettenberg Bay at the end of the year. Daddy has said that we will go there directly after the schools close. I won't even go all the way to Cape Town. They'll fetch me from the George station."

Douglas ambled up the hill, his hands behind his back, his absent-minded fly undone. He caught her eye. "I have been thinking what I said about the Marbles. Perhaps I should review my position. I want to be fair. But for them to be in London is not such a bad thing."

Garnett finished his coffee and lay on his back. He pulled his hat over his eyes, and gave a satisfied sigh. Frances looked at Douglas and put her finger over her lips, tilted her head to one side and put her palm against her face to signal that they should let Garnett sleep. She beckoned to Douglas to lie down with his head on her lap. He obliged but felt uncomfortable having his face so close to the lower part of her body. Her stomach rumbled. She turned on her side. "This will be better." She arranged his head so that it was between her hip and her ribs. She stroked his hair, and tickled his forehead until he fell asleep next to her fragrance. She disentangled herself, lowered his head gently, and lay down next to him.

Garnett was the first to wake. He squinted as he searched to see where the sun was and fumbled for his fob watch. It was just past four. The sun had caught his forearm, and the skin was tender. He tapped Douglas' leg.

"Shh… Let's put the things in the car. Let her have a few more winks. She really is so beautiful."

Frances woke from the sound of the boot opening and found herself alone on her rug. "Are we going home?" She asked.

"It's already past four," Douglas said.

"Golly gosh, I've had a lovely sleep. I've had such a nice day."

They drove slowly back to Graaff Reinet into the afternoon sun with the windows of the car open and the warm Karroo air blowing through their clothes, too preoccupied with thoughts of their lingering sensations to say much. They dropped Frances at a seemingly deserted Marshall's boarding house and made arrangements for Douglas to fetch her at seven that evening.

"I love that woman," Douglas said.

"We are programmed to love women. We should be grateful for that. It leads to fulfilment."

"What kind of fulfilment do you mean?"

"Human fulfilment. The woman is your other half. She was created to complete you. That and procreation."

"Did you study much of that?"

"Much of what?"

"Procreation."

"I'm not sure what you mean?"

Douglas stopped the car outside the hotel. "The physical thing."

"We had to learn how everything works, if that is what you mean?"

"It must have been interesting."

"The studies were pretty clinical I would say, but interesting, nevertheless. It helps to understand how things work. If you like I will explain it to you sometime."

"Do women enjoy it as much as men?"

"In some cases more than men. But women are delicate creatures and they need to be properly coaxed. For them it's a more emotional thing than with men. Always remember that and you'll never go wrong. We'll talk more about it in the car tomorrow, if you like."

"Ja, that would be good."

Shortly before seven Douglas set off on foot to fetch Frances. She was waiting for him in the entrance hall of the boarding house. The sun had caught her face and made her forehead and her nose quite pink. "When you arrived here last night, gosh it seems like an age ago now, my face was swollen from crying, and look at me now with my reddened brow," she said. "And I did take my hat along and stupidly left it in the car. I was so excited to be with you that I was a bit irrational. It feels as though we are on holiday. Isn't that a gorgeous feeling? Shall we go? It is a splendid evening. Can you smell the jasmine?"

"Yes, it reminds me of going to the dance. When I first kissed you."

"How romantic of you to remember that now. Jasmine will always remind me of that night. Let's not walk too fast – it is so pleasant outside. I want to savour the time I have with you, and do things perfectly deliberately and slowly to extend the pleasure as much as possible."

Garnett was on the veranda of Brunton's Hotel. He had had a long leisurely bath. Mr Brunton appeared next to him. "Waiting for the others, are we?"

"Yes, thank you Mr Brunton."

"I trust you've had a pleasant day and that the victuals for the picnic were to your satisfaction?"

"Yes, thank you. The food was excellent."

"The dam is quite something. Been good for our area, made farming more reliable. Good for business. Had some of the engineers staying here."

"Mr van Yssen mentioned this morning that Miss Rose's father, Judge Rose stayed here."

"You know him then?"

"Yes, reasonably well. Has he often stayed here?"

"Twice. The first time was shortly after the trial of that poor unfortunate boy in Swellendam. And then more recently when he and his wife were on their way to Bloemfontein."

"I don't recall the trial."

"It was about four or five years ago."

"I've been overseas for the last six odd years, studying."

"That is why you don't know about it. My brother owns the hotel in Swellendam and attended the trial in the Circuit Court. The Judge sentenced the fellow to death."

"What happened?"

"The boy was tried for murdering his mother. She was a widow. He was only nineteen. Kid and his mother often quarrelled violently. The neighbours gave evidence to that effect. I gather there was only flimsy circumstantial evidence. The boy admitted that he and his mother had quarrelled on the night in question but claimed that he was so upset by the quarrel that he went for a walk in the veld, and returned in the early hours of the morning. He found his mother in the passage, near the back door, in a pool of blood, stabbed to death. Knife was never found. He was a frail boy. The district surgeon in his evidence said that the wound was so deep, and because some bone had been fractured, that the wound must have been caused by a very strong person. You're a doctor yourself. You'll know what I'm saying. The good Judge felt otherwise. From all accounts, at times during the trial he was so nasty to the boy that he no doubt intimidated the jury. He said in his judgement that the boy's rage had given him the strength to inflict such a cruel wound. It was a sad affair, a sad affair indeed. The boy was hanged in Pretoria. Old Reverend van Rooyen from Bredasdorp went up to Pretoria to be with him. He had christened the boy and held him in his arms when he was a baby. The boy protested his innocence right up to the last moment. The Reverend was so disturbed by it all that he took to drink, and was driven out of his parish in abject poverty. Some relative of van Rooyen who farms here in the district gave him a room. He was here in the bar one evening, maudlin, and in his cups. He was alone in the bar when I went to close up and could hardly walk. He sobbed bitterly as he told me about the gallows. When the boy stood on the scaffold the Reverend was so distraught at the injustice that was about to happen that he collapsed and instead of being able to comfort the boy who was about to die, the boy tried to comfort the old man by saying that all was well because he was going to meet the Lord. The angels in heaven must have wept. Two years ago the police in Caledon arrested some scoundrel for burglary, searched his dwelling, found some of the dead woman's trinkets hidden in a drawer. The man mistakenly thought that the police knew more than they did and confessed to the murder of the boy's mother. What an utterly, utterly dreadful affair. When the Reverend heard the news he took a shotgun and went into the kraal of the farm where he was staying. He sat down against the stonewall of the kraal and before anyone could get to him, he cursed the Judge in a loud voice, put the barrel into his mouth and blew his head off. He was a man of God."

Garnett was pale. "I don't know what to say."

"I apologise if I have upset you. I suppose it is none of my business, except that I have found it very disturbing. It was queer to look the Judge in the eye when he stayed here, and to see him sitting at the table happily talking to his wife, seemingly unconcerned. I sometimes cannot sleep when I think of the injustice that was done, and poor old van Rooyen. Here your friends are now."

Frances skipped happily onto the veranda holding Douglas by the hand. Garnett watched Brunton's departing shoulders and his sad apologetic podgy head tilted to one side.

"Hello Garnett!" Frances exclaimed.

"Hello Frances."

"You seem subdued," she said.

"I'm just a bit preoccupied."

"Shall we go and have dinner?" Douglas asked.

Garnett stood up and straightened himself. "That's a good idea."

The men had soup but Frances decided to skip the first course.

"Douglas mentioned that you were planning to leave at about eleven thirty tomorrow morning, Garnett."

"It might even be a good idea to leave a fraction earlier. The weather is changing. We could encounter rain along the way. It will slow us down."

"You are so perceptive. How do you know that it will rain?"

"Well, one cannot be absolutely sure, of course. The wind has changed direction and the barometer has started to drop. That's a sure sign."

"Will I see you in the morning?"

"Of course, I'll come along to say goodbye."

"That sounds horrible. I mean 'goodbye' sounds so final. It has been so wonderful to have the two of you here. I gather it was Daddy's suggestion for Douglas to visit me. I am indeed fortunate that he admires Douglas as much as he does. I got a bit sunburnt today."

"So did I," Garnett said.

"You seem awfully preoccupied, Garnett?" She asked.

They all ordered fish.

"Garnie is thinking about his patients, I am sure."

"It is difficult to get away when one is practising on one's own. I find it easier to cope when older people become ill – one would expect that – but when young people become seriously ill it seems so unjust."

"I have often wondered why there should be imperfections in our world," Frances mused. "Why was everything not simply created perfect?"

"This is nice fish," Garnett said.

"Very good fish," Frances agreed.

"Think how boring it would have been if everything was perfect," Douglas remarked.

"Surely the beginning must have been perfect?" Frances said.

"We don't know what the beginning was like," Douglas replied.

"It must have been perfect, surely?" Frances persisted. "What do you think Garnett?"

"I don't think it helps too much to speculate about such things. We've just got to try and make things better. Take my work for instance, there's little point in seeking the philosophical origins of disease. I just have to accept what is presented to me, and the knowledge that is currently available, and make the best of it all."

Two overdressed women and a man entered the dining room. The women were arm in arm and giggled naughtily. The man embarrassedly nodded a greeting and the women seemed not to notice anybody else.

"Where were we?" Douglas asked.

"I was asking why we should have an imperfect world," Frances said.

"Conventional wisdom is that it is the consequence of the Fall of Man," Douglas suggested.

"What do you think, Garnett?" Frances asked.

"I don't really know what my position is. It seems to change depending on my mood. There is something in me that opposes the notion of a Fall of Man. I once made that remark in catechism class, and was told by the minister who taught us that my attitude was the clearest illustration of the Fall of Man – my refusal to accept the teaching showed to what depths I had fallen! I think we have an infinite capacity to do good. And if we try to do as much good as possible, and we show other creatures kindness and compassion, we can't go far wrong. It is too easy simply to accept a theory like that, and then to say, 'I am fallen, I am a sinner, and it's not my fault, something has caused me to fall, let the church dig me out of the hole.' In my better moments I feel that there is so much more good than evil."

"Aren't we becoming a trifle serious?" Douglas asked.

"I do apologise."

"It was entirely my fault," Frances said. "I broached the subject. Let's talk about something really jolly."

On the veranda yellow light from oil lamps lit the surfaces of the tables. The wind had dropped and the air was warm, filled with the thick sweet fragrance of syringa blossoms. In the distance a turtledove chortled in the light of the moon. The crunching wheels of a shiny Hupmobile rolled past slowly. "What a night," Garnett said. He looked up at the sky. "Come and stand here," he said as he stepped off the veranda. "Come and stand here in this shadow, and look at the sky." Above them was the firmament. "The air is so clear tonight. At times I want to choke with emotion when I see the sky like this. The Milky Way is so densely filled with heavenly bodies that it looks like a band of continuous vapour. The entire sky seems to be pressing down on us. Just imagine what a magnificent entity it must have been that made all of this. It is so wonderful." His voice trembled with emotion and he sniffed. Frances put her hand on his arm.

"If you two don't mind I am going to turn in. I'll see you in the morning then, Frances. I have had a lovely day," Garnett said. "I have become very fond of you."

"And I of you, Garnett." She leant forward and kissed him on his cheek.

"Goodnight Garnie, see you in the morning."

"It means a lot to me that we all get on so well," Douglas said when they left the hotel.

"And to me."

He took her hand. "Let's go the same way as last night," she suggested, "to our secret place. I don't want to compromise your reputation."

"We'll make sure nobody sees us."

"The houses have eyes."

"They will be shut by now."

When they turned the corner to go towards the cypress trees they heard piano music, and saw shafts of light stretching across the road, opposite their secret place. There was a party across the street.

"What utterly rummy rotten luck!" Frances exclaimed.

"Let's cross the road anyway. It will be better to go directly to Marshall's. I have had an uneasy feeling."

"Drat, and I wanted us to be completely alone, just for a while. It will have to wait for the end of the year. Can you imagine what it must be like to be secluded in one's own house, the doors barred, the shutters closed, completely alone, just the two of us, completely private. What a privilege that must be."

"Yes it must be wonderful."

"To explore each other as modern liberated people should do. To be free from stuffy social constraints."

"The constraints do serve a purpose."

"I acknowledge that. But our turn has now come to enter the romantic realm of intimacy. I am so excited."

They arrived at the door of the boarding house. "I am so sad that you are leaving tomorrow, and yet I am so very happy that you came to see me Douglas. I am thrilled that all has turned out well. If we are going to be together forever, a few moments now will not matter. I love you."

"And I love you more and more each day."

They kissed, and she watched as his figure went off into the distance and faded into the night.

Chapter Twenty-six

Saturday 3 December 1927

MRS VAN YSSEN woke at five, washed herself, and put on a light floral cotton dress for the journey to Plettenberg Bay. She went into the garden and picked figs and early spring peaches. The car had been packed the night before. Van Yssen had made a list of things to remember. Betta's wages, and money for Jafta, their Christmas presents, put off the main switch, reminder to water the garden, remind them to make full use of the water turn next week. They were to let Madame Jacquard have as much fruit as she wanted.

Van Yssen pointed to the mountains, "We could be in for cloudy weather."

"Or some rain," Douglas suggested.

"That won't be very nice," Mrs van Yssen said.

"It's better for it to happen now, dear, at the beginning of the holiday, besides it never lasts at this time of the year."

They gradually ascended the Montagu Pass. Vaporous condensate swirled and billowed and darted at the car and came and went. Van Yssen let the car slow down. Rivulets ran down the windscreen and he turned on the windscreen wipers.

"Shouldn't we put the lights on?" Douglas asked.

"That is good thinking." Van Yssen chuckled.

"At least it is cool weather for travelling. Roads can be a bit slippery though. You'll have to watch the passes on the other side of George."

When they began their descent van Yssen put the car into second gear. At times the mist and fog became so dense that he had to bring the car to a halt. "I hope there's not too much traffic coming up."

As they approached George an hour later, angry squalls of rain flung themselves onto the car. A wild south-westerly wind relentlessly drove fleeing storm clouds up into the dark violet blue mountains.

They arrived in Plettenberg Bay just after two in the afternoon. To the south thick metallic grey clouds threatened. To the north patches of blue sky appeared.

"You know where the house is, Douglas," van Yssen said. "What about the keys?"

"They will be at the police station."

"And the maid?"

"She's probably there already."

It started drizzling again when they arrived at Hurter's house. Sienna had taken shelter in a leeward corner of the veranda that was partly overgrown by a milkwood tree. Dry leaves swirled and scraped about in the wind, mixed with cobwebs and seeds from the surrounding trees. Douglas stopped the car as close as possible to the front of the house. They heard the sound of the sea and smelled the sea air mixed with the fragrance of coastal vegetation, and the creosote of the timbers under the veranda.

"Good afternoon Sienna, let me introduce you to my parents."

"We are grateful that you were willing to come an help us, Sienna," Mrs van Yssen said.

"I hope madam will be satisfied."

Douglas unlocked the front door. The air was stale and filled with scents of linseed oil, floor polish, paraffin from the lamps and carbolic.

"We should clean the house before we take the things from the car," van Yssen suggested. "If we could get the primus going we could make some tea. I think we should have something to eat, do some justice to the picnic basket. While you help the women, Douglas, I will go and get supplies. I made a list last night with the help of your mother."

By five that afternoon the house was ready. The rain had stopped and the sky was clearing. Sienna stood waiting at the side of the house with a brown paper packet of food under her arm. "Come along, Sienna," Douglas said. "Let me fetch the keys to the car."

"The tea is ready," van Yssen called to his wife as he proudly carried a large wooden tea tray into the dining room. "It is too cold to sit outside. There will be plenty of sunny days ahead. I am looking forward to having Garnett here, and Madame Jacquard. It will be quite festive to have a house full of people, to see you decorating the Christmas tree. Let the tea draw for a minute."

Douglas was back. "Sienna says there's a leak in the kitchen. She put a basin down."

"I was just saying to your mother how much I am looking forward to the holiday. I'm pleased we've come, and I am glad that Garnett and Madame Jacquard will be joining us. At what time do you think the Roses will arrive on Monday?"

"If I know the Judge they'll get here early, soon after lunch.

"Are we going for a swim in the morning?"

"Let's see what the weather does. We'll get up when we wake up."

"You said you and Garnett visited the Leibners on your way here last year?"

"It must be awkward to have to take everything across the river to their house," Mrs van Yssen said.

"They seem to like the idea, but I agree with you, Ma. Gee but it is really nice to be here. You have no idea how I have been looking forward to coming here."

"And seeing Frances," his mother said.
"Yes."

Van Yssen was the first to wake to the sounds of Sienna chopping wood for the stove. The wood was dense and dry. First there were big solid chops, then changing notes of pieces of wood falling onto a growing pile, then the smaller sounds of thin bits to get the fire going. He wondered if she could bake bread. He put his large hand on his wife's warm rump, and heard Douglas' bed creaking, and then his footsteps in the passage. His wife took his hand and kissed the back of it and pressed it against her face. "Your bathing costume is in the cupboard with your other things, Albert."

The air was still fresh when Douglas and his father went down to the beach in their bathing costumes and dressing gowns.

Breakfast consisted of bacon and eggs, fried tomatoes, fried bananas, thin mutton sausage, bread and marmalade, and strong coffee. Van Yssen cleared his throat. "When you were in Graaff Reinet, Douglas, did you and Frances talk about a wedding date?"

"What makes you think of that now, Albert?"

"I have actually thought a lot about it since Douglas got back."

"You haven't said anything."

"They were just thoughts, really. But now that we are here, and are likely to see more of the Roses it might be a good thing if we could be prepared and have certainty, in case anything is broached."

"No, we did not discuss anything specific. It is fair to say that we both probably felt that it should not be delayed too much. But even if we feel that way, there are of course the practicalities. Financial practicalities, where to stay, Frances would have to give up teaching in Graaff Reinet, or I would have to go where she is, and give up teaching here, I mean Oudtshoorn, you know what I mean. So in the circumstances I don't think we should force anything. I would be more comfortable if I were to establish myself – I have not even taught for a full year."

"It will never be possible to give her everything she is used to now," his mother said.

"She is an only child, Anneke. Her mother is well-to-do in her own right. Her father is wealthy. They will make sure that she does not lack for anything. They know we cannot compete; yet they have welcomed the prospective marriage. They are fully aware of Douglas' circumstances. We have enough. We are respectable professional people, of standing in the community, from a good background and I am sure they respect that. These are things that cannot be measured in money, and we should not even really discuss them. I respect your point of view, son, my only concern is that your engagement should not become drawn out interminably for the wrong reasons. I have had quite a lot of profitable work in recent years, and I no longer have your university costs, so what I am saying is that I would be quite willing to help you. Also, I have accumulated some capital, and we can only live in one house so I would be quite prepared to help you to buy a house."

"Gosh Dad, you've just had a huge expense sending me to England!"

"I have factored that all in, Douglas. Your mother and I have modest needs. Let's see how things unfold."

"The weather is improving. It would be so pleasant to go for a walk along the beach before lunch. I haven't put my feet into the sea for years," Mrs van Yssen said.

Monday 5 December 1927

The van Yssens had lunch early. Van Yssen and his wife lay fast asleep, their window open to the sounds of the surf. Their curtains occasionally flapped in the sea breeze. An easterly wind made white horses on a pale blue sea. Douglas sat on the veranda, with his book. He saw the printed words but read nothing. He kept glancing for the Roses' car to arrive. It was already two thirty. He had been past the house that morning and found the front door ajar and the windows open. There had been no sign of Martha. He heard Sienna filling a galvanised bucket with water from the tank at the back of the house. He went to the back of the garage. The grass was long and he trod warily for snakes. Beyond their fence was a small abandoned graveyard. A piece of broken gravestone lay at an uncomfortable angle in faded grass. What did Pheidias think about while he urinated on the Acropolis? He buttoned his fly. Should have had sheep here. He rounded the corner of the house. The Roses' car was at the side of their house. Martha fetched a suitcase from the back seat. He waited a while. There was no sign of anyone else.

"When will the young lady be arriving?" Sienna asked.

"They have just arrived," Douglas replied.

"Master must be very glad. Madam told me you are engaged"

Douglas smiled and nodded. He went back to the front of the house. There was still no sign of activity at the Roses' house so he tiptoed into the dining room, finished his tea, took his shoes off and lay down on the chaise longue. It was after four when Douglas woke. The taste of tea was still in his mouth. His parents were on the veranda. "The Roses have arrived," his mother said.

"I think I'll stroll down there in a while and go and say hello. I know the old chap likes to have a sleep in the afternoon when he is on holiday, and the more so I'm sure after driving a long way, so I'll wait a bit first."

Just after five Douglas put on a clean shirt and flannels and went to the Roses' house. He picked yellow daisies on the way and tied them together with a few strands of grass. The early evening was mild. He felt the sun on his back and his neck. The sea air was thick. The tide was going out and exposing the beach. Reflections of people on the beach made colourful shimmering movements.

He knocked on the front door. Mrs Rose held her arms out. "Douglas! How delightful of you to come." She threw her head back to one side. "You look so well! Not as pale as when you returned from England." She saw the flowers in Douglas' hand. "Frances will be thrilled with those. We're about to have afternoon tea. Do join us, and tell us all your news. Are your parents comfortable?"

"Yes, thank you Mrs Rose."

"Jeremy has had a sleep, and I'm not sure whether Frances has woken up. It will be a pleasant surprise for them to find you here. Let's sit down. Martha is busy with the tea. I'll get something to put the flowers in. I find it hard to believe that a whole year has gone by since we were last here. So much has happened. There was so much anticipation, which will no doubt turn into reflection. Just being here at this place at the sea, I have always since I was small loved places at the sea; they restore me. I could hardly sleep this afternoon. You must think I am quite silly."

"How could I ever think that Mrs Rose, you have always been so kind to me."

"Dear Douglas. I think we should start. No, let me go and wake Frances, she will never forgive me if I don't. Excuse me for a moment."

Douglas thought of the time he and Garnett had spent there.

"Frances was fast asleep. As soon as I said your name she sat bolt upright, she'll be with us presently. I will let Jeremy sleep for as long as possible. He's quite fatigued. It would seem as though he had a very difficult trial before we left. He desperately needs the rest here. So now tell me how you all are?"

Before Douglas could reply Frances appeared, pink sleep marks on her cheek. "I'll go and see what's happened to the tea," Mrs Rose said.

"My darling Douglas," Frances said, and they embraced and held one another. He kissed her and they only let go of one another when they heard the clinking teacups approaching.

"Afternoon Master," Martha greeted Douglas. "It is good to see master again" She put the tray down on the table and Mrs Rose appeared.

Frances yawned. "Gee I have had a wonderful sleep. I always seem to sleep so much better here, and I am quite ravenous. What are we having for supper?"

"We are going to have cheese omelettes."

"That sounds yummy."

"When did you arrive, Douglas?" Frances asked.

"On Saturday."

"Yes I know that my dearest man, what I meant was at what time did you arrive?"

"We had some really bad weather in the Montagu Pass, so we only got here after two. It was still raining when we arrived. The weather has been improving ever since."

"Frances tells me that you are staying for Christmas?"

"Yes we are. We have invited a friend from Oudtshoorn to spend a few days with us over Christmas. Mrs Jacquard, she has no family here, and has become a good friend to my mother. Garnett is arriving after New Year and will take her back with him."

"Douglas has told me about her, she's an artist, is she not?"

"Frances has told me about her. What brought her to these parts, Douglas?"

"It's a bit of a mystery. She has only told my mother, and I don't know whether we ought to talk about it, that her husband because of 'a matter of honour' ended up in the Foreign Legion. Judging by her cultured ways, they must be people of good social standing, but that is all I know. In the circumstances she was unwilling, or unable I suppose, to remain in France. She is a trifle eccentric."

"How interesting. I would very much like to see her paintings. When is she arriving?"

"Only on the twenty-second."

"That's after we leave."

"What do you mean when you say she's eccentric?" Frances asked.

"Perhaps I should have said unconventional. She studied in Paris and lived there until she came here."

"Come, come now Douglas," Mrs Rose teased. "You cannot wriggle out of that. Tell us about her – an artist with a husband in the Foreign Legion, an art student in Paris, Paris in the early twenties. What does she look like?"

"She's typically French, dark hair, blue eyes. Oil paint under her nails. She's a bit untidy at times. She has a wicked sense of humour; calls a spade a spade, if you know what I mean. To start with she was ostracised in Oudtshoorn."

"Why?" Frances asked.

"Possibly just because she is different. We know of no other reason. My mother felt sorry for her. My father initially kept his distance but has grown to like her. We have introduced her to our friends. She is like a breath of fresh air in Oudtshoorn. Of course there are the bigots, who would behead her just because they imagine she is Catholic. She can be unpredictable, and although she does not have much, she is quite generous."

"Sounds as though she will be an entertaining guest," Mrs Rose said.

The Judge entered the room. "Ah Douglas, my good fellow. Good to see you again." They shook hands. "How are you getting on?"

"Fine, thank you Judge."

"I take it your parents are well?"

"Yes they are indeed, thank you."

"You're staying on for Christmas, then?"

"Yes we are."

"I wish we could have done that," Frances remarked.

"It would be so much simpler," Mrs Rose observed.

"Tradition is tradition, dear," the Judge chided.

"Did you have a good journey, Judge Rose?"

"Tolerably. Getting too old for this now. Weariness drives away my sense of adventure."

"You need more exercise, dear."

"You could be right, you know, Elizabeth. Tell me Douglas, does your father have any interest in hiking?"

"His work requires a lot of walking. He enjoys it."

"Then he and I should go hiking sometime."

"It is getting late, and I think I should be going home." Douglas got up from his chair.

"I'll walk with you, and say hello to your parents."

"Is it not a bit late for that Frances?" her mother asked.

"Not at all, Mrs Rose. We don't stand on ceremony, especially not on holiday. Everything is quite informal. That's what makes it special to be here."

"That's what I like to hear!" The Judge exclaimed. "Elizabeth, we should go for a brisk walk before supper. The tide is out and the evening is begging."

Douglas and Frances walked arm in arm across the scrub covered sandy slope to Hurter's house. Sienna was in the kitchen. "Do you know where my parents are?" Douglas asked.

"They have gone to walk along the beach."

"Let's go and find them."

The beach lay under drifts of vapour illuminated by the declining sun. Several groups of people were discernable along the shore: a family with small children, a father carrying a little one already in his pyjamas, an elderly couple with their West Highland Terrier that barked at and attacked small hissing waves, a young very pregnant woman and her husband, ahead of them the unmistakable figures of the Judge and Mrs Rose.

Frances let go of Douglas' arm, skipped up to her parents and tapped her father on his shoulder. "We've come to find Douglas' parents, everyone in creation must be out on the beach this evening."

"Unless they've gone in the other direction," the Judge said.

A seagull shrieked to frighten away a competitor for the early-supper crust that a small boy had thrown towards them.

"They are likely to have walked towards the Robberg," Douglas said. "My dad avoids the area near the whaling station."

"Walk with us anyway, we're bound to encounter them if they have gone this way," Mrs Rose suggested.

The van Yssens had turned and were on their way back when they met them.

"Well, well, well, how splendid to see you, Albert, Anneke," the Judge exclaimed.

"Hello Anneke, Albert," Mrs Rose shook their hands.

"Good evening Jeremy," van Yssen shook his hand. "My, but you look so well Frances."

"I assume all is well in Oudthoorn?" the Judge said. "We must make some plans to get together. We'll get the women to arrange it."

"We should be getting back, Albert," Mrs van Yssen said.

"No need to rush when on holiday, Anneke," Mrs Rose said.

"I have to help our servant with the supper, she's not used to cooking."

"A good cook is the most important thing when you are on holiday," the Judge pontificated. "I learnt that from my father. They always took the cook with them to the south of France or Italy. He wouldn't go on holiday without the fellow. Also, he could not stand foreign food. Had to have what he called English Food."

Mrs van Yssen moved about uneasily. Van Yssen took her hand. "I am sure Anneke is right, we ought to get going."

"Would you like to have drinks with us tomorrow evening?" Mrs Rose asked.

"That's a splendid idea," the Judge responded.

"Yes, thank you very much," van Yssen said.

"Shall we make it seven, or shortly thereafter?" Mrs Rose proposed.

"That would suit us very well, thank you, Elizabeth, Jeremy," van Yssen said.

They said cheerful goodbyes. "Why are you in such a hurry to get back, it almost seemed rude?" van Yssen asked his wife.

"It's the tea, and the chill in the air, I need to go to the toilet."

"I am feeling a bit cold," Frances said after a while. "I think Douglas and I should turn back."

Tuesday 6 December 1927

Douglas arrived at the Roses' house at eleven. Mrs Rose was on the veranda in a wickerwork chair, reading a book underneath a straw hat with a colourful scarf tied around the bowl.

"Hello dear boy! What a smashing day for a picnic. I hope you and Frances will have a lovely day. How romantic. You know by now that I am an incurable romantic. I would have liked to meet your French woman. Perhaps some day when we visit Oudtshoorn we could meet her."

"I am sure you will like her."

"Whom are you talking about?" Frances asked as she stepped onto the veranda.

"Hello Frances," he kissed her on her cheek. "Your mother was just enquiring after Madame Jacquard. I was saying your mother would enjoy her company."

"Your basket has been prepared Douglas."

"That's very kind of you Mrs Rose. I should have offered to bring the things. It was quite shabby of me not to suggest it."

"Oh, come now dear boy, your mother said your maid was not much of a cook. All I had to do was to give Martha instructions. I am afraid it's not much of a spread. Provisions here are limited, really just sandwiches and fruit and something to drink. The basket is on the dining room table, if you would collect it, please. Jeremy has gone to the village to buy paint for the windows. We have a man coming tomorrow – always some wretched repairs to be done. He was saying it is really much smarter to rent a holiday house than to own one. But, let me not detain you, off you go, and have a wonderful time."

She watched Frances and Douglas strolling hand in hand, their heads moving in conversation, along the beach until they virtually disappeared into the sea air.

"How did your exams go?" Frances asked.

"Fine, I think, judging by the papers. We should have good results. I won't be able to take much of the credit. Mrs Archer did an excellent job while I was away. And your exams?"

"It is difficult to tell, but I think fine. The standard of Latin has always been high, which made it easier for me."

"It is really good to be on our own, don't you think?"

"It is so thrilling. We should find a secluded place."

"What will people say if we disappear into the dunes on our own."

She pretended to scan the beach. "I don't see anyone who will mind. Apart from our parents I have not seen anyone I know."

They wandered further and further along the beach, each reluctant to be the first to seek seclusion, she because she had suggested it, and he because he first wanted to get as far away as possible from other people. He looked back. The houses were almost indistinguishable now and there was not a soul in sight. He put his free arm around her waist and felt the soft upper part of her hip moving in the palm of his hand. Her cotton dress slid back and forth over her underwear. She put her arm around him. He stopped and put the picnic basket down on the beach. He drew her towards him and began to kiss her until she was quite limp from passion. They continued to walk for a while. Her face was flushed. "May I tell you a secret, Douglas, a very special secret? And promise that you will never let it out?"

"I promise."

"After we became engaged, Mummy told me how wonderful the physical relationship between a man and a woman can be. Of course she stopped short of being explicit in any sort of way, but it was the manner in which she said it that said it all, and I am beginning to learn what she could have meant. That night in Graaff Reinet under the cypresses when we loved one another, something inside me, my womanhood, was awakened. It asked to be fulfilled. I thought about it as time went by and began to understand, in a very abstract sort of way the real meaning of being a woman. God, how I would love to be a mother to children. I am so fortunate to have you."

"That seems like a nice place," he said looking to his right.

He assisted her up the slopes. She took her shoes off when they became filled with sand. He searched for the best place. Better to go further in. The folds between the dunes became deeper as they went. A bit further they found a copse of shiny-green milkwood trees.

"This seems perfect," Frances suggested. "How fortunate to have shade."

Douglas spread the tartan rug that they had had at the dam at Graaff Reinet and put their basket down in one corner. He lay down with his hands behind his head.

"I brought something to read. Daddy does not like it."

"What is it?" he said absent-mindedly, looking at the patterns made by the milkwood leaves and the spaces between them.

"Virginia Woolf's new novel."

"What is it called?"

"'To The Lighthouse.' I have been reading it in my room."

"Why does your dad not like it?"

"He does not like the Bloomsbury crowd. I am sure you will recall what he had to say about Lytton Strachey when you and Garnett were here last year."

"I remember well."

"Well, Strachey is part of the Bloomsbury group, and he says if they embrace him they are all suspect."

"Are you enjoying it?"

"Yes, very much. You said you enjoyed 'Mrs Dalloway.'"

"It was different; quite different. I have since often thought how much can occur in our minds in a single day. What is the Lighthouse about?"

"It is in three parts. I have just started the second. The first has a central character, Mrs Ramsay, and is about her Victorian life and that of her family."

"What is she like?"

"You mean Mrs Ramsay?"

"Yes."

"She is intuitive and considerate. Her husband is an uncompromising, cerebral man. Ever since I first read Virginia Woolf, I think it was 'Jacob's Room,' I am utterly compelled by her technique. Her distinction of style is now more refined. She exposes the subtle dimensions of her characters, the Ramsays, their children, and their guests, as they anticipate going to the lighthouse. She captures the divisions and diversity in the family; how the children go to lengths of inventing differences when there are already too many differences among them. And as though that is not difficult enough to do, she still manages to set it perfectly in Victorian time and idiom. You must read it yourself; it is so saturated with meaning that it is quite hard to describe. She is able to isolate the essential symbols of human existence and present them in a form that makes you feel that you have understood them for the first time. What a genius she is."

Douglas closed his eyes and as he turned his head towards the sun he seemed to be able to see through the pink tissues of his eyelids. He smiled as he listened to Frances.

"Are you listening to me?"

"Of course I am."

"Then why are you smiling?"

"Because I am pleased to be with you. I love listening to you. You're almost as intense about your subject as I am sometimes. It's like hearing myself speak."

"You are mocking me."

"Now why would I want to do that when you are so serious?"

"There, see, you are mocking me. Would you rather that I should be frivolous?"

"If you kiss me I will tell you."

"I am not going to be bribed."

"All right then, read me a bit from your book."

"I am not in the mood to read now."

He pushed himself up on his elbow and smiled at her. "You are so beautiful." She blushed, and sidled over to him. He lifted her hair at the back of her head and kissed her on the nape of her neck. She gripped his thigh and turned her face towards him. They lay on their backs and observed the canopies of the trees. He turned onto his side and looked at her. He kissed her. She took his hand and put it on her breast. "Wait," she said and sat up. She undid the buttons of her blouse and lay down again. "Try again now." Not fully understanding what he was meant to do he slipped his hand into her blouse and held her breast. He could feel her nipple under his palm. "Wait," she said, and sat up again. She pulled her spencer up above her breasts and lay down. He kissed her again and put his hand in under her blouse. He held first the one breast in his hand until he could feel the nipple stiffening and then went to the other breast to feel it responding, and then gently back to the first. "Do you like that?" she said between kisses.

"I love you Frances."

She pressed his hand down on her breast. "Do you like that, my love?"

"It is amazing."

"I don't think I could ever have done this with anyone else."

"Do you really like it very much?"

"Of course I do."

They lay like that for a while and he kissed her some more. She put her hand against the front of his trousers. "May I feel?" She said.

"If you want to. I'm a little shy."

"This is so lovely," she said and gently stroked him. "I've wondered what it would feel like. I'll have lovely dreams tonight. Can you imagine what it will be like when we are married? To be able to take all the delight we want in each another. Don't you think it is an extraordinary concept: for two human beings to take delight in each another. Just think of that – to give pleasure to another and in doing so to be rewarded by receiving even greater pleasure until you reach an unbearable crescendo. We must really start putting our plans together. Let's have something to eat, and talk." While she buttoned up her blouse he saw her glancing at the swelling in his trousers. "We could carry on again later on if you like. Shall we start with some fruit, or shall we have it afterwards?"

"What would you prefer?"

"I am going to start with a sandwich."

"I'll join you, thank you." He sat up and crossed his legs in front of him.

She knelt at the picnic basket and turned her head and smiled as though she felt his eyes on her body.

"This sandwich is excellent," he said. "I think I'll have a peach. Makes a good combination. What kind of cheese is this?"

"It's an imported Swiss cheese Mummy ordered for Daddy. He loves it. Gruyere or something like that."

"It has a nice tangy taste."

"Would you like some tea?"

"In a moment, yes, please."

"Isn't it a lovely day. We should go bathing when we get back. Mummy bought me a new bathing costume. It is quite fun – all stripy, blue and white wool with a matching cap. Daddy said he saw you and your father in the surf this morning."

"The weather might be changing." Douglas tilted his eyes towards the sky. She saw reflections of low clouds from the west in his pupils. A shadow passed over them. "It is amazing how quickly the weather can change. Gee this sandwich is really good."

"Have another one, there are plenty. Wait, there are also boiled eggs."

"I beg your pardon?"

"I said there are lots of sandwiches, and also some boiled eggs."

"My ears have been a bit clogged. I went to see Garnett. He said it is possibly just a bit of catarrh. Is it not strange how one can sometimes have such happy days, when you seem to be in harmony with everything. From the time you wake up, until you go to bed everything seems to work out well. Today is one of those days. Each time we are together I discover things about you that I could not have imagined. The way you let me touch you."

"I wanted you to touch me, to give you pleasure, but also so that I could experience pleasure."

A sharp gust of wind whipped up sand and flung it into them. Frances hurriedly covered the basket with a napkin. The trees around them shook wildly and the fynbos was ruffled by the grasping air.

"This often happens here at the coast after the weather has been so perfect," he said.

"Do you think it will improve?"

"It is possible but I doubt it."

"What time is it now?"

He looked at his watch. "Nearly half past two."

More gusts shook their trees and the sky darkened. "I suppose we will have many other days," she said as she began packing away their picnic things. "It's is not even worth having tea now, or would you like some?"

"Not unless you're going to have some."

Once they left the shelter of the dunes the full force of the wind struck them. It was blowing offshore and made the incoming waves steep and blew their frothy manes from their tops. Fearful shivers darted wildly across the surface of the sea. The tide was in and Frances found the soft sand of the beach difficult going. She steadied herself holding onto his arm and took her shoes off. "That's better." She hesitated, "I should take my stockings off. I laddered the one earlier on." She smiled as she looked at him while she fidgeted under her dress and undid her suspenders. She deftly took her stockings off and put them into her pocket. "There, that's better. I suppose my parents will be asleep if I know them. It is strange to think of them doing what we will be doing when we are married. I wonder why we can never imagine our parents being intimate?"

"Yes it is odd. Garnie and I once discussed that when we were younger. It seems as though all children find it hard to imagine their parents making love."

Frances had a problem keeping her hat on, and took it off. She undid her scarf from around her neck and tied it around her head.

"Avoiding thinking about it is almost like denying where we come from."

"Would you bath in front of our children?"

"Well, I am rather shy…"

"I mean would we bath together in front of our children? Modern thinking is that it is a good Idea. Perhaps if children grow up in that way they won't find it so strange to think that their parents make love."

"I don't think my parents even undress in front of each other."

"At least my parents do that. I have not seen mine completely naked together, but I recall my dad walking around in their room in his all-together when I was younger, and my mother sitting on their bed in her underwear. It was quite sweet. Seeing him naked was little different from seeing a large naked male dog. We don't ever seem to find that strange; or other animals without pants on."

"You had better come to our house if your parents are resting."

"I would like that. Mummy reminded me that you're all coming to us for drinks this evening."

It was raining when the van Yssens arrived at the Roses' house. Douglas stopped the car as close to the front of the house as he could. The Judge had on a Burberry and a large brown hat. He opened a black umbrella and assisted first Mrs van Yssen and then van Yssen onto the veranda. Douglas briskly ran up the stairs before the Judge could get to him.

"Who would have thought we could have such a sudden change in the weather?" The Judge exclaimed. "I am afraid it will be better to sit inside. I'll tell Elizabeth you are here. Come Anneke, let me find you the most comfortable seat.

"Hello Frances," Mrs van Yssen said, admiring her. "My, but you do look fetching. Douglas tells me that you had a lovely outing. At least you had good weather to start with."

Mrs Rose entered in her most elegant finishing-school bearing. She wore a grey pleated woollen skirt, its hemline just below the knees. A blue and white silk scarf was tied carelessly around her neck. Anneke van Yssen looked down at her own dress. Yellow primroses, pink poppies, purple delphiniums and green leaves wilted on the dark blue silk fabric that lay across her lap. Her hemline was just above her ankles. "Heartiest greetings to the van Yssens! What I hoped was going to be a grand evening, watching the light fading on the shore, will now have to be an indoor affair."

"We shall have to make the best of our circumstances. What will you have to drink, Anneke?" the Judge asked.

"I'll have some sherry, thank you, Jeremy."

"And you Albert?"

"Sherry will be fine for me thank you, I would prefer dry."

"I am having gin and tonic water, Albert, if you would like to change your mind?"

"No, no, sherry will be fine, thank you."

"What is it going to be Elizabeth?"

"The weather suggests that I should have a very dry vermouth with a teeny dash of lemon."

"And what about you young man? I have some excellent beer from Belgium."

"That sounds very good, thank you Judge."

"Frances is awfully predictable. She'll have ginger ale with a smidgeon of bitters, eh my girl?"

The Judge falsely hummed some or other little melody while he prepared the drinks. Mrs van Yssen looked about the room.

"Are you enjoying your stay Anneke?" Mrs Rose enquired.

"Yes, yes we are. One forgets how different it is at the coast."

A vigorous squall flung itself against the house and drove clattering rain onto the tin roof and the windowpanes.

"Here you are Anneke." The Judge handed her a glass of sherry. "And here is your vermouth, my dear. Tell me if you need more lemon. Should we open the front door, Albert?" He handed Frances her drink.

Mrs Rose took a sip of her drink. "This is just utterly perfect, Jeremy."

"Shall we have a toast then? Here's to a sparklingly good time at the seaside. And to the families." The Judge was hearty.

"Hear, hear," van Yssen responded.

Mrs Rose raised her glass demonstratively. "Savouries will be served presently. We should have some music Jeremy, nothing too dreary if you don't mind, something festive and jolly."

The Judge examined the pile of records on the table where the gramophone stood. "What about some jazz?" He peered over his spectacles.

"That sounds jolly," Mrs van Yssen said enthusiastically.

"You might not like my taste in music, Anneke." The Judge cast her a mischievous sliding glance.

"We have got used to the modern music," van Yssen said.

"Very well then, I have new recordings of jazz music, sent out to me by my brother." He held up a record. "*On the Sunny Side of the Street* played by Bernie Cummins and his orchestra." He continued to look through the records. "*Big City Blues, I'm Just a Vagabond Lover, I've Made a Habit of You*. Here we go then!" The music began to play.

"Chin, chin," Mrs Rose said holding up her glass. She swayed in an ungainly way to the music and grinned. The Judge joined in with clumsy movements of his hand that failed to keep time. Frances cringed. "This is so utterly jolly," Mrs Rose said. "We should get Florrie to show us the blackbottom!"

"You need something faster than this Mummy."

"We'll just do it slowly, Frances," her mother replied. "Frances tells me that you had a marvellous picnic Douglas. What it is to be young, and in these rollicking times. When Jeremy and I were courting it would have been unthinkable to go anywhere without a chaperone. We had a marvellous evening when Douglas and his friend Doctor Nel were here last year, Albert. We sat outside on a perfect evening and Jeremy played Italian opera music. So romantic. What a lovely night that was. Do you remember, Douglas?"

"How could I ever forget Mrs Rose."

"I had hoped that we would be able to recapture that atmosphere this evening. But alas it was not to be."

Mrs van Yssen had a sip of sherry. "It is so difficult to recreate special moments, almost impossible really. They have a habit of happening on their own."

"There's much philosophy in what you say Anneke," the Judge complimented. "Talking about the opera music, will Nel be coming down?"

"Yes," Douglas replied.

"Jolly good, then he can sing for us," the Judge said.

"He'll only arrive after New Year, Judge, and only for a few days," Douglas replied.

"He is such a charming young man," Mrs Rose said. "We should tuck into the savouries, won't you pass them around, please Frances."

"When will you be returning to Cape Town, Jeremy?" van Yssen enquired.

"On the twentieth, my good fellow. It's a Tuesday."

"I could really get to love your jazz, Jeremy," Mrs van Yssen's cheeks were flushed from the sherry. "Your savouries are delicious, Elizabeth."

"Frances, my dear daughter, you are very quiet this evening?"

"I wish we could have stayed for Christmas," Frances said. "It is so pleasant here. And Daddy enjoys a good rest here."

"We have a tradition dear."

"We could start a new tradition, Mummy. Just imagine, we could all have had a jolly festive time."

"Not if the weather was like this," the Judge said. "When shall we go for a hike?"

"Whenever it suits you Jeremy, just give me a day or so warning."

Mrs Rose's drink made her jolly. "Are you having any guests, Anneke?"

Van Yssen glanced at his wife. "We are having a French woman, who now lives in Oudtshoorn, over for Christmas."

"That's rather decent of you, Albert. Has she been there for long?" Mrs Rose asked.

"For some years. She has been a good friend to Anneke."

"Where is she from?" The Judge asked.

"The Paris area," van Yssen replied.

"We gather she had to leave France on account of her husband," Mrs van Yssen interrupted.

"Why would that be?" the Judge asked.

"Yummy, a scandal then!" Mrs Rose sat forward in her chair.

"Well, not quite," van Yssen said. "A scandal; that would be too harsh. She is an artist, an accomplished woman, well educated, and well read. She is just different." van Yssen wanted to change the subject. "From what we understand there was what is termed, shall we say, a matter of honour. That is all we know. She has not told us more than that. She is very proud. As a consequence of the 'matter of honour' her husband joined the Foreign Legion."

"The Foreign Legion, how romantic, how utterly romantic," Mrs Rose exclaimed.

"When individuals seek the shelter of the Legion, dear, it is because they have committed crimes, often heinous crimes, and as I always say, evil should know no probation." There was a hint of asperity in his voice. His bushy eyebrows were dissonant.

Van Yssen squared his shoulders. "Madame Jacquard is an interesting person, to say the least. We have introduced her to our friends and they have accepted her. In fact she has been like a breath of fresh air in the town."

"My Albert has such noble principles. He will not flinch. He felt that Madame Jacquard was being treated poorly, because of ignorance, prejudice and hypocrisy, and he set about putting things right, as he always does. It goes well beyond appearances for him. He is respected in Oudtshoorn for his independent views and as a man of principle. Now she is the soul of social gatherings."

"What are her paintings like?" Mrs Rose asked.

"They are after the Impressionist style, mostly landscapes. They are beautiful, and as Doctor von Essellen of the college remarked when he opened her exhibition, done with competence, which shows that she was classically trained." Mrs van Yssen was pleased with the quality of her statement.

"That sounds reassuring," the Judge cleared his throat. "What about another drink?"

"We should get one of her paintings," Mrs Rose suggested.

"That sounds like a lovely idea, and it would help her no doubt," Frances contributed.

"It's so cosy in here now. I am having a lovely time. Life is so much less complicated here," Mrs Rose said in a languid voice as she leant back in her chair. "I ought to have another drink, Jeremy. Just a teeny one."

The Judge looked to see how van Yssen and his wife were doing with their sherry, but their glasses were still nearly half full. "We had some interesting discussions last year, did we not, Douglas?" The Judge prepared his wife's drink and poured himself another.

"Yes we did indeed Judge."

"Hand me your glass Douglas, for the other half of your beer."

"I don't know whether I should."

"Come now, if your father and your mother won't join us in another round, you should at least come to our rescue."

Frances handed round more savouries.

"Talking about Nel, I am reminded of what I said about the 'Black Shirts' when he was here. I meant to remind him of what I said when he was in Cape Town, in the light of what happened in America in May."

"What happened dear?"

"The Memorial Day incidents when two Italians who went to join the Fascist march were attacked and killed by anti-Fascists. I must admit it seems like a bit of an irony – killing in the name of peace. And talking about killing, the Ku Klux were there too, no doubt proud of their feast of lynchings. That's one thing about this country: we have never seen people taking the law into their own hands as they have in America. And do you want to know why that is Albert? I'll tell you. It is because our courts have been tough on criminals, so if anything, public sympathy has been for the criminal, and the public are less inclined to take the law into their own hands. Sometimes we may seem a bit harsh, but in the greater scheme of things it is inevitable that a few flowers will get cut down when you harvest the wheat. Would you not agree Albert?" the Judge asked.

Van Yssen smiled embarrassedly.

"Don't be afraid to speak your mind, Albert, I really respect a strong debate."

"I'm not sure what you are asking me to comment on Jeremy."

"The philosophy of having a tough justice system and the salutary effect that such a system has on society at large. Erring on the side of being tough results in a more stable social order."

"It is an interesting approach, I have not really thought too much about it."

"Then would you agree with me?"

Van Yssen lifted his steady clear blue eyes. "Something in me always pleads for fairness. I cannot see how unfairness, in any single instance, can be justified. I cannot see how administering a system that could be unfair to one individual ought to benefit others. To me justice has to be applied evenly to each separate individual. We cannot say that if one innocent man is convicted and one guilty man goes free that the one cancels out the other, it is not some currency that can be distributed in a way that leaves some poorer and others richer. We may inspire fear by being tough, but that does not earn respect. If we want to underpin the foundations of society we have to be seen to be fair. To my mind it is better for guilty men to go free than for one innocent man to be convicted. I agree that we have been spared the barbaric behaviour of the American South; but that may be for other reasons."

"Such as?"

"An innate sense of what is fair and just that our settlers brought with them, together with their great Roman Dutch legal tradition."

Frances cleared her throat. "Daddy, in purely logical terms, it is near impossible to draw any meaningful conclusion from the absence of a certain kind of social behaviour."

"You have lost me Frances."

"If we find that in certain countries people do not beat their children at home it would be spurious to suggest that it is because the children are treated harshly at school."

"I think I understand Judge Rose's point," Douglas said, "and it is a good point. It must be evident to all that a weak judicial system will lead to frustrations."

"I haven't finished, Douglas," Frances said. Douglas tried to hold her hand but she refused. "Let me finish, please. What I am trying to say is that it is not sound reasoning, Daddy, to conclude that we have been spared lynching in this country because our judicial system is harsh. There is no scientific way in which to connect the two things. To do so would require an immense amount of research in conditions that are forever changing. At best a conclusion of the kind that has been drawn really tells us only what the person who is expressing the opinion is thinking."

"Well said, Frances," her father said.

"Don't patronise me, Daddy."

"You wanted to say something, Douglas," the Judge said.

"I think I see your point, Judge, and I agree with the essence of it." Mrs Rose admired Douglas. "If we examine history we do find greater social stability, as well as political stability, in countries with well-developed judicial systems. At the same time I must point out that there is the possibility that a sound judicial system is a function of a well-developed and stable society. The two things go hand in hand. Like the chicken and the egg it is impossible to say which comes first."

"And I still maintain that you cannot produce a better society by being intentionally harsh in the courts," Frances said.

Mrs Rose tilted her head to one side and smiled condescendingly at Frances, "My but you are fiery this evening. Your picnic and the fresh air seem to have renewed your spirit."

"Oh, Mummy!"

"Well, that was refreshing," the Judge said. "Please don't spare my feelings, for I am indifferent to much, except the law. It is a characteristic of most members of my profession that they will speak to any brief. What is more it is perfectly reasonable for us to plead one way in the morning and another way in the afternoon, and if asked why that is so, you would answer that you were wrong in morning, and right in the afternoon."

"I feel we should be getting home," Mrs van Yssen moved about in her chair.

"The evening is still young," the Judge said.

"It has stopped raining," van Yssen said. "Anneke is right. We have had a lovely evening, and we look forward to having you over for lunch. I would like to go for a walk, Jeremy, whenever you are ready."

"That's a corking good idea, Albert."

The air on the veranda was fresh. The wind had died down. Out in the night, beyond the curtain of water beads dripping from the edges of the veranda, a vast multitude of crickets and frogs transmitted their screeching and burping signals into the ether in search of their own kind. Van Yssen looked up at the sky. "The stars are becoming visible. Tomorrow promises to be a lovely day,"

Friday 9 December 1927

At ten in the morning the Judge and Mrs Rose left Plettenberg Bay for Knysna. They had been invited there to have lunch with friends and had decided to leave early so that Mrs Rose could first do some shopping. Frances elected to stay at home so that she and Douglas could spend time on the beach and have lunch together.

It was a sunny day. A gentle breeze came from the west. She watched him striding across the loose dune sand. He wore his woollen bathing costume, and had a change of clothing tucked under his arm. His legs were irresistible. He was lost in thought, his head bent forward. But then he always was. He looked up. She smiled and waved at him. He waved back. He stamped his feet on the steps to leave the sand behind. She embraced him. "I am so excited, dearest heart, to be alone with you today. I suggest we take our beach umbrella, and the two canvas chairs, Martha will help us, and she'll bring us some tea later on. I have it all planned. Then we will have lunch on our own, when she rings the bell for us. Mummy and Daddy will only be back quite late I imagine."

He could see the outlines of her bathing costume under her loose cream coloured linen dress with bright red buttons. She smelt delicious. She held the back of her hand away from her hip and admired her ring. "Come let's go!"

From their house the van Yssens could see the figures of their son and his fiancé strolling along the beach. Frances was frolicking, running ahead of Douglas, stamping in the shallow water to make splashes, putting her arm through Douglas' and leaning her head on his shoulder. Behind them, at a respectful distance, Martha followed with a folded canvas chair in each hand.

Douglas planted the umbrella in the sand, unfolded the chairs and placed them in the shade of the umbrella.

"Thank you Martha," Frances said.

Douglas settled in his chair. He yawned.

"Are you tired my love? Have you not had enough sleep?"

"I think I've had too much sleep. The more I sleep the more I want to sleep, especially here at the seaside. I feel so relaxed, and so relieved at the way things have turned out."

She put her hand on his arm.

"Be careful, Frances, the whole world is watching."

"I don't care. We are engaged after all. People are allowed some physical contact when they are engaged. Putting my hand on your arm is hardly overstepping the bounds of social decency. We can overstep those bounds when we're alone inside later on."

"I think I shall go for a swim," he said and jumped up. "I hope the water's cold."

"I'll read my book."

Douglas stood dripping next to the umbrella. Frances handed him his towel. He dried himself, folded his towel and sat down on it on the sand. She passed him his tea once he was settled.

"Still enjoying your book?"

"It's quite nice not to be confined to my room with it. Daddy has been muttering some more."

"About what?"

"About all sorts of things. He spotted my book and fulminated against the literature that is emerging overseas. I suggested that he read it to see for himself how brilliant the woman is but he just grunted and waved his hand dismissively. He is comfortable with his prejudices and does not want to risk having them disturbed. It is like wearing an old garment that is a bit uncomfortable, a bit too small for you, but familiar, and which you suspect probably does not even really suit you, but you fear changing it for something else, even though it could be better, could leave you worse off."

Douglas laughed. "There has been a real change in you."

"What on earth do you mean?"

"Your mother said it the other evening: a sort of a feistiness."

"To be truthful, I sense a restlessness in myself. It is as though an ancient instinct that came with me when I was born, that has been lying dormant, has been aroused. It is quite a pleasant sensation really. It is difficult to describe. In one way it is vague and in another way it is real. It is quite subtle. I have amazing physical sensations when we touch one another. Oh what am I saying? To be plain, I am desperately in love, and utterly frustrated. I wish we could get married."

Douglas thought of his room at home, of his bicycle, of his monthly income. "If only you knew how much I want to be with you Frances."

"I am not talking about being together, I am talking about getting married."

"You know my circumstances, you know how much, or should I say little, I earn. I don't have a house."

"Mummy has her own means, she could help us."

"I believe I should accumulate something first."

"Why? If we love one another enough things will take care of themselves."

"My most dearest love, many a marriage has been wrecked by financial difficulties. Ours deserves to be given the best possible chance. What difference will a year make? I'll come and see you as often as I can."

"A year! That seems like an eternity!"

"Just think of it. Garnett and I visited here a year ago, and it has gone by like a flash. Next year will be just like that."

"Will you kiss me now and kiss me after lunch when the maid has gone to her room?"

"Well… we'll have to see about that. Aren't you going to swim?"

"I'll swim in my own good time, if you please." She got up from her chair, and began unbuttoning her dress. He looked out to sea. "Have a look if you wish." She waited for him to respond and watched his uncertain eyes. She stroked his head playfully and skipped off into the waves. He watched her girlish lissom body and her long legs as she lent forward to catch water in her hands and splashed her shoulders and her face, and then her thighs. She had tied her hair up. Her shoulders were straight. She beckoned to him to join her.

They heard the bell. Martha was on the veranda. Frances waved to indicate that they had heard.

Frances went to her room to change, and Douglas into the spare room. He peeled his damp woollen bathing costume off and hung it out of the window by its straps. He dried himself. Frances' nipples will be cold and salty and her mouth warm. He stood with his feet apart and dried the areas between his legs. He heard Martha putting the dishes onto the table.

Frances still had her last hair clip in her mouth and was tying up her hair when she entered the dining room. "Won't you please carve the meat, dearest?" she said through clenched teeth. "You must sit at the head of the table. I've told Martha to go and swim. She loves it, and the white flag is already up. They've only got until three." She looked at him when she put food into her mouth and she saw him watching the succulent movements of her mouth.

She put her fork down. "What are you thinking about, my love?"

"How wonderful it is to sit here with you just the two of us at the table."

"I know. I won't let Martha go, in case my parents get back early. She won't disturb us. I'm rather hungry, must be the swimming and the air. Let's not rush."

He paced himself, watching her plate, so that he would not finish before she did.

"I shall have another helping, if you would carve some more meat, dearest," she said. "What about you."

"Yes, thank you, I too am quite hungry."

"How much do you love me?" She tilted her head playfully.

"How does one know by what to measure it? I know that I love you with all my heart. I have felt attracted to other women, which I am sure is quite natural, just as you have been attracted to other men I'm sure. And although I am smitten with your exquisite physical appearance, totally smitten in fact – you looked so attractive on the beach today – it is almost as though we have met before." His hands trembled.

Tears welled up in Frances' eyes. "Oh my love!" She stroked his forearm reassuringly. The surf crashed loudly. "The wind must be changing," she said.

"Why do you say that?"

"Did you not hear the surf?"

"No. I must have got some water into my ears."

After lunch they sat on the veranda for a while, holding hands. "Let's go and sit inside," he suggested.

"Yes."

He took her arm and closed the front door. He pulled her towards himself and smelled her face cream. She put her arms around him. They began kissing. They were becoming better at it and could contemplate their intimacy. He put his hand inside the top of her dress and felt her breast. She pressed her pubis against him and he could feel himself swelling. She pulled her mouth away from his and tilted her head back. "May I feel?" He nodded. He expected her to put her hand against his trousers but instead she slipped it into his trousers. She gasped as she got a hold of him. "Oh my word, how lovely this is!" His knees began to tremble. "May I feel?" he asked. "Yes." He looked around to make sure that they had enough privacy. With her hand still inside his trousers she moved away so that he could lift her dress. He first considered putting his hand on the outside of her pants; instead impulse prompted him to put his hand inside. She started shaking. She was slippery. She started sobbing. He took his hand out. "No it's fine, it's fine, carry on," she said. "I'm crying because it's so nice." She still held on to him inside his trousers. They stood like that and listened to their heartbeats. They heard the back door closing and Martha's steps in the passage and hurried out onto the veranda.

Martha followed them outside "Can I make some coffee now Miss Frances?"

"Yes, that would be nice thank you, my mother left some mince pies."

"Did you enjoy your swim, Martha?" Douglas asked.

"It was very nice, thank you, Master. Sea water is good for the gout."

"Please excuse me for a moment, I need to do my hair," Frances said, and went inside.

Douglas sat down. White horses were on the surface of the sea. He put his hands up to his face and smelt his fingers. All he could smell was perfume and talcum powder.

Sunday 11 December 1927

Douglas woke early and went outside. The air was already warm: berg wind conditions. It would be a scorcher. Frances had sent a note the day before to say that she was not well and would spend the day in bed. He thought better of it than to ask Martha why Frances was not well. She must be upset about something. In the early hours he made up his mind that their intimacy of the previous day was to blame. He should have restrained himself instead of yielding to temptation. He should not have allowed the snake to beguile him; he should not have picked the fruit. You think it's going to be pure and noble and perfect while your passions deceive you and then it turns out to be a disaster and spoils a perfect relationship. He hated himself. No gratification, no form of ecstasy, can be worth this wretched misery.

His father appeared, cup and saucer in hand, in his bathing costume, his towel around his neck. "What's going on with you Douglas?"

"How do you mean?"

"You've seemed distracted since yesterday. Is there a problem? You must tell me if there is."

"It's just that Frances is not well."

"Then shouldn't you go and see her?"

"I suppose I should. Her note just said that she was not well."

"At least reply, if you have not already done so."

"That would be a good idea."

"Do it now, before we go swimming. I'll wait for you. There is some writing paper on the dining room table. Sienna can take it down there."

When Douglas and his father returned from the beach, Sienna had returned from the Roses' house with a reply from Frances.

> *Dear Douglas,*
> *I am so sorry that I was not feeling myself yesterday, please do come and have tea with me at eleven, if at all possible.*
>
> *All my love, and more*
> *Frances.'*

"What is it?" van Yssen asked.

"She wants me to have tea with her at eleven."

"Ah! There you are Douglas," Mrs Rose hailed. "Our little girl has been under the weather, I'm afraid."

The Judge lowered his newspaper and looked at Douglas over his spectacles. "Hello Douglas. Infernal hot day. Should really be inside with the hatches battened down."

"Good morning Judge."

"I'll tell Frances that you are here. She'll be pleased to see you." Mrs Rose said and went inside. "Frances will join us presently."

Frances was pale. "Hello Douglas, how good of you to come." She kissed him on his cheek and held his hand. She gave him a wan smile. He put his arm around her shoulder.

"Let's sit down," Mrs Rose suggested.

"I am afraid we will be having more rain after this heat. It always happens. I should go for a swim. And then just a very light lunch, and a jolly good sleep afterwards. A bit of brawn would have been perfect, and some fruit."

"It won't be easy to make brawn here, dear, Martha would not know how to do that."

"What have the van Yssens been up to, Douglas?" the Judge asked.

"My father is having a good rest. My mother has been writing letters. She seems to do that interminably. I've been reading."

"What are you reading?" the Judge asked.

"I am still gnawing at Gibbon."

"You have been reading that for quite a while now. Many people have started it and few have finished it. When I was young and ambitious I once thought of tackling it. Where are you now?"

"I am at chapter forty seven which deals with certain theological influences during the period four hundred to about five hundred and sixty."

"What is that about?" Frances asked.

"There was a lot of discord among the Christians of that time, even after paganism was extinguished. There were all kinds of disputes; about the Trinity, about Incarnation, all kinds of currents. The very early movements; the Ebionites and Gnostics. Gibbon was a religious sceptic, but then I think good sceptics make good historians."

They watched the Judge and Mrs Rose setting off along the beach, he in his blue and red striped towelling dressing gown and slippers and she a few paces behind him in the loose sand, holding her hat down on her head.

"You look pale," Douglas said with concern.

"I'm fine really. Come and sit close to me, move your chair up."

"I was worried."

"I can see that you're not yourself."

"How do you mean?"

"You seemed awkward with my parents."

"I didn't realise that."

"Is something troubling you?"

"I was worried about you, I did not know what was wrong."

"Then you could have written a note and asked."

"I was afraid to, and procrastinated. I mean you were quite fine, in excellent health, on Friday."

"You are a real old procrastinator, Douglas van Yssen."

She lowered her voice and lent her head towards him. "I suspect that my condition was partly brought on by our intimacy."

Douglas' stomach went into a knot. She held her head away from him, to look at him more sharply. "You poor beast, you have no idea what I am talking about!" He did not know what to say.

"You will have to learn much more about a woman's body if we are to get married, my dearest. About once a month a woman's body starts preparing itself to conceive. I have been blessed with a mild menses, Douglas, but our explorations of each other encouraged my body to prepare more thoroughly than usual, and caused me quite a lot of discomfort. But it is all fine now, I am a little tired, but I am fine, and I just need your warmth and your love."

He kissed her on her forehead, and put his arm around her shoulders. "I am so relieved that you are well. I had the most dismal and wretched thoughts, that I might have offended you with my enthusiasm; that you were sick with regret for what we did."

"Your enthusiasm thrills me."

They sat for a long time looking out to sea, holding hands until she felt the warmth returning to his anxious hand.

Saturday 17 December 1927

Van Yssen heard the groaning sounds of the Roses' car as it haltingly heaved its lumbering way past the front of their house, across the uneven grass and fresh molehills, and crawled in under the shade of the milkwood tree.

"Here they are," he called to his wife and went outside to welcome the Roses.

"You have picked a corking good day, Albert. Always a good sign," the Judge said as he eased himself from the car. "Still dashed stiff from our walk, or should I say climb."

"Hello Albert," Mrs Rose had a basket in her hand. The contents were covered with fig leaves. "I have brought you some peaches. There was a farmer here yesterday, you no doubt saw him, selling fruit from his wagon, very good peaches, and watermelons, lovely fragrances. There you are Anneke, hello my dear."

Frances had a broad smile. She had on an apricot coloured cotton blouse with a v-shaped neck, and a pale Prussian blue pleated knee-high skirt that rested on her hips. A loosely tied scarf tied around her neck matched her skirt. "Where's Douglas?"

"He'll be here in a few moments," van Yssen replied.

"Where have you been?" Frances asked when he arrived on the veranda.

"Oh just at the back of the house. The tap of the water tank seems to be dripping."

"What can I offer you to drink, Elizabeth? I could not get any vermouth unfortunately but I did manage a bottle of white wine. I have put it into water to keep it cool."

"That was very thoughtful of you, Albert. I shall rather wait, and have some at the table, thank you."

"We have some gin, Jeremy, but only lime juice to go with it, and I have some beer if you prefer."

"I haven't had gin and lime for quite a while. On a day like this it would be perfect." The Judge rubbed his hands together enthusiastically.

"Could I have some lime and water, please, Mr van Yssen?" Frances asked.

"This house is very comfortable," Mrs van Yssen heard Judge Rose say.

"We are quite happy here. It is good of Hurter to let it to us," van Yssen said.

"Especially at this time of the year," Mrs van Yssen added.

"This is such a lovely large table, and a wonderful room," Mrs Rose said as they entered the dining room.

Mrs van Yssen seated her guests. Sienna carried in a tray with a large ornate white porcelain soup tureen and matching ladle. She was dressed in a new overall and starched cap. Van Yssen removed the lid of the tureen. A bouquet of sherry blended with sapid chicken stock wafted from the swaying surface of the chicken consommé and spread into the room.

The Judge threw his enthusiastic hands up in delight, "By Jove, this smells delicious. How exquisite to sit here in this house at the seaside and to experience such culinary excellence." van Yssen proudly dispensed the soup with the air of a chemist who had prepared a concoction, making sure that the number of loose chicken flakes per volume was more or less equal in each plate.

"I have tried my best to make some very thin toast," Mrs van Yssen said enthusiastically.

Mrs Rose tasted her soup. "What a lovely treat, Anneke. Where on earth did you learn to make this?"

"Madame Jacquard taught me. She has a secret way. She loves making soup. She even has it for breakfast."

"Good God, imagine that!" The Judge laughed. "Of course I don't wish to detract from your outstanding consommé, Anneke, I am just thinking of having thick bean soup or pea soup for breakfast. Give me bacon and eggs any day. Sometimes I feel we make too much of their cuisine."

"It certainly is unusual," van Yssen said. "I get the impression that much of it came about through necessity. Traditionally they ate a lot of cereals and pulses, and comparatively little," he took a sip of his soup, "Madame Jacquard tells us, animal products."

"This is so nice," Frances said. "You must tell us how you made it Mrs van Yssen. I would like to learn to cook."

"Oh! Now really Frances, what an outlandish thought," her mother exclaimed.

"Judging by the excellent taste I could tell that it was not a simple affair to make this," the Judge complimented.

"You've excelled yourself Ma," Douglas said.

"You shouldn't say that Douglas, you should make it appear that this is simply par for your mother's cooking," Frances said cheerfully.

"I thought I would prepare things that we do not often eat, so we are having bobotie as our main course."

"What a lovely touch, Anneke, French soup and then a Malay dish." Mrs Rose dabbed her mouth with her napkin.

The Judge had a second helping of consommé that he fairly slurped from his spoon while he crunched pieces of liberally buttered toast. He started to perspire, and his nose ran from the pleasure of eating. He mopped his forehead with his handkerchief. Frances had a small second helping, "just a soupcon, if you will forgive the pun."

Douglas opened the wine bottle with considerable difficulty because the cork was brittle, and in the end fragments of cork were left floating in the neck of the bottle.

"Never mind old boy," the Judge chuckled, "we'll just have to spit out the cork, or swallow it! Ha! Ha!"

"This is lovely wine. Lovely fruity flavours," Mrs Rose said approvingly.

"It should really be a little colder, but it is so difficult to keep things cold here," van Yssen said.

"I think you have done very well, thank you, Albert," she replied. "Our holiday is now almost at an end."

"Oh, Mummy, do you have to make me sad. I cannot bear the thought of going home."

"I know my dear, but it will not be too long before the two of you are married, and then you and Douglas will be able to spend lovely long holidays together at the seaside. The house is there for your use. I realise how much you have enjoyed this holiday. I can see the change in you Frances, and in you dear Douglas."

"Do you play Mah Jong, Albert?" the Judge asked.

"Friends of ours in Oudtshoorn are quite keen players – it's all the rage there – but I have somehow not had an opportunity to play."

"Damn good game. We brought a set down with us. It would have been a good way to pass the time. Pity we left it until now. Lots of jolly good fun. Anyway, we'll have other occasions I am sure."

Sienna cleared the table and returned with bobotie and yellow rice with raisins. There was also a green salad and a bowl of thick salad dressing that Mrs van Yssen had made in a glass jar that Sienna had shaken until her forearms were numb and all the oil was emulsified.

"I absolutely love yellow rice," Frances said.

"Douglas," the Judge said, "Remember what we said about the Flag? At least it was laid to rest last month."

"Yes, Hertzog's speech was excellent." Douglas said. "Simple and direct, no flowery diction, no exaggerated sentiment; it was fitting and served to lift what had become a veritable cloud of impending disaster that hung over the entire country. We should learn from the affair. Whoever said sentiment was an amorphous thing! One underestimates its power. No doubt there will be lingering resentments. But at least there is a tangible sense of relief."

"You said the other day, on our walk, Albert," the Judge said, "that you are reading Philip Gibbs' *Realities of War*. I thought about it afterwards. He was quite controversial, during the early stages of the war, arrested, and probably lucky not to be put up against a white wall and shot."

"Why was that?" Frances asked

"A conflict between the Foreign Office and the War Office about news from the Front. The War Office wanted to black out all the news and allow only official communiqués to be made public. Gibbs fell foul of Kitchener and instructions were given to arrest him if he went to France. He was duly apprehended in Havre and accused of wandering about the war zone smuggling uncensored nonsense back home. He was quite fortunate really, for one of the Scotland Yard men who guarded him, became a good friend and took a letter back to England, as a result of which Lord Tyrell at the Foreign Office exerted his influence to liberate Gibbs. Eventually war correspondents were accredited and allowed to operate, about five of them if I remember correctly. The amazing thing was that Gibbs was one of them." The Judge turned to Douglas. "What do you think of him, Douglas?"

"I have not read much of his work. Garnett is very keen on him. His style is quite interesting if a bit hesitating, like someone snapping away with a camera. I remember reading an account of a conversation he had with a French soldier on a train soon after the outbreak of the war. The conversation could as well have been from a poor theatre piece. It was touching in some ways, but so distorted by sentiment that it became detached from reality, and in the end one had little feeling for what was described; the account was meant to move, but failed because it was a caricature."

"You would make a marvellous critic, Douglas," Frances said.

"Perhaps I have been unfair to Gibbs. He has made a valuable contribution by describing, the horrors and futility of war. He seems to be persuaded that there will never be another war, but I cannot see how that will be when we examine history. Why should it suddenly stop now, after thousands of years of conflict?"

"He was entirely wrong about the outcome of the tensions between the Triple Alliance and the Triple Entente," van Yssen observed.

"He was educated at home by his parents. I find that strange considering that his father had a job at the Board of Education. Doesn't say much for the man's faith in the education system if he did not send his own son to school. Gibbs seems to be in love with the idea of being a writer." Douglas laughed, "Like someone who is tone-deaf but wants to be a great conductor. Like grasping the zeit but not the geist."

"I think you are being a bit harsh, Douglas," his father interrupted, "after all the man has been knighted, and he is the first journalist ever to obtain an interview with the Pope."

"That was because he is a Catholic, Dad, and because he has made himself conspicuous by protesting at Lloyd George's reprisals."

"His protest really only started after he interviewed the Pope, Douglas."

"Fair enough."

"Only one more day and then our packing will start. I dread the thought," Mrs Rose lamented.

"I could arrange for Sienna to go over and assist you," Mrs van Yssen suggested.

"That would not be necessary, we have always managed in the past, Elizabeth."

"Some help would be most welcome, Jeremy, we're not getting any younger you know."

"Then it is agreed," Mrs van Yssen said, "I shall send her across to you as soon as she has done the most essential things."

"You are very quiet, Frances," her mother said.

"You should know her well by now Elizabeth, it is the prospect of leaving that has begun to take hold of her."

Frances smiled sadly at Douglas and tilted her head to one side. He took her hand. "I don't know why I always spoil the end of the holiday by being so miserable," she said. "If you all must know, I feel truly wretched at the prospect of leaving here, and the more I think about it the worse it becomes." She was close to tears. "So we had better change the subject, if you don't mind."

"We have had a lovely time, Frances," her mother tried to comfort her.

"Yes, that is so but I have nearly three weeks of holiday remaining, and I would much rather have spent it with Douglas. But I understand, as we said earlier."

"The weather has improved so why don't the two of you go for a picnic tomorrow." Mrs Rose suggested.

"My, but I am having a good meal. I'll have forty winks this afternoon, and be fresh as a daisy tomorrow." The Judge yawned.

"What you should do, Frances," Mrs Rose suggested, "is to go by car to the river, and take the rowing boat. I can just imagine your reflection, with your large white straw hat, in the dark water of the river, and the sound of the oars and water against the boat."

Frances put her patted hands together eagerly. "Do you think that will be possible, dear Douglas?"

"Of course. I must confess that I am not much good at rowing, but I watched Leibner at Kaaimans River."

"There's nothing to it my good fellow, you'll have the hang of it in ten minutes."

"I suggest you leave at ten, to give yourselves time to get to the river," Mrs Rose proposed.

"I have made Douglas' favourite dessert, from the time that he was little: banana custard with little white ducks," Mrs van Yssen announced sentimentally.

Sunday 18 December 1927

Douglas arrived at the Roses' house just before ten. Frances was adjusting her hat to the most attractive position when she heard the car arrive. A picnic basket and a rug stood ready.

"Jeremy has gone for a walk, Douglas. Frances will be ready in a minute. I trust you are well today?"

"Good morning, Mrs Rose. Yes I am very well, thank you. I hope you are well?"

"I am mostly always well, dear boy. There is not much that gets me down, and besides, being miserable serves little purpose. I have much to be thankful for. Life has been extraordinarily kind to me."

Frances held her arms out to Douglas. "Isn't it a lovely, lovely day! Not a cloud; not a breath of wind. Shall we go?"

"We will expect you when we see you, Frances. I shall write to your dear mother, Douglas, to thank her for the excellent meal. She went to so much trouble on our behalf."

"It was our privilege to have you at our house, Mrs Rose."

"You are so kind."

The transmission of the car whined as they drove uphill. Douglas glanced at Frances.

"I hope I shall never disappoint you."

"I am sure that there will be times when we will be disappointed, but it will be about little things, not about things that really matter. When I was poorly last week, I am completely well again now, and lay on my bed I thought about the way in which we explored each other. It was so perfect."

"The credit should go to you, for the clever way in which you encouraged our relationship to develop."

"Oh, my dearest, it is hardly my doing, it is your endearing way that has encouraged me, and made me love you. At times, the other day when we were touching one another my emotion was so strong that I feared that it would burst out of me. Instead it turned into a spiritual experience."

"I have a great responsibility towards you, Frances. I was so concerned when I received your note to say that you were not well, I feared that you did not want to see me because of what we had done."

"Oh, my love, it is your Calvinist guilt."

"I know, I know. I wonder whether I will ever be rid of that."

"It is such an unnecessary burden. Carrying it around is the real sin because the guilt constantly threatens to corrupt. Let's open the windows so that we can feel the wind on our faces and smell the fragrances of the vegetation. The sun is encouraging them to give up their scent."

Douglas parked the car in the shade of some trees away from the water's edge. "That's our boat over there, I think." Frances pointed to a clinker built rowing dinghy lying upside down, a safe distance from the edge of the river. In the days that it had been out of its boathouse, strands of grass had grown past the gunwales, and when Douglas turned the boat the right way up the grass underneath was yellow. "You should take care when you do that, Douglas, there could be a snake underneath, or scorpions. Be careful when you pick up the oars. We should wipe the seats: they have mould on them. I'll get the things from the car."

A tall young man with blond hair and blue eyes, his trousers held up by a college tie, emerged from the trees. "I say, I shouldn't wonder if you could do with a hand, the boat's bound to be a trifle heavy. I'm Hadley we have a house over there," he said waving his hand vaguely to his right. "We're quite isolated, starved for visitors, really. My parents bunker down here for the entire holiday, and I am left to forage for myself. I'm a damn nifty rower of a boat, you know, could take you up the river." He watched them narrowly. Douglas introduced himself and Frances. "Did you say Hadley?"

"Yes Hadley Stockwell. Dashed cumbersome name if you ask me!"

"It is so kind of you to offer your assistance, Mr Stockwell, we would welcome it if you could help us get the boat into the water," Frances said.

"Getting it in down the slope is the easy part. It's the getting out of the boat that's the problem."

"The tide should be in when we return," Douglas replied.

Stockwell wagged his index finger at Douglas in mocking admonition, "Very clever, now."

"It was so kind of you to offer to take us up the river but we'll manage, thank you."

They pushed the reluctant boat down the grassy embankment. Stockwell held onto the bow while Douglas and Frances brought their things on board. Douglas slipped the oars into the rowlocks and held the blades out of the water while Frances arranged herself in the middle of the seat at the stern so that she faced Douglas. "There we go," Stockwell cried at he pushed them away from the bank into deeper water. The boat drifted and turned so that it pointed the wrong way. "Put the portside blade in the water!" Stockwell called. Douglas put the wrong oar in the water and the boat swung around until it pointed in the right direction. "Lucky manoeuvre!" Stockwell slapped his thighs in amusement.

"It will be fine, Douglas, just ignore him," Frances said under her breath.

"I'll wait for the two of you to get back."

"We'll be quite a while," Frances waved at him.

Douglas thought of Leibner's rhythmic movements and measured his hand positions. He dipped the blades into the water and pulled as evenly as he could on the oars. The boat began to move. "Feather the blades!" Stockwell called.

"What is he saying?" Douglas asked.

"Something about 'feathering,'" Frances said. "Just ignore him, he is just trying to show off."

Douglas began to get the hang of what he was doing. He started to realise what he had to do to prevent the oars from slipping out of the rowlocks and to stop himself from falling backwards when he did not dig the blades in deep enough. He wedged his feet in under the corners of the seat in front of him and decided not to watch the movement of the oars.

"How far should we go?" he asked.

"We have been quite far up the river on occasions. There are good picnic spots further up, and the scenery is quite spectacular."

He smiled at her as his confidence grew.

"I knew you would manage."

The mouth of the estuary and its marshes and fens lay behind her. Ahead of her were tall steep sides of the river gorge. He saw the pale greens and fawns and oatmeal colours of the dune vegetation and pale blue hazy sea beyond. She witnessed the silent calm surface of the dark brown waters of the river ahead. The water was so still that the sides of the gorge were mirrored perfectly. It seemed as though there was a world above the water and a world below. There was no seam between the two worlds. The sound of the sea disappeared and all that they could hear were the sounds of the oars and the chatter of birds in the trees.

"Gosh, you are doing well now, Douglas."

He had beads of perspiration on his forehead. "The tide is still going out, and when we go back it will be coming in. So we will be going against the tide both ways. Not very clever."

"Further up it does not flow strongly. Isn't it beautiful here?"

"You look so beautiful Frances, in that hat."

She touched the wide brim of her straw hat. Light from the water reflected by the brim brightened her face. Part of her bottom lip stuck to her teeth as she opened her mouth to smile at him through her bright green eyes.

They rounded the second bend in the river. Vegetation on the upper reaches of the hillsides became more arid as they went. The gorge was silent. They were alone on the dark water of the river. A penetrating cry of a fish eagle startled Frances and she looked in the direction of the sound. "What an excellent idea to come up the river. The water and the sky. And we have the whole day ahead of us."

"We shouldn't return too late."

"Let's not even think of that. What are you thinking about?"

"Nothing in particular. I wonder how this year will turn out. I sometimes have quite gloomy feelings. At times it is as though I want to prevent myself from being happy. That's badly put, but it is how it is. It is almost as though I cannot convince myself that human beings are meant to be completely happy. I want to be happy but I am not sure that I deserve to be. I feel guilty when I am too happy. As I said earlier, how do you shake it off?"

"If you want to get rid of guilt you must yield to temptation. Don't resist it. The problem lies in the very nature of temptation. If we do not feel restrained by the thought that it would be wrong to do something there is no temptation. If we want to do something and we think that it would be wrong to do it that is temptation. Notions of right and wrong are at the root of the problem."

"But there is a right and a wrong."

"Is there really, in every sense?"

"Your question seems cautiously qualified?"

"Of course we know that there is right and wrong in a sense of good and evil, but I must say that I sometimes also have a problem with those concepts. Intuitively it appears to me that the meaning of life is indivisible."

"This is a new tack?"

"I have always been scared to air these ideas – which I have had as long as I can remember – for fear of being ridiculed. You know what Daddy is like. It is either black or it is white. The subtle shades in between are a pure indulgence. I fear that what my intuition suggests to me might be misinterpreted because it is so far removed from the main streams of thought. I have even been reluctant to discuss it with you lest it should drive a wedge between us. But now that we have grown so close it is easier for me to reveal to you the most intimate places of my mind." The green clear eyes searched his face.

"Gee, I must collect my thoughts," he said.

"If we go back to the issue of right and wrong and the discussion we had the other day, after I had been poorly. You seemed to have difficulty with what we did – when we touched one another. And you seemed to think that I suffered remorse. Why should the most natural thing yield remorse? Why should it arouse feelings of guilt? How can it be possible for any part of what we did to be wrong? If we really surrender ourselves fully to our love we will experience the indivisibility of that love. If it is undivided it cannot be subject to a notion of right and wrong." She stroked his hand. "Do you understand what I am trying to say, Douglas?"

"I think so."

"You don't sound convinced."

"I'll have to think more about it."

"That's the point. That's the whole point, the undivided lies beyond reason."

He kissed her on her temple. She did not respond.

"It is very important to me that you should understand how I feel about these things, Douglas. I trust you to understand. Especially now that we have crossed boundaries that neither one of us could have imagined we would do. And we have crossed them with such ease. I don't want you to have any feelings of guilt about us, particularly if we are going to be separated for a while. Guilt will disfigure our relationship. It is a destructive thing. We must get it out of the way. I love you more than you could ever imagine, and I want our relationship to be strong because of its openness and honesty. Just as there must ultimately be nothing that separates us physically, so there must be nothing that separates us emotionally."

At times Douglas rowed the boat, and at times they just drifted about. Eventually faded colours in the distance became the dunes lying under a lazy Sunday afternoon haze at the mouth of the river. There were hardly any clouds, and only mild breezes drifted in from the west. They ate sandwiches, and fresh peaches. There was cheddar cheese that went well with green grapes, and more tea and small biscuits with almonds pressed into their centres.

She sat close to him as they drove home. The picnic plates and cutlery rattled on the back seat. The streets of the village were deserted. The houses were inscrutable. The windows of her parents' room were shut, and they tiptoed about on the veranda.

"I think you should have a rest," Douglas suggested.
"Only if you will come and see me later."
He kissed her on her forehead.

Monday 19 December 1927

Mrs van Yssen helped Douglas to wrap Frances' Christmas gift.
"When are you going to take this to Frances?"
"Later this afternoon. They will be having an early night because they are leaving very early."
"Be careful of the scissors on the table, Douglas. It is such a lovely day, you should have spent some time on the beach with Frances."
"I would like to, but the arrangements have already been made."
"Then change them."
"I'll see."

The Roses' house had been prepared for its long rest. It appeared embarrassed. Its interior had been rearranged and its furniture covered in drapes and it waited resentfully for its occupants to leave.

"I am afraid we are camping now, Douglas," Mrs Rose announced. "We will have to leave some things behind, and I would be glad if you could please take the basket that I have put on the table for your mother. Jeremy is exhausted and has been having a snooze before the long drive tomorrow." A yard broom had been left standing against the veranda wall.

"I have brought Frances a little gift for Christmas."
"You're spoiling her rotten, dear boy."
"Yes, I am a very lucky girl," Frances said from the front doorway. "Douglas won't tell me what it is."
"And so he shouldn't, Frances. Why don't you go for a walk along the beach, you two, while I get things ready?"
"Let me just put my present in my room."

They held hands tightly, holding onto each other more firmly, because they did not know how they would say goodbye. They were separate from their surroundings – the afternoon sun that was still high in the sky, a calm sea. A few holidaymakers on colourful towels were scattered at discrete distances. A man sat with a large white handkerchief on his head, its four corners tied in knots to make a hat, reading a heavy book. A toddler doggedly carried small buckets of water to a dam he had made, determined to transfer more water than that which continued to soak away.

"Will you write to me, Douglas?"

"Of course I will."

"I mean soon?"

"Yes, I promise."

"Soon we shall be together all the time; all our waking hours, and at night, loving each other. And when you go off to work in the morning we will know that I will still see you that same day." Her voice wavered. "It was a pity that we could not find a suitable place on the shore. Weren't you disappointed?"

"More than you could imagine."

She let go of his hand and put her arm through his. "How I love you. I am so very happy."

"I am also very happy."

During tea the atmosphere on the veranda was heavy. Little was said lest the wrong things be said. The Judge and Mrs Rose said their goodbyes to Douglas, wished him a merry Christmas, and went inside on some pretext so that he and Frances could be alone.

Frances had tears in her eyes, and sobbed when he kissed her goodbye. She blew her nose on her hanky and wiped tears from her eyes. "I am so silly!"

"No you are not." Douglas had a lump in his throat.

"I always spoil things. I don't want you to remember me like this!" She laughed a silly sniffing laugh.

He held her in his arms and hugged her gently. They stood holding one another, unwilling to let go.

"I will telephone you on Christmas day," he said. "Please travel safely." He went down the steps of the veranda and looked back before he rounded the corner of the house. She was watching him, her hands held together clutching her handkerchief, her eyes red with sadness.

Chapter Twenty-seven

Wednesday 11 January 1928

Dearly beloved Douglas,

It is hard to credit that Christmas and New Year have been and gone. Although some events of our holiday are more distant now, others remain as vivid as if they happened yesterday. Surrounded by my most happy memories I fondly think of you now.

Thank you for telephoning. A thousand thanks again for the exquisite gift you gave me for Christmas. I polished the silver myself and have transferred all my jewellery into it. It has taken place of pride on my chest of drawers, and I have watched as Mummy glanced enviously at it when entering my room. Daddy grunted approval when I opened your parcel on Christmas morning. "Damn fine antique jewellery box," he said. "Wonder what else the young man has up his sleeve?"

I feel secure in the knowledge that my parents are so fond of you.

It was wonderful that we could all holiday together, and that our fathers went for a lovely walk. Daddy said afterwards, and I forgot to tell you, that he had found his conversations with your father most stimulating, in fact when he sat down, on his return, to get some sand out of his boots, he said, "What an interesting man. I envy him his profession, to be out in the open and to have the mental stimulation of doing mathematical calculations." He nodded as though he agreed with himself and added, "Like his son, van Yssen wears his learning lightly."

I would love to know how the rest of your holiday went. Every time I think of Plettenberg Bay images of our picnic in the dunes appear. I shudder with delight when I think about the way we loved when my parents went to Knysna for the day. You have awakened such passion in me. Think, think, think of some plan so that we may be together as soon as possible, please. I trust that you will come and see me at the station on Saturday. I shall telephone before I leave.

Please write and tell me about Madame Jacquard's stay with you. She sounds like a jolly interesting and colourful person.

Did Garnett catch any fish? Do write and tell all. I have had my photographs developed, and will show them to you on Saturday.

On Christmas day we went to church as usual and had our usual Christmas luncheon, with the usual people, except that Florrie and Christopher were unable to attend on account of being overseas. They went to stay with Florrie's aunt in Surrey, in the hope of having a proper white Christmas. We should do that one day, and go to London for Christmas. We could stay with the Chisholms. Just imagine it, having a traditional Christmas dinner, fires, me in a fur coat in the bleak cold outside, and then the two of us snug at night, together in bed.

As usual we stopped with Daddy's cousin, John Barry, in Swellendam. The trip was quite exhausting. I don't know how Daddy manages to drive such long distances in one day. We had two punctures, but managed to get help on both occasions, and only arrived at Swellendam after five in the afternoon, covered in dust and parched. Daddy says that the more sensible thing to do in future would be to put the car on the train and drive from George. Mummy said it sounded like a fetching idea to her. Fortunately the stays in Swellendam always only last one night, and consist of a soaking bath, drinks, dinner and a long night's sleep in a feather bed. Barry is an ill-tempered brute with an Irish chip on his shoulder. Heaven knows how we came to be related. (He is daddy's second cousin.) Anyway to his credit he did try to be as pleasant as he can be and the stay was tolerable.

I miss you my most precious darling. I am desperately starved for your love. I cannot wait to see you on Saturday.

Lots and lots of love,
Frances.

Douglas wrote to Frances on Tuesday February 28, 1928.
Dearest Frances,
Thank you so much for your letter. I am glad that you are well. You are constantly in my thoughts. It is frighteningly hot here. As Garnett says, even the crows are yawning.

So far school has been fine. I have a very enthusiastic standard nine class, and it should be gratifying to teach them.

I mentioned to you when we were at Plettenberg Bay that my ears seem to be blocked. I told Garnett about it when he was there and he suggested that I should see him once we were back in Oudtshoorn. It did not seem so bad when we got home but last week it was worse and I went to see Garnett yesterday. He did a thorough examination, and could not find any clinical reason for the dullness I am experiencing. When I expressed my relief, he looked quite distressed. I could see that he was having some emotional difficulty. At first I thought that it could be that he wanted to discuss some personal problem unrelated to my condition. He sat for a long time in an uncomfortable silence looking down at the surface of his desk. When he finally lifted his eyes to look at me his expression was grim. The news is not good. He explained to me that the treatment I had in London may only have brought temporary relief, and that there is a possibility of nerve damage. He said that we are not to give up hope, but taking my family history into account the prospects are not very encouraging. I could not believe what I was hearing. He and I had such a jolly time on holiday. We had so much fun playing cards with Madame Jacquard, and now this. I could not get up at first. My body felt like stone. We sat there looking at one another. Garnett had tears in his eyes. He pretended that he had an emergency at the hospital and left his patients waiting while he drove me home.

I have not told my parents what Garnett said, and when they asked I tried to show as little emotion as possible and merely remarked that Garnett could not find anything wrong. I know that I shall have to deal fully with the matter sooner rather than later, but there it is. I thought you should know. I feel quite sick at the prospect of going deaf. I am quite numb and irrational and in class I imagine that my hearing is becoming worse when I see mouths moving at the back and hear nothing, but it is of course the boys whispering inaudibly. In the circumstances I would like to ask your permission to cancel my visit to Cape Town so that I can get my bearings. Dear God, how unpredictable life is. To think how everything has changed. In a matter of a few weeks the bright colours that adorned my hopes for the future have been extinguished and my prospect utterly dimmed by grey misery.

Last night I dreamt that I was sobbing.

It grieves me profoundly to send you this dreadful news. I will always love you Frances.

With my deepest love,

Douglas.

Saturday 10 March 1928

The van Yssens had barely finished their supper when their telephone rang. "I will answer it, I am expecting a call from Beaufort West." van Yssen said as he got up.

"Frances!" He was pleasantly surprised.

"Is that you, Douglas?"

"No this is his father speaking. How are you, Frances?"

"I'm fine thank you Mr van Yssen. I hope you and Mrs van Yssen are well."

"Yes we are very well my dear, but let me not waste your money. I'll call Douglas."

Douglas closed the interleading door. "Hello Frances, how are you."

"As well as can be expected in the circumstances." She was crying. "I decided to come and telephone from the hotel, at least there is some privacy here. I want you to know darling man that however disturbing your news is, and whatever may happen, my love for you can never change, and I will give you every support. I feel so helpless, I want to be with you and comfort you. Please do consider coming to Cape Town. We will be together on the train, and we can discuss the future with Mummy and Daddy. They will give us every support. I have not said anything to them, please reconsider."

"Things are very difficult. I have not told my parents. I go to bed every night resolving to tell them the next morning, and when morning comes I don't have the courage."

"Schools close on Friday, I will be leaving on Saturday. We only have a few days left. I understand your predicament, but you have to be courageous. Grasp the nettle. Speak to them tonight and be resolute so that we may plan our future. I have been in quite a state since receiving your letter and I went and sat in the church so that I could be alone. I was lonely there. Please, please reconsider. I love you, Douglas, and I understand how you must feel. Can you hear me, Douglas? Douglas?"

She heard his choking sobs. "One moment," he said through his tears. He held the telephone mouthpiece to one side, and blew his nose. "I'm alright now."

"We need to be together now, Douglas, not apart."

"I know, I know. It is difficult to speak. I will telephone you tomorrow afternoon. I love you, Frances."

"I love you too. I am praying for you."

Douglas put the receiver down and tried to compose himself. His parents were outside and had left the light off so that it would not attract mosquitoes.

"Frances sounded upset?" van Yssen asked.

"I am sure she's fine, Dad."

"You have also not been yourself, Douglas," his mother said. "Is there a problem?"

Douglas sighed.

"There is nothing that cannot be solved," his father said.

"You have never hidden anything from us, my child."

"My ears felt clogged when we were at Plettenberg Bay. I told Frances about it, and then I told Garnett when he arrived. He suggested that I see him when we got back. At first it seemed to get better and I thought it might just be a bit of water from all the swimming, but then I had a problem in class. So I went to see Garnett after school the week before last. He told me that it is possible that Yearsley's treatment may after all only have brought temporary relief, and that there is a possibility of permanent nerve damage which may result in deafness."

Mrs van Yssen's cup rattled in its saucer and smashed onto the floor. "Oh my goodness, oh my goodness."

Van Yssen sat slumped with his head in his hands.

"I wrote to Frances and told her what has happened. That's why she rang. No matter how hard I tried, I could not bring myself to tell you. After all you have done for me, and the sacrifices you have made." His voice broke and he took his handkerchief from his pocket.

The sounds of the night vanished. The darkness was denser. The warmth that had remained in the air after the sun had set vanished. They, the three of them, were forsaken by hope and even by their misery.

"You should have told me Douglas," his father said.

"Yes, I know, but I did not want to disappoint you."

"I cannot let you endure this on your own, my son." van Yssen got up and went to where Douglas was sitting. He put his hand on his son's shoulder. "We will deal with this as a family. As long as we preserve our honour. How certain is Garnett of his diagnosis? Should we not get a second opinion?"

"I asked him that. He said that Yearsley had written a report to Dr Roux. Yearsley was very pleased with the outcome of his treatment but had a caveat as a result of the final hearing tests he performed. Evidently he had hoped for a better result, and he warned Roux that the lack of improvement might be a sign of nerve damage. Yet Yearsley said he could not be sure."

"And Garnett knew this all along?" van Yssen's brow was confounded. "Why did he remain silent?"

"What good would it have done if he had told us Dad? It would have made no difference. See it from his point of view. He would have taken away hope. Even now he says that we should remain hopeful for no one can tell how far my deafness will progress."

"Hope and faith are so important Albert."

"I told Frances that I will not be able to go to Cape Town in the holidays."

"But you have already bought your ticket," his mother said.

"That is of no consequence Anneke. Why don't you want to go Douglas?"

"Dad, I do not want to be with other people, especially not Frances' parents. I need to be alone to come to terms with this. To get my bearings. Just when everything seemed so promising, when there was clarity about the future. Believe me, this has been an enormous shock to me. Frances and I were so happy at Plettenberg Bay."

"You must also see it from her point of view, Douglas," his mother said. "It must be a shock to her."

"She said so this evening. She was distraught."

"I will go and see her at the station. It is better for me to be alone for a while. I was going to see Garnett, but I think I'll go for a walk, and then turn in early. Garnett was pretty upset himself. He cried when he told me."

"He's been a very good friend to you," his mother's voice trembled with emotion.

"We should all have an early night, we need rest to clear our minds," van Yssen suggested.

The van Yssens watched as Douglas went down the garden path into the gloom until he was a ghostlike figure whose head floated past the pittosporum hedge. Van Yssen and his wife sat and looked into the night while grief dissolved their energy and distorted their features.

"I will wait for Douglas to return." van Yssen's voice was bereft of emotion.

"I will wait with you. I will be back in a moment." She rose slowly, straightened her dress and shuddered as she sighed.

Out of habit his eyes followed the rocking movements of her hips as she went down the passage. In the distance a train hooted twice. The coaches swayed and clattered, the reciprocating pistons hissed and thrust them towards the graduation. The sun was beginning to set near Great Brak River and restored the surface of the sea to mother of pearl. Images of her suspenders and her thighs and the rest of her revealed themselves and he drove them from his mind. That is why the dark machine, brought to life by fire and brimstone, hooted twice – a cock announcing betrayal. They betrayed themselves that night. His own conscience had forsaken him then. He allowed his lust to drive him, as it had done so many times before, but never like that, in public, on a train. It was woman who first ate of the fruit and because I hearkened unto my wife's body I am now being punished. We, the both of us, are being punished now. Because I was born in sin I was granted knowledge of good and evil. Huge restless forms threatened his understanding. A vortex of tumultuous guilt, an irresistible gravitational field of remorse, drew him away from his God. A sense of destruction compelled him to pull the pillars of the temple down on himself so that he could conceal himself under the rubble. From the kitchen his wife heard his sound, a groan of ominous despair that came from inside his large frame, as his faith left him.

Mrs van Yssen put the tea tray down on the veranda table. "I will let it draw for a while Albert." She did not look at him. She did not sit down but went and stood at the railing of the veranda.

"I am not so sure that Garnett has told all," he said.

She did not reply.

"Perhaps Douglas should have gone to someone with more experience."

"Isn't that why he sent him to Dr Roux?"

"I shall telephone Garnett tomorrow and have a private discussion with him."

"I would inform Douglas if you have such an intention."

"I will think about that, but I would prefer to have a confidential discussion with Garnett."

"Douglas is his patient, Albert."

"And I am his father. I have a responsibility to our son. I need to make plans. If Garnett is not prepared to tell Douglas the whole truth for fear of discouraging him, he should fully disclose the prognosis to me so that I can plan for the future. If Douglas follows in the footsteps of your father, then he will have to follow a different profession. He will no longer be able to teach. I will have to speak to Archer. We do not want even a hint of a scandal. Then there is Frances. She deserves to know what Douglas' prospects are. We owe it to her, and to her parents. I find it strange that Douglas kept us in the dark for so long."

"He has been behaving strangely but I thought it was his work or because he is in love. I got the impression at Plettenberg Bay that he and Frances were becoming more intimate. After the first picnic he was different. It is not always easy for young people to explore the unknown. Little tensions and misunderstandings are bound to arise."

"Just what has that got to do with the present difficulties?"

"Just that he has not been himself."

Van Yssen looked at his watch. "It is nearly half past nine. I wonder when he will be back?"

"What could he do if he did not teach?"

"There are possibilities. He could edit books, all kinds, history works. He could do research. It is a dreadful affliction. I'll go and see Garnett on Monday morning while Douglas is at school. I will leave for Prince Albert after that."

They heard the garden gate and saw Douglas approaching, his hands in his pockets, his head low.

"I have made some fresh tea, my son."

"Thanks Ma that will be nice." Douglas sat down heavily.

"Will you be coming to church with us tomorrow, Douglas?" His mother asked.

"Probably."

"It will be hot tomorrow," van Yssen said.

Monday 12 March 1928

Van Yssen dropped Douglas off at school, bade him a good day, and proceeded to Garnett's surgery. He had telephoned Garnett early on Sunday morning while Douglas was out. Garnett was alone at the surgery. He had left the door of his consulting room open and got up from his desk to receive van Yssen when he heard his footsteps. "Good morning Mr van Yssen. Come and sit down." Garnett closed the door.

"Douglas told us of his problem on Saturday night."

Garnett raised his eyebrows.

"Yes, he only told us of his visit to you on Saturday. So for nearly two weeks he has carried the news around with him. In his defence he did write to Frances after he saw you and told her. She telephoned on Saturday night. I want you to be frank with me. I want you to be completely honest with me. I know that Douglas is your patient and that there is medical etiquette to be observed but I am his father and in the circumstances I feel that I have a right to know how serious his condition is. His entire future, and for that matter the future of our family is at stake."

Garnett leant back in his chair. "This has been very difficult for me."

"I understand that."

"We have known one another our entire lives. I love Douglas as though he were one of my own brothers. I am not sure if you realise, but Douglas and I have never had a serious disagreement in our entire lives. I am so proud of his achievements. He is so much brighter than I am. To see this happening has been difficult. And I think of you and Mrs van Yssen, and your only son. Soon after he came to see me for the first time I learnt about his grandfather. The colour of the whites of his eyes gave me my first clue."

"What do you mean?"

"They had a bluish tinge. That is often an indication of otosclerosis. I did not know what to do. I could not believe it. The only way out was a second opinion. And if we were going to seek a second opinion I wanted the best second opinion available. Roux is the best ear nose and throat specialist there is in the Union, and Douglas was going to Cape Town. Roux suggested Yearsley, although I had read about his work. What Yearsley is doing is truly revolutionary. There is no doubt about that. Roux told me that it was only after weighty consideration that he decided that Douglas should see Yearsley. The probability of total and permanent deafness was so great, and Roux was so certain that he had made the correct diagnosis, that he felt that Yearsley's treatment would offer the only possible cure. The prospect that irreversible nerve damage may have occurred before Douglas left to see Yearsley was never mentioned to me and I never considered it. But even if I had known of the possibility, I would still have taken the risk of finding a cure. Roux wrote to me after Douglas returned from England, and sent me a copy of Yearsley's report."

"May I see the report?"

"You are welcome." Garnett opened Douglas's file. "All that it says is that Yearsley had hoped for a greater improvement in Douglas' hearing and that a lack of improvement suggests nerve damage. Here it is." He passed him Yearsley's report.

"Then there is still some hope."

"There is always hope, and I am foolish enough to believe in miracles. It may not please you for me to say that, since you are a Logical Positivist. However, I must be realistic. And unless we have a miracle, the prognosis is grim, especially if we take into account his grandfather's history."

"How did you learn about that?"

"I am not sure. Roux might have told me."

"I thought you said earlier that you were aware of it before you sent him to Roux?"

"I am really not certain Mr van Yssen. People talk. I listen. It could have been my dad, or Uncle Charlie. I am not sure. If you are concerned about my professional conduct, I can assure you that I am utterly conscious of the need for the utmost discretion."

"No, no, you misunderstand me. I have the greatest respect for your professional conduct."

"Is there anything else?" Garnett asked.

"I did not mean to offend."

"I understand."

"I am just terribly upset about my son."

"I understand."

"Thank you for all you have done Garnett. I have to go to Prince Albert now."

Garnett stood up and took off his white coat. He gathered his suit jacket. "I will be going to the hospital now to do my morning rounds. I postponed them so that I could see you."

Mrs van Yssen put on her straw hat and went outside with her shallow flower basket and secateurs to cut roses for Madame Jacquard. She arranged the flowers loosely in the basket, and set off briskly.

"I expected you Anneke. Shall we sit in the studio? The garden is looking so beautiful."

"I brought these for you Guillemette."

"They are beautiful, thank you." She kissed Mrs van Yssen on her cheeks.

"Is it Douglas?"

"Yes." Mrs van Yssen started crying.

"Is it the girl?"

"It is everything. He is going deaf."

Madame Jacquard gasped and held her throat. "Mon Dieu! Are you sure?"

Mrs van Yssen nodded.

"But the man in England cured him. He was fine just the other day, in front of my eyes. Why do you say this now?"

"He went to see Garnett because he was not hearing so well. There is nerve damage. He will become just like my father. I have given it to him. He has inherited it from me, his mother. As I have told you, my father could not hear a thing. He was the same age as Douglas when he started going deaf."

"How is Albert?"

"Douglas went to see Garnett two weeks ago but he only told us on Saturday evening. I fear that Albert will only really feel the shock in the days to come. He has gone to Prince Albert. He did not say a word when we went to bed on Saturday night. He was strangely calm. I was awake most of the night and at times I got up to pray. I am not sure whether he was awake or asleep."

"And Douglas?"

"It is hard to tell. He bottles everything. He feels sorry for us and we feel sorry for him, and none of us knows what to say. We are all numb and very tired. I don't know what will become of Douglas. My father once said that he would have preferred to be blind than deaf. I found that strange."

"Come and sit down my dear. What terrible news you have brought me with your flowers. I do not know what to say, and you know how much I like talking. Is there nothing that can be done?"

"Albert went to see Garnett early this morning. Please do not say anything about this to Douglas, because he does not know. Albert has now gone to Prince Albert and will be back tomorrow afternoon, so I will only know then what they have discussed. I will never stop praying for my son, and who knows, the Lord may hear my prayers."

"Let's have some coffee. I have made a marzipan and almond tart. You need something sweet, it will make you feel better. I have not been to church for many years but I will also pray. I too had a son, but I will tell you about that another day. So while you have your son you must thank God, even if your son is deaf." Madame Jacquard sat proudly erect, her eyes filled with tears. She wiped her tears away with the hem of her smock and began pouring their coffee.

"I did not know you had a son."

"My son is dead."

"Oh my goodness, I am so sorry."

"Mothers sometimes suffer a great deal. We make love to our husbands and conceive. We carry our sons inside us. We learn to love them while they kick inside us. We endure the pain of birth with much joy. Then we suckle them. We do not expect them to die before we do. I will tell you one day, not now."

"I am so very sad to hear about your son. Who am I to complain."

"Do not give up hope Anneke and if you do, then at least pretend that you still have hope."

"I came here for comfort and now I feel I must give you comfort."

"No one can take away my sadness, Anneke. Only I can deal with it. Each one of us is really like an island. If we seek a solution outside of that island we will not find one. Will Douglas have to find another occupation?"

"Yes, I am sure he will."

"There must be many possibilities for a man who is so clever as he. He is lucky. He is fortunate too that you are well connected."

Mrs van Yssen ate some of the almond tart. "This is delicious."

"Forgive me for saying it but you will have to be very strong. Albert will try to find something to blame. He is a fine man, and a good man to be sure. He is a man with a great deal of cerebral activity. His first passion is the passion of the mind. To him everything is the result of the intellect, and in that way you do not always solve all the problems that you find in life. His brain will ask questions that his brain will not be able to answer. He will look for his reason to answer what can only be answered by some other part of him, and if he cannot find the answer he will reason that he must have done something wrong to deserve this. For a man like that there must always be cause and effect. But life is not that simple. Sometimes when I stand and paint and I see into the essence of the colours on my canvas, or when I see a beautiful landscape in front of me, I know that there is something so beautiful, and my experience is so pure, that I have no doubt. When I am in that condition, or should I perhaps say in that suspension of the mind, only in that condition can I deal with the death of my son, and the absence of my husband. When I am like that I have no desire to reason and then I do not grieve."

"You are lucky that you have that gift."

"I am glad you call it a 'gift' because the experience is granted to you. You cannot demand it. Yet it is there, waiting, eager to respond if we desire it enough. Please do not misunderstand me Anneke, I like Albert, he is a good man but he will find this very difficult. Because he will not surrender himself to his passion, because he will not let go, it will be difficult for him to come to terms with this tragedy."

"I also find it difficult."

"I understand. Would you like some more coffee?"

"Yes thank you. We were all so happy, so relieved when he came back from London. We had such a lovely holiday, and now this cruel blow. I cannot imagine how Frances' parents will react."

"It will be a test for them. Their reaction will tell us much about them. It is in difficult times that our characters show themselves. If there is enough love we can fix anything. If there is pretence it will expose itself. I like your friend Garnett very much. He is authentic. He has beautiful eyes. They are the windows of his soul. I had such a good time at your beach. It must have been a romantic time for Douglas and his Frances."

"Douglas was meant to go to Cape Town on Saturday, but he does not want to go anymore."

"He should go."

"I also feel that he should go, it cannot be easy for Frances."

"Yes, she must be very sad, he should be with her."

"He does not want to face her parents. He says he has a defect. He says he wants to be alone so that he can come to terms with his condition. Frances will be on the train on Saturday, he said he would go and see her at the station. Douglas can be very stubborn."

"His stubbornness has made him successful. Beethoven was a very stubborn man."

"Sometimes it can also lead to one's downfall."

"I have often, how do you say, speculated whether his music would ever have been so good if he had not gone deaf."

Saturday 17 March 1928

The rain started during the night. Van Yssen woke several times to the musical sounds of water in the down-pipes. Could Douglas hear the rain, the patterns of sounds of drops falling on the different kinds of vegetation in the garden? The air was cool. He got out of bed and pushed the top half of their sash window up. Anneke was asleep. He looked at his watch. It was already past six. It was still dark. It was nearly the end of March. Unseasonable rain. He had dreamt a great deal: all sorts of things from his past, flotsam floating past. The images had been vivid. Why could he not remember them? The images had left their effect on him so that he could see and feel but could not recall what had caused the effect. He could feel the images but not see them. He tried to recall them. A pale gravel road, a large piece of bright green water with reeds growing in it. There were no people. Anneke spoke about Beethoven the other day. Deafness must be the worst thing possible for a musician. Someone said, or did I read it, that his later works were the most spiritual, the quartets. Douglas will see Frances this afternoon. He must go on his own. We will sort something out. There are many possibilities. I'll go and have a bath now.

A misty soaking rain continued to fall the entire day. Ensconced in his room Douglas started preparing for the next term. Van Yssen went to his office to complete some work and to buy himself a new pair of boots at Hepworths. Mrs van Yssen was at the dining room table writing letters. The grey striped cat slept in a corner of the settee, his head under his paws to shield him from the inclement weather.

Douglas thought of Frances on the train. Was she in her floral dress, or in her pleated grey-blue woollen skirt? He remembered how her lip had stuck to one of her teeth when she opened her mouth to smile. To feel the nipple stiffen between his thumb and his forefinger. Her scent as the warm air of her body escaped when she unbuttoned her blouse. There was a knock at his door.

"Did you not hear me?" His mother asked.

He got up and opened the door.

"I have made some scones. Your father will be back soon. We might as well start otherwise they might get spoilt."

They sat down at the dining room table. Mrs van Yssen had moved her writing things to one side. Betta had polished the furniture the day before and the odour of their special mixture of linseed oil and methylated spirits hung heavily in the room.

"Your father and I spoke this morning, my boy, and we feel that you should go on your own to see Frances. It is really a great pity that you cannot see your way clear to go with her to Cape Town."

"It probably will be better for me to go on my own. The scones are very good."

"What have you been doing?"

"Oh, just getting ready for next term. The holidays aren't long."

"I wonder what's keeping your father?"

Douglas stared at the rain.

"Douglas?"

"Yes I can hear you. Betta tells me you went to see Madame Jacquard. She was quite taken with Garnett, at Plettenberg Bay. I wonder what her whole story is."

"She has had a difficult life. She told me, and I have not even mentioned it to your father, that she had a son."

"A son?"

"Yes, he died. She did not say how, and I did not pry. She was quite upset when she told me."

"How strange life is. You would never say it when you consider how cheerful she is."

"She is very courageous. I hear the car."

Van Yssen walked into the dining room with a large shoebox wrapped in brown paper. "Have a look at these Douglas." He produced a brown boot from the box. "Flack and Smith. Mr Tracey managed to get me a pair – genuine Spanish leather. They should last a good time."

Douglas examined the boot. "Marvellous quality. Would almost be a pity to put dubbin on them."

"What time do you plan to leave?"

"Oh, about three thirty."

"It would be poor form if Frances arrived before you. Rather go a bit earlier."

It was still mizzling steadily when Douglas arrived at the station. He wore his raincoat and held an umbrella over his new fedora. The platform was deserted. People were packed into a steamy waiting room. He would sit with Frances in her compartment. He could not remember whether he had closed the window of the car and hurried back through the mud to see. It was closed. He stood under the canopy of the platform, half closed his umbrella, banged his hat against his leg to get drops of water off. He looked at his watch. Still about quarter of an hour. What if the train was late? He could not remember ever travelling in the rain. You can't even open the windows. Could get all fogged up in there. Damn nice boots. Cordwainers. He sauntered towards the stationmaster's office. The stationmaster was putting his jacket on. The engine appeared around the last bend. People poured from the waiting room. He put his hat on. The sky had become lighter. There was only very faint drizzle now.

The brakes of the train screeched piercingly as it came to a shuddering stop. He could not see Frances. Windows opened. He looked for a waving arm. It was unlike her. Then he saw her, her back to him, climbing from the train struggling with her suitcase. He ran up to her.

"Frances!"

"Before you say anything," she said, "please help me with the rest of my things. There is no point in arguing. All the necessary arrangements have been made. I will not be a burden. No, don't say anything, I have discussed it with my parents and they agreed that I should see you. Please help me, take this." She handed him her suitcase. "The other things are in my compartment – G. I have booked at the Queen's Hotel."

A barrow arrived. "The car is at the back."

"Daddy managed to change my booking. I shall continue my journey on Monday afternoon. I knew there was no point in asking your permission. I understand what you are going through, and there is a need for us to discuss things quite calmly. It is better this way since you decided not to go to Cape Town." She was out of breath.

"I am sorry about that. I need to resolve things within myself."

"I fully understand the position you have taken."

Douglas drove slowly along George Road. "My parents will be so pleased to see you. They, both of them, urged me to go to Cape Town. Shall we go to my house first?"

"Yes, let's go to your house. We can let the hotel know that I have arrived. Is that your school?"

"Yes."

"What a magnificent building! The town is larger than I expected."

"I'm glad." Douglas was confused. His equilibrium was disturbed.

"Is that the river you wrote about in your letters?"

"Yes, we only have one river."

"You seem detached, my love. I know you don't like the unexpected. I regret springing this on you. It was not easy for me but we cannot leave serious matters up in the air. I want you to know just how much I care about you. Mummy actually suggested that I come and see you when she heard how miserable I was. I have cried myself to sleep every night since I received your letter, and I want to be with you, my dearest man. Who's that woman waving to us?"

"Where?"

"Over there."

"That's Mrs Jacquard. I wonder why on earth she's out and about on a rainy Saturday afternoon." Douglas waved.

"She seems nice. You must take me to see her work if there is time."

"She is nice."

Patches of blue sky began to make openings for the sun.

"He's back soon," van Yssen said to his wife.

"What's going on now?"

Van Yssen peered through the living room window as the car turned into the driveway. "Dear Lord, it's Frances."

"Oh my word, Albert. Go and meet them, I need to straighten my hair, to make myself presentable." She trotted to their bedroom.

"Frances, what a pleasant surprise," van Yssen shook her hand and kissed her. "Come inside, Anneke will be with us in a few winks."

"This is a lovely garden. What a lovely house," Frances said as she looked about.

"Do come inside, my dear."

Van Yssen guided Frances into the drawing room.

"I'll sit where I can see the garden, if I may."

"You may sit wherever you please, my dear."

Mrs van Yssen arrived. "What a wonderful and completely unexpected surprise!" She embraced Frances warmly.

Van Yssen observed Frances. She looked tired. She had rings under her eyes, and it was evident that she had been crying. And here she was now, miserable and on her own in a strange town to see his son. His heart bled for her.

"Daddy made a booking for me at the Queen's Hotel. I felt that I had to come and see Douglas. Even if it is just until Monday."

"We cannot let you go and stay in a hotel, Frances," Mrs van Yssen said. "You must, and we insist, you must stay with us."

Frances opened her mouth to protest.

Van Yssen shook his head severely. "We could not possibly let you stay in the hotel."

"We have a comfortable spare room. I will make up the bed when we have had tea. I will ask Douglas to bring your luggage inside. You must be with us, and have some rest."

Mrs van Yssen was in the kitchen when Douglas came in through the back door. "Your father and I have asked Frances to stay with us, so if you would be so good as to get her luggage and put it in the spare room, I will make the bed. We cannot let the poor thing go to a hotel. It must have taken a great deal of courage for her to come here to see you Douglas. She looks haggard. She needs a lot of rest. Your father and I will go and play cards at the Elleys this evening, as planned. We'll have supper early and the two of you will have the whole evening to chat. I think you should ask your father to telephone the hotel and ask them to cancel the booking. Mr Robinson won't mind, I am sure. Get some biscuits from the pantry. You must be thrilled that she is here. I would have liked to show her off to our friends. Aren't you thrilled that she is here?"

"It was quite a surprise."

"For heaven's sake be enthusiastic, be affectionate towards her. She loves you, as no one else will ever love you Douglas."

"I know. I feel a great responsibility towards her. That is why I need time to resolve the issues facing me."

"Well, she's here now and there is no better way to deal with the issues than to do it together. That is clearly why she has come."

"I need to restore my balance. I am of no use to anyone at present. At times I feel so destructive that I fear what I might say. I should be alone at a time like this."

"Go and be with Frances."

Douglas practised a smile as he approached the living room. Frances was looking out of the window when he entered the room. "You have such a lovely garden," she said. "I imagined it quite differently. I imagined succulents and rocks, not a well-manicured lawn, and such splashes of colour. The roses are beautiful, and the walnut and peach trees with Kentucky blue grass under them. I love the ash tree. How civilised."

Van Yssen returned, "I have cancelled your booking, Frances. Perhaps you would like to telephone your parents to tell them that you have arrived safely? Douglas will show you where the telephone is. Douglas will show you your room."

Mrs van Yssen took out her Royal Doulton cups and used the silver teapot. There was no knitted cosy today.

"My parents send their best regards," Frances said. "Daddy said a special thank you for putting me up. I think he was actually jolly relieved that I am with friends, and not on my own."

"It is the least that we can do," Mrs van Yssen said. "We are so very pleased to have you with is."

"Did you have a good journey?" van Yssen asked.

"Yes, yes indeed. I had a coupê to myself, which is always a privilege."

"Frances, Albert and I have been invited to play cards with friends this evening. Apart from that we have nothing planned for the rest of the weekend. I would like to suggest that we have an early supper, and leave you and Douglas to enjoy one another's company this evening."

"I hope I am not putting you out?"

"Oh, my dearest girl, of course not. I cannot begin to tell you how pleased we are to see you."

The van Yssens excused themselves from the supper table and left Frances and Douglas to finish their meal in their own time.

"I'll get some fruit," Douglas said. He kissed her on her head. "I love you very much."

The telephone rang and he went to answer it. "Hello Garnie. No, they have gone on their own, I'm not going. Frances is here. Yes, here at our house. Yes, it's wonderful. On Monday afternoon. Yes come and say hello tomorrow morning. We won't be going to church. See you then, bye."

"That was Garnett."

"So I gathered. Nice fruit," she said as she cut a piece of peach and put it into her mouth with her fork. She sprinkled salt on the next piece. "Delicious."

"His parents have made some or other arrangement. He asked whether he could come tomorrow afternoon instead. I suggested late afternoon."

The early autumn dusk grew stronger. What was left of the daylight assumed a bluish hue that made their faces pale. They looked at one another. Her tired eyes shone with sympathy and hope. He could not hold her gaze for long.

"Yes?" she asked.

"I feel terrible Frances." His voice wavered.

"I know."

"I am no good to anyone, as I am now."

She put her hand on his. "We have our future."

"I cannot believe what is happening to me. As I said to my mother in the kitchen this afternoon, I feel such destructive resentment, that I feel at times as though I have taken on evil proportions. I feel as though I am watching all the sounds that I have ever heard becoming smaller and less distinct and disappearing into the distance. I cannot imagine what it must be like never to hear again. I shall have to give up teaching, and I fear that it will happen soon."

"Why soon?"

"There is no telling how rapidly my disease will progress. It was what Garnett did not say that said it all. I could tell from his face and his eyes. Already I strain to hear certain sounds."

"But it could happen slowly and they could find a cure."

"There is no cure, and there will never be. Once the nerves are damaged, the damage cannot be reversed."

"Then we will find another way."

"There is no other way."

"I know how wretched you are feeling, and I understand better than you may think what you are going through, Douglas. I have not come here to make things worse, but to try and give you my loving understanding and support. It would be quite inappropriate to quarrel with you." She stroked his arm.

"I know, and I apologize for my behaviour. It is just that I feel so helpless. I cannot understand why this should happen to anyone. Why in heaven's name are we born with hearing, or for that matter with sight, only for that ability to be lost because of disease? In fact why should there be disease at all? What went wrong with the creation? Why is it out of joint? I have been betrayed. I look at the trees and they are flawed. I look at the flowers and they are imperfect. The whole creation is a mess, a whole concoction of errors. For me all the beauty has gone, and it proves to me that what I perceived to be beauty was a figment of my imagination. It never existed objectively. It is all a great big deception. That's what it is. There is no justice. What have I done to deserve this?" She withdrew her hand from his arm. "I did not want you to see me in this state. I do not want anyone to see me like this. I have put a brave face on for the sake of my parents because I do not want them to suffer more than they are already suffering. I cannot talk to them like this. I should not talk to you like this. Garnett is the only one to whom I can bare everything without feeling guilty. I have spoken to him, but he has no answers. My mother speaks of Beethoven. Madame Jacquard put the idea into her head – how he overcame, or transcended, his deafness. How his disability inspired him to greater heights. What poppycock."

"You frighten me."

"I do not mean to. It is dreadful of me to have done that. I have a great responsibility towards you Frances, and I am fighting with myself to prevent my remorseless anger from reaching you. I am infected with resentment of huge proportions and I do not want my contagion to reach you."

"What are you saying? You are my life, for better or for worse. I shall stand by you even if you were insane. I can never be separate from you. This cup will pass. Time heals everything. I know that you will still do great things. I am very tired now. I think I should go to bed. Please come and kiss me goodnight."

She left him sitting at the dining table.

Sunday 18 March 1928

Betta prepared a huge breakfast of scrambled egg, bacon, sausages, fried tomatoes and fried bananas. There was toast and marmalade and percolated coffee and green fig preserve.

"Were you comfortable last night, Frances?" Mrs van Yssen enquired.

"More than comfortable, thank you. I was exhausted. Douglas was understanding and let me go to bed quite early. I feel much refreshed. The food looks very good. I am famished."

"What can I give you Frances?" van Yssen asked.

"I'll have a bit of everything if I may, not too much egg, please."

"I would like to suggest that we go for a walk after breakfast," Douglas said. She nodded affectionately with her head to one side.

"I would like to look at the French woman's paintings, if that would be possible?"

"Let me go and give her a ring right now, in case she wants to go out." Mrs van Yssen got up from the table.

"Yes that would be a good idea," Douglas said. "And then we can go to the suspension bridge. The river is quite beautiful down there."

"Why don't you take the car, after lunch, and go up to Rust en Vrede, Douglas."

"That sounds like a good idea Dad."

"What is Rust en Vrede?" Frances asked.

"It is the source of our drinking water. There is a magnificent waterfall."

Mrs van Yssen returned to the breakfast table, "She would be delighted to see you, she said the sooner the better, but there is no need to rush. It is Sunday and we should have a leisurely breakfast."

"I love my room, it is so peaceful, and the night was cool, which was a blessing after the blazing heat we have been having. One sleeps so much better. My aunt Jemima, on my mother's side, loved houses. She said they had their own personalities. She always talked about the feel of a house. Your house has a wonderful feel. It is a happy house."

Douglas smiled sadly at her. "We saw Mrs Jacquard yesterday when we drove from the station."

Frances put her hand through Douglas' arm as they walked along the deserted Sabbath roads towards Madame Jacquard's house. "I should have put my hat on," Frances said.

"She won't mind. She is quite informal, Left Bank informal."

An easterly wind exposed the rustling undersides of the leaves of the trees. Hints of autumn. Summer green was turning into copper colour. Reluctant shadows now fell in different places and the sunlight was thinner.

"How is your hearing today?"

"Not too bad. Sometimes it is better than at other times. I cannot understand why that is."

"I am looking forward to seeing Garnett."

"My mother is going to invite him to have supper with us, so that we will be able to go to Rust en Vrede after lunch."

"I like being here with you and your family. I am happy here. Your house, the books, everything." She pressed his arm against her body.

"That means a lot to me."

"Where does Garnett stay?"

He pointed to the northeast. "Over there, beyond the river. This is Mrs Jacquard's house."

"How quaint, a bijou!"

"I'll go ahead," He said as he opened the garden gate. An acorn clattered loudly on the tin roof of the house. He tapped the knocker on the front door.

"Ah, my Douglas! And his Frances!" She kissed Douglas on both cheeks. "My, my, my so this is Frances." She took Frances' hands in hers, "What a beautiful fiancée you have Douglas. I am so glad to meet you Frances."

"I have not even made formal introductions," Douglas said.

"You know me by now," Madame Jacquard laughed. "I am just a little bit different, Frances. But come inside. Besides I feel as though I have known you for a long time, so there is no need to introduce. Anneke tells me you want to look at my paintings?"

"Yes, I have heard so much about you. My mother said she too would like to see your work."

"Please do not expect me to be, how would you say Douglas, coy? Is that right?"

"That depends on what you want to say, Madame Jacquard."

She led them into her studio. The garden doors were open. There was sunlight on the wooden floor. The soft scent of pink and white dog roses put loosely into a glass vase mixed with the odour of oil paint. Frances wandered about. The last of the zinnias, marigolds and marguerites, grown from seeds brought from France, were visible behind two stoneware jars. Geraniums overflowed from a raised flowerbed.

"I got up very early this morning to make something to have with our coffee. It is in the kitchen. I will be back now."

"May I help you?" Douglas asked.

"No, no, Douglas, you stay with Frances. I will manage."

Frances made a sweeping movement. "This has such a special atmosphere. I have never been into an artist's studio before. The untidiness, the splotched with paint, brushes, the wine bottle with turpentine, her smock hanging there, the odd pieces of furniture, the pink couch, and the large windows and light. The lampshade with its cobwebs, the dusty black umbrella with its curved brown wooden handle, in the corner. The piece of sculpture on its side."

Madame Jacquard returned with a tray. "I have made a Genoa cake, a Pain de Genes."

"How exciting I have never had that before!" Frances exclaimed.

"Monet loved Pain de Genes, my dear. I thought it appropriate."

Douglas took the tray from her.

"Thank you Douglas, we will sit over there at the table, I have cleared one corner, if you will forgive the mess. One day I shall tidy it. I don't know when that will be."

"Did you spend much time in Montparnasse?" Frances asked.

"Yes, and no. It was inevitable, as a student, but I was never comfortable with the excesses."

"How do you mean?" Frances was intrigued.

"It is all very well to search for meaning, and I suppose all young people do. Something compels us to try and find meaning. People were wild, they did everything in excess, they did silly things also with art and their excuse was that they were experimenting with new forms. To experiment is good, we must go to new frontiers, but we must have a balance if we are going to recognise what is of value. In art it is only the universal that has lasting value."

"I take it you are talking about Expressionism?" Douglas asked.

"On the contrary. I am an Impressionist at heart."

"But then you are not talking about something that comes from inside?"

"As an Impressionist I am a mirror that reflects what I observe. If the mirror is flawless what I reflect is pure. Remember, photography greatly influenced Impressionism. If the lens of the camera is flawed, or if the film does not properly record, the image will be imperfect. My mind is the film that records what I see and how I see it. If I will allow my mind to function perfectly and if I am honest, you as the viewer of my work will see what I see. 'Correspondence' we call it in French. But enough of that, I have not even cut the cake!"

"Why are your paintings covered?" Frances enquired.

"So that they will not distract you. Believe me they are waiting to look at you. First we shall concentrate on our conversation, and then we shall visit the paintings."

Frances laughed happily. "What an amazing way of seeing things. I have been so happy since I arrived here in Oudtshoorn. Everything just seems right." She took a bite of the cake. "Oh, my goodness how delicate, how exquisite, no wonder Monet liked it. I could never have imagined Oudtshoorn like this. I would love to live here."

Madame Jacquard looked at Douglas. There was no emotion in his eyes.

When they had had their tea Mrs Jacquard got up. "It is now time for you to look at my paintings." She walked to the nearest easel. "Let me first show you some work in progress. The canvas was prepared last month. I have to be at the scene itself. Sometimes I have to walk for hours, sometimes the taxi comes to fetch me." She removed the cover. "This is near the Olifants River."

"I recognise the area. The train passes by there," Frances said.

"It is important to go at the same time each day, and the seasons are changing, so I will have to hurry." The tall reeds near the river were fresh pale green. Beyond the reeds terracotta hills displayed bright green scrub. In the distance a succession of hills progressively assumed deeper shades of blue until their colour transformed them into mountains. Madame Jacquard uncovered another painting. "This I finished last month. It is on a farm near Calitzdorp. We have our own haystacks here. It is early in the morning and the sun is rising, as you can see."

"Why do you say we have our own haystacks here, surely there are haystacks wherever you go?" Douglas asked.

"Monet did a series of paintings of haystacks. His pupils copied him.

When I drove with your parents to Ladismith early one morning, I saw some haystacks with the early light on them and a row of trees behind them, just like in his scene near Giverny, so I returned one day and here it is. And now let us look at some of the others." There were two still lives of flowers and one of a bunch of purple grapes, and some more landscapes. There was a painting of a white farmhouse set against a copse of poplar trees, in the Cango valley.

"I absolutely love your paintings. What an extraordinary, overwhelming surprise."

They sat down again at the table. Madame Jacquard watched as Frances observed Douglas. Her eyes were desperate. A cloud moved past the sun and the room darkened.

"For how long will you be visiting, Frances?" Madame Jacquard enquired.

Frances was lost in thought and the question startled her. "Oh, tomorrow afternoon. I shall be leaving tomorrow afternoon, I'm afraid."

"What a pity that it is so short, your visit. I like you very much. But, there will no doubt be other times."

"Yes, I will be sad to go, but that is how things are. No doubt there will be other times."

After leaving Madame Jacquard, Frances and Douglas went towards the river and the suspension bridge. "When Madame Jacquard asked me how long I would be staying, I realised how little time I have left here, and I wonder whether you would mind very much, my love, if we stayed at home this afternoon?"

"You mean instead of going to Rust en Vrede?"

"Yes."

"Yes, that would be fine."

"I would prefer to be with you in a way that has no distractions."

"How do you mean?"

"I mean I want to be alone with you and preferably in a familiar place. And I like your house. I want to be with you where I am comfortable. All this has been a great shock to me and I don't want to be in public, among strangers."

"I just thought you would like to see the place, it's quite extraordinary."

"Perhaps another time."

"This is the suspension bridge. There aren't many of them in the Union."

"I certainly have never seen one. It is quaint, let's go onto it."

The bridge swayed as they walked. From the middle they looked down at the sluggish brown-green waters of the river below. Intrusive movements told them that there was someone else on the bridge. When Douglas looked up he saw Mr and Mrs Edmeades approaching in their Sunday best, she with a pale pink parasol for the sun.

"Fancy finding you here Douglas!" Edmeades exclaimed. "It was unusual for the van Yssens not to be in church. I wondered about that. But now I can see why."

"Let me introduce you to my fiancée Frances Rose."

"How do you do Miss Rose," they said and took turns to shake Frances' hand.

"How do you do," Frances said.

"Douglas is a lucky young man, Miss Rose, to have bagged such a prize as you," Edmeades said as he took off his hat and Mrs Edmeades smiled in her most religious way.

"I must concur with my husband," she added and looked at him for demure approval.

"Will you be staying long, Miss Rose?" Edmeades asked.

"I am afraid only until tomorrow afternoon. It is really much too short."

"You're telling me! Much too short," Edmeades guffawed. "We must be on our way now or the cook will scold us, and we can't have that, can we now? I bid you good day, and hope that we shall see more of you, Miss Rose." Mrs Edmeades smiled and nodded and took her husband's arm as he led her away along the swaying bridge to have her lunch and their afternoon sleep while he anticipated her generous body adorned in flesh coloured lingerie.

"Charming people," Frances commented.

"Perhaps we should go home now," Douglas suggested. "We'll go into town tomorrow morning."

Van Yssen was in his study when they arrived. "So? You've been gone a long time. What was your visit to our French woman like?"

"We also went for a walk down to the river," Douglas said.

"She is awfully interesting, quite charming, and her paintings are exceptional. She has so much style, and from all accounts has had a most colourful life," Frances said.

"She's colourful all right," van Yssen remarked.

"She made us a lovely cake," Frances added.

"Dad, we have decided that we would rather stay here this afternoon, rather than to go out to Rust en Vrede."

"In that case your mother and I will probably go for a drive."

Mrs van Yssen appeared in her apron. "Lunch is nearly ready."

"Thank you for arranging for us to go and see Madame Jacquard, Mrs van Yssen."

"It was a pleasure my dear. I have found her company delightful. I still have a few things to do."

"We also met Mr and Mrs Edmeades at the suspension bridge," Douglas said.

"He's such a jolly man," Frances smiled.

"Let's go to the dining room," van Yssen suggested.

There was a large roast chicken amply surrounded by roast potatoes; finely grated carrot salad with bits of pineapple and orange juice; fried eggfruit, small squashes and baked red sweet potatoes with cinnamon sticks.

"Yummy," Frances said as she observed the food.

"Ordinary country fare, my dear." van Yssen started carving the chicken.

"Is Garnett still coming?" Mrs van Yssen asked.

"Yes, late this afternoon," Douglas replied.

"I love it here," Frances said.

"We are so pleased about that," Mrs van Yssen smiled at her.

"I am sad to be leaving tomorrow, but I am glad I've come. I had to come and see Douglas. I have prayed a great deal and my prayers have left me with a lot of hope. I want you to know that the reason why I decided to come here is that I will face any challenge with Douglas." Mrs van Yssen had tears in her eyes. Van Yssen stopped carving the chicken. Douglas looked down into the polished surface of the table and saw the distorted reflections of his ears.

"Well, it did not quite come out as I meant it to, and I am rambling, I know, but I have come to terms with Douglas' condition, and I will give you every support, my love."

Douglas took her hand. "Thank you, Frances."

"Well, as I was saying," Frances continued, more cheerfully now, "I really love it here. I love the atmosphere of your house. Douglas said we could go into the village tomorrow morning. I am looking forward to that."

"I don't know how to respond." Mrs van Yssen sniffed as she wiped her eyes and her nose. "We love you Frances, dear child. It has taken a lot of courage to come here at a time like this. Douglas is very fortunate to have you. You are a very special person."

"We'll have forty winks, and I mean only forty winks, Douglas, it's still early, and then your mother and I will go for our drive."

"If you don't mind, Douglas, I too shall have a rest," Frances said.

"Now tell me about your visit to Madame Jacquard," Mrs van Yssen asked.

Douglas opened his mouth but Frances spoke first. "She must have had very good training. She's no amateur. Does she sell much of her work?"

Douglas cleared his throat. "She had a small exhibition at the library last year, in the middle of last year, and it was reasonably well received, but I do not think that there is yet a sufficient appreciation of modern art here in Oudtshoorn. There was a review of the exhibition in the *Courant*, by Mrs Hemple, the wife of the Anglican priest, and it was not too kind. Mrs Hemple does some watercolours herself, and perhaps she was not the most suitable person to do the review. Madame Jacquard found the article quite amusing and pinned a copy of it up in the kitchen for a day and then destroyed it. She has a remarkable ability to ignore the opinions of others."

"Because she is at ease with herself," Frances commented.

"That's an interesting comment," van Yssen said.

"It's true Mr van Yssen, if you think about it. If we have certainty, opinions of others cannot influence us unduly. If there is uncertainty we tend to seek the approval of others and let their ideas influence us. And it is almost always certainly the kind of influence we least want. Quite apart from the fact that she is foreign, meaning French, and they are odd in many ways – Daddy says they are leftovers from excesses of the Revolution – she has a formidable presence. She is uncanny."

"She's not in the least religious," Mrs van Yssen contributed.

"I'm not surprised," Douglas remarked.

"What do you mean by that?" His father asked.

"Religion can obstruct spirituality."

"We must be careful now, Douglas, it is Sunday," his mother chided.

"Unless we are superstitious, Ma, it does not matter on what day we tell the truth."

"Madame Jacquard is a good woman," Mrs van Yssen replied hastily.

"It was interesting for me to meet someone like that. I don't think I have ever before met someone quite like that. She has passionate energy that charges her awareness. It is as though she sees more than other people do, as though she understands what you are about to say even before you say it."

"You are very quiet Douglas," His father said.

"What Frances says is intriguing. She must have been stunningly attractive when she was young."

"She has a past," van Yssen said.

"We don't know much about that, Dad."

"She has a sad past." Mrs van Yssen wanted to deflect any difference of opinion. "She told me that she had a son once."

"When did she say that, Anneke?"

"On Monday when I went to see her, when you went to see Garnett."

"You went to see Garnett, Dad?"

"It was more of a casual meeting Douglas."

"What happened to her son?" Frances asked.

"She did not say, except that she would tell me one day. That's when she spoke to me about Beethoven, Douglas."

Douglas stared ominously at his father.

"And I have been thinking about Helen Keller," Frances added.

"Let's just change the subject. Let's just pretend that all is normal, which it is, in a sense." Douglas was irritable.

The sound of cutlery on crockery grew louder. They heard themselves chewing. "I have made a plum pudding, and we have some cream," Mrs van Yssen announced while Betta cleared the table.

Douglas remained in the living room when his parents went for their nap, and Frances retired to her room to have a sleep. His eye fell on the gold lettering on the cover of a new green unfamiliar book. He got up to fetch it. *Bismarck* by Emil Ludwig. He opened the book and read a quotation by Bismarck: 'That which is imposing here on earth... is always akin to the fallen angel; who is beautiful, but lacks peace; is great in his plans and efforts, but never succeeds;

is proud and melancholy.' The weather had improved greatly. A mild westerly wind stirred the trees in the garden and made the patterns of their shadows play on the windowpanes and the Chinese carpet. The aroma of coffee was still in the room. He turned the pages of the book and looked at the pictures of Bismarck from his youth to the end of his life. How he changed as he grew older! Why is it that some people always strive? He too was ambitious once, about his studies. There seemed to be purpose then. His one tooth was sensitive to heat. He should go and see Leibner. Why did he not have the same desire for physical contact with Frances? He put his index fingers into his ears and pushed hard to seal off all sound. His nails hurt the canals but he pushed more. Someone could be entering the room and he would not know about it. He felt anxious: someone could be standing behind him and he would be unaware. His stomach turned. They all expected him to behave differently, to behave better. It was not like a common cold that would go away after a while. And if his grandfather gave it to him what was to say that his children and his grandchildren would not be afflicted? That was the worst of it all: that it would not stop with him. 'Accept it' she said. I cannot accept it. Never to hear any sound again; to have your head permanently bunged up. 'Make the best of your circumstances, Beethoven, Helen Keller.' If only they knew what it was like. 'Is great in his plans and his efforts, but never succeeds.' If You are taking my hearing away from me how do You expect me to succeed? Bismarck and Leibner. At Kaaimans he never mentioned Bismarck. With his new moustache they look quite alike. Is this the world of the fallen angel? Did we pass Kaaimans on the way home? We must have. It is beautiful there: the hills and the rugged cliffs, the hoarse sounds of the waves. To smell the sea again. His disillusionment emptied him. Would I one day be able to remember what sounds were like? The book slipped from his hand and he put it down next to him. He closed his eyes. Bismarck spoke to him, but he could not hear. They were together in a horse drawn coach in a grey wet cobbled London street.

"Your mother and I will be leaving now, Douglas. Don't forget to wake Frances."

Douglas went to Frances' door and knocked softly. There was no response and he knocked again. He opened the door cautiously and went inside. She was fast asleep, poor thing. Some blond hair was stuck to her creased temple. She must have lain on that side. He sat down on the chair next to her bed and observed her. She did not belong to him as he was now. He felt sorrow. He wanted to weep. The wetness that he needed to weep was gone. He touched her on her shoulder. "I have made you some tea."

"Thank you my love," she held her arms out to him.

He sat down on the side of the bed and hugged her.

"Kiss me," she said.

He kissed her on her cheek.

"No, properly."

He kissed her on her mouth and she drew him closer to her. She smiled bravely at him. "Let's go and have tea, just give me a few moments to make myself presentable."

"I have had the most wonderful rest. I was exhausted when I arrived," Frances said as she entered the dining room. "I dreamt of pictures and paintings in a different world, in which easels walked about with stiff wooden legs on broad plank floors. It was so nice, just like a pantomime. Have you ever thought of writing a history book?"

"There would not be much of a demand for it."

"Yes there would, you have such a talent to make the subject interesting. Just think, if you could make history popular, there would be a demand for it."

"It's a thought."

"You are just trying to fob me off by agreeing."

"No, really, I am not. I shall consider it, but there is a lot to sort out. I'll have to go and see Dr Archer about my future. I must examine all my options."

"It's good to hear you talking like that."

"It is one thing to talk and another to succeed. I don't think anybody can grasp how I feel. It is as though vital threads inside me have been severed. That which seemed to be my guide, that directed my conscience, that improved the beauty of the things I saw and felt, that which seemed to be unwavering, that sometimes made me say, 'what made me do such a stupid thing?' that thing has been driven away by my resentment."

"I understand."

He stared at the surface of the table.

"You must not lose your faith Douglas."

"I don't think I ever had any. I don't know what it means. Philosophically I have a problem with the notion of faith. What does it mean to 'believe' in something? In what?"

"In that thing you say you have driven away. You said it gave meaning to your life, that without it you are disillusioned. You should summon it, and it will return."

"Dear, dear Frances, I am so unkind to you. My conduct deserves reproach, forgive me. I am disgusted with myself. It is terrible. I feel worthless."

"Should I not have come to see you?"

"I am not implying that."

"I know you are not. I was impulsive."

"You were spontaneous. You were yourself. I am glad that you are here. What scares me is that I feel so resentful. I do not want you to be exposed to my resentment. I want to take revenge by hurting everything around me, and the only way I can prevent myself from hurting you is to avoid my impulses."

"I shall be patient. Let's go for a walk. The fresh air will do me good."

The van Yssens turned left at Selansnek and headed towards the eastern Outeniqua mountains, in the direction of Mossel Bay.

"You seem to be in a better frame of mind, Albert, since Frances arrived."

"I am pleased that she has come, and I am putting on my best face. To do otherwise would just make things worse, if that is possible."

"Garnett has known for some time that his hearing would again deteriorate."

"One would not have thought so judging by his behaviour at Plettenberg Bay."

"He masks his feelings well. Doctors learn to do that. But, when I think back, I realise that there were telltale signs. The way he sometimes looked at Douglas when it appeared as though Douglas did not hear something that was said. It all comes back to me now. I should have told Douglas that I was going to see Garnett. I don't want to harm his trust in me. Garnett can be quite touchy."

"Why do you say that?"

"He thought that I was criticising his professional behaviour when I asked him when he first knew that Douglas' condition was irreversible and how he knew about your father. He was quite touchy. He bridled. I have not seen him since. It may be a bit awkward this evening."

"You cannot imagine how I feel about my father's deafness. It has been passed on through me. I am the one who has given it to my son. Can you comprehend what that feels like, Albert?"

He demurred.

"I think of that little boy with his dark hair and his grey eyes looking up at me when I suckled him; of all the promise throughout his life and the wonderful, absolutely wonderful young woman to whom he is engaged, and I cannot believe that this could have happened to us. How was I to know that I would pass my father's deafness on to him? And if I had known, how would that have changed things? Would I rather have had no son at all than to have my deaf Douglas?" Her voice wavered.

Van Yssen stopped the car on the side of the road. He put his forehead on the top of the steering wheel and sobbed. "It is also my fault. We are being punished for what I am."

She put her hand on his shoulder. "No, no, you are a good man Albert you have never done anything wrong. You are just and fair. You are a man of principle."

"It is my lust. I am being punished for my lust!" he cried bitterly. "I should not have done what we did on the train."

She gasped in dismay. "Oh, good Lord, that was the most precious experience we ever had."

"You do not know what thoughts I had, what I thought when I saw your nakedness, how unashamed I was when you put your face against my eager manhood. I knew it was wrong but I succumbed. You do not know how often I have recalled the images of your privacy, and how I have had to restrain myself from taking you again in that way. And now I am being punished for my lust. I have always been filled with lust."

"I loved you more that night than I could ever have imagined. I felt closer to God than ever before."

"Oh my goodness, what have I done! I have defiled your innocence with my lust. I have sinned."

"You have not sinned, Albert."

"Yes I have. If only you knew how readily I yielded to my most base animal instincts, my venereal perversity. I have practised a deceit towards you by pretending to be normal while the animal rages inside me. All that remains for me now is constantly to pray for forgiveness, God's forgiveness and your forgiveness."

"Perhaps we should go home."

"No, we will carry on as planned, and allow the young people more time together."

Anneke looked up at the metallic-blue mountains that towered ahead of them, their highest peaks shrouded in mist and clouds. *I will lift up my eyes unto the hills*

Garnett arrived at the van Yssens' house shortly before six. He parked his car in their driveway, put on his Trinity College blazer, straightened his cravat and went to the open front door. He knocked and waited. He saw Frances approaching along the passage.

"Garnett, dear friend!" she exclaimed. "How good to see you." She gave him a hug.

"Hello, Frances."

Douglas arrived, "Hello Garnie. Come inside, we're in the drawing room."

"Good evening Garnett." Van Yssen shook his hand. "Anneke will be with us presently."

"Gee Frances, it is so good to see you. Let me have a good look at you. You are as beautiful as ever. Have you had a good first term?"

"From a teaching point of view, it was quite satisfactory, and as uneventful as Graaff Reinet can be. Apart from the little bit of tame local scandal, life there is humdrum. And how is your practice getting along?"

"More work by the day, very busy. By the way Douglas, we would like you to play tennis with us this Wednesday."

"I don't know, Garnie."

"I insist. It's a prescription. Don't argue. We will see you there at four, and that's all there is to it. So what's this that I hear, that you're continuing on your way to Cape Town tomorrow, Frances?"

"I am afraid so."

"Great pity," Garnett said. "Not much time for Douglas to show you off. It's not often that we are privileged to have such a stunning girl in this town. We should make the best of it."

"You really are a rascal, Garnett Nel!"

Mrs van Yssen had tried her best to conceal her red eyes. She had splashed them with cold water and held tealeaves on the lids. She smiled unconvincingly when she entered the living room. "Hello Garnett. It's just a light supper, a Sunday evening supper if you please."

"I had such an enormous lunch Mrs van Yssen, the less I have this evening the better."

"How was your holiday at Plettenberg Bay, Garnett?" Frances tried to make conversation in the uneasy atmosphere of the darkening drawing room.

"I had an excellent rest there, thank you."

"Most importantly, did you catch any fish?"

"Small ones."

"Garnett kept us in fish while he was there." Mrs van Yssen tried to match Garnett's jolliness. "Would you like a beer, Garnett?"

"That would be very nice thank you."

"I met Mrs Jacquard this morning. We went to look at her paintings."

"She's really quite different."

"Oudtshoorn is such an unusual place, I should have come here sooner. Have you lived here long Garnett?"

"I was born here, Frances. My dad came here when he was about six, so we're old inhabitants. My mother is from this district. It is interesting place and strange in some ways. I think the ostrich feather boom, or should I call it ostrich feather madness, attracted many unusual people. It was like a gold rush. All sorts converged on the town in the space of a few years. Would you say that's correct Mr van Yssen?"

"I've never thought of it in gold rush terms. You could be right. It certainly did not grow as gradually as other towns did. It certainly did attract the fortune seekers, and those who thought that they could make money from the fortunes of others. This house was built with ostrich feather money, and virtually abandoned when the boom turned into bust."

"When was that?" Frances asked.

"When war was declared. There were large consignments of feathers on the high seas when war was declared; consignments that immediately became worthless because feathers were no longer fashionable. And we were left with all the immigrants to our town. So when the 'French Woman', as she became known, arrived, the town had become accustomed to having odd people washing up on its shores," Garnett said. "To call her odd is perhaps harsh. Let me rather say a trifle eccentric."

"I liked her, Garnett."

"So did I Frances, we had a lovely time at the seaside, by the kind courtesy of the van Yssens, of course. She amused us, sometimes without meaning to. She swam every day and exercised her upper body vigorously while she stood on the sands."

"I think she is a wonderful person. She has given me a great deal of very good advice. She has shown me that there are many different ways of looking at things," Mrs van Yssen said. "We should go through to the dining room, please. Albert has a long day ahead of him tomorrow."

"Where are you going, Dad?"

"To Ladismith. Fortunately the weather is cooler. I have given Fourie a ring and he will fetch you and Frances at three tomorrow afternoon."

Monday 19 March 1928

Frances woke early, did her ablutions as quietly as possible, and went outside. The garage doors stood open and the car had gone. The air was bracing. Heavy dew lay on the grass. She walked down the garden path. At the gate she stopped and turned to look at the house. There was no sun on it yet. She decided to go for a walk and set off in the same direction she and Douglas had taken the day before. In the east the sky was light. The air was filled with the sounds of birds. She wondered whether Douglas could hear them. She felt alone. At least she would be home tomorrow. She cried a little, and felt better afterwards. She walked around the block and saw no one. When she got back to the house the front door was ajar, and some of the sash windows had been opened. Betta was sweeping the veranda.

"Mister Doulgas has gone to look for Miss Frances," Betta said. "I has made coffee for Miss Frances. It is in the dining room."

"Thank you so much, Betta."

She poured herself coffee and heard Douglas' footsteps in the passage.

"Ah, there you are. I went to look for you."

"Good morning my dear man, am I not going to have a kiss?"

"Of course! We'll have our breakfast, and go into town."

"That sounds like a glorious idea."

"Where did you go?"

"Just around the block. I did not want to get lost."

"You can hardly get lost here." He was amused.

Fourie fetched them at half past ten.

"Which way should I go so the young lady will have the best views of the town?"

"Along van der Riet Street, along the top," Mrs van Yssen requested.

"Where are we going, Ma?"

"I thought the Waldorf would be a good idea. They have such nice little snacks there, and it is spacious."

Fourie turned into Queen Street and headed south.

"There's one of our synagogues," Douglas pointed to the right.

"Is there more than one?" Frances asked.

"There is another one further down in St John Street," Douglas replied.

"It's quite something for a town this size to have two synagogues, isn't it?" Frances asked.

"We have a very large Jewish community here. The ostrich feathers attracted merchants and traders. There are even Jewish farmers in the district," Douglas commented.

Mrs van Yssen entered the Waldorf with great pride, followed by Frances and Douglas. Sitting in one corner was Mrs Liebenfeld, her flushed face under a large trembling brown felt hat, in emotional conversation with her friend and confidante Jayne Atlee. Mrs Liebenfeld cast furtive conspiratorial glances and saw Mrs van Yssen. She straightened herself to protest the innocence of what she had just said, and smiled with a little wave of her hand. Then she saw Frances. She stretched out her arms to Mrs van Yssen in a gesture of great welcoming, "Anneke, come and say hello to us! And introduce us! Hello Douglas, you rapscallion, so this is the girl you went to visit at Plettenberg Bay?"

"Hello Anneke." Jayne Atlee was uncomfortable.

Mrs van Yssen introduced Frances. The women took turns to examine Frances.

"How long will you be staying Miss Rose?" Mrs Liebenfeld asked.

"I shall be leaving this afternoon."

Jayne Atlee gave Frances a warm smile. "We have heard much that is complimentary about you, Miss Rose. It is really good to make your acquaintance. No doubt we will see much more of you. Anneke and Albert should have arranged a party to introduce Douglas' fiancée to Oudtshoorn society. You should think of that Anneke, you really should, it is never too late for that."

"And you, Douglas? Just standing there and grinning. What have you got to say for yourself?" Mrs Liebenfeld taunted.

"What can I say?" he responded embarrassedly.

"It's a beautiful lass," Mrs Liebenfeld said. "What it is to have the bloom of youth."

"You look very well yourself, Antoinette," Mrs van Yssen responded.

"Sometimes life is cruel, Anneke, but I will just have to bear my burdens with equanimity."

A waiter guided them to the other side of the tearoom.

"The town is quiet. It's the school holidays," Mrs van Yssen observed when they were seated. "The weather is still good enough for people to go to the coast. But first, what are we going to have? They have excellent waffles."

"That sounds jolly good," Frances said, "and tea, please."

They had hardly started their waffles when Mrs Hops and Alice Kuys entered the tearoom. Douglas got up to greet them.

"Frances? How nice to see you again," Mrs Kuys said.

"Frances, let me introduce you to Mrs Hops," Douglas said.

"She surprised us all, it is a wonderful surprise visit, Alice."

"How long will you be staying, Miss Rose?" Mrs Hops enquired.

"Only until this afternoon."

"Well, we won't take up any more of your precious time, Anneke. It was so nice to meet you Miss Rose," Mrs Hops said, as she and Mrs Kuys went to their table.

Douglas glanced at Mrs Liebenfeld. "Within hours the whole town will know that you are here."

"Now, now Douglas, she is not as bad as you make out," his mother chided.

"The waffle is delicious," Frances said with a half full mouth.

"I am in a better frame of mind," Douglas announced.

Frances affectionately tilted her head towards him and conspicuously put her hand on his sleeve. "I am so thrilled to hear that. I shall leave more happily this afternoon."

"I'll make an appointment to go and see Dr Archer in the next few days and explain my position to him, and see what comes from that. That is all I can do for now. I have decided to deal with it one day at a time."

"How did you learn to cook, Mrs van Yssen?" Frances asked. "I shall have to learn, because to start with we will not be able to afford a cook."

"I suppose I always helped to do things on the farm, helped in the kitchen from an early age. My mother used to bake a great deal, for church functions and various bazaars and I would help with my apron on when I was little – beat the eggs, mix them with flour, and help to prepare the cake mixes. I learnt to knead bread so that enough air got into the dough. It was pleasant in the kitchen, especially in winter time. It was large, with scrubbed wooden floorboards, had a huge black woodstove, an assortment of scrubbed tables and surfaces to work on. We made our own sausage, smoked our own hams. The pantry was the best, situated on the cool side of the old house. The mixture of smells in there was glorious – spices and dried herbs and ground coffee and cinnamon cookies and fruit – summer peaches and plums and muskmelons. We had large galvanised sheet metal bins in the pantry that contained maize meal and wheat meal and one for bran, and other grains. It was wonderful to put your head into the bins and to smell the meal. I loved to sit on the lap of one of our servants when I was small and have some of their food. They had a special way of frying sausage and mopping its juice up with bits of bread. Even now, at my age, I can transport myself back into the old house, back into the pantry, or out into the garden and relive again the things of my childhood. But, alas, I am getting carried away. You asked about cooking. The best thing to do is just to do it. Acquire a good cookbook, follow the instructions and you will be surprised how easily you will learn, and how much enjoyment it will give you."

"You're so encouraging."

Douglas laughed. "What are we having for lunch?"

"A pot roast."

"That sounds delicious," Frances said.

"Mrs Liebenfeld and Mrs Atlee are waving goodbye, Ma."

"I wish I didn't have to go," Frances lamented.

"Then why don't you stay for another few days?" Mrs van Yssen suggested.

"Mummy arranged for us to go to my uncle's farm when Douglas said he could not come to Cape Town. I cannot cancel that arrangement now, I'm afraid. Douglas could always come with me?"

"I feel I should sort my own matters out here, Frances. I'm sure you'll understand."

Mrs van Yssen looked away. "My, how time flies, Mr Fourie is at the door."

After lunch Frances packed her things, and brushed her teeth. She went into the kitchen and gave Betta ten shillings and thanked her for all her help. It was nearly a quarter to three. She went to the drawing room, took a copy of the Ladies' Home Journal from the shelf next to the bookcase and began paging mechanically.

Mrs van Yssen arrived. "Where is Douglas?"

"I have no idea, Mrs van Yssen."

"Let me go and see if I can find him." She found him straightening his fly as he entered the kitchen. "Remember to wash your hands Douglas. Frances is waiting for you in the living room."

Mrs van Yssen embraced and kissed Frances on her temple. "May God bless you my child." She started to cry. Douglas stared at the flowers in the garden. Betta wiped her eyes and Fourie stood with his back turned to give them privacy. Mrs van Yssen waved to them with her small white handkerchief and smiled through her tears as they left.

Frances and Douglas sat close together in the back of the taxi. They waited on the platform while Fourie sat at the counter of the waiting room. "Thank you for coming to see me Frances. I apologize for being such bad company. I feel better today, and I must thank you for that. Please write to me. Give my regards to your parents, and ring me when you get home, please."

She patted his knee. "I love you dearest. I know these are dark moments but we shall overcome them, together. That is all that matters."

Douglas stood on the platform and looked at Frances until the train gave its first squealing jerk and began to move. He looked at her while she was carried away framed in the window of her compartment, until he could no longer see her, and then he looked at her image as he remembered it while he stared at the railway tracks.

Chapter Twenty-eight

Tuesday 20 March 1928

THE NELS had just finished supper when Douglas arrived. "Come inside, Douglas," Mr Nel called. "Pull up a chair and come and sit down with us. We were just talking about that Scottish bloke who claims that he can send pictures by wireless. Garnett says he thinks it's not a hoax, but I think it is just a huge joke. He's been saying for years now that he can do it, but if it is true why is it that he has not yet put it to proper profit?"

"Gosh, I really would not be able to comment, Mr Nel."

"Was nothing said about it when you were overseas last year?" Louis asked.

"Not that I am aware of, Mr Nel."

"We can only speculate Dad, we just don't have enough dope on it."

"I still think it is a hoax. It's stuffy in here, let's go and sit outside."

"I need to go to the surgery to look at my appointments for tomorrow. I was in the district the whole afternoon and came straight home."

Garnett parked his car at the surgery door. "I could not stand all the senseless quarrelling any longer, just had to get away. Come inside, Douglas."

"So Frances has been and gone," Garnett said.

"Yes."

"It was damn good of her to come and see you."

"Yes it was."

"Hell, I would have thought there would have been a stronger reaction from you."

"I would have thought so too."

"What's the matter?"

"I don't know. I seem to have no emotions. I am numb. I'm neither happy nor sad. I'm incapable of reacting. I am so preoccupied with my condition that everything else is excluded. I cannot remember how it felt to be in love. I tried yesterday morning to be as affectionate as possible to Frances, I tried to pretend that I was cheerful, and the worst was when I took her to the station. Despair has invested me with impotence. How long will it be before I go completely deaf?"

"Gosh! I don't know. Nobody knows."

"I mean, is it a question of months or years?"

"It is impossible to say. Even Yearsley could not predict that. How is your hearing at the moment?"

"At times it is a strain. I have problems in class. I've made an appointment to see Dr Archer tomorrow, to discuss my future. I'll have to quit soon."

"There's surely no need to be hasty?"

"Yes there is. I need to have certainty. I just cannot continue to travel in hope."

"I know it is easy for me to talk, but you should guard against being self destructive."

"I just want to shut myself off from the world."

"What will you do if you stop teaching?"

"Frances has spoken about doing editing, or writing history."

"That sounds excellent."

"Ja, but I don't want to do anything like that. I don't want charity, her father finding a job for me."

"For heaven's sake, why not?"

"I don't want to be beholden to anybody. I will make my own way, even if it is along a desolate road."

"But what will you do?"

"I'll go farming."

"Farming? You must be off your rocker, Douglas. Have you lost your marbles? You're an intellectual. You could be one of the great historians of your time, and you want to squander your life on farming? For heaven's sake man, that would be worse than suicide."

"If I'm as brilliant as you all say, I can figure out what to do. If other people can do it, so can I. It can't be that difficult."

"It is more difficult than you think. You're dependent on the weather, on markets; pests and diseases attack crops and animals. I go into the district regularly. People are struggling. And they are people with a lot of experience, tough people, who have farmed for generations."

"Perhaps that is their problem."

"How do you mean?"

"Could be in a rut, the same old rut as their fathers and their grandfathers, that's why they don't make money. They need new ideas and new methods. I'll start with an open mind."

"When did you get this idea?"

"I have always liked the idea of a farm."

"You've never said anything about it to me before."

"Fair enough, but I have always had the thought, I promise you."

Garnett shook his head in disbelief.

"You might well shake your head, Garnie, but I can make this thing work."

"Have you told Frances about this?"

"No."

"Have you told your parents?"

"No, but I will speak to my dad, when I have seen Archer. Now there is something that I need to ask you, Garnett. I need to know what the probability is of my children inheriting my condition, in view of my grandfather."

"Now you're asking me! We did study a little Mendelian inheritance, mostly in first year botany, but I must admit that I was not very good at it. We know there are conditions that are carried by the mother, and inherited by the son, for example haemophilia. The sons can pass the condition on to their daughters who will in turn pass it on to their sons, and so on. The mechanisms of inheritance are not simple. A lot of work will have to be done to refine the accuracy of predictions relating to inheritance. That's about all I can say. But why are you so interested in this?"

"I don't want to give Frances deaf children."

"I see."

"I cannot bear the thought of using her to pass this condition on to my offspring."

"I cannot make a prediction upon which you can base a decision. And if I read you correctly, judging by your present state of mind, the decision you want to take is one that could change other people's lives. Don't be impulsive, Douglas. Be patient. Get over this awful shock first, before you do something you will regret for ever."

"Garnett, as I become more and more deaf things will become worse. I had a foreboding once after I came to see you about my ears. Then my passion for Frances prompted my reason to dismiss the foreboding. Now that my faith has been destroyed, I am left only with belief in the foreboding. Isn't that an irony? The worst is still to come."

"We should go away for a few days. We should go to Herolds Bay. I could rent Raubenheimer's house for a few days. It will do you good. I'll do some fishing and you can contemplate the way ahead."

"It's a thought."

"When will you see Frances again?"

"On Saturday at the station. I promised her I would be there."

"And when do the schools start again?"

"On Monday."

"I don't know what to do about Frances."

"In what way?"

"I cannot expect her to be part of an uncertain future."

"Surely that is for her to decide?"

"She is not rational."

"I totally disagree. She is most rational. But I can understand that you cannot see that now."

"My circumstances are not normal. I cannot expect her to lead an abnormal life."

"What is a normal life, Douglas? People get married and their spouses become ill or disabled. Is someone who is ill or disabled normal? But they live through that, and often adverse circumstances serve to strengthen their love. The challenge brings out the best in them."

"I cannot explain myself Garnett. The whole thing has been made worse by our intimacy at Plettenberg Bay."

"Your intimacy?"

"We touched one another."

"You're forever holding hands, fiddling with one another."

"Not like that. In other ways, under our clothes."

"That is perfectly normal for people who are engaged."

"While we were there, and even before that, I sensed that there was something wrong with my ears, I knew that something was wrong, and yet I said nothing, I could not stop myself. I deceived her. I pretended to myself that it was just catarrh, or seawater or something. She thought she was being intimate with someone who was normal."

"Did she consent?"

"She encouraged it, and I just could not help myself. She was so enthusiastic."

"Then you are hardly being fair to yourself by saying that you deceived her."

"She could not know what I felt and thought at the time. I was a cad."

"And if you had not had your ear problem, would you still consider yourself a cad?"

"The fact is that I have my ear problem."

"And now you feel guilty because of that, and to add to everything else it is making you angry from embarrassment, and destructive."

"Yes."

"What are you going to tell Archer tomorrow?"

"I am going to tell him that I am going deaf. I am going to tell him that I shall have to stop teaching."

"And what if he asks you to continue?"

"I will tell him that that would just be putting off the evil day. He has nothing to gain from that, and neither have I. At most I shall agree to carry on for another term to give him time to find a replacement."

"And then?"

"I have to find a farm and borrow money from my dad and the Land Bank to buy it."

"I have to get going early tomorrow, come, let me take you home."

"I would rather walk, if you don't mind. It will give me time to think."

Wednesday 21 March 1928

"Come inside, come inside," Dr Archer hailed. "And sit down. I won't be a minute."

Douglas looked about the headmaster's spartan office: the books in the glass fronted bookshelves, a funny little Persian rug that unsuccessfully tried to give the place a better tone, an amateurish painting of aloes on an arid hillside, and the inevitable framed Latin quotation – *Per Laborem ad Astra*. He should present Archer with another one – *sumus semper in excretum sed alto variat*.

Archer returned briskly, carrying papers. "The next newsletter, Douglas. I would like you to proofread it for me in the next few days if you don't mind?"

"With pleasure, Dr Archer."

Archer sat down. He put his elbows on the edge of his desk and clasped his hands. "Now, what can I do for you?"

"Dr Archer, I have a very difficult matter to discuss with you."

Archer frowned, leant back in his chair and put his hands behind his head. "You seem very serious. It is holiday time young man."

"It's difficult. I don't know how to start, or where to start."

"The best is always to start at the beginning."

"As you know I had to go to England last year for treatment of my hearing problem."

"And now you have to go again?"

"If only it were that simple."

"What do you mean?"

Douglas ran his hands over his head. "I am going deaf."

"And you want leave of absence to have further treatment?"

"Further treatment will not be of any use. All the options have been exhausted. The treatment last year, as it turns out, was a long shot. It provided only temporary relief."

"Surely there must be something that can be done in this modern day and age?"

"I am afraid there is not. There is nothing that can be done for me."

Archer leant forward with his elbows on his desk and put his mouth against his hands, his eyes cast down. He sighed several times. He put his hands together in prayer-like fashion and held them against his forehead. He groaned. He fidgeted with his face. He sighed again. He scratched his nose. He leant back in his chair. "Do you realise how proud I am to have you teaching at my school, Douglas? How much of an inspiration you are to the rest of the staff? You give stature to my school, man, and now this. I can see what is on your mind. It is hard to imagine how devastating it must be for you. I don't want to use trite little phrases. Before you say anything more let me ask you not to be impulsive. I will help you as much as I possibly can. I have grown to admire and respect you. Please think again. Stay on for as long as you wish."

"My hearing deteriorated quite a lot last term. I have been to see Garnett Nel. It is impossible to predict at what rate my hearing will be lost. I want to be fair to you, and to the boys. If things continue as they did last term I will not be able to go beyond next term, and that will be touch and go. I am so sorry about this."

"God, don't apologise to me, it is not of your making. What can I say! I am shocked beyond belief."

Douglas had tears in his eyes and his lips quivered.

Archer got up, walked round his desk and put his hand on Douglas' shoulder and began patting his back gently. "Oh my goodness." He went and stood at the window with his hands behind his back while Douglas composed himself. When he eventually turned around he saw Douglas putting his handkerchief into his trouser pocket. He shook his head. "Why you of all people?"

Douglas walked along Queen Street and turned into Church Street to his father's office. He could see his father sitting at his desk through the half open door. He knocked.

"Ah, it's you Douglas, come inside. How was the meeting with Archer?"

"About as one would have expected, I suppose."

"What did you say to him?"

"I was perfectly direct. I told him that I was going deaf and that I shall have to stop teaching at the end of next term."

His father held his head in his hands. "Is that not a bit extreme? Surely we do not know how long it will take?"

"I went to see Garnett last night, and he also said that there was no way of telling what will happen to my hearing. I sense that it will probably happen sooner than we think. I might as well face that fact."

"And when you stop teaching, what then?"

"I'll have to find an alternative."

Saturday 24 March 1928

Douglas woke early after a restless night. The holidays had begun to bore him, and his boredom sapped his energy. The house was still asleep and filled with stale air. He went into the kitchen to make coffee. He opened the back door and the window to let fresh air in. He smelled the odour of fermenting figs that had fallen to the ground. The train was due at nine. He went to the woodshed to find kindling for the geyser. There was dew on the grass between the paving stones of the path. The lid of the coffee pot heaved and clattered from the boiling water. This is what it would be like on the farm: a simple honest life, in the autumn. The irritating hissing, whining noise in his ears would not matter on the farm. There nothing would depend on his hearing. The crops would grow by themselves, and the animals can't talk anyway. Humans are the problem. He did not hear his mother enter the kitchen.

"You should put your dressing gown on, Douglas."

"It's not that cold, Ma."

"If you go outside you should have your dressing gown on, my boy. The neighbours might see you in you pyjamas. That would lower the tone. Miss Rubenstein is easily offended."

"I have made coffee."

"You must be pleased that you will be seeing Frances."

"Ja, I am."

Douglas had nearly finished his breakfast when his father joined him at the table. "The weather has improved a lot."

"I beg your pardon?"

Van Yssen raised his voice while Douglas stopped chewing and looked at him. "I said the weather has improved."

"Yes, I'm pleased about that. I think I should get going; I don't want to be late. Thanks for letting me have the car. Please excuse me."

"That's an old jacket, Douglas, put your new one on," His mother suggested.

"This is fine Ma."

"No it's not Douglas, and you know it. Why are you so otherwise?"

He went back to his room and put on his new jacket. It was a clear day. There was no need to rush. He parked the car under an ash tree outside the station building, and went to the stationmaster's office to see when the train would be arriving.

"There has been a problem Mr van Yssen, with one of the lines near Worcester. The train has been delayed by about three hours."

"What is going on now?" van Yssen exclaimed when the car drove in through their gate. He put down his newspaper and went round the side of the house to the garage where Douglas was just getting out of the car. "And now?"

"The train has been delayed, for three hours. I'll have to go back later on."

"Why has it been delayed?"

"Something to do with the rails near Worcester."

"Poor Frances."

"She must be approaching Mossel Bay. I am sure she'll ring."

When the telephone eventually did ring it was nearly ten o'clock. Douglas went to answer it.

"Douglas, thank goodness you are at home, I was so worried that you might be sitting at the station. Then you must realise that we have been delayed. We should from all accounts be at Oudstshoorn a trifle after twelve. But how are you my dearest man?"

"I'm just fine, thank you, and you?"

"I'm disappointed not to be with you, but I've had a good rest on the farm. Mummy and Daddy send their very best wishes to you, and so do the Sterlings. I must not speak too long, there are others waiting to use the telephone, see you in about two hours. Lots and lots of love."

"All my love to you too, I'll be seeing you."

Douglas took up his position on the platform. The day had become warmer, and he perspired slightly. He saw Frances. She wore a cream summer dress with a dainty green and pink floral pattern. Her fair hair was shoulder length. Her hand with the ring was on the windowsill of the coach. She was nearly upon him before she saw him, "Douglas!"

He smiled shyly. "I am so glad that you have arrived at last." They kissed through the open window. She went to the end of the carriage and stepped onto the platform. They hugged and she kissed him again.

"How are you my dearest man? How have you been this week?"

"I'm bearing up. I have missed you. I went to see Garnett and I went to see Dr Archer on Wednesday."

"The latter sounds ominous?"

"It isn't meant to. I just had to go and discuss my future with him."

"Let's walk along the platform, I need to stretch my legs. I don't think the train will stop for as long as usual on account of the delay. What did you say to Archer?"

"I said that I shall try to see out next term."

"And then?"

"I cannot see myself teaching beyond the end of next term."

"What will happen then?"

"I'll have to find something else."

"I told you that Mummy and Daddy send their best regards, I spoke to them about your condition and Daddy put forward some jolly interesting ideas. He spoke to Mr Wainright at the *Times*, and it would seem as though they are desperate to employ a good leader-writer. Mr Wainright was excited at the prospect of offering you a position on the paper. Isn't that marvellous?"

"It was very kind of your dad."

"So? What do you say to that, my love?"

"I'll have to get my affairs in order here."

"But you will at least consider it? It is a very good position. More lucrative than teaching. And right up your street."

"It is tempting, I must say."

"And there will be other opportunities too, once you're in circulation. Of course it will mean moving to Cape Town."

"How was your visit to your uncle's farm?"

"It was lovely." She squeezed his arm. "What have you done with yourself?"

"Not much. I started preparing lessons for next term. I did some reading and not much else."

"You said you saw Garnett."

"Ja, on Tuesday evening."

"How is he?"

"Well, and jolly as usual. I asked him for an indication of what I can expect. He said it was impossible to predict. He said not even Yearsley could make a prediction."

"I still have a secret hope that your hearing won't get any worse."

"If only it were so. Will you ring me when you get to Graaff Reinet?"

"I shall."

"How has your journey been? I mean apart from the delay? What actually happened?"

"I'm not sure. The conductor said there was a problem with one of the tracks, on this side of Worcester. Some plates came loose at a level crossing, or something like that. A farmer spotted it and alerted the railways. They had to fix the line. Beside that the journey has been uneventful. I'll arrive quite late. But it is so very good to be with you my dearest man. I love you more than you could imagine Douglas. You appear a bit distant, but I understand why, and I will give you all the space you need to come to terms with things. Please write to me often. Easter is in two weeks' time, perhaps we could do something then?"

"I had not thought of that. I love you too, Frances."

When the conductor's whistle blew she clung desperately to him. He could feel her hot tears on his face. "I love you, look after yourself, give my love to your parents." She clambered aboard. They held hands through the window. He stood with a sad smile and watched her as tears continued to stream down her face. "Silly old me," she tried to laugh, but sobbed instead.

Douglas drove home slowly. His father and mother were in the living room.

"We waited for you, lunch is ready," His mother announced.

"So, how did it go?" His father asked.

"All right. Frances sends her regards to you."

"Would you like to help me by bringing the plates to the table, Douglas, they are in the slow oven, please." His mother was on her way to the kitchen.

"For what we are about to receive, Lord, please make us truly grateful, amen."

Van Yssen carved the leg of lamb and they helped themselves to vegetables.

"This meat is really tasty, Ma."

"So you say it went all right? How was Frances?"

"She was a bit tearful when she left."

"Poor thing," his mother said.

"She said her father has spoken to Wainwright, the editor of the *Times*. He is looking for a leader-writer. She said Wainwright felt that I would be ideally suited for the position, and that he would like to offer me a job."

"That sounds marvellous, Douglas, congratulations!" His father was clearly relieved.

"Thank the Lord, my prayers have been answered." His mother put her knife and fork down and clasped her hands together.

"Except that I don't want to go and work for a newspaper, and I don't want the Judge to find a job for me. It's demeaning."

"Now, now Douglas, we have to keep our heads."

"Are you saying I'm now also losing my marbles?" Douglas was irritated.

"I don't like your tone Douglas," his father warned.

"What tone?"

"Let's just try and reason this through as calmly as possible, please," his mother pleaded.

"Douglas, I don't know how you can say that what the Judge has done demeans you. There is another way of looking at it. Judge Rose knows what you are capable of, he knows the potential you have, and he wants to make sure for your sake and for the sake of his daughter, to whom you're engaged, I might remind you, that you have the best career opportunities possible. That's hardly demeaning."

"That depends on how you look at things."

"We have never had unpleasantness in this family. We are only three."

"I have also never been deaf, mother."

"The best thing to do is to deal with facts," van Yssen said. "Let us try not to let the emotions cloud our reasoning. Don't you think that you should at least examine the possibility of an offer from the newspaper?"

"How would I go about it? Telephone the Judge and say, 'Frances tells me that you have spoken to the editor of the *Cape Times*, Judge, in an effort to find me a job. Thank you very much, Judge, now where do we go from here?' Or something like that? I could not do that. Never."

"We don't have to rush, Douglas." His mother tried to smooth things. "I understand that this is a difficult time for you, and for us all, at the moment. You still have the whole of next term to plan."

"But don't let good opportunities go begging. Don't make it difficult for those who are trying to help you," his father said.

"Now how would I be doing that?"

His father sighed heavily. "My dear man, if the Judge is trying to help you, you should at least show the greatest civility possible. At least give the appearance that you are grateful for his efforts."

"He would respect me more if I made my own way."

"Have you any specific thoughts, my boy?" his mother asked.

"As a matter of fact I have. I mentioned to Garnett the other evening that I have for a long time thought of having a farm."

"A farm?" His father put his knife and fork down loudly. "A farm? Good God, Douglas, a farm?"

"Yes, a farm, Dad."

"And where would you get a farm from?"

"I could borrow money from the Land Bank. And perhaps if you could give me a hand."

"Whose idea is this, has Frances suggested it?" van Yssen asked.

"No, I have not even discussed it with her."

"It must be Garnett's idea." Van Yssen was determined to find a scapegoat.

"No, when I told him about it he said I was off my rocker to consider it, but I think he's wrong. It would be a perfect thing for me to do."

Van Yssen shook his head in disbelief. "I cannot credit what I am hearing. You're a scholar Douglas. Farming requires special skills, of a practical nature; of a physical nature. Your talent would be squandered. Apart from that it is not easy to make money farming. I see it all the time, not only here in this district but in other districts too. Farmers find it hard to pay me for the work I do for them. You have no experience of farming. The only people who survive are the ones without debt. Go and speak to some people in the district. I can arrange it. Ask Garnett to introduce you to some of the more successful farmers and discuss it with them."

"I think that most farmers are handicapped by traditions. They're in a rut. They don't think of new, smarter ways of doing things. I looked through some *Farmer's Weekly's* at the library yesterday afternoon. There are exciting things happening in the agricultural field. There was a story about almond trees. There is a very good demand for almonds at present and the demand is increasing annually. Just imagine that, nobody here has made a serious effort with almonds. People plant lucerne in abundance but no one seems to be aware of a species of melonitis that carries more nodules than lucerne and grows faster. People are chained to their old ways. Frances' uncle farms near Paarl so they know about farming and are unlikely to be opposed to my idea. The Judge might even like it, who knows?"

"What about drought, poor weather conditions?" van Yssen had lost his appetite.

"The government has initiated an experiment with prickly-pear as a stock feed and it is reported to have been a resounding success. You know how drought resistant those things are. All one has to do is to create several options and to position them strategically, so that if one thing fails, another can take its place. In other words spread risk."

"It is good to see you so enthusiastic, Douglas," his mother said.

"I heard the other day when you told Frances about your childhood on the farm Ma, and what a wonderful life you had."

"I spoke about our kitchen."

"But an abundant kitchen from all accounts."

"At times things were very difficult. There was always food, enough food. But in other ways we really struggled at times."

"But not all the time?"

"No, not all the time."

"Let's not go off at a tangent now," van Yssen warned.

"I don't think we are, Dad."

"The best I can say Douglas, is that you should think very carefully about this idea of yours. At best it is romantic. It is not practical. Fortunately we do not have to make any firm decisions for some months. Let's agree to change the subject for now, and talk more about it some other time."

"I thought of wandering down to the recreation grounds. Rugby season is about to start and the first team is playing a friendly, more of a warm-up match, against Beaufort West."

Saturday 12 May 1928

Douglas writes to Frances

Dearest Frances

Thank you for your letter of the 30th. It means a great deal to me that you have written so regularly. In three weeks time the term will end. My hearing is quite bad at times, and the die is now finally cast for me to quit teaching at the end of the term.

Dr Archer has arranged a farewell function, which is quite embarrassing. I would have much preferred to simply slip away quietly and gone my way.

Let me reassure you that I will take up your father's kind offer to arrange an interview for me with Mr Wainwright. I have a lot of clearing-up to do at school so I will only be able to go to Cape Town towards the end of June, and I hope you will forgive me for not travelling with you on your way home. Please let me know when you'll be returning to Graaff Reinet so that I can arrange to be on the same train. I shall let you know when I will be leaving for Cape Town – it does depend when Wainwright will be able to see me. I am examining some other options, in case the newspaper position does not materialise, and although I have not mentioned it to you before, and I hope that it does not come as too much of a surprise – as it did to my parents – but I have contemplated going farming. To say the least, my parents, particularly my father, are hugely against the idea, and would like me to consider the newspaper, so is Garnett, but I feel certain that I can make a success of farming. I would very much like to talk to your uncle when I go to Cape Town.

For the rest, things have been pretty dull. Teaching, now that I see it for what it is, is a bit of a bore. I think farming will be much more exciting and I have been spending a lot of time reading *Farmer's Weekly's* at the library. I appreciate that it will be a challenge and I have few illusions. I have been looking at the advertisements for farms, and there is a lovely farm that is being sold out of a deceased estate. The farm is situated on the slopes of the Outeniqua Mountains in the direction of Mossel Bay.

It is on a river that from all accounts is a reliable source of water.

The climate is quite different from that of Oudtshoorn. Being closer to the mountain it is more temperate, yet being on the northern side of the mountain means that there is plenty of sun in winter. The asking price is quite reasonable but I still have to persuade my father to lend me some money, and I'll have to approach the Land Bank for a loan. Clearly I will have to do my sums carefully but the best is that I will have quiet periods when I will be able to pursue my interests in history, and maybe even do some writing as you have suggested. I hope you like my idea.

I will naturally come and see you at the station on your way through on Saturday the second. Please do not think that my enthusiasm for the farming venture will influence my consideration of the newspaper option. I promise you that I will give the newspaper really very serious thought. And it would be quite nice to live in Cape Town again.

We had some friends over the other evening to play rummy, Mrs Jacquard among them and she affectionately asked after you, and asked me to send you her best regards. She has taken a fond liking to you and impressed upon me how much she would like to see you again soon. Now what else is there? I need to tell you that I love you, and that I very much look forward to seeing you.

Lots of love
Douglas.

Sunday 20 May 1928

Mr and Mrs van Yssen drove home solemnly after church. Autumn was well advanced. Overhead the sky was a clear thin blue and the horizon was pale. Colourful leaves blanketed the roadsides and crackled as they swirled frivolously after the passing car.

"I'll make us some tea. There is still some sponge cake left over from Friday."

"It was a good sermon," he remarked.

"Yes, it was a good sermon."

"I have been thinking a great deal about Douglas' idea to go farming."

"And?"

"All my life I have steered him in directions of my choice. All his life I have regarded his achievements as my own achievements. What he achieved academically I proudly considered my own. I have had such great expectations of him. But they were really hopes for me. I have been selfish. I have been vain."

"Oh Albert, don't keep on punishing yourself."

"I have to be honest Anneke, I want to bare my soul. Yes, I have been selfish. I have been so scared of letting him be his own man. I have always thought that I wanted to protect him, but in actual fact I wanted to control him, and now when I come to stand naked before the truth, I feel that I should change my ways. I have come to realise that the shock of what is happening to him must really have been far worse than my shock, and I have been feeling sorry for myself instead of comforting him. I woke up during the night from a dream in which he approached me with a smiling face, and suddenly realised that he is showing enthusiasm, which means that he is emerging from his despair. Perhaps it is right for him to go farming. What is the worst that can happen? If it turns out to be a disaster he will have learnt his lesson, and we could sell the farm, possibly even at a profit. I have a bit of money tucked away."

"He told me that he has agreed, and he has let Frances know, to have an interview with the editor of the *Cape Times* towards the end of next month."

"That is good. It will mean that we have options. If he goes to the interview knowing that I am no longer opposed to the idea of a farm. It will make for a better interview."

Garnett dropped Douglas at his gate a little after five, said goodbye and went on hurriedly to the hospital to do his evening rounds. He and Douglas and a new young woman teacher at the Girls High School, Miss Zietsmann, had been for a picnic at the Kammanassie dam. The van Yssens were on their veranda and waved to Garnett.

"Hello," Douglas said. "I am parched. We did not take enough water along."

"I need to talk to you, Douglas," his father said.

"I beg your pardon?"

"I said I need to talk to you."

"I'll be one minute, have to see a man about a horse."

When Douglas returned his father patted the seat of the chair next to him. "Come and sit down here."

"Douglas, I made a discussion with your mother this morning, are you listening?"

"Yes, I can hear you."

"I explained to her that I have had second thoughts about the farm. Now please don't rush to conclusions. Listen to me carefully." Van Yssen raised his voice to make sure that Douglas heard him. "I still want you to go to the interview in Cape Town. I understand that you have conveyed to Frances that you will go. I think you should telephone the Judge and thank him, and ask him if it would be appropriate for you to telephone or write to Mr Wainwright directly. Do that tomorrow, or even telephone the Judge this evening. Yes, rather this evening. Now coming back to the issue of the farm. If you should decide, after the interview with Mr Wainwright, and only after that mind you, if you should decide that you still desperately want to go farming, and if you are certain that you could devote yourself, and commit yourself completely, to such an enterprise, I shall do all I can to assist you. We would have to find a suitable farm, one that will offer the best prospect of success. We will have to do quite a lot of investigation and research to see what is available in the district and we'll have to get really good unbiased advice."

"There is a farm advertised in the *Farmer's Weekly*, up in the mountains towards Mossel Bay, that is being sold out of a deceased estate. It is about a hundred and fifty morgen, with plenty of water from the river."

"That is a good area," van Yssen said. "But let us first get the interview out of the way. On the other hand we might lose it if it is really good. I'll find out from Hugo Pocock who the executor is. Perhaps we could get a first right of refusal."

"I cannot tell you how much I appreciate what you have said, Dad. Thank you so much. I'll telephone the Judge this evening."

Monday 21 May 1928

Van Yssen returned home from his office earlier than usual. He hurried inside and knocked on Douglas' door.

"You're home early, Dad?"

"I saw Hugo Pocock this afternoon about the farm. It turns out he is the executor. He has agreed to grant us first right of refusal, but he says there is someone else interested in the farm and he wants us to go and view it as soon as possible."

"Gosh."

"When do you finish school tomorrow?"

"At quarter past two."

"Good, we'll go there then. I'll drop you off in the morning and pick you up at two fifteen. Hugo is not prepared to wait too long; he would not want to go beyond the bounds of his professional ethics. And I don't blame him. He said it is a good property."

Tuesday 22 May 1928

Van Yssen waited for Douglas to emerge from the school building.

"Good afternoon, Dad."

"Where are your books and your papers?"

"I've locked them in my cupboard."

"I hope you're not losing interest in your work. It won't do to leave a bad impression."

"No, no, not at all. You can be sure that I shall give my best until the last."

"I hope so. I have brought some sandwiches. I spoke to Mr Hudson at the bank. He's going to try and find out whom to speak to about the farm. Hugo Pocock said it was a good thing that it is being sold out of a deceased estate, which means that at least it was not a bankrupt farm. I have written down the directions. It is about twenty five miles from here from what I can gather."

Clouds were drifting in on a fresh north-wester that brought hope of rain. They headed towards the towering blue Outeniqua Mountains. Beyond the turnoff to Bakenskraal they entered the last level stretch before the start of their ascent. Both of them had travelled the road many times before but observed the landscape with new interest. Vegetation began to change. They left the uncomfortable dryness of the plains and welcomed the appearance of more restful ericaceous vegetation and grasses. They crossed the causeway over the Kandelaars River. Distant wisps of pale wood smoke turned into copses of young poplar trees that had shed their leaves. Brilliant green lucerne fields stretched along the banks of the river. They drove ever upwards towards the mountain that lay in the shape of a huge slumbering dragon. The colours of the mountain changed as they went: pale Prussian blue shadows became metallic greys and pinks in the afternoon sun. Before them the highest peak grew taller, a sentinel of striking clear manganese blue, prominent glistening wet facets of rock and a bright sky. Douglas looked into the valley below and noticed a row of four old pepper trees.

"I wonder who planted those?" he asked.

"We'll have to ask the way at the shop."

The man at the shop looked them up and down. "You are nearly there, Sir. It is about a mile or so up towards the mountain. The house is close to the road, only one with a red roof. Anything else?"

"No thank you. We have come to view the farm."

"Are you thinking of buying?"

"We've just come to look."

"It is good soil."

"And water?" Van Yssen asked.

"More than enough. I see you have an Oudtshoorn car."

"We are from Oudtshoorn."

The storeowner extended his hand. "Van der Byl."

"I am van Yssen and this is my son, Douglas."

"Only the old shepherd is up there now. He's hard of hearing. Have a good look and feel free to come and see me on the way back. I'll make some coffee in the meantime."

They found the house without difficulty. The area around it had become overgrown. Unruly vines were tangled over a trellis. A small flower garden in front of the house contained neglected rosebushes that had gone to seed and a large variety of enthusiastic weeds. The house was shut. It was rectangular and of modest proportions. The tin roof was in good condition. The paint on the window frames was powdery and cracked. Two chimneys with blackened nostrils indicated where the fireplaces were. The rough-plastered walls were dusty. Some distance below the house, in the direction of the river, loose wood smoke crept from the chimney of a small cottage. A mongrel dog was tied up next to the cottage and began to bark so loudly that its voice echoed in the valley. A small grey-bearded man with a crooked back appeared from the side of the cottage and stared at them. He shook his head and swayed from side to side as he started towards them on bandy legs. When he was about twenty yards away he stopped and stared some more from under bushy eyebrows, and then he continued cautiously towards them. His khaki trousers were patched and so were the uppers of his brown boots. He hesitated.

"*Ek is van Yssen van Oudtshoorn.*"

The man cupped his hand behind his right ear, and turned that side of his head towards them. "Mister will have to speak louder."

Van Yssen moved closer to him. The man moved away.

"I am van Yssen. From Oudtshoorn."

"Mister need not shout quite so loudly."

"What is your name?"

"Jan Willemse."

"Have you been here long?" van Yssen asked.

"I was born here and grew up here and I'll probably die here. Is Mister going to buy the farm?"

"I don't know. We'll first have to have a look."

"The old lady has been dead for about six months. The old fellow has been gone for quite a few years." He wrung his hands and sucked his grey unshaven hollow cheeks in further. "I don't know what will happen to me. I am living off the veld and the few pence the attorney gives me, and I have to care for everything here. There's more than a hundred and fifty sheep."

"I'll see what I can do."

"Mister doesn't by chance have any tobacco?"

"I don't smoke."

"Perhaps Mister could leave me a small bag at the shop. When Mister has finished looking."

Van Yssen nodded.

"Take your time and ask whatever you wish."

There was an orchard with peach and apricot trees that had not been pruned for some time. Stone furrows were proof of irrigation. An unevenly cut lucerne field bordered the river.

The shepherd followed them for a while. "I'll have to go now. I have put the dog's food on the fire."

Douglas and his father went to the bank of the river. Steady water flowed silently through pools and between large round boulders. "I'm glad that Hugo Pocock has agreed to give us first right of refusal," van Yssen nodded in a satisfied way. "I will check the beacons one of these days. You'll have to give me a hand." They drove back to the store. There was a carpentry workbench at the one end of the veranda at which van der Byl was repairing a stinkwood chair. He had put some chairs ready next to an empty packing case that served as a table. He fetched a blue enamel coffee pot and three enamel mugs. He fetched sugar and a porcelain jug of milk.

"And? What do you think of the farm?"

"Interesting," van Yssen replied.

"There are also others after the farm. It is not the biggest farm in the whole world but good soil and enough water are hard to beat."

"I would like to buy some tobacco for the shepherd."

"How did you hear about the farm?"

"An attorney friend is administering he esate."

"Always the best way. But you will have to strike while the iron is hot. The old woman struggled after her husband's death."

"We could see the place has been neglected."

"Have you farmed before?"

"I grew up on a farm in the Free State."

"This is a different kettle of fish, this is mixed farming."

"If we buy the farm my son will come and farm it."

The storekeeper turned to Douglas, "And what are you doing now?"

"I teach."

"And now you want to start farming?"

"It will be a new challenge."

"At least it is a good farm."

Van Yssen paid for the tobacco, and they said goodbye to van der Byl.

"May you prosper!" van der Byl called as he waved to them. He watched as the car disappeared in a cloud of dust, and shook his head.

"So what do you think, Douglas?" van Yssen asked.

"It is a nice place, don't you think?"

"Yes I agree, I think it has possibilities. Of course price is important."

◆

Chapter Twenty-nine

Wednesday 20 June 1928

THE RAIN that had been falling for two weeks over the Peninsula continued to descend in large diaphanous sheets as Douglas' train made its way slowly and respectfully past the graveyards at Woltemade. He looked in the direction of Woodstock. Wolraad Woltemade. The movements of the train transported him back onto the *Trafford Hall*, riding out the hostile dark storm in Table Bay before its anchor. The large German on his horse, plunging into the furious surf off Woodstock, to rescue strangers trapped on a stricken sailing vessel, going into the sea again and again when the owners of the ship had already abandoned its crew, until Woltemade and the horse were exhausted and drowned in the icy Atlantic water, never to see his wife and their children again. Douglas pulled his overcoat tighter around himself as he stood in the passage of his coach. Drizzle drenched the windows and an invisible cold grey wind rattled the glass.

Frances and Doyle were on the platform. She had done her utmost to make herself attractive. She wore her favourite cloche hat and a new jade-green woollen military style coat. She ran up to him and embraced him. Doyle took his bag. "Darling, darling man," she said as she kissed him all over his face, "You look so well!"

He smiled and hugged her again. "I am well, and you?"

"I am all right. But I have missed you terribly. And the weather has been wretched. We have sat by the fireside and read and played cards; only once or twice did we go out to tea."

Arm in arm they followed Doyle to the car. "I'm struggling with my hearing. I hope it won't hinder the interview."

"You'll be just fine. We'll leave your bag at the hotel, and then go to our house. Mummy is dying to see you. Then Doyle will deliver you to the *Cape Times* offices. Mr Wainwright said to Daddy only yesterday that he is much looking forward to seeing you. Isn't that grand? Afterwards we'll have lunch somewhere as you suggested, and then dinner at our house this evening. Daddy has invited the Searles for this evening and Mummy has invited Uncle James and Aunt Ethel over for Friday evening so that you can talk about your 'farming endeavour' as Daddy calls it. I can't wait to hear about the farm."

"I beg your pardon?"

"I said I want to hear about the farm."

"It is quite charming, in a valley on the slopes of the mountain. I'll tell you as we drive."

Mrs Rose waited for them in the living room. "Douglas, my dear boy, how are you, how lovely to see you."

"Good morning Mrs Rose." She stood on her toes to kiss him on his cheek.

"Come and sit down next to me, Douglas, and tell me all your news." Mrs Rose sat on the side of his better ear. "Did you have a good journey?"

"Yes, quite pleasant, quite uneventful, thank you."

Douglas looked at his watch. It was nearly ten o'clock.

"There's still plenty of time," Frances said.

"I am so sorry, I'm quite preoccupied with the thought of my interview."

Mrs Rose took his hand. "You will find Mr Wainwright a very pleasant man. Silly me, I've just remembered, you met him at your engagement. He knows all about you. You have nothing to be concerned about. If you don't like his offer, there is always the farm. Tell us all about the farm you went to see."

"Gee, let me see where to begin. Hugo Pocock, the attorney who is administering the estate out of which it is being sold, gave us an option on the farm until the end of this month. So we have barely more than a week to go. My dad insisted that I consider the newspaper option, and said he would not make a decision about purchasing the farm until I had been to see Mr Wainwright. You know what it is like. I have always thought that farming would be nice. I admit I never spoke about it, because it seemed so farfetched, but now that the possibility looms I am a bit nervous, and at times wonder whether a good solid salaried position would not be more prudent. So you see, as usual, I am betwixt and between."

"You wrote that it is a nice farm," Frances said enthusiastically.

"Exactly where is it?" Mrs Rose asked.

"Yes it is rather nice. It is situated on the slopes, that is the lower slopes, of the Outeniqua Mountains, in the direction of Mossel Bay from Oudtshoorn. It is about twenty-five miles from town; more or less half way between Mossel Bay and Oudtshoorn, but on the Oudtshoorn side of the mountain."

"What kind of farming do you have in mind?" Mrs Rose asked.

"They do mixed farming in that area: lucerne, some tobacco, potatoes, sweet potatoes, fruit, sheep, some wheat. And there are lots of other possibilities."

"And the climate?" Frances enquired.

"Much kinder than in Oudtshoorn, because of the altitude."

"And the house?" Frances asked.

"It is rather modest, to say the least, but is has possibilities and my dad thinks one could make more of it with a bit of imagination. The structure is sound."

"It sounds like a grand adventure Douglas!" Mrs Rose tried to encourage him.

"I am looking forward to talking to Mr Sterling," Douglas said.

"My brother can be a bit of a Job's comforter, Douglas. It has been a constant struggle for him. So don't be discouraged by what he has to say."

"Frances tells me that you have had rather poor weather, Mrs Rose."

"It has been absolutely horrid, rain, rain and more rain. It is about as bad as it can be at this time of the year. Nothing wants to dry. The bedclothes are damp at night. What would I not give for the lovely sunny weather that we had at Plettenberg Bay. But it is what the farmers need, or so James tells me. How are your parents?"

"They are fine. They have not had an easy time, what with all my difficulties. It was a great shock to all of us"

"And to us. You have become as a son to us Douglas. It has been most distressing."

"Do have a biscuit, Douglas, you must be starving." Frances said.

"I had an enormous breakfast. I do feel much more positive about the future. Quite apart from farming I have decided to do some history research, and I might very well do some writing. It would possibly be a good combination of activities, farming and history."

"It would suit you absolutely!" Frances exclaimed. "I could see, when you arrived this morning that you had undergone a change for the better. I am so pleased."

"How does your father feel about the farm?" Mrs Rose asked.

"Oh, gosh, he was strongly opposed to the idea. And he made no bones about it. But then his position began to change. It means a great deal to me to have his support. He has been quite ambitious for me. I think he saw the sense of it all, considering my condition."

A sudden burst of wind drove the rain against the windowpane and forced smoke down the chimney.

"Oh my word!" Mrs Rose exclaimed.

"How is Judge Rose?" Douglas enquired.

"He's fine, thank you Douglas. Hard at work as ever. It never stops. Books, law journals, reference works, papers, it never ends. It must be very exhausting to use one's brain all the time. And recently he has not even been able to play his beloved golf, on account of the weather. But I do suppose that spring will be here sooner than we expect and everything will look different again. It's hard to imagine now that the sun will ever be visible again, or that we will have cloudless skies."

Hope appeared. "Doyle is here Madam."

"The car is here for you, Douglas," Mrs Rose said. "Frances tells me that the two of you are going to lunch in town when you've been to Mr Wainwright? I am going to bridge this afternoon. Doyle will come and fetch Frances when he has dropped you. Lots and lots of good luck, dear boy."

Wainwright's secretary, efficiently clad in a tight-fitting green and oatmeal hounds-tooth tweed suit, complete with brogues and small darting eyes, made Douglas comfortable in her oak panelled office which adjoined the office of the great man. "Mr Wainwright will see you presently, Mr van Yssen." She knew why he was there. What was more, he was Miss Rose's fiancé. She studied him as he sat and read the *Cape Times* of the previous day. He scanned the front page and went straight to the leader page. Clever man. Quite handsome too. Would not mind his slippers under my bed. Strong fellow. She had heard the Judge say to Wainwright how awfully clever he was.

Wainwright's door swung open. A young cherub-faced reporter, notebook and pencil in hand, made a polite gesture as he greeted Douglas, winked at the secretary and left the editor's offices. Douglas got up. Wainwright extended his hand warmly, "Damn rotten weather we have arranged for you Mr van Yssen. Come inside."

"How do you do Mr Wainwright."

"Come and make yourself comfortable my good fellow." Wainwright arranged himself behind his desk. "You do realise of course that you come to me very highly recommended. I was aware of your distinguished academic career, and indeed told Judge Rose at the time that you decided to go teaching that you would be better served coming to work for me. And now you are here, albeit for different reasons and in different circumstances. I am aware of your condition, so we don't have to deal with that." Wainwright was talking deliberately loudly and making slightly exaggerated movements with his mouth that irritated Douglas.

"Now to come directly to the point, Mr van Yssen, I am prepared to offer you a position as leader-writer, and you may start whenever it suits you, but I would prefer you to start sooner rather than later. Judge Rose tells me that you have ideas of going farming – I gather that the Judge has discussed matters with your father in that regard."

"I was not aware of that."

"Oh my goodness, I have let a cat out of the bag. Oops, as we would say in our modern world of psychoanalysis, what a little Freudian slip, I mean bag." He smacked himself on the wrist. "Tut, tut, naughty boy." He grinned sheepishly. "Anyway, let me tell you nevertheless, farming is a very hazardous occupation. You would be much better off here among us on the newspaper. I have not a shred of doubt about your abilities. We need a man of your intellect, a man who has a sense of history, someone with perspective of the issues of our time, someone with balanced views, who can give additional dimensions to the opinion of this newspaper. I have no doubt whatsoever that you will be able to fill the position with distinction. Well?"

"You seem to have more faith in me Mr Wainwright than I have in myself."

"Don't sell yourself short, my good fellow. And what is the worst that can happen? If it does not work out, there's always farming to fall back on. Believe me this is the least risky way."

Douglas moved about on his chair. "What you have said is most flattering Mr Wainwright and I am potentially interested in your kind offer."

"Jolly good. Your salary will be better than a teacher's pay. I gather that you are leaving again on Saturday. Discuss it with your father when you get home. And let us see how we go from there. You will have your own office as behoves your position. Let's go for a walk around the paper so you can get a better feel of the environment in which you will be working. Most of the staff will only come in this afternoon."

"This is the newsroom, where the reporters work. That is the news editor's desk. All local news passes through his hands and he arranges assignments for reporters. They wandered through to the next room. The sub-editors sit next door to him, in here. Before the news reports get to the chief sub-editor they go to the copy taster, local as well as news from the wire services. The sub-editors edit the various pieces of news and send copy to the works department for typesetting and proof reading." They went down one floor. "This is where the pages of the paper are made up, in this frame called a chase, by the way. A papier mache-like impression is made of the completed page and a curved plate is cast from the cardboard impression. That plate fits onto a cylinder of the printing press. As simple as that."

"Thank you, Mr Wainwright it is most interesting."

"It gets into your blood my boy, you will have ink in your veins before long." He steered Douglas towards the front entrance of the newspaper and stood for a while searching Douglas' eyes for a response. "Do come back to me when you have spoken to your father. It was good to see you again, Douglas. I hope you'll join us."

"Thank you."

Wainwright left Douglas outside on the pavement. The rain had stopped and the sky was lighter. He looked at his watch. It was after one. Frances would be waiting at Cartwrights. He hurried down St Georges Street.

Frances was seated in the far corner of the tearoom. The foppish maitre d', Malone was near the door, a menu folder pressed against the lapels of his suit with a pale hand. He swept towards Douglas in an extravagant way. "How nice to see you again Sir. Let me take you to Miss Rose." Douglas smelled the sickly sweet hair gel that Malone had used to make his head look like a shiny black patent leather cap.

Douglas kissed Frances on her cheek and took off his coat.

"I'll put it on a hanger Sir, it is a little damp," Malone suggested. "A waiter will be with you presently. The fish is very good today."

"So, my love, how did the interview go?"

"You could hardly call it an interview."

"But you must have been there for an hour."

"First I had to wait a while. Mr Wainwright did all the talking. He never asked me anything about myself. Evidently he and your father have had discussions and your father has even been speaking to my dad, which is something I was not aware of. It would appear as though everything was pre-arranged. The 'interview' was just a formality. The good news is that he has offered me a job, and would like me to start as soon as possible. We then walked about the premises and he showed me where things happen. So at least I have more than one option. That will in some ways make the choice easier, but in other ways more difficult."

A waiter appeared next to their table.

"Shall we order?" Frances asked.

"Have you decided what to have?"

"I like the idea of having fish. What kind of fish is it?" she asked the waiter.

"Sole Madam, Sole Bon Femme."

"That sounds excellent," Frances said.

"I'll also have that, thank you," Douglas said.

"It is a pity that Wainwright did not ask me anything. He never gave me a chance to ask anything. He has made up his mind and intends pushing a square peg into a round hole."

"I am sorry if things did not go as you expected."

He took her hand. "It is hardly your fault, Frances."

"In a way it is, I must confess that I encouraged Daddy to speak to Mr Wainwright. But then Daddy also thought that it was an excellent idea."

"I am not sure that Wainwright has thought this thing through properly. I don't mind telling you that the idea of being a leader-writer for a major newspaper has more appeal than I have admitted. There was something exciting about the newspaper atmosphere. You could feel it in the air, even though there were hardly any staff yet. But I have two problems. The one is that in order to be a successful leader-writer it is absolutely essential to have a serious interest in politics. And I have virtually none. As an historian I may have an interest in international affairs, but in the local stuff virtually none. The other problem is that to be a leader-writer I would have to have my finger on the pulse of both local and international affairs – I would have to visit parliament when it is in session, listen to the gossip and whispers in the corridors. Similarly I would have to follow provincial and municipal affairs. My handicap, as you well realise, precludes all that."

"Surely Mr Wainwright has thought of all of that, he is a very smart man."

"I am not convinced he has. He is helping the future son-in-law of a prominent friend. Such a contract, Frances, does not have sufficient substance, and therefore cannot endure.

"Frances, make no mistake, I know that farming will be hazardous, and the thought of being assured of earning a good salary every month, which, by the way, he said would be better than a teacher's salary, greatly appeals to me. I like the idea of writing, and of expressing the kinds of views you find in leader pages. And the research aspect would appeal to me. All my life I have had an academic leaning. It is very difficult. I don't want to disappoint your father. He has gone to a lot of trouble on my behalf, and I am most grateful for that, I shall have to make up my own mind."

"How did you leave it with Mr Wainwright?"

"Inconclusively, I suppose. I got the impression that he thinks it's a done deal. I did say that I am potentially interested in his offer but that was to relieve the pressure. He said to discuss it with my father."

"You poor thing, I can see that it is difficult for you."

He sighed heavily. "My instinct tells me that a man with a defect like mine should make himself as independent as possible."

"I don't understand?"

"What I mean to say is that someone with a defect should avoid being dependent on others. He should be as independent as possible."

"Why do you say that?"

"Very often help stems from pity. People with defects don't like pity or charity. It harms their self-esteem. They want to help themselves."

The fish arrived.

"This looks yummy," Frances said.

Douglas tasted the fish. "It is very good. Good choice. Let's change the subject. It is my problem and our future and I have to solve it as best I can. I just want to forget about it all, and sleep on it, and see what the morning brings, step away to get a better perspective."

"It seems as thought the weather is starting to clear," Frances looked out of the window.

"Pardon?"

"I said the weather is starting to clear."

"There was a shepherd with very poor hearing on the farm we went to look at, what a pair we would make!" He laughed so heartily that the heads of people around them turned. For the first time she was embarrassed by him.

"Doyle should be waiting," Frances said. "He has to take Mummy to bridge. What I think would be a really nice idea is to walk up through the Gardens. It would be lovely to take the fresh air and to be in the sunlight. So I'll let him first take Mummy and then meet us at the top, in Orange Street."

"Yes, it would be good to go for a walk."

The wet surfaces of roofs, pavements, windows, the branches of barren oak trees and the evergreen leaves of Java fig trees glistened in pale sunlight. They were more conscious of the dripping trees and water flowing in the gutters now that rain had stopped. Lions Head was clear. Pointing in that direction Frances said, "That is a good sign." She put her arm through his. "You have brought us good weather. It must be a good omen." She squeezed his arm. "I love you." Swishing car tyres prevented him from hearing.

They strolled through the Gardens. The air was bracing. "It is good to be back here," Douglas said. He breathed in deeply and savoured the scent of damp bark and leaves decaying in soggy flowerbeds. Vapour lifted from the hard surface ahead of them. "It is good to be back here. I realise now how I have missed it. It would be pleasant to live here. Earlier I smelled sparks from the overhead cables of a tram, and it brought back memories of my student days. One forgets how much more activity there is here, the bustle of people going to work, the number of motor cars, the ships in the docks."

"I hope tonight will not be too awkward," Frances said.

"Too forward?"

"I said I hope it will not be too awkward."

"It should not be, I'll listen as carefully as I can."

"I don't mean it like that, I mean about the interview with Mr Wainwright."

"Oh I'll be discreet. You can count on that. I'll just say that the offer is a most attractive one and that I have agreed, that's a nice positive word, I have agreed to speak to my father, since he will be my partner in our prospective farming venture, and that it is the only correct thing to do, and that I have given Mr Wainwright an undertaking that I shall then come back to him."

"We are likely to have a late night, and I suggest that we both have a sleep this afternoon."

"That's a good idea. We must decide what we are going to do tomorrow."

"I have nothing planned. If the weather is good we could go around Cape Point and we could have lunch somewhere."

Frances had just woken when Mrs Rose returned at five in the afternoon. She heard her mother arrive. The front door opened and closed. "Where is Miss Frances?" her mother asked Gladys. Then there was a gentle knock on her door.

"I'm awake," she called, "Come inside."

"Are you all right?" Mrs Rose asked.

"Yes, very much so. I have had a delicious sleep." She yawned.

Mrs Rose sat down in Frances' easy chair. "How did Douglas' interview go?"

"He said the whole thing seemed pre-arranged. Mr Wainwright offered him the job, without asking him a single question."

"That's jolly dee. I hope he has accepted?"

"He has doubts."

"About what?"

"About what he should do. He wants to be his own man."

"But Daddy has gone to so much trouble."

"That's part of the problem, I think."

"You speak of a problem? What is the problem to which you are referring?"

"There has been a change in Douglas."

"That is to be expected."

"Possibly, but I find it disconcerting. It is difficult to define. He seems oddly assertive and yet does not have as much purpose as before. He wants to do everything only his way. He is uncompromising. He was never like that. I suspect that he formed an idea of how Mr Wainwright would conduct the interview, and when what he hoped for did not materialise as he expected, he reacted unfavourably. Coupled to that is a resentment that others are intruding. I could see that he really did not like it that Daddy and his father had discussed the prospect of joining the paper without his knowledge. He reacted with restraint but his resentment, it was almost disdain, was quite apparent. He was otherwise and irritable – quite out of character."

"Don't you think it is just because he has a very difficult decision to make?"

"Possibly."

"Poor darling."

"I shall have to be very patient, Mother. I'll need a lot of wisdom."

"We must understand that Douglas is suffering a great deal. Can you imagine being in his position?"

"It is impossible to imagine. Coming back to Mr Wainwright, it is clear to me that Douglas feels that he has not been offered the position on merit. He believes that it puts him at a disadvantage. He says that a leader-writer needs to be in touch with events as they unfold around him, he needs to be aware; to listen to what is going on. And he will not be able to do that. He has a point. There is no sense in embarking on a career if you know, before you start, that your journey will be a brief one, and that it may end in the disgrace of failure."

"His farming venture could also fail."

"Yes, that is so, but if it does he will fail on his own, and not at something of Daddy's making. Don't you see, failing at something of which our family is part, will be so much more acute? On top of that everything is made more complicated by his reluctance to disappoint Daddy. He also feels that a leader-writer should have a passion for politics and he has little if any interest in that. What a mess."

"I hope this evening turns out all right. I hoped that by inviting the Searles we would create an air of normality, a sense that things are just as before."

"I know. All we can do now is to make the best of it."

"I hope your father gets home before Douglas arrives so that I can brief him. I will leave a message at the club for him to telephone me as soon as he gets there."

"I asked Douglas to come over early, I said about six."

"Gosh, that is early. Daddy likes his evenings at the club."

When Douglas arrived, the telephone had not yet rung and it was nearly half past six before Mrs Rose heard it ring.

"Hello dear," the Judge said, "I have only just arrived here. I was delayed by a last minute application. I was asked to ring you. Rest assured that I have remembered about the Searles, and I'm just going to have a drink with Basil. He's been waiting quite a while."

"I needed to talk to you about something. Douglas is here. I need to speak to you as soon as you get home please."

"You sound anxious."

"I need a private word with you before you speak to anyone else. Just say a quick hello and pretend that you have to rush off to your study to make an urgent telephone call."

"Your cunning impresses me, my dear." He was clearly in a jovial mood.

The Judge arrived home after seven, and nearly collided with Douglas who was coming out of the cloakroom. "Douglas my good fellow! How very good to see you. I've just had a drink with Basil Wainwright, and I think there is every reason for celebration. He tells me that you and he had a most fruitful meeting. Congratulations. Just the formalities to be sorted out with your father. I have to rush, I have an urgent telephone call to make. Dashed sorry about this, see you in a moment."

"Thank you, Judge."

Mrs Rose was waiting in the study and closed the door. "We need to talk Jeremy. It's about Douglas."

"I have just spoken to him; now when I came in. I told him I had a drink with Basil Wainwright and congratulated him, and he thanked me."

"I heard what you said to him. I had a lengthy discussion with Frances this afternoon, and things may not be as they appear."

The Judge frowned.

"Frances and Douglas met for lunch today, after he saw Basil, and Frances fears that Douglas may not be as enamoured of the idea of joining the newspaper, as we may have hoped."

"She must be mistaken. I'll speak to him about it. I'll make it plain to him what an excellent opportunity this is. I've gone to a great deal of trouble on his behalf." The Judge's voice rose.

"Steady on now dear. We need to have the wisdom of Solomon. Assume a passive position. Too much enthusiasm on our part might make him feel that we are cornering him."

"But I discussed it at great length with his father."

"Basil said as much to Douglas, which was not awfully correct since Douglas did not know about that."

"I can't help it if van Yssen does not inform his son of our negotiations."

"Let me get you a drink dear. I'll say you're still busy on the telephone."

Mrs Rose returned with her husband's drink. He took a large sip. "It is time for me and Douglas to have a good direct man to man chat to get this whole thing sorted out."

"It would hardly be appropriate this evening, the Searles are about to arrive. Let things be for the moment. Let's not put Douglas in a difficult position. He is going through a very difficult period. Let's just try to have a normal happy evening, and be as supportive of any ideas that Douglas may have, just for tonight, please?"

The Judge harrumphed. It was going to be difficult for him to change his expression.

Mrs Rose left her pensive husband with his drink, sitting in his study. "Daddy will be here presently Frances. I need to see what is happening in the kitchen. Hope forgot to order chives from the greengrocer."

The Judge remained in his study until he heard the front door bell. He got up stiffly from his chair and made his way to the front door.

"Greetings Jeremy!" Searle exclaimed. "Thank you for inviting us."

"Hello Malcolm, good evening Margaret." The Judge kissed her on the cheek. "Do come through to the living room, the others are there."

Douglas got up when the Searles entered the living room. "You do remember Sir Malcolm and Lady Searle, Douglas," Frances said.

"Of course he does Frances. Hello Douglas?" Sir Malcolm shook his hand vigorously.

"Good evening Sir Malcolm, Lady Searle." Douglas shook hands.

"I trust you had a pleasant journey, Mr van Yssen?" Lady Searle asked.

Douglas did not reply, and merely nodded his head in agreement.

"What can I get you to drink, Margaret?"

"Sherry would be fine thank you, Jeremy."

"And the usual for you, Malcolm?"

"There's nothing like a really good single malt, Douglas, especially in the winter, before the fire, after a hard day's work." Searle noticed the beer in Douglas' hand. "You should try it sometime. Once you have acquired the taste it is like heaven's nectar."

Douglas smiled politely. "Thank you Sir Malcolm, alcohol does not do much for me. We tried it as students. Some of us enjoyed the sensation but I really didn't. In fact I found it a nuisance to become befuddled."

"One doesn't have to become befuddled, as you call it, my good fellow. The stuff's medicinal if used with discretion, makes you relax a little and certainly promotes sleep. Besides, it has different kinds of effects on people. I had a friend, when we were students, a chap who studied mathematics, and he in fact became better at doing the most abstract calculations the more he drank. Damn remarkable it was. It certainly didn't befuddle his brain." Sir Malcom took a large draught of his whisky. "Perfect stuff, Jeremy, outstanding flavours." He turned to Douglas. "I hear whispers in the corridors of the powerful, Douglas, that you are thinking of a career change, perhaps even settling here in Cape Town. Quite apart from the fact that newspaper folk drink a great deal, my advice is not to live in the same place as your parents-in-law. Ha, ha!" He laughed and laughed at his own joke while his wife tried to catch his eye to give him a disapproving look but Searle was too clever to look in her direction. Douglas moved about embarrassedly from one foot to the other.

Mrs Rose returned to the living room. "I am so glad that you have brought your delightful mirth with you Malcolm." She gave Mrs Searle a welcoming embrace. "My, my Margaret, but you do look lovely."

"I was just warning Douglas about living in the same town as his parents-in-law, Elizabeth," Sir Malcolm was in full cry. "And about the way in which newspaper chaps drink. Don't you see how funny that is?" And he laughed some more. "It must be the whisky, Douglas! But jokes aside," he was more serious now, "what made you interested in a newspaper career?"

Douglas did not know where to begin. "I shall have to give up teaching, in fact I have given up teaching, because of my hearing difficulties, and I'll have to start a new career." The Judge watched him narrowly, as he would a man giving evidence. "At one time I considered a newspaper career, before I decided to go teaching, so this is probably somewhat of a natural progression one might say, returning to the original idea."

"Douglas is also considering buying a farm, and spending his free time doing research and writing," Frances added hurriedly.

"That sounds absolutely fascinating, Douglas," Lady Searle exclaimed enthusiastically. "A gentleman farmer and historian, how romantic, it would suit you absolutely! And you could raise your children on a farm, and tutor them at home, how lovely."

"Before you plunge into an oration, dear, let's hear what Douglas has to say about it," Searle suggested.

Douglas looked at Frances. "As Frances said, farming is an alternative."

"It can be a very risky one, mind you," Judge Rose commented.

"Nothing ventured, nothing gained, Jeremy," Searle said in a put-on fatherly voice and slowly shook an admonishing index finger at the Judge.

"I am sure Douglas will make the correct decision. He has been very successful at whatever he has tackled," Mrs Rose said encouragingly.

"Unfortunately I do not have the luxury of much time," Douglas said. "Perhaps that is a good thing."

"Douglas went to see Basil Wainwright this morning, Malcolm, and he has made him an offer to join the newspaper as a leader-writer," Judge Rose explained.

"What a lovely position to be in," Mrs Searle enthused. "Everybody is after you, job offers, a farm waiting for you, how fortunate, how very fortunate."

Hope appeared and nodded her head.

"It would seem dinner's ready, shall we go through?" Mrs Rose suggested.

They started with green pea soup. Searle turned to Douglas, "Elizabeth always spoils me. She knows what I like. There's nothing like this on a cold winter's evening. It's the smoked Dutch sausage that she adds that I really like. The sign of a perfect hostess: she spoils her guests in special little ways. Apart from the fact that it flatters, it shows careful consideration. There's a lot to learn from that."

"Oh go on Malcolm, you old flatterer. Sir Malcolm is shrewder than you think, Douglas, he's already preparing me for the next meal."

"Elizabeth makes it very difficult for me, Douglas. She spoils my husband rotten. He loves coming here, and thinks that it is so much better than eating at home."

Douglas had difficulty following what Lady Searle said because of the sounds of the cutlery.

Sir Malcolm laughed so much that he nearly choked. He laughed at himself. "I simply let the two of them compete, and I am guaranteed to emerge as the winner. Now Douglas, pray tell me, what will you farm with, assuming of course that you choose that option?"

"The farm on which my father and I have an option, or perhaps I should call it a right of first refusal, is situated, as I told Mrs Rose earlier today, on the slopes of the Outeniqua Mountains on the Oudtshoorn side of Mossel Bay."

"That must be near the Robinson Pass?" Searle asked.

"At the foot of the Pass, on the left hand side, overlooking the river."

"Which river is that?" Lady Searle asked.

"The Kandelaars River."

"And the kind of farming?" Searle looked at Douglas from under his eyebrows while he wiped pea soup from his moustache with his napkin, and inspected the napkin to see how much soup he had removed.

"Generally mixed farming. There are sheep on the farm, I'm not sure how many, we will establish that when the time comes, lucerne, tobacco, sweet potatoes, fruit, and there are no doubt other possibilities."

"What other possibilities?" Searle enquired with a full mouth.

"I beg your pardon, Sir Malcolm?"

"I asked about the other possibilities." He spoke more loudly.

"I have been doing quite a lot of reading. It seems to me that most farmers are unwilling to experiment. Take as an example a species of lucerne known as melonitis that carries more nodules than lucerne, and grows more rapidly. Vetches if sown at the rate of twenty-five to thirty pounds per acre would store fully one hundred pounds of nitrogen per acre. The traditionalists scoff at new things. I am prepared to have an open mind. By the way, vetches have double the feeding value of oat hay. They will fatten stock and produce more milk, besides enriching the soil. Just think of that – you get more out, and at the same time you put more back into the soil, so that you can grow a subsequent crop without fertiliser. If you tell the traditionalists about it they just laugh and shake their heads."

"It sounds so exciting," Frances could hardly conceal her enthusiasm.

"It is not always easy to find a market for new farming products. That is why people have a tradition of producing certain crops." The Judge was now prepared to add his considered opinion.

"We have to have enterprising people in this world, Jeremy, otherwise we will make no progress," Lady Searle suggested.

"What is the significance of nitrogen, Douglas?" The Judge asked.

"I beg your pardon, Judge?"

"The significance of nitrogen?"

"In the air?"

"No, no my good fellow, in the soil."

"There are plants that are capable of taking nitrogen from the air and transferring it to the soil."

"I know that much, Douglas. What I am asking is what the significance is of having it in the soil?"

Frances glanced anxiously at her mother.

"It acts as a fertiliser." Douglas waited for a response. "It is an essential component in the production of protein. It is what one might call a protein building block. Legumes take nitrogen from the air and transfer it to the soil. Then if you grow another crop in the same soil, a crop that cannot take nitrogen from the air, the subsequent crop benefits from the nitrogen left by the first crop. You would have no need to put nitrogenous fertiliser into the soil. In a case like that you reap the benefit of producing a highly nutritious crop by taking something out of the air, and by doing so you introduce a protein building block into the soil for subsequent crops."

"It almost sounds too good to be true, like perpetual motion, and we know that's bunkum," the Judge said.

"What are we having next, Mummy?" Frances asked.

"It was going to be a surprise for Sir Malcolm."

"Out with it Elizabeth," Searle said pleasantly.

"I know how you like duck, Malcolm, so I thought we should have pork!"

"I also enjoy pork, and you know that, lovely crackling, and apple sauce."

"Well, we are having duck."

"Now there's a thing for you to think about, Douglas; producing ducks. I'm told they are hardy things, easy to raise. There is likely to be an increasing demand for them."

"I do not wish to give the impression that I will definitely go farming. I shall retain an open mind. I am aware of the risks of a farming venture."

"Which reminds me of the whispers. I take it that Wainwright has made you an offer? He would be a fool if he didn't," Searle continued.

Douglas hesitated, and looked at Frances. "I do not want to put Mr Wainwright in an awkward position, and I don't want to be presumptuous."

"Come on now Douglas, I shan't give anything away, and besides Basil Wainwright has the hide of a rhinoceros. Don't be fooled by his gentle manner. He's quite shrewd. He needs a man of your ability more than you need him, and he knows it. I respect your reluctance to say too much. It would be a damn interesting job. Forming the opinions of the populace. Very powerful if you ask me."

Hope arrived with a large covered dish. "Frances has been showing a keen interest in cooking, thanks to your mother, Douglas. We are not having the usual roast duck this evening; we are having Peking duck. She taught Hope to make it, from a recipe book that she bought herself."

"My goodness, this is delicious!" Sir Malcolm said as he tasted his first mouthful.

"Excellent, my dear," the Judge said to Frances.

"You must tell me how you achieved this, it is exquisite," Lady Searle added. "Cooking like this can really spoil the best of men."

Frances blushed. "It was a lot easier than I thought it would be."

Douglas gave Frances a complimentary look. "I think this is the best food I have ever eaten."

"Careful what you say now, Douglas, you don't want to offend your prospective mother-in-law," Searle joked. "You're unusually quiet and pensive, Jeremy. Work on your mind?"

"I have all sorts of things on my mind. At least the weather has improved, and if it continues like this we'll have some golf on Saturday. Haven't played in weeks. The duck is very good Frances."

"Hope must be given the credit, Daddy, I'm so pleased that you like it."

"What's for dessert?" Searle asked.

"Bread and butter pudding," Frances replied.

Searle patted his ample tummy fondly. "I hope I'll have room for that. We must not be too late, tonight. I have an appeal to hear tomorrow morning. We'll give you a lift home Douglas, if you like?"

"That is jolly kind of you, Sir Malcolm."

"Saves you the walk, dear fellow."

The Roses returned to the living room when the Searles and Douglas had left. "I'll have another cup of tea," the Judge said.

Mrs Rose poured the tea.

"What did Douglas say to you after his interview, Frances?" the Judge asked.

"It is quite late, dear, shouldn't we go to bed?"

"Not before I know what Douglas said."

"He did not say very much, Daddy."

"That's not what I understood from your mother."

"I am sorry if I have created a problem. Much of what I said to Mummy was drawn from inferences I made from what Douglas and I discussed at lunchtime."

"There's no point in being evasive, Frances, we need to get things straight. Inferences won't do. I have gone to a devil of a lot of trouble to help Douglas. He never even thanked me this evening."

"I thought you said he thanked you when you spoke to him after you arrived, Jeremy?"

"Well, it was just a cursory, a little, rather casual thank you, if you like. Nothing sufficiently formal to be properly deserving of my efforts."

"I feel that we should be as unselfish as possible," Frances ventured.

"Who's being selfish?" The Judge asked irritably.

"I am not accusing anyone, Daddy."

"It rather sounded as though you did." His eyebrows were in disarray.

"Daddy, I have never, in all the time that I have known Douglas, seen him as enthusiastic about anything, as he is now about farming."

"It's just a passing fad, Frances, it's an escape. Did you not see how he thrashed about when I asked him about nitrogen? I wonder whether he really knows what nitrogen does. And he wants to go farming?"

"It is a foregone conclusion that he has no farming experience, Jeremy, but he can learn, and Frances makes a very good point. I agree with her, I have never seen the man so enthusiastic, one could even say passionate, about an idea. What is important is that it is his idea. If we consider what he is going through, he should be encouraged at all costs."

"He imagines he is interested in farming. He has no idea what it encompasses. He has no idea of the risks, no idea of the hard work. He is an intellectual. I am creating an opportunity for him to do what he does best. I have promoted his cause because I believe he should use his head, not his hands. And to be perfectly direct, Frances, he is not treating my efforts with the respect that they deserve. There is no gainsaying that. I am sorry." He heaved and breathed heavily and pursed his mouth. "Now if you have nothing more to say, I shall take myself off to bed. Goodnight."

Mrs Rose put her arm around Frances' sobbing shoulders. "Let me make you some Horlicks, Frances. It will make you sleep better. I will speak to your father tomorrow. We cannot let things go on like this. His pride is at stake." They went to the kitchen. "The sad thing is that he cannot stand not having his way, even if he is wrong. That is why he has been criticised for some of his judgements. He will only see things his way. There is no other way. He is disappointed that Douglas might turn down Basil Wainwright's offer. He would rather save face and send Douglas down the wrong road than to admit that he has made a mistake. He won't easily forgive Douglas – you must prepare yourself for that. Here, help yourself to sugar. Instead of having to deal with only one man, you now have two. Do go to your room now, I shall wait till he is asleep. I'll sit and read for a while."

"Friday evening could turn into a disaster. Daddy does not get on with Uncle James at the best of times, and if farming discussions are going to dominate, heaven alone knows what could happen."

"Perhaps I should arrange for Uncle James to plead indisposition, or something. Perhaps we could even go and visit Uncle James on Friday afternoon. I'll tell Daddy that he telephoned to say that he is not feeling well. Then I'll suggest that instead of seeing James here on Friday evening, we could go and visit him, so that Douglas can see at first hand what things are like on the farm – the pretext being that he might be discouraged. I only hope the car will be available. Besides it would be a nice outing for Douglas, and for us, and it would be interesting for him to visit the farm."

"That would be better. Thank you so much for being such a good friend and ally, Mother." Frances kissed her goodnight and went off to bed with her cup of Horlicks.

Friday 22 June 1928

Douglas waited at the front entrance of the Helmsley Hotel for Frances and her mother. As it entered the grounds he skipped down the red polished steps. "Good afternoon Mrs Rose." He opened the back door on Frances' side and kissed her. "Hello Frances. Good afternoon, Doyle." He got in next to Doyle, and immediately swivelled round to face Frances and Mrs Rose. "I am looking forward to visiting Mr Sterling's farm. Where exactly is it, Mrs Rose?"

"I have decided that we should go via Stellenbosch, Douglas," Mrs Rose announced.

Douglas cupped his hand and held it behind his right ear. "I understood that Mr Sterling's farm is near Paarl, not Stellenbosch?"

Mrs Rose spoke more loudly. "Yes it is near Paarl, or should I say the Klein Drakenstein area, we are merely taking the Stellenbosch route. We're going over Hellshoogte, it is quite spectacular; there are lovely views."

"Mummy likes outings by car almost as much as Daddy does, Douglas." Frances leant forward to get closer to Douglas.

"I must apologise," he said, "I'm having a bad day with my ears."

Frances patted him on his arm.

"I am grateful to you, Mrs Rose, for arranging this visit. I have agonised about my future, and there is no point in beating about the bush, and pretending. The more I think about it, the clearer it is becoming to me that it may not be the best thing to join the newspaper. My intuition is that I should make myself as independent as possible. If I am going to be handicapped I must create my own resources. I know it may sound like a contradiction. One cannot always rely on help. People's intentions change; their willingness becomes exhausted. I do not have as many opportunities now as I would have had if I had not developed my condition. Things will never be the same again and I must face it. We must all face it. That is why I am pleased for this opportunity."

"We should also not be too gloomy, Douglas," Mrs Rose's voice was firm. "I realise that it is impossible for me to grasp what you are going through. I will give you all my support, whatever you decide. I would like to suggest that you have lunch with us tomorrow. My husband is going to play golf and will not be going with us to the station. He likes to start early at this time of the year."

"That would be very good, thank you."

The car groaned up the steep inclines and narrow bends of Hellshoogte. Doyle was hunched over the steering wheel in intense concentration and pre-emptively hooted loudly before each bend. Beads of sweat crept down his face from under the edge of his cap. The car shuddered noisily over the corrugations of the corners and drifted towards the precipitous edges of the road. "It's quite exciting!" Mrs Rose exclaimed as she looked at a ravine below.

"I could do without this excitement," Frances shouted as she observed a sheer slope on her side. Their descent was cautious and the surface of the road became smoother. They had to stop to let a farm lorry pass.

"It won't be too long now," Frances said into Douglas' ear. He smiled and nodded that he understood. The winter valley below them was stark. In the distance some of the mountain peaks were snow-capped. In damp dark brown soil of lands recently sown, surprised young bright green translucent shoots of wheat and barley stood eagerly in the afternoon sun. Bare pinkish grey fruit trees stood frigidly in the blue light of the shadows of the hills. Snot-nosed urchins played in squalor outside mouldy labourers' cottages where red and blue and yellow and white washing hung on rickety washing lines. Ahead of them a donkey cart accelerated under a cracking whip and swayed drunkenly to make way for the threatening car.

The entrance to the Sterlings' farm was unprepossessing. Two white gateposts that posed as sentries were in need of paint, their feet covered in green algae. Attempts at planting blue gum trees along the driveway to the farmstead were in evidence. The farmhouse was more reassuringly imposing. Figures in relief on the Cape Dutch gable told that it had been built in 1782. The front door was ajar and the irregular reflections on the small panes of the mullioned windows confirmed the liquid nature of glass.

Douglas assisted Mrs Rose from the car. James Sterling appeared at the front door, followed by his wife Ethel with a small child on her hip. Sterling wore brown woollen whipcord trousers and a grey-green Harris Tweed jacket. He kissed Mrs Rose, "Hello Elizabeth, Frances, so nice to see you so soon again."

"Dashed good to see you again, Douglas. I'm sure you remember Ethel."

"Yes of course, we've met several times." Douglas smiled at her and they shook hands.

"We've made a fire, and brewed some tea. Ethel has made some muffins, come inside, come inside."

A spacious living room was permeated by a strong odour of wood fires. A newly made fire roared furiously in a generous hearth. The floor was paved with terracotta tiles worn hollow where the glaze had departed. Two oil paintings hung on either side of the fireplace: one of a haughty man in a white eighteen-century wig and the other of a woman of the same period who wore a sad sour look. Douglas could not decide whether the two of them could have been capable of producing offspring or perhaps the paintings had emanated from an auction room. There was a dining room table and two couches with loose, well-worn covers in faded floral patterns. A threadbare Persian rug in one corner served as the sleeping place for an enormous stinking untidy brown Irish wolfhound who refused to acknowledge the arrival of the visitors. A dark green wooden toy train, whose one red wheel was missing, lay on its side under a small table. A large glass fronted bookshelf stood against one wall.

"Please sit wherever you please," Ethel Sterling suggested. "I'll see to the tea." She disappeared and promptly returned followed by two coloured servants who carried wooden trays. "On second thoughts, shall we rather sit at the table? It is more comfortable for the men."

Frances observed Douglas inspecting the room and peering through the windows. She went and stood beside him. "It is nice here, don't you think?"

"Wonderful house," he said.

"I confess it is a trifle untidy, but then that's the way we are," James Sterling commented. Ethel Sterling poured the tea and handed Mrs Rose her cup before serving the others. Douglas studied her. She was slovenly and in her thirties. Her fingernails were dirty and she was slightly plump. She had a vague unworldliness, about her, an uncaring air that almost bordered on self-assurance. Bright blue eyes, fair hair tied back, good features and soft pink earlobes.

"So now Douglas, my good fellow, my spies tell me that you are thinking of taking up farming?" James Sterling asked.

"I am considering it."

"Few people make money from farming, and as must be clear to you, when you observe our circumstances, we certainly don't." He chuckled embarrassedly. "So if yours is not solely a commercial purpose, and if you are prepared to accept it as a way of life, you might well find it attractive. Elizabeth has explained things to me, and I want to say that I am devastated to learn what has befallen you my dear chap. It's a really very rum deal I must say, very rum." He took a sip of his tea and glanced at Douglas over the rim of his cup to see what his reaction was. "However, we should be chivalrous and not bore the women with farming talk, so what I suggest is that you and I take a walk around the farm when we've had our tea. We'll leave the mothers to natter."

"I would like to come along," Frances said.

"You are most welcome, dear girl," Sterling said. "This niece of mine is most spirited," he said and put his arm around her shoulders and squeezed affectionately.

"You smell of pig-pooh, James," Frances said.

He recoiled and started smelling his hands and his sleeves, and looked under his feet.

"Only joking!" Frances laughed and clapped her hands together in delight.

"Wicked girl," Her mother said. "She's always so full of mischief here, Douglas."

Frances laughed and laughed. "It is because I so love it here."

"It seems as though you have good rains?" Douglas asked.

"Yes, it has been good, but we now need really cold weather – admittedly there has been some snow on the higher peaks, but we need really cold weather for the vines and fruit trees to become properly dormant, and to kill off all the ruddy pests. That can sometimes really get to me, the way the damn things invade my property and help themselves to what I am struggling to produce. Darn good muffins these, Ethie; as usual you have excelled yourself. She's a marvellous bird Douglas, couldn't be shackled to a better woman, and a better mother to my children I could never have found."

"I love the farm," Ethel ventured, encouraged by her husband's approval.

"I know you do, my dear," Mrs Rose smiled.

"How long have you been farming?" Douglas asked.

Sterling produced a careworn frown. "Let me see, how long have we been married now, Ethie?"

"Twelve years next month."

"I came here three years before that. I was twenty-eight when we got married, and Ethie was twenty-two. Gosh, how time flies. But I am getting off the track as usual, yes about fifteen years, now, Douglas. Can't believe how the time has flown."

"How did it happen that you started farming?" Douglas asked.

"Oh well, you know, one thing leads to another, I was never much good at the books. I caught the last two years of the war. Gave me a sense of adventure. Was difficult to settle down after that."

"James was decorated; he is always so self effacing," Ethel said.

"Go on Ethel, I would have done that for anybody. After the war I thought of making the military a career but my father would not hear of it, and instead bought me the farm as a kind of sop. So here I am, or should I say, here we are, Ethel? The kids have a marvellous life. Young James is playing Rugby football this afternoon, pity he is not here to be introduced to you, Douglas. I think we should get going, I'll find you a pair of wellingtons Douglas, spare your shoes that way. Ethel, do get Frances some wellies."

Mrs Rose remained with Ethel. Outside the air was bracing and shadows were beginning to lengthen. Some labourers were making their way to their cottages with containers of wine and some provisions and their wages and lifted their hats respectfully to the visitors. "We mostly produce grapes, and fruit, Douglas. I recently put in some almond trees. There appears to be a growing demand for almonds. Admittedly it takes some time for them to bear fully, what, up to six years, but it is a good long-term investment, and they aren't too much trouble. The grapes go to the co-op, most of mine are used for brandy, but those over there, Muscat de Frontignac, are for muscadel wine. Interesting wine. Our stock came from Languedoc. Some say that the grape could well have been the original grape used centuries ago on the Greek Island of Samos. If produced by fermentation it makes an excellent dry white table wine. Today we add wine spirits to the sweet juice of muscadel, and by fortifying it the *geur*, as my neighbour calls it, is preserved forever. This can be a hell of an interesting business, old man. From a historic perspective, since that is your subject, the great dessert wines of Constantia were popular with royalty as early as the late eighteen hundreds. Napoleon enjoyed them in exile. The Afrikaners also use them as communion wine. Some of my grapes also go to port making." He pointed in the direction of the orchards. "There is a good market for fruit in England, now that shipping has become so advanced, what with cooling facilities. We keep some pigs up there in the valley, and a few sheep. Most important thing is to be organised, and to plan. I've had quite a lot of help from the neighbours over the years, as I'm sure you will have. One's got to take some of the advice with a pinch of salt. Chaps around here are pretty set in their ways. There are one or two progressive blokes, and then of course there are the government's efforts at agricultural extension work. I say getting the right information and using it is just like blending wine, it is best to blend tradition and modern ideas."

"My farm, if we do purchase it, is quite small by comparison to what I see here. Quite modest really."

"Where is it?"

"On the slopes of the Outeniqua Mountains on the Oudtshoorn side of Mossel Bay."

"I don't know the area. What do they farm there?"

"Generally mixed farming, a bit of fruit, lucerne, a few sheep, some grapes for raisins and sultanas, tobacco, that sort of thing."

"There's a lot to be said for mixed farming, spreads the risk, but one has to be careful not to do so many things that you master none. And water? Do you have enough?"

"I forgot to mention, they also grow a bit of wheat in our area. The farm is on a river that flows most of the year, so we will irrigate. The mountains to the south of us are tall and are the source of streams. The rainfall in our area is also quite a lot better than in Oudtshoorn itself."

"Sounds dandy. And what does my lovely niece think of all of this?"

"I will support Douglas in whatever endeavour he chooses. When I think of the wonderfully happy times that I have spent here, I could not think of anything nicer than to live on a farm."

"There's my girl, what a star you are, Frances." Sterling looked affectionately at her.

"Douglas will also do research and write history books." She put her hand through Douglas's arm and drew closer to him. "Dearest man, I knew it would all turn out well."

Sterling pointed to the mountains to the northeast. "That's where most of our water comes from, and timber. The pigs are also up there; Ethel would not have them near the house on account of the stink. Coming to think about it, Douglas, when I started I knew sweet blow-all about farming, and I have survived, so if the property you're thinking of getting has any potential, you should be fine. It is not as difficult as some make it out to be, and if you are prepared to read, and take advice from the people at the agricultural colleges and the university, and if you are willing to be progressive, you should be fine, really fine, eh Francie?"

"What are those?" Douglas asked.

"A state secret really." Sterling put his index finger over his lips. "Those, my dear fellow, are olive trees, believe it or not. Just a few, as an experiment. If they grow in Europe, in Mediterranean areas, why should they not do well here? Anyway, we'll see how they go. Nothing ventured, nothing gained."

"James is a great inventor, Douglas."

"Now don't you start, Frances," Sterling said.

"No really, he has made all kinds of such very clever things. You must show him your staircase that folds from the ceiling."

"Well, even I must admit that it is a damn good contraption that."

"And your special plough for the vineyards."

"It's not really a plough, it is just meant for gentle tilling of the soil in the vineyards."

"It is so clever Douglas, and so convenient to use."

"Stop it Frances, it is just that I am able to impress your innocent mind."

"Absolute twaddle, and you know it very well. Stop being so modest. You should advertise you abilities and sell your ideas."

When they got back to the farmhouse, Mrs Rose was reading in the living room in front of the fire. She put her book down.

"Well?"

"It was most enjoyable," Frances replied. "Where's Ethel?"

"She's bathing the little one."

"I think I shall go and have a peek."

Douglas warmed his legs in front of the fire.

"Did you enjoy that, Douglas?"

"I beg your pardon, Mrs Rose?"

"I said did you enjoy that?"

"Oh yes, very much, indeed, thank you."

"I think we should get going soon. It is a long way, and we want to avoid driving in the dark."

Ethel dried the little one in front of the fire. "We don't stand on ceremony, as you can see," Sterling said. "Ethel likes to be 'natural' as we say."

"Victoria is just like a little cherub," Frances said adoringly.

"Come now you two," Mrs Rose was standing clutching her handbag and agitating to go. "James, won't you tell Doyle that we have to leave."

"Next time you're in town, Douglas, the two of you should come and stay for a few days."

They said goodbye to Ethel and the little one, and went outside to the waiting car. "Thank you so much, my dear brother." Sterling watched the black car gently pitching and rolling as it went along the uneven driveway and become smaller when it turned through the gate. He waved, not sure that they were watching. He went inside to his wife and their child.

"I hope you enjoyed that Douglas?" Mrs Rose asked.

"Yes thank you, Mrs Rose. I really appreciate all your effort. It was most interesting."

"Well?"

"In some ways it has confirmed how daunting farming can be. It is good that I am going home tomorrow. I feel a bit unsettled to be honest, the prospect of the newspaper and a fixed income has appeal, and on the other hand I have sentiments that make farming seem attractive. Perhaps it is the romantic in me. There are the practical realities: the farm we have in mind is a lot smaller than Mr Sterling's farm, much more modest in every way."

"James started with much less land, and bought more from the immediate neighbours as he generated income and time went by. You could do that," Mrs Rose suggested. "I could see again how happy Frances is on the farm. Time will provide us with the wisdom to make the right decision. I have arranged for Jeremy and me to go to the Gilbert and Sullivan evening at Hiddingh Hall. We'll have supper there. I have arranged for you and Frances to have supper at home, if that will suit you?"

"That's very kind of you Mrs Rose, thank you."

Frances gave her mother a little hug. "That is so clever of you!"

Mrs Rose's jaw was set firmly. "I don't want to involve Daddy in any further discussion at this stage. We'll take you to the hotel Douglas, and then Doyle can fetch you when he has taken us to Hiddingh Hall."

Saturday 23 June 1928

Mrs Rose and Frances fetched Douglas at a quarter past three in the afternoon. "Jeremy sends his best regards, Douglas, and asked me to say how much he regrets not being able to accompany us this afternoon. I hope you understand. He is quite exhausted from the pressure of work, and getting out into the fresh air will be therapeutic."

"Thank you Mrs Rose, of course I understand," he said with a sense of relief. He glanced at Frances who looked a little embarrassed and smiled uncertainly.

At exactly four o'clock the train gave its first lurch towards departure. Mrs Rose, with Doyle standing a few steps behind her, waved until the train disappeared, and went briskly to the car.

The train seemed to have less respect for the graveyards at Woltemade on its way from Cape Town. It was not very full and Frances had a coupê to herself by courtesy of the influence of the Judge's new registrar. Douglas was in a four-bunk compartment in the adjoining coach and had a companion, an elderly military officer, on his way to see an ailing brother at Molteno in the North Eastern Cape.

"Let's go and have some tea," Douglas suggested.

Frances took his hand. "It's good to be near the saloon."

"I'll book for dinner this evening."

"That would be very pleasant."

"I am beginning to come to terms with the prospect of a new career."

"I'm glad to hear that."

"Sit on this side, so that you're facing the engine. It's easier to see, and you'll be looking away from the sun."

"You are so considerate, my dear. My Uncle James is a nice fellow, don't you think?" She said, her mouth full of cake.

Douglas frowned and looked at her in an enquiring way. "The noise of the train is drowning out your voice."

"I said my Uncle James is a nice person."

"Yes he's a terrific chap, younger than I remembered."

"He's just turned forty." Douglas nodded but she knew that he had not heard. She leant forward. "We'll go and talk in my compartment, when we've had our tea."

Frances observed him when he was not looking. She loved him even more now. Yet he was different. Something ineffable threatened the strands that held the two of them together. Perhaps it was just an altered perception. It could be that their relationship was assuming a new form. Or were the happy illusions created by their romance departing, like ghosts, at the approach of the first light of their new reality? Which was more real: the starkness of his condition or the dreams that had preceded it? Her father. He knew how to send a message of his discontent and how to drive others to choose, to choose between agreeing with him or not, which meant choosing between him and others. The romantic anticipation that had invested their family with so much happiness was evaporating, leaving a dry residue.

"What are you thinking about?" he asked.

"Oh nothing really. I am just thinking about the term that lies ahead. I can't believe that we are already in the middle of the year."

"Let's go to your compartment." He spoke so loudly that heads of other passengers turned.

He opened the door of Frances' coupé. She made herself comfortable next to the window and he sat beside her. He took her hand and kissed it gently. She put her head on his shoulder. "Have you thought any more about what you want to do?" She asked.

"I am confused. At one moment my mind is made up that I want to go farming – when I think of how happy you were on your uncle's farm. Then I wonder whether you would really want to live like that. And I think of all the difficulties of farming. That then makes the idea of having a fixed income and living in civilised Cape Town appear more attractive. When I remember my stay in London I want to be a city person. And then there is your father. I don't want to incur his displeasure. He would be a formidable foe. It would put a terrible strain on our relationship. The two themes of what I should do are like harmonies that keep changing. Beyond the two harmonies an intuitive phrase keeps on insisting that the newspaper job is the right thing. My instinct tells me that at best it would be a compromise, at the very best just a temporary thing, and when it comes to an end, as it surely must, it will not be a happy end."

"When I hear you speak like this, it tells me that you should be a writer.

Isn't it an irony that you should turn yourself against the opportunity of writing with such eloquence."

"My resentment is so strong, because of what is happening to me, that I feel at times that I want to destroy my own abilities."

"That would only make things worse."

"In my better moments I know that."

"You must not consider Daddy in this."

"I cannot do otherwise. He is involved. We cannot unscramble the egg now. We are all involved – my parents, your parents. We cannot separate ourselves from them. We will be tied to them forever."

"I think you should do what your heart tells you to do, and I will support you in whatever you decide."

"But what do you feel I should do?"

"Go farming. If it does not work out other options remain."

"What about your father?"

"It is your future, Douglas, not his. He will have to learn to accept that. Mummy, in her subtle way, will use her wiles, her feline wiles, to manage him. She has good instincts and she has a way with men. She will be so nice to him that he will not be able to resist, and he will come round to seeing things her way without knowing how he came to change his mind. It won't be easy but she'll manage. She is so very fond of you, Douglas. She has told me that you are the son she always wanted. She will make sure that you are protected."

"I hope you understand that we'll have to postpone any ideas of marriage for a while."

"Why on earth would we want to do that?"

"Because there is too much uncertainty at present."

"Marriage will bring greater certainty."

"The kind of uncertainty that I am referring to is financial uncertainty, the worst kind to have in a marriage. It will produce strain and wretchedness."

"My parents will lend us support."

"That should be the last thing to consider in the present circumstances. I could not entertain financial assistance from your father when I am going against his wishes. Also I don't want to be beholden to anyone. I want to be independent; that is the very reason why I feel that farming is the best choice. Let me start and see how it goes."

"Do you still love me as much as before?"

Douglas turned, took her by the shoulders, and looked her straight in the eye. "I love you more than you could ever imagine, Frances. I shall never love anyone as I love you." He held her hand tightly. They sat, comforted by the reliable rocking of the train and its rhythmic clattering over the joins in the rails. "Why do you ask?"

"You seem distant at times, disconnected. No, wait, don't say anything." She held her finger over his lips. "I understand, as I have said before, I understand what you are going through. I cry myself to sleep at night I understand so well. I know that you must be devastatingly pre-occupied, not only with your condition but also with the difficult decision you have to make. It must have been a miserable wrench to stop teaching, I know all that, but there is something else, something that is impossible to define, that is concealed in the shadows between us, something that is threatening. Are you aware of it?"

"No, I am not."

The winter landscape raced past. Long shadows of trees made the last thin sunlight flicker in the compartment. The train hooted exultantly as it left the mountains behind and sprinted along the level section towards Worcester.

"Is it that there is something that is worrying you that you are not telling me?"

"My deafness is inherited. I will pass it on to my offspring. Garnett thinks that it is transmitted through the mother, like haemophilia. So my mother carried the disease without being affected by it, and gave it to me. She got it from her father who was as deaf as a doornail. Garnett is not sure exactly how my children will be affected and what the probabilities are, but either they or their offspring will likely be affected. Do you have any idea how miserable it makes me feel to think that I have a defect that I am going to transmit to my own children or their children?"

The train freewheeled, preparing to slow down. The carriages were loosely connected and seemed to float. The sounds of movements were hollow. The green leather seats creaked. The window rattled. They felt the brakes being applied.

"We could agree not to have children," Frances whispered. "Or we could adopt a child."

Douglas sighed profoundly and held his forehead in his hand. He looked out of the window. Tall bluegums with smooth white trunks glided past. People on the platform were dressed for the cold, in overcoats and scarves and gloves.

"I forgot to book for dinner," Douglas said.

"And I need to go to the toilet."

"I'll go and make the booking in the meantime."

"Kiss me. All that really matters, my love, is for us to be together."

Frances sat on the toilet. The sensation of urinating transported her into some of her daydreams: their stone house on the hill; their chubby baby in his cot, standing holding on to the side and falling onto his bottom when he let go to hold his arms out to her. She would have to detach herself from what she had hoped for. May one flush the toilet while the train is in the station? It is only wee. The image of the baby presented itself again. She could see the features of the child. She could smell him. She could feel his warmth. His eyes were blue, his hair the colour of Douglas' hair. She took some paper to wipe herself and looked down at her pubic hair. Tears filled her eyes. She could feel that baby's face against her cheek. She kissed his temples through her tears. She pulled up her pants, straightened her dress and splashed cold water onto her eyelids.

Douglas was waiting outside her compartment. He nodded. "I think I got the last table."

"That's very good, I am looking forward to having dinner with you."

In the dark the train made its way towards Robertson with renewed vigour. The moon had not yet appeared and the reflection of the lights in the empty passages of the coaches made it almost impossible to see anything outside. Frances had put up the shutter of her window and sat on the navy blue railway blanket of her bed, holding her handbag on her knees. She had changed and was wearing an elegant plain drop waist dark green velvet dress with long sleeves. She had put on a little lipstick and used a hint of eyeliner. Her fair hair was tied back. The heater was on and helped to release the scent of her perfume. She heard Douglas knock and got up to help him open the door. She put her arms around him and pressed herself against him. "We will be alone tonight," she said. He held her until he felt that she wanted to be released and closed the door behind her.

"I'll lead the way," he suggested as they set off along the swaying passageway. He opened to the door of the saloon. Heads turned as the handsome man and his beautiful fiancée entered.

"I will have some wine this evening," she said, leaning forward when they were seated. He raised his eyebrows and frowned quizzically. She stroked his hand. "You don't have to say anything."

"Conversation is becoming more difficult for me," he said. "Especially when there are other sounds."

"It's fine, I understand." She patted his hand. "I'm as hungry as a horse. I hardly had any lunch."

"I'm glad you're hungry. You'll enjoy your food more. The menu looks good."

"I'll start with soup."

"This is very pleasant," Frances said, as she tasted her wine. She buttered a small piece of toast. "The soup is good too. They must have used fresh tomatoes."

Douglas nodded and smiled. "It seems they used fresh tomatoes," he said.

"It's just fine. Everything will turn out well, Douglas." She leant forward and made exaggerated movements with her lips.

He thought of the other journeys that they had had. The atmosphere in the dining saloon was festive: the formal behaviour of the stewards in their white jackets and black bow ties, the white damask napkins and table cloths, the shining glasses and silver cutlery on the tables, lights reflected in the window-panes, the excitement of going towards a destination. We are all nomads, stimulated by the anticipation of new destinations, whether on a spiritual journey or a physical one, or on a journey of a developing relationship.

"What are you thinking about?" Frances asked.

"I was thinking that we are all nomads, on an eternal journey. We are always going somewhere, travelling through our own minds, with our thoughts as pieces of luggage. We are part of a dynamic universe; that is why it always seems as though we have a destination, perhaps many destinations? Who knows why things happen as they do? We seek permanence and certainty, but that is impossible to achieve. Certainty can only be attained by unconditionally accepting uncertainty." He was talking fairly loudly so that she could hear.

She put her finger over her lips. "We'll talk in my compartment."

The hot food had made Douglas perspire. Frances' cheeks were flushed from the wine. Her features were soft and her eyes dreamy. She giggled when he put his arm around her to help her across the open landing between the coaches. "We have the whole night to ourselves," she said into his ear. "We could pretend that we are alone together in our house on your farm."

He let her into her compartment and she flopped down on her bed and lay back. "Close the door Douglas and come here." She sounded a little silly. "Make sure the door is properly shut and come and lie on top of me. I want to feel what it is like."

"We can't do that."

"And why not, may I ask?"

"Not on the train. The conductor could arrive. Men aren't supposed to be in women's compartments at this time of the night. It would be most embarrassing if we were caught."

"I couldn't give tuppence."

"Come now Frances, let's not be silly."

"Who's being silly, dear man? I am never silly, and you should know that."

"I'll sit with you for a while and then you should prepare for bed. The conductor will be doing his rounds."

She sat up and put on a serious look. "We'll make ourselves look oh so respectable, and wait for him. And when he's gone we'll carry on. How's that?"

"First things first. You sit in your corner and I'll sit in mine until he comes. Agreed?"

"But first give me a sloppy kiss."

"Where on earth did you get that expression from?"

"Florrie told me, that's where I get it from, silly."

"You're quite amusing, Frances."

"Don't patronise me." She yawned slowly until her pink tongue curled upwards at the end and she had tears in her eyes that made her eyeliner run. "Come now Douglas, do as you promised and kiss me. I hear the dreadful little man in his shiny blue serge uniform rattling his key in the doors at the other end."

Douglas kissed her quickly.

"That was a rather mean little kiss, and not at all sloppy or wet."

The conductor's key rattled intrusively in the metal recess of the door. Douglas sat as far away from Frances as possible. The conductor opened door. "*Goeie naand*, good evening," he said. "Tickets please." He looked over his spectacles at Douglas. "I was wondering where you were at this time of the evening Mr van Yssen."

"How do you know his name?" Frances asked.

"I make a point of studying the passenger list Miss, so that I will know who my customers are, and where they should be."

"We are betrothed to be married, you know," Frances said in a precious voice and held out her hand to display her ring.

The conductor nodded disinterested approval. "Your ticket, please, Miss."

Frances fumbled in her handbag and proudly produced her ticket. "See, here it is!" She waved it about.

The conductor clipped the two tickets and handed them back. "I wish you a pleasant evening. Goodnight."

Douglas closed the door and sat down. "I think I should be going soon."

"First lie on top of me, you promised."

"I never promised anything of the sort."

"Yes you did." She flopped back on her bed and held her arms out to him. "Come now dear boy."

Douglas sat down next to her. "I think we should try it some other time, Frances. I love you so much that I feel that we ought to let it happen in different circumstances." He lent over her and gave her a long intimate kiss as a compromise.

"That was so yummy," she said dreamily. He could smell the wine on her breath.

"We'll have breakfast together tomorrow morning. I'll fetch you at seven." He kissed her again. "I hope you'll sleep well."

She held on to his hand as he got up to leave. "You are so dear, Douglas. You are my protector. Will you always be constant to me?"

He smiled. "I shall try my best."

Sunday 24 June 1928

The van Yssens waited for the train.

"I dreamt about Douglas last night, Albert. It was an uneasy dream. I can't remember exactly what it was that I dreamt. I have tried in vain to recall it. All I remember is that Frances and Douglas were on a beach holding hands, walking along. They let go of each other. She walked deeper and deeper into the water and he just strolled on as if nothing had happened. As though he could not hear her cries for help. I had a desperate feeling when I woke. I took some Phospherine before we left."

"You should not pay too much attention to your dreams, Anneke. Don't attach too much importance to them. Trust in the Lord instead. The last thing you want to do now is to let on that you have anxieties."

"The Bible is full of dreams."

Van Yssen shook his head disapprovingly. "Things were different in those days."

The bell at the level crossing announced the approaching train. He drew his wife away from the edge of the platform to make way for the heat of the locomotives. Douglas was the first to disembark, suitcase in hand, followed by Frances. She embraced Mrs van Yssen.

"How are you my child?" Mrs van Yssen asked.

Frances put on a brave face. "I am quite well, thank you. And how are the two of you?"

"We have missed both of you, my dear," Mrs van Yssen replied. "I wish you could have stayed with us for a few days. I so much enjoyed having you here."

"I love it here. Perhaps there will be a time, hopefully in the near future, for Douglas to show me the farm. We went to visit my uncle's farm. I love it there. I even made butter there once."

The conductor came past. "The train will be leaving soon, it will not be a normal stop, we have some time to make up. So please board soon, please." He repeated his message as he went along.

Frances took Douglas' hand. "I will telephone you this evening. Please write to me dearest?"

He kissed her and hugged her while his parents pretended to be interested in other things. They said goodbye to Frances. Then they waited for the train to leave. When she blew Douglas a kiss she was crying.

"You were rather abrupt, Douglas," his mother said as they went to the other side of the tracks.

"Excuse me?"

"I said you were rather short with Frances. Has anything happened between the two of you?"

"No, not at all. I just have so much on my mind. I'm sure she understands."

"How did your interview with the editor go?" His father asked.

"It was fine, thank you, but as you know from your discussions with Judge Rose, Dad, it was rigged." Van Yssen moved about uneasily and Mrs van Yssen glanced sideways to see what his reaction would be. "Rigged by the Judge. So it was hardly surprising that Wainwright offered me the job without really interviewing me at all. He was like a lapdog. The net result is that I just have to say 'yes', and I'll be a leader writer for the Cape Times."

"And how do you feel?" His father enquired.

"It won't work. You cannot be deaf and do that job. You have to have your ears wide open for that kind of work. You have to go parliament and hear what is going on there. You have to pick up all the subtleties of social and political life around you, all the time. There will be news conferences to attend. And if the thing does not work out, can you imagine what that will be like? I would have to move to Cape Town. The Roses will be watching me like hawks, especially the Judge. I don't want to make an enemy of him. He has already taken an unpleasant tone because I did not jump at the opportunity. I think he can become quite nasty. He went to play golf yesterday afternoon on a flimsy pretext and did not even come to the station to see us off as usual. There is too much at stake to make impulsive decisions. In point of fact the Judge has unwittingly shown me that it would be foolish to put myself into a position over which he has too much influence. I have thought long and hard about things. Someone with my difficulty needs to be as independent as possible, not reliant on others. Can you imagine if the editor had to sack me, because I could not do the job? It does not bear thinking of. I have not given my decision to anyone, but I know in my heart of hearts that the farm is the only practical solution."

"Farming is not easy, Douglas," his mother said.

"I realise that. We went to Frances' uncle's farm on Friday afternoon. I could see that they were struggling. But they were happy despite that. Much as I will try to make the farm succeed commercially, I fear that farming is more of a way of life. And it may suit me. At least I have my qualification. I intend to do research and to write history when the seasons permit. So it will not just be the farm."

"Will Frances be prepared to come and live on the farm?" His mother asked.

"I think so, but we will have to put any ideas of marriage to one side for the time being. I have made that clear to her. I need to handle this transition. I need to establish myself first."

"How did Frances respond?" His father asked.

"You know Frances, Dad, she is a romantic creature. She wants to get married and help me on the farm, but it is not time for that right now."

"She is so loyal. Lengthy courtships are not ideal. They lead to frustrations," his mother said.

"I know that Ma, but I have a great responsibility towards her, and I have to do the correct thing for her sake and mine."

"So how will you handle the Judge?" His father asked.

"I have thought about that. I will let a good few days pass so that he will think that I have considered the matter thoroughly. Then I will write to him and thank him profusely for his generous assistance and explain to him why it is impossible for me to take the newspaper job. Beyond that I cannot do anything. If he does not want to be appeased I cannot help it. It is my future, not his."

"It is his daughter's future," van Yssen grunted.

"With respect Dad, no one is more aware of that than I. I have deep concerns for Frances' future, our future. Do you think that I want to do anything that is not in her interest? I love her, I value her love for me, and I must think of what is best for her. It will not be in her interest to make a foolish short-term compromise, especially not one designed to please her father. So, if you are prepared to help me I would like to go farming, and the sooner I get started and begin to live the rest of my life, the better."

"I promised to help you, and I will do so, Douglas. We'll go and see Pocock tomorrow morning."

Chapter Thirty

Monday 10 September 1928

MR HARTMAN, the carting contractor, arrived at the van Yssens' house at seven in the morning. He knocked on the open front door, his hat in hand.

"Good morning Mr Hartman. We are ready," van Yssen called from the passage.

"It is good that the weather is cool. There's still a little snow on the Swartberg. I went to Prins Albert yesterday."

"We will have to be careful with the books. They are valuable."

Douglas appeared, two suitcases in hand.

Hartman and his two helpers carried Douglas' bedroom furniture, consisting of his bed, his desk, his chair and his cupboard to the waiting truck. Other items had been purchased to furnish the farmhouse and were stored in the garage. Cutlery and crockery, kitchen utensils, pots and pans, cups and saucers, had been wrapped in newspaper and packed tightly into cardboard boxes. Douglas' bicycle stood conspicuously against the side of the house so that it would not be forgotten. Food supplies had been bought: an assortment of tinned food, corned beef, glass jars of preserves and jams, dried pulses, meal for bread, eggs, oats for porridge, potatoes, meat, salt ribs, dried sausage, smoked ham, biltong and milk and biscuits of various kinds. A large cage containing white Leghorn chickens with bright red combs stood ready. Bunches of beetroot and carrots had been placed in wet hessian sacks so that they could be put back into the vegetable patch on the farm. Douglas and his parents had made lists for weeks. Matches were important and paraffin for the lamps, and the lamps themselves, and candles. Shoe polish and dubbin for his boots. Linen and towels and new clothes and spare boots. Each box was labelled in pencil.

Douglas travelled with Hartman and his helpers. Mr and Mrs van Yssen followed in their car. "I am sad that he's leaving home," his mother observed wistfully. Betta waved from the veranda and wiped her tears away with her apron. In front of the van Yssens the shaking large white canvas canopy of the truck was contrasted against the blue sky and the grey-green scrub of the surrounding veld.

"It had to happen sooner or later; I left home, you left home, Anneke. I'll let them get ahead so that we won't drive in their dust."

Although he was hardly a talkative man, Hartman tried to make conversation with Douglas. Douglas could only hear bits of words because of the noise of the vehicle and gesticulated that he could not hear. Hartman looked at him out of the corner of his eye, and shook his head. There was a rumour in town that the fellow was going deaf.

"I hope we thought of everything," Mrs van Yssen said.
"It is impossible to think of everything, but I am sure we have the essentials. He won't starve. It's a start."
"The sheep have started lambing, isn't that exciting."
"It will encourage Douglas. There's a good demand for wool at present. I think we have made a very good buy with the farm. We were lucky."
"I hope so. I really hope so. Just imagine him all alone there tonight. Soon he will be all alone and in complete silence. We should get him a dog."
"It will have to be suitable for the farm. You don't want a dog causing problems with the sheep. The shop is not too far away from him. They have a telephone."
"What happens if he becomes ill?"
"He's young and strong, Anneke. He'll manage. Our forefathers had to manage. And there's Garnett. He'll go and see to him should the need ever arise. There are also the neighbours of course."
"I did not like the look of those Ellis people. Douglas should also have a cat to keep the mice and the snakes away."
"Yes, that's a good idea. There is nothing wrong with them. It is just that they don't have much. But they are decent God-fearing folk."

Douglas looked at the towering mountains ahead of them. There were patches of cloud over the peaks. A haze over the lower slopes gave an air of mystery to the place where his farm lay. Along the roadside drifts of spring flowers formed brightly coloured carpets. When they reached the first farms, fruit trees were blossoming and a copse of poplar trees had small soft new green leaves. They drove across the Kandelaars River causeway. Clear mountain water meandered through round boulders. The road became steeper and Hartman changed into second gear. Hartman slowed down and waited for van Yssen to catch up. "It would be better if Mr van Yssen could now go ahead to show me the way," Hartman suggested.

Near the general dealer's store two small coloured children, a flimsily dressed boy and a girl waved hopefully. Van Yssen turned onto the road leading to the farm. He could hear the grass on the raised central part of the road brushing the underside of the car. One of Hartman's helpers jumped from the truck and ran to open the farm gate. The area around the house had been cleared, the house whitewashed and the roof painted dark red. Willemse was sitting on the kitchen steps. He got up when the truck caught his eye. He had chopped a huge amount of firewood and stacked it against the wall outside the kitchen as a token of his willingness. Kindling waited in a wooden Laurel paraffin box. He had also cleaned both chimneys but would keep that announcement for a time when he needed a favour. He decided to reserve the news of the caracal killing two lambs until they were more settled. Otherwise the sheep were doing well. They would have to shoot the caracal if further losses were to be prevented. Hartman and his men carried Douglas' furniture and boxes into the house. Douglas and his father helped with some of the things. His mother indicated how to arrange the furniture. The windows had not been cleaned properly. Douglas would need some domestic help. They could ask van der Byl about that.

Hartman had another assignment and could not stay for coffee. He took off his hat to say goodbye and wished Douglas everything of the best, turned his truck in the farmyard and left.

"We'll have coffee Douglas, and then we'll help you to unpack," van Yssen offered.

"I'll manage, Dad."

"We would like to help, Douglas." His mother's tone was insistent.

They sat at a table on the veranda and looked into the valley below. The mountain air was crisp. In places the grass was still fawn from winter. On higher ground swathes of soft pink heather quivered in the breeze. The fruit trees had blossoms. It was a good thing that they had come to prune them when they did. It was a good time to extend the orchard. They would put in apricots and yellow cling-peaches for dried fruit. Sheep bleated intermittently. And almond trees. The branches of the pale grey oak tree at the end of the field below the house had begun to bud. No doubt a late starter. Van Yssen finished his coffee and ate his rusk. "Well we can't sit here all day as though we're on holiday. There is much to do."

Douglas and his parents arranged his things as they thought best. His bookshelf was unsteady on the uneven floor of the living room and van Yssen cut little wooden wedges to make it more secure. "One thing we completely forgot, Douglas: the tools. We'll have to make a list before we go and I will bring them here in the next few days. The bookshelf should not be too close to the fireplace."

Mrs van Yssen unpacked the kitchen utensils while Willemse cleaned the windows. He showed a reluctance to enter the house and had to be coaxed inside while he left his hat on the step outside. Mrs van Yssen unpacked Douglas' suitcases and packed and hung his clothes in his bedroom cupboard. He had few things. They would get him some more. She remembered the paintings that Madame Jacquard had secretly sent along as a gift. She found Douglas on his hands and knees in the living room trying to straighten his Persian carpet whose corner had become caught up under the leg of the settee. "Mrs Jacquard sent along a gift for you, Douglas."

"I beg your pardon, Ma?"

"Guillemette Jacquard sent you a magnificent gift, my boy. It's in the car."

"What is it?"

"Go and have a look."

Douglas found the two paintings wrapped together in brown paper on the back seat of the car, and carried them into the house. He unwrapped them on the table of the living room. One was of the haystacks near Calitzdorp and the other of blossoming peach trees in a field in the Cango Valley. "They are magnificent. I would like to hang them here in the living room."

"She can ill afford to give paintings away, especially her best work. It is like the parable of the poor widow."

"I know; it makes me feel quite sad. I don't even have a hammer. I'll have to wait for Dad to bring the tools. How silly it was not to think of that."

"We should have lunch. I'll boil water. You can warm the soup for supper. I sincerely hope that you will feed yourself properly. Try and start the day with a good breakfast. It is easy to make porridge, and you have fresh milk, and cook some eggs."

"I'll be perfectly fine Ma. I'm looking forward to being on my own. It will give me time to sort things out. And I have a great deal to do here, as you well know. We are fortunate to have Willemse, he knows everything around here, and he seems to be quite a loyal sort. Judging by what he has done he really has made an effort to please. That is a good sign."

Van Yssen appeared at the kitchen door. "Just remember one thing Douglas, old retainers are not always the best people to have. One is reluctant to let them go because one fears that one will not be able to find better people, but there are always better people. Efficient people cost less. I am not saying we should let him go, on the contrary, but it is just something to bear in mind for the future. He was quick to get down to his cottage as soon as he sensed it was lunchtime."

"It will be all right, Dad."

"Get him to put the vegetables into the ground as soon as he returns, and let him water them well, Douglas."

"Yes, Dad."

Mrs van Yssen put supplies onto the shelves of the pantry.

"I think we should see to the lamps, Douglas, get paraffin into them, and put them ready," his father suggested. "Make sure your flashlight is handy in the night. Put some paper into the latrine. Put some chlorine ready and the scoop. You want to keep the place as hygienic as possible. I'll purchase tools tomorrow and bring them out here on Wednesday."

It was past four in the afternoon before the van Yssens said goodbye to Douglas. He opened the gate for them. His mother looked back at him while he shut the gate.

Douglas resumed unpacking. He started with his books. It was a good time to arrange them in proper order. When he went to unpack his clothes he found that his mother had made up his bed. Some things would have to wait for the morning. He walked to Willemse's cottage. Smoke came from the chimney. A large axe stood in a chopping block. Wood splinters were scattered around. A few white hens clucked in their coop. He would have to remember to feed his chickens. They would have to stay in their cage until he could make a proper coop when the tools arrived. He knocked on Willemse's door. There was no reply. He knocked again and waited. Willemse appeared from behind the cottage doing up his fly.

"Thank you for the wood." Douglas said.

Willemse nodded.

"We'll have to get started early tomorrow morning," Douglas suggested.

Willemse nodded. "I'll be ready even though I'll have to sleep in the kraal with the sheep tonight. The caracal took two lambs last night."

"Two lambs?"

"Yes, two lambs."

"Why did you not say so when we arrived this morning?"

"I did not want to upset the old man. It would not have been a good start."

Douglas broke out in a sweat.

Willemse nodded. "We'll have to acquire a gun. Preferably a good shotgun. I must now first go and eat something and prepare food for tonight. It keeps the cold away." He went inside his cottage. The door had been newly painted, with some of the leftover red roof paint.

Douglas walked back to the house in the gloaming, his hands in his trouser pockets. He looked at his watch. It was nearly six. Higher up in the valley wood smoke rose from the chimney of a neighbour's house. Two lambs gone, even before he got started. He must write to Frances. He looked at his modest house. A pit latrine. Almonds would be better than livestock. Animals are always a problem. He patted his back pocket. The best would be to hide the money in one of the jars in the pantry. It only takes a few minutes to warm the soup on the Primus. It's good that they filled it with paraffin. His father said not to over-fill it. Once the garden improves the place will look better. A fire would be cosy. He carried wood into the living room. The scent of the wood gave him comfort for a reason he did not understand. Garnett was good at that sort of thing. Have hot soup in front of the fire and read a little, and start his letter to Frances. Garnett knows about guns. He would ask him. Perhaps he could even come and shoot the *rooikat*. He walked around the house and undid the shutters so that he could close them. The air was cold.

Once the fire was started he lit a lamp and carried it to the kitchen. He placed it on the kitchen table and lit the Primus stove. His mother had poured the pea soup into an enamel saucepan. He stirred it and placed it on the Primus. He turned the flame down a little so the soup wouldn't burn. He looked about while he waited. He fetched bread from the pantry and the breadboard, rummaged about in the drawer of the kitchen table for the bread knife. There was no sign of it and he had to cut the bread with one of the meat knives. He buttered the crust. He stirred the soup and went to see how the fire was doing.

The room felt warmer. He was pleased to see how well the fireplace drew. The flames darted on the wall. Willemse needed a better overcoat. And boots. He had forgotten to put the money into the jar. Two lambs.

    Douglas buttered more bread and ladled soup into a plate. He carried his food and the lamp to the living room. The dining room would have to wait for guests. He'd have to tell his father about the caracal and the lambs. He would prefer not to own a gun. Garnett could come and shoot the caracal. Jackals could also be a problem with sheep: poison them. Strychnine does the trick. He nearly burnt his tongue on the soup. He put some more wood on the fire. In town they use coal. This is better. He examined the room and thought of Frances and tried to remember where he had put his writing paper and pen. He was certain he had brought ink. Better to wait until morning, easier to write in the daytime. He washed his supper things with blue soap in an enamel basin and dried them with his stiff new dishcloth that smelled of shop. He made sure that the back door was locked and walked back to the living room with the lamp. The light and the shadows that followed him leapt about on the walls of the passage. He suddenly felt weary. Damn, he had not fed the chickens, or given them water. They must be asleep by now. Better not to disturb them. They were safe in the barn, if the door was properly shut. He went to his room, took the flashlight from the drawer of his bedside cabinet and went out through the front door. At least there won't be snakes about in this cold. The barn door had been closed and the hasp tied down with a piece of wire. Good for Willemse. Possibly even fed the chickens. He looked at his house as he walked towards it. The light of the lamp shone through the slits between the shutter louvres. He went inside and locked the door, then went to see that everything was secure. He put more wood onto the fire, turned the lamp up a little, looked to see how much paraffin was left, took his copy of Pickwick from the bookshelf and settled himself in his easy chair next to the fire. There was not enough light so he placed the lamp to his right on the mantelpiece, and being familiar with the work, began to look for a chapter that he was likely to enjoy again. He looked up at the ceiling. He saw Frances, getting off the train in Graaff Reinet. He smelled the sulphurous smoke of the engine. What would she be doing now? Surreal images of the journey to the farm that morning appeared before him with startling clarity: the gravel road, budding trees, pink and white blossoms and a blue sky. He felt the movements of Hartman's truck and saw the mountains. Douglas and his father had drawn up a list of things to do, and made an outline of plans for the next six months. His father would be here with the tools tomorrow. Maybe Garnett will come along one of these days. He wondered about Willemse. Was he asleep in the kraal? How could he hear the *rooikat* if he was so deaf? The two of them. He felt lonely and sad. A cup of tea would be nice. What about his washing? He had never thought of that. The newspaper job might not have been so bad. It is too late now. The Judge would never forgive him. God, if he could see me now, sitting here in the dark in this modest abode, these circumstances. Have to make it work. Find one or two labourers tomorrow, get a woman to help with the housework. Dig the holes for the almond trees. They could arrive any day. The sheep have to be dipped. It is good to have objectives. It would have been nice to have an Aga stove. Fag to light the Primus each time you want to make tea.

He carried his lamp to the kitchen and made some tea. He helped himself to assorted biscuits. The clock said eight. There was a long night ahead. He balanced the book on his lap and held the one side down with his elbow while he drank his tea. He had spilt some in the saucer and drops fell from the bottom of the cup onto the pages of his book. He wiped the pages with his handkerchief and held the book up to the light to make sure that it was as clean as he could get it. Pity to mess up a first edition like this. His father would not be pleased. Should he wipe it with a wet cloth? It wasn't too bad. Could make it worse by wiping it. It's only the first day. Bound to be unsettled. Things will get better. Get to know the neighbours. How the hell will I wake up in the morning when I am no longer able to hear the alarm? He put his book down and fetched the latest *Farmer's Weekly* from the top of the bookshelf. The cow will be here on Wednesday. His father did say that they could get a small tractor. They could plough the field near the riverbank and put vetches in for better milk production. In the meantime there is enough grazing. They would have to get the chicken coop ready as soon as possible, and make it caracal-proof. He needed a better lamp if he was going to read properly at night: a pressurised mantle lamp, preferably one with twin mantles. His right ear was itching. He got up to fetch a match and settled down to scratch his ear with the tip of the match. He dug some wax out and smelled it, then let out an enormous fart. He laughed out loud. What a luxury to be able to do exactly as he wanted. He could walk about without any clothes on for that matter.

He tried to concentrate on his reading to little avail. Start again. Chapter Nineteen. 'A pleasant Day, with an unpleasant Termination.' 'The birds, who happily for their own peace of mind...' The coop would have to be well constructed. It would be better to go to bed, and to start early. Tomorrow will be different.

He took one of the fire irons and moved the burning logs to the back of the pan, tapped them so that they would burn faster and put the fire screen in front of the hearth to prevent sparks from getting onto the wooden floor. With his lamp in his hand he went to the bathroom and brushed his teeth before unlocking the door at the end of the passage. He stood on the edge of the veranda to urinate. The bedclothes were cold and he shivered when he climbed into bed. There was more moisture in the air up here, that's why. He lay and looked at the *Farmer's Weekly* for a while, studied the knots in the wooden ceiling boards and scratched his testicles. He turned his lamp down, blew out the flame and began to think of the intimacies that he and Frances had at Plettenberg Bay. He had fluid oozing from him the one time. Goodness knows what might have happened. He started to get an erection; strange that it always happened more readily in new or unfamiliar places. We are nomads.

What a thing it was to touch her there. It was unbelievable. She liked it. Imagine being in bed with her, here under the eiderdown, naked. The stern face of the Judge looked disapprovingly at him, wig and robe and all. There was no way he could expect Frances to come and live here. His erection was gone, withered by the reality of his circumstances.

Douglas woke several times during the night. He had gone to bed too early. In the early hours of the morning he dreamt of a leopard stalking him in the back of Hartman's truck and of falling off onto the road with the leopard clinging to his back. The Judge found it highly amusing as he observed what was happening from the side of the road, bent double with laughter and slapping his thighs with delight. Then Willemse was in the barn, his pipe in his mouth, drunk and bleary-eyed, axe in hand, methodically pulling the chickens from their cage and chopping off their heads while he prayed for them. Douglas woke in a heavy sweat and pushed the eiderdown away so that he could cool down. That was terrible. It was still dark in his room and he lit a match to read the alarm clock. It was quarter to five. He got out of bed and put on his dressing gown. He unlocked the passage door and walked a few yards from the house to relieve himself in the grey dawn. Heavy mist lay in the valley below him. Smoke came from Willemse's chimney and there was yellow light in his dull window. He shivered He selected suitable kindling and thin pieces of wood and rolled old newspaper into balls to start the fire. He would make himself a good breakfast. Once the stove was going he lit the Primus to boil water for coffee. There was enough milk. He measured two tablespoons of ground coffee into the flannel bag of his white enamel coffee pot. He would make some oatmeal porridge and fry eggs and sausage and have bread and apricot jam. He warmed milk on the stove in a small grey enamel saucepan, poured it into his coffee and placed the rest on a cooler part of the stove for his porridge.

He wasn't sure how to open the eggs and managed to break the yolks of both eggs. The pan was not hot enough and the broken eggs stuck to it. He managed to scrape all the egg out and heaped the broken pieces onto a slice of bread. The sausage was easier. He had seen Betta cooking sausage in a pan. He opened the kitchen shutters while the sausage cooked. The pear tree at the back of the house was full of white blossoms luminous in the early light. His porridge was sputtering, lifting the lid of the saucepan he let out steam. He had more coffee. He would get the hang of eggs in time. Damn nice food even if he must say so himself. He sat down and ate his porridge. The eggs and sausage followed. He mopped the last of the juices up with a bit of bread using his knife and fork. He had promised himself that he would not allow his table manners to deteriorate.

He cautiously touched the side of the stove's copper hot water tank to see if the water was hot. He put some more wood into the stove. He opened all the shutters and some of the windows to let light and air into the house. Willemse's dog barked at him when he went outside. The sky was cloudless. Not a leaf stirred. He carried jugs of hot water to his bath, added a little cold water and lowered himself into the bath. He looked out through the open bathroom window at the fawn hillsides on the slopes of his mountain, radiant in early sunlight. He soaped himself thoroughly, rinsed himself by pouring water over his head with a large enamel mug and got out to dry himself. There was a nip in the air. He dressed in khaki's, put on his new working boots, and a warm blue jersey and went out to see to the chickens.

Willemse was already in the barn, feeding the chickens. "Thank you for seeing to them last night."

"What does Mister say?"

Douglas raised his voice. "I said thank you for seeing to the chickens last night."

"That is what Mister is paying me for."

Douglas could barely hear Willemse's voice, hoarse from the night in the kraal.

"How was last night?" Douglas enquired

"It was quiet. We did not lose anything. I'll just have to keep watch at night until we can shoot the caracal."

"I am expecting my father later."

Van Yssen arrived shortly before eleven to find Douglas and Willemse digging holes for the corner posts of the chicken coop. Douglas had marked out the area and decided to put it against the northern wall of the barn so that only three sides would have to be built. Douglas looked quite pleased with himself and smiled as he looked up to greet his father. "Well? What do you think?" He asked.

"It looks like a good job, my boy. I've brought you some mail. The tools are in the back of the car. Let's go and have tea. I'll explain to you what I have bought."

Van Yssen waited in the kitchen with Douglas while he made tea. "Dad, we've had a bit of a problem. Willemse only told me about it yesterday after you had left. He said he did not want to upset you. There is evidently a *rooikat* about, possibly more than one I would imagine. The night before last two lambs disappeared. Willemse is convinced that they were taken by the *rooikat*."

"That's not good news."

"We need a gun, or someone to shoot the thing. Won't you ask Garnett what we should do? He and Uncle Charlie are forever going hunting, perhaps he could be persuaded to come and shoot it?"

"Yes I'll do that. Those things are a pest Douglas. We used to get our dogs to chase them up a tree, and then shoot them with buckshot."

"Willemse has taken to sleeping in the kraal with the sheep. I can't expect him to do that for ever."

"Shepherds like him are tougher than you think. It would be a mistake to let him think that you feel sorry for him. He expects to do what he's doing, that's why he does it. How was your first night?"

"It was different but fine."

"I realised as we sat at home how lonely it must be. It would be ideal to get married."

Douglas looked at the floor. "That won't be possible, Dad."

"I understand that you wish to postpone things, Douglas."

"I am glad for the opportunity to speak to you alone about this, Dad. I do not wish to upset Ma, but I have thought for some time now that it would be better if Frances and I did not get married."

"What on earth are you saying?"

"It's complicated Dad. Let's go and sit outside in the sun, it's a little cold in here."

Douglas carried the tray to the veranda.

"You say it's complicated? Complicated in what way?"

Douglas put his hands behind his head and leant back in his chair. "Where shall I start? Let me start with what is my most important consideration, namely Frances. Frances has on occasions spoken about having children. I am concerned about passing my defect on to my children or their children, and for that matter, Frances' children. I have said so to her. She spoke about adopting a child. I could not bear the thought, although I did not say so to her. I could not have somebody else's child and pretend that it is my own. Then, what is more, there is the question of my changed circumstances. I could not expect her to come and live here. Please don't misunderstand me. I am enormously grateful to you for having bought this farm. It is what I wanted, and still want. It is just that I will have to make the farm a success first, make it more than it is now, before I could think of having a wife, especially Frances, considering her background and the wealth and luxury that she is accustomed to, also considering the social standing of the Roses. Believe me she would come and live here tomorrow if I let her – she has said as much. She is enough of a romantic to think that she could make anything work."

"She is a woman of character, Douglas. People like that have an inner power to alter circumstances."

"I am sure you are right Dad, but I think it would be a mistake to bring her here now."

"You will never find another companion like Frances. If you pull asunder what destiny has ordained, you do it at your peril. Just think how she came to Oudtshoorn to see you when she received your news. I have witnessed how much she loves you. A woman's love is a miraculous thing, Douglas. Men cannot understand it. It is a purer form of love than the love we are able to give. It is unconditional. Our love is always conditional. It always has something attached to it. We always expect some form of counter performance. Women are not like that. They are unselfish creatures. Their loyalty is boundless. Don't throw that away. If you push Frances aside, for whatever reason, you will damage her irreparably. Don't do anything in haste. You have been here for one night. Let some time pass, start developing the farm. You will have much time to contemplate. The best time to contemplate is while you work."

"Destiny has not exactly been kind to me."

"I know, but who knows what it still has in store for you. It may be taking your hearing from you but it has given you a woman of extraordinary quality who will inspire and assist you to reach great heights."

"There are social differences, Dad, and we all know that. Even in the most ideal circumstances it is difficult to cope with social differences. In my circumstances it has become impossible."

"Yes there are differences, but they are not important. If there were differences of social class it would have been another matter. But there are not. We may come from different backgrounds but our people, both from my side of the family and from your mother's side, were prominent in society. There may be language differences, or little differences of social custom, or even different political views, but not of social class. We have read the same literature, studied the same subjects at university, played the same sports. We might eat different food, but then the Dutch and the English eat different food. And let me tell you something Douglas, you are more learned, better read, and in that sense better educated than Judge Rose. He may know the law, but he is not a particularly well-read man, and as for Mrs Rose, I don't think she has read a really serious piece of literature in her life. She has breeding all right, and that allows her to cope socially and have confidence, and she is a really very nice person, but there is no reason for us to stand back. The Judge and his wife may have travelled a lot but if you listen to their descriptions of their travels, they are quite shallow really. People like the Roses – Frances is a refreshing exception – have an inbred knack to give the appearance of social superiority. English boys acquire the skill at an early age and it is silently nurtured at their public schools, it is a form of social armour designed to conceal what they really are. But, if you strip away the veneer of pretence you will find little substance. We must not let the tragedy of what is happening to you be influenced by the Roses, Douglas. Ignore the Judge's feelings, and the way he is behaving because you have decided not to take the newspaper position. Don't let him dominate. If you allow him to, he will dominate, and he will not respect you. Be your own man. Let Frances' love for you be your first consideration. If she wants to come and live here, and help you, let her. Don't squander the opportunity to spend your life with the one person who recognises your potential better than anyone else. Could I have some more tea, please?" Van Yssen sipped his tea and looked across the valley below. "I will speak to Garnett this afternoon. If he cannot come and see to the *rooikat*, I will ask Grady for the use of a shotgun, or a rifle and come and shoot it myself. We might have to set a trap for the animal. But we will have to kill it soon. I have been thinking about our plans here. You should concentrate on the sheep. We can acquire some more sheep and purchase a really good ram to improve the herd. And concentrate on lucerne production. I have thought of tobacco, but it is finicky and it may not be hot enough up here. The cow is coming tomorrow. There is more than enough grazing. There are lots of things we can do. We can purchase a pump to get water from the river onto the higher areas. We could even consider getting a lighting plant. You mentioned melonitis: experiment with a small patch. And we'll get a tractor, but it will have to be a second hand one. So have faith, work hard, plan carefully and we could make a success of our venture."

"I really appreciate this discussion, Dad, and all you are doing for me, I really do. I wonder whether I could please ask you a favour? I found it difficult last night to read by the light of the oil lamp, and I wondered whether it would be possible for us to get a pressure lamp with a mantle."

"I have seen Swedish Aladdin lamps at Prince Vintcent, I'll get one. We should have thought of that, my boy. I ought to get going. I'll speak to Garnett. We'll come out here again over the weekend, your mother and I. If there's anything you desperately need, ask the shop to let us know."

The week went by without unusual events. The chicken coop was completed, another lamb was lost, the cow arrived and Willemse showed Douglas how to milk it in the barn. Van der Byl introduced Douglas to a neighbour, Mr Ellis. Ellis found Douglas a young coloured labourer named Gert and a maid named Martie, who was the sister of the woman who worked for the Ellises. The maid was quiet and energetic, and industriously cleaned and washed and polished and dusted with an ostrich feather duster; and baked bread and filled the lamps with oil without having to be told.

The weather improved, the oak tree started getting its first new leaves. They started with the construction of a sheep dip. Douglas found great relief in physical work. At night he was pleasantly tired and after reading by the fireside went to bed early. There was fresh milk each day. The chickens laid sufficient eggs. The almond trees from Britz were delivered by railway truck and Gert and Douglas planted them according to the written instructions contained in a large window envelope that accompanied the consignment; all twenty-four of them in a straight line along the border of the field below the house. The holes, the instructions said, had to be square so that the roots could penetrate the corners and not go round and round, and diluted kraal manure was to be added.

Saturday 15 September 1928

Douglas became accustomed to having the doors and the windows open and ceased to lock up at night. When the van Yssens arrived on the farm in the afternoon, accompanied by Garnett, they found the whole house standing wide open and Douglas fast asleep face down on his bed, his feet, still in their boots, dangling over the edge. His shirtsleeves were rolled up, his forearms brown. His braces had slipped from his shoulders. His father beckoned to Garnett to have a look at Douglas, and his mother put her hand over her mouth in amusement. Garnett chuckled and shook his head.

"Let him sleep for a while, he seems exhausted," his mother suggested.

"I'll go and fetch the things from the car," van Yssen said.

Garnett had brought a twelve-bore shotgun and a box of Eley smokeless cartridges containing buckshot, and a kit for cleaning the gun. "I'll show him how to use this a little later."

"He has done some shooting," his father replied.

Mrs van Yssen made coffee and van Yssen unpacked the pressure lamp. He put paraffin into it, tied the mantle on, filled the receptacle below the mantle with methylated spirits from a small copper can with a curved spout and set it alight so that the pipe leading to the mantle could heat up sufficiently to turn the paraffin into gas. The mantle turned to ash. He pumped the lamp just before the methylated spirits gave out. The mantle turned bright white and emitted enough light to illuminate the kitchen. "There we go!" He was pleased with himself. "Douglas will enjoy this, he'll just have to be careful not to bump the lamp."

"I feel we should wake him," Mrs van Yssen prompted.

"I'll go and see to him,' his father said.

Mrs van Yssen and Garnett were in the dining room when Douglas staggered in, yawning and stretching himself and looking wild. "Hello everybody. Sorry about this. Had a tough week."

"The house is spick and span," Mrs van Yssen said as she got up to kiss him.

"Ja, the place looks good, Douglas." His father said.

"And you, Garnie! It's really good to see you. I'm still confused from sleeping. Give me a few moments, I need to wash my face." Douglas disappeared.

"Don't you think he's looking well, Garnett?" Mrs van Yssen asked, when Douglas was gone.

"He's a different person, Mrs van Yssen, completely different. And for the better."

When Douglas returned there were spots of water on his khaki shirt and the front of his trousers. His hands were still wet between the fingers. He sat down at the dining room table and grinned sheepishly.

"Your father tells me that you have had some trouble with a caracal, Douglas," Garnett said.

"You'll have to talk a little louder, Garnie. Ja, we're having trouble with the *rooikat*. It has killed three of our lambs."

"I have brought a shotgun and cartridges. When we've had tea we can do a bit of practice shooting. Caracal are nocturnal. You might have to wait for the cat at night and catch it in the light of a torch. Or put some bait out, or even tie a lamb up outside the kraal."

"I noticed that everything is most tidy, my boy."

"I have a labourer, Dad."

"That is good." Van Yssen nodded approval.

"We'll take a walk a bit later, Garnie. It's quite pleasant down at the river."

"I brought a pressure lamp, Douglas. I lit it in the kitchen. I'll show you how to light it before we go," van Yssen said.

"Is the maid, what is her name, Douglas, is she able to wash and iron?" Mrs van Yssen asked.

"Absolutely, Ma. She even bakes bread. She's a real find."

"What is her name?" Mrs van Yssen asked.

"Martie. My labourer is called Gert."

"Where do they live?" van Yssen asked.

"In cottages on the other side of Ellis' farm. Even though he has so little he is generous to others."

"And your man Gert?" His father enquired.

"He is remarkably energetic and has endless stamina. He can dig for hours. He has not an ounce of fat on him. He's like a whippet. It makes me realise how soft I am. We work together, and at night I am so sore and stiff that I can hardly move. But I must say that the combination of physical activity and my books at night is the best thing I could have hoped for. The weather has been good, and the days are getting longer. It is quite inspiring to see things waking up after the winter."

"Shall we go and fire a few shots then, Douglas?" Garnett asked.

"Ja, that's a good idea. Heaven knows how I am going to find the *rooikat*."

Van Yssen was pensive. "I would like to take a walk around. I would like to thank Willemse for his good work with the sheep. It's a never-ending job, really. We should consider increasing his wages."

When his parents and Garnett had left Douglas went about the farm. Willemse was milking the cow in the barn. "I see Mister has arranged for the shotgun to come. Now we'll be able to shoot that rubbish." Willemse looked past the side of the cow. "We'll just have to have a good plan."

Douglas fed the chickens and made sure the door of the coop was secure. The weather had begun to change. Clouds were coming in from the southwest and the wind increased in strength. He closed the shutters of the house and made sure that the windows were shut before he carried firewood into the kitchen and the living room. It is nice to have proper light. Imagine a lighting plant. He looked forward to the chicken pie his mother had brought. There was no need to heat it. Tomorrow is Sunday. Have a good rest. Perhaps walk over to the Ellises later in the morning. Ask him about pumping water from the river. The previous owners were quite clever getting water to the house. Just a little weir further up and a two-inch copper pipe to the tank. Don't know what one would do if the river ever dried up. You'd be finished. He made a fire in the living room and lit the new lamp in the kitchen and carried it to the living room. The light transformed the room. The gloom of previous evenings was gone. His afternoon sleep had done him good. He felt energetic. He reviewed the happenings of the past week.

Sunday 23 September 1928

Douglas woke early. He lay and looked at the patterns of light on the ceiling made by the louvres of his shutters. The week had gone well. He had spent three nights with Willemse, waiting for the caracal, to no avail. Garnett was coming to visit today. So the message at the shop had said. He would be there for breakfast. Douglas got up and went to the kitchen to light the stove. He opened the kitchen shutters. He was about to enter the kitchen when he saw Willemse rushing towards the house, beckoning to him. "Come, mister, come, my dog has chased the caracal up the tree. He is sitting there now. Bring the gun."

Still in his pajamas, Douglas ran to his room and took the shotgun from his cupboard. He put on his dressing gown, shoved his bare feet into his boots, took some cartridges, put them in his pocket and ran after Willemse. The caracal was high up in the swaying branches of a Cape ash. Its defiant eyes were bright yellow. Douglas hesitated. The animal was larger than he had imagined. It was beautiful. The tips of its ears had long tufts. He lowered the gun.

"Mister must shoot. Shoot!" Willemse urged. "The creature has caused us a lot of damage."

Douglas opened the breech and put in two cartridges. He took aim while the cat watched him. 'Squeeze the trigger,' Garnett had said. The shot went off. The cat was gone, falling through the branches of the tree.

"Watch him, Mister!"

Douglas had hit the hindquarters of the caracal. Bloody and badly injured as it was, it tried to crawl away, making an unearthly howling noise and looking resentfully at the two men. "It is a female, shoot her again," Willemse shouted in a high-pitched voice.

Douglas took aim close up and shot the caracal's head off. What was left of it lay still. Willemse clapped his hands with glee. "That's good. It looks as if she had young." He pointed at her teats. "I'll have to go and find them." A piece of ear, its tuft still intact, lay next to the caracal. Douglas nodded and walked back to the house. And this on a Sabbath morning. High up in the valley a raptor soared in pure blue early morning mountain air. He went to the kitchen and lit the stove so that he could warm water for his bath. He boiled water on his Primus for coffee. He would cook the eggs and bacon when Garnett arrived. That's why she was killing the lambs: to feed herself and her young.

When Garnett arrived Douglas had opened the house and was tying his bootlaces on the veranda. It was a bright sunny day. Faces of the mountain glistened from recent rain. Spring flowers turned their faces towards the sun. Douglas had not heard him arrive and Garnett observed his friend as he stood with his one foot on the edge of a chair. He had grown leaner and looked stronger. Garnett's movement caught Douglas' eye.

"Garnie! I shot the *rooikat* this morning! Wow, it was quite a business!"

Garnett walked up to him and shook his hand and patted him on the shoulder.

"Fantastic, well done. Tell me about it."

"Let's go to the kitchen. I'll tell you while I make our breakfast."

Douglas put more wood into the stove and took a frying pan from its hook above the fireplace. He cracked six eggs and emptied them into a cream coloured earthenware bowl. He put bacon into the pan. "Have some coffee Garnie."

The aroma of fresh coffee mixed with that of the frying bacon. "It is pleasant here," Garnett remarked.

"Not bad."

"Now tell me about the cat."

Douglas recounted the story. "And Willemse is now determined to go and find the young."

"I wonder where he's going to start looking."

"Shall we go and eat in the dining room?"

"That would be a civilised thing to do."

Douglas removed unopened mail from the dining room table, tossed the mail onto a chair standing in the one corner of the room and spread a brightly coloured blue and yellow and red and green floral tablecloth over the table. Early morning sunlight made the room cheerful. He laid knives and forks and side plates. He brought a wooden breadboard from the pantry and freshly baked bread. He put jams into jars and took jam spoons from the sideboard drawer, and a butter knife.

"I'm most impressed, Douglas."

"Something my dad drummed into me, Garnie. Always keep the standards up, no matter where you are. For your own self respect, not for others. Although if you want to impress others, like you for instance, it helps." Douglas laughed loudly.

Garnett's eye fell on the mail. It was the same mail his father had brought to the farm the week before. Sticking out from under some other items was the corner of a letter with a Graaff Reinet postmark. Douglas had made eggs and bacon; he had also fried tomatoes and a generous amount of sausage.

"Please help yourself, Garnett. I'll cut some bread. I know you like the crust."

Both men attacked the food with enthusiasm. Douglas poured more coffee. "You've become very quiet, Garnie?"

"It's none of my business, but you seem to have ignored your post." Garnett glanced in the direction of the mail.

"I've been so preoccupied with things here."

"Even Frances' letter?"

Douglas looked away.

"Is there a problem?"

"I wish you hadn't asked."

"What is the problem?"

"My father and I had a long discussion here the other day, on the Tuesday after I arrived here. I told him that I no longer want to get married."

"What on earth has got into you, Douglas?"

"Nothing."

"That's nonsense."

"What has got into me, Garnie, is that I am going deaf. And it is happening quite rapidly now. If you did not talk as loudly as you obviously do to accommodate me, I would not hear very much."

"What has that got to do with not opening Frances' letter?"

"Everything. My father pleaded with me to reconsider my position, and I have, and I have come to the same conclusion. It is quite simple. I am not prepared to let Frances bear my children in the knowledge that I may pass this cursed affliction on to them or their children. Without this it would have been difficult enough, considering our different backgrounds. But now with this, I realise that it has become impossible. My prospects have changed, Garnett. I am stuck here now, and must make the best of it. You yourself can see how modest my circumstances are. I cannot guarantee any woman a reasonable living here."

"You could have taken the newspaper job."

"No, I could not."

"Why not?"

"First of all the Judge arranged the whole thing. It was rigged. To my dismay I even discovered that there was communication between my father and the Judge. At the time I could not make an issue of it with my dad, although I felt like it I assure you, because I feared that it would harm my efforts to persuade him to buy the farm. In other words I was too cowardly. But I resented the fact that he went behind my back and at the very least encouraged the Judge to get me the newspaper job. By the way, that went on while we were discussing buying this farm. Anyway, I was not prepared to take charity from the Judge. It just felt wrong. Besides, I feared that if I did not succeed at the newspaper, and was living in Cape Town, that it would be the worst of all situations. Rose would have behaved as though I had let him down etcetera, etcetera. It would have been a right royal mess. It would have been the worst kind of embarrassment for me. I was very tempted to take the newspaper job believe me. But to be a leader-writer one has to have ears. You need to know what is going on around you. You need to hear society's whispers. I came to the conclusion some time ago, and I still feel that way, that someone with my kind of disability should make himself as independent of others as possible. People in wheelchairs resent being pushed around by over-eager strangers."

"The Judge is hardly a stranger, Douglas. And he greatly admires you. Mrs Rose adores you, and Frances loves you more than you can imagine. Do you realise what you are throwing away? Do you realise what this will do to Frances?"

"I cannot help it Garnett. Fate has dealt me a bum hand and I now have to play it as best I can."

"I don't believe what I am hearing. You're only thinking of one thing, Douglas. Yourself. Fate may have dealt you a bad card, but not a bad hand. Fate gave you a colossal intellect; fate gave you the best girl imaginable. It dealt you some extraordinarily fine cards, but you focus only on the one."

"I have always lacked a certain decisive element, Garnett. I am decisive about negative things, and yet I am indecisive about positive things. I just want to cut myself off from the world, from everything and everybody. The people that have been part of my life when I could hear need no longer be part of it. Deaf Douglas will make new friends, friends that deaf Douglas deserves." Douglas pursed his lips. His hands trembled. His face was white with emotion.

Garnett scratched an itchy place behind his right ear. "Does Frances have any idea how you feel?"

"I think she has a suspicion."

"Good God, a suspicion!"

"I have hinted at it. I did not want to hurt her."

"She deserves better than that."

"I know. I don't want to be dishonest with her. She thinks that my behaviour is a function of my shock at going deaf, and that it will pass. She thinks that this is just a temporary phase. I hate myself for letting her labour under that illusion. The poor thing is trying to be so understanding and so accommodating. She thinks there will be a reprieve, when there can be none. God, I hate myself. Today was going to be such a happy day here with you. No emotions. And now, although the sun is shining, this bright room has become dark."

"So what do you plan to do?"

"I must go to Graaff Reinet and tell her."

◆

Chapter Thirty-one

WHEN HIS PARENTS visited Douglas on the last Sunday in September they told him that they had decided to spend a few days at the mineral springs in Montagu and had invited Madame Jacquard to accompany them. The obligation to visit Frances had nagged and troubled him constantly since his conversation with Garnett and the need to act had reached such proportions that he could no longer procrastinate. He prevaricated each time his mother mentioned Frances and the more he equivocated the more insistent his mother's tone became, which put upon him the idea of secretly visiting Frances. The announcement that his parents would be going away, made him decide to use the opportunity of their absence to go to Graaff Reinet. When he asked when they would be going his father said that they would be leaving on Thursday the eleventh, and returning on Monday the fifteenth of October.

Saturday 13 October 1928

Douglas hardly slept all night. At five o'clock he got up and warmed water for his bath. The night before he had taken his blue-green tweed jacket from his cupboard, a cream Viyella shirt, a tartan tie, his grey flannels, socks, and had polished his brown brogues. Once he was dressed he made himself coffee and buttered two slices of bread. Van der Byl went into town each Saturday morning and had agreed to take him to the station – even though it meant leaving earlier than usual. How he was going to get back to the farm he did not know, unless he put his bicycle on the back of the truck and left it somewhere in town. Or Garnett could give him a lift back. He went to the dining room to have his coffee and bread. Frances' letter lay on the sideboard, still unopened. He took it and put it into his shirt pocket, to read it along the way. He took it from his shirt pocket and looked at the postmark: Thursday September 6. The day before the start of the last school holidays. He had not gone to the station to see her. To atone for his omission he should now open the letter. He looked at her handwriting. How he had looked forward to her letters. How the patterns of her handwriting had enchanted him. Her face, her fair hair, her green eyes, her lovely eyes, all that she is was captured in her handwriting. It has so much character. Would he be able to smell her if he opened the envelope? While he remembered his memories he opened her letter.

Thursday 6 September 1928

My dearest Douglas,
Tomorrow is the end of term. You must be close to moving to your farm. I

have decided not to go home for the school holidays, so there will be no need for you to interrupt your preparations to come and see me at the station. I am missing you terribly, and I constantly think of you. When I am in class, teaching, the words that I use are your words. The subject matter conjures up associations of you, of us. The irregular Latin verbs make me think of your clever ways of remembering exceptions. As you know, I am doing The Mill on the Floss with the standard nines.

The descriptions of country people make we wonder what it is like on your farm. When Maggie speaks of her feelings for Philip Wakem, I compare my feelings for you. Every moment produces an association that reminds me of you. You have changed my life forever. My spirit can never be separate from yours, no matter what happens. When I came to understand that, I realised that time has become irrelevant. Knowing that I can never really be separate from you gives me extraordinary freedom. I am free because I no longer have a choice, which brings me to the purpose of writing to you.

I have come to terms with the nature of your condition. It was a great shock to me when I received the news that your deafness had not been cured in London. Until then I had every faith that my prayers would be answered. I now realise that God does not necessarily single us out for special treatment; we cannot expect Him to respond to our individual requests. I also realise that He, in His flawless way, creates challenges for us. Difficulties are part of our world. How we deal with them is what matters. At first I was angry because of what has happened but came to understand that there is no point in that. I realised that it would be better to use the energy that I expended being angry to try and make things better.

I want you to know, my love that I will give you as much time as you need to come to terms with your new circumstances. I will give you the freedom to decide in your own good time what our future should be. I realise that it was wrong of Daddy to try and influence you to take the position on the newspaper. How I am going to deal with my parents, especially Daddy, is a different matter, and that is why I decided to stay here for the holidays, on the pretext of having so much preparation to do before the start of the last term. You must please try to understand Daddy. He has been so proud of your achievements, and has spoken so much of your great ability to all our friends, that he now fears that he may have to save face. And that is not easy for him. His pride has always been a dreadful obstacle. Mummy will be bitterly disappointed if there is to be an extended engagement, but if that is how it must be, she will come to accept it.

The real point I want to make is that I feel as though we are linked in a way that makes temporal issues irrelevant. I fully understand that you need time to adapt to your new career; after all it is quite different from *what you anticipated. I fully support what you are doing. Upon mature reflection, it makes a great deal of sense. Please write to me and tell me all that is happening, what you are doing, what the farm is like, what your house is like, everything, please. I would like to come and visit you at some stage, perhaps at the start of the December holidays? We could ask your delightful Mrs Jacquard to be our chaperone!*

Please know that I love you with all my heart and that I will wait patiently for you to decide our future.

Lots and lots of love
Frances.

Douglas was numb. He groped for the ear of his coffee cup. The coffee was cold. He looked at his watch. Van der Byl would be getting ready to leave. He ran to his room, collected his Gladstone bag, shut the house and hurried along the road to the shop. Van der Byl was waiting for him next to a cheeky looking bright yellow Essex Terraplane pick-up truck. "I thought you had over-slept."

"No, not at all. I aplogise for being late."

The truck was noisy and conversation was impossible. Empty wooden crates clattered on the back. It was the first time Douglas had gone to Oudtshoorn since moving to the farm. The features of the landscape seemed different now. He turned to look at his mountain. It was a clear day except for wisps of mist in some of the valleys. Willemse would look after everything and Gert had promised to help to keep an eye. He had hidden the shotgun in the ceiling of the pantry and made sure that there were no marks to show that he had opened the trapdoor. The blossoms on the fruit trees had vanished. Poplar trees on the banks of the Kandelaars River were dark green. Their leaves trembled in light early morning breezes. Douglas felt quite sad at leaving his house, and his things, up there on the slope of the mountain. The almond trees were looking good. One of these days they would be able to start selling a few lambs, and generate income. That would be good. Van der Byl had spoken of someone who wanted to buy lucerne. Willemse had not found the young of the caracal. He thought of Frances' letter. It would be wrong to go to Graaff Reinet. It would be better to write to her. He noticed that his trousers were creased just above the knees. They must have slid to one side of the hanger.

The journey to Oudtshoorn seemed brief. It felt to Douglas as though he had been away from Oudtshoorn for a long time. Early summer had transformed the trees and vegetation into lush green. There was hardly anyone about. He saw Mr Bailey taking his dachshund for a walk and avoided making eye contact with him. He patted the bag on his lap. Van der Byl turned into George Road and headed for the station. Douglas looked at his watch. It was just half past seven. The train was only due to leave after nine. Van der Byl stopped his pickup outside the main entrance to the station and turned the engine off. "Will you manage now?"

Douglas nodded. "Thank you very much for the lift Mr van der Byl. I appreciate it."

"See you back at the farm."

Douglas stood and waited for van der Byl to depart and waved goodbye to him. He had decided to have a cup of coffee in the waiting room before walking back to town to see if he could find Garnett. In any case Garnett would still be at the hospital now. He would not wait for the train to arrive; there was no point in that. He had a second cup of coffee and a sickeningly sweet koeksister, paid the waitress in her black dress and small white apron and studied her figure and her legs as she walked away. Not bad. He felt a bit nauseous when he got up. Not having had proper breakfast, or the fumes from the pickup, or perhaps the koeksister? Should rather have had a sausage roll. He picked up his bag and started the long walk to town. It would have been dreadful for Frances if he had turned up in Graaff Reinet. Whatever could have possessed him to think of that? A moment of madness. What a shock it would have been for her: first the surprise at seeing him, then the embarrassment of a broken engagement. How could he have thought of that? How could he have imagined that it would be the noble thing to do to face her? What an aberration. He must have been insane. Maybe his ear thing had gone into his brain. If his judgement could have been so misguided it was just as well that he did not take the newspaper job. It was a good thing that the weather was cool. He did not need to take his jacket off. The thick sweet scent of a pittosporum hedge transported him back to their house. If he could not find Garnett he could always go to Madame Jacquard. But she had gone with his parents. She was an attractive woman. He liked the way she walked, and the loose movements of her buttocks under her dress. He saw her tit at Plettenberg Bay when she washed her hair at the back of the house and had loosened the top of her bathing costume. All that sunlight and hard work on the farm makes one randy. Too many eggs can also make you randy. He nearly walked into a pepper tree that leant towards the pavement. It would be a good idea to go to Prince Vintcent, to see what they have there. There was no need to be furtive anymore. He'll just say that he had the opportunity to get a lift with van der Byl. He'll tell Garnett the truth though.

The door to Garnett's surgery was open. He put his head inside. Sister de Wet was polishing the wooden table. He knocked and smiled at her.

Her lips said, "Why is Mr van Yssen here so early?"

"Good moring, when will Doctor be here?"

She looked at her little upside-down watch attached to the chest part of her white uniform. "He's at the hospital, operating. Probably only about ten thirty."

Douglas scratched his head.

"It is rather strange that Mr van Yssen should arrive here now, because I heard Doctor say only yesterday that he was going to visit you on the farm tomorrow."

Douglas only caught snatches of what she said. "Please tell Doctor that I am in town and that I would very much like to see him before I go back to the farm. In the meantime I'll wander down to the shops and drop in again after half past ten."

The idea of a secret visit to Frances had embedded itself so firmly in Douglas' mind that he still felt quite furtive when he walked towards Prince Vintcent. Going past the dressed sandstone building that housed the Magistrate's Court aroused a sense of guilt for deceiving his parents and when he got to the door of the police station he entertained the thought of being arrested for having salacious thoughts about Madame Jacquard. He had not hung her paintings up yet. How could Dostoevsky have known so much about guilt? He was startled by a tap on his shoulder. He turned to find Hugo Pocock standing next to him.

"Hello, Douglas." Pocock smiled amicably. "Good to see you. How are things on the farm?"

"Hello Hugo. Everything's fine, thank you. Yes, fine, just fine. But it's early days. We have lots of plans. It all costs money you know."

"Come to see your parents?"

"No, well actually, they have gone away to Montagu for a few days. I unexpectedly managed to get a lift into town, so I thought I would use the opportunity, get back to civilisation, see the bright lights, see what the shops have to offer. I am in fact on my way next door. I want to look at their lamps and I want to see if they have a spring-trap. We're having a problem with caracal and jackals."

"Best thing to do with jackals is to poison them. Don't mess around with traps. You still have to shoot them when you catch them. I think you people made a good buy with that little farm."

"We also think so. And we owe you a great deal of thanks for assisting us."

"I did nothing really. Anyway, good luck, I must be going now." Pocock shook Douglas' hand vigorously and disappeared into his rooms.

Douglas wandered into the Church Street entrance of Prince Vintcent, his Gladstone bag in his hand. He was a bit peckish. He reminded himself that he liked coming to the department store. He liked the scent of newly unpacked things. He noticed Mr Schmidt the owner, dressed in a dark pin-striped Saturday-morning suit, a white shirt and a yellow child welfare rose pinned to his lapel, conscientiously and energetically inspecting various departments, looking here and there, directing his shop assistants to display merchandise in the most tempting way, rearranging this and that. Schmidt the Industrious, who had started work in the store as a messenger and now owned it, greeted Douglas hurriedly, shunned his eyes, and moved his shoulders about uncomfortably as if to say that it was an inconvenient time and that it was all very well for Douglas to saunter about early in the morning, but he, being as conscientious as he was, had no time to make idle chatter on a busy Saturday morning. He went from Haberdashery to Ladies Clothing, to Hairdressing to

Men's Outfitting, to Furniture, to Crockery and Cutlery, to Hardware, from Glassware to Materials. He went outside to make sure that the window displays were as they should be and straightened his tie when he caught his reflection in a bevelled glass window. Recurring thoughts of Madame Jacquard's buttocks enticed Douglas towards the women's clothing department – a month on the farm, deprived of the sight of women, made him seek the wonder of feminine things. He pretended that he was looking for someone. A young woman behind the haberdashery counter smiled at him. She was well built, athletic, some would say. She wore a pink and turquoise blue dropped waist dress of cotton foulard that fitted closely. He could tell that she had good legs from the way she stood. She had dark hair and a fair skin, and clear dark blue eyes. He saw her mouth moving. He put his hand behind his right ear and leant forward. "You are Mrs van Yssen's son," she said. He smelled her perfume. "I am glad to make your acquaintance," she said.

"How do you do," Douglas replied.

"Oh, I'm all right, thanks. My name is Maggie Thompson. I work here."

Douglas smiled and nodded as though she was a new pupil in his class. He held out his hand. "Oh my!" she giggled. She shook his hand reticently. Her hand was warm and soft.

Mr Schmidt walked over to them. "Can we help with anything, Douglas? I apologise for not giving you the attention earlier. This is an important time on a Saturday."

"I would like to look at the lamps, Mr Schmidt."

"Well, you know where they are, my boy." He turned to Maggie Thompson. "It appears Mrs Dease needs some attention, Miss Thompson. Come let me take you to Hardware, Douglas."

"Good morning, Mrs Dease," Douglas smiled at her.

"Hello, Douglas. Fancy meeting you here. Your parents have gone away, haven't they?"

"Yes, to Montagu."

"I am sure they will enjoy that. I am told it is quite therapeutic."

"I don't recall seeing Miss Thompson here before," Douglas said to Schmidt as they walked towards the hardware department.

"They are new in town. People from Natal. Father's a builder, bit of a vagabond from all accounts. Puts his daughter and his wife out to work. Rough fellow by all accounts."

"She seems like a nice person."

"Time will tell, my boy. I can bet you she does not know what therapeutic means. It is hard to get good employees these days. How are you getting on, on the farm?"

"Fine, thank you. It is still early days."

"All days are the same Douglas. The effort at the beginning has to be the same as at the end. Run the farm like a business, my boy, like a business. Here are the lamps. Now please excuse me."

Douglas ambled about in the hardware department and looked at the assortment of lamps. There was no doubt that his father had bought the best. He looked at his watch. It was nearly half past nine. Breakfast at the Waldorf would not be a bad idea. He strolled into Church Street. As he passed the door to the haberdashery department he glanced inside. Maggie made a small tentative movement with her hand, fearful that Mr Schmidt would see. He waved back at her. Poor thing. At the Waldorf he chose a window table to observe the passing Saturday morning parade, bought a copy of the *Oudtshoorn Courant* and settled down contentedly while his breakfast was prepared. It was strange to sit here and eat when his home was just on the other side of the river.

When Douglas arrived at Garnett's rooms at a quarter to eleven, there was only one patient in the waiting room. Douglas sat down and nodded his greeting. The woman looked familiar but he could not place her. Douglas' eyes followed the woman as she left but he still could not place her. When he turned his head Garnett was standing in the door in his white coat. He shook his head playfully and beckoned Douglas to come inside. "Do sit down," he said, "I must wash my hands."

Sister de Wet brought a tray of tea and some biscuits and closed the door firmly behind her.

"What on earth are you doing here in town, Douglas?"

"I was on my way to Graaff Reinet."

"Are you saying my rooms are on the way to Graaff Reinet?" Garnett spoke quite loudly.

"Not quite. As I told you, I could not let things carry on the way they were, and decided that I should go and see Frances. I don't want my parents to know, and when they told me that they were going to Montagu for a few days I thought I would sneak away to see Frances. But my courage failed me. Besides I thought that it would be terrible for her if I arrived there, unannounced, and broke off the engagement. Imagine the embarrassment."

Garnett sighed. "I hoped and prayed that you would change your mind. Please don't be in a hurry. Give it some time. Don't act in haste. Drink your tea, it is getting cold. How did you get into town?"

"Van der Byl gave me a lift. I had made up my mind to go to Graaff Reinet. In fact this morning I was still going. Then I read Frances' letter. I had not opened it. It was just as well I did. I want you to read it." Douglas took the letter from his inside pocket and handed it to Garnett."

"I would rather not. It is a private matter."

"You are my friend Garnett, you are my doctor. Please read it."

Garnett looked at the letter that lay before him. He had not seen Frances' handwriting before. It had so much character. If it would improve things he should read it. If it could buy time he would read it. If it would lead to dialogue that would change Douglas' mind he should read it. "Why do you want me to read it, Douglas?"

"So that you will understand why I could not go to Graaff Reinet."
"Is it important for me to understand that?"
"Yes."

Garnett removed the letter from its envelope and unfolded it. He moved about uncomfortably and made his chair creak. Douglas watched, vigilant for any response. Garnett read the letter slowly for a second time. When he finally put it down he blinked hard to stop his tears. He drank some cold tea. He fiddled with his one ear. He got up and walked about the room, his hands behind his back. "So when you read this you decided not to go?"

"I beg your pardon?"

"I said, and when you read this you decided not to go?"

"Yes. But I had already made arrangements with van der Byl, and he was going especially early so I couldn't let him down. He dropped me at the station and I walked here. I had breakfast at the Waldorf. Bertie Hurford and David Rivett saw me through the window and came to say hello. I saw Mr and Mrs Hops. I had a little chat to Hugo Pocock at Prince Vintcent. He said we made a good purchase with the farm. It is good to be in town. One or two of my pupils said hello. It was quite nice."

"Aren't we avoiding the real issue, Douglas?"

"In some ways it has been settled, if you read between the lines."

"In what way has it been settled?"

"It is clear to me that Frances does not want any further immediate action. That's why I did not go. It has given me more time. She has moved the issue of our future from a temporal level to something much more abstract. Our relationship now has a new dimension that allows it to function in a new reality. I was thinking about it when I walked from the station and realised what she was saying: we are now two spirits that are joined together, not two people. Time has ceased to have the significance it had before. Don't you see it? It is such an elegant solution. I have to give the female intuition the credit for being so creative."

Garnett sat in silence, his chin on his one hand and shook his head slightly as though he was disagreeing with himself. "How are you getting back to the farm?"

"I'll have to find a lift, or walk. But don't you agree with me? I mean about the letter?"

"I'll have to think about it. I was planning to come and see you tomorrow. I could cancel my tennis this afternoon and take you home. Perhaps stay the night. Or we could go after tennis. Why don't you join us?"

"Hell, I couldn't do that. No, I don't have any kit. I'll go to the library while you're at tennis. I would be most grateful for a lift, and it would be really good if you could stay over."

Garnett fetched Douglas from the library at five. He had bathed and shaved and packed some things for the night and smelled of shaving cream. He wore his brown corduroy hunting jacket with leather trimmings and leather on the elbows. "Don't you need any supplies, Douglas?"

"No thanks, I have everything. Plenty of milk, eggs. We can have some ribs and sausage for supper, if that's all right with you? The shop has most things anyway."

It was still quite light when they got to the farm. Willemse was surprised to see them when they walked into the barn where he was sitting on his little stool, milking the cow. He got up and stood about uncomfortably, not knowing what to say in front of Garnett.

"I hear you got rid of the caracal?"

"Yes, Mister shot her dead good and proper. It is now just the jackals that are bothering us."

"I am glad to see things are going well," Douglas said.

"They must go well."

"I must say it is really pleasant here," Garnett observed as they walked back to the house.

"We'll make a fire later on."

"Is it cold enough?"

"It will suddenly get cold up here, later on."

Douglas lit the new lamp and then the stove and Garnett helped him to make their supper. The aroma of the food cooking made Douglas realise that he had not had any lunch. He offered Garnett some bread and butter. They ate their supper in the dining room and after washing the dishes Douglas carried more firewood into the living room. He went down on all fours and made the fire while Garnett watched. He had become quite adept at it. They sat on either side of the fireplace and watched the flames. "I have cheese and watermelon preserve."

"That sounds like an excellent idea. And some tea. I'm a bit thirsty from the tennis."

"I find the salt ribs make me thirsty."

Douglas went to the kitchen. Garnett looked around. Madame Jacquard's paintings still stood against one wall. A book lay open on the table. He could not see what it was. There was ash on the tiles in front of the fireplace. The room was cosy with the shutters closed and the curtains drawn. The fire roared. The old people really knew how to design a fireplace. There was something sterile about the room. The carpet was nice enough. It would look better with the paintings. He felt pleasantly weary. Turn in early. Not start any discussion now.

Douglas returned with a tray. "Please help yourself, Garnett."

"Do you think I could have a slice of bread, please?"

"Of course. You've been quiet about what we discussed this morning. I nearly said 'yesterday.' It feels as though I have been away for days."

"Let me sleep on it. I can't think clearly now. I am just relaxing a little.

Have had a tough week. There is so much to learn. I just hope it is not at the expense of my patients. I delivered a lovely baby last night. A little boy. Obstetrics is something I enjoy. To see new life coming into this world.

"When we were at Plettenberg Bay you said you would explain to me some of the workings of the human body. You know, to do with reproduction. I have often wondered whether women really enjoy the physical aspects of their relationships with men. You intimated that they do."

Garnett chortled mischievously. "Douglas, let me ask you, if your ear itches and if you push your pinky into your ear to scratch it, which has the most enjoyment? Your pinky or your ear?" He burst out laughing.

Douglas bellowed so loudly with laughter that Garnett could feel the vibrations of his voice.

"I mean women even have a masturbation problem."

"What! You can't be serious."

"I'm quite serious. I promise you. I was reading a Lancet article about treating masturbation in young women only recently, after a young girl of about nineteen, was brought to me for treatment. I must say that I don't have profoundly strong feelings about the matter, but the habit appeared to produce strong feelings of guilt in the patient, and the idea that she was committing a heinous sin, but she could not stop herself. Goodness knows how her mother found out. Having said that, there are some encouraging signs in the modern psychological attitude towards masturbation to see it not as a sin but purely as retarded development."

"How do they suggest it be treated?"

"Ag, all sorts of ways: relieving constipation, cold morning plunges, exhilarating walks, avoiding enervating atmospheres, moral as well as material. The article said that many women have found that intellectual work that had not proceeded smoothly was apt to provoke sexual feelings. Many authorities advocate manual outdoor labour. I cannot help feeling that the harmfulness of masturbation is grossly exaggerated, and I wonder whether the so-called treatment offered by wrong individuals cannot do more harm than good. What I found quite amusing in the article was the suggestion that marriage is not a solution for the simple reason that some women receive greater satisfaction from masturbation than from normal intercourse. It doesn't say much for the men, does it? Ag, and then the article goes on and on about duties towards society and injuriousness of the habit in a social sense, and so on and so forth. Quite frankly I would rather practise surgery and deliver lovely babies than to become involved in what are really silly psychological matters."

"It is absolutely amazing. Females are not that different from us I guess."

"It is important to know how to give a woman pleasure. If you know what to do they will eat out of your hand."

"Do you know how to do it?"

"In theory, I do."

"I am listening."

"I think you're a bit young for this, Douglas. Perhaps we should leave it for another day. When you're a little older."

"Don't be like that Garnie. Just give me some broad outlines."

"The most important thing is to take your time at the start of things. Don't rush. Tease the woman, I mean physically. Tickle in the right way in the right places. Be romantic. They really like that. You must make her so excited that she can't stop herself. Of course, there are women who are more enthusiastic than others. It has always been so. There are willing horses, in a manner of speaking. And there will always be the cold ones. Don't waste your time on the cold ones; there are more than enough who are enthusiastic."

"Have you heard about new people in town called Thompson?"

Garnett sat up. "What makes you ask that?"

"I was at Prince Vintcent this morning and a girl who works there, called Maggie Thompson, introduced herself to me. She knew I was 'Mrs van Yssen's son.' I don't recall seeing her before. She was behind the haberdashery counter."

"They are recent arrivals. What made you think of the girl, now?"

"She was quite fetching in a physical sort of way. Not that it is of any real interest to me. It is just interesting how some women can give you a wee twitch in the nether regions. Old Schmidt was quick to lead me away from temptation and made disparaging remarks about the family. Said her old man is a bit of a drifter."

"Schmidt is no angel, from all accounts. Maybe he is saving the bit of meat for himself. To have in the storeroom after hours."

"That never occurred to me, but you could be right."

"I think I should turn in, if you don't mind. We have lots to talk about tomorrow. I would be interested to know all that's happening out here."

"I was going to write to Frances, but I think I'll also go to bed now. I'll write to her in the next day or two. There are candles and matches in your room. I've put some spare blankets on the chair."

Sunday 14 October 1928

Garnett was the first to wake. The rest of the world was still asleep. First light approached tentatively, and illuminated the louvres of his shutters. The air in his room was cold. It was warm in bed. He pulled the bedclothes up to his face, turned on his side and put his hands between his knees. He was thankful to have slept well. It must be the mountain air. He was hungry. He thought about Douglas and was suddenly engulfed by such dissonant presentiments that he felt as though he was in a place without dimensions, a vast colourless plain of spiritual desolation. He was uncomfortable and began to perspire. Douglas was disconnecting himself from the conventions that made ordinary life intelligible. He no longer spoke quite the same language as other people. He was establishing his own rules. Why do injustices like this happen; like the injustice that her father handed down? Why does God let such things happen? He does not let it happen. We let it happen, because we become disconnected from Him.

Garnett could not stay in bed with his forebodings. He got up and put on his dressing gown, then his slippers, and went outside through the kitchen not disturb to Douglas. But Douglas was unlikely to hear him anyway. The early morning sky was grey. He wondered who had planted the row of pear trees that stood along the barbed wire fence. He would light the stove so that there could be hot water for a bath. They could do the lamb chops he had brought along. That would be nice.

Douglas shuffled into the kitchen while Garnett was busy making coffee. The wood in the stove burnt cheerfully and sent heat into the kitchen. Douglas stretched his arms above his head and yawned audibly. "The weather looks fine, Garnie. We should go for a good walk after breakfast."

"That's an excellent idea. I've brought my walking boots. Always have them at the ready for farm visits. I hope you don't mind, I put some water into the tank for a bath."

"I can't hear you."

"I said I am warming some water for a bath, if you don't mind."

"I can't install a geyser unless I have running water."

Garnett nodded. "We should have the chops for breakfast."

"Great idea."

Garnett and Douglas sat on the veranda after breakfast. Willemse trundled up the slope with a bucket of milk and a basket of eggs. He lifted his hat to say good morning and went around the house to the kitchen.

"I like it here," Garnett remarked. "I like it very much. I think you have made the correct decision, Douglas."

"Frances' old man does not think so. I fear I have made an enemy of him."

"It is such a pity."

"What?"

"I said it is such a pity."

Douglas shrugged his shoulders. "Well, the die is cast. There is nothing that I can do about it now. I shall write to Frances tomorrow."

"As I said before, don't do anything in haste."

"I am grateful for the way in which she is accepting what has happened to me. What everyone seems to be missing is that I am also thinking of her future, that I am concerned with her well-being. It is not as though I am pushing her aside out of selfishness. I am not the person that she was going to marry. I am different now."

"She does not see it like that. To her you are the same person. The fact that you are losing your hearing simply means that something has happened to the man she loves. Once her love for you was formed it could not change. In her mind the two of you are bound together. Nothing can ever sever that bond. And she is right. That enables her to come to terms with what has happened.

She does not perceive that you have become blemished. To her nothing can tarnish her affection for you. If there are difficulties she will try to find a way to overcome them. She won't run away from them."

"Are you saying that I am running away from my difficulties?"

"No, I am not saying that."

"But you are surely implying it?"

"Douglas, please understand, I am not implying anything, and I am not trying to say that one of you is right and the other is wrong. All I want is for the two of you to be happy, and I don't want you to squander the opportunity to marry a wonderful girl. It is your great good fortune to have Frances. Don't you see that she can compensate for your difficulty? She will be such an inspiration to you, an inspiration that will make your handicap seem quite insignificant, and allow you to go to great heights. I beg of you, don't throw it all away. Let her make her own choice. Don't choose for her. You say that you do not want to be unfair to her, yet if you choose for her you would be unfair to her."

"I really don't know."

"I realise that you must have had your mind made up when you decided to go to Graaff Reinet yesterday. It is good that you did not go, even if it was for the wrong reasons. Something pulled you from the brink."

Douglas and Garnett hiked along the banks of the Moeras River and up the slopes of the mountain towards Engelseberg. The wind came from the west. It was a clear day. Pink heather swayed in the breeze. Obstinate tall pale green grasses ducked and weaved and struggled to stay upright. On the higher slopes wet platinum coloured rock faces glistened in the morning sun. They stopped at times to admire the views. In the distance, to the north, the Olifants River valley lay in a haze, beyond that the mighty blue-black Swartberg lay motionless under a blanket of white fleece clouds. In swales and hollows sheltered from the wind, the sun released delicious herbal summer fragrances. Garnett's physical exertion made him contemplative. His eye fell on the tiny pink flowers of a branch of heather that shone with numinous clarity and what he saw had such pure meaning that he stopped and looked up.

"It seems you are far away, Garnie," Douglas chuckled.

"Yes, and yet I'm here."

"It's nearly lunch time, I think we should go back."

Garnett left the farm in the late afternoon, in time for his evening hospital rounds.

Tuesday 16 October 1928

Dear Frances
I must apologise for taking such a long time to respond to your letter. I have been extremely busy on the farm. It was neglected for many years and needs to be rehabilitated. The only good thing is that because much

of the ground has lain fallow for a long time it has regained fertility. I have the prospect of making lucerne sales and my sheep are doing well. My father and I are planning to purchase a ram of good quality to improve the herd. I have acquired a cow and my chickens are producing lots of eggs. (I built the chicken coop myself – with some help of course – and realised again how clumsy I am!) I have engaged a young coloured woman servant and a labourer, and the old fellow who came with the farm, Willemse, who is of indeterminate race, is a real pillar of reliability. Having someone to do the house makes a world of difference. She is willing and intelligent and bakes the most delicious bread and only yesterday offered to make me a lamb stew. We have our own meat, and vegetables from the garden, and the flavour of the fresh ingredients is so intense – one forgets what it is like to eat really fresh things when one lives in towns and cities. We have put in almond trees and they have taken well, and promise to produce a lucrative crop in a few years time. I am pleased with that for they are not easy to plant.

Garnett came to visit me on Saturday and stayed over. We hiked in the mountain on Sunday morning. It is quite beautiful up there. My river, the Moeras River, has quite a lot of water. It never ceases to amaze me how water just continues to seep out of the mountain and fill the streams and rivers.

I am grateful that you understand my difficulties. In some ways it is not easy being here on my own. In other ways the solitude is welcome. My father purchased a good lamp that enables me to read more easily at night. I am able to spend the evenings reading and planning my activities on the farm. I have much time to contemplate and it is becoming ever clearer to me that the newspaper position would not have been the right choice. Even though I might have enjoyed it initially, it would not have endured. To be perfectly honest I have had pangs of regret when I imagine the stimulating Cape Town newspaper atmosphere,

I remember the unique smell of the newspaper offices and the printer's ink in the room where the presses were. Wainwright is such an affable man and turning him down was not easy.

Yet I know that I would not have coped. My hearing is deteriorating quite rapidly and at times I have difficulty following conversations. No doubt I shall have to learn to lip read. I am told that some people become quite good at it. Hope I am one of the lucky ones.

However, coming back to your letter, and as I said earlier, I am deeply grateful for your understanding. We shall have to see what the future holds. As I said to you before, I have to think as much about your future as about my own. Please understand that I am not the same person as before. I have spoken about us as travellers through time. I am still such a traveller but my destination has changed. The hopes and the aspirations that I once had of living a normal life are gone. I can never again be normal. My deafness has disfigured my future, and in that sense has disfigured me. You must have no illusions about that. It would be wrong of me to pretend that all will be well, just as before. That would have been an easy way out.

The point you make, when you say that you feel as though we are linked in ways that make the temporal issues irrelevant, is important because it says that our relationship has already become more abstract. How I wish that it could have been different. So much has been taken away from me that I walk about the farm and grieve at my loss. Nothing can be the same as before, and we must face it. How we should proceed from here I cannot tell. Perhaps I should come and see you, but it will be difficult in Graaff Reinet. I have no means of transport other than my bicycle and until such time as I am able to make a sufficient profit here to buy a car, the bicycle will have to do. I do not want to be dependent on others, like Garnett, so perhaps I should arrange to visit you in Cape Town at the end of the year, before you leave for Plettenberg Bay.

Lots of love
Douglas.

Chapter Thirty-Two

Cape Town, Sunday 9 December 1928

THE JUDGE and Mrs Rose waited grim faced on Platform Two for Frances' train to arrive. A fierce south-easterly wind rattled glass panels in the station roof and chased pieces of paper and loose debris and dust along the areas around platforms and the tracks. Frances had written to her mother and told her of her concerns about Douglas, and that she did not hold out much hope that their engagement would continue. Since his suggestion to visit Frances in Cape Town in his letter of October 16, Douglas had not answered any of Frances' letters.

The Judge looked sideways at his wife to see how she was. She glanced at him to make sure that they were not within earshot of anyone, "I can see that you are concerned about Frances, Jeremy, but we must be very careful how we handle this. It is a very difficult time for all of us. Not knowing exactly what is going on makes it harder. We tend to prejudge things in such circumstances, to form conclusions that are written all over our faces. We will need the wisdom of Solomon." The wind carried the sound of the approaching train towards them. Mrs Rose gripped her husband's sleeve. "Please be patient."

He glared at her. "I know what to do, Elizabeth."

The train wheels came to a dry screeching, uneven halt. At first there was no sign of Frances. Then they saw her familiar hand waving to them. She wore no hat. Her blonde hair was longer than when she left. She smiled broadly and disappeared from the window of her compartment.

"She seems quite cheerful," the Judge observed.

"She's trying to make it easier for us, dear."

Frances ran up to her father and hugged him. He held her by the shoulders and looked at her. "My, my, what it is to have such a beautiful woman in my arms. I am so pleased to have you home, my dear."

Frances embraced her mother, and kissed her on her cheek. "Dearest Mummy, how lovely to see you. I cannot wait to be home, in my happy place, in my room. Jolly nasty old summer wind that is blowing."

"The beastly wind has been blowing for five days and nights," her mother replied.

"I saw the cloth over the mountain, from the train."

"Well then, let's gather your goods and chattels and make our way home," the Judge proposed.

Doyle was next to the car when the Roses and the porter arrived with Frances' luggage. "Good morning Miss Frances." He lifted his chauffeur's cap.

"Hello Doyle, you're looking very smart. A new uniform?"

"I am grateful to have a new uniform, Miss Frances."

"I trust you and your family are all well?"

"Yes, we're all fine thank you Miss Frances." Doyle's sympathetic face said that he knew.

"Home James, and don't spare the horses." The Judge's contrived humour served only to charge the atmosphere.

"Have you had breakfast, Frances?" Her mother asked.

"No, I wasn't hungry enough earlier, Mummy, but I must say I am a bit peckish now."

"We'll have a grand breakfast then, shall we!" the Judge exclaimed jovially.

"That sounds lovely, Daddy."

"We have not asked anyone to lunch, Frances," her mother informed her. "We don't want to share you with anyone."

"I am rather tired, I would like to sleep this afternoon. I am looking forward to being at the seaside."

"We all need to get away. Daddy has had a very busy time."

"Did you not say that Joan Peacock was going to be on the train with you, Frances?" Her mother asked.

"She was indeed, but she got off at Paarl to go and see her relatives. I was relieved to see the back of her. She can be quite nosey and nasty at times, well actually most of the time. She really has to make an effort to be pleasant, it does not come naturally."

"She'll pay the price," the Judge said. "She'll end up a frustrated spinster."

Though it was Sunday, both Gladys and Hope were on duty. Doyle carried Frances' luggage from the car to the front door and the maids took it from there.

"If you don't mind, Mummy, while breakfast is prepared, I would very much like to have a bath. I feel as though I have the grime of the train on me."

"That would be fine, Frances, but don't be too long. Breakfast is nearly ready."

"I'll be in my study, Elizabeth, send for me when you are ready."

"That's such a lovely dress, Frances, I'm so glad that you're wearing it again," Mrs Rose said when Frances entered the dining room. "Won't you please tell Daddy that breakfast is ready? I'll ask Hope to serve it."

The Judge put his arm around Frances as they walked along the passage to the dining room. "You've lost a bit of weight, my dear?"

"I was not aware of that, Daddy. It must be all the hard work I suppose."

Mrs Rose was seated, waiting for them.

"The food smells yummy," Frances said. "By the way, how is James doing? Have you heard from them?"

"Confounded farming," her father sputtered, "there always seems to be a problem. If it is not one thing then it is another. Cannot understand why people get involved in it. There are much better and more lucrative occupations."

"What will you have Frances?" Mrs Rose asked.

"I'll have cereal to start, thank you."

"And you Jeremy?"

"I'll plunge straight into the scrambled egg. I'll have bacon and some fried banana, also a little sausage. I'll help myself to toast."

"You asked about James, Frances; he's well and so are Ethel and the children. He tells me the vineyards are looking particularly good after the rains and our rather severe winter cold, and promise to deliver a good crop. The fruit trees blossomed well, so there's much promise."

"Even if this year's good the next one will be bad. It's always like that," the Judge mumbled with a full mouth. "James should have gone into business. Been a merchant or something instead of investing all that money in an enterprise that is full of risk. Too many variables in farming, biologically too complex."

"Someone has to do it, Daddy, otherwise we won't have food to eat."

The Judge's colour rose, and he grunted.

"Tell me about your last term, Frances," her mother suggested.

"Well, let me see, what can I say. From a teaching point of view all went well. I think my results should be good."

"I am sure they will," her father said.

Frances was suddenly close to tears. "From every other point of view it was dreadful." She started crying.

Mrs Rose looked reproachfully at her husband. He glared back at her and slammed his knife down on the table with such force that it startled Frances. She looked up at him through her tears. "Now look here," the Judge roared, "I think it is time that we stopped beating around the bush. Even if the branches are full of thorns we must now grasp the nettle and admit that van Yssen has treated you, has treated us, shamefully."

"Jeremy, please."

"No, I am not prepared to sit here and pretend otherwise. I shall call a spade a spade. What good is it to sit here and behave as though we are all happy? Who are we fooling? We certainly are not fooling ourselves, and there's no one else in the room." Frances started getting up from her chair. "No, you sit down, and let me finish."

Mrs Rose's face was white.

"I looked forward to coming home, and now I wish I hadn't," Frances said between sobs. "I hoped that there would be kindness and sympathy here, but it seems there is none."

"There can be none of that while we deceive ourselves. Van Yssen is a ne're-do-well. I had my suspicions about him when he first darkened our doorway."

Frances ran from the room.

Mrs Rose began weeping softly. "I cannot believe that you have just said that. I know that you are angry, that is plain for all to see, but to be so vicious and so unfair, Jeremy. There is clearly a dark side to you that you have managed to conceal from me all these years. I am bitterly disappointed in you. A real man would not behave like this."

The Judge turned puce and slammed his fists on the table. He threw his napkin down and stormed from the dining room leaving a distraught Mrs Rose alone at the table. She looked at his plate of unfinished food, his napkin on top of the pile of yellow scrambled egg with its bits of green parsley. His toast had jumped off the side plate when he banged the table. She put it back on the plate. It was a good thing his coffee had not been poured. Something in her had snapped, been severed, and made her feel paralysed. She felt her heart pounding but had no sensation in the rest of her body. Had a monster always lurked inside her husband, that he could have been so vicious. Not many months before he could not say enough good about Douglas. Now this.

Mrs Rose found Frances sitting slumped forward on the side of her bed. Her eyes were red. She was pale and made no sound. She held her wedding finger in her right hand and fiddled with her engagement ring. When Mrs Rose sat down next to her Frances started so that her mother moved to the easy chair next to the bed. "I am so sorry, Frances."

There was an interminable silence. When Frances eventually spoke her words were measured, her hollow voice was raw, the sound that came out of her was visceral. "Only God knows how much I have suffered. That is how it is with humans. Others can never fully grasp how we feel. It is innocent to imagine, or to hope that they are capable of that. Each one of us is totally separate. The closest I ever came to feeling that I was one with another human being was with Douglas, and now I wonder whether it was really so or whether it was merely an illusion. I wonder what sin I must have committed to deserve this. My remaining hope was to find refuge here in the house in which I grew up, and to discover warmth and understanding, some support, or at least the pretence of it, and now I have been betrayed for the sake of pride and vanity, for thirty pieces of pride. The man I have loved and respected since I came into this world has feet of clay. Even if Douglas were to change his mind, things could never be the same with my father. He has broken something in me. It would be like trying to glue pieces of china together. The cracks and the little missing fragments will always remain when you put it back on the mantelpiece. I shall never be able to trust him again. It meant so much to me that he admired Douglas. Now it seems it was all humbug. God, I cannot believe it, why he had to be so destructive. Any hope that I could still have found happiness has now finally departed."

"His pride is hurt, Frances. He was angry for your sake."

"His pride Mother? His pride? What does his pride matter in all of this? Is a father's pride more important than his love for his daughter? Is his disgusting vanity more important that an understanding of what I am going through, what I am suffering? I see it now. I never realised it before. You knew all along that he was flawed and you have silently conspired to conceal his errors. In his language you have been an accessory after the fact. There is also a doctrine of common purpose. If you don't mind, I would like to be alone now, save for me to say that I shall wear this ring for ever in memory of all this and in memory of the man I shall love for the rest of my life, and I make a solemn vow today that I shall never marry, unless I marry Douglas."

"We should somehow try to patch things up. We cannot go on holiday like this, it will be too ghastly," Mrs Rose said nervously and fidgeted with her amber beads.

"If you don't mind, I would rather stay at home. I could not bear to go along. Besides it is only for two and a half weeks."

"But the staff have been told that they may have their holiday, before we start preparing for Christmas."

"I'll manage on my own. I would prefer that. Wild horses could not drag me into the car with him."

"And if I could get him to apologize?"

"Mother, the damage is done. Nothing could undo what he has done to me. I can never feel the same about him. What he has done is not something we can now sit and bargain about. Let it just be. What he said is what he really feels. When I needed him most he deserted me."

◆

Chapter Thirty-three

The years 1929 – 1933

FRANCES CONTINUED to write to Douglas. Sometimes her letters remained unopened for many weeks, and the longer he left them the more difficult it became to open them. When he did find it in him to reply, he wrote with strained difficulty and mostly in vague generalisations and about his activities on the farm. By 1931 he was completely deaf.

The depression that started after the collapse of the New York stock exchange in 1929 spread like a contagion over the world, and also reached the Union of South Africa in the early 1930s. Everywhere financial stability was threatened. In the Union the collapse of the American market resulted in a steep decline of diamond prices, and together with the decline in the price of wool, major exports were on the brink of collapse. To make matters worse, South Africa of the early thirties saw the most severe drought in living memory. Worst affected by the depression and the drought, were the farmers. During times of prosperity many farms had been over-capitalised and owners could now no longer cope with their interest burdens. Commercial banks and other institutions started calling in loans, and foreclosing. By 1932 large rural areas were in distress. Many individuals had to abandon their farms and fell into abject poverty. These unskilled people migrated to cities and towns in search of employment in a labour market that was already saturated. There was virtually no demand for agricultural products. Desperate attempts were made by the authorities to prop up the farming industry. Although the prices of maize and wheat were fixed, it was of little value, because of the lack of demand.

In 1931 England abandoned the gold standard. As the world's most important gold producer, the Union refused to follow England's example and at a special sitting of parliament in November 1931, the Government resolved to maintain the gold standard and to curb the massive outflows of capital to London. Exchange controls were introduced and anti-dumping measures established against those countries that had abandoned the gold standard. In 1932 at the Imperial Conference in Ottawa the Union Government made desperate attempts to establish preferential trade agreements within the British Commonwealth, but they proved to be to little or no avail. Later that year pressure increased for South Africa to abandon the gold standard, and on December 27, 1932 the authorities relented. The effect immediately became evident. The gold price rose overnight, gold share prices increased in value, and the gold mining industry promised to enter a boom period. Money flowed back into South Africa and material welfare revived.

The van Yssens had paid in cash for the farm, and therefore had no interest burden. Yet they could sell very little. Money was scarce and barter was sometimes the only means of acquiring what people did not produce. Albert van Yssen's land surveying practice relied heavily on rural work and the lack of demand for his services severely strained his resources. He closed his office in town to save the rent and began working from home where he used his study and Douglas' room. He and Mrs van Yssen visited the farm once a week, usually on a Friday, to fetch fresh produce and so were able to live on very little.

Frances had begun to correspond with Mrs van Yssen and formed a silent agreement with her not to mention their correspondence to Douglas. Van Yssen knew of their correspondence but gave the appearance that he was unaware of it. Although she did not say so to Frances, Mrs van Yssen gave up all hope that the relationship between Douglas and Frances would be resuscitated. In her turn Frances reconciled herself to her fate. She continued to teach in Graaff Reinet and continued to wear her engagement ring. She treated her father with distant courtesy and relied on his unrepentant pride to be a natural barrier between them. As for her mother, her physical needs ultimately determined her loyalty. She contrived several times to bring about reconciliation between Frances and her father but never succeeded because she could not bring herself to negotiate in honest faith.

Frances bought a small house in Graaff Reinet and acquired her own car. She visited Cape Town infrequently and preferred instead to spend some holidays on her own in the family house at Plettenberg Bay where she could relive her happier moments.

───────◆───────

Chapter Thirty-four

Thursday 18 February 1932

DOUGLAS ROSE VERY EARLY, saw to essential things on the farm, gave instructions to Willemse and Gert, strapped his Gladstone bag to his bicycle stand with pieces of red inner tube rubber and rode to Oudtshoorn. The largely downhill journey of about twenty-five miles took a little more than three hours. He arrived at his parents' house before the heat of the day. He had a bath followed by a generous breakfast with his parents after which his father drove him to town for his lip reading lesson. When his lesson ended he stopped at Garnett's surgery, but Garnett was out and not expected back until late afternoon, so he proceeded to collect his mother's dress-making material at Prince Vintcent.

When in Oudtshoorn he made a point of visiting Prince Vintcent in the hope of seeing Maggie Thompson. From the first day he saw her something intrigued him: she was very different from Frances. Whereas Frances inspired all that was delicate and virtuous, and had filled him with such pure emotions that he found it difficult at times to imagine physical intimacy, Maggie exuded a quality that aroused a raw compelling desire in him. And he had come to enjoy having that desire aroused.

When he entered the department store he immediately looked to see if she was at the haberdashery counter. She was bending forward over the counter, in conversation with a customer. Her dark hair was tied back, the pale skin of her neck exposed. He moved to one side so that he could look past the back of the counter and see her legs. He loved her legs – must be the best legs he had ever seen. And what a rump she had. She turned towards him as if she could feel he was looking at her, and smiled. He was embarrassed. Her customer left. She beckoned to him with her index finger. As he approached she turned her back towards him and bent over slowly to take his mother's parcel from under the counter. The back of her dress came up above her knees and he saw the edge of her petticoat and the ribbing of her stockings. She knew what he was looking at. She gave him the parcel and placed a piece of paper on the counter. She indicated to him that she wanted to write something. 'I am going to the bioscope tomorrow evening, on my own.' She looked up, tilted her head enquiringly to one side and raised her eyebrows. His mouth was dry. His parents were going to a bridge drive. "What is showing?" He whispered. She took her piece of paper. "A seven reel comedy, *Hold that Lion*." "That sounds like fun," he said. He took the parcel, grinned at her and hurried from the store. He looked inside through the window. Maggie was smiling and lifted her hand.

He turned around and found Madame Jacquard standing in front of him. She raised herself onto her toes and kissed him on both cheeks. He smelled her perfume and looked down her cleavage. She put her arm through his in a motherly sort of way and guided him in the direction of High Street. She stopped, disengaged her arm and made signs of drinking from a cup. "You and I," she indicated and lifted an imaginary cup from her hand made in the shape of a saucer. "Yes, that would be nice, thank you," he said. The town was quiet. There were sales everywhere. Some signs in shop windows told the lie that merchandise was being given away below cost. They encountered several people they knew as they proceeded to the Waldorf Tearoom, the Warrens, the Luscombes, Garnett's mother and father, and Mrs Taute. Douglas said hello awkwardly and pretended that he understood all that was said to him with exaggerated well meaning mouth movements, and Madame Jacquard, having by now held several successful exhibitions of her work, acknowledged their acquaintance a trifle condescendingly.

There were hardly any people in the Waldorf. Madame Jacquard ordered a waffle with cream, and a pot of tea. "No coffee?" Douglas asked. She beckoned to him to pass his notepad and pencil. "The coffee here is bad," she wrote. "It is more difficult to ruin tea."

"How long are you staying, this time?"

"I am going back on Sunday afternoon. I'll also have tea. Nothing to eat. Had a huge breakfast."

"How are things?"

"Fine. Still very dry. At least there is still a trickle of water in my river."

"They will end, these terrible times. The worse things become the closer we are to the end. Life is like that. I will come and visit you again some time. This time I will stay longer, and make some good landscapes. I enjoy where you live. You need a woman there. A man should not live on his own, like you are doing now. It is not good."

Douglas read the words as she wrote them in her peculiar French handwriting. What could he say? He would not mind taking her to bed. He remembered how she was on the farm. How she washed her underwear and her stockings in a colourful enamel basin on the back veranda and hung them on the washing line behind the house, a faded pink scarf tied around her head to keep her hair out of the way. She had seen him watching her through the pantry window, and stared at him playfully while she attached her pants and suspender belt to the line with washing pegs. She had encouraged him to have some wine with their supper and afterwards sat in a coquettish way next to the fire so that he could see more of her thighs, her cheeks flushed. He thought of Maggie. He would just casually mention that since they were going to play bridge, he felt like going to the bioscope. After all he needed some distraction.

"We can walk home together, if you like? I have done what I had to do."

"Yes, I thought it would be hot today, but it is not too bad, I would like that. If you don't mind I would like to look at something at Hepworths." She agreed. Douglas never had any intention of visiting Hepworths and when he discovered that Mr Tracey the manager was out, he used that as a pretext to come back another day. His plan was to walk back past Prince Vintcent once more. He looked through the window to see if he could catch a glimpse of Maggie, but there was no sign of her. He and Madame Jacquard walked down the hill towards the suspension bridge. On the bridge he let her go ahead. The bridge swayed. He observed her closely as she walked. She had shapely legs, the strong straight back of a dancer. She had on a floral cotton dress in the colours of a Renoir landscape – fields of washed-out green, dark green hedgerows, orange and yellow and red flowers in a meadow. Below, the murky water of the river seeped slowly through reflections of the vegetation on the banks and waving branches of green slime. Beyond them lay the lucerne fields that were in her painting. Her buttocks moved athletically as she strode ahead of him. If he looked carefully he could see the definitions of her underwear and the little lumps made by the attachments of her suspender belt on the sides of her thighs. He tried to imagine what was underneath that. A puff of summer air blew her perfume towards him. The wind moved the dry reeds on the riverbank and he thought about his cousin that day she had made him touch her. Madame Jacquard was right: he needed a woman. Jesus, it must be nice to do that. What if he were to put his arm around her? What would she do? Garnett said that some women are more enthusiastic than men. That's hard to believe. She's been without a man for years. Imagine putting his arm around her when he got to her door. It was not far now. But imagine if he had it all wrong, if his fantasy had distorted reality. Would she understand his need, or would she be insulted? Would she tell his mother? Why had she said she would come and stay on the farm, for longer?

On the bridge a man and a woman approached them. The bridge swayed more than before. Madame Jacquard and Douglas stood to one side to let the strangers pass. The man seemed to enjoy making the bridge sway. Madame Jacquard shook her head disapprovingly, and put her arm through Douglas'." He looked at her. Her breast lay on his arm. She disengaged herself once they were off the bridge and straightened her dress. She shook her head again. "That was damned inconsiderate," Douglas said.

At her house Madame Jacquard indicated to Douglas to pass his pad and pencil. "Thank you for being so gallant, Douglas, for walking me to my home. Come and visit me when you want to. Say hello to your mother, please. I have not seen her for some time."

Douglas thought it wise to spend the evening at home with his parents in order to build up credits to justify going to the bioscope the following evening. They had supper consisting of brawn, coarse brown bread, fruit from the garden. Douglas drank two glasses of milk and had a second helping of brawn. His father watched him eat. He had grown strong and lean. His face and his arms were tanned. He seemed greatly preoccupied. He had all the energy that accompanied the insensitivity of someone who was disabled. Van Yssen wondered how the lip reading was going. He touched Douglas' arm. "How was your lesson?" He mouthed the words carefully.

"The lesson was good, thank you. Don't speak unnaturally, Dad, speak normally. It makes it easier for me."

His mother waved her hand to catch his attention. "How are things on the farm?"

"Fine, thank you. I saw Mrs Jacquard in town today. We had tea at the Waldorf, and I walked her home. She said to give you her regards. I nearly forgot. Are you still playing bridge tomorrow evening?"

"We thought of cancelling it," his father replied.

Douglas shook his head to say that he did not understand, and pushed his pad and pencil towards his father.

"We thought of cancelling it," van Yssen wrote.

"No, no, you must not do that on my account." He held his hands up in protest. "I would feel awful. I should have stayed at home. You must go, please go."

"What will you do?" His mother enquired.

"Oh, something or other. Visit Garnett, stay here and read. I thought I might even go to the bioscope."

"The bioscope?" his father asked. "You never go there!"

Douglas shook his head and pushed his pad towards his father. "Why do you want to go to the bioscope when you've never shown much interest before? All on your own?"

"Ag it's not important. I just thought it would be nice light relief for me. I've been doing some heavy reading. I have started the last volume of Gibbon. I have also decided to learn German. I want to read the great poets, Goethe, Schiller."

"Let him be Albert. Let him do as he pleases. He has few pleasures."

"Your mother says you must do as you please and go and enjoy yourself."

"I saw what Ma said, Dad." He smiled at his mother.

Friday 19 February 1932

Mr and Mrs van Yssen left for the Elleys' house. Douglas wolfed down the rest of the omelette and went to brush his teeth. He grabbed his jacket and hurried down the garden path. The walk to the Gaiety Theatre took about twenty minutes. There weren't many people at the cinema, which suited him, no one he knew. He could not see Maggie anywhere, and went to buy his ticket. What to do now? He stood about, looked at the poster advertising the film 'Douglas MacLean's Paramount Comedy, *Hold that Lion*.' Sounds pretty corny. If she did not pitch up he would go home. People entered the theatre. The usher, grey haired and with a nicotine-stained moustache, his poverty camouflaged by his long burgundy coat with gold braiding, shuffled over to him. "The picture is going to start," his mouth said. Without asking he took Douglas' ticket and guided him to the door. The lights were already dimming and the serial was about to start. He waited for a few moments so that his eyes could adjust to the dark and find a seat. He looked about. Maggie was in the back row, to his left. She made an embarrassed gesture. His heart was pounding. He left through the door he had entered and went in through the opposite door, closer to where Maggie was, and sat down next to her.

Each serial episode started with the end of the previous episode. One car was chasing another along a winding road through arid hills. Presumably the car that was being chased carried the baddies and the one in pursuit the good guys. The pursuing car hit a rock and overturned violently, rolled down a sleep slope and exploded. There was no hope of the hero surviving. Now in the replay of the scene, and looking from another angle, it became evident that the hero had been flung from the car. He lay still for a few seconds, stood up stiffly, picked up his hat and dusted it against his thighs, put it on his head and marched off shaking his head, his striped double breasted suit still neat and unmarked, ready to continue his pursuit. It was so ridiculous that Douglas burst out laughing. Maggie patted his arm to quieten him. Without thinking he put his hand on hers as though to reassure her. She put her fingers through his. Her hand was soft. He turned to look at her. There were no other people near them. She had on a sleeveless navy blue cotton dress with a square cream coloured collar. A small black leather handbag rested on her lap. She indicated that she wanted to write something. He took his pad and pencil from his jacket pocket and handed them to her. It was difficult to see in the dark. When brighter images flashed onto the screen she could see well enough to write, and handed the pad to him. He held it so that he could see. "My father is very strict. He does not know I am here. I am becoming nervous. Let's rather go for a walk to the river? Nod if you agree. I will leave first and then you can follow me."

Maggie got up and squeezed past him. He could feel the backs of her legs against his knees. He waited a while before he left the bioscope. She was standing a little distance down the street, pretending to look at display window of the pharmacy. When she saw him she started walking along St John Street in the direction of the shoe factory. He followed at a distance. She turned right into Queen Street and headed for the corner of Church Street and down to the suspension bridge. It was going to be full moon in three days time and the summer evening was bright. She stopped at the bridge and lit a cigarette. He smelled the sweet smoke she exhaled. "Well, here we are," he said. She smiled sweetly and held out her packet of cigarettes to him. He put up his hand to decline. "I don't smoke, thank you." She shrugged her shoulders. She indicated that they should walk along the bridge. To their left on the opposite bank there was a copse of pine trees, their dense branches black in the moonlight. The mixture of perfume and tobacco smoke that came from her was so unusual that it excited him. She skipped along the wooden boards of the bridge, and leant back against the cables and mesh that formed the sides. She threw her half smoked cigarette over the side and watched the glowing end as it fell. She put her arm through his and they walked together in step like two people in a three-legged race, their common legs touching at the thighs. He put his arm around her and felt her back muscles moving against his arm. She put her arm around him. At the end of the bridge she turned towards him and kissed him. He could taste the tobacco in her open mouth. She motioned that she wanted to write something. "Please do not think that I am being forward, don't think badly of me. I have seen you often but you did not see me. I liked you from the first time I saw you. I know you were engaged, and that you now live alone. I like you very much. I knew that if I did nothing you would never come to me. I was also engaged once, and am not innocent. I think you are a very attractive man."

"I think that you are most attractive, Maggie. As you clearly know I have a great problem. I am completely deaf. I will never hear again. I am trying to make a living on a small farm in these difficult times. I expect that I shall remain a bachelor for the rest of my life."

She started shaking her head and tears came into her eyes. She opened her handbag and wiped her tears away with a small handkerchief. "I feel so sorry for you. I can hear from the way you speak that you are a very clever man. I am not clever, but I think that you are a very kind person. Will it be possible to see you again?"

"Yes, I would like that."

"My brother has a car, he can bring me to your farm one day?"

"Yes, if you would like to. It sounds like a good idea to me. It is quite primitive."

"I am used to that. We have had very hard times." She took his hand and led him across the road into the clump of pine trees. She indicated that she wanted to sit down. Douglas found a thick patch of dry pine needles. He stopped her from sitting down, and took his jacket off. He spread it over the pine needles and they sat down next to one another. Maggie lit a cigarette and threw her head back to blow the smoke up into the night air. The frogs certainly sounded very happy she thought. The river had a fishy smell. She leaned towards Douglas and kissed him on his cheek next to his ear. He looked at her. There was something sad about her, something tragic. She was quite courageous though. Would she be hurt if he did nothing? He did not want to hurt her. Or would she think that he was taking advantage of her? He put his arm around her shoulders and held her tightly against him. She tilted her head until it touched his shoulder and put her cigarette out on a piece of flat stone. He kissed her. She made small sniffing gasps through her nose and put her hand on the inside of his thigh. He unbuttoned the front of her dress. Her nipples were stiff and she started to tremble. She lay down and he lay next to her. She pressed herself against him and moved her hand further up his thigh, and then slowly further and further. He began to shake. He let go of her breast and started pulling up the hem of her dress. It slid over her petticoat and she parted her legs. It was hot under her dress. Slippery moisture had seeped through her pants. She started unbuttoning his fly and held her breath while her hand struggled to find its way through his underwear, careful not to hurt him with her nails. He struggled to contain himself. He tried to think of something else, of fishing, of hunting, of working on the farm, but it was too late. She held on to him and milked until his convulsions ended and then sat up to assess the condition of her dress. He shook his head apologetically. "I'm so sorry about this." He was breathing heavily. "No, no," her lips said. He wanted to say more but she put her finger over his lips and kissed him again and again on his forehead, and on his face and his mouth. She went to the edge of the river and splashed water onto her dress to remove his semen while he buttoned his trousers. When she returned she lay closely against him with her back so that they could fit together better. He put his arm over her hip and touched the wet front of her dress. This was not at all like masturbating. It was made more complete by her presence and their spontaneity. His spine felt loose and he had a dreamy satisfied sensation of being spent. He could feel the warmth of Maggie's body and her buttocks against him. He lay and looked at her neck and the shape of her head, and her bare arm. He lifted his head to look at her face. Her eyes were closed and she breathed contentedly. He looked up into the trees. The moon was quite bright. What he found remarkable as he let his mind wander was that he found no trace of guilt.

Maggie turned over, kissed him on his forehead and sat up. She motioned that they ought to get going. "I shall walk you home," he suggested. She nodded in agreement and stood in front of him so that he could brush errant pine needles from her dress. She did the same for him. They walked with their arms around one another from the trees and went in the direction of the town. "Where is your house, Maggie?" He had said her name. She loved the way he said her name. "At the top of St Saviour Street. We must not let my father see you. I will go in alone."

He watched from a distance as she knocked on the door of the house. A light came on at the front door. A woman in a pink candlewick dress dressing gown opened the door and held her arm out to welcome Maggie. Douglas stayed until the door closed and started his walk home.

"What happened to your dress?" Her mother bent over with concern to inspect the front of the dress. "Oh my, it is such a lovely dress. You need to keep it for work."

"It must be something I ate. I felt a little sick, and brought up on it. I tried to wash it off at the bioscope."

"Give it to me, I'll rinse it in cold water."

"I'll manage Ma, not to worry."

"No, you have had a busy week, and you have to get up early. Let me do it for you. You can take it off right here. Pa is asleep. He was in his cups when he eventually got home. Johnny has gone to Mossel Bay to see that little bitch of his. She left a message at the garage for him, so of course he hurried off as soon as he had washed himself. God knows where he gets the money for petrol. He keeps pleading poverty when he has to pay me for his board and lodging.

At least they let him use a garage car." Maggie handed her mother the dress. "You go to bed now my child. I'll see to this and then make myself a cup of tea. I don't want to wake Pa up, he might get ideas, and I'm not in the mood for his nonsense. Johnny takes after Pa; he can't get enough of that little tart. She'll end up in the family way if he's not careful." Maggie kissed her mother goodnight and went to her room. She slept on an iron bed with a coir mattress. There was a framed print of the Mother of Jesus, holding her hands together in prayer, above her bed. A heavenly light shone from one corner of the print and illuminated the back of Mary's head to give the effect of a halo. In the distance the gates of Heaven stood, and beyond them sentimental symbols of everlasting peace and happiness adorned a radiant sky.

Mrs Thompson tossed Maggie's dress over the back of a kitchen chair and filled a basin with cold water. She held the dress away from her to see it better. She frowned and smelled the dress, expecting the sour odour of vomit. Instead there was something else. At first she was not sure. Then she smelled again. A familiar alkaline odour. She smelled it again and sat down at the kitchen table, with the dress across her lap. She quickly removed it lest it contaminate her and put it into the water of the basin. She smelt her hands and washed them in the kitchen sink. She sat down again and lit a cigarette. There was no one in Maggie's life. Ever since that rubbish left her because she found him screwing someone else. She acted oddly when she went out. Takes a mother to know a daughter. A married man, or that bastard Schmidt. There were plenty of stories about him and the girls who worked there. But Maggie had too much sense to let a fat slob like that near her, unless of course there was a promotion on the cards. Even so, she was too principled for that. She had her faults, but once her mind was made up she would not do anything foolish. Good thing she got rid of that fiancé of hers. Now there went a real rubbish, as Johnny summed it up so aptly at the time, a real piece of shit. Well never mind, at least it's on the outside of the dress and not inside of her. Shows how clever she is.

Douglas strolled along in the moonlight, past the houses that were the town, their tin roofs reflecting silver moonlight. Most lights were off by now. What a remarkable thing a town was: a collection of people in shelters, burrows really, containing hopes and aspirations, fears and disappointments. There were the good houses, modest ones, grand ones, well built ones and badly built ones. He went past Swart the barber, lying in his bed next to his large wife who was so knock-kneed that she looked as if she had two left legs, the pencil that was used to hide the grey in his moustache smudged at the corner. On past Schoeman-on-the-corner where he turned left, past Diemont's house and the house that Jan Plan built, opposite Leibner. The streets were deserted. The inky shadows cast by the moonlit buildings and trees had a sharper contrast than the shadows of the day. The dark places were darker. He crossed the suspension bridge again and looked at the pine trees below. The gland of his penis was glued to the front of his shirt that he had mistakenly pushed into his underpants. He would have to be careful when he took it out. Would have to make a plan the next time. The chaps at varsity spoke of that. If you are certain you're going to get lucky, eat a lot of cheese in the afternoon, and have a little wine. Then go and have a sleep, but first give it a good wank so that you won't get ahead of yourself when it really matters and disappoint an eager girl. Sounds contrived, but they vouched it worked, and there were one or two really fancy studs in College House.

In the distance the lights of a car went past. Could be his parents. He was going to sleep in the spare room, in Frances' room, where she slept that time. She liked the wallpaper. He felt sad. She tried so hard. He would always love her. He recalled the way she looked the day she arrived in Oudtshoorn, her eyes red from crying about him. Women are remarkable. She now belonged to his former life, to the time before the silence came. He tried to remember what sounds were like. There could be someone behind him right now and he would not know. He looked around. The moonlight enchanted the fields. A breeze transported the innocent scent of maturing seeds and wheat stubble and stirred the leaves of an ash tree and he tried to imagine what that sounded like. The lights of a car fell on the trees in front of him and cast his walking shadow before him. He stepped off the road onto the verge. It was fine at night, but hell, in the daytime it was dangerous, especially on his bicycle. Going home on Sunday. Fortunately did not have clothes to wear to church. What would he do with Maggie's brother if they came to visit him on the farm?

Douglas was relieved to find that his parents were still out when he arrived home. He went straight to the spare room, made sure the one window was open, drew the curtains properly and began to undress. He folded his shirt and underwear very tightly, sniffed at the bundle and stuffed it into the corner of his bag under the other things. Once he was in his pyjamas he went to the bathroom to clean his teeth. He inspected the bookshelf in the passage for something to read. A small volume bound in red linen with gold lettering lay on top of the other books. He picked it up: *Anne of Geierstein or the Maiden of the Mist* by Sir Walter Scott. He pulled the blankets to one side and began reading the Editor's Introduction. A quotation from Scott's 1829 diary was marked in pencil in the margin. It read, 'I can very seldom think to purpose by lying perfectly idle, but when I take an idle book, or a walk, my mind strays back to its task, out of contradiction as it were; the things I read become mingled with those that I have been writing, and something is concocted'. What contradictions Maggie and Frances are. He had grown idle. Did not read enough. What could he concoct out of his idleness? Her pants were wet. That's what did it. Would she have gone the whole way? The trouble with someone like that is that you don't know where you are in the queue. Unless it is that she really likes me. It was not as if she was unwilling in any way. What a body. They could swim together in the river on the farm. It would give him chance to inspect the merchandise. He read the quotation again. That's what he had promised himself, to combine his life as a farmer with his academic interests. To let his mind stray creatively while he carried out his physical work and then to plunge into his reading of history, and write his own book. But you need to have access to a decent library. He paged through the book. He must learn German. The old man has a German dictionary. That's a start. Should keep up his Latin. Catullus would have been proud of him tonight. It would be nice to do a history of Rome. From a new perspective. That would properly fuck old Rose in the eye. What was it like inside her house? Would she be asleep by now? It was a pretty modest house. You would think a builder would have a better house. Times are not easy. Puts his daughter out to work. What an attractive daughter she is too. What would his parents say if they found out? Like Flavius' girl. 'Flavius, unless your delights were tasteless and inelegant, you'd want to tell, and couldn't be silent. Surely you're in love with some feverish whore: you're ashamed to confess it.' The old bastard was testing him. He was both asleep and dreaming when he entered his Elysian plains, speckled with brightly coloured flowers that sang with joy as Frances came running towards him, her blonde hair flowing and he began to cry in his sleep.

Saturday 20 February 1932

Douglas' father had to wake him to get ready for his lip reading lesson. He had a bath and a hurried breakfast. Mrs van Yssen signed to him that she would be going along to town, and then wrote on his pad that they could meet after his lesson and go home together.

"What was the bioscope like?" she asked.

He shook his head and she had to write. "It was a lot of nonsense. I did not stay, went for a walk and early to bed instead."

After his lesson he strolled to the shops. They had agreed to meet at the Standard Bank, where his father had to attend to some business matters. Douglas found his mother waiting in the reception area outside the manager's office. "I want to go to Prince Vintcent quickly, to see to something," he said, and left. He skipped across the street and went into the store. Maggie was not at her counter, and he sauntered through the store to the hardware department where he pretended to look at the tools. He took up a vantage point from where he could see the haberdashery counter. Some women entered the store and when they disappeared Maggie was back. He had picked a rose in the garden of Mrs Botha after his lesson and stuck it into the inside pocket of his jacket. He walked up to Maggie's counter, smiled at her, and said, "This is for you." He put the pink rose down in front of her and turned to go. Maggie held the rose in her hands and followed him with her eyes. A middle-aged woman was standing at the entrance. It was his mother.

Mrs van Yssen frowned at Douglas. "What was that about?"

"She dropped her flower. I picked it up for her."

Saturday 5 March 1932

Douglas had had a busy week. He had been to the shop earlier, made himself lunch of bully beef and baked beans and relished it on the veranda in the late summer sun. He was reading Saki's *The Unbearable Bassington* when he fell asleep in his chair. Something was tugging at his chair or perhaps his arm and his book fell to the floor. He stooped to pick it up and saw the feet of a woman. It was Maggie. To her side stood a young man. Douglas was not sure whether he was awake or dreaming. He nevertheless decided to get up. Maggie picked up his book. "This is my brother Johnny," she indicated. "Johnny this is Douglas." Johnny stepped forward weaving his torso embarrassedly and held out his hand palm down. His fingernails were short and the stained cuticles ingrained with grease. The cracks in the rough skin of his fingertips were filled with dirt he could not remove. He had fair wavy hair, dark eyebrows and green eyes.

"How do you do, Johnny," Douglas extended his hand.

"Nice of you to ask, but I'm just fine."

Maggie made a writing motion with her hand. Douglas took them into his living room and presented his pencil and paper.

"Johnny is on his way to Mossel Bay to deliver a car for the garage and visit his girlfriend. We told my parents that I was going with. I have come to visit you. Johnny will come and fetch me tomorrow afternoon, if that's OK?"

Douglas' parents had been there the day before and were not due to return for another week. There were no prospects of other visitors. "That would be fine, I think," he stammered.

"Right, well that settles it Sis, I must be on my bicycle, as we say in the classics."

Douglas grasped only snatches of what Johnny said. Johnny took the writing pad and wrote, "Make sure Sis is on her own in the spare room tonight." He shook his finger in naughty admonishment. "Nice to meet a gentleman like you. She says you treated her very nicely." Johnny trotted off to the car parked beyond the gate and brought back a small pillbox red cardboard suitcase with Maggie's things, and a brown paper parcel. He waved to Maggie and Douglas, and ran back to the car with exaggerated pretence of urgency.

Maggie stood next to Douglas on the veranda and looked out over the valley below. In the distance the sheep grazed peacefully and occasionally bleated plaintively. She tapped him on his arm and held her hands out, palms upwards in admiration, and raised her eyes heavenwards to say how beautiful she thought it was there. Douglas showed her to the spare room. She sat down on the bed and bounced up and down playfully on the innerspring mattress, and patted it with her hands. They went to the kitchen where Douglas lit the Primus. "Would you like tea or coffee?" he asked.

"Tea, please." She pointed to herself, "I will make it."

"No, it's fine, I am quite capable."

She shook her head assertively. Douglas fetched biscuits from the pantry. They sat on the veranda and had tea. Maggie went inside to get the writing pad. "I was paid on Monday and brought you some neck of lamb for a stew. I can make a very good stew. We will have it tonight. You can show me where everything is. We can take vegetables from the garden and light the stove early so that it will be hot. My brother and I have been past here before, on the way to Mossel Bay. I saw you near the road once, and knew this was your place. We waved and hooted but you could not hear us." Douglas smiled at her and nodded in appreciation. "Show me your farm," she wrote and made a sign of walking with her index and middle finger. "That's a very good idea," he said.

They traversed the slope below the house and headed in the direction of the river. Willemse's dog barked in the distance. Maggie pointed at Willemse's cottage. "Who lives there?"

"It is my man Willemse. He's a simple creature, not quite as deaf as I am. Minds his own business. He's bound to be asleep now. Guards the sheep at night. When we came here we had comparatively few sheep. The flock is now nearly three times its original size – careful of the stones." They went through a gate in the fence and walked into the pale green light of a copse of poplar trees. The silver furry undersides of leaves fluttered like decorations. Maggie heard gurgling water below. The path through the trees was overgrown. They came to another barbed wire fence with well-weathered grey wooden stays. At one end there was a gate that Douglas held open. Maggie stopped and looked about. "It is so beautiful here."

"Yes it is beautiful. I am glad you appreciate it." He took her hand. She made coy girlish steps to show that it pleased her. Her hair had been cut shorter since the last time he saw her and was held back with ivory clips. She wore a brightly coloured cotton dress printed with small innocent flowers. Her one stocking had become badly laddered. He would buy her a new pair when the opportunity arose. When they emerged from the trees the river lay before them. There was not much water. Douglas took her hand and led her along the bank. They came to a place where there was a large pool. A stretch of biscuit coloured dry river sand stretched along the edge of the pool. They sat down on the sand. "This is like being at the seaside," she wrote in the sand with her finger. "I have been to the seaside with Johnny, to Mossel Bay." She smoothed the sand with the back of her hand so that she could write some more. "Before that we lived in Durban. You could catch the tram and go to the beach there."

"I love it here," Douglas said. "There is not much water now, but the pool is quite deep enough to swim."

"I can't swim," she wrote.

"You can stand in it; it only comes up to the middle of my chest." Douglas lay back on the sand and felt the sun on his face and his chest. What would his parents say if they knew the girl was here, for the night? Imagine if Garnett pitched up. It was bad enough that Willemse would find out. He could say that her brother was meant to fetch her that same evening on his way back from Mossel Bay, but that he was delayed unexpectedly. So what else could he do? He could not turn her away. *Honi soit qui mal y pense.* Why was she there in the first place? He pointed to the ladder in her stocking. She nodded. "I'll buy you a new pair."

She shook her head, pulled back her dress and began taking off the laddered stocking. He ought not to watch. When she caught his eye he blushed. She laughed and lent forward to kiss him playfully on his forehead, then took off the other stocking. She had strong legs. He recalled what it had felt like when he put his hand under her dress. There was no need to rush anything today. They had the whole afternoon and the whole night. She put her stockings down next to her on the sand.

Maggie smoothed the sand. "What made you go deaf?"

"It is an inherited condition. I got it from my grandfather."

"Can the doctors not make it better?"

"They tried. No, there is nothing that can be done. It will never get better. I have come to accept that."

"That is so very sad. I feel so sorry for you. I saw you come into the shop with your mother, already some time ago. I saw you walking in the town with that strange French woman. You are very handsome. I liked you from the first time. I could see that you come from a gentleman's world. We are just ordinary people who have struggled all our lives to make ends meet. My father is a rough man and times are very hard for him right now. I knew that if I did not do anything you would not have come to me. It does not matter to me that you are deaf. It is not necessary for you to hear me to know that I am sincere. You must feel it. If you don't love me, I will understand, but I think that I love you, and I must tell you that so that you will not think I am bad, or that I sleep around. Even if you chase me away eventually, I can see what you are like inside. Your eyes tell me that you have suffered. I saw all your big books in your house, and I heard that you are the best teacher in the whole world. You must be very clever."

Douglas studied her as she wrote sentence after sentence in the sand, and smoothed the sand to continue. She was refreshingly authentic. He looked at her hand as she wrote: the reddish roughness of her fingers said that she did her own washing. She had good features. Her dark blue eyes were bright; her teeth were clear and strong. She smelled fresh. He looked at her stockings lying next to her on the sand. Social conventions did not constrain her. She had no ulterior motives; no preconditions separated her from him. There was nothing hidden. She slid her bare toes in under the hot sand. She had come to see him because in a childlike way she wanted to be with him. She did not expect any counter performance. She sought nothing material. If he liked her that would be a greater reward than she had ever received from anyone else. He looked at her and took her hand. "I like you very much, Maggie. I am glad that you have come to visit me. Thank you so much for the meat you brought. You must let me pay you for it. I cannot wait to have the stew. Let's go back to the house."

She put her stockings into her pocket, and he helped her up. He put his arms around her and began kissing her. She responded and pressed herself against him. She raised herself onto her toes so that their pubic areas could make amorous contact, and they became so excited that it felt as though they were eating one another. Maggie could hardly breathe, and when he sensed her excitement, Douglas' emotions became so feverish that he felt as though he was losing control of his senses. His passion inspired hers and her passion eclipsed his, each wave mounted upon the next. She disentangled herself and squatted so that she could write in the sand. "I will go and make your food now. A good stew takes a long time. We will love each other tonight."

They got back to the house just after four. Douglas lit the stove and went to the vegetable garden with Maggie to pick green beans and carrots. She washed the beans and the carrots, took a few potatoes from the pantry and peeled them. Douglas sat down at the kitchen table to keep her company, and to see if he could help. She unwrapped her brown paper packet and cut the meat into neat pieces. She sliced the potatoes and the onions into a large cast iron saucepan, added the meat, water and seasoning. She waited until the water boiled, removed the scum from the surface and moved the saucepan to a cooler part of the stove. "We must let it simmer for about an hour and a half now, then I will add the rest. I will cook the beans and carrots on their own later on." She smiled broadly at him in a self-satisfied way and rubbed her hands together proudly. She turned his left wrist to see what time it was. "Can we make hot water please. I would like to have a bath."

"Yes, I will do that for you. Do you want to bath now?"

"In a little while please."

"When is Johnny returning?"

"Only late tomorrow afternoon. He goes there most weekends."

Douglas filled the copper tank of the stove with water from a bucket and nodded to her that the water would be ready in a while. She went to her room. Douglas went to the living room and flopped down on his couch. He tilted his head back and closed his eyes. He felt his intestines bubbling ominously. It was the beans and bully beef. Trotters du Toit, what a funny bugger he could be, once said you had to be very careful of beans. He said they could assassinate love. What a stuff-up it could be. He'd have to be bloody careful not to let off a stink. The more he thought of it the more bloated his abdomen felt. Shit, what a stuff-up. And if you poured the stew on top of all that stuff that is already there, it could lead to a right royal explosion. Damn. He needed to fart. Perhaps that was a good sign. If he could have a good crap a bit later on, the day, or should he say night, could still be saved. It's a good lesson to learn. Always be prepared. But he could not have anticipated this. He decided to go and see what Willemse was doing. He went to Maggie's door and knocked lightly. "I am going to see to a few things. Will be back in a while."

Douglas found Willemse sitting on the bench in front of his cottage. An enamel plate was at his side. Remnants of food told him that Willemse had had his afternoon meal. He only ate twice a day. He was smoking his pipe; his dog at his feet. He indicated that he was going to milk the cow. A small bunch of mountain flowers lay on the bench next to him, tied together with strands of grass. He gave Douglas the flowers and pointed towards the house to say it was for her.

Douglas went with Willemse to the cowshed, and then strolled about to delay his return to the house. The almond trees had grown remarkably well, and had begun to bear, albeit in small quantities. This year there were more green furry fruits, like small green peaches and next year there would be more, and more the year after that. He felt movements in his stomach and hopped up and down on the pretext of exercising, in case someone was watching, in the hope of hastening the passage of the contents of his gut. The trick would be to have some sour figs. Those things can clear your insides out in half an hour, if you eat enough of them. The more conscious he became of it the more uncomfortable his stomach felt.

When he got back to the house Maggie was in the kitchen. She stirred the contents of the iron saucepan and added the remaining potato pieces, and more stock. He could swear his sense of smell had improved to compensate for his loss of hearing. The food smelled good. His stomach rumbled. He put more wood into the stove. He had left Willemse's flowers on the veranda, and went to fetch them. When she saw him returning with the flowers in his hand she smiled. "These are from my man Willemse," he said. "I gather he picked them for you. It is a touching sign of his approval."

Maggie took the flowers and embraced Douglas. 'This is the nicest thing that has ever happened to me," she wrote on Douglas' pad. She fetched a small glass vase from the dining room for the flowers. She stroked the little flowers.

Douglas pointed to one, "These are called *sewejaartjies* because they almost last for ever."

She took his hand, led him to the spare room and opened the cupboard to show him that she had hung her clothes. A towel lay neatly folded at the bottom end of the bed. Modest makeup things and a small bottle of perfume had been arranged on the bedside cabinet next to her candle. Her shiny red suitcase stood in one corner.

"The water for your bath will be ready in a while, come and sit with me in the living room."

They sat closely together on the couch, holding hands. "There's a knock at the back door," she said and got up. Douglas motioned to her to wait and went to the kitchen. Willemse had brought the milk. Douglas thanked him and gave him some tobacco he had bought that morning, and a loaf of bread. He put a few more sticks of wood into the stove and Willemse carried wood into the kitchen. From the way he shuffled about it was clear that he was hoping to have a closer look at Maggie.

"It was Willemse, he brought the milk. He's a good man." Douglas sat down next to her and took her hand. She snuggled up to him and put her head on his chest. He put his arm around her and without thinking cupped her breast in his hand. She sighed contentedly. He let go of her breast after a while, and fondled the curves of her hip. He felt her breast again to challenge her willingness. She turned on her side, kicked off her shoes, drew her legs onto the couch, and covered her legs and feet with her dress. "The stew smells very good," he said.

She pushed herself onto her elbow to get hold of the writing pad. "You must be hungry, your tummy is rumbling."

"No, not at all. I'm not hungry at all. It must be my lunch."

"That is just as well. The longer the stew cooks the better. We must eat at your dining table. I will set the table, if you show me where everything is."

Douglas held her shoulders and carefully pushed her down on the couch. He lent over her and kissed her. He inspected her face and her hair while she looked happily up at him. She was most attractive. Quite different from Frances. Her dark hair grew out of her clean white scalp. Her skin was unblemished. Her innocent eyes were trusting. He manoeuvred himself so that he ended up on top of her. They started rubbing themselves together. She opened her legs and pulled up her dress. He looked down as she lifted her dress and saw her pink pants. A few curly hairs protruded from the edges. Drops of fluid escaped from him. She was breathing heavily. She put her hand over his mouth, and pointed towards the kitchen. He got up. She straightened her dress and her hair and put on her shoes. When Douglas got to the kitchen the back door was opening. It was Willemse with a basket of fruit. He pointed in the direction of Ellis' farm and motioned that it had arrived when he was securing the gate for the night. He had told Ellis that Douglas was asleep. Maggie appeared at the passage door. Willemse greeted her with a large nod of the head and a servile bow. "Thank you so much for the flowers."

"You have to speak quite loudly to him, he's a bit deaf," Douglas said.

It was plain that Willemse approved. Maggie noticed that the front of Douglas' trousers was damp and stood between him and Willemse.

Dusk was settling over the farm when Douglas went outside to close the shutters. He lit two lamps and helped Maggie to carry her hot water to the bath. He put some more water into the copper container, and added wood to the stove. They were alone now, the two of them, in his house. He was not sure whether to make a fire. It was not very cold. The woman had made food for them. She was having a bath. Would she sleep in his bed with him? He needed to fart again, and went outside to the privy. He loosened his trousers and sat down in the hope that he would be able to rid himself of his flatulence. All he could produce was more wind. Maggie was already in the kitchen. She had bathed and washed her hair and wore the same dress she had on earlier, except that she had put on a green hand knitted cardigan whose sleeves were pushed back half way along her forearms. She cut up green beans and sliced the carrots. She inspected the stew and stirred it. Douglas kissed her in the nape of her neck and she giggled. It was cosy next to the warm stove. "I am going to lay the table," Douglas announced.

He took a stiff white starched tablecloth from the bottom drawer of the sideboard and spread it over the table. He decided that they should sit opposite one another, and arranged the place settings accordingly: knives and forks, butter knives, a butter dish with its own butter knife, a wooden breadboard, salt and pepper pots with real silver caps, napkins. He put the vase with her flowers at the one end of the table and took two dinner plates to the kitchen for warming.

Maggie measured two cups of rice. He fetched a jar of preserved yellow cling peach halves from the pantry and tipped the contents into a Pyrex dish. He opened a tin of cream and emptied it into a small bowl. Maggie looked at him and licked her lips in approval. Her pants and her thighs appeared in his mind. He had an urge to grab her and carry her to his bed. Ever since she arrived his desire had continued to mount and he did not know how much longer he would be able to restrain himself. Yet he was mindful that the consummation of what he had lusted for and dreamt of from the time that he had emerged from puberty with an exquisite collection of rare and valuable fantasies, was now at hand, and the way he managed the situation would determine the quality of that consummation. He would like to explore her body unhurriedly, to savour its delicacies slowly. An opportunity like this was indeed rare. It would be a sin to waste it because of impatience. Besides, there was the question of his flatulence.

Maggie wanted to take the saucepan with the stew to the dining room, but Douglas transferred the stew into a serving dish, and carried it to the table. She followed with the rice. He drew her chair out for her and helped her to sit comfortably. He placed the lamp to one end of the table so that it would not shine into their eyes and dished up for her and then helped himself. He could see she was hungry. The stew was hot and she blew on the first few mouthfuls before cautiously holding the pieces of lamb between her teeth and fanning her mouth with her hand. Her lips were generous and their well-defined edges gave them an amorous shape. He liked that. She held her knife and her fork in a peculiar way, but that could be sorted out. Lips are more difficult to sort out.

"This food is absolutely delicious," he said. "Thank you for preparing it." She smiled happily, pleased at the compliment. He watched her feeding her female body. She had no bra on, possibly not even pants. He felt movements in his stomach. "I am very glad you came to see me Maggie. You are making me feel very happy. I have not felt happy for a very long time. It is nice to be here alone in this house with you. I think you are most attractive."

She wrote on the pad and slid it across to him. "You are such a nice man. I feel safe with you. I want to make you happy. I am happy."

She had an attractive way of chewing her food. She never put too much into her mouth. She chewed in a patient rhythmical way and did not hurry to have the next mouthful. She had made herself at home and seemed quite comfortable. As though she knew the house. She carried no unwanted baggage or psychological burdens. She did not ask for anything. She had brought her own meat for the stew, purchased with her own hard-earned money. She was too busy giving to think of asking for anything.

He helped her to carry the dishes to the kitchen. He indicated to her that he had to go outside and lit a storm lantern. He left the back door standing open and she watched the swaying lamp and Douglas' lurching shadow heading down the well-worn grass path for the privy.

He was gone for quite a while. After he had washed his hands in the bathroom he went to the dining room to find Maggie sitting there, waiting to serve dessert. It pleased him to see how much she enjoyed the peaches and cream and enthusiastically had a second helping. She sighed contentedly, sat back in her chair and let her arms hang loosely at her sides to show that she could not eat any more.

Maggie would not let Douglas wash any of the dishes or even help her and insisted on doing them herself. She led him to the living room and made him sit down with a book while she saw to the kitchen. It was still not cold enough to make a fire. His visit outside had produced great relief and he started contemplating what lay ahead with greater confidence. Her pants from whose sides a few dark pubic hairs revealed themselves. White thighs. Her lips opened when she put food into her mouth. She had a way of walking, not unlike Madame Jacquard: a strong straight back, shapely legs like a dancer, good hips. Firm breasts that sat high. When Maggie had finished in the kitchen she went to her room to make a wee, put a little perfume on the insides of her forearms, and behind her ears and joined Douglas in the living room. He held out his arms to her. She kicked her shoes off and sat down close to him. He did not want to appear too eager for he realised that there would be no stopping once they got started. He kissed her and she lay back on the couch. Her dress was a little above her knees. Because she had no pants on her dress rested unevenly on her freshly washed tuft of pubic hair. Her nipples were stiff. He lay down next to her on his side and kissed her some more. He put his leg over hers and pressed his thigh into her. She unbuttoned the front of her dress so that he could see her breasts. He kissed the nearest one and she giggled. He slid his hand in under her dress. He cupped his hand over her and looked into her dark blue eyes. Such excitement was hard to imagine. He tickled her and stroked all the little folds and fissures and brushed her soft pubic hairs while she writhed against his hand and his finger. She half sat up and wriggled away from him. She kissed him on his temple and got up from the couch. She held out her hand as a sign that they should go to the bedroom. He walked behind her to his room. She had gathered her dress up above her hips and held it in front of her and in the half light of the passage he could see the creamy pink cheeks of her rear, separated by a shadow line, moving as she walked to his bed.

The first time did not last long and he remained lying on top of her. He felt her sobbing and touched her face. Her eyes were wet. She took her dress off and walked to the dining room to fetch the writing pad. She lit the candle next to his bed. "I am so very, very happy."

"I thought you were upset, or that I may have hurt you?"

"NO, NO. I had that feeling that some women talk about."

They lay together in one another's arms. With their desire spent they were innocent again. Douglas thought of the sensation he had of entering her, expanded by her willingness and her enthusiasm. He kissed her forehead and tasted the saltiness of her perspiration. He held her one breast and then the other as he had done as a little boy with his mother and felt her nipples taking turns to become stiff.

He still had his socks on and decided to take them off. He needed to have a leak and went outside completely naked. He looked up at the myriad of stars and stood with his hands behind his head while a mountain breeze cooled his damp nether regions, and he urinated leisurely. Drops of urine splashed from the grass onto his bare feet. On the kitchen steps he wiped the tops of his feet against the backs of his legs. He shivered as he went down the passage. Maggie had got into bed and he jumped boyishly in next to her and hugged her. When he started kissing her again she played with his testicles. She pushed the bedclothes away so that he could have greater freedom of movement and they began making love again. It was more deliberate and measured. He could stop for a few moments and look at her in the twilight of the candle that swayed slowly on the wall. Then they would lie completely still to see how long they could remain like that. She suddenly pulled his buttocks in towards her with some force and then he felt her nails digging into his back. Her convulsions were so captivating that he felt no discomfort. She looked as though she could hardly breathe. Her face became soft, her eyes dreamy. The hair next to her temples was matted. He could no longer hold himself back and felt the stealthy approach of delirious ecstasy.

Douglas and Maggie slept in one another's arms and in the early hours of the morning they made love again. At about nine o'clock while Douglas still slept Maggie made coffee and lit the stove for hot water and their breakfast. She sat naked in the chair next to his bed while they had their coffee, and he propped himself up on one elbow. "You are wonderful," he said. "I wish you could know how happy I am. As most boys do, I have thought a great deal about making love, but I would never ever have thought that it could be like this. I could start all over again."

She took the writing pad. "You made me have lovely thrills. You cannot believe how nice that is. I cannot wait to come and visit you again. We could do it all the time until we are tired of it. I think I love you."

Douglas put his coffee cup down and held his arms out to her. "Come and kiss me, Maggie."

When the bathwater was hot they bathed together. She soaped and washed him and he did the same for her. She fried eggs and made toast on top of the stove and after they had eaten they went for a walk up the slopes of the mountain. Her shoes were not quite suitable. She picked a few mountain flowers. On their return they made tea and sat on the veranda and looked at one another. He liked her. He could grow to like her more. The Easter weekend was barely three weeks away. "When will you be able to come and visit me again?"

"Easter weekend," she mouthed.

"Easter weekend?"

She nodded.

"That would be lovely."

"What will your parents say?" she wrote.

He pursed his lips and pulled his mouth down at the corners and shrugged his shoulders. "Hell, I don't know. We'll have to cross that bridge when we come to it, I suppose. I was engaged to be married a few years ago. Then I became deaf. I think my parents are still hoping that it will be salvaged. But there is no hope of that."

"She must be very sad. I feel so sorry for her. It is easy to love you. I will never ask you about your past."

Johnny arrived shortly after four thirty, as he had promised. Maggie and Douglas waited on the veranda next to her red suitcase. Johnny shook Douglas' hand and picked up his sister's suitcase. "Come on Sis, Ma will become suspicious."

Douglas kissed Maggie goodbye and held her hand as they walked to the car. "Thank you for coming to visit me, Maggie, and thank you Johnny for bringing her here. We have had a lovely time. I will close the gate." He shook hands with Johnny, kissed Maggie again on her cheek and watched them drive off.

"I can see from the way you look Sis, what you've been up to. You'd better do something or Ma will know. I feel pretty relaxed myself. What a pair we have turned out to be, hey? Fornicators of the first order."

"Don't talk like that, Johnny."

"So the gentleman is teaching you some smart manners?"

"He's a very decent man. A very nice man. And I am not a fornicator, and you should know that. Yes I did it with Cecil, but only after we were engaged to be married. And he was not up to much. He was a pig. Always in a hurry. Once he had grunted through his bushy moustache he had little time for me. And he cheated on me. I am glad to be rid of him."

"I never liked him. I still think he is a piece of shit."

"I like Douglas very much. We had a lovely happy time. I don't mind that he is deaf. He is a very learned man. I have never seen so many books except in a library. He has read them all. He studied at a university. People in town say he was the best teacher that there ever was at the Boys High School. He was also engaged once but broke it off when he became deaf. They are genteel people. I want to go back to him. I want to care for him, Johnny. I feel safe with him. I never told anyone, but Cecil smacked me once or twice."

"What! Why did you never say something? I would have given him a fucking good smack or two. Why did you not tell me, Sis? You know how much I care for you. We might have our differences and I do sometimes tease you, I know, but you mean a lot to me. Cecil smacked you? Christ Almighty, if he ever crosses my path I'll teach him a fucking lesson he'll never forget."

"You must never speak like this in front of Douglas. He might think we are rough people."

"He can't hear any way."

"He is learning to read lips. Some words are easier to read."

"We must get our story straight. You stayed with me at Moira's house. I have filled her in. Her mother's quite a sporting gal. Gets up to a bit of fun herself from what Moira says. So they're not going to bust you. I told them where you were. Put your head out of the window so you can get some wind in your face. I made a mistake once in the hot weather when I visited Moira and did not wear my pyjamas and left them folded up in the bottom of my case. Ma wanted to know why I had not worn them. I said I fell asleep in my clothes. But I could tell that she knew I was lying."

"Easter is just around the corner."

"Yes, I know. I must be clever about that. I am going to try and borrow one of the cars from the garage. Old Nel is a bit of a piker. You have to be smart to outwit him. But I'll find a way, to be sure. If you can get the Saturday off and I can manage a car, we'll take a little trip. Moira is getting pretty serious."

"What do you mean, serious?"

"I think she imagines she is beginning to hear wedding bells."

"And you don't hear any bells?"

"Marriage is a hell of a business, Sis. A hell of a business. You're stuck for ever like a fox with your tail chopped off, Sis. With a troop of snotty crying kids."

"I like children."

"Yes I know. Womenfolk are different."

"I don't care if Ma finds out what I am up to."

"She's not your biggest problem. It's Pa you have to be careful of. He could give you a bloody good hiding, and you don't want that. Best may be to take Ma into your confidence. It may be a little risky, but it is the only way to get her on your side. Then she will protect you from Pa. He's so fucking difficult and unreasonable at times, or should I say impossible. Ma can be a bit treacherous when she's had a tipple or two."

"He's not having an easy time, Johnny."

"Why the hell do you want to defend him when he has treated you the way he has?"

"I only want to be fair."

"The sooner you can get out of that house the better, Sis. You're a good person. You deserve a lot better. Anyway let's go over some of the things you and Moira and I did in Mossel Bay this weekend so that we'll talk the same story."

Chapter Thirty-Five

Thursday 10 March 1932

BY TEN O'CLOCK Douglas had seen to most things on the farm and strolled to the shop to buy a few essentials. Van der Byl had written him a note. "Doctor Nel telephoned to say that he would be visiting on Sunday – at about eleven."

Sunday 13 March 1932

Douglas woke early. He lay in bed for a while and thought of Maggie, then went to the kitchen to heat water for his bath. Vapour floated carelessly from the surface of the warm water that stirred above his breathing stomach as he soaped and washed Maggie and she lathered his pubic hairs while she kissed him. For reasons he could not understand his physical experience with her had dislodged and brought to the surface things deeply hidden in his psyche. Was it that the act was so primal, so original in its nature that its innocence could not be corrupted? The pleasure she had given him refused to be tainted by moral guilt or scruple. He loved Frances so, and his love for her was so elevated that he found it difficult to imagine having intercourse with her. Yet when they had touched one another he had felt guilty. Why did he not feel that now? Was it because there were no conditions? Now even his rare collection of prurient fantasies, of which he was so fond, was in danger of becoming worthless. He had carried his fantasies into every room of the whorehouse of his mind. Now as he emerged from that mansion into a lush green field with a single oak tree, blue sky, delicate white flowers standing in the grass, he could not remember where he had left them.

Wherever he went, in the paddocks with the sheep, in the barn, looking at the steep peaks of his mountains, everything contained something that reminded him of Maggie. Willemse caught him staring at the rear end of the cow, much to his embarrassment. What it was to be so innocently uninhibited as she. The way she sat naked on the chair in his bedroom, drinking her coffee, while she allowed him look at every crevice. This is what must be meant by free love. Less than two weeks before the Easter weekend. If he could last that long. It would be rather pleasant to go down to the river if the weather was good. They could swim and lie naked on the sand. Would she come? How would she let him know? How could he find out? If things were different he could send a letter with Garnett. If she did manage, how would he keep his parents away? Tell them he was going away with Garnett. Going to Herolds Bay with him. Would be tricky because Garnett would not want to be part of a deception, but it could work, as long as Garnett did not know.

When Garnett arrived Douglas had had breakfast and was sitting outside in the sun reading Joseph Conrad's *Typhoon* and recalling his experiences on board the Trafford Hall. When he saw Garnett he got up and they shook hands with exaggerated boyish vigour. Garnett held a large basket in his left hand. 'I've brought you some goodies,' his mouth said.

"Thanks, very much but you should not have bothered. I'm going to make us a roast chicken." Douglas looked at his watch. "I have prepared it and I should really put it into the oven now. Come with me, and I'll make tea at the same time." He put his book down on the seat of the chair.

"So how have you been?" Garnett wrote on the pad in the kitchen. "Tell me all."

"I have been very well, extremely well really. Things are looking up here. My sheep are doing well. As you already know, the wheat crop was better than expected, except that I still do not know how I am going to get it sold. Thank goodness for the farm. At least I can live off it. The present state of affairs cannot last. Demand should begin to pick up soon."

Garnett shrugged his shoulders and made a who-on-earth-can-tell expression.

"And what is your news Garnie? Have you managed to find a woman yet?"

Garnett grinned and picked up the pencil, "There's a new girl in town. A Miss Weber, Irene Weber. She teaches at Girls High. Started at the beginning of the year. She's really very attractive."

"Have you asked her out?"

"She's a bit snooty. I have invited her to the tennis dance. Said she'd let me know. Plays hard to get I think. She's a real madam. Very proud, aloof, bit of an intellectual. Not the kind you would think of fooling around with."

"Sounds interesting."

"What's happening with Frances?"

"Nothing. She belongs to my past."

"It is a pity."

"I opened one of her letters the other day. She wrote it quite some time ago. She spoke of a rift between her and her father. She did not go into detail but it seems as though it began when our engagement ended. I always thought he was quite a heartless bastard. I was always uneasy in his company."

"Funny that you should say that, I also felt uncomfortable in his presence."

"There were stories in Cape Town that he was quite harsh in court, a bugger to appear before him, evidently. Young advocates literally shook and trembled in front of him. They say he enjoyed that. Yet I must be fair and say that he treated me very well."

"He had a healthy respect for your intellectual capabilities."

"You flatter me."

Garnett shook his head.

"You've always championed my cause, Garnie, and that is extremely kind of you, but look at me now. Be realistic. Here I am on a small farm, penniless, in the midst of a worldwide depression and stone deaf."

"All of that says nothing about your intellect."

"I had a girl here last weekend."

Garnett frowned. "What?"

"Ja, I had a girl here. We had a wonderful time. She slept here, in my bed with me."

Garnett made circular movements next to his temple with his index finger.

"No, I'm not mad. I'm quite serious."

"She came out here, to the farm?"

"Yes."

"She just pitched up out of the blue?"

"No, we went to the bioscope when I was last in town."

"What on earth are you up to? Who is she?"

"Her name is Maggie Thompson. She works behind the counter in Prince Vintcent. Remember I asked you whether you knew of her?"

"And your parents?"

"I'm thirty one. It's my business."

Garnett sat down on one of the kitchen chairs. Douglas stood next to him so that he could see what Garnett wrote.

"Is this some bad joke?"

"No, I'm serious."

"You had her in the sack?"

"Yes, correct. I had her in the sack."

"And."

"We did what people do in the sack, the whole night long. What else would you like to know? It was the most remarkable experience I have ever had. Prodigious."

Garnett held his despairing head in his hands.

Douglas carried the tea tray to the veranda and they sat down in the autumn sun. The leaves of the oak tree at the bottom of the field and of the poplar trees near the river were beginning to turn. The most distant parts of the mountain were pale blue. The morning was windless. Every now and then Garnett heard wavering bleats of the sheep. Perhaps Douglas was simply fabricating a story to see what his reaction would be, to be otherwise. So Garnett waited for his tea to cool. Douglas sat down next to Garnett. Garnett said nothing and began to drink his tea slowly.

"I forgot the biscuits, let me get some." Douglas returned with a biscuit tin, opened it and put it on the table so that they could help themselves. He chewed loudly and slurped some tea. "I can see you don't believe me. You think I've made it up. No, no, don't protest, it's written all over your face."

Garnett smiled and took the writing pad. "You're a very good actor. You should have been on the stage. You're just trying to shock me. And you have failed. So let's stop talking bullshit."

"I am not talking bullshit Garnett, I am deadly serious. I really am. Listen to what I have to tell you. For a while now, whenever I went to Prince Vintcent, I saw the girl. I told you about her. She was friendly and I began greeting her. She is attractive. When I last visited my parents I had to go and fetch a parcel for my mother at the shop; that was on the Thursday. Maggie had been asked to keep the parcel, and when I collected it from her, she wrote me a little note asking me, or suggesting is probably the better word, suggesting that we go to the bioscope the following evening. My parents were going to the Elleys so I decided to take up the offer. We stayed in the bioscope only for a while and then went for a walk down to the river where we had a bit of a cuddle. I walked her home afterwards. I felt very comfortable with her. She is a kind and wholesome person. Then last weekend, last Saturday morning to be precise, I was sitting here on the veranda, reading. I must have fallen asleep because I woke from a slumber and found her standing right here next to me. I thought I was dreaming. Her brother was on his way to Mossel Bay to visit his girlfriend and he dropped Maggie off here to spend the weekend. She brought a neck of lamb and made me a delicious stew. It was quite unreal. Imagine pitching up here with a little red suitcase and a packet of meat to make me a stew. You don't expect such things to happen in real life. In some ways I still can't credit it. I keep on thinking that I must have had some kind of delusion, from a piece of mushroom or something, or mould in my barley soup. I know it sounds really weird. But the most incredible part of it is how well we got on. It is as though the gods have delivered her to me. She is completely artless, completely lacking in guile, devoid of all deception. She is utterly innocent."

"She could not have been so innocent if she went to bed with you."

"I have thought how I would describe her innocence. By the way, she was engaged once but broke it off. It is as though she is almost detached from the ordinary ways of the world. She has nothing yet she wants to give. She demands nothing in return. You don't find many people like that. She is completely open. There is nothing hidden. She simply said, that first evening, that she liked me from the first time she saw me. She knows about my condition and now that she has been to the farm, understands the circumstances in which I find myself. It does not seem to matter to her. What we did was most exciting but I am not smitten as I was with Frances. I am not in love or something silly like that. It is though I skipped the crazy stage."

Garnett indicated to Douglas to sit closer to him so he could see what he wrote. "From what you have told me, you have met this girl exactly twice. The first time you cuddled as you say. The second time you went to bed with her. You have not met her parents; you have no idea what they are like. You know little if anything about her past, about her education, anything. You are playing with fire."

"You don't understand, Garnie. Wait till you meet her. Will you take a letter to her for me? I want her to come here for the Easter weekend. She indicated that it might be possible."

Garnett took a deep breath. "I have a professional reputation to protect. I cannot be party to a reckless dalliance. I cannot be a messenger."

"Then just mail it, please. I'll address it to her care of Prince Vintcent."

Garnett nodded. "Do forgive me for sounding so surprised. I don't mean to offend you. Our friendship means a lot to me. I don't want to meddle in your private affairs, but you have to consider this thing extremely carefully. Let's go for a walk."

"I need to add wood to the stove. I'll do the potatoes when we get back."

When Douglas returned from the kitchen Garnett took his arm to show him what he had written. "I know the girl you mean. Her father is a builder and a speculator. Rough character. What does her brother do?"

"He's a motor mechanic. Works for Uncle Charlie it would seem."

"Odd thing to come and drop your sister off for the night at the house of a man you've never met, don't you think?"

"Maybe not if you know your sister well enough."

"What do you expect from the relationship?"

"Simply put, it is what it is."

Garnett frowned. "And what do you imagine she expects?"

"To be happy and well treated. You know Garnett, when one has been through what I have been through, having your whole life changed, having most, if not all, of your aspirations and hopes and dreams destroyed, when you have experienced life that raw, that harsh, you come to realize that there is really very little to be romantic about. You realize that even when the happy anticipation of something glorious is gone, there still is meaning to life, and what remains when all the crap is stripped away, quite ironically, has more substance. She and I have both had our disappointments. What remains for us is to share our honesty."

Thursday 24 March 1932

Douglas waited for Maggie to arrive. The maid had cleaned the house as though she knew a visitor was coming, or perhaps because she thought that it was going to be a holy weekend. Douglas picked mountain flowers and put them into a vase on the dining table. He stood outside the house in the roadway from where he could see the open gate. It was becoming dusk and he started having doubts. A white butterfly fluttered past, moving randomly in the thick mauve evening air. The lights of the car were suddenly there. Johnny jumped out and hopped about from one foot to the other with one hand in his trouser pocket. "Jees, I need to make a pee." Douglas pointed to the back of the house. "Just do it in the bushes." Douglas kissed Maggie hello and helped her with her suitcase, and a wicker basket lined with a checked white and blue cloth. She flung her arms around him and hugged him once he had put her things down.

Johnny shook Douglas' hand shyly and wrung his hands. "I must get going before it gets too dark, Sis, the mountain is dangerous. Please give apologies to your friend for being so hurried." He kissed Maggie on her cheek. "See you on Monday afternoon." He shook Douglas' hand again rather self-consciously and hurried to the car. Maggie and Douglas stood with their arms around each other as they watched him leave.

While Douglas went to close the gate, Maggie unpacked. The basket she had brought still stood on her bed. In it were pork chops, and a large chocolate cake that she had baked on the pretence that it was for Johnny's girl. She hung her dresses in the cupboard and put her underwear onto the shelves. She had brought shoes for walking and her bathing costume for the beach at Mossel Bay. She heard Douglas approaching. The shutters were still open. He put his arms out to her and embraced her. "I am so pleased that you have come, Maggie. I cannot tell you how much I have looked forward to seeing you. It is wonderful to have you back."

"Me too," her mouth said.

He kissed her. He felt his penis expanding and put his hand down the front of her dress. He felt her gasps and pushed her down on the bed. She undid the front of his trousers and put her hand inside. He pushed her pants down and touched her. While he took his trousers off she removed her pants completely. He climbed onto her. He felt the vibrations of her voice box against his cheek and her breath fluttering in his eyes as they tried to get ever closer together. When they were done he kissed her and kissed her and kissed her all over her face and she kissed him back. They lay joined together in front of the open window until the fluids that seeped from them evaporated and became cold.

They fried the pork chops that Maggie had brought, in a pan, and cooked rice and vegetables for their supper. Douglas made a fire in the hearth and they lay on the carpet in front of the fire. He read to her from *David Copperfield* while she had her head on his lap. They made tea and ate biscuits. When she started yawning they went to his room and undressed by the light of a candle. They stood naked against one another before climbing into bed. They made love as if they were saying goodnight, and fell asleep.

In the morning he made coffee for her and warmed water for their bath. They ate breakfast in the dining room and went for a walk in the mountain. After lunch she asked him to read some more to her and he had to explain the meaning of some words. She then wanted to go and say hello to Willemse who was pleased to see her.

For supper Maggie made thick green pea soup flavoured with strips of bacon. When the soup was ready they ate it with thick slices of fresh brown bread generously spread with yellow salty farm butter.

"The girls at the shop say Dr Nel is your friend?"

"Yes he is. He was here last weekend."

"Does he know about us?"

"Yes."

"What did he say?"

"He was surprised."

"Did he not disapprove?"

"It is not his business. It is our business. I could not give a rat's tail what other people may think or say. You have made me very happy. What you have given me is so honest, so authentic, that nothing that other people may say or do can devalue it. You are very special Maggie. When we first made love I became innocent again. You are the first person to whom I have ever made love. Before that happened all sorts of fantasies of what it would be like to have intercourse with a woman stimulated me and aroused me. The first time we did it, it felt to me as though I had entered a place where there is no time or space – a mystical world – where all my old fantasies ceased to have any meaning."

She held up her hand. "What does mistica mean?"

"The way that I am using it means understanding things better than we as humans ordinarily understand them."

"I think I know what you mean. When I was little I had a friend that no one else could see. Yet he was real. I think I was about three. He was my husband, his name was Bela and we had two children. My mother told me so often that there was no such person that I eventually believed her and said goodbye to Bela. I still remember him sometimes. He was a good man. I missed the children for a long time afterwards. They must be grown up by now. I have not told anybody else this. They will think I am mad but what I had with Bela made a lot of sense."

"Coming back to what people might say, I shall have to tell my parents about us. And you will have to tell your parents. I don't want to spoil what is good and wholesome with deceit."

"I love the way you talk. When you speak you rise like a great giant before me. I like the big words you use. They just roll off your tongue so easily. Have you always been able to speak so well? How did you learn to do that?"

Douglas laughed. "I would not say that I speak well but it helps to read a lot."

"I enjoyed the books at school. The books we had to read."

"What do you remember best?"

"I cannot remember really. Let me think. The last one we did before I left to go and work was *Treasure Island*."

"What is your age, now?"

"Twenty-four. I was sixteen when I went to work. How old are you?"

"I am thirty-one."

"How old is your friend?"

"Dr Nel?"

She nodded.

"Same age as I am."

"He looks like a nice man. He came to see my father when he was ill."

"What was wrong with your father?"

"I think it was his lungs. The doctor came to our house a few times. He has a nice car. Johnny works at his uncle's garage."

Saturday 26 March 1932

In the morning Maggie decided to tidy Douglas' cupboard. Two of his woollen jerseys had moth holes in them and she found mothballs in a packet in the pantry. She washed some of his things and her underwear as well as her stockings and hung them on the line behind the house. When she had finished they had tea and Douglas suggested going to the river. Willemse saw them disappearing hand in hand into the poplars. What it was to be young and virile. He had had a common law wife, before the great flu took her from him. That was a terrible time. What could a man do? When the woman died their child left him, blaming him for her death. He had not heard of him since and he often wondered what had become of his son.

Douglas and Maggie lay on the sloping sandy shore of the river, holding hands. The sun was hot and Douglas took off his shirt. Maggie stroked his hairy front as if her fingers were a comb and teased the hair so that it stood up in tufts. "I think I am going to have a swim." Douglas stood up and took his shoes and the rest of his clothes off. She watched his muscular legs and white buttocks walking down to the edge of the water and when he squatted to splash water onto his chest she saw his penis dangling below him. He plunged into the water and swam a few bold strokes. "It's quite cold," he called out of breath, "but refreshing. Come in."

Maggie took her clothes off and tiptoed to the water's edge. He could see she was shy. She tested the temperature with her foot. She shuddered and held her arms across her breasts. She had goose bumps on her thighs. Poor thing, she wanted to please him. "I think it is too cold for you. I'm coming out now, get dressed." He watched as her lovely rear end, with pink creases from her underwear, trotted back to her pile of clothes. She bent over to pick up her pants.

Willemse was surprised to see them returning so soon. From Douglas' wet shirt he could see that he had been swimming, but not she. They waved to him. He waved back and watched them going up the house.

They had the leftovers of their pea soup for lunch and afterwards slept on Maggie's bed until well after four in the afternoon. Maggie was first to wake and staggered barefoot and yawning to the kitchen. While she waited for the water to boil she took their washing off the line and folded it on the dining room table. When their tea was ready she went to her room and sat down next to

Douglas. He was still drowsy and she stroked his hair. She made the motions of drinking from a cup and he groaned playfully as he got up. She cut him a generous slice of chocolate cake. "You are spoiling me," he said. After tea he read his book on the veranda while she ironed their clothes in the kitchen. Willemse brought milk and eggs to the kitchen door.

In the evening Douglas read more to her from *David Copperfield* and they sat staring into the fire before going to bed. Maggie washed herself and put on a pair of Douglas' pyjamas. She held the bedclothes to one side so that he could get in next to her and snuggled up to him. He wet his fingers with saliva and extinguished the candle. They lay silently for a long time. The moon had been full a few days earlier and its indirect pale light filtered through the shutters. He looked at her and saw that she had fallen asleep. He was still wide-awake and when he eventually fell asleep he dreamt that he was in a foreign restaurant. He did not know where, but it was foreign all right. There were people that he imagined were Gypsies. They played violins and made music that he could not hear. Maggie was at his side. They ate strange delicious food from plates that had hand-painted brightly coloured borders. The men wore dinner jackets and there was a Chinese painting of a misty lake in the one corner, partially concealed by a bamboo screen. A beguilingly attractive dark haired woman appeared from behind the screen in a scarlet Spanish dancer's frock. Her lipstick was dark shiny red and she had small blue and red patterns tattooed all over her bare tits. She cocked her index finger at Douglas and said in a chalky seductive voice that he could clearly hear. "You have won the raffle, Sir. I am your prize. You may spend an afternoon of your choosing with me, and do anything with me that will please you." All who were present clapped their hands and the band struck up to play a foxtrot. It felt to him as though he was not completely asleep, as if he could interact with the characters and events in his dream, as though he could choose what he wanted to experience next. He woke up and put his arm around Maggie. She sighed contentedly in her sleep and muttered something. He comforted himself by holding her breast and thought about his dream.

Sunday 27 March 1932

Easter Sunday morning arrived with the sun. Willemse carried a can of milk up to the sleeping house. He tried the back door but it was locked and he put the milk down on the top step. Inside Maggie and Douglas were fast asleep. It was past eight o'clock before Maggie woke. She got out of her side of the bed, took her pyjama trousers off and squatted over the chamber pot to urinate. She got back into bed without the trousers on and put her arm and her one leg over Douglas. He groped about as he woke and found her naked buttock. At first it felt to him like a giant breast but it had no nipple and when he realised what it was he turned towards Maggie and took his trousers off. He lay on his back and pulled her onto him. She was embarrassed to be on top of him but he smiled at her and held her playfully so that she couldn't get off. Once they were engaged she sat up, put her hands on his shoulders and began riding him like a horse. He unbuttoned her pyjama top and watched her breasts quivering as she wriggled her hips, her eyes glazed, experimenting to see how she could find the greatest pleasure.

They made love twice before they had a bath. She tidied the kitchen and made breakfast of fried eggs, fried tomatoes and sausage. Even in their remote location the sense that was Sunday had reached them. Everything was resting. He wondered what her voice was like and how she pronounced her words. He thought about the woman in his dream and her tattooed tits. What a raffle to win. They smiled at one another while they ate. Their lower regions had become sensitive. No doubt the tissues would revive as the day wore on. It would be nice to have her here all the time but he was not sure how practical that would be. Not to mention what his parents would say. He could not imagine how he would introduce the subject, or how he would introduce her to them. They would have to be careful that she did not get pregnant. He had been quite reckless. If they were going to continue like this they would need prophylactics. He could prevail on Garnett to bring him some. "We must be careful that you don't become pregnant Maggie."

She wrote on the pad, "This is a good time of the month. I will have my period any day now. Don't worry. I will be fine."

"How do you know that?"

"My auntie is a nurse in the hospital. I listened when she explained to my mother because my father makes demands. The doctor at the hospital told the nurses that there is a time when it is safe. If we are clever it will be fine."

"You are clever. What would you like to do today?"

"Just to be with you. I love it here on this farm. It is a happy place. This is a friendly house. You are a very nice man. I love you for being so kind to me. You are also very handsome and you are gentle."

Monday 28 March 1932

Douglas' father woke very early after a night of disturbed sleep. It must have been something he had eaten. He had perspired heavily during the night and woken with his heart thumping against his ribs. Through the night his thoughts had constantly turned to Douglas. The weather had become nasty and he was concerned about Douglas' journey back from Herolds Bay. At eight o'clock he telephoned the Nels to ask when Garnett was expected back.

Mr Nel answered the telephone.

"This is Albert, Louis, good morning, how are you?"

"I'm just fine thank you. To what do I owe the honour?"

"I apologise for ringing so early. I just wanted to know when Garnett will be coming back from Herolds Bay?"

"I know he's got to pick up something for Bailey, on the way back in George, and from there he'll be coming straight here. Is there some problem?"

"No, I thought if they were going to be back early, I would go and see Douglas this afternoon. I haven't seen him in a while."

"I don't understand. What has Garnett's return got to do with visiting Douglas?"

"Because he's gone along."

"There must be some misunderstanding, Albert. To the best of my knowledge Garnett went by himself. He was going to meet Rodgers there, to do some fishing. He left on Thursday afternoon. Are you sure Douglas was meant to go along?"

"So I thought. You've got me worried now. I dare say I am a trifle confused."

"I'm sure Garnett went on his own. He told me he was going to purchase fishing tackle in George, on the way to Herolds Bay. He never mentioned picking Douglas up. That would have meant going via Mossel Bay."

"I am so sorry for having troubled you. I must have misunderstood things. Thank you very much. Goodbye, and all the best."

"I'll have to go out to the farm, Anneke," van Yssen's forehead was puckered.

"You seem troubled, is there a problem?"

"I rang Louis Nel to ask him when Garnett would be back because I thought of visiting Douglas, and he tells me that he thinks Garnett went on his own. I thought Douglas was going along. I wonder what's going on? Maybe he is sick or something."

"Then I should go with you."

"No, it's fine. I just had such an uneasy feeling during the night. You've been looking forward to seeing Joan. Stay here. I will be fine. In fact I'll just have some toast and coffee and then go immediately."

"Are you sure?"

"Yes."

Van Yssen drove to town to put in petrol. Perhaps Douglas went along after all. Louis could be confused. It would nevertheless be good to go to the farm, to see that all was well. He was so preoccupied with concern that he saw little on his way to the silent world of his son. He started looking for signs to reassure himself. If he did not encounter a car in the next five miles Douglas would be fine. If smoke came from the next farmhouse chimney, Douglas would be fine. Perhaps he was watching the sea at Herolds Bay. He reached the shop near the farm before he knew it. The shutters of the farmhouse were closed. Down below near the river pale grey smoke drifted from Willemse's chimney. At least he was there. Van Yssen went to the flowerpot on the veranda to find the front door key. It was not there. He tried the door but it was locked. He went to the kitchen door. It too was locked. Douglas must be away. He walked down to Willemse's cottage. Willemse was sitting on his bench with his dog at his feet. He started when he saw van Yssen.

"Good morning," van Yssen said loudly.

Willemse got up. "Good morning, Sir."

"Is my son here?"
Willemse nodded. "Ja." He pointed hesitantly at the house.
"Why is everything still shut? Is he ill or something?"
"He's not ill."
"Is he inside the house or has he gone for a walk, or something?"
"I don't know, Sir."
"What is going on?"
"Nothing."

Van Yssen stood for a few moments with his hands in his pockets and rocked back and forth. He turned and walked back up to the house. Willemse was behaving oddly. Maybe he's been drinking again. He would leave a note for Douglas. But he needed some paper and a pencil. He looked again in the flowerpot in case he had missed the key. He had not tried the door at the other end of the house. He walked around the back of the house to see if any of the shutters were unlatched. Opposite Douglas' window he heard sounds. Almost as though a bed was creaking. He stopped and listened. He heard a faint moaning. Douglas was ill. The door at the end of the passage was unlocked. He went down the passage and peered into Douglas' room. Maggie was on top of Douglas moving up and down, making slow circular movements with her hips. They were completely naked. He could see the glistening where they were joined. The floor creaked and Maggie turned her head in the direction of the sound. An elderly man was standing at the door. She jumped from Douglas and grabbed a sheet to cover herself. Initially Douglas remained on his back, confused at what was happening. He lifted his head to see what was going on and saw his father turning away from what he had witnessed. His erection vanished. He rushed to shut the door. Maggie sat on the side of the bed, sobbing bitterly. Douglas put on his dressing gown and went to find his father.

Van Yssen sat slumped at the dining room table, his large despairing forehead supported by the palms of his hands. As much as he tried to dispel the image of how they were joined, it refused to leave. This was graphic proof of punishment for what they had done on the train. Fate had a way of calculating these things. If you disturb the fundamental rules of the universe you do it at your own peril. Now this. As if the depression was not bad enough. This disgrace. His only begotten son.

Douglas appeared on the opposite side of the table, in his dressing gown. Van Yssen could not lift his eyes. Douglas stood with his hands on the back of a chair. What could he say? The element of deceit was worst. How much had his father seen? No matter. Van Yssen was aware of the motionless shape of the red tartan dressing gown in front of him.

Without looking up he wrote on the pad left on the table. "Why, Douglas," his hand wavered, "why did you have to tell me that you were going away for the weekend with Garnett?"

"I thought it would be better that way, Dad."
"Who is the woman?"

"She's a girl, Dad. Someone I like."

"Where does she come from?"

"From Oudtshoorn, from Prince Vintcent. She works there. I met her there."

"A shop assistant?' He heavily underlined the words 'shop assistant."

"Yes Dad, a shop assistant."

"How long has she been here?"

"Since Thursday afternoon."

"What will the neighbours say?"

"They are away."

"So this was planned?"

"Not really."

"It either was or it wasn't?"

"Yes it was."

"How did she get here?"

"Her brother was on the way to Mossel Bay. He will fetch her again this afternoon."

Van Yssen shook his head in disbelief. "What kinds of people are these? What kind of person would deliver his sister to the house of a man? To stay over for the night, nights?"

"She is really a very good person, Dad. She has been very kind to me. She even brought meat to cook and a cake that she had baked."

Van Yssen looked up at his son. "When did all this start?"

"When I was last in Oudtshoorn. I have known her, her name is Maggie Thompson, for quite some time. Whenever I went into the shop I saw her and we exchanged pleasantries. She has more good in her than a lot of people I know. I regret that I have made her party to my deceit. She does not deserve it. It is my fault. I encouraged her. She is the victim of these circumstances."

Van Yssen stroked his forehead with his fingers and looked down at the surface of the table. He looked for meaning in the patterns in the grain of the wood. He rose slowly from his chair and gathered his hat. "I should get going," he said.

"I am so sorry that you had to find out like this, Dad." Douglas opened the front door for his father and watched as his father's shoulders and his hat, skew on his head, went down the steps of the veranda. Van Yssen did not look back and instead lifted his left hand in a feeble farewell gesture. The emptiness of the gesture made the silence worse.

Maggie was still sobbing when Douglas returned to his shameful dishevelled bed. She had put on her green hand knitted jersey. Apart from that she sat naked on the edge of the bed. He sat down next to her and put his arm around her. She turned so that he could see her mouth, "Who was that?"

"My father."

She started sobbing again.

"It is all right Maggie. It was unfortunate that it happened like this, but there is nothing we can do about it now. The deed is done. I feel sorry for him.

He is a true Victorian. I will warm some water for our bath and make coffee. Come with me. I do apologise to you for the embarrassment, for my father's intrusion. I am really very sorry for what has happened to you."

She sniffed as she dried her tears and shook her straggling hair. "It was all my fault."

"No it is not your fault. Come, let us go and make some coffee." He took his dressing gown off and put it over her shoulders, and with a towel around his waist led the way to the kitchen.

For Douglas the experience began to have cathartic qualities. He hummed as he lit the Primus stove, feeling vibrations in his throat and not knowing what it sounded like. Maggie sat at the kitchen table for a while and then went to fetch the writing pad. She saw van Yssen's handwriting but turned the page so that she could not read what he had written. "Everything was so beautiful. I was so very happy here. Now everything has been spoilt for ever."

Douglas smiled. "I'm glad that it happened. It sends my dad a clear message. The ice is broken now." He took her by the shoulders and kissed her on the forehead. "I love you for the happiness that you have brought me, Maggie. I know it was embarrassing for you, and for me, but there is nothing that we can do about it now. We have our own lives to live."

"I feel so sorry for that man. He must be very hurt inside. It will be best for me to go away so that I will never be there to remind him of what he saw." She started crying again.

"You will do nothing of the sort. When he gets to know you he will grow to appreciate what a lovely person you are. What would you like for breakfast?"

"I am not hungry. I want to have a bath, please."

The tears in van Yssen's eyes blurred his vision. The sides of the road were indistinct and when a car passed him going in the opposite direction his wretchedness made him wonder what it would have felt like to drive into it. 'O my son Absalom, my son, my son Absalom! Would God I had died for thee.'

Mrs Hops was leaving when van Yssen arrived. "Is everything all right, Albert?" his wife enquired. Mrs Hops tilted her head for his response.

"It seems he went with Garnett."

"Oh thank goodness, Mrs Hops exclaimed. "Douglas is such a wonderful son. I so wished he would have married his Frances. Anneke and I were talking about that just now. But I must be going now. I have to see to Jimmy's lunch. He becomes most irritable when it is late. Such a man of habit." She kissed Mrs van Yssen on her cheek and trotted down the garden path.

"You seem upset, Albert?"

"You'd better come and sit down with me." They went into the living room.

"What is the matter?"

"Douglas did not go with Garnett."

"How do you mean? You said he did go along. Is he all right?"

Tears welled up in van Yssen's eyes.

"Oh Albert, what happened? Is he hurt, what?"

"You must be very brave, Anneke."

"Oh, Lord!"

"What I am going to tell you may upset you very much."

"What!"

"I found Douglas in bed with some hussy."

"Thank God, I thought something had happened to him. But how terrible!"

"The woman has been there the whole weekend. The house was shut, all the shutters still closed, when I arrived there, but the door at the end of the house was unlocked, so I went inside and found the two of them." His hands trembled and his head began to shake. He was pale.

"Try not to upset yourself too much, I'll get you something sweet to drink."

"No, wait. Or, yes, ask Betta to make some tea. I'll put honey into it."

Mrs van Yssen returned to the living room.

"I am just so relieved that nothing happened to him."

"Something did happen to him, Anneke. He was in bed with a strange woman. I don't know how to tell you this, without offending your sensibilities, but she was completely stark naked and sitting on top of him, doing, moving herself around. Douglas could not hear me. She must have become aware of my presence, and jumped off him, and there he lay on his back in all his shame. It was unspeakable."

"Did you speak to him?"

"Yes."

"And what did he say?"

"He said he was sorry for what had happened."

"Was that all, no explanation? Who was the woman? How old was she?"

"She's young."

"Did he say who she was?"

"Some shop assistant who works at Prince Vintcent. God in Heaven! Can you believe that! What a mess. What a terrible mess our lives have turned out to be. What have I done, what have you done, to deserve this? Can you imagine the disgrace when this gets out? What will people say?"

"Could you see what she looked like?"

"Dark hair, blue eyes, well built, fair skin. That's all I remember. She was terrified when she saw me. Serves her right."

"I know the girl you mean. She is very sweet."

"Sweet! Sweet? For God's sake Anneke, if you saw what I saw. Two people devouring one another like animals. One of them my son. My own son. She did not look very sweet or innocent to me. She knew what she was doing, all right. I saw everything imaginable. For God's sake, it was terrible."

"Keep your voice down, dear. Betta will be bringing the tea anytime now."

"For how long has the girl been working at Prince Vintcent?"
"For quite some time, now. I'm not sure."
"Have you spoken to her?"
"Yes, often."
"What does she sound like?"
"They are ordinary people, Albert."
"Why don't you just say it? Common people."
"Why do you say it like that?"
"Anneke, when I questioned Douglas – and I must say that I was bitterly disappointed in him because it came out that he deceived us by telling us that he was going with Garnett while planning the whole affair – because I could not understand how the woman got there, he informed me that her brother, her brother mind you, had, as it were, delivered her to Douglas' doorstep, to go to bed with him. What kinds of people do things like that, Anneke?"

Betta carried in the tea. She had heard van Yssen's raised voice.

"Thank you Betta." She waited till Betta had gone. "I realise that you are upset Albert, but we must keep cool heads. We must not make things worse than they already are."

"Things cannot get worse, Anneke."

"Don't say that Albert. Douglas is alive and he is well. He is a man, and he has his needs. At least he has been discreet."

"Discreet! How can there be anything discreet about having a woman in your house for the entire Holy Easter Weekend? Willemse knows about the whole thing. He was a co-conspirator. Just think of it, Anneke, our son Douglas conspires with a common man who works for him to have a woman in his bed."

Mrs van Yssen put a generous amount of honey into her husband's tea.

"That is a bit extreme, Albert. We cannot tell whether poor old Willemse had anything to do with it."

"I could see that he knew what was going on. Whose side are you on?"

"I am not on any side, Albert. I love you and I love Douglas. I just want us all to be as happy as possible. What has happened has happened and we must do our level best to make the best of our circumstances."

"What will people say?"

"Go and speak to Garnett tomorrow. Perhaps he can talk to Douglas. It could be that it is just something that will pass. Then at worst there will be few rumours. Kings and heads of states have had mistresses, Albert. It is not as terrible as you imagine. Guillemette was saying just the other day how common it is for French men to have mistresses. Douglas has not committed a crime."

"How you can make so light of it astonishes me. He has committed a sin. He has sinned before God. He has had intercourse out of wedlock. We are being punished. Guillemette has strange ideas about a lot of things; her judgement is not always to be trusted. She does not even go to church."

"She is a good person Albert. She has been a very good friend to us."

"Everybody and everything is good in your eyes. Douglas is just like you. He had the temerity to say to me, standing naked in front of me in his dressing gown, that the woman was a good person. How can you be a good person when you are sitting on top of a man, writhing like a snake? I saw my son like that, Anneke. In all his nakedness. And the woman."

"She's just a girl Albert, a really sweet girl. She is generous to a fault. When she measures out material she always errs in my favour."

"Then she's stealing from Schmidt."

"Oh Albert, life is not always a matter of black and white, it is not built up of precise little blocks of right and wrong."

"If we lose our sense of morality, of what is right and what is wrong, we will lose everything. What does it benefit us to seek earthly pleasures only to lose the Kingdom of God?"

"I realise that you are very upset, but spare a thought for Douglas. How do you think he must feel, and the girl? Drink your tea"

Van Yssen could hardly hold his cup. "Just imagine what Judge Rose will say."

"We should not let him influence our lives, Albert."

"He is a man of great stature."

"Douglas thinks he has feet of clay."

"He would. Who is he to judge others, considering his own behaviour? Judge Rose has great influence in important circles."

"You are making too much of him. Frances hardly even speaks to him because of what he said about Douglas."

"How do you know that?"

"Frances wrote to me."

"I was not aware of that."

"I thought you were, Albert. Anyway, there is really no need for us to discuss Judge Rose. More important matter is how we are going to handle Douglas."

"I really don't know. It might be worthwhile to speak to Garnett."

"I would like you to take me to the farm in the next day or two, if your work permits, for me to have a word with Douglas. In the meantime I shall avoid going to Prince Vintcent because of Maggie."

"So you know her name?"

"Yes, everybody does. I'm sure you've seen her."

"I don't recall anybody like that. What did the Judge say about Douglas?"

"Frances did not say, except that it was so unkind that she lost all respect for her father. She said that she always thought that her father admired Douglas, and that her father had betrayed her by what he said."

"Then this will only make Douglas worse in his eyes."

"With the greatest of respect, Albert, I cannot see why Judge Rose should even enter into the present discussion. He is irrelevant in this, and considering him will merely distract us. When you go and see Garnett I shall consult Guillemette."

"I would prefer you not to do that, Anneke."

"As you wish, Albert."

"I can't believe that this has happened. I mean what sort of people are they?" He got up with difficulty and shuffled off to his study, guided by the glistening vision of where Douglas and Maggie had been joined.

Johnny picked Maggie up at the farm shortly after four that afternoon.

"What's wrong, Sis? The two of you look as though you have been to a funeral?"

"Douglas' father found us in bed together this morning."

"Holy shit! You mean?"

"Yes."

"You mean you were?"

"Yes."

"Holy double shit! What happened?"

"Douglas spoke to the old man in the dining room while I stayed in the bedroom. It was terrible Johnny." She started to cry. "It was awful, awful, awful. You cannot imagine how terrible it was, to be seen like that."

"Better stop howling, can't go home like this. Ma will want to know why you look like this. Jesus, I once nearly got caught with my pants down. It wasn't funny. What did his old man say?"

"Hardly anything as far as I understand. He just sat there staring at the table. Then he left without hardly saying goodbye."

"What does Douglas say?"

"He just shrugs it off. Said he loved me."

"You must be careful about getting involved with toffs, kiddo. You'll get hurt."

"Douglas is not one of those. He is a decent man. He is sincere."

"They're always sincere while they are hunting for a bit of crumpet. Trouble starts when they've had enough."

"It's not like that, Johnny, not at all. It is special."

"So what now?"

"He wants me to come back the next time you go to Mossel Bay." She sniffed and blew her nose loudly. "How was your weekend?"

"I had the time of my life. Now let's get our story straight in case we get interrogated separately."

Wednesday 30 March 1932

Douglas and Willemse were dipping sheep when his parents arrived at the farm shortly after three in the afternoon. Without thinking, his father knocked on the front door, and shook his head stupidly when he realised what he was doing. He heard the sheep bleating louder than usual and walked towards the kraal. Mrs van Yssen remained on the veranda – the house had become another woman's domain. She sat down with her handbag on the lap of her buttercup coloured shirt-waister. She examined her face in the mirror of her compact.

When van Yssen saw Douglas, suntanned and strong, absorbed in manhandling reluctant sheep and plunging them into the dip, his disappointment was momentarily eased. Willemse tapped Douglas on the shoulder and pointed at his father. Douglas nodded. His father waved in reply. Douglas indicated to Willemse to carry on while he went to the house.

Before Douglas could get to him, van Yssen turned and walked back to the house. On the veranda his mother held out her arms and embraced him while his father stood uneasily to one side. "Come inside with me ma, while I put some water on."

"I'll go and see what Willemse is doing," van Yssen suggested.

"I see Dad is still mightily upset?"

His mother nodded.

Douglas and his mother sat side by side at the kitchen table. "I really very much regret what happened, Ma. I am not going to make any excuses. The worst of it all, the very worst of it all is that I lied about going with Garnett. I shall never do that again. I realise that it has done a lot of damage to my relationship with Dad. I'll have to mend that as best I can. I must also tell you that Maggie had no part in my deceit. She is honest to a point of naivety. Please try and impress that upon Dad."

Mrs van Yssen sat and listened without looking at Douglas. "I know that Dad feels that Maggie's family does not have the right social standing. He said they're common. I've never met them. For all I know he might be right. Everything happened so naturally that I have not the slightest feeling of remorse or regret. I feel no guilt. The only thing, as I said earlier, that has spoilt what happened is that I lied about going with Garnett because I wanted to avoid having visitors. I wanted to be alone here with Maggie. It was the second time she visited me here. I told Garnett about the first visit. As far as the social implications are concerned, I no longer have any normal social life. I live here as a virtual recluse, cut off from the world, barely existing. I have no prospect of marrying Frances. God knows how I loved her. When my relationship with her ended something in me died. I will never again be able to love a woman as I loved Frances. It is difficult to describe what I feel for Maggie. She is completely natural. She makes no demands, and as I said to Garnett, she is so busy giving that she has no time to ask for anything. She has not had an easy life. The best of all is that we are able to communicate without saying a word. It is a sort of intuitive exchange. It is as though the gods on Olympus have relented for what they did to me and sent me an offering. The poor thing, she even brought a neck of lamb, that she purchased with her hard earned money, and made me a stew. She washed my clothes and tidied my cupboard. I had time to read. I can't live here on my own for ever, Ma."

His mother indicated that she needed to write something. "I know the girl. She is sweet. She has an inborn decency that deserves a decent response. I don't know how we are going to solve the social issues. They present great difficulties. I don't know how we are going to deal with your father. He will not be able to understand what you say about being natural. He is heavily burdened with Calvinistic guilt. One day I will explain to you why I say this. "She took the page on which she had written, tore it up and put it into the stove. "What did Garnett say when you told him?"

"His reaction was not favourable. He said I was playing with fire. Whatever that meant. I assume he was also talking about the social implications. Poor old Maggie, she was also worried about what you and Dad might think. I said to her that I don't give a rat's tail what people say. I can't hear them anyway. I will do whatever I please with what I have left of my life."

"You must try to respect your father in this. He made a great financial sacrifice when he bought the farm for you."

"If he wants to sell the farm, I'll find some other way."

She shook her head vigorously to avoid misunderstanding. 'I am only saying this because I want you to respect his position. There is no threat. Please just be sensitive to his needs.'

"I wish I was not dependent on him, Ma. But unfortunately I am. I have always had to do as he dictates."

"He is the head of our family. You are his only son. He loves you. He has always admired you so, and your achievements. Please don't disappoint his remaining hopes." Mrs van Yssen heard her husband approaching and put her finger over her lips to warn Douglas.

They had coffee in the dining room. Douglas said nothing and leant back in his chair his hands confidently behind his head, his legs stretched before him, a self-satisfied impenitent expression in his eyes. The atmosphere was fraught. The only sounds were the clinking cups and creaking chairs. Van Yssen took the writing pad. "The sheep are looking jolly good." He pushed it towards Douglas. His mother smiled.

She hugged and kissed Douglas before they left and his father shook his hand.

"What did Douglas have to say to you, Anneke?"

"He is most contrite about telling you an untruth. Said he did it so that he and the girl could have privacy."

"And so he should be. If I cannot trust my own son, who can I trust?"

"Douglas is not a dishonest person, Albert."

"He lied to me."

"You must learn to forgive more easily."

"If it means that I must compromise my principles I cannot do that. To forgive certain things only means to encourage them. I ask very little of Douglas. Does he ask for forgiveness for what he did out of wedlock?"

"No, he is unrepentant about that. He refuses to see anything wrong in what he has done. He implied that what the girl has to offer him is compensation for what fate did to him, something about the gods on Olympus bestowing an offering upon him. He says the girl is natural and innocent."

"Innocent! Good Lord Anneke, if you saw what I saw."

"What exactly did you see?"

"I cannot tell you. It would offend you."

"Was it unnatural?"

"No, but they were having intercourse."

"That is a natural thing to do."

"But it is not natural to see your own son like that. And the little hussy."

"We cannot undo what has happened Albert. All that matters now is the future."

"We must persuade Douglas to abandon this liaison immediately. That will at least limit the damage already done."

"He told me that Garnett knows."

"How did he come to know?"

"I think Douglas told him when Garnett visited."

"What did Garnett say?"

"He told him that he was playing with fire."

"And so he is."

"Douglas will not easily let go of the girl. He would want to do the honourable thing."

"He did not do the honourable thing towards us."

"The two things are different."

"No they are not."

"He says there is an intuitive bond between them. As though she is the right person to fit into a deaf man's life."

"He is compromising."

"He has no alternative."

"He is taking second best."

"What alternative does he have?"

"God in Heaven, Anneke! What are you saying? That our son cannot find a woman of suitable social standing because he is deaf? That he must take second best. A man so brilliant?"

She said nothing.

"And now we must stand by and watch in silence while he humiliates us, and himself, by entering into what can at best be called a misalliance? What a scandal it will be. What will people say?"

"They will get used to it Albert."

"What will become of our name?"

"People know us for what we are. Our good friends will understand. The others will have their friendship tested and reveal their true natures. You attach so much importance to matters of principle, Albert. Now is your opportunity to live up to that. Examine every aspect of this affair honestly and objectively.

Forget about what people will say. Consider only the underlying principles. Strip away your pride, and see what remains. You have not even met the girl. I have met her. My intuition tells me that she is a good person."

"I have seen her. She is a flirt."

"Do you say that because she was friendly?"

"She was forward."

"Douglas was quite defiant, Albert. The more we oppose this relationship the more obstinate he will become. And we will drive him away from us. I have noticed changes in Douglas since he became deaf and began his cloistered life. He is difficult at times, and you cannot blame him. He is a man. You cannot expect him to be celibate forever. Can you think of a single girl you know who would want to marry him?"

"That is a dreadful thing to say, Anneke. Frances would have married him."

"Yes, and she would still marry him today. But Douglas will not subject her to that. Nothing will ever change his mind. I see it from his point of view. And I see it from Frances' point of view. There is no purpose in debating what would have been or what could have been. We have to deal with present realities. I will invite the girl to have tea with me."

"You cannot do that. It will signal some form of approval."

"Not necessarily. It depends on how I handle it. It will be for the better. Please leave it to me."

"I will think about it."

Thursday 31 March 1932

Van Yssen had some business matters to attend to in town and took his wife along to do her grocery shopping. She arranged for the groceries to be delivered and met Madame Jacquard at the Waldorf so that they could walk home together.

When the two women reached Prince Vintcent, Mrs van Yssen went inside and handed Maggie an invitation to have tea with her the next Saturday afternoon. Maggie took the envelope nervously. Mrs van Yssen smiled in a friendly way. "Don't be afraid of me, Maggie. I sincerely hope that you will come and visit me. Tell your mother that one of your customers has invited you to tea. Our address is inside."

Chapter Thirty-six

Saturday 2 April 1932

UNSEASONABLE RAIN had begun falling during the night. When Maggie set off to see Mrs van Yssen it was still drizzling. She had found an old black umbrella among the brooms in the kitchen cupboard and Johnny helped her to repair the place where fabric was undone from its frame. She wore a camel-hair coloured woollen coat that her mother had bought second hand in Durban and the blue dress she had worn the night she went to the bioscope with Douglas.

Rain blurred the otherwise arid town and made it seem uninhabited. The wooden boards across the suspension bridge were fungus slippery. She glanced at the pine grove where they had had their first encounter. Water dripped from the autumn leaves of ash trees that lined the road. It was not that far really. She knew where the house was. Johnny had taken her past there so that she would not get lost. It was a smart house. They must be rich people.

Her father again had no work. The landlord would be on their necks. There would also be a lot of screaming and shouting at home. Douglas would never do that. Mind you, there would be little point. He was deaf. The rain became heavier and she had to hold her umbrella at an angle to protect herself. She lifted it every now and then to measure her progress. Her feet were wet. She stood under a tree for a while, and then pressed on because it would be rude to be late. It would be nice to get out of the house for good.

He would never have her. He is too smart. All those books. She was not even sure how to spell certain words.

Mrs van Yssen had made a fire in the living room. She had baked a large ginger cake after lunch. Albert said he thought that it would be a good idea to spend a rainy afternoon in the library and left while she was still mixing the cake.

Mrs van Yssen heard Maggie's hesitant knock on the front door.

"Oh my goodness me, you're so wet. My dear girl, we'll leave your umbrella out here, come inside. I have made a fire. Let me take your coat. I'll hang it in the kitchen. Come and sit down next to the fire."

"Thank you very much Mrs van Yssen."

When Mrs van Yssen took Maggie's coat she realised that she was shivering. She fetched a hanger and hung it from the edge of a kitchen cupboard.

"I've put the water on to boil. Oh my, your shoes are wet. Let's take them off, and your stockings, we'll put them in the kitchen to dry. There's just the two of us. My husband has gone out for the afternoon, to do some work in the library."

"Does he also read a lot like your son?"

"Like father, like son, Maggie. They are both bookworms."

"Your son read to me, from a lovely book. Copperfield. It is a lovely story. I want to get one of those books for myself. Do you read a lot?"

"Not much, I'm afraid."

"Why have you invited me to come here?"

"My son told me about you."

"Is it to tell me to stay away from him?"

"No, not at all. I would never do that. He has his own life to live."

"I am to blame. I liked him from the first time that I saw him. He is a good man but he hurts inside. He puts on a laugh, and the way he walks tries to hide what he is suffering. I don't know why I like him. I can't help it. It does not matter that he cannot hear. He speaks with the way his face changes and his body moves. He is a kind man. I know it cannot work. We are working class people. You are rich. I can see it from this house, even if he does not live like this I can see that he is used to better. You must not think that I will make demands. I am really very sorry for what happened. I felt so sorry for your husband. It was so sad. I should never have gone to see your son the way I did. He is an innocent man. I have been engaged. It did not work out. Going to your farm was all a big mistake. That is all I wanted to tell you. That is why I came here today in the rain. Please try to forgive me."

"Come with me Maggie. Let us go and get the tea. I will lead the way."

Maggie followed in her bare feet.

"Is this what people call an ostrich feather palace?"

Mrs van Yssen smiled. "Not at all. It is what they call a town house. It was built by an ostrich farmer when he made a lot of money from the feathers."

"It is grand. The paper on the walls is so pretty. And the tiles on the floors. I need to go to the toilet. It must be the rainy weather."

"The toilet is next to the bathroom."

"Inside?"

"Yes the outside one is for the servants."

"I have never been to a toilet inside a house."

"There you go." Mrs van Yssen opened the door for her. "When you have finished, pull the chain downwards and water will flush. The kitchen is over here. I will wait there for you."

Maggie entered the kitchen. "That was so very smart. How nice not to have to go out into the rain."

"I grew up with outside toilets, Maggie. It was quite a surprise to me to have this luxury. We managed to buy this house quite cheaply after the war. It was designed by one of the architects who built the Boys High School where Douglas was a teacher."

"They say he was the best teacher there ever was."

Mrs van Yssen smiled. "He did enjoy his work there."

"My father is a builder. He hates to work for architects. Says they give him a devil of a hard time. He knows more about building than they do. Times are very hard right now. We should not have left Durban. Then all of this would not have happened." She warmed her hands over the shiny domes that covered the plates of the Aga stove. "I have never seen a stove like this."

"We acquired it only recently. We used to have an electric stove. This one is very nice in the winter. It keeps the whole room warm. If you would like to bring the cake."

"I will take the tray, Mrs van Yssen."

Mrs van Yssen put more coal onto the fire and riddled it. The new coal crackled. A thin gust of wind rattled the sash windows of the living room.

"Do you think it will snow on the mountains?" Maggie asked.

"I doubt it very much. It is hardly cold enough for that."

"It must be cold where your son is."

"Yes."

"Why did you want me to come here?"

"Because I like you."

"After what I have done?"

"You were not alone in this Maggie. Douglas must accept his responsibility. Without his participation nothing would have happened."

"Yes, but I was too forward. It was difficult for him. I asked him to go to the bioscope with me. I should not have done that."

"When was that?"

"When he last came into town, I think, in February. I remember because it was still so warm."

"I have been to see Douglas. He told me about you. He spoke very well of you. He has no regret about what happened. I am not here to judge you, or Douglas. I do not intend to scold you, Maggie. I will not take my husband's side against you. I must be equally fair to the both of you. That is what being fair means. I have to admit that my husband is very upset. He has always worshipped his son. Douglas went to university in Cape Town where he was one of the best students. He has a Master's Degree in history."

"What does that mean?"

"It means that he has studied further than most people. My husband is a good man. He has always had very high hopes for Douglas. It was a great shock to him when Douglas became deaf. And to me. Douglas was engaged to be married to the daughter of a judge in Cape Town. He broke it off when he became deaf because of his diminished prospects. His fiancée still loves him. She and I still correspond, and I know she still occasionally writes to Douglas although he does not reply to her letters. It was a great shock for my husband to find the two of you."

Maggie began to cry. "I should never have come here. I knew you were going tell me how bad I am."

"I don't think you are bad. I told my husband what a sweet person you are. I can tell what you are like. I just want you to know what my husband is like. He is older than I. He grew up at a different time, in different circumstances. I grew up on a farm where we had lots of animals. For me what happens between a man and a woman is natural. For him it is not. Things that I regard as natural are sinful to him and make him feel guilty. It is very sad. It makes him unhappy. I don't think God wants us to be unhappy, but I do think that we should behave in a responsible way. I have not asked you to come and see me to hurt you or to make you unhappy; on the contrary, I want to be your friend. I know my son. There is now a bond between the two of you. We, the two of us Maggie, must try to make things better, not worse. We will have to work together at that. Now let's have some tea and cake. I have a friend I would like you to meet. She is a French woman."

"I know the one you mean. I am feeling much warmer now. Your cake is very nice."

"Douglas told me that you baked a cake for him. A chocolate cake."

She sniffed and nodded. "It is a nice fire. Do you want me to stop seeing your son? Because if you want me to go away, if that will make everybody happy, I will do that. Although I must say that I really do like him very much. I have always liked someone like him, my whole life."

"I don't want you to go away. Why should you do that on anybody's account? You and Douglas are both grown up. You must make your own decisions."

"We were very happy on the farm. I have never before been so happy in my life. Not in the way that you may think. I mean happy in my soul. I told him that when he speaks he rises like a giant in front of me. I think I should go home now."

"It is still raining and it is early yet. I cannot let you go out in this cold. We will wait for my husband and then take you home by car."

"I am scared of seeing Mr van Yssen again. I have seen the two of you together in the store. He looks like a very strict man to me. Although he did smile at me one time. I did not know who he was then. He saw what we were doing. I cannot look him in the eyes again. I had better get going."

"It will not help to run away. Let him see how nice you really are."

"Did you plan for it to work out like this?"

"No, not at all, not at all. The idea was that he would go out for the afternoon so that you would not be embarrassed by his presence. I promise you that."

Maggie nodded. "I know that you are sincere, but I am scared of him."

"You have nothing to be scared of. You are an honest person Maggie. He should see that for himself. Who knows, perhaps we were meant to have this weather so that you could meet him. Please stay. Quite apart from anything else, I cannot let you walk home in the rain. Coming here was bad enough. Let's go and make some fresh tea." Mrs van Yssen put more coal onto the fire and placed the screen in front of the fireplace.

Maggie was startled by the sounds of van Yssen's car as it went past the window of the living room. He did not expect her to still be there. He wiped his muddy shoes elaborately on the mat outside the kitchen door before he entered. He saw a tea tray on the kitchen table and the half eaten cake. From the coal smoke that came out of the living room chimney he knew where to find his wife. They heard him approach and before he entered the living room he called dissonantly, "Did she come?" Before his wife could reply he saw Maggie sitting by the fire.

"Albert, let me introduce you to Maggie Thompson."

He hesitated before he held out his hand. "How do you do Miss Thompson."

She shook his hand firmly and said nothing.

"Albert, Maggie got terribly wet walking here. I am drying her coat and her shoes in the kitchen. I said we would drive her home. I will add water to the teapot for your tea." She left the two of them in the living room.

"I need to take my coat off," van Yssen said brusquely and followed his wife to the kitchen.

"What on earth are you up to Anneke?"

"I am not up to anything, Albert. I am merely doing what is right."

"She does not even have shoes on. Such unseemly familiarity. Did I have to meet her in a state of undress? What has happened to our propriety? What next? Where is all this going to end? It was not a good idea to invite her here in the first place, now we are going to take her to her house? I have a good mind to refuse."

"Do as you please, Albert. Do as your conscience dictates. But act with honour and dignity. The girl has an inborn decency that even her difficult circumstances could not corrupt. Do you know what that is worth? Just see her as another human being who needs to be treated decently, to whom we should be fair. As we do to one of God's children we do unto Him."

"I would be pleased if you would not lecture me Anneke."

"Let us not squabble about this my dear husband. It will serve no purpose."

Van Yssen carried the tray back to the living room. Maggie sat watching the fire, one bare foot on top of the other, seeing little blue, yellow and orange flames dancing above the bed of coals. The images he had captured at the door of the bedroom replayed themselves; her quivering buttocks, the colour of ripening early spring peaches, drawn apart where Douglas was entering her. The pleasure of his recollection angered him and made him resent her for leading him into temptation. And to be in his own house with the woman. Maggie looked out through the windows. The rain had stopped. The trees were still dripping. Van Yssen stood close to the fire to warm himself. The library had been cold. Mrs van Yssen handed him his tea. "I nearly forgot about the cake, Albert." She went to the kitchen.

"The rain has stopped Mr van Yssen," Maggie said. "I can walk home now. It is not so far. If I could just have my coat and my shoes, please."

He was surprised at her accent. It was better than he had expected. "I will take you home. My wife and I will take you home. When your things are dry. Where did you live before you came to Oudtshoorn?"

"In Durban. I am so sorry for what happened. It was my fault. I told Mrs van Yssen everything. I said to her that if you want me to go away, I will. I don't want to be the cause of unhappiness. I have prayed and prayed and prayed that you will forgive me because I do not want to hurt other people." She held his gaze with steady clear blue eyes.

She certainly was not hurting Douglas when he saw them. She was attractive. He nodded abstractly, as if to say he would in due course consider the merit of what she had said. In her simple way she had a mind of her own.

"Here we are, Albert. I brought you some cake."

He sat down at the table in the corner, with his tea and his cake. Maggie turned her head and caught Mrs van Yssen examining her. Mrs van Yssen had put on fresh perfume; ready to leave when her husband was ready. "Shall we go and see how your things are getting on in the kitchen Maggie?"

Mrs van Yssen sat in front next to her husband and Maggie in the back. The skirt of her coat was still a little damp and so were her shoes. Her small brown handbag sat at her side and the old black umbrella rested against the seat.

"How far up St Saviour Street are you?" van Yssen asked.

"Just a little way above High Street Mr van Yssen. I will show you the house."

Van Yssen stopped on the opposite side of the street and opened the car door for Maggie. Mrs van Yssen got out and shook Maggie's hand. "Thank you for coming to see me Maggie. Please see that you do not catch a chill."

"Goodbye Mrs van Yssen, Mr van Yssen." She shook his hand, looked left and right and trotted across the street to the front door of their house. She went inside without looking back.

Van Yssen started the car and put it into gear.

"Thank you Albert, it could not have been easy for you."

"She has a surprisingly strong presence. But I cannot for the life of me understand what a girl like that would want with Douglas?"

"How do you mean?"

"They cannot have anything in common. When I think of Frances, how compatible they were. How their minds soared when they were together. How absorbed they were in one another. That was so perfect, so unique."

"I know."

"At least the girl is not quite as common as I thought. She does not speak too badly. Who knows what might have become of her if she had had a better chance in life."

"I don't know what to think. Perhaps it would be better to let things settle before making further judgements. Whenever she served me in the shop I thought she was sweet. I still think so. She has a disarming manner. As Douglas said, she is completely unaffected. She told me that she liked Douglas from the first time she saw him. But there was more than just words. There was something intuitive in her manner. I don't know how to put it. I don't know what to do. She said that she would go away if we wanted her to."

"She also said that to me."

"What did you say in reply?"

"I did not know what to say."

"It required a lot of courage on her part to come and see me, Albert, and then to face you. Your presence can be quite formidable."

"I know."

"We should go to the farm tomorrow."

"We'll go after church."

"I'll take some lunch along."

Sunday 3 April 1932

When Mr and Mrs van Yssen returned home from church he changed into grey flannel trousers and a sports jacket. It still drizzled lightly at times and the air was cold. Mrs van Yssen carried a picnic basket to the table on the veranda and waited for her husband to lock the front door. The mountains ahead of them were shrouded in cloud and mist. The wind direction had changed. It was coming from the east, which meant that the weather was going to clear. The rain had made the soil darker in places. The colours of the landscape were softer than usual. The late summer greens of the poplar copses on the banks of the Kandelaars River were showing signs of autumn yellow. And in the distance the moving clouds revealed facets of the ageless mountains. The rain had made the surface of the road firmer and free of dust.

"It is hard to believe that less than a week has passed," van Yssen observed.

"Yes, but I am glad that we are going to see him. Difficult as it may be for me, I am slowly coming to terms with the fact that things have changed for ever. At times I cannot believe how much he has changed. Sometimes when I look at him I see an older person. He has grown apart from me. I suppose that would have been inevitable, no matter what happened. But at least it would have been with Frances. We probably would have had grandchildren by now. I sometimes imagine the two of them together in a charming cottage in Cape Town, sitting in front of the fire while their toddlers play at their feet, of them visiting us and showing off my grandchildren to our friends. Now that is all gone, forever. And I don't know what to do or what to say about the Thompson girl."

"Once he develops a taste for the woman, it is like drink, Anneke."

"I know. I am fearful of showing too much disapproval. It will just drive her more into his arms. I will tell him that I invited her to tea. It will be interesting to see what his reaction will be."

'It will be interesting."

When the van Yssens drove up to the house they found Garnett's car parked underneath the sparse shade of the stooped wizened pear tree outside the kitchen. Wisps of smoke came from the chimney.

"This will complicate things a little," he said.

They walked around the house but there was no sign of Douglas or Garnett.

"They must have gone for a walk, I know Garnett likes to walk on the mountain."

"I'm sure Douglas won't mind if we go inside. Let's put the basket in the kitchen."

The stove was hot. The lid of a big black pot sputtered and released a delicious odour of pot-roasted lamb.

"I've not had any tea today," Albert remarked. "I'll boil some water."

Douglas and Garnett found the van Yssens at the dining room table. Mrs van Yssen embraced Douglas. "Hello Garnett, how lovely to see you. You are such a good friend."

Garnett smiled. "Hello Mr van Yssen."

Van Yssen shook Douglas' hand and managed a faint grimace.

"We have brought some things," his mother informed him.

"It is nice of you to come. There's plenty of meat. We have been for a long hike up the mountain. Garnett arrived early. The rain will do wonders for the grazing." Their boots were damp.

Garnett left soon after lunch to give the van Yssens an opportunity to be alone with Douglas. The weather was clearing rapidly and van Yssen suggested that they should sit outside. His mother took along the writing pad and pencil.

"I invited Maggie Thompson to have tea with me yesterday afternoon."

"Did she accept?"

Mrs van Yssen nodded. She looked away.

Douglas did not know what to say.

"She walked all the way to our house in the rain. Her shoes and her coat were soaked. We took her home in the car, afterwards."

"Why did you do that?" Douglas was irritable.

Mrs van Yssen frowned. "What do you mean?"

"I mean, why did you invite her to tea?"

"She has served me often in the shop. There is something decent about her. She must have been terribly upset about what happened. I felt sorry for her. We have to resolve this problem in a dignified way."

"I do not see it as a problem. I am quite happy to be completely open about it. I discussed it with Garnett this morning. I told him everything."

Van Yssen took the writing pad. "Was that wise? Don't blurt everything out. Keep some powder dry."

"Dad, I deceived you over going to Herolds Bay with Garnett. I made my affair with Maggie a clandestine one. You took me to task for not telling you the truth, and I sincerely regret doing so. Now you are asking me to be discreet at the expense of being economical with the truth?"

Van Yssen closed his eyes in denial and shook his head. "That's not what he meant." Mrs van Yssen wrote on the pad. "We don't have to make any hasty decisions. The girl has some very endearing qualities, genuinely good qualities. We are merely asking you not to rush things, and not get yourself into a position from which you cannot extricate yourself. Be patient."

"Then you must also be patient, Ma."

"When I said that she has an inborn decency, I really meant it. You have a responsibility to behave decently towards her. Don't take advantage of her."

"That is really clever, Ma! And I don't mean to be nasty in any way, to get me not to see her on the pretext of treating her decently! I understand very well how both of you must feel. I understand your embarrassment. I understand how our friends will view the liaison – I have already had to endure Garnett's censure the whole morning. I cannot explain how I feel about Maggie. I am fully aware of the social consequences."

The van Yssens braced themselves.

"Why must I consider what others may think of me, in my state? I sit here, stuck in the middle of nowhere. I don't even have a dog to keep me company. Willemse is hardly intellectually stimulating. My life is not normal. Why should I pretend that it is? Apart from the two of you and Garnett, who has taken the trouble to visit me? One or two of the neighbours but even they find it a strain. Who has taken the trouble to come here from town? Nobody gives a damn, so why should I?"

"Frances would happily have married you. She still would." Mrs van Yssen showed him what she had written.

"Have a heart, mother. We have been over this so many times, one way or another. I could not have subjected Frances to this. The longer I live here the more plain it becomes."

Van Yssen took the pad. "So what you're implying is that you now have to settle for second best?"

Mrs van Yssen saw what he wrote and held her hand up in a restraining gesture.

"No Anneke, what has to be said has to be said."

"I've had to settle for second best as far as my hearing is concerned, as far as a career is concerned. What difference will a little more second best make?" Douglas had a wry smile. "What I must tell you in all honesty is that the second best that is Maggie has made me very happy. The ineffable simplicity of what she is has a great deal of meaning. It has made me see quite clearly how we compromisingly entangle ourselves in the strands of social conventions. For me there is no longer any need for that. I can never be part of so-called normal society again. I don't want to be part of that again. Two unlikely ingredients, my deafness and the girl's authenticity, have combined to set me free. I understand at last what a huge comical farce most of life is. And the worst is that when you drive home you will shake your heads and lament what you see happening to me when you should really be rejoicing."

Chapter Thirty-seven

Saturday 7 May 1932

AFTER MAGGIE had had tea with Mrs van Yssen Douglas wrote several notes to her, delivered by van der Byl, inviting her to visit him, all to no avail. What remained was to visit her.

He got up early, informed Willemse that he would be away until the following evening, and pumped his bicycle's wheels. With his bag strapped to the carrier, and his muddy green tweed sports coat on backwards, a scarf around his neck, to protect himself from the early cold he began his journey into town. The first stretch was downhill and the cold morning air bit into his hands. He took turns to put one hand into a trouser pocket but the bicycle was difficult to control that way.

He had not let his parents know of his visit. He expected to reach town at about nine. He would go straight to see Maggie, and arrange to meet her when shop hours ended at one. Then he would go home. He and Maggie could have something to eat at the Central Café. It could be that his parents had scared her off. It could be that she was embarrassed about what had happened with his father, or at tea with his mother. It could just be that Maggie was uncomfortable with them as a family. Not that he did not trust his parents. But they were clearly disenchanted with the relationship. One must never underestimate the power of disapproval or the lengths people will go to, to manipulate others. He planned what he would do. Go and see her first. Confront her in public so that she could see that he was sincere. He would take her home after their lunch. He would tell his parents what his intentions were. Nothing would be concealed. The back end of his bicycle swerved dangerously as he went down a slope. He looked down to see what was happening. The rear tyre was punctured. Shit. He carried the bicycle to the roadside and unpacked his puncture repair kit. He located the hole in the tube and prepared a patch. Once he had inflated the wheel sufficiently he wiped his hands on a bush and continued on his way. A few miles further a truck with a Mossel Bay number plate stopped and offered him a lift. He hefted his bicycle and bag onto the back and climbed into the cab.

"I am Liebenberg." He held out his hand to Douglas. He was a man of Douglas' age, well dressed.

Douglas put his hand to his right ear. "Douglas van Yssen. I am sorry, I am deaf."

The fellow smiled kindly, shook his head sympathetically and nodded.

"I was on my way to Oudtshoorn," Douglas said. "I farm up on the slopes of the mountain."

The fellow nodded.

He would get to town much earlier, now. He would go home first. And announce his intentions. It would be really nice to have a car or a small truck of some kind. A truck would be better. The fellow had strong hands. There were rugby boots and a bag in the foot well where Douglas sat.

"Are you going to play rugby?"

He nodded and pointed downwards with his finger to say that he was going to play that day. Probably Mossel Bay versus Oudtshoorn.

Liebenberg dropped Douglas at his parents' house. Douglas thanked him, wished him good luck with his match. It was just after seven in the morning and the house was still asleep. He knocked on the front door. His father was in his dressing gown and pyjamas. "What brings you to town?" He frowned.

"I have come to visit."

"Come inside. I will tell your mother that you're here."

"Shall I put my bag in the spare room?"

His father nodded.

"Douglas is here, Anneke," van Yssen called as Douglas disappeared towards the spare room.

"My, my how lovely." She hurried from their bedroom. Douglas had put his bag down on the bed and was opening the curtains. She saw his large frame illuminated by the white morning light as he stood in front of the window, looking out at the familiar garden. She hesitated to admire him, reminding herself how much she loved him. He should have a haircut. She held out her arms. It was nice to embrace her. She was soft and she smelt of night cream. He better understood her physical attributes, and the way she felt, now that he knew what a woman was capable of. He was reluctant to kiss her on her mouth – it would reveal how much he had learnt – so he kissed her on her cheek. When she put her arm through his he could feel her breast. They walked to the dining room. "I'll get some coffee. Make yourself comfortable."

His father appeared. Douglas took his writing pad from his jacket pocket and pushed it towards his father.

"You must have left very early?"

"Ja, I did, but I also got a lift, with a fellow from Mossel Bay. He's come to play rugby."

"There is a match on today. How are things going on the farm?"

"As usual. We have ploughed and sowed the wheat. Now it's a matter of providence. Almonds were better than expected. We've again noticed caracal spoor. Willemse has set a trap."

Mrs van Yssen arrived with the coffee. She sat down next to her husband and took the writing pad. "This is rather unexpected. What made you decide to come into town?"

"I tried to make contact with Maggie. I sent several notes with van der Byl but I got no response. I thought she might be ill."

"She is not ill. I noticed her on Thursday."

"I wonder why she has not responded. I have heard nothing from her since she came to have tea here with you."

Van Yssen tried to conceal how pleased he was. Perhaps the storm had passed. Mrs van Yssen had the guilty look of the innocent.

"I'll go and have my bath," van Yssen wrote.

Mrs van Yssen thought of something to say.

"Have you spoken to her since she came here?" Douglas asked his mother.

She shook her head. 'I have done the necessary shopping at J. D. Jones, but I have not avoided Prince Vintcent.'

"I need to behave in an honourable way, Ma. I cannot just leave it at this. If she does not want to see me, there is nothing that I can do. I must be frank though, and say that I have missed her. If you don't mind I will have some breakfast with you and then go into town and see her."

"At the shop, with the whole town watching?"

"Yes, with the whole town watching. Except that I may be disappointed at the turnout!"

"Don't be so frivolous. What will people say?"

"I have no idea what they might say. What do you think they will say, Ma?"

She blushed. "They might wonder why a man of your stature should be interested in someone like that."

"Someone like what?"

"You know what I mean."

"I have forgotten, Ma, please refresh my memory."

"You know it is difficult to express exactly what I feel in writing."

"We are going around and round in circles Ma. Let's just keep things simple. I feel that I owe it to Maggie to make contact with her. There might be a misunderstanding."

"But you could be discreet. She may not want to see you anymore and going to Prince Vintcent could cause a scene."

"I will not cause a scene. I promise you. I will ask her to have a bite with me when she finishes work at one."

"Where will you take her?"

"I thought of the Central Café."

"That's very public."

"Ma, with the greatest respect and affection, you persist in trying to make my meeting with her clandestine. I do not want to do that. It is quite simple: I will walk into Prince Vintcent this morning, I will go right up to her, kiss her on her cheek, while the whole of Oudtshoorn watches me, and invite her to have lunch with me. As simple as that."

"Do you have enough money?"

"Ellis paid me last week for lucerne he took some time ago. I'm quite careful with the pennies. I will not waste any money."

It was a pleasure for Douglas to have food that someone else had made. He felt comfortably replete as he headed for Prince Vintcent. The feeling of grit in his eyes from getting up early had disappeared. He could always have a sleep later in the afternoon. It was pleasant to be in town again. The trees were preparing for the winter. Some people were saying that it would be a cold one. It would be good for the fruit trees. Make them dormant. Kill all the pests. Sudden cold is not good for the lambs. He wondered what Maggie would be wearing, how she would react when she saw him. The streets were quiet. Two boys in their school uniforms were ahead of him. Probably on their way to rugby. He pictured how he would find Maggie, how he would approach her. Before he knew it he was on the pavement outside the store, next to his reflection in the bevelled windows. He became nervous. Perhaps he should wait a while. She could be busy. He might embarrass her. While he was standing there contemplating what to do, the power of his earlier resolve propelled him into the shop.

She was standing at her counter, one foot behind the other. The toe of the navy blue shoe on her back foot pointed to the ground. She seemed to be daydreaming. She had on a long-sleeved hand-knitted pale pink jersey with buttons down the front over a dark blue dress with a printed light blue and white flower pattern. Her hair was slightly longer than when he had last seen her. She looked up and saw him. She stepped back. He held out his hand to her. She looked around nervously. She found some paper and a pencil and began to write, as though she was taking an order. He took her by her shoulders and kissed her on her cheek. She started crying softly. "I thought you would never come."

"I wrote you several notes."

"I know, but I wanted you to come to me." She tried to suppress her tears.

"I am embarrassing you. I will meet you here at one, and we will go and have some lunch." He kissed her on her lips and left.

She watched him leave, and sobbed with relief. Schmidt, the canny merchant, who never missed a thing, saw it all. He did not know what to make of it, but the Van Yssens were valuable customers, and she was a very good worker. He walked over to Maggie. "Go to the ladies room, my child. I will watch your counter until you return."

Douglas emerged from Prince Vintcent with a sense of relief and strode purposefully towards Garnett's rooms. There were only three people in the waiting room. Sister de Wet announced that Douglas had arrived. It could be a medical matter for all she knew. Douglas was happy to sit and read the *Courant* while he waited for Garnett.

"What can I do for you?" Garnett mouthed.

"I decided to visit town. Haven't seen you for a while."

"Yes I know, I have neglected you."

Douglas frowned. Garnett wrote, "I have neglected you. I apologise."

Douglas laughed. "It must be the new girl in town. How did the dance go? Did she go with you?"

"Yes." Garnett beamed.

"Have you grabbed her yet?"

"How can you ask me a thing like that?"

"The same way you asked me about Frances. Does she like you?"

"Hard to tell. She's pretty difficult to fathom, as I said before."

"I've come to see Maggie."

"I thought that was all over? Just a passing thing."

"What on earth made you think that? I can't just abandon her after what happened between us. And besides that, I don't want to. I want to do the decent thing, and quite apart from that, I want to have a relationship with her. I have informed my parents that I came here this weekend to see her. I have not seen her for well over a month. I have sent notes to her to invite her to visit me when next she had an opportunity and she failed to reply. So I thought I had better come to town and see her myself in case there was a misunderstanding of some kind. I have just been to the shop and invited her to lunch. I kissed her in full view of everybody and she cried. She said she thought I would never return. It was quite pathetic. I will meet her at one when the shop closes and we'll go to the Central Café. My parents must have scared her off. I don't mean deliberately, just that they probably intimidated her. She needed reassurance. And here I am, now. As I told you, I don't give a stuff what anybody thinks. I will follow my own head and do what I know is right for me, and Maggie."

"I hope it's your head you're following. How did you get into town?"

"By bicycle."

"I will take you back tomorrow after lunch, so we can have a good natter."

Douglas took that as an indication that Garnett wanted to get on with his work. "That would be absolutely marvellous, Garnie. Thank you very much."

"See you at two-thirty?" Garnett wrote.

Douglas gave him a thumbs-up. "Thanks."

Douglas had some time to kill and decided to visit the library. Three years earlier the sinecure of librarian had been bestowed on Beatrix Kuys. She was more gauche than ever. Her mousy hair was parted in the middle. Elaborate fine plaits were coiled over her ears to resemble raffia coasters. The ends of the collar of her cream coloured blouse were held together with one of her father's tiepins. Her biscuit brown cardigan was drawn in around her waist with a matching belt. She wore a tweed skirt that matched the polished floorboards of the library, lisle stockings and brogues. She had become a part of the furniture and fittings and only a trifle more animated than her sombre surroundings. She smelled of bookbinding glue and printed paper. She was reading, and looking sternly over her spectacles at two young children whose whispers were too loud, when Douglas' figure caught her eye. She jumped up involuntarily and blushed. She flattened the front of her skirt with her hands and to her embarrassment nearly touched herself where she shouldn't. Would Douglas think that she was being suggestive? Heaven forbid! She prepared a simpering smile.

"Hello Beatrix!" Douglas said in a loud voice.

"Shsssss." She put her finger sternly to her mouth, satisfied that she was able to reprimand him.

"I have some time to spend," he continued loudly. A man in the corner where the newspapers were shook his head disapprovingly.

Beatrix again put her finger over her lips. Douglas grinned at her. "You look quite silly like that Beatrix." She examined her clothes and looked at her feet to see whether he meant the way she was dressed. When she looked up he was strolling among the bookshelves. He always started at the History section even though there was nothing new, then to English Literature. Then he went to look at the Magazines and Newspapers. The new *Manchester Guardian* had arrived. He looked at the book reviews. After that he contented himself with the *Farmers Weekly*. It might be a good idea to plant some Irish potatoes. There was some crap that someone asked about a ten brake horsepower crude oil engine exploding, and a reply that did not answer the question. He should look again at the issue of heavy versus light pruning.

He was bored and could think only of Maggie. The image of those legs behind the counter. To think that he had been all the way up those legs, and beyond. She undid her stockings from her suspenders while she sat on the edge of the bed, and rolled them down her thighs. Imagine getting an erection here in the library and calling Beatrix Kuys to come and explain to him what it was and asking her how he could get rid of it because it was so utterly uncomfortable. There was an advertisement for Mr R H Dent's Ardente for deaf ears, specifically fitted to suit the individual. Wouldn't help. He looked at his watch. It was a quarter past twelve. His eyes wandered as he contemplated what to say to Maggie. He noticed Denis Kuys whispering to his daughter. She pointed in Douglas' direction and Kuys turned around. Douglas got up to greet Kuys. They shook hands and went outside to converse in greater comfort.

"How are you?" Kuys lips said.

"I'm just fine, thank you Mr Kuys."

"And the farm?"

"My father's fine, thank you."

Kuys shook his head. "I said the farm."

"Oh the farm. No, everything's fine out there, considering the circumstances."

"What brings you to town?" Kuys tried to clarify what he was saying with hand movements.

"This and that. It was time to take a break, but I'll be going back tomorrow. Garnett's taking me back."

"Nice to see you Douglas. Good luck." They shook hands and Kuys went back into the library.

Douglas took a long breath of cool autumn air and exhaled through his nose. It was always good to do that. The morning was dragging. He sauntered towards the Anglican Church, ever closer to Prince Vintcent. Mr Luscombe the attorney suddenly appeared around the corner. He grinned when he saw Douglas. No doubt his head was full of very confidential legal things for he always wore a little smile that said, 'I could not possibly divulge any more, so there is no point in asking me.' Even the way he said hello was meant to convey that it would go no further. That superior little smirk. What a prick. It is amazing what perspective a really good fuck had given him.

"Good afternoon, Douglas." Luscombe always knew precisely what time it was so that his charges would be correct. He tilted his hat.

"Good afternoon, Mr Luscombe."

"It is good to see you again."

Douglas nodded and smiled. Condescending shit.

"How are you getting on?"

"Just fine, fine, thank you."

"The Circuit Court is sitting here at present. Judge Rose is here. You might like to see him."

Douglas could not understand all he was saying and frowned. Luscombe had been to collect the mail and took a pencil from his pocket. He wrote on the back of one of the envelopes. "Judge Rose is in town with the circuit court. We're having a reception this evening at the Queen's Hotel. I'll tell him I saw you. Perhaps you would like to visit him? He's a fine man."

Douglas' stomach turned. Of all the rotten luck. Imagine if the Judge saw him with Maggie. God Almighty. He broke out in a sweat under Luscombe's penetrating stare. He was in the dock face to face with that stupid bastard with the powdered wig. "I'll only be in town until tomorrow, Mr Luscombe. I have many things to attend to. I'll have to see whether I shall be able to find the time, although I doubt it."

Luscombe enjoyed his discomfort. "I'll convey your best regards," he wrote, and bared his long regular bone-coloured teeth to show that he was pleased. He nodded to himself as though something of greater importance had suddenly captured his imagination, and went on his way.

Douglas expected to see the Judge's figure around every corner, his face appearing from every doorway. What a wretched time for him to be here. There was nothing to do. Stuff him anyway, and anyone who looks like him. It was nearly one o'clock when Douglas positioned himself outside the main entrance of Prince Vintcent. The doors were already closed. A few straggling customers came out, then the staff began to leave. Two women shop assistants emerged and giggled when they saw Douglas. He turned to have another look at them only to see that they were having another look at him. More people left the shop. At last he saw Maggie. Behind her was the large looming figure of Schmidt. The little pink rose in his buttonhole had begun to wilt. He opened the door for Maggie and gave Douglas a sly wink, a little gift from a great philanderer.

Maggie had composed herself during the morning. She looked radiant. They walked towards Hepworths on the High Street corner. He let her go ahead at times to let oncoming pedestrians pass and enjoyed the movements of her hips and the good way she carried her shoulders. He chose a table at the back of the Central Café, and next to the wall, so that they could have as much privacy as possible and be as unobtrusive as possible. There were few people and he saw no one he knew. Maggie made a gesture to one of the waitresses. He pulled out a chair for her and helped her to sit down. He sat down next to her so that he could see what she wrote. "I have missed you," he said. She looked different from the last time he had seen her. There was a soft look in her eyes. Her skin was radiant, her colour good.

She patted his hand. "I have missed you. You are talking very loudly. Try to whisper."

He nodded and patted her hand. "Did you get my notes?"

"Yes."

"Why did you not reply?"

The waitress appeared. "What will you be having?"

"Please give us a little while to decide," Douglas said. Maggie enjoyed the confident way in which he said that.

"Why did you not reply?"

"I wanted you to come to me." She started to cry softly. "I think I am pregnant."

Douglas' head swam. He felt giddy. Dizzy images of early childhood insecurities swayed unsteadily before him. The anticipation of taking her to a secluded place along the banks of the river that afternoon went limp. He tried not to show his panic. She dried her eyes and tapped his sleeve. "Please do not be upset. I will find a way."

He gripped her thigh. "What do you mean?"

"I will not get rid of the baby. It is mine and I will raise it as my own, no matter what happens."

Beads of perspiration accumulated on his forehead. "Does anybody else know?"

She shook her head. "My mother has a sharp eye and may suspect. She has said nothing."

"Will you tell her?"

"What else can I do. You must please believe me if I say that I did not trick you. I swear to God in Heaven that I did not do that. I love you too much."

Douglas put his arm around her and kissed her on her temple. "You must come and live on the farm. I will care for you."

"I don't know what my father will do when he finds out. He will give me a hiding I think."

Jesus wept. How can people think like that? "When can you come to the farm?"

"When Johnny next goes to see his girl."

"How soon?"

"A week or two."

"Will you come to me?"

"Yes."

"I give you my word that I will not abandon you, Maggie. I have grown extremely fond of you. Although this is clearly a shock to me, I must stay calm, and together with you, I must find the best solution." His mouth was dry and he had difficulty moving his tongue. "You have no idea how you have changed my life. You have given my life meaning that I never dreamt would be possible. I want you to be with me all the time. I would like to see the baby grow up with the best chance in life. I am not so hungry anymore, but I think we should eat."

"I have been craving for bacon and eggs? Would it be wrong to have that this time of the day?"

He laughed and shook his head. "I'll have the same. But let's do better, let's have a mixed grill?"

He examined her face. There was relief in her eyes. Warmth returned to her hands. She still sniffed a little. She met his gaze. His eyes were kind. You can trust a person like that. She was careful not to be too demonstrative in public. She managed to smile a little to say that she felt more settled. The food arrived sooner than expected. Douglas noticed that she had started to copy the way he held his knife and fork, and that encouraged him to decide that he would inform his parents and visit her parents as soon as convenient. The poor thing. "I am so sorry that you have had to suffer all this on your own," he whispered.

"It's all right."

Maggie offered to pay for her lunch but Douglas would have none of that. Oudtshoorn rugby supporters were buying tobacco and cigarettes at the one end of the counter. They had clearly had a beer or two. The leader of the pack was particularly vocal and made noises under his breath about a sporting gal, while the others laughed. Maggie responded by putting her arm through Douglas' arm, and turned her back on the ruffians. There was much mirth and a muted wolf whistle when they saw her behind and her good legs. Maggie tugged at Douglas' arm to get him outside and away from the embarrassment, and nearly stumbled as she did so. The laughter was more raucous. One of the revelers turned to the rest, "She's also had a toot!"

"It is such a nice sunny day, I think we should go for a walk anyway," Douglas suggested.

She beckoned for his writing pad. "Wait for me on the corner. I will go home and put other things on. I will tell my mother I am going to visit a friend."

Mossel Bay supporters on the back of an open truck came past. The driver's elbow extended from the window of the cab as though he was hugging the door. They whistled at the striding Maggie and sang, "She'll be coming round the mountain when she comes, she'll be coming round the mountain…"

Douglas waited on the corner. The air was cool but it was pleasant in the sun. He studied her as she approached. She had an interesting way of walking. Her lengthy strides made her attractive hips movements more pronounced. Her back was straight. The air pushed her dress against her so that all her contours were visible. She smiled. They walked along van der Riet Street towards the river. They took turns to examine each other, searching for signs of reactions and reassurances. At the river they mounted a raised narrow wooden footbridge. The railing was rickety and he was anxious when she let go of the railing. "Be careful, Maggie." They walked along the bank of the river and found a place to sit where the vegetation was dense. He kissed her and she put her arms around his neck. He squeezed her upper body against him, and then let go for fear of hurting her tummy. "It's fine," she insisted. He reclined on the grass. "What a beautiful day." She lay down next to him and put her hand into his jacket pocket to get out the writing pad. "I wish we were on the farm. I love it there."

They reclined on the grassy riverbank in the pale autumn sun. She held his hand and snuggled up close to him and entertained herself by studying his face. The pores of his skin were clean. His dark beard was beginning to show. His eyelids looked as though they had been anointed. His scalp was clean. Crow's feet had begun to form at the sides of his eyes – from laughing so much. The top of his forehead was white from his hat, and could easily get sunburnt. When she fell asleep with a contented sigh he felt her warm breath on his cheek.

When Maggie woke, Douglas was asleep. She pulled up the sleeve of his jacket to see what time it was. It was already past four. In the distance she could hear the roars of the rugby crowd. It was time to go home. She still had all her washing to do, for Monday. She shook Douglas' shoulder. He sat up. She knelt next to him and kissed him. "We must go." They kissed goodbye before they left the seclusion of the riverbank. "You must come and see me as soon as possible, please so that we can make our plans for the future," he said.

She nodded emphatically.

"Garnett Nel has offered to take me back tomorrow after lunch, for which I am grateful."

"Please do not say anything," she wrote.

"I won't. Even though he won't ever repeat anything I tell him. We have been friends since we were quite small, and he is a doctor."

Her face said she trusted him.

"You can always ring the general dealer, van der Byl, and leave a message for me." He tore a page from his writing pad and wrote down the number. "If you have any problems or difficulties please let me know. From now on I am responsible for you." He kissed her again. "I am a little shell-shocked but I am happy."

"So am I."

Douglas left Maggie on her corner and began his walk home. He found his parents in the living room. They had made a fire. Mrs Van Yssen was reading and her husband was asleep with the newspaper on his lap, his mouth open to reveal a molar with a gold crown. He did not hear Douglas enter, and his mother got up quietly. Douglas accompanied her and put water onto the hot plate. He was desperate for good hot tea and something sweet. He peered into a brown paper packet, spotted shortbread and helped himself.

"Did you have a good day?"

"Ja, rather interesting. I saw Maggie, and we had lunch. Nobody seemed to notice us. I visited Garnett, and went to the library where I encountered our dear schoolmarmish Beatrix. She's really become an old woman. So much so that I can't remember what she was like when she was young. I think she was born old." His mother shook her head with amused disapproval. "Her father popped in, and I said hello to him. He did not give me much time of day, and I think I know why, because I met Mr Luscombe a little while later and he informed me that Judge Rose is in town with the Circuit Court. Luscombe is going to a reception for Judge Rose and offered to convey my regards."

"What did you say?"

"Nothing. What could I say? I'm sure he wouldn't want to hear from me, or us. I'm sure that is why Mr Kuys was so short with me – he did not want to say anything about the Circuit Court being here."

His mother took the writing pad. "Is something troubling you? You seem to have something on your mind."

"No." He shook his head and shrugged and pulled his mouth down at the corners. "Maggie was very relieved to see me. I enjoyed seeing her. She is well. I have invited her to visit me."

His mother shook her head despairingly.

"Don't worry Ma, it will be all right. Garnett has offered me a lift back to the farm, after lunch tomorrow. Damn decent of him."

Sunday 8 May 1932

Garnett arrived at the Van Yssens a little after two- thirty. Douglas was waiting for him at the gate. They had had lunch early and his parents were asleep. Garnett had brought along an old blanket to wrap around the bicycle so that it would not scratch the back of the car when they tied it onto the luggage rack.

"Thanks awfully Garnie. I need to talk to you. But that will have to wait until we get to the farm."

They drove in silence. Garnett was reminded of the conversations they used to have on their trips, the time they went to Plettenberg Bay when Douglas was so madly in love. Here he sat now in his silent world, frowning to himself, going back to his farm with his bicycle strapped to the back of the car. Living there day in and day out, deprived of normal social intercourse. Douglas sat with his arms folded across his chest, staring ahead. The baby must be smaller than a shrew. When would a woman first feel it? She was carrying around a tiny little creature inside herself. Would it be a boy or a girl? There was a strong smell of petrol. Garnett stopped the car to see what the problem was and found that the cap of the spare petrol can had come loose and allowed petrol to spill. He screwed it down tightly and they continued on their way. Garnett felt tired. He had had a demanding week, visits to the district until late at night, a difficult operation to remove a colon tumour, a delivery after an unusually lengthy labour, it never seemed to end. What did they do before he arrived? The car was performing smoothly. It's important to have the correct tyre pressures. Fishing was not good at this time of the year. In a few months it would be hunting season. He would like to know how Douglas's meeting with Maggie went. Miss Weber would have enjoyed Frances' company. Birds of the same feather. Maggie was socially illiterate.

Douglas closed his eyes so that he could see Maggie more clearly, striding towards him down St Saviour Street, her hips with strong strides, her dress pressed against her pubis. It would be nice if she could come to the farm next weekend. She seemed quite keen. The road was quiet.

Douglas held the farm gate while Garnett drove in. He undid his bicycle from the back of the car and carried it onto the front veranda. He unlocked the front door and went from window to window opening all the shutters. It was good to be back at home. He looked out over the valley below and the mountains to his right. The air was different here. Must make a list of what to do tomorrow.

Garnett yawned and sat down on one of the folding canvas chairs on the veranda. He could have a little zizz right here. Douglas made the movements of drinking from a cup and raised his eyebrows in an enquiring way.

Garnett shook his head. "Later." He took some notepaper from his inside pocket. "How did it go with Maggie?"

"Fine, thanks. I bumped into old Luscombe who told me that Judge Rose is in town with the Circuit Court. That was a bit of a shock, and Luscombe enjoyed telling me. Those buggers are able to decide whether to go on Circuit Court or not and I wonder why Rose chose to come to Oudtshoorn. I was terrified that he would see me with Maggie. I don't know why, it's none of his business. He had quite an intimidating effect on me at times. I'm bloody glad I'm rid of him. It's strange how long the effect of a person like that can last. And to think that I could have had him as a father-in-law! Shit, what a pun, I mean the law part."

Garnett beckoned for Douglas to come and sit down next to him. He put the notepad down on the veranda table, and started writing. "Remember when we went to Graaff Reinet that time?" Douglas nodded. Garnett looked serious. 'The owner of the hotel, what was his name again?"

"I don't remember either."

"Starts with a B. Anyway, he told me a terrible story about Judge Rose. It has haunted me ever since. I did not want to tell you, and I won't go into all the gory detail. What happened is that he convicted and sentenced to death a young fellow from Caledon. Also a Circuit Court case. The youngster was hanged in Pretoria and an old clergyman who had known the kid from birth went to Pretoria to be with the boy before and during his execution. The boy maintained his innocence to the last. The old man had baptised the boy and held him in his arms as a baby, and was so overcome with emotion when the boy stood on the scaffold that he collapsed and the boy tried to comfort the old man. Jesus Christ, can you imagine that? Some time later, the police, when investigating another case, by chance found the real murderer, and the old reverend, when he heard that, went into a kraal on the farm where he was then living as a drunk, cursed Rose and shot himself."

"Jesus, Garnie, why have you not told me this before?"

Garnett's hands were trembling. "I did not want to burden you. I need a cup of coffee."

Douglas put his elbows on the table in front of him, clasped his hands and rested his nose against his fingers. "I always felt that bastard was flawed. There were rumours of his unfeeling cruelty, the way he treated people in his court. One always gave him the benefit of the doubt, which is more than he seems to have given others. I can't believe that he would have done something like that."

"Brunton, that was his name, said that there was forensic evidence that suggested that the boy could not have murdered his mother, but Rose was not prepared to consider it."

"Does Rose know what he did?"

"I'm sure he does. The case received a lot of publicity. As did the subsequent trial of the real murderer."

"I'm stunned. I'll go and make your coffee."

Garnett accompanied Douglas to the kitchen. The excitement of telling Brunton's story had taken away his sleepiness.

Douglas lit the Primus stove and put a saucepan of water onto it. "Maggie thinks she's pregnant."

"What?"

"Yes you heard correctly. Maggie thinks she's pregnant."

Garnett began shaking his head. He put his hands deep into his trouser pockets and strode about the kitchen in exaggerated noisy steps, as though he was trapped. He went to the veranda to retrieve the notepad. "What on earth are you going to do?" He held it up for Douglas to see.

"Nothing, what can I do? She wants to have the baby. She says she loves it. Even if she has to raise it on her own. I won't let her do that. I told her to come and live on the farm."

"As a common law wife? What about the child?"

"It's quite simple. I will marry her. That will give fucking Judge Rose a thing or two to think about."

"It will hurt Frances terribly."

"I know, and I feel dreadfully sorry about that, but that is how it will have to be. Anyway he will probably tell Frances, 'I told you so'. Nothing's ever his fault. When did it happen?"

"What?"

"That the boy was hanged."

"I'm not sure. My dad thinks about seven or so years ago."

"It is funny that I never heard about the case. I wonder why. I'm glad I never encountered him in town. He must have known all the time that I courted Frances that he had sent an innocent man to the gallows. And all the time he behaved quite normally. He used to joke, he was pompous, he was proud, a prig to be sure. God, how can you live with yourself after something like that? The worst is that he was always so critical of the misdemeanours and little transgressions of others. He would be quite intolerant of the smallest suggestion of an untruth. He once said to me with a satisfied smirk that the law was not about justice, there was no such thing as justice he said. It was a figment of imagination. The law he said, is a game, a game that like all other games has winners and losers. Sometimes you win and sometimes you lose, like in cricket. You can't always rely on the umpire. He makes mistakes. He gave me quite an eloquent sermon about that, as though he had thoroughly prepared it; I see the import of that now. I can see how disturbed you are, and you never said anything. Poor Frances, to live with a miscreant like that."

"Let's change the subject."

They went outside with their coffee and ginger biscuits. Douglas stood and stared into the distance, and shook his head. "Sometimes, just sometimes, I wonder whether I am not better off the way I am now: deaf and penniless. I live in a world of my own. It is a much simpler world than the one I once lived in. I don't mind telling you that it was such a shock when Maggie told me that I nearly fell over."

"Would you be happy to marry her?"

"Yes, I suppose so."

"Do you love her?"

"What is love, Garnett? I once thought that I loved Frances so much that my feelings at times suffocated me. I could not imagine then that I would feel differently. Now it is gone. I cannot even remember exactly how I felt. Looking back it all seems a little silly to me. We read of great enduring loves in history. What were they? I don't know. I look at Mrs Jacquard, at her singular love for her husband, and I find it remarkable. The bugger is somewhere, she does not know where, fighting for France, or lying on an iron bed in a North African desert fort, and I wonder whether her love for that man will ever diminish. When I think about that I feel shabby. I think I am shallow when it comes to love. Why did I love Frances? It all seemed like a fairytale. The two young intellectuals, so perfectly suited, the families so much in harmony socially. The elders spoke of great futures, of how we were absorbed in each other. The prospective grandmothers already had toddlers on their knees. And now there is Maggie. What difference will it make to me whether I marry her or not? At least I will have a companion. There's more to her than you think. She has sound instincts, lots of kindness and plenty of sharp common sense. Physically she's a ravishing woman."

"Let's see how things unfold. For all we know she might not even be pregnant. Sometimes women miss a period after lots of sexual activity."

Monday 9 May 1932

When Maggie returned home from work just after five thirty in the afternoon her mother was waiting for her in the kitchen. Her father was doing work on a farm in the district and would be away for a few days.

"I need to talk to you young lady," her mother said without first greeting her. "Come and sit down here." Her mother pointed to a chair, stubbed her cigarette out in an old oyster shell that served as an ashtray, and pouted her bottom lip as she blew the smoke out. Maggie sat down apprehensively. She knew the tone of voice.

"Kitty Strydom was here this morning. She came here specially. She told me that she saw you and a man going into the bushes next to the river. No, no wait, don't say anything; let your mother finish what she has to say. Kitty says it was an older man. He was dressed like a real toff. She says she can't be sure but she thinks you were holding his hand. So what I am saying to you my dear girl, just what the bloody hell is going on? And don't try and fool me, I am much to sharp for that. I'm an old hand. And just before you try and lie to me, let me tell you that I have noticed for a while now that you have a different look in your eye. I hope it's not what I suspect it is. So think very carefully what you say. You have a good job, Mr Schmidt thinks well of you, you have a reputation to protect. You cannot afford to be seen with all sorts of men who have no morals, who would take advantage of you, and then throw you away when they have finished with you. To think that a daughter of mine will sneak into the bushes next to the river in broad daylight! To do what there? What sort of man does that? What sort of man does not have the decency to first meet your parents, to introduce himself? Christ Maggie, what will people say? You know what a gossip Kitty is."

Maggie blanched. She started trembling.

Her mother was getting into her stride. "And before you try to explain yourself, before you think I am setting a trap for you, let me remind you of the night you came home after you said you were going to the bioscope, when you said you got sick over your dress. It was not the kind of sick you wanted me to think it was. I know what was all over your dress. That sick came from somewhere else, didn't it? I know what I smelled when I washed your dress. So what the bloody hell is going on?"

"I have met a very nice man."

"A nice man you say? A very nice man who sneaks into the bushes with you, who does not have the guts to come and introduce himself to me!"

"Please listen to me, I will tell you everything."

"It had better damn well be everything. You're lucky your father's not here. He would have given you a damn good hiding by now, all over that tail of yours that sneaks around in the bushes."

Maggie had tears in her eyes. "If you will listen to me mother, I will tell you everything." There was resolve in her voice.

"Well go ahead then, but be careful. I am not going to be tricked."

"As I tried to say to you, I have met a very nice man. He used to come into the shop from time to time. He was a teacher here in town and now lives on his farm. He is a very kind man. It was all my fault, I fell in love with him when I first saw him. I asked him to go to the bioscope with me. He is an innocent person."

"You, you asked him to go to the bioscope with you?"

"Yes, I did. I wrote on a piece of paper. He is deaf, but he is a very clever man."

"Did I hear right, Maggie? You say he is deaf. How deaf?"

"Completely."

"How often have you seen him?"

"I have been to his farm."

"How do you mean you have been to his farm? How did you get there?"

"Johnny took me."

Her mother nodded slowly. "Now it all begins to make sense, you deceitful little bitch. And to think that your brother had his hand in this. I'll teach him a lesson he's likely to remember for a long time. How many times did you go there?"

"Three times in all."

"And Johnny pretended that he was going to visit that floozy in Mossel Bay, and all the time he stayed on that farm with you and that man."

"Johnny did not stay there, he did go to Mossel Bay. He just dropped me there."

Her mother lit a cigarette with trembling hands. "Are you telling me that you slept over on a stranger's farm, alone with the man? He could be a monster. He could have raped you. He could have slit your throat and nobody would have been any the wiser. Have you lost your mind?"

"He's not like that, mother."

"That's what they all say, until it turns sour."

"I think I am pregnant."

"Oh my God! What are you saying to me! That's why I could not sleep last night, that's why I had such a bad dream. We must get rid of the baby."

"No, I will not do that."

"We will make a very hot bath for you, this evening. I will put lots of mustard into the water and we'll see if it will get the baby loose."

"I will not do that mother. I want the baby."

"Are you crazy? What will people say? You will have to quit your job. We need the money. What will people think? Just think what it will do to your father's reputation, to my reputation?" Mrs Thompson straightened her bodice and steadied the curlers in her hair. "And may I ask, what is his name?

"Douglas. Douglas van Yssen."

"That's a fancy name."

"He went to the university, his mother told me."

"His mother told you? How did you come to talk to her?"

"She invited me to have tea with her. That's where I went that Saturday afternoon last month when it rained."

"How did she know to invite you to tea?"

"Douglas told her about us."

"Where do they live? Are they decent?"

"They live in what they call a town house. It is a very smart house."

"Do they have money?"

"I don't know, I suppose they must have some."

"Douglas was engaged to be married to the daughter of a judge, but he broke it off when he went deaf."

"He was no longer good enough when he went deaf, but now he is good enough for you?"

"It is not like that. His mother told me that the girl still wants to marry him."

"She told you that because she wants to scare you off."

"It was not said like that."

"What a fine bloody pickle we are in. Your father will be like a wild boar. He'll be as mean as shit. He'll bugger up Johnny for sure for aiding and abetting you. You can take poison on that. And your job. You can't go and stand there with a fat stomach and large eyes like a cow that is expecting to calve. Thanks a lot. Thank you very much for making such a bloody mess. I nearly said something else, but that would have been bad language."

"I am sorry for the trouble that I am causing you, Mother. I have never in my whole life felt so happy than when I am with Douglas. We don't even have to speak."

"There's little point in speaking to someone who cannot hear, is there?"

"He was in town on Saturday. We had lunch at the Central Café. He fetched me at the shop, for everybody to see, and we went for a walk afterwards. I told him that I thought I am going to have a baby."

"What did he say?"

"He said he would never abandon me. He said he would care for me."

"Did he say you must get rid of it?"

"No. He would never dream of that. He said I should go and live on the farm with him. He would care for me."

"What about your wages?"

"I would not need them on the farm."

"We have rent to pay."

"Yes I know."

"Who else knows about this?"

"Only Douglas' friend."

"Who is that?"

"Doctor Nel."

"Let me get this straight. You say Doctor Nel and your man friend are friends?"

"Yes, they have been good friends all their lives, they grew up together."

Her mother became calmer. She sighed. "The Doctor is a classy man. Help me with the supper. We will find a way."

Maggie was peeling the potatoes when Johnny skipped cheerfully into the kitchen. "Hello Sis, hello Ma. I have some good news. The Colonel gave me a raise."

"At least you have something to be cheerful about, you common little shit."

"What do you mean Ma? What am I supposed to have done?"

"You're an accomplice after the crime, you little rubbish. And you know it. Taking your sister to that man, and now she's pregnant, you filthy little rat. I wouldn't be at all surprised if you have been dipping your own little wick in somewhere. That's all you men want to do."

"Jesus, Sis."

Maggie did not look up.

"We're going to have to make a plan. Maggie does not want to get rid of it, and I am not the kind of mother to suggest she should, so, as I said, we'll just have to make a plan. Your father will be as mad as a snake. I won't let him touch a pregnant woman. The best is for her to go to the farm and to stay there for a time. Your father will only be back on Friday. If you can ask the Colonel for a car you can take us to the farm. Maggie can go and see Mr Schmidt in the meantime and tell him, I don't know what she'll tell him, we'll think of something."

"Tell the old man that Maggie has been transferred to the Mossel Bay branch. Sweeten it by saying that she's got a promotion. So instead of pissing him off, he'll be pleased."

"Just watch your language young man," his mother said. "You scare me, you're such a smooth little liar."

"You've trained me well Ma."

His mother threw some potato peels at his face. He ducked like a boxer. "Pick it up Johnny, we can't make a mess in here," she said.

Wednesday 11 May 1932

Douglas went to van der Byl's shop just before lunchtime to buy tobacco for Willemse. There was a note for him from Maggie. "I am coming to see you tomorrow." A week day. How odd!

Thursday 12 May 1932

When Douglas had seen to the most essential farm matters, he made sure that the house was tidy and put on clean clothes. At about eleven thirty a maroon Chevrolet lumbered over the uneven road from the gate and came up to the house. Despite some dust its chromium-plated parts gleamed in the sunlight. Johnny was at the wheel. Next to him in the front sat a thin stern looking woman, her mouth puckered in anticipation of what to say. Her piggy eyes darted about taking in as much as she could. She had assumed an air of affected importance, of someone who wanted to appear as though she often rode in a car. At first Douglas did not see Maggie in the back of the car, and expected a confrontation. "This is not what I expected Maggie, I thought it would be more grand," her Mother said.

"Don't say things mother. Although he cannot hear he can sometimes read lips. He can see what you are saying."

"Oh go on, don't be silly, now."

Johnny was the first to jump out. He shook Douglas' hand in a familiar way and held onto it longer than usual while he grinned. Mrs Thompson was next to get out. She had her finery on, to impress Douglas, complete with her second hand snakeskin shoes. She straightened her brown linen dress and shook her head to give her hair its best appearance. "This is our Ma," Johnny said.

Douglas was larger than she had imagined. She was sure she had seen him before. She looked him up and down because she had convinced herself in the early hours of the morning that he should be reprimanded for the liberties he had taken with her precious.

"How do you do Mrs Thompson." His voice was deeper than she had imagined. He must have a big pair of balls. He was a bit of all right. She'd had an eye for the lads herself before she lost her figure.

"Nice of you to ask. I'm just fine thank you."

Maggie got out of the car. Douglas went over to her and kissed her. "I am so glad that you have come, and that you have brought your mother." He embraced her and looked in the direction of Johnny and Mrs Thompson. "Do come inside." He showed the Thompsons to the dining room and went to the kitchen. Maggie followed him. She started writing, "I told my mother. She is scared my father will give me a hiding. She was not pleased when she heard but is calmer now. I have told Mr Schmidt that I have to go back to Durban urgently on family business and my mother will tell my father that I have been transferred to Prince Vintcent in Mossel Bay. I have brought my things and will stay with you for as long as you will allow me."

"I am so glad. I have missed you."

Douglas carried the tea tray to the dining room. "Do you think I could have some black coffee, please?" Mrs Thompson asked.

Douglas frowned. "Coffee?"

Maggie nodded. "I will go and make it."

"She knows her way around," Mrs Thompson said to Johnny.

"You must write down if you want to speak to him, Ma."

"I feel that I owe you an apology, Mrs Thompson. I wish I could say that I am sorry about what has happened with Maggie, but I do not regret it. The way in which it happened was perhaps unfortunate, but she has brought me great happiness, for which I will always be deeply grateful. I have explained to Maggie that I will care for her and I am glad that she has come to stay with me. I will look after her and care for her as best I can. My circumstances are modest I'm afraid, as you can see, but I don't lack for anything. Maggie has met both my parents, but I have not yet told them that she thinks she is pregnant. I will inform them at the earliest opportunity. I have told my friend Doctor Nel but his professional position does not permit him to disclose such a confidence. I have no doubt that there will be a lot of gossip in town. I regret that but there is nothing we can do now. I'll just have to face the music. I think your daughter is a lovely person, and I am proud to be associated with her, and to tell you the truth I feel as though we, that is Maggie and I, have nothing whatsoever to be ashamed of."

Douglas' eloquence took the wind out of her sails. She put her palms down flat on the surface of the table as though she was going to push herself up. "Well, well, well, that was a fine speech, we'll have to see if you can live up to your promises."

"I don't understand." Douglas said.

Maggie wrote on the notepad. "My mother says she hopes all will turn out all right."

Douglas smiled.

"Let me see that, Maggie. And tell him that I am damn cross with him, and that he'd better behave himself when I'm around. I am not going to sit around and make polite conversation. You must also explain why I have brought you here so that he does not think I will ever approve of indecency. Explain to him what your father will do to you if he finds out. Explain that we will have to get him used to what has happened very slowly. We have to get back because Johnny has to return the car." She slurped her coffee, munched a few of Douglas' ginger biscuits and got up stiffly. She dusted the crumbs from her lap. "Where's the toilet, Maggie?"

Douglas shook Mrs Thompson's hand while she looked the other way. Johnny said an over familiar goodbye. After all they were nearly relatives now. Maggie and Douglas watched as the car crawled and heaved to the open gate. Next time Johnny should close it behind him. Douglas bent down and grabbed Maggie around her thighs and picked her up. She squealed as he carried her towards the house.

"Well I never, not much of a farm, but he's quite posh. We'll have to think of the best way to handle your father, Johnny." He glanced at his mother. The old lady looked quite satisfied judging by her smirk.
Douglas went to give Willemse his tobacco while Maggie saw to her things. When he returned he found her in the spare room unpacking her things. "Why don't you come to my room?"

She shook her head. 'There will be visitors. Your parents and others. I will sleep with you in your room.'

He took her in his arms and kissed her. "You have made me very happy. I will go in to town as soon as possible and tell my parents our news."

Chapter Thirty-eight

Friday 13 May 1932

DOUGLAS WALKED to the shop as soon as he and Maggie had had their breakfast. He asked van der Byl to telephone his parents to ask them if it would be convenient to visit them the following day. Van der Byl wrote on a piece of wrapping paper that he was planning to go in to town the next morning and that Douglas would be more than welcome to travel with him.

Saturday 14 May 1932

Douglas had told Willemse the day before that he would be leaving Maggie on her own on the farm, and asked him to take care of her. He kissed Maggie goodbye while Willemse watched from a distance. Van der Byl was not quite ready to leave and was quarrelling with one of his labourers about not tying a tarpaulin down properly over the back of the truck. When the tarpaulin was eventually tied to van der Byl's satisfaction they put Douglas' bicycle down on top of it and left for Oudtshoorn.

Van der Byl dropped Douglas off outside his parents' home and half saluted, half waved goodbye as he watched Douglas pushing his bicycle down the driveway. Strange fellow, they say he has a girl on the farm. Would never have thought he had it in him.

Mrs Van Yssen had prepared a hearty breakfast for Douglas. His father appeared to be in a better state of mind. Douglas ate enthusiastically. It was rewarding to feed him. Douglas did not say a word while he ate. His father could tell he had something on his mind, probably money, of which there was not much at the moment, or some implement for the farm.

"How are things on the farm?" His father wrote and held it up to him.

"Things are going well." He continued to butter his toast.

"Will you have enough winter fodder?"

"Plenty." He slapped spoonfuls of marmalade onto his toast, and slurped his coffee.

Mrs van Yssen shook her head. His table manners had deteriorated since he lived on his own.

A piece of toast stuck in Douglas' gullet and he had to swallow hard before he could talk again. "I trust you haven't encountered our friend Judge Rose?"

"No we haven't. We are not likely to. The days of mixing with the Roses are gone for good." He held the paper up long enough for Douglas to see.

Douglas washed the last of the remaining crumbs from his mouth with coffee. "That's no real loss."

"Why do you say that?"

"After what Garnett told me I wouldn't have anything to do with that bastard if you paid me."

"Douglas!" His mother exclaimed, horrified that Douglas could show such wanton disrespect.

"I always thought he was a bit of a fool."

Van Yssen held up his open hands, to flag down Douglas' excesses. "What has got into you?"

"Do you remember when Garnett and I went to see Frances in Graaff Reinet that time? Well the owner of the hotel where we stayed told Garnett that Rose had previously stayed there. The owner, a chap by the name of Brunton, told Garnett about a young fellow who had appeared in front of the Judge, charged with murder. Rose treated the boy cruelly and was quite unfair to him and sentenced him to death. He ignored vital medical evidence that might have raised reasonable doubt, and the boy was subsequently hanged in Pretoria. An old dominee who had known the boy since birth attended the execution and when the police by chance found the real murderer the old dominee committed suicide."

"Where is all of this supposed to have happened?"

"Not supposed to, Dad, it did happen. In Caledon."

"When?"

"Garnett's dad thinks about seven years ago. Mr Nel knew about the case."

"Why did Garnett wait until now to tell you?"

"I asked him the same question. He said he did not want to upset me, and let it influence my relationship with Frances."

"How utterly dreadful." Mrs van Yssen wrote.

"As I said to Garnett when he told me on Sunday, I always thought the Judge had feet of clay. There was something lacking in him. He was not half as good a jurist as he would have us believe. Great people are not pompous or vain, as he is. He's a downright prig. His trick is to make people believe that there is more to him than there actually is. I told Garnett how cynically he once lectured me about justice and the law. And the worst is that the boy's unjust death probably ran off his duck's back like drops of water. I'm glad to be rid of him."

Mrs van Yssen turned to her husband, "Now that I think about it, I did hear something about that awful affair. Alice Kuys mentioned it, she heard about it from Denis."

"What was that, Ma?"

She wrote down what she had said.

"You see, Dad."

Betta cleared the breakfast plates and Douglas treated himself to a second cup of coffee and more toast. "My visit here is not without purpose. I have a rather awkward announcement to make, well actually two announcements to tell the truth." He sounded almost reckless. He sipped his coffee. "Let me get straight to the point. Maggie thinks she's pregnant. We are going to have a baby."

Mrs van Yssen's upper body swayed under the weight of what she heard. Van Yssen went white; he held the palms of his hands upwards as if to question the heavens and shook his large sad head. He leant back in his chair. He sat forward and rested his elbows on the table. He exchanged glances with his wife. His body felt heavy with despair. This is what Job must have felt like. He looked at Douglas. He saw again the little boy that he had held in his arms, the little boy unsteadily taking unsure steps in his nappy, the academic achiever, going off to university for the first time, the graduation ceremonies. And now this, the decline and fall. He felt as though a piece of his soul had broken off. His left hand had a cold feeling and began trembling. The clock above the fireplace ticked loudly.

"I wish I could say that I am sorry for what has happened, but it would be dishonest of me. Maggie has said to me that no matter what happens, she will have the baby. She'll not give it away for adoption. If she has to she will go away with the child and she will raise it on her own. She has told her mother, but not her father. Her mother fears what her father might do to Maggie, and at my suggestion brought her to the farm on Wednesday. She is staying in the spare room. I wanted to tell you that so that it would not come as a surprise if you visited me, which I don't suppose you would want to do, now. I won't send her away. I want to have her on the farm. After all it is also my child. I need a companion. You have absolutely no idea what it is like to be there in utter silence, cut off from the rest of the world. It is like being in solitary confinement. Sometimes I have felt as though I was going mad. I said nothing, because I did not want to upset you. After all it is not your fault that I am like this. There is no point in pretending that things are going to get better. They are not. I am already over thirty. I know that I am a disappointment to you, Dad. I thought I would farm, and read and study and write something worthwhile. I thought my physical activities would complement my intellectual ones, but it has not turned out like that, and on top of everything, the last few years have been a desperate struggle for survival. Maggie has made me very happy. Even though she has had little education she is intuitive and practical. She is good and she is honest."

"It says something for her that she wants to keep the baby," Mrs van Yssen said.

"What Ma?"

"It says a lot for her that she wants to keep the child."

"That's the kind of person she is."

"What are you going to do?" his father asked.

"What can I do? I have to take responsibility for what I have done. I have to do what is right and what is honourable. I have a responsibility towards the child."

Van Yssen got up stiffly from the table and walked about the room. His left arm felt numb and he flexed his shoulder to try and relieve the discomfort. They were down at bedrock now. Things could hardly get worse. On top of everything the Judge was in town. What a time for all this to come together. As though by Design. The disappointment was greater while he still had hope. Now that there was no longer any hope to which he could cling, the disappointment too was gone. He had hardly any feeling left. He sat down again and continued to shake his head.

"We will find a way, Albert."

He shook his head. "Douglas must do what he has to do. We have sheltered and protected him for too long. He must find his own way."

Douglas raised his eyebrows, "I can't understand?"

"I said that you must do what you have to do."

"With your blessing?"

"Whatever. You did not seek my blessing when you decided to have this alliance, why would you need it now?"

"Because I am your son." The earlier recklessness was gone.

"You will always remain our son," his mother wrote.

Van Yssen felt such futility, so forlorn, such resentment for what had happened to his hopes that he wished Douglas would leave. He felt short of breath.

"I think I should go. I sincerely regret that I have disappointed you."

"Do you need anything?" his mother asked.

"No thank you. I'm fine." He shook his father's hand.

"I'll come outside with you," his mother said. She took the writing pad and pencil with her.

She sat down at the outside table while he put his bicycle clips on. "You must give your father some time to get over this. He has been very good to you. I understand your circumstances better than you think. We will come and see you next week. If necessary I will ask Garnett to bring me. Take some drinking water with you."

"No it's fine, I'll drink from the river." He kissed his mother and rode off through the gate. He looked back and saw his father standing in the doorway.

Scattered clouds cast shadows on the hills. He headed for his mountains. Past the turnoff to Bakenskraal, the mile long straight began and thereafter the long climb. A car made invisible by its silence nearly knocked him over, and when he felt its air he almost slipped on the gravel verge. A cloud of dust swept over him. He stopped and got off his bicycle, wiped the dust from his eyes. He looked at the mountains as he again mounted the bicycle. His sight had improved as his deafness became worse. What would Frances have been like in bed? How Maggie likes it. Balls fit better on the saddle now. His thigh muscles were already feeling strain and there was still a long way to go. Being highly sexed is attributable to mothering instinct, Garnett once said. Being highly sexed because of mothering instinct is surely a virtue not a vice. Will sleep well tonight next to her warm soft body. Go to bed early. Have some beans and lamb chops, unless she's making something else. Read a bit. Get up early tomorrow and take her for a walk. The vegetation began to change. There was more greenery now and grasses were visible among the scrub. The sun was on his back and he began to perspire freely. At the causeway over the Kandelaars River he stopped to drink water. He knelt on a large round boulder and filled his hat with water that he poured over his head. He scooped up handfuls of clear icy water. It was cool in the shade of the trees. Further up along the banks of the river, groups of young poplar trees, the colour of pale grey wood smoke, stood against brilliant green irrigated lucerne fields. He dried his hands on his handkerchief and resumed his journey towards the mountains. Did his father expect him to remain celibate forever? Sexually deaf? The colours were changing almost imperceptibly. Metallic greys and pinks in the afternoon sun, pale Prussian blue shadows in the gullies. The highest peak was illuminated, clear manganese blue, prominent against the other glistening facets of the mountain and the sky. How on earth would he have found a wife? What would she be doing now? He felt as though he was forever riding away from his father. They had become separated. He could never redeem himself. He was nearly at the place of the four pepper trees. Mossel Bay was on the other side of the mountain, where Johnny's girl is. Probably a real goer. Madame Jacquard enjoyed her stay there. She would have been a good lover, probably knows all the little tricks. What would the old man have said about that? Feel sorry for him, but what could he do now? He looked down onto a paddock where a flock of Merino sheep stood silently, all pointing the same way. Smoke rose from Ellis' chimney.

 Douglas arrived at the farm shortly after three. Maggie heard him stamping the dust from his shoes on the kitchen steps and opened the door for him. She had been kneading dough. He picked her up as he hugged her, while she held her hands away from him, and pretended to dance with her. He kissed her. "Wow, I'm so thirsty. It was a hard ride. It was hot. He put his hat down on the kitchen table and sat down. What are you making? I'm hungry."

 "Bread," she said. At times he understood her. The stove was hot, waiting for the bread.

 "I think I'll fry some eggs."

 "I'll do it for you." She patted the air to indicate that he should remain seated. "How did it go?"

 "How did it go?"

 She nodded.

 "As was to be expected; maybe a bit worse. My father is clearly very upset. My mother did not really commit herself. I think she likes you. It's the woman thing. It is interesting that men always think they have better morals than women. We are certainly less forgiving of transgressions. It will take time for my Dad to get over this. I can see it from his point of view. My fiancée's father, the Judge, is in town at the moment, with the Circuit Court. It makes things worse for them. We have not had contact with him since 1928, and he's not a very pleasant man. Ja, so it all complicates matters. Nevertheless, I'm glad that I have told them. My parents and I now have to find a *modus vivendi*."

"What is that?"

"A way of living together. It is a Latin expression. I thought we should go for a walk in the morning."

"That would be so nice."

Saturday 21 May 1932

The van Yssens had let Douglas know earlier in the week that they would be visiting him. Maggie cleaned the house meticulously and polished the floors. The weather was good and she left the doors and the windows open so that the house could air. She picked wild irises and put them into a vase on the dining room table where she expected they would have tea. Douglas had coached her how to arrange things on the table and how to serve the tea. She had baked a chocolate cake, and put it ready on the table. She put on a Chinese lawn dress printed with little pink roses and put stockings on. She cleared the washing line so that her underwear would not be on display.

Van Yssen stopped the car opposite the kitchen door. They walked to the front of the house and knocked on the open front door. Douglas appeared, still fastening the front of his shirt.

"Do come inside."

His mother kissed him, and his father shook his hand without saying anything.

"Let's go to the dining room," he suggested.

"This looks very nice, Douglas." His mother swept her hand over the waiting cups and the cake. She pointed at the flowers and smiled. Van Yssen sat down heavily and held his hat on his lap, as though he was ready to leave. His mother opened her bag and took out her little notebook. She had written in it. "Your father does not want there to be ill feeling between the two of you. Although he is bitterly disappointed, it was his suggestion that we visit you. You are our only child and we must stand by you. That is more important than what people might say. He says he understands how difficult it must have been for you these past years."

"Thanks Dad. I appreciate all that you have done for me. I really do. Let me see where Maggie is."

Maggie apprehensively entered the room. "Good afternoon, Maggie," Mrs van Yssen said. Van Yssen rose from his chair. "Good afternoon, Miss Thompson." He shook her hand.

"I will put the water on," Douglas suggested and disappeared.

Maggie stood about uneasily.

"Where does the cake come from? My husband loves chocolate cake."

"I baked it. It is the only cake I know how to bake."

"Douglas tells me that you can make a very good lamb stew," Mrs van Yssen said.

"That is really very easy to make, Mrs van Yssen."

Douglas returned with the teapot in one hand a cosy in another. He let the tea draw for a while. Maggie was still standing. He pulled out a chair for her next to his father and she sat down cautiously.

"Could I have the notebook Anneke," van Yssen asked. He wrote: 'I would like to take a walk around the farm, if you would like to accompany me?' He handed the notebook to Douglas.

"I would like that, Dad."

"The flowers are lovely, Maggie," Mrs van Yssen observed. "Did Douglas pick them for you?"

Maggie shook her head. "No I picked them myself. I like flowers. They are nice things. It is a pity that they live for such a short time. As the Good Lord said, we should become like them. I have often thought about that, what it could mean. And I think it means that we must be more natural. The flowers don't think. We think too much and what we think often spoils what should be natural."

Van Yssen looked at her from under his bushy eyebrows. How could one ever think too much! If we did not think we would not exist. She could not have heard of Descartes. What a combination! Douglas the arch-intellectual, and this waif who thinks it is undesirable to think too much. How sadly little she understood.

Mrs van Yssen poured tea, and cut the chocolate cake. At first van Yssen was reluctant to have cake, but relented. The cake was light and not too sweet. His first mouthful convinced him that it was the best chocolate cake he had ever had. He sipped the strong flavoursome tea while he still had chocolate residue in his mouth. "Your cake is excellent, Miss Thompson."

Douglas and his father strolled in the direction of the almond trees. "It is hard to credit that these have been in for a little less than four years."

"Yes they have done very well. The soil is good."

"How is the lucerne?"

"All right. If I had a pump we could give it more water."

"When things pick up we'll get a pump. You should be careful that pumping will not interfere with water rights."

"From what I can gather those rights have been sorted out in terms of an agreement between the neighbours. Water always gives rise to quarrels so they had to be careful."

"What are you going to do about Maggie? How long is she going to stay here?"

"I don't know, to be fair. I presume her mother will break the news to her father in due course, and when he calms down, I suppose I will have to meet him. I'll wait until then."

"What about her job?"

"Schmidt thinks well of her, from what I gather. He has been told that she has taken ill. At some stage he'll have to be told that she'll not be going back for a while. He has been trimming staff because of the depression, so I'm sure he'll not mind too much. It won't do for her to stand behind the counter with a fat tummy. As I told you and Ma, Maggie will keep the baby. I realise that a scandal is threatening, and I apologise for that. I have to face the music."

The faces of friends appeared before van Yssen. How is Douglas? He's fine. What happened to that lovely fiancée of his? You mean Miss Rose? Yes, the Judge's daughter. Well, Douglas thought that because of his condition… What a pity. Maggie Thompson? The girl who was the shop assistant? Yes? She's pregnant. What has that to do with Douglas? He is the father. How on earth did that happen? An illegitimate child.

"What are you thinking about Dad?"

Van Yssen waved his hand dismissively. "Nothing. Let's go and look at the sheep."

Maggie added boiling water to the tea, and she and Mrs van Yssen each had another cup. "Has Douglas been very busy?" Mrs van Yssen asked.

"Oh yes, quite busy. He has also been reading a lot. I am also doing some reading. He and Willemse have been mending some fences. One can see that the winter is coming. He said he would prune the trees in the middle of the winter, when they are asleep. I will start a new vegetable garden soon. I would like to grow vegetables. I know how to do that. My father grew vegetables in Natal. The soil here is very good. It would be best near the back of the house."

"When do you think the baby will come?"

"Two months have gone by, so it must be in seven months. Douglas thinks in the middle of December."

"It is better to have a baby in the summer than in the winter. How are you feeling?"

"I have never felt better in my life. I have so much energy."

"Have you not had morning sickness?"

"What is that?"

"Some women get it. They feel nauseous, usually in the morning."

"No, not at all."

"I apologise for asking such personal questions. Are you sure that you are pregnant? Should you not go and see a doctor?"

"I have missed two months now. I feel there is a change inside me. My breasts have felt a little ticklish."

"Perhaps you should see a doctor. Someone is going to have to deliver the baby."

"I don't know who to go to."

"We should ask Doctor Nel to come and see you."

"Won't he tell my father?"

"No, he would never do that. He is not permitted to do that. The rules of his profession forbid that."

"But he has been to see my father, when my father was sick."

"That makes no difference. If you agree I will speak to Douglas and with his permission I will ask Doctor Nel to come and see you. We will pay for that."

"Are you hoping that he will say I am not going to have a baby?"

"No, my dear child, I am not. I want you to have the best care. After all, it will be my grandchild. And besides, I like you. I have seen the change that has come over Douglas, and it is for the better. He needs a companion."

Douglas and his father strolled up the slope towards the house. Van Yssen had to stop from time to time to regain his breath. "What is the matter, Dad, you have always been so fit?"

Van Yssen shook his head. He tapped his chest. 'I don't know.' He sat down on the veranda and breathed heavily.

"You should go and see Dr Diemont."

"No I will be all right. I think we should get going, it is getting late."

The van Yssens said goodbye to Douglas and Maggie. "Please come and visit us again, soon," Maggie asked.

"I need to see you alone for a moment,' his mother wrote. They went into the living room. 'I feel we should ask Garnett to see Maggie. To examine her and to see that she is well. That there are no complications. If you agree I will speak to him and ask him to come here?"

"If you think that is necessary."

"Yes, I do."

"What was that about?" van Yssen asked as they turned into the main road.

"I suggested to Douglas that we should arrange for Garnett to examine Maggie, to make sure that all is well."

"What did he say?"

"He agreed."

"Do you think he will marry her?"

"I think he should."

"What are we going to tell people?"

"Just exactly what there is to tell, my dear, that Douglas is going to get married."

"If it does happen, it should be a quiet affair, a civil wedding. Denis could come to our house and conduct the ceremony there. I dread meeting her parents and her brother. I've seen him at Charlie Nel's garage. He's a common looking little fellow."

Chapter Thirty-nine

Tuesday 24 May 1932

AS SOON AS SHE had had breakfast, Mrs van Yssen asked Betta to take a note to Madame Jacquard asking if it would be convenient to call on her later that morning and asking what time would suit her. Shortly before eleven Mrs van Yssen put on a hat and with her handbag under her arm left for Madame Jacquard's house. The front door was open. Mrs Van Yssen knocked quietly. She heard a door closing at the back of the house. Madame Jacquard held her hands out as she strode down the passage. "How lovely to see you Anneke. It has been some time!"

"Yes, and I do regret it, I should have come to visit you sooner."

"Do come inside. It is such delightful weather. Winter is late this year. A little cool at night, but the sun is so warm, and the trees are losing their leaves. Autumn can be so beautiful. I will show you what I am working on. At present there is not much money to buy what I paint, but I carry on. Times will be better again."

"You are always so optimistic."

"If I did not have hope, what would I have? Nothing. If I did not have hope, life would have no meaning. When I think of the beautiful art that I have seen, when I think from what ultimate source that beauty must come, I do not doubt that life has meaning."

"You inspire me so Guillemette, I love you for that. You have been such a wonderful friend."

"Let me fetch the coffee."

Madame Jacquard carried a tray into the studio.

"I don't want you to think that I only come to see you when I have a problem." Mrs Van Yssen sat with her knees together, her handbag still on her lap.

"Is there a problem? I do not sense one."

"I told you about Douglas' dalliance with the shop assistant."

"Yes, and the more I thought about it, the more I said to myself, good for him. The man is over thirty years now. He probably never had a woman before. That is unnatural. Did you think it would go on forever? That he should live like a monk on that little farm, with his head in his books, castrated by conventions? I often saw the girl in the shop, just as you did. She is attractive. Admittedly she is uncultured, but that gives her a certain charm. She has a good comportment and that shows that she has a good instinct. The poor man has been living like a recluse. He has become separated from his normal society, what else was he supposed to do. I can understand that he was attracted to the girl. And he is a strong attractive man; she probably could not resist him. So there!"

"If only it had stopped there. The girl is pregnant."

"Oh my, how exciting, you have a grandchild on the way. I am sure that it will be a beautiful baby."

"I am afraid it is affecting Albert's health."

"I am sorry to hear that."

"He fears a scandal."

"There will be a scandal all right, as soon as the news gets out. The ones who will scandal most will be the self-righteous. I hope they will keep the baby."

"Maggie is determined to raise the child. She will not let it be taken away from her."

"That is a very good sign. Are they going to get married?"

"Nothing has been said in so many words, but reading between the lines, I would think that is what Douglas considers honourable. When we visited them on Saturday she spoke about making a vegetable garden. That at the very least means that she is planning to stay on the farm for some time."

"She is staying on the farm, making a vegetable garden! How charming. I must give her some garlic. He has a woman in his house. That will make a big scandal in this town. It will be fun. Oh, how exciting. At times it is so dull here, at least on the surface. But underneath the surface lots of things are going on."

"Nothing like this."

"How innocent you are, there are lots of goings on in this dry dusty puritanical place. I went for a walk the one evening, when the weather was mild, and what did I see? I saw the German dentist crawling along in his car next to the curb, in the nocturnal shadows of a tree. And who should jump in? You will never guess. Mrs Liebenfeld. Yes, Mrs Liebenfeld. She sat down close to him and they started kissing as if they were devouring one another. Her hand was between his legs, stroking him like a woman possessed. It was quite erotic to see, and the sounds they were making! Their grunts could have woken the whole town."

"Oh my goodness, you mean Dr Leibner?"

"Yes, you see?"

"Surely not? They are such prominent people."

"That is my whole point. They, and the likes of them, will cast the first stone, I assure you."

"But that does not help us."

"Anneke, there is absolutely nothing you can do. Nothing. You and Albert will simply have to put courage on your faces. It will go away. These things do. In time the scandalmongers will find tastier morsels."

"But to think that our son will marry a shop assistant. We had hoped for so much more. Poor Frances, what will become of her?"

"I like Frances and I feel bitterly sorry for her. They would have been an ideal couple, but it was not meant to be. I could sense all these years that you and Albert still had hope that the impossible would happen. What has happened now has brought an end to that hope. Now we must turn our backs and look into the future."

"You make it sound so simple."

"It is simple, Anneke. Two people are attracted to one another. They are adults. They have had an affair. It is their private business. That is it. Once a man gets a taste of a woman, especially an attractive enthusiastic woman, he can be completely transformed. What his body has experienced will be for some time the uppermost thing in his mind. He will be fascinated by what he is experiencing, almost as though he is watching what is happening to him. What has been kept from him, what he has dreamt about since he changed from being a boy into a man, is now suddenly there for him to have whenever he wants to. How do Douglas and the girl behave when they are with you?"

"They certainly show no regret. They do not seem embarrassed. Douglas was quite matter of fact about it all. The girl has an openness, as though it was just a natural thing to do."

"And it is."

"Albert says it is sinful to have intercourse out of wedlock, and I must say that I too have had pangs of conscience. To make matters worse he found them naked in bed together, while they were joined together. He saw everything. That is all he would say to me. It shocked him a great deal to see his own son like that. On top of it all it was Easter time."

"Yes that is unfortunate, but it has happened, and we must now look forward. How far is she?"

"A little more than two months."

"If they are going to get married they should get married soon, before it shows too much. It will look better that way."

"What shall I say to people?"

"Tell them that the two of them have known one another for some time, and they have decided to get married. What else can you say?"

Mrs van Yssen's hope of receiving comfort had been disappointed. She had hoped for miraculous advice. She sat embarrassed now, lost in thought, not knowing what to say.

"Come, let me show you what I am working on, Anneke."

Thursday 26 May 1932

As soon as they had eaten, van Yssen drove his wife to town. He left her at the greengrocer and went to the bank. There were few people about. Taboni, the personification of a greengrocer, large moustache, cigar in his mouth, was standing in the doorway of his shop, a white apron of coarse cotton tied around his bulging girth.

"Good morning, Mrs van Yssen."

"Good morning Mr Taboni." She went inside.

"Ah, Anneke," a familiar voice said. "Fancy finding you here so early. Expecting guests?"

Mrs van Yssen turned around and came face to face with Mrs Edmeades.

"Good morning Denise."

Mrs Edmeades leant towards her conspiratorially. "I saw Douglas and that perky shop girl from Prince Vintcent coming out of the bushes near the river a few weeks ago. I was going to mention it to you. I said to Charles that I could not imagine what the two of them were doing there." She looked furtively around the shop and put her face closer to Mrs van Yssen. "They were holding hands! In broad daylight mind you, quite brazenly. I said to Charles that I thought you should know. Charles said that it could not have been Douglas, and I said I was quite sure it was. It won't look good if something like this got out. I went to the shop to make sure that it was the girl I thought it was, only to discover that she has mysteriously gone on sick leave. My, my, I said to myself now that's a coincidence."

Mrs van Yssen could feel her colour rising. They could not have been seen by a worse gossip. The shock of the confrontation made her feel faint. She tried to brace herself. The colour left her face.

"Goodness Anneke, are you all right?"

Mrs van Yssen held onto the cheese counter.

"I think you should sit down," Taboni suggested. "I'll get you some sugar water." He brought a bentwood chair.

"Oh dearie me, what have I done? Anneke I am so sorry. I should not have said anything."

Mrs van Yssen struggled to compose herself. She desperately wanted to flee. Taboni brought the sugar water. Van Yssen appeared in the doorway of the shop. He rushed forward. "What is going on?"

"Anneke nearly fainted. It was all my fault. I told her that I had seen Douglas and that girl coming out of the bushes near the river."

Taboni raised his eyebrows.

Van Yssen's anger mounted. He helped his wife to her feet and led her to the door, and helped her into the car. "I have not bought anything, Albert."

"Never mind, we will get what we need later. I will telephone the order through to Taboni. I'll give the butcher a ring. They can deliver what we need."

"It will be all over town before we know, if it is not already doing the rounds, Albert."

Mrs Edmeades went straight home and told her husband. "The plot thickens," Edmeades said, "I saw Louis Nel earlier and asked him whether he knew if Douglas had a new attachment. He asked why, and I told him what you had witnessed. Nice way of putting it to a lawyer, don't you think? He appeared quite surprised. What a turn-up for the books."

Taboni closed his shop at one o'clock and went home for lunch and told his wife what had happened to Mrs van Yssen, and what he had overheard. Later that afternoon Mrs Taboni told Mrs Hops, in great confidence of course. Mrs Hops put on her hat and scuttled off to Mrs Bowles. Mrs Taboni's maid told Mrs Gordon's maid who in turn told Mrs Gordon. By the time the Elleys had a bridge drive at their house two days later it was the whispered, head shaking, disbelieving subject of conversation. The story travelled from house to house and gathered colour as it grew, and was referred back to Mrs Edmeades for corroboration. Douglas had been seen doing up the front of his trousers. Could he not just have relieved himself? No it was not that kind of buttoning-up. Besides, the girl was straightening her dress and the back of her dress was creased. She was also rearranging her hair. They were seen embracing each other. Now she was gone from the shop. The story eventually reached Schmidt and he nodded as though he had solved a difficult riddle, a riddle that only a philanderer could solve. When his wife cross-examined him he admitted, not quite under oath mind you, that he had seen Douglas in the shop, several times, and yes, he did see him talking to Miss Thompson. The fact that she was ill did complicate matters he admitted, but he reassured his wife that he would send a note to her mother and ask her to come and see him at her earliest convenience.

"What shall we do Albert? Wherever I go, whomever I meet, I am conscious of an atmosphere. There are insinuations hidden in their faces, eyes that want to exchange sympathy for more information."

"We'll batten down the hatches and ride out the storm. To hell with what people think. Bitterly disappointed as I am that things have turned out like this, there is nothing we can do but to make the best of it. If Douglas wants to marry the girl then so be it. It would be a damn lot better for him to act with decency than to heap on us the greater disgrace of an illegitimate child. I am at the end of my tether, Anneke. I was a fool to think that I could control Douglas' life. I cannot. I have done my best. I can do no more. I had unrealistic expectations. But to think that it could have come to this, I would never have thought possible."

"I think you should go and see Douglas. He may be thinking one thing and we another. Discuss with him what he is planning to do so that we can act accordingly. If you would like I will go along."

"That is a good idea. I will look at my diary, and if possible go tomorrow afternoon."

Wednesday 25 May 1932

Van Yssen left for the farm shortly after lunch. He opened the gate and looked about. He drove slowly to the farmhouse fearful of finding Douglas and Maggie in some compromising situation. As he got out of the car a movement at the back of the house caught his eye. He heard her humming to herself as she raked the dark brown soil of a newly made vegetable patch. There was Maggie, the skirts of an old cotton dress with a printed pattern tucked into her pants to raise the hem, her glossy dark hair tied back with a mauve and blue scarf, totally absorbed in what she was doing, oblivious of his arrival. She had stuck seed packets onto twigs to indicate what she had sown. A shiny bright green watering can stood to one side. She continued to sing to herself as she worked.

Her dress showed patches of perspiration under her armpits. She had her back to him and he saw her rump quivering from her movements. Her shoes were muddy. He cleared his throat and she started.

"Oh my goodness, Mr van Yssen, you gave me quite a fright."

"Good afternoon Miss Thompson. Is Douglas here?"

"He's gone with Willemse, to set a trap for the caracal cat. They won't be too long. Do come inside and let me make you some tea, or coffee if you prefer?" She led the way to the kitchen door and took her shoes off before she entered. "If you would like to make yourself comfortable, I'll put the water on."

"Coffee would be nice, thank you."

Van Yssen settled himself in the living room. He preferred to be where the books were. He took his hat off.

Maggie arrived with his coffee and a few almond biscuits on a plate. She had made herself more presentable and combed her hair, and washed her hands. She sat down opposite him. He looked at her. She held his gaze for a few moments and then looked away. "What vegetables have you sown?" he asked.

"All sorts of things. Beetroot. I love beetroot. Carrots, squashes, although it is really the wrong time for them, but you never know, beans, they always reward you. I thought the other day of growing flowers. There must be a market for them. I'm going to try asparagus one of these days. It is so fulfilling to see the little shoots making their way through the soil and growing stronger. It is quite amazing to think that all you need to make food is sunlight, water and soil. Apart from the seed, everything is free. It is not as though the good Lord put us here without anything."

Van Yssen sipped his coffee. He could not contain his smile. "Well, the soil is not free. One has to own it, and to own it you have to purchase it."

"The first people did not buy it. There was no such thing as money then. But they could plant seed, and pick fruit from the trees."

"Yes, I suppose you are right. The coffee is very good."

"I roast the beans myself. It has to be done patiently in an oven that is just the right temperature. I keep the roasted beans in a jar with a tight lid. And then I only grind as many beans as I need for each pot of coffee. It is better that way."

Douglas saw his father's car as he walked up towards the house. Van Yssen heard him stamping his feet on the veranda. "Hello Dad. Have you been here long?'

Van Yssen shook his head. He pointed to the coffee cup.

"I'll fetch the writing pad, and leave the two of you to talk. I have some work to do Mr van Yssen."

"I need to discuss a few things with you. Shall we sit at the dining table?"

"Yes, that would be fine." Douglas sat down next to his father.

"Your mother and I have had a discussion. Stories of you and Maggie are all over town. Mrs Edmeades saw the two of you coming out of the bushes near the river. She is the worst. We cannot undo what has happened. We will stand by you no matter what. But we must present a united front. That is essential. In order to do that we need to know exactly what your plans are. So that we will not end up saying one thing while you say another."

"Is that why you have come to visit me today?"

"Yes. We cannot leave things to meander along."

Douglas sat back and his chair creaked violently. He put his hands behind his head. "I have told Maggie that I would like to marry her."

"What did she say?"

"She said that she wants me to be absolutely sure. She does not want me to marry her if I have any doubt. She says she wants her baby to grow up happily, not in an atmosphere of regret and recrimination. She says she would rather go away and raise the baby on her own, because she will make sure that the child is happy. That is all that matters to her. She says she was as much to blame as I am, if not more, which I somehow doubt."

"How do you feel?"

"Dad, if I must be perfectly honest, I am so happy here with Maggie. She loves me. She is authentic. She's intuitive. She will be a very good mother, of that I am certain. My life has changed since she has been here. You have no idea what it means to me to have another human being here that I can touch and feel and smell."

"Then you must marry her, and the sooner the better. Discuss it with her and let me know what she says. You must go and meet her father. I will come and fetch you when you are ready. She must ask her mother to tell her father that she is expecting. We must face things now. The sooner you are married the sooner the rumours will stop. Rumours are always worse than the facts. Her coffee is very good, do you think I could have another cup?"

"She knows how to make really good coffee."

"I like the way she has made a vegetable garden. She's plucky. I respect pluck."

Van Yssen had another cup of coffee and gathered his hat. He went outside with Douglas and walked to the back of the house where Maggie was caringly watering her rows of seeds with the green watering can. "I must be going now Maggie. Thank you for the coffee. Until next time then."

He had said her name. "Goodbye Mr van Yssen," she called and waved to him, the watering can in her other hand.

Douglas walked to the gate and shook his father's hand. "Thank you Dad."

Van Yssen turned the car into the main road. It was as though a great sadness had departed from him, as though he had survived the delirious crisis of a severe illness and was now recovering. Seeing the girl in the vegetable patch had done something to him. The dark depression that had weighed down upon him was gone, driven away by her simple virtue. There was not enough sin in the whole universe to extinguish her virtue.

The speed with which he came into the driveway told Mrs van Yssen that something had happened. She hurried to the garage. "Is everything all right Albert?"

He smiled as he got out of the car. "Yes everything is fine, Anneke. I am glad I went to see Douglas."

"You look happy. What happened?"

Van Yssen walked to the drawing room. His wife followed. He flopped down in an easy chair and gathered his breath. "When I arrived, Douglas was out in the veld with Willemse and I found Maggie busy in a vegetable patch that she had made. She had sown her seeds and was raking the soil. She was in rapture, oblivious of my arrival and was singing absentmindedly to herself as she raked. She had put the seed packets on sticks to mark what she had sown. She looked quite fetching as she worked and mused contentedly. As I stood and watched her I saw something in her that I had not seen before. On the way back here I contemplated how I would describe it to you. It is difficult to put into words. She had an effect on me. Seeing her standing there, I could see the world as she sees it, with her clarity and directness, without artifice, free from the trammels of social devices. She told me about her vegetables. She made coffee for me while we waited for Douglas. Her coffee tasted different. She explained how she makes it. She understands how things work, as though she is in tune with them. I looked at her while I drank my coffee, and she looked at me. I no longer cowed her. I could sense that. It was as if she could see right into me. When Douglas arrived she went back to her vegetable garden so that Douglas and I could have privacy. We had a discussion and we agreed that he would speak to her about getting married. He acknowledged that they had already spoken about it. He said that she had told him that she would only consider marrying him if she knew that it would bring happiness to her child. She told him that she would rather look after the child on her own than to risk an unhappy upbringing. I said to Douglas that I felt if it is going to happen, the sooner the better. And quite frankly my dear I don't give a cat's whisker what people may say. I am happy that Douglas has a companion. God works in mysterious ways. I realised as I drove back that she has no sinfulness in her, that I am not there to judge her. She has no malice. There are not many people like that. What I saw them doing now seems innocent enough. It was my wrong thinking that defiled it. I feel as though I have been freed from my guilt."

"I love you, Albert. What must we do now?"

"Wait to hear from Douglas."

Thursday 2 June 1932

On a clear cold early winter morning van Yssen drove to the farm to fetch Douglas and Maggie. It had been arranged that Douglas would meet Maggie's father. He had been informed of her condition and her circumstances and had taken the news better, in fact much better, than his wife and Johnny had imagined he would. It was agreed that Maggie would stay with her parents for the two nights that she and Douglas were planning to be away, and that Douglas would stay with his parents. Van Yssen would take them back to the farm on Saturday afternoon.

Douglas shut the house. Maggie was ready with her little red suitcase. Van Yssen invited Maggie to sit in the front of the car with him. Douglas was in the back. Willemse attended to the gate and doffed his hat as they drove past. He wished he knew what was going on.

"There's a rug on the back seat Maggie," van Yssen said. "Put if over your legs, it will keep you warm."

"Thank you Mr van Yssen." She leant over the seat to get the rug. Douglas smiled at her.

"I will drive to our house, where we will have something to eat, and then Douglas can take you home Maggie." Some doubt returned to van Yssen. "Will that be all right?"

"Yes that would be splendid," she replied.

Douglas was enjoying himself. He moved to the sunny side of the car. It pleased him to see his father and Maggie in conversation.

Mrs van Yssen was ready to welcome them. They left Maggie's suitcase in the back of the car. She shook hands with Mrs van Yssen and thanked van Yssen for fetching them. Betta peered from the kitchen window while she wiped soapsuds from her forearms.

"You know where the bathroom is, Maggie, if you need anything." Mrs Van Yssen knew that the bladders of pregnant women could be impatient, even though it was a bit soon to think of that.

Betta carried a platter of scrambled egg to the dining room. Mrs van Yssen introduced her to Maggie. Betta had not abandoned her loyalty to Frances and glared at the impostor. Douglas was searching his father's bookshelves for something to read and had to be fetched. He had shown Maggie the classically correct way of holding her knife and fork, and had coached her in the finer aspects of table manners. His father was a stickler for correct manners and knowing what to do would further ingratiate her to him. She sat erect in her ladder-back chair and spread her napkin over her lap as soon as she had sat down. She broke her toast into small pieces and buttered them individually. She ate her egg with her fork and offered her host and hostess salt and pepper. She did not ask for anything and waited for it to be offered to her. Her behaviour did not escape Van Yssen's attention and it pleased him.

"My husband tells me that you have made a wonderful vegetable garden, Maggie."

"It is hardly a wonderful garden, with respect to Mr van Yssen, it is just a simple little patch. And we'll have to see what I manage to produce. I hope it will work."

"I'm sure it will be a success," van Yssen said.

Douglas turned his eyes from one mouth to another to follow the conversation. He could make out that they were mentioning the garden. "Maggie has made a nice garden," he said.

His father nodded.

"It felt strange coming into town. It felt as though I have been away for months," Maggie said. "I like it up there, on the farm. I do not like being with a lot of people. People interfere with everything. The silence up there says more than all the jabbering in town. I can hear the wind blowing through the tall grass up there, making whispering noises. You have no idea how nice that is. Everything up there is alive, it makes you think that everything is alive, even the rocks of the mountain."

"That is beautiful, Maggie," Mrs van Yssen said.

"When is your father expecting you, Maggie?"

"My mother said he would be at home the whole day. He is waiting to start his next job."

Douglas and Maggie arrived at her house shortly before lunch. Her father was waiting for them, leaning on his elbows on the narrow white wall that separated the small front veranda from the pavement. A cigarette dangled from the corner of his mouth. He saw the car stopping on the opposite side of the street, and at first did not realise who it was. He stared at Douglas, getting out of the car. Douglas walked round the car and opened the door for Maggie. He retrieved Maggie's red suitcase from the back seat and carried it for her as he helped her across the street. Thompson stood up straight and stretched his stiff builder's back. In an act of uncharacteristic wastefulness he threw his half smoked cigarette down onto the ground and stamped it out with his foot. He watched as they approached and tried to remember what he had decided to say. Even though his wife and Johnny had done their best to describe Douglas, this man was different. His face showed that he worked outside. This fellow was larger than he had imagined. He moved with the grace and confidence of a heavyweight boxer. He had prepared to lecture him. But he would not be able to do that.

"Daddy, this is Douglas." She kissed her father cautiously.

"I am Douglas van Yssen. How do you do Mr Thompson," Douglas said and held out his hand.

Thompson only nodded his head because he thought it would not be courteous to speak to a deaf man. "We'll go and sit inside, Maggie."

Her mother was in the passage examining her own reflection in the glass of a picture, adjusting her hair. "There you are my little girl."

"Good morning, Mrs Thompson," Douglas said.

"Good morning Mr van Yssen."

"Bring some coffee," Thompson ordered. "We'll go and sit in the lounge."

Strands of tobacco smoke floated in the air. Thompson indicated to Douglas to sit down. He had dealt with deaf people before. One thing was for sure, there would be no point in scolding the chap for what he had done. Some of the springs in the seat of Douglas' easy chair had come loose and poked his buttocks. He resisted the temptation of moving about for fear of admitting his discomfort. Thompson knew what that seat was like. Mrs Thompson stood leaning against the post of the doorway, to see what was going to happen.

"Ask him what he has got to say for himself, Maggie."

She opened her handbag to get out her pad and pencil.

"I understand what your father said, Maggie. Mr Thompson, I wish to apologise most sincerely to you for not introducing myself earlier. I also want to apologise unconditionally for what has happened. I regret that I have embarrassed you and your family. I will take all the blame. However, the fact of the matter is that Maggie is expecting our baby, and I feel a great responsibility towards her and the child. I have been living on my own on the farm for about four years now. I was engaged to the daughter of a judge before I became deaf and broke off my engagement because of my condition. Apart from that I have not had any close relationship with any woman. Maggie is the first woman with whom I have had any form of intimate relationship. She has made me very happy, and to come straight to the point, I would like to marry her. I have grown to love her, and if you would agree, and if she will have me, it would mean a great deal to me if she would become my wife. I do not have much to offer Maggie, times are difficult, but she will not want for anything. My parents know that I wish to marry Maggie, and if you and Mrs Thompson should agree, they will proceed with the all necessary arrangements."

Thompson had not expected such directness. He stubbed out his cigarette in a brass ashtray and distorted the lower part of his large ruddy face with a rough freckled hand. Mrs Thompson had heard enough and went to the kitchen to make the coffee. Thompson moved about in his chair and scratched some scales from the back of his hand. He heaved and breathed out heavily through his nose.

"Tell him I don't want him to say that he wants you now, while the gilt is still on the gingerbread, if you know what I mean, only to throw you aside like a rag doll when he gets tired of you."

"He is not like that Pa."

"How can you tell? I can see the way you look at him. I wouldn't be surprised if you took the lead in this."

"I love Douglas, Pa. He is a good man."

"That is the trouble with you. Everybody is always good according to you. And then you end up in trouble. And what about your job, and our board and lodging? Next thing Johnny will get too cosy with that hussy of his and it will be only your ma and me to care for ourselves. Times are hard. Now this. I cannot afford a wedding. You know that."

"Douglas and his family will take care of that. We will just have a small private wedding at their house. We have discussed it."

"Small and private because they are ashamed of us. We are the workers. You will never fit in there."

"I do not want to fit in anywhere, Pa, I just want to be with Douglas. He does not want to fit in anywhere. He will take very good care of me. I know that with my heart."

"Your heart is in your pants."

Maggie started crying. "It is not like that," she sobbed.

Her mother returned with a tray. "What is going on now?"

"I love Douglas and he has asked to marry me, but Pa says my heart is in my pants. It is not like that. I have been so very happy with Douglas, so happy on the farm. I want Pa to be happy, I want you to be happy. I want everybody to be happy. Please just give us a chance."

Thompson glared at her. She passed him his coffee and handed Douglas his cup. Thompson poured coffee into his saucer and slurped it from the edge. "Why don't you put the kid up for adoption?"

"I will not do that," Maggie said firmly. "I will never do that. I would rather die first. I would never consider that."

Thompson looked at Douglas who sat impassively. Douglas had caught only snatches of the conversation. "I am perfectly sincere, Mr Thompson. I don't know what else to say. If you feel that you need time to consider my offer, I understand."

Thompson began nodding to himself. He grunted, took another cigarette from his box of fifties, elaborately tapped the one end of the cigarette on the box, put it into his mouth in his special way that he thought looked smart. He took his matchbox, removed a match, looked to see whether Douglas was watching, held the box in position between his last fingers and the base of his hand and struck the match with the thumb and forefinger of the same hand. It had taken a lot of practice to learn to do that. A man who could do that had other tricks up his sleeve. An old crocodile – only the eyes were showing. He exhaled the cigarette smoke through his nose, and spat out a small piece of tobacco.

"Ask him if he would like a milk stout."

Maggie wrote on her pad. "My pa wants you to have a beer with him. Say yes."

"That would be very nice thank you, Mr Thompson."

Maggie fetched two bottles of milk stout.

"Tell him I say it is good for the blood. The Doctor said so."

"Pa says Dr Nel told him it is good for one."

Douglas smiled.

"Douglas and Doctor Nel have been friends all their lives Pa. He will be at the wedding if you let us get married."

"He is a good man, the Doctor," Mrs Thompson observed. "He did not even want to charge us. He said we could pay when things got easier. My husband had ammonia."

"Douglas can't hear you Ma."

"Then write on the paper."

Thompson poured his stout down the side of his glass in order to avoid having too much of a head. He put the glass down for a few moments to conceal his eagerness to start drinking. He took a huge draw from his cigarette that lit up the end in the gloom of their dingy room, and while he was still exhaling the smoke took his first draught of stout. He wiped his mouth with the back of his hand and smacked his lips as he felt the cold liquid flowing through his chest. "My late ma used to say that if there's bugger all you can do about a thing, don't do anything about it. Now I can do bugger all about the fact that you are pregnant Maggie. I do not want to have a bastard around me, so if you have to get married, then it must be so. But warn this fellow, and I really mean it, I am not stuffing around, if he as much as puts a bloody foot wrong I will give him a hiding like he's never thought possible. You know me, I don't like my kith and kin to be buggered around. I nearly said something else. There is one condition. You must stay at home, and go back to work until the wedding. After that, you can do as you please, and also, I want to warn you: don't come crying or begging to me."

"I have made a vegetable garden on the farm, Pa. Douglas is busy with other things. I need to be there to water the seedlings when they come up."

"That is too bad. I have made a condition, don't press me. Take it or leave it. He is big and ugly enough to do that little job for you."

"My father has agreed that we can get married. But I have to stay here and go back to work until the wedding."

"Are you happy to do that?"

"Not really, but I know him, he will not budge now. We have no choice. Speak to your parents and try and arrange the wedding as soon as possible."

"Thank you very much Mr Thompson, thank you Mrs Thompson. I am very happy the way things have turned out. Thank you for your hospitality. I should be going now."

"Tell him to stay and have another stout."

"Pa wants you to have another beer. Please say yes."

Douglas burped and nodded in agreement.

It was nearly half past one before Douglas was able to extricate himself. The stout had gone to his head. He said goodbye to Thompson and his wife. Maggie accompanied him to the car. "Will you be all right here?"

"Yes."

"I will speak to my parents and come and see you tomorrow afternoon. I am so happy the way this has turned out." He gave her a lingering alcoholic kiss while her parents watched, and hugged her.

"He's not a bad fellow," Thompson commented. "Pity about the money."

Chapter Forty

Thursday 10 March 1932

DOUGLAS DROVE HOME cautiously from the Thompsons because of the effect of the alcohol. His face was flushed when he walked into the dining room. His parents had nearly finished their lunch.

"I'm afraid I have been drinking," he looked a little sheepish.

"How did it go?" His mother asked.

"Fine. He's a difficult rough man. Insisted that I have a drink with him, two bottles of milk stout in fact. He drinks milk stout in the belief that it is good for you. He said Garnett told him that. Good excuse. He has agreed but wants Maggie to stay here and to go back to work until the wedding. I was worried about her safety because he can evidently become violent but he seems to have accepted the situation with equanimity. He's more concerned really about losing the money Maggie brings home every month."

"Your mother and I have been talking. I will go and see Denis Kuys and ask him to conduct a civil ceremony here at home. I'm sure he will agree. Do you have a date in mind?"

"The sooner the better, as you said."

"We will invite Alice Kuys, and Mrs Jacquard, and Garnett, and Maggie's family. It all depends on Denis' schedule."

Friday 3 June 1932

Van Yssen telephoned Denis Kuys early in the morning and asked to see him some time that day. Kuys suggested three thirty. He asked van Yssen what it was about. Van Yssen said it was a private matter and would rather not discuss it over the telephone.

Kuys was removing his robes when van Yssen arrived. "You look rather severe Albert. What is it that is troubling you?

"Thank you for seeing me, Denis. I have a delicate matter to discuss with you. No doubt you have heard the rumour?"

"There have been whispers, but you know me, I don't brook gossip. So I am afraid you had better enlighten me. Is this a legal matter?"

"No, no not at all."

"What is it then?"

"To come straight to the point, and I must say it grieves me to have to tell an old friend this, and especially someone who saw my son growing up. Douglas has had an affair with a girl who works at Prince Vintcent, and the girl is pregnant."

"Adoptions do not fall within my province, Albert."

"We are not considering an adoption Denis. Douglas and the girl want to get married."

"He must have lost his senses. A shop assistant? Who is she?"

"Her name is Maggie Thompson. They are people from Natal."

"I don't know them."

"I'm sure you will have noticed the girl. She is fetching."

"How did all this happen?"

"We think at the beginning of March. They just got together somehow; you know how these things are. You have seen so much going through the courts. They have happened since the beginning of time. Carnal infatuation is a powerful thing. Anyway it has happened, difficult as it is to believe. I realise that it was unrealistic of me to think that Douglas could sit up there on the slopes of the mountain, celibate for the rest of his life."

"What will the Roses say?"

"They must say whatever they wish, Denis. I cannot do anything about that. My reason for coming to see you today is to ask you whether you would consider conducting a civil wedding ceremony for us, at our house."

Kuys opened his diary. "Do you have any date in mind?"

"In the next two weeks or so."

"Give me a day."

"What about a fortnight from today?"

"Fridays are difficult, unless it is in the afternoon."

"That would be fine. What time will suit you?"

"Half past four?"

"Thank you very much Denis."

"Don't mention it my dear fellow, that's what friends are for. Let me order some tea." Kuys returned after a few moments. "I don't want to pry, but this must have been very difficult for you and Anneke."

"More difficult than you could imagine. Socially it is a disaster, but we have to face the facts. The blessing is that the girl is a wholesome person. She has a kind heart. She has lots of common sense and she's practical. Who are we to judge others. She's open and direct to a fault. And she is attractive and physically strong. So we did not get the daughter-in-law we hoped for, but then neither did Douglas get the life he deserved. We don't always get what we want, and sometimes there is a reason. Frances would have been the most ideal companion. They were perfectly suited. She would still marry him today, but Douglas is uncompromising. Between the two of us Denis, Frances and Anneke still correspond. Anneke will have to write to her and tell her what has happened. I dread to think how Frances will receive the news. I think she still occasionally writes to Douglas but he does not even open the letters."

"Do you want me to tell Alice?"

"Yes, if you would. We would like her to be at the ceremony, she will understand. Anneke will invite her formally. And we will invite Garnett Nel."

"Gosh, Albert, you have been through a lot. My heart goes out to you and

Anneke. Such a brilliant man is Douglas. The girl, this Maggie Thompson, do you know whether she has a past?"

"From all appearances not here in Oudtshoorn. She was engaged once. That much we know. I find it difficult to get through to Douglas. We used to have wonderful conversations. We enjoyed each other's company. We were friends. As he became deaf he grew increasingly distant. It is understandable that communication became difficult, that stands to reason, but it was more than that. He withdrew; he kept everything inside long before this affair of his. He seemed odd at times."

"It must have been a great shock to him to go deaf. I don't know how I would have managed. It can affect the mind."

"The strange thing is that he showed little resentment. I suspect that more went on inside him than he was prepared to show, and the sad thing is that he probably kept it inside to spare us grief. It is as if he no longer allows himself to experience any emotion."

"How has he reacted in this matter?"

"How do you mean?"

"About the girl."

"Quite unconcerned, tame as a baboon. As if nothing has happened. No matter what I said, it was like water off a duck's back."

Kuys shook his head.

"Anyway Denis, I must not detain you any longer. Thank you very much for your assistance." Van Yssen took his hat and left.

Kuys watched him through his window, as he walked down Church Street. The strong strides of the land surveyor had become shorter, his shoulders more stooped and more bony, his sad head to one side.

Van Yssen found Douglas and his wife in the drawing room. She was knitting a jersey and he was reading.

"I have been to see Denis and he has agreed to conduct the ceremony on the seventeenth, at four thirty, that's a fortnight from today." He wrote the information down for Douglas. 'I suggest you arrange for us to meet the Thompsons. Have them over. Tomorrow afternoon would be a good time. Make contact and see if it will suit them. You can go and fetch them and Maggie, and take them home again afterwards.' "It is all settled, Anneke. I will go and see Garnett and invite him. Denis will speak to Alice tonight and I said you would invite her yourself."

"As I said, I would like to invite Madame Jacquard, Albert?"

"Yes that it a good idea. She will handle anything and make the best of the situation."

Saturday 4 June 1932

Mr and Mrs van Yssen watched through the lace curtains of the drawing room for Douglas to arrive with the Thompsons. Thompson was in front next to

Douglas. Mother and daughter in the back. Van Yssen waited until movements were discernable through the stained glass window before he opened the front door. Thompson stood boldly in front. He wore a black blazer with large golden M.O.T.H. pocket badge, complete with its circle of stars and rifles crossed over a symbolic tin hat, a white shirt with an open upturned collar. His greying hair was slicked down and parted in the middle. He held his hat in his hand. He had cut his chin shaving and pasted a piece of cotton wool onto the cut to stem the bleeding. He snorted and swallowed to get the phlegm of his post-nasal drip from his vocal chords before he introduced himself. "Jack Thompson. I am pleased to make your acquaintance." He thrust his hand towards van Yssen. "This is my missus, Beulagh. Maggie you know."

"How do you do Mr Thompson, this is my wife. How do you do Mrs Thompson. Hello Maggie. Do come inside. It is nice to have you over."

"I can see where Douglas learnt to be such a gentleman," Mrs Thompson remarked.

Thompson looked around and up at the ceilings as he strode stiff wide-legged into the house, assessing the quality of the workmanship. A lot of money was spent here all right. They did not build many like this. Architects who design places like this can be fucking difficult when it comes to contractors. Better to stay away from them. Van Yssen showed them to the drawing room.

"Please do sit down," Mrs van Yssen suggested.

"Is there any special chair that is reserved for the guv?" Thompson asked as he took his box of cigarettes from his jacket pocket.

"No, not at all, I'm quite happy to sit anywhere," van Yssen replied. "Make yourself comfortable. It is quite nice here next to the window, Mrs Thompson."

The Thompsons sat down. Thompson took a cigarette and started tapping the end on the box. "I hope we are not going to smoke by ourselves, Jack, offer some cigarettes around."

Van Yssen held up his hand to decline the offer. "Thank you very much for your kind offer Mrs Thompson, but we don't smoke."

"Hope you don't mind if we do, Jack and I. Maggie never liked the idea."

"Of course we won't mind. There are ash trays, as you can see."

Douglas' eyes went from mouth to mouth. Mrs van Yssen wrung her hands and fidgeted. "It is the maid's weekend away. I'll go and see to the tea," she announced.

"Maggie can go and help," Mrs Thompson offered.

"That won't be necessary."

"No, she must help," her mother insisted.

"Come along then, my dear, let's go and make the tea."

Mrs van Yssen and Maggie went to the kitchen. Mrs van Yssen put a saucepan of water onto the hot plate. "How have you been, Maggie? My husband was impressed with the work you have done on the farm, your garden."

"It is nothing really. I enjoy it, so you can't really call it work. I am sorry about my parents. I am embarrassed about them. I do apologise."

"My dear child, don't say that. We cannot choose our parents, and besides, I am sure they are very good people."

"I do not want to end up like them, Mrs van Yssen. I want to make something of my life. I want to go forward. Douglas has shown me how to conduct good manners. I like that. I have a lot to learn, but I am trying hard. You must also help me. Your kind of life is much better. There is a peacefulness in this house. It is not like that at home. Struggling the way we struggle brings out the worst in people. My parents are forever blaming each other, trying to hurt each other in little ways. Life should not be like that. I look at the dresses in the shop. Some of them just look better than others. I say to myself why is one design better than another? Why is one coat more elegant, as Mr Schmidt would say, than another? Why are some people more genteel than others?"

"We don't know why that is. I think education has a lot to do with it. To read a lot is important. Abraham Lincoln the great American President had little formal education but he read and read and read, much of it in the back of a caboose, and he educated himself that way, and he became the president of his country. I will help you in any way I can."

The back door opened and Betta appeared.

"What are you doing here, Betta?"

"I knew you would have people, and I thought I would help."

"Do go back to the drawing room, Madam, it will look better if a servant brings the tea."

"Yes I was in Flanders," Mrs van Yssen heard Thompson saying as she and Maggie returned to the drawing room. He pulled the lower part of his blazer out so that he could better display his M.O.T.H badge.

"I have read about events there. It must have been terrible," van Yssen remarked.

Thompson blew blue smoke out towards the ceiling and settled himself more comfortably in his chair now that there was a familiar topic. He assumed an air of self-importance and authority. He skilfully flicked ash off his cigarette into the ashtray with his little finger. "Terrible is not the word." He paused and drew on his cigarette. "Nothing can describe the hell we went through. I was thirty-two when I joined up in 1915. Maggie was seven and Johnny nine. I saw them standing on the docks in Durban, the three of them in the miserable rain when the tugs pushed the troopship, that took us north, away from the quayside. You don't know what that does to a man when he thinks, what they are thinking, saying goodbye while they are crying. They know that you are not coming back and you know that you are not coming back but no one wants to say it. And you wonder to yourself what the hell you are doing but it is too late and there's nothing you can do, because if you did you would be a deserter and they would shoot you anyway."

"Why did you go?" van Yssen asked.

Thompson frowned. "Why did I go? Because other people went. They said you were a coward if you did not go. I also thought it would be an adventure. My life had been quite hard. My father was a carpenter. He worked day and night. He took me out of school when I was fourteen to go and work for him. The two of us worked day and night to scrape enough together. He died while I was away up north. He did not leave a bean. When I came back my mother was by herself in the house. She did other people's washing to stay alive. When she died we sold the house and came here, because they said there was work. I should have stayed in Durban."

"What were conditions like in Flanders?"

"Bad."

"In what way?"

"The trenches were terrible. The way it stank in there. We stood and lay amongst the corpses. The whole thing was stupid. You just sat there in the mud and rain and cold or scorching heat and waited for Fritz to shell you. After the way the Germans behaved in Belgium we knew they could use gas at any time. There was a rumour that they were using a new kind of gas, green stuff. They wiped out a lot of people with it did those sausage-eating pigs. I felt sorry for the youngsters in the trenches. Many of them suffered from mutism and tremors. We later called it shell shock. The worst experience I had was in the battle of the Somme."

"Stop talking about it Jack, you will start having your nightmares again," his wife chided. "I also don't want to be reminded of it. My stomach turns when I think how I went with the two little ones to look at the casualty lists, to see who had fallen. It was the only time I was glad not to see your name, while the other women shrieked and sobbed and went home to pack away their husbands' things. Jack says he can still to this day smell the inside of those trenches."

"Let's talk about happy things. Albert loves talking about the war. Tea will be here presently. Betta has come in to help me. It was so nice of her."

"Were you in the war, Mr van Yssen?" Thompson asked.

"No."

"Why did you not go and fight?"

"Well I suppose there were several reasons."

"Such as?"

"I don't think they would have had me because of my age, but apart from that I am a pacifist, Mr Thompson, a conscientious objector if you will."

"Ah, here the tea is, Mrs van Yssen exclaimed happily. "How do you take your tea Mrs Thompson?"

"As it comes out of the pot, but nice and strong and with milk. Jack also has milk and two sugars."

Van Yssen was eager to reach finality about the wedding arrangements. "I went to see my friend Denis Kuys, the Magistrate, yesterday afternoon, to explore the possibility of having a wedding ceremony here at our home. He is quite happy to do that for us, and has suggested a Friday afternoon. We looked at some dates and he said Friday the seventeenth, which is a fortnight from now, would suit him, at about four-thirty in the afternoon, when he has done with his court work."

Thompson put his cup down loudly in his saucer. "This whole business has jumped on us out of the blue, Mr van Yssen, I have not got used to it yet. Besides there is the matter of my self-respect. What will people say, people like Mr Schmidt at the shop? Then there is the question of money. I cannot afford a wedding."

Van Yssen waved his hand dismissively. "Oh, you need not worry about that. I will pay for everything."

"It is generous of you, but I have my pride to think about."

Mrs Thompson took her cup of tea from Douglas. She glared at her husband. "We have been over this Jack, and you gave me your word that you would behave. I think Mr van Yssen has gone to a lot of trouble on our behalf, and Maggie is as much to blame for the reason we are sitting here, as that fellow over there. Maggie says she loves him and he loves her, so there is no point in beating about the bush, we will leave it to the two of them to do that, ha, ha, so let's cut the nonsense and agree to a fortnight from now, and get it over with. This is a grand house to get married in. And to get a Magistrate to come here to marry our daughter, well, I've never heard of that in my life. I'll have to get a new dress."

Mrs van Yssen wanted to make progress while the mood was right. "Would you like to invite anyone? We thought of making it a small intimate affair, and of only inviting Mrs Kuys' wife who has been a good friend since Douglas was quite small, and Mrs Jacquard, a friend of the family as well as Douglas' friend Dr Nel."

"We don't know many people in town. Johnny, Maggie's brother, will come and Beulagh's brother might be visiting us then," Thompson replied.

"Please think of anything special that you might want us to do, and give us a ring."

"We don't have a telephone," Mrs Thompson said.

Thompson had another cigarette and asked whether he could have another cup of tea. He skilfully dunked his biscuits in his tea to soften them, and lowered the sodden pieces into his eager mouth.

Thursday 16 June 1932

Van Yssen fetched Douglas from the farm in the morning. Douglas had tried his suit on earlier and was pleased that it still fitted well. It needed pressing, but Betta would see to that. It had been agreed that he and Maggie would sleep in the van Yssen's spare room the night of the wedding and that his father would take them to the farm the following day.

In the late afternoon he used his father's car to visit Maggie. By the time he arrived at the Thompson's house, Thompson had consumed several bottles of stout and was in quite a jovial mood. Maggie was so glad to see Douglas that she cried when she embraced him. He kissed her fondly and held her hands as he looked at her tummy. "What has it been like at work?" he asked.

"I missed you," she mouthed.

"I missed you too. From tomorrow we will be together."

Douglas informed Thompson that he would fetch them the following afternoon, but Thompson said that Johnny was going to borrow a car. Douglas did not stay long, on the pretext of having to go and see Garnett. He said goodbye to Mr and Mrs Thompson and Maggie went to the car with him. "Are you all right? Do you need anything?"

"I'm a bit nervous, that's all. The girls at work made a collection and bought me a present. Mr Schmidt was quite decent and gave me some money in an envelope and said I could have tomorrow off on full pay. He said he would like me to come back and work for him anytime I feel like it. It made me feel better that he is not cross. My uncle is here. He is sleeping."

Friday 17 June 1932

Mr and Mrs Kuys arrived early at the van Yssen's house. Kuys, van Yssen and Douglas went to the drawing room to discuss proceedings. Kuys had taken the trouble to write out on cards what he was going to say and explained that he would hold them up for Douglas to see while he spoke. "It will only take a few minutes. Does Douglas have the ring?"

"Yes. I have."

It had been arranged that Garnett would pick up Madame Jacquard, and they were next to arrive. Van Yssen went outside to welcome them. "How good of you to come Guillemette, Garnett. The women are in the dining room, Guillemette." Mrs van Yssen had put lots of flowers in the house so that their scent would lessen the sadness she felt towards Frances; instead the flowers reminded her of the funerals she had attended. From the time she woke up that morning she could think of nothing else but Frances. She saw her fair face, her sensitive troubled clear green eyes, the refined movements of her innocent hips, her pitiful sobs when she realised that Douglas' deafness was irreversible. Frances' spirit went with her the entire day. When she put a vase of flowers down in the drawing room, where Douglas would be married that afternoon, a cloud passed before the sun and darkened the room. She was close to tears and had to bite her lip to conceal her misery from the others. She and Betta and Guillemette had spent the morning making canapés. Douglas had wandered about, his hands in his pockets, picking a book from a bookshelf, reading a little outside on the veranda, strolling back into the kitchen with an irritating self-satisfied grin. All he could think about was Maggie's body next to him that night. The anticipation of having a woman in bed in his parents' house, with their full knowledge and consent, aroused him. Earlier when his mother had gone to put flowers in the spare room she had found him putting his new flannel pyjamas ready under his pillow and for the first time she had a feeling of dislike for her son. It was good to have Guillemette there.

The Thompsons arrived. Johnny parked the car in the driveway next to the house. He looked uncomfortable in a suit and fiddled with the collar of his shirt. Mrs Thompson had borrowed money from her brother and bought a new fashionable bright red dress that did not match her brown snakeskin shoes. She wore a small porkpie hat with a veil. Her brother was a small serious looking man with a pencil-thin moustache. Thompson dusted flakes of ash from his lapels and stamped his cigarette out on the gravel of the driveway as though it was a dangerous insect he was trying to kill. Maggie wore an elegantly tailored dark green woollen suit that Schmidt had given her as a wedding present and a large white hat that lighted up her face. Van Yssen stood on the veranda to welcome them.

"Good afternoon Mr van Yssen," Thompson said. "As I warned you, my brother-in-law has come to visit. Merrill, this is Mr van Yssen, father of the groom. Mr van Yssen, this is Merrill Taylor from Springs." The procession climbed the steps to the veranda and traipsed into the house. Introductions were made. Alice Kuys had taken a liberal dose of Phosferine to calm her nerves. She had often seen Maggie at the shop, and had been to take another look at Maggie after the news broke, but she needed to be adequately prepared for Maggie's parents and her brother, judging by the rumours. Now they were there. Denis was used to dealing with all sorts of people, not she. Van Yssen made the introductions. The Thompsons stood about uneasily. Taylor stood to one side, his hands behind his back. Douglas appeared in the doorway of the drawing room and went over to Maggie. He took her hand and kissed her. Mrs Jacquard arrived from the toilet smelling of French perfume. Garnett, smartly dressed in a dark-grey Saville Row suit, went to talk to Thompson and asked him how he was; he said hello to Mrs Thompson, and asked her how she was; he introduced himself to Taylor.

Denis Kuys cleared his authoritative throat. "I would like to suggest, if it pleases everybody, that we let the wedding ceremony begin?" Thompson looked at van Yssen who was nodding and he also nodded. Mrs van Yssen hurried to the kitchen to fetch Betta. Kuys waited until they were present. "Shall we begin? Douglas, Maggie, if you would please come forward. We are gathered here today to join this man and this woman in marriage. The ceremony is a brief and simple one. We will begin with Douglas." Kuys held up the card that he had prepared for Douglas.

Douglas took the card. "I do solemnly declare that I know not of any lawful impediment why I Henry Douglas van Yssen may not be joined in matrimony to Margaret Jane Thompson."

Kuys turned to Maggie and smiled. "Please say after me, 'I do solemnly declare,'

"I do solemnly declare,"
"That I know not,"
"That I know not,"
"Of any lawful impediment,"

"Of any lawful impediment,"
"Why I may not be joined in matrimony,"
"Why I may not be joined in matrimony,"
"To Henry Douglas van Yssen."
"To Henry Douglas van Yssen."
"Now we will say the Contracting Words." He handed Douglas a card.

Douglas cleared his throat. "I call upon these persons present to witness that I Henry Douglas van Yssen do take thee, Margaret Jane Thompson, to be my lawful wedded wife."

"Please say after me, Maggie."
"I call upon these persons present to witness,"
She repeated the words.
"That I Margaret Jane Thompson do take thee, Henry Douglas van Yssen to be my lawful wedded husband."

Kuys held a card to indicate that Douglas should produce the ring. He already had it in his hand, and slipped it onto Maggie's finger.

"You may now kiss the bride." Douglas took Maggie in his arms and kissed her lovingly. Kuys continued, "By the powers vested in me I now declare that Henry Douglas van Yssen and Maggie Jane Thompson here present have been lawfully married. There are some formalities. I have brought along the register and I would be glad if we could complete the formalities before we let the celebrations begin."

Mrs Thompson started sniffing and scratched in her handbag for a handkerchief.

Once the register had been signed and witnessed, Mrs van Yssen announced that tea and coffee would be served in the dining room. Madame Jacquard went over to Maggie. "You look so radiant, Maggie. And your husband looks so handsome. You must come and visit me some time. I hope Douglas will invite me to stay with you on the farm. It is so lovely there. There are beautiful scenes to paint."

"I am sure we would love to have you, you are so kind."

"I have brought you a little gift. I will leave it with Anneke."

Van Yssen had cornered Mrs Thompson's brother. "May I get you anything, Mr Taylor?" Garnett joined them.

"I'll have some tea, thank you."

"There is something stronger, if you would prefer?"

"It is good of you to offer but I don't drink."

"A little drink is sometimes good for you," Garnett suggested jokingly.

"I'm sure it is," Taylor said cheerfully.

"Will you be visiting for long," Garnett asked while van Yssen fetched the tea.

"For a few days only, I have to get back to my parish."

"Your 'parish'? What do you mean by that?" van Yssen asked.

"I am a Baptist minister, Mr van Yssen."

Mrs Thompson overheard the conversation. "Merrill has always had a liking for the Bible. He's as poor as a church mouse but that's all he ever wanted. His only fun is making kids."

Taylor's smile said, she's a bit rough at the edges but she has a good heart.

"How long have you been in the church?" van Yssen asked.

"I worked until I had enough money to put myself through my studies. I was a shipping clerk to start with. I have now been in the church for seventeen years."

Kuys was in conversation with Thompson. "Albert tells me that you are a builder, Mr Thompson?"

"That's right your honour."

"Please call me Mr Kuys. I gather you are from Durban."

"Lived there all my life. I was told there was work here so we upped and left. Now we are stranded here. I will just have to make the best of things."

Johnny stood to one side eating a flapjack. Maggie sat next to Mrs Kuys at the dining room table. Douglas had refined the way Maggie held her cup and drank her tea. Mrs Kuys studied her closely. It was strange to be so close to the subject of all that gossip. At first Maggie seemed unreal to her. The picture she had built up of Maggie, even having seen her so often in the shop, was different. She was attractive. She had good features. She was kind, and as Anneke had described, without airs. She wore no makeup – that would have detracted from her natural fresh beauty. Her tissues had become vitalised by her pregnancy. Her hands were almost translucent. "I believe you like it on Douglas' farm?"

"Yes I do. I like it very much."

"Will you not be lonely there?"

"I never feel alone, Mrs Kuys."

"Never?"

"No, I have too much to do. Besides as long as there are animals and birds about and I can see things growing, I can never feel lonely. There is too much life around me for that."

Douglas had seated himself at the top of the table, his arms folded across his chest. He surveyed the scene. Alice Kuys looked as if she was expecting Maggie to bite her. Alice Kuys was in the close proximity of a sinful woman and she could not credit that the girl was so nice. Wonder what she told that Beatrix of hers? Should have brought her along. Garnett was having a good chat to Madame Jacquard. It wouldn't do the way he looked at her tits. He would tease him about that. Maybe Beatrix masturbated. Should he tell Thompson that they had bought some milk stout? Stuff him, he'll misbehave. He felt a hand on his shoulder and looked up. It was Denis Kuys.

"When are you planning to go back to the farm?" He wrote on the back of one of his cards.

"Tomorrow, Mr Kuys."

'How are things going there?"

"Things are still tight. I wonder how long this depression will still last?"

"I spoke to some people at the bank the other day. They think it will still last for years."

"That will bankrupt a lot of people up there. My neighbours, the Ellises, have turned to riding transport to earn cash."

Mrs van Yssen turned on the lights. "Alice and I should get going, Anneke. We have a longstanding appointment to have dinner with the Pococks. I could not change it, I'm afraid. I still have one or two things to do at home."

Mr and Mrs Kuys took leave of everybody. Thompson got to his feet rapidly, to shake Kuys' hand. Douglas and his father accompanied them to their car. "I would like to thank you most sincerely, Uncle Denis for what you have done for us," Douglas said. "Thank you Aunt Alice." He kissed her on her cheek.

"Good luck Douglas," her mouth said. "She's a very sweet girl."

The Thompsons were determined to overstay their welcome. Van Yssen put more coal on the fire and riddled it. "I think I'll have a gasper now that the Magistrate has gone," Mrs Thompson announced.

"I'll have one too," Garnett said.

"It's nice and warm in here," Johnny remarked.

Garnett walked over to him. "Douglas tells me that you work for my uncle."

"Yes I do, Doctor, he's strict but he is a good man, always ready to let me have a car. I'm a mechanic there."

Mrs Jacquard went to the bathroom to take her hat off. She tidied her hair and returned to the drawing room where she took Mrs Kuys' place next to Maggie. "It has been such a lovely evening Maggie."

"Thank you Mrs Jacquard."

"You have a most exciting time ahead of you. I want to send you some of my special garlic, and I will teach you how to plant it. My father taught me how to do that. Anneke told me how impressed Albert was with your vegetable garden."

"I will go back there tomorrow and see how my seedlings are doing. I can hardly wait. Douglas says they are doing fine."

"When I come to visit, I will bring the garlic. I love children."

"Where is your husband?" Mrs Thompson asked Mrs Jacquard.

"How should I say, he is somewhere. He enlisted in the French Forces and he moves from place to place, mostly North Africa."

"I was near Ypres during the War. Do you know the place?" Thompson burped. "I'll have one more for the road, and then we must go."

"My husband tells me that you are a minister of religion, Mr Taylor?"

"Yes I am, I'm in the Baptist Church, in Springs."

"If we had known you could have conducted the wedding ceremony, but it all happened so suddenly," Mrs van Yssen responded.

"These things happen Mrs van Yssen."

"Something more to eat?" She asked.

He patted his stomach. "I've done really well, thank you."

The van Yssens and Douglas and Maggie saw the Thompsons to their car. Johnny shook van Yssen's hand vigorously and respectfully and cast another glance at the house.

"Goodnight, Mr van Yssen. Thanks for everything," Thompson said.

"Please call me Albert. I think we should be on first name terms."

"It was so good to meet you Mr Taylor," Mrs Van Yssen said. "May God speed."

Maggie kissed her mother and father. Her father gave her a playful little slap on her bottom. He winked at her. "Now don't go and do anything tonight your old man wouldn't do!" Thompson helped his wife into the car, got in next to Johnny who was at the wheel, and turned the window down. The old van Yssens and the young van Yssens stood as Thompson's arm came out of the window to say goodbye.

"I'll go and take my hat off now," Maggie said.

"And I'll go and see to the soup," Mrs van Yssen responded.

"I think we need more coal," Douglas said, "I'll go and get some."

Garnett and Madame Jacquard stayed for soup. It was clear that Maggie was exhausted. She had expended much nervous energy in anticipation of her parents' behaviour. Now that they had gone and she was married, the resilience with which she had fought her fears was gone and replaced by fatigue.

"I think we should all go to bed early tonight," Mrs van Yssen suggested. "I will make you a hot water bottle Maggie, and prepare some warm milk. I think you should say goodnight to our guests and prepare for bed."

Maggie got up from the table. "Thank you so much for honouring me with your presence."

Madame Jacquard patted her hand. "Sweet dreams."

"I am glad I was able to come tonight, Maggie," Garnett said, and shook her hand.

Douglas and his father escorted Madame Jacquard and Garnett to Garnett's car. "Thanks a lot Garnie, thank you Madame Jacquard," Douglas said. "Do come and visit, and bring along that girl of yours Garnett."

Douglas helped his mother to clear the dining room table and thanked his father for making the arrangements. When he eventually got to the spare room, Maggie was fast asleep. She lay on her right hand side, her hand with her wedding ring against her face.

◆

Chapter Forty-one

THE WINTER OF 1932 was severe. At times there was snow on the mountains. Douglas put the spare room bed into his room so that Maggie could be more comfortable next to him as her tummy grew. They made fires at night. He read to Maggie in the evenings. Mrs van Yssen brought her maternity clothes. Maggie worked in her garden. She sowed new seeds when the moon was right and harvested her vegetables. She made Douglas' favourite lamb stews with fresh ingredients. When there was enough water in the river, Douglas irrigated the fields where wheat was to be sown, and ploughed with a pair of horses that Ellis lent him.

The van Yssens visited regularly, and so did Garnett. Towards the end of August Madame Jacquard came to stay for a few days and showed Maggie how to plant garlic. She also showed her how to make onion soup. Maggie watched Madame Jacquard paint.

One Saturday afternoon, towards the end of September, Garnett invited Miss Weber to accompany him on a visit to the farm. Garnett had purchased supplies as a gift for Douglas: dried beans, coffee beans, soap, rice, boot polish, tins of sardines, tea and a few treats such as butterscotch and chocolate.

"I assure you, you will enjoy his company very much, Irene," Garnett reassured Miss Weber as they drove towards the farm. "He's poor, but rich in intellect. He obtained his Masters Degree *Cum Laude*. Best to use the writing pad to communicate with him. He's able to lip read well but I have found that he has to get used to an individual's lip movements."

"And his wife, what is she like?"

"She's practical, has a lot of common sense, good intuition. Not much education."

"How does he cope with that?"

"They are an interesting combination, an utterly unlikely combination."

"How do they communicate?"

"He knows exactly what she is saying, and of course, she can hear him."

"What I mean how is she able to satisfy him intellectually?"

"Oh that is out of the question."

"Does he not get bored with her then?"

"Strangely enough not, or so it would seem. He has always lived in a bit of an inner world, always been introverted at times. His thoughts are his real companions. He can be quite jolly though, to be fair. He has an unusual sense of humour. Ask him about his favourite Scottish poet. He'll love that. She makes his life constant. She is attractive, as you will see. Her lack of intellectual demands gives him a certain freedom. In fact she makes no demands, as he has said to me, because of her propensity to give."

"I like that, what you've just said. I have never thought of it like that."

"You will see that there is a remarkable connection between them. Together they enjoy the simplest things. She loves him. She loves the sight of him. He belongs to her. I have seen her face light up as she watches him when he walks up the slope to the house."

Miss Weber stubbornly insisted on opening the farm gate for Garnett. They drove up to the house. Douglas was in his chair on the veranda, book in hand. He had decided the week before that his Latin had become rusty and had started re-reading Vergil's *Aeneid*. He rose when their movements caught his eye and put a bookmark into the book. He had not met Irene Weber before.

"Hello Garnie! How decent of you to come."

"Douglas this is Irene Weber."

"How do you do Miss Weber." They shook hands. He was handsome and his eyes had a boyish smile. She had expected a serious man with sad eyes. He was much taller and his shoulders broader than she had anticipated. He had a confident loose athletic bearing. His forehead was pale from wearing a hat. Although his hands had become rough their movements were refined. She glanced at the book he was reading. Vergil – *Aeneid* – Book Six.

"Do come inside, I will go and fetch Maggie. She's having a little rest."

Garnett held his hand up to get Douglas' attention. "I've brought a few things for you."

Douglas frowned. When Garnett took a cardboard box from the car Douglas realised what Garnett had said. "Really Garnie, you shouldn't have. We're doing fine."

Garnett carried the box into the kitchen and put it on the kitchen table. Miss Weber waited in the living room. There was a strong odour of wood smoke. A copy of *The Pickwick Papers* lay on the mantelpiece. Volumes of *The Decline and Fall* reclined to one side in a large busy bookshelf. The Judge's gift, ten volumes of George Grote's *A History of Greece*, bound in leather, stood lower down. The room was plain except for two impressionist style landscapes. She walked over to the paintings to see who the artist was. She heard the rattling of cups and Douglas' loud voice approaching and turned lest she appeared too inquisitive.

"I thought we should have our tea in here," Douglas said. "Maggie will be with us in a few moments. Do sit down, Miss Weber."

"Please call me Irene."

Garnett took the writing pad. 'She says please call her by her first name."

Maggie appeared in the doorway. She was visibly pregnant now. She had sleep creases in her temple and her cheek. "Good afternoon," she yawned. "I'm Maggie. Hello Garnett. How are you?"

"I'm very well, thank you. Let me introduce you to Irene Weber."

"How do you do, Maggie."

"How do you do." Maggie looked her up and down disarmingly while she stifled a little yawn. "We need some biscuits, let me fetch them."

"I did not know your wife was going to have a baby?"

"He could not see what you said, Irene. The baby is due in December. The plan is for me to deliver it."

"Oh, that is wonderful! You said you and Douglas have known one another for a long time?"

"Virtually all our lives. We grew up together."

Irene took the writing pad. "I noticed that you are reading *The Aeneid*."

Douglas laughed. "I really enjoyed Latin at school and university, and I recently thought that it had become rusty, so I have decided to revive it. Did you do Latin?"

Irene nodded. "At school and first year at university."

"Did you enjoy it? Where were you at university?"

"At Stellenbosch. I enjoyed Latin moderately, but it was not one of my favourites. I preferred German. My father is German. My real love is literature; German, Dutch as well as Afrikaans and English for that matter."

"Are you familiar with *The Aeneid*?"

"I would not say familiar but I know the story. I always felt sorry for poor Dido. That Aeneas could have abandoned her was wretched."

"I suspect you know more than you are prepared to let on."

"I love the classics."

"Vergil had an interesting life. Do you know the *Georgics*?"

Irene shook her head, "I only know of it."

"Then you will know that it was the second of his great works. In it he describes Roman farming methods, crop production methods, cultivation of vineyards and olive trees, animal breeding and beekeeping. The remarkable thing about the poem is that it is, in reality, a textbook for farmers. I mean, can you credit that! And besides being a textbook it contains some of the finest Latin poetry ever written. The mind boggles. Can you imagine one of our modern day agricultural textbooks in poetic form?" Douglas guffawed loudly. "I had a romantic idea once, when I decided to come here, that I would read and write and farm like the old Romans. But then the depression came along and I had not bargained on that; now it is just a matter of survival."

"Garnett told me your first interest is history?"

"Yes."

"Do you prefer any specific period?"

"More recent periods of European history do interest me. My real love is Roman history. What people they were: warriors, farmers, jurists, orators, statesmen, conquerors, poets, engineers, one can go on. I have at times been so carried away by my thoughts of their history that I have dreamt that I heard the clashing of weapons and the excited breathing and whinnying of horses in battle. For someone who is deaf it is remarkable to hear again, even if it is only in a dream."

Garnett had not seen Douglas so animated in a while. His eyes were sparkling. Maggie watched him admiringly. She was glad that the woman had excited him so. Garnett asked Irene to pass him the writing pad. 'I told Irene that you have a favourite Scottish poet. Tell her about him."

Douglas snorted with laughter. "Maggie also enjoys him." He got up and dug out a small faded red volume from the bookshelf.

"It must be Burns," Irene encouraged.

Douglas grinned from ear to ear. "A trifle more obscure than that. Also a Robert, but this time it is Robert Henryson." A piece of paper served as a bookmark. "This is Maggie's and my favourite bit:

> Upon ane tyme (as Esope culd Report)
> Ane lytill Mous came till ane Revir side;
> Scho micht not waid, hir schankis were sa schort,
> Scho culd not swym, scho had no hors to ryde:
> Of verray force behovit hir to byde,
> And to and fra beside the Revir deip
> Scho ran, cryand with mony pietuous peip.

"Don't you think it is fantastic! Maggie cries when I read it – just look at her." Maggie wiped her tears away and giggled embarrassedly. "I can't help it, I feel so sorry for that little mouse."

"Don't you think it is fantastic, Irene?" Douglas asked.

"It is unusual."

Douglas was enjoying himself. "It is wonderful stuff. The way he selects his detail. There is not too much, not too little, just enough to create gentle ironical humour. He has an extraordinary sense of the ridiculous that is so delicate and so exact that the faintest emphasis is enough to indicate it. Listen to this; it is not as subtle, just downright funny. A fox kills a lamb at Lent, dips it in a stream and fishes it out, crying: *'Ga doun schir Kid, cum up schir salmond agane.'*"

"Hell that's bloody funny, don't you think!" He laughed and laughed.

Garnett shook as he laughed at Douglas' amusement. Douglas wiped his eyes with the back of his hand. His amusement was infectious. Irene laughed and so did Maggie.

"What a happy time we're having, I've never seen him like this. I'm glad you came to visit Miss Weber." Maggie exclaimed.

"Garnett tells me that you are expecting your baby in December?"

"Yes it's not too long from now. I can't wait. Then there will be three of us here. It is a good thing to have a baby in the summer. Douglas' mother said she would get me a cot. Our spare room is empty. The baby will go in there when it is old enough. Although I can't imagine how I will be able to separate myself from my baby. Would you like to go for a walk?"

"That would be very nice thank you."

Maggie got up and tapped Douglas on the shoulder. "Miss Weber and I are going for a walk." He nodded his approval.

"Please call me Irene."

"Thank you, I shall." Maggie fetched her straw hat, and the two women went into the garden.

"Irene's a lovely girl, Garnie," Douglas said when the coast was clear.

"She's pretty smart. It frightens me. As you well know I'm neither an intellectual nor an academic. The books always presented a real challenge, doing matric twice and all that. Irene matriculated when she was barely fourteen. She graduated when she was eighteen. I was still on the school benches at that age."

"Where is she from?"

"Robertson-McGregor area. Her father is a Dutch Reformed clergyman."

"I thought she said he is a German?'

"He is."

"What does she teach?"

"Currently history and German."

"She's good looking. Good legs. You've always liked that, haven't you?"

Garnett grinned.

"I must thank you again for the supplies, but you should really not do that. We are managing quite well. We don't want for anything."

"You said the wheat is looking good."

"Yes, there was enough water this year, fortunately. Water is always a problem. I borrowed two horses from Ellis to plough the land."

"And the other things?"

"You mean here on the farm?"

"Yes."

"Lucerne looks good, but always needs more water. The sheep are fine. I will put in potatoes and onions. I am thinking of putting in some citrus, but they need lots of water, so I'll have to consider it very carefully."

"You often mention the Ellises. I don't know them. What are they like?"

"They're as poor a church mice. Maybe even poorer, like Henryson's little mouse. They can hardly ever afford to employ labourers. The kids are kept out of school when it is time to plough. When they get home from school they have to work in the fields. They do everything by hand. There's no machinery. They till their soil with spades. The kids hoe the potato and onion lands. It's a hard life. You should see how they live. It's penury."

"How is Maggie feeling?"

"She says she has never felt better in her life."

"That's good. I will come and see her in the next few weeks."

"I would be glad."

Garnett wanted to get back to Oudtshoorn before dark. He still had hospital rounds to do, so he and Irene left just before half past four. "What an interesting man," Irene remarked when they were out of earshot.

"He's remarkable. He's become a bit odd since he grew deaf, as I intimated on the way here. Mind you though, he's always been a trifle eccentric."

"He's a very handsome man."

"Yes."

"He has an heroic face."

"I never thought of him in that way, but yes, he's good looking. What did you and Maggie talk about?"

"Nothing much. She's preoccupied with her pregnancy. I asked her how she enjoyed living on the farm. She said they loved it, wouldn't exchange it for anything. She touched the tall grass affectionately with her hand as we strolled along and said how excited she was because everything around her is alive. Quite charming. Why did Douglas become deaf?"

"We think it is an inherited condition, known as otosclerosis. The little bones in the middle ear become calcified and fused together. The mechanism that is meant to transmit sound to the audio nerve becomes jammed."

"What was his fiancée like?"

"A bit like you."

"A bit like me! What does that mean?"

"Frances is a beautiful intellectual."

"Where does she live?"

"In Graaff Reinet, where she teaches."

"What does she teach?"

"Latin and English. She graduated with distinctions in those subjects."

"Why did they not get married?"

"It is a long sad story. When it was clear to Douglas that his deafness was irreversible he felt that he did not want to subject her to his circumstances. It was a terrible blow to her. He said he did not want to run the risk of their children inheriting his deafness."

"But he was prepared to run that risk with Maggie?"

"They had to get married."

Miss Weber blushed. "Was there not something else he could have done besides farming?"

"He was offered a newspaper job in Cape Town. It was arranged by Frances' father and because of that he refused it."

"How did the engagement end?"

"I think he wrote to her."

"The poor woman. And Douglas' behaviour in all this?"

"He showed no emotion. He no longer allowed himself that. He was very much in love with Frances. I think he set about extinguishing his feelings for her when he realised what was happening to him. Let's be fair, it must have been a terrible shock to him, a terrible thing to come to terms with. He has changed a lot. I mean this whole affair with Maggie. From what I can gather, he came to town one weekend to spend time with his parents and ended up going to the bioscope with her. The next thing she arrived on the farm with her brother and she stayed there for the weekend while her brother went on to Mossel Bay. She then spent the Easter weekend with Douglas, and Bob's your uncle, she was expecting. The van Yssens are prominent people, highly respected. It was a terrible scandal. Socially Maggie's family and the van Yssens are utterly incompatible. And throughout it all Douglas was as cool as a cucumber. He seemed quite pleased with what he had accomplished and behaved as though nothing unusual had happened. He told me he couldn't see what all the fuss was about."

"When did they get married?"

"In June. I was there. It was a private ceremony at the van Yssens' home. Just a civil marriage."

"I feel sorry for him. I like Maggie. I also feel sorry for his fiancée."

"She is the daughter of a judge in Cape Town. From all accounts her father will never forgive Douglas for what has happened. I never liked Judge Rose. He's a hard man. Arrogant too. I don't think he liked me very much. I'm sure Frances must know by now that Douglas is married."

"You can see he is a true academic."

"What do you mean when you say a true academic?"

"Such people have special qualities. An intuitive academic like Douglas sees more in what he reads than most other people. When he reads the *Aeneid* he understands Vergil's thought processes. That way he builds up a latticework of essential detail that he is able to use whenever he wants to. It is a waste for him to sit on that farm."

"He appears to be much happier now that he has a companion. I have not seen him as animated as he was today, for a long time."

"He will surely tire of her."

"I have at times thought so. He has defined what he wants from her. Their intuitive relationship is good, and dare I say it, they probably have a good physical relationship. That is very important in a marriage."

Irene did not reply.

"I hope I have not offended you?"

"No." She sat further away from him. "Have you seen his fiancée since the engagement ended?"

"No, I haven't. Her father was in town recently with the Circuit Court, but I did not see him."

The van Yssens visited regularly. Van Yssen's admiration for Maggie's enterprise grew and a bond formed between them. He came to see her marriage to Douglas as a blessing. Mrs van Yssen looked forward to having a grandchild.

Saturday 10 December 1932

Douglas and Maggie were having lunch in their dining room when Maggie had her first contraction. She thought at first that it was a stomach cramp. "What is the matter?" Douglas asked.

"Just my stomach, I think. It's nothing."

They continued their meal. When they carried their plates to the kitchen about twenty minutes later, Maggie nearly dropped her plate as she had another contraction. She put her plate down on the kitchen table and sat down. Douglas knelt down next to her. "Are you all right?"

"Yes. I think it's the baby."

"I must go to the shop. I'll call Willemse." He ran down the hill to Willemse's cottage. There was no one there. He ran back to the house. Maggie was where he had left her. "He's not there," he gasped. "I'll go to the shop." He ran along the farm road and crossed the main road. The shop was closed. He peered in through the window in the hope of finding that van der Byl was still there. The inside was deserted. He ran to van der Byl's house. There was no one there except for a small coloured boy who was chopping firewood. "Where is Mr van der Byl?" he shouted. The boy pointed in the direction of Mossel Bay and imitated handling a steering wheel.

"I must use the telephone, immediately!"

The boy shrugged his shoulders.

"Where are the keys?"

The boy patted his pocket to say that van der Byl had them with him.

Douglas ran to the back of the shop. He picked up a stone and smashed the glass of one of the sash windows. He contemplated asking the boy to telephone but when he turned around the boy was running away so that he would not be implicated in breaking and entering. He pushed the lower half of the window up and climbed inside. He turned the handle of the phone vigorously to ring the exchange and lifted the receiver. "*Dit is Douglas van Yssen van Moerasrivier, dit is Douglas van Yssen van Moerasrivier,*" he shouted several times. "I am deaf, I am deaf, and cannot hear you. Please, please telephone doctor Nel at two six seven, two six seven and tell him the baby is coming. My wife's baby is coming. He must come immediately."

Douglas had no way of knowing whether the woman at the exchange had heard him and kept on repeating his message. When the call was put through to Garnett's house, Mrs Nel answered the telephone and quickly handed the receiver to Garnett. All he could hear were Douglas' wild shouts, "The child is coming, the child is coming!"

When Garnett arrived on the farm Maggie's contractions were less than a minute apart. Douglas frantically wrung his hands. 'Boil some water,' Garnett scribbled on a bit of paper, and put on his white coat. Maggie was in their bedroom. She was lying on her back on the bed, her knees slightly raised. Garnett lifted her dress. Her water had broken. She still had her pants on. "We'll leave your dress on Maggie. We'll have to take your pants off." She lifted her hips and he helped her. Another contraction came while Garnett was putting on his latex gloves. He lifted her knees and parted her legs. She looked anxiously at him. She was dilated to four fingers. He patted her knee. "It looks very good indeed Maggie. It won't be difficult." She had another contraction. She was more dilated.

Garnett could see the top of the baby's head. It was a welcome sign that it was in a good position. She groaned and Garnett looked at his watch. Thirty seconds since the last one. He pushed a red rubber sheet in under Maggie, and pulled its edges towards the sides of the bed to make it taut.

Douglas rushed into the room. "What must I do with the boiling water?" Garnett indicated that he should leave it in the kitchen.

Maggie groaned again. Sweat poured from her face. She looked at Douglas with wide pleading eyes. He took her hand.

Garnett indicated to Douglas to leave the room. "I want you to give a big push when the next contraction comes, Maggie, just as we discussed, there, now push, push. That's excellent, more, keep it up, here it comes." The baby, covered in buttery mucus, slithered out of Maggie. Garnett grabbed it by its feet and dangled it upside down to get the mucus out of its breathing passages. He slapped the baby on its bottom and it let out an offended scream that filled its lungs with air. Maggie cried with happiness. "It's a bonny girl, Maggie, a beautiful girl. I will pass her to you in a few moments but I first have to see to the chord." Garnett tied the umbilical chord off and snipped it. He wrapped the baby in a little blanket that Maggie had put ready and passed her to her mother.

"She's so beautiful," Maggie murmured, "So beautiful."

"It's a good idea to put her on the breast as soon as possible."

"Will she know what to do?"

"I am sure she will."

When the baby felt Maggie's nipple next to her mouth, her mouth opened and she tried to find it. Maggie was surprised how strongly the baby sucked. Her breasts felt as though they had pins and needles as colostrum was released. She felt her womb contract to expel the afterbirth.

There was a slop pail next to the bed and Garnett put the afterbirth and what remained of the umbilical chord into it. He fetched the boiled water and washed Maggie. He wiped the rubber sheet and replaced it with a towel. He got more water and washed Maggie's face. Then he went to find Douglas. He was standing on the veranda. Garnett extended his hand towards Douglas with a wide smile. 'It's a girl!' He took him by the arm and led him to Maggie.

When she saw Douglas she burst into joyous tears. He kissed her. He looked happily at the baby, and as he kissed it on its head, smelt the organic amniotic fluid.

"I think we should all have some tea," Garnett suggested. In the kitchen he wrote on Douglas' notepad: "Maggie should have complete rest for ten days. She will need help. I have made arrangements for a nurse to come and assist her. She will be here later this afternoon. I will stay here until she comes."

"Where will she sleep?"

"On the spare bed next to Maggie's. You can sleep on the couch in the living room."

"Thanks Garnie but we will manage. Everybody around here does. Besides I cannot afford it."

"I have made arrangements to pay her. She's very experienced. She will run the house for a week or two. Regard it as a gift from me. You go and make the tea, I'll go and see to Maggie. It is a lovely healthy baby."

"It is a miracle. I am sure many before me have thought that."

That night while the nurse and Maggie and the baby slept Douglas lay on the couch in the living room. He read from *The Aeneid* and eventually fell asleep. In the early hours of the morning he dreamt that he had come to the Mourning Plains, the abode of unhappy lovers. Forlorn hills stood in the distance as he flew towards them with massive feathery wings. He must not go too close to the sun because the wax could melt. Dido stood alone in the distance, a wreath in her hair. She was glasslike and transparent. She turned around to follow the shadow that he cast as he circled the desolate place, and when she did so he saw it was Frances. He descended and shed his wings. She looked tearfully at him while he tried desperately to justify his desertion of her. He cast his eyes down to the ground in shame and when he had enough courage to look up she had removed herself from his presence.

◆

Chapter Forty-two

The years 1932-1938

MAGGIE DECIDED to name their child Jane. On the last Sunday in January 1933 Jane was christened in a simple small whitewashed church with a red tin roof that stood in a pale green field not far from Kleinmoerasrivier. The van Yssens attended the service, as did Maggie's parents and Madame Jacquard. Garnett was there, accompanied by Irene Weber. Madame Jacquard arranged the flowers in the church.

For those who had survived the cruel Depression of the early thirties, a period of economic prosperity was at hand. In 1932 the Minister of Finance of the Union, N C Havenga, attended the Imperial Conference in Ottawa. There he negotiated a preferential trade agreement for South African products within the British Commonwealth. Although prices of agricultural products continued to decline for a period after that, the trade agreement ultimately led to expanded markets for South African products, and by 1934 the prices of primary agricultural products began to rise, much to the benefit of farmers. By 1934 the growth in poverty that had increased so dramatically during the depression began to decline. The government subsidised interest on agricultural loans and saved many farmers from bankruptcy.

Jane was a thriving child. Her intelligence was above average. Douglas read to her a great deal, from an early age. When she was five van Yssen began showing her how to do elementary arithmetic, whenever he visited. Madame Jacquard taught her how to draw and to paint. Maggie taught her how to garden and keep chickens. She learnt to ride a pony and played with mud and water in the furrow behind the house while she sang to herself in her soft white cotton hat held down by an elastic band under her chin. She climbed trees and learnt to shoot. At night she fell asleep easily and dreamt of the happy things she had done that day.

In 1934 Garnett married Irene Weber in the small town of Maclear. Douglas and Maggie were unable to attend the wedding for financial reasons. After their wedding Garnett and Irene travelled to Port Elizabeth and boarded the Dresden of the Nord Deutcher Lloyd Shipping Line, bound for Europe, where they spent an extended honeymoon of six months. While they were in Bavaria they visited Oberammergau, and by chance met a man called Alois Lang in a tavern. Lang it turned out had played the part of Jesus in the 1934 Passion Play. Garnett was so moved by the experience that he decided to name their first born after Lang. In

1936 Garnett's and Irene's first child, a girl, was born. They named her Aloise. Towards the end of 1938, Irene became pregnant with their second child, Paul

During the years 1934 to 1938 there was considerable economic progress in the Union. Roads were built, railways expanded, harbours modernised, air services were improved. In 1937 legislation was introduced to regulate agricultural marketing which resulted in much improved stability in the agricultural industry. By 1938 there was little unemployment; commerce and industry flourished.

Van Yssen turned sixty-three in 1938. As economic conditions improved, his land surveying practice again prospered, but his health was failing. The nagging disappointment at what had become of Douglas, and the social embarrassments he had suffered at the time of Douglas' marriage, had taken their toll. Although he grew increasingly fond of Maggie, he could not detach himself from thoughts of what could have been. He grieved for the loss of Frances. He often thought of Douglas' last graduation, of the luncheon afterwards with the Roses, meeting the Earl of Athlone and President Reitz, and the grand time they had when Douglas and Frances became engaged.

Towards the end of 1938 van Yssen had a mild heart attack. Dr Diemont diagnosed cardiac insufficiency and prescribed a prolonged period of rest. Diemont explained to van Yssen that each case of the disease had to be judged on its merits and prescribed digitalis and a change in diet to include more meat, eggs and cheese, farinaceous puddings and six to eight ounces of wine in the evening. Mrs van Yssen, as she had done through all their tribulations, continued to do her best to support her husband.

On many occasions Madame Jacquard accompanied the van Yssens on visits to Douglas' farm. Although there was no news of her husband, her positive attitude to life never wavered and Mrs van Yssen took that to mean that Madame Jacquard knew that she and her husband would one day be united.

During the late thirties the influence of Afrikaner cultural leaders, supported by an influential press, began to inspire the political and nationalistic consciousness of large numbers of Afrikaners. The growth of nationalism in Europe, especially in Germany, only served to give impetus to Afrikaner nationalism. Furthermore, the economic rebirth in the Union provided enormous energy that fuelled a cultural renaissance. Even though signs of division within Afrikaner ranks began to appear, inspired by issues such as the National Flag and the National Anthem, unity within the ruling United Party proved so remarkably durable that only profound emotional eruption within the psyche of Afrikanerdom, or unpredictable external factors, could provide a spark to destroy that unity. Yet the circumstances that had produced unity gradually became eroded, leaving the political landscape tinder dry and it was only a matter of time before a spark would be provided to set alight the landscape.

The Centenary Celebrations of 1938 provided that spark. At the centre of the celebrations was the commemoration of the Great Trek. On the sixteenth of December 1938, in remembrance of the Battle of Blood River, the corner stone of the Voortrekker Monument was laid just outside Pretoria. The old rebel leader, and member of the Cabinet, General J C G Kemp announced there that the military headquarters 'Roberts Heights' would in future be known as Voortrekkerhoogte. This was not the only sign of danger to the United Party. In 1938 the Prime Minister, General Hertzog, decided that *Die Stem van Suid Afrika* would be sung at all official occasions and that *God Save the King* would be regarded as a prayer for the King of South Africa, and would be played only on those occasions when the Governor General represented the British Monarch. Only Smuts' stubborn unwillingness to confront the inevitable, allowed tenuous unity to be maintained.

The growing political division in the Union seeped into every aspect of social life. Deep-seated acrimonious sentiments, that had become subdued after the Boer War and the First World War by the comfort of political unity, were revived and given fresh character by the new political division; these new sentiments informed old differences and imbued personal animosities. There can be little doubt that the political climate helped to inflame emotions in a dispute over water from the Saffraan River between Douglas' neighbours the Ellises and their immediate neighbour, Gert Laubscher. Rumours that the Ellises had given refuge to Boer rebels during the Boer War, and Laubscher's pro-British stance made the two parties more antagonistic.

◆

Chapter Forty-three

Friday 8 April 1938

IT WAS TIME to tidy the barn. As the morning dragged on, Douglas felt more and more hungry. He started peering from the large double doors to see whether Maggie had hung the white cloth over the balustrade of the veranda to signal that lunch was ready. When it was eventually there, moving lazily in a midday breeze, Douglas wiped his hands on a piece of towelling and made his way to the farmhouse. The sky was pale hazy blue above the house. The trees had autumn hues. A donkey cart with two people approached the side of the house. An ear of one of the two donkeys stood erect while its other ear irritably flicked at pesky flies. Six-year-old Jane ran towards him, her thick flaxen hair bobbing, dressed in a pale blue smocked dress that Douglas' mother had given her, her arms outstretched towards her father while her mother doted from the veranda. He caught her as she leapt into his arms and clung to him like a monkey. He moved closer to see who was on the cart. It was old Cornelius Ellis and his son Izak.

Izak tied the reins to the pear tree behind the kitchen. Old Cornelius climbed stiffly from the cart. He straightened himself, took off his hat and smacked it against his thigh to remove dust, and silently held out his hand to Douglas under enquiring steady pale blue eyes. He motioned that they should go inside. Izak followed dutifully.

"Good afternoon Missus van Yssen," Cornelius said. "I know it is a bad time to come and visit, but we are on our way to town and we need to consult with Mister van Yssen."

Maggie looked at the dust on Cornelius' shoes. "It is such a lovely day, let's sit outside. Would you like some coffee, or tea?"

"Coffee, thank you Missus van Yssen," Cornelius replied. Izak nodded self-consciously, hat in hand.

Douglas sat down with Jane on his lap. She had her arms around his neck and tried to kiss him on his mouth, as she had seen her mother do. Douglas kept his head turned to one side to encourage her to kiss him on his cheek. Maggie brought the writing pad and pencil to the veranda and carried a reluctant Jane off to the kitchen.

Cornelius took the pencil and paper and moved his chair closer to the table so that he could write. He licked the end of the pencil and wrote slowly and deliberately in trembling copperplate. "We have come to see you about the water. We are still having problems with Laubscher. The water from Saffraan River. I have been to see him to ask him if we cannot reach an agreement. This thing has been going on too long. When we came here in 1911 I asked Olivier for water. Laubscher says again we may not touch the water. As it belonged to

Olivier and now belongs to him. You know what it is all about. We have spoken before. You are a learned man. We need help from you. He says our predecessors in title abandoned their water rights in the notarial document of 1906. Can you look at the document, please, and tell us if that is the truth."

"I will gladly peruse it, if you could let me have it."

Cornelius nodded. "I will send it with one of my sons. They must know what is going on. I will not be on this earth for ever."

Maggie returned with a tray and poured coffee.

"Have you spoken to an attorney yet?" Douglas asked.

"They are reluctant to help, Laubscher is a wealthy man, they are not keen to go up against him. Whatever he says around here, goes."

"That makes me all the more keen to help. Let me have the document."

The men drank their coffee in silence. Cornelius wiped his large grey moustache with his sleeve and gathered his hat. He bent over the table, licked the end of the pencil again, and wrote, "The document will be here tomorrow."

"That was a quick visit Oom Cornelius?" Maggie said.

"Yes my child, but I am glad we came to see your husband. He is a clever man and says he will help. He can tell you the whole story, we have spoken about it before." Izak had not said a word. He found Maggie so attractive and so clean that he dared not look at her body for fear that it would give his thoughts away. He shook her hand, his head averted lest he have sinful thoughts so close to Sunday.

Cornelius went back to the table. "There was some division of water by arbitration somewhere between 1920 and 1922."

"Let me have the document, Oom Cornelius. I will do my best."

Douglas went to the cart with Cornelius and Izak. He patted Izak's shoulder farewell and assisted Cornelius onto the cart.

Maggie carried the lunch dishes to the dining room. Jane stubbornly tried to get into her baby chair. "You're a big girl now, Jane, you won't fit into that. Perhaps if you have a brother or a sister, they'll be able to get into it. It is meant for small babies."

"I am a baby."

"Yes you are my baby, but you are a big girl now. One of these days you will go to school."

"I don't have to go to school, Daddy will teach me everything there is to know. Why is he deaf?"

"We don't know."

Douglas entered the dining room. Maggie kissed him. "What was that all about?"

"It is the perennial old thing about water rights. In the ten years that I have been here, and as I have mentioned, before that, people around here have been fighting about water; they have been doing that forever. The Romans fought about water. It causes lots of ill feeling. Laubscher is a difficult man. He maintains that his predecessor, Olivier, made Old Cornelius understand quite clearly that he was not entitled to water from the Saffraan River, even though Ellis' farm is above Laubscher's farm. I have noticed that Old Cornelius is scared of Laubscher because of Laubscher's wealth and power in the district. Cornelius told me some time ago that a fellow called Mayer, who worked for Olivier, subsequently worked for Laubscher for a while, after the Laubschers acquired the farm, and that Mayer claims that he was present when Olivier told Cornelius to keep his hands off his water."

"When was that?"

"Oh, ages ago, 1910, 1911 or thereabouts. Anyway, that's what it's all about. Laubscher, from what I gathered this morning, is again intimidating Cornelius by referring to a legal agreement that was drawn up between groups of previous owners in terms of which the water is divided among the riparian owners."

"What is riparian?"

"It comes from the Latin *ripa, ripae*, meaning a river bank. So when we say riparian owners we mean the owners of land along a riverbank. Riparian law can be quite intricate. The impression I have is that the Ellises don't have a desire to fight with Laubscher, and that they would rather try and come to a peaceful agreement, but they do feel quite strongly, and probably justifiably, that they have a right to take water from the Saffraan River. The mutton is jolly good, my dear. I like the way you have done the sweet potatoes. Your mint sauce is exceptionally tasty."

"Don't they get their water from the Moeras River?"

"Yes that is their main source of water. The way they share it with the other upper owners is well regulated. Cornelius told me some time ago that there was some agreement about Moeras River water in 1927. However, they also have some land on the other side beyond the ridge, towards the west, they call it Elandskloof. They started clearing land there more than twenty years ago. Elandskloof borders on the Saffraan River, and they feel that they are entitled to some of that water. Laubscher bluntly refuses. He has threatened Cornelius with legal action if he touches the water. That is a daunting prospect for a man who has no money, and Laubscher knows it."

"Do you think they are entitled to the water?"

"My instinct says yes. They are decent people. And although they are simple folk they are not stupid. Old Cornelius is more shrewd than you may think; just look at his handwriting." Douglas held the notepad so Maggie could see. "If a man like that had had proper education, who knows what might have become of him. He discussed the matter with me before. I feel they have a good argument. I would like to see what the document says. They will let me have it tomorrow. It will be interesting to read it."

Maggie cut up Jane's mutton. "Would you like me to help you eat, darling?"

"No thank you, I'm a big girl now."

Jane reminded Douglas of his mother. He smiled at her. "When my parents come to visit tomorrow, I will ask my father what he thinks about the water. He knows the area reasonably well."

Saturday 9 April 1938

Izak Ellis arrived on horseback at Douglas' farm at about eight o'clock in the morning. He tied the horse to the pear tree, took off his hat and knocked on the open front door. Maggie appeared.

He nervously produced a brown paper parcel from his jacket pocket. "Good morning Mrs van Yssen. This is the document Mr van Yssen asked for."

"My husband has gone to the shop. He will be back any minute now. Would you like to wait for him? Do please sit down." Jane appeared in the doorway holding a rag doll. She looked at Izak and pulled her mother's skirt aside to hide her face.

"Thanks."

Douglas saw the horse and went straight to the veranda. Izak put his cup down to greet Douglas.

"Morning Mr van Yssen."

"Morning Izak."

Izak handed him the document. "Stay for a while," Douglas suggested. He opened the parcel. The deed, a Notarial Contract, was written in Dutch. It started in the usual way, *'voor mij ... notaris publiek ... compareerden,'* and then the names of the parties followed, as owners of the farms in question. First twenty-three names *'ter eene zijde hiernamaals genoemd die onderste bezitters,'* and then several names *'ter andere zijde hiernamaals genoemd de bovenste bezitters.'*

Izak watched him read. Douglas flicked through the pages. At first Izak thought that he was able to read that fast. Douglas put the document face down on the veranda table and nodded to himself. "We are expecting visitors this afternoon. I will read it tomorrow morning, and let your father know what I think. Thank you." He put his hand on the document as if to protect it.

Izak said goodbye and rode home.

The van Yssens arrived at the farm shortly before four that afternoon. Maggie had washed Jane's hair and dried it in the warm yellow autumn sun at the back of the house. To Maggie's disappointment Jane insisted on wearing a pair of faded pink calico dungarees. "I tried my best to persuade her to put a dress on, but she wouldn't hear of it. So I let her be. I hope you don't mind," she said to Mrs van Yssen.

"You are a good mother Maggie, I'm sure your judgement is sound." She kissed Maggie on her cheek. "I have brought Jane some new shoes. Let her open the box."

Jane grabbed the box and hugged her grandmother. "Say hello to Oupa, Jane." Maggie said. Jane put the box down and affectionately hugged van Yssen's leg. He loved her. Sometimes when he looked at Jane, memories of his little sister returned and he felt his throat tightening and tears threatening. It was uncanny how similar Jane's expressions, her gestures, were. She looked so familiar. Van Yssen embraced Maggie and kissed her on her forehead.

"Where would you like to sit Pa?" Maggie asked.

"Let's sit outside, if you don't mind, my child. There will not be many days like this left before the winter comes – let's make the best of it. I love autumn. The colours of the trees are so beautiful up here." A breeze rustled the drying leaves of the trees near the house. "Where is Douglas?"

"He has had his head buried in a document that the Ellises asked him to read," Maggie answered.

"What is it about?"

"The never ending quarrel about water. You know how it is, Pa. Douglas says Mr Laubscher will not allow Oom Cornelius to use water from the Saffraan River. Mr Laubscher says that there is a contract that divides the water; it goes back to 1906. Douglas is reading the contract to see if what Mr Laubscher says is correct."

"Why does Ellis not go to an attorney?"

"Douglas thinks that the lawyers in town are scared of going against Mr Laubscher because of his position in the district, and even if they were to act for Mr Ellis they will do it half heartedly."

"If that is so it will be a sad day. If Ellis is entitled to water then he should have his fair share."

"Douglas says Mr Laubscher is a bully."

Van Yssen smiled wryly.

Douglas appeared. "Hello Dad, hello Ma." He had that cross-eyed look he always had when he had been studying.

"I have just been reading a document Cornelius Ellis asked me to peruse."

"Maggie mentioned it."

"It is quite interesting. I must look at it more carefully, but it seems to me that it contains nothing that should prevent the Ellises from having water from the Saffraan River."

Van Yssen took the writing pad. 'Why does Ellis not consult an attorney?'

"The lawyers are scared of Laubscher."

"It does not say much for their courage."

Douglas shrugged.

"I once did work for Laubscher in town, at his town house. He had a dispute with a neighbour over a boundary line. All was well until I found that Laubscher had exceeded the boundary, not the neighbour. Well, was he furious! He accused me of siding with the neighbour, as though I would compromise my professional integrity. He threatened me and took more than a year to pay me for my work. He is not a pleasant man. He is arrogant. What are the elements of the issue between the Ellises and Laubscher?"

"At present Ellis relies entirely on water from the Moeras River.

Laubscher does not use any water from the Moeras River. He only gets water from the Saffraan River which is a tributary of the Moeras River. Ellis' property lies above Laubscher's property, and the Saffraan River cuts across a small triangle of their land known as Elandskloof. From there the river flows through Laubscher's farm. Ellis has been clearing land at Elandskloof for many years and done dry land farming there. He has always wanted water from the river where it goes through his land, and Laubscher has persistently said no. Laubscher claims that his predecessor, Olivier, forbade Ellis from using water, and says that the notarial contract, the document I am reading, drawn up in 1906, excludes Ellis from using any water."

"Is that what it says?"

"For the life of me I cannot see where it says that Ellis is not entitled to water. I will have to look at it more carefully, but my first impression is, unless I am missing something, the agreement only regulates the division of water between one group of upper owners on the one hand, and another group of lower owners, people towards Armoed, on the other hand. No mention is made of the way in which water is to be divided within each group. A Rider to the agreement was registered a few months after the original agreement. The Rider regulates the use of water between two individual upper owners. The need for a Rider strongly suggests that the original agreement was not intended to regulate the division of water between individual members within a group. If my conclusion is correct, it means that Laubscher is either ignorant or he is bluffing. Either way he's wrong."

"You must be careful about getting involved, Douglas."

"Why?"

"Laubscher is unpleasant. If you are going to be seen to take sides in a matter like this, you must prepare yourself for a long tough fight with people with a lot of money and influence."

"You know me Dad. If I believe in something I will hang on until they chop my head off, like Martin Luther."

"I respect that. I am like that myself, but don't say I didn't warn you. You must also think of the Ellises. They have very little. If they become embroiled in a legal battle it could cost them everything. The law is a treacherous thing. You will have lawyers on both sides telling their clients that they are right. But only one side will win. And both lawyers will get paid. My father always warned: 'you go to court to defend your shirt and you leave without your trousers.' Remember too that water law is pretty tricky."

"I am aware of that. Do you know the area up there?"

"Where?"

"Elandskloof."

"Not at all. I still think that Ellis should get proper legal advice."

"I agree. I asked him about that. I will continue to press him, I assure you. Nevertheless I will tell him what I think and prepare him as best I can. If necessary I will go with him to see someone in town."

"One wonders whether Laubscher has already sought legal advice. Maybe that's why he is so cocksure of himself. If he has, it would be interesting to know whom he approached."

"I will ask Ellis if he knows anything."

"What are you and Daddy talking about Oupa?" Jane asked. She admired her new t-strap brown shoes as she sat on a chair and swung her legs to and fro.

"How shall I explain it, my dear child? Since the beginning of time."

"It sounds like my *Just So Stories*."

"From the very beginning people have always quarrelled about things, Jane. It is always about things. In this case one farmer wants water from the river and his neighbour does not want him to have the water."

"Mummy says we must all share. Why can they not share?"

Van Yssen laughed. "If only it were that simple, my child, we would not need so many lawyers."

"What are lawyers?" she asked.

"Laws are just like the rules here at home. Things you may do and other things you may not do. The lawyers are the people who explain what those rules are and how they work."

"I know our rules. They need not tell me what they are."

"If everybody knew the rules, Jane, the world would be an easier place."

Van Yssen tapped Douglas on the sleeve, "Aren't children wonderful! They ask us the simplest of questions and we find it difficult to give the answers. We adults take so much for granted, but when we have to explain the simplest of things we find ourselves sadly wanting."

Wednesday 13 April 1938

Old Cornelius Ellis and his eldest son Cornelius arrived at Douglas' house shortly before ten in the morning. It was a chilly day, made more so by dense cloud cover and a thin breeze that came from the mountain. Maggie and Jane were in the living room, busy with Jane's reading and writing lesson, as Douglas had shown her to do. Douglas had gone with Willemse to see to an injured ewe.

The knock on the front door startled Maggie. She glanced through the window to see who it could be and found two tall erect Ellis figures standing with their backs to the front door, hats in their hands, looking out over the valley while they waited for the door to be answered. She tidied her hair and straightened her dress.

"Good morning Oom Cornelius, Cornelius."

"Good morning Missus van Yssen. We have come to talk to Mister van Yssen."

"He's gone with Willemse to see to the sheep."

"We will wait," Old Cornelius replied. "We can just sit outside."

"No, no, that won't do. Come inside, to the dining room."

"Thank you."

It was nearly noon before Douglas returned. Old Cornelius sat and cracked his knuckles while Douglas washed his hands so that he could handle the notarial contract. He had made notes, and a summary of the most important points. Old Cornelius swayed uncomfortably in his chair, his arms crossed over his body, bracing himself for bad news. His face was red.

Douglas set out the contract and his pieces of paper on the table. "Oom Cornelius, I have examined the contract thoroughly. Unless I am missing something, and I don't believe I am, unless I am missing something, I cannot find any reason why Laubscher should deny you the right to use water from the Saffraan River. I am of the opinion, and remember that I have no legal training, that the contract," he tapped his fingers on the document, "that the contract is essentially between two groups of individuals, namely one group described as 'upper owners' and another group known as 'lower owners.' The contract does not say how the apportionment of water should occur among a specific group of owners. What is more, the contract uses the plural when it deals with those who receive water from the Moeras River, and uses the singular, when it deals with the Saffraan River. The singular upper owner was Olivier. I can find nothing in the contract that either expressly states or implies that your predecessors in title waived their rights to water. They probably did not even know that the Saffraan River flowed through their land. That is probably why, when the contract was drawn up in 1906, it did not include a provision to say how the Saffraan River's water had to be divided between your predecessor and Olivier. *Om dit reguit te stel*, Laubscher is talking shit. Either he's stupid, and I don't think he is, or he's trying to bluff."

Cornelius put his hands on his thighs and rocked back and forth with his upper body. The tissues around his eyes relaxed. Cornelius looked at his father and grinned. Old Cornelius lifted his hand. "We must remain calm, Cornelius, there's a long road ahead." Old Cornelius took Douglas' writing pad. 'What must we do now?'

"The best thing to do in these matters is always to try and be reasonable. Try to settle this with Laubscher in a friendly way. Go and see him. Tell him that you have studied the contract and cannot see from what is written in it that you have no rights. Ask him to show you where it says that. He may not like that. Pretend to be ignorant, make it sound as you have come to ask him to help you to interpret the contract."

Old Cornelius smiled. "We will do that. Thank you for your help. We will not stay any longer, I have already used too much of your time. Thank you very much."

Douglas handed the contract to Old Cornelius. He insisted on saying goodbye to Maggie. "Your husband is a very clever man, Missus van Yssen." Douglas walked with them to their donkey cart. Old Cornelius shook Douglas' hand repeatedly to show his gratitude. Douglas waited while Cornelius junior turned the cart around and watched as they rode towards the gate, their heads together in animated discussion.

"They seem happy enough, what did you say to them," Maggie said.

"That there is nothing in the agreement that deprives them of their right to share the water."

Monday 25 April 1938

Cornelius Ellis wrote to Laubscher immediately after receiving Douglas' opinion, and asked for an interview. Laubscher replied to say that he was very busy and suggested the Monday after Easter at ten in the morning. At half past nine on the appointed day Old Cornelius and Cornelius junior arrived in a light drizzle on Laubscher's farm.

Laubscher was waiting for them at the front of his house, his ample girth thrust out ahead of him. "He looks as if he's swallowed a sheep," Old Cornelius remarked. Laubscher had put on a new jacket and trousers to intimidate them, and arranged for several servants to be conspicuous near the front of the house. He invited them inside and took them into a gloomy drawing room with burgundy coloured wallpaper. Laubscher's manner was stiff, his jaw set, his lips pursed defiantly. "Sit," he said abruptly. The Ellises sat down cautiously to show respect. "I trust you haven't come begging."

Old Cornelius smiled as though Laubscher had made a joke.

"What do you want to see me about?" Laubscher asked.

"About the water."

"Will you never learn Cornelius? That matter has been settled, and you know it. Why do you carry on as though it has not been settled?"

"I have not come to fight with you Gert. I was hoping that we would be able to sit down as civilised people and come to a fair arrangement. I don't think that it is right to chase us away like dogs every time we ask for fair treatment. Let us open our minds and look anew at this whole thing."

"There is nothing more to look at, Cornelius. Thirty-two years ago our predecessors carefully determined how the water should be divided, neither you nor I had part in that, and they decided that your predecessor in title did not have a right to water from the Saffraan River. You are bound by that decision. It is as simple as that."

"We don't agree with that."

"Oh, you don't agree! It does not matter whether you agree or not, that is what the notarial contract says. You can stand on your head and it will not change what is written there."

"The contract does not say that we are not entitled to water." Cornelius took the contract from his pocket.

"Now you're disguising yourself as a lawyer."

"Not at all, Gert, I have come to you to appeal to you to be fair to us, in the name of the Lord please be fair to us."

"I take exception that you should imply that I am not a fair man. I am being fair. I am simply applying the terms of the contract. You are the one who wants to bend the rules, Cornelius."

Cornelius unfolded the pages of the notarial contract. "With respect,

Gert, I disagree. If what you say is correct would you be so kind as to show me where in this contract it says that we do not have a right to water."

Laubscher waved his hand disdainfully. "I am not here to teach you how to read. If you don't understand what is written there, go and ask someone who can read properly."

"We have done that."

"Oh, and may I ask, who was so kind as to do your reading for you?"

Old Cornelius and his son looked uncomfortably at each other. Cornelius nodded to his father to proceed. "We asked van Yssen to look at the contract."

"Van Yssen? The land surveyor? I've already had a set-to with him."

"We are talking about his son, Douglas, at Kleinmoerasrivier."

"That deaf ne're-do-well who had to get married in disgrace."

"There is no need to insult him. He is a good man. And he is cleverer than all the people in the district put together. He is a learned man. They say he would have been a professor if he did not become deaf."

"If he is so clever why is he sitting up there in poverty?"

"Douglas van Yssen has read the contract and he says it does not say that we have no rights. If you think we have no rights, please show us where it says so, so that we may put this thing to rest for once and for all, Gert."

"Do you think I am stupid, Cornelius. You come here with a witness, while I am on my own. You ask me to dig a hole for myself? What do you think I am? Someone who must explain to a man like you what is clearly there in black and white? If this is how you want to come and conduct what you call a civilised negotiation, you are sadly mistaken. You are wasting my time. And tell that van Yssen to stay out of my affairs. He does not know what he is tampering with. He will get a bloody good hiding if he sticks his nose in my affairs and I would not be surprised if his father put him up to this. What does van Yssen think he is, a bloody lawyer?"

Old Cornelius was red in the face and started trembling. Cornelius put his hand on his father's arm. Let's rather leave, Pa."

"I've held out my hand in peace to you, Gert, and you strike it aside." Cornelius shook his head sadly as he stood up to leave.

Thursday 28 April 1938

Old Cornelius and Cornelius junior arrived at Douglas' farm late in the afternoon. Old Cornelius had been reluctant to go and see Douglas again but was persuaded by his son that it would be unfair to leave the matter in the air, and not let Douglas know what had happened at the meeting with Laubscher. From the way old Cornelius lumbered up the veranda steps it was clear how things had gone. He put his silent hand out to Douglas while he took his hat off. Douglas bade them sit. He offered refreshments but Cornelius shook his head and held his hand up to refuse. Maggie came to say hello and fetched the writing pad.

"It did not go well," Old Cornelius wrote. "He treated us badly. I have come to say sorry to you. I told him that you had read the contract. I am sorry about that. To drag you into this. He said you must keep your nose out of his business otherwise he'll give you a hiding. I apologise. I should not have mentioned your name. It is our fight. I am not even sure if we should carry on. He will never change his mind."

"I have thought a lot about this matter Oom Cornelius. I have read the contract several times. I have no doubt that you have a case against Laubscher. You should go and see a lawyer. I will go along if you wish. Call Laubscher's bluff; let a lawyer write him a letter."

"We cannot afford legal costs right now. It may have to wait. It has been going on for so long, a little longer will not matter."

"Let me know when you are ready. I will assist you as much as I can."

Chapter Forty-Four

The years 1938-1941

AS THE THIRTIES drew to a close political issues in South Africa became increasingly acrimonious and threatened the unity that had prevailed since 1933. Matters came to a head when war was declared on September 3, 1939.

At the outbreak of war, the Prime Minister, General Hertzog, proposed that South Africa should remain neutral. He argued that the Union did not have the same interests as Britain, and to the dismay of some of his cabinet colleagues attempted to justify Hitler's actions. Smuts vehemently opposed Hertzog's stance and declared that the Union should not remain neutral. When Hertzog's motion was put to the vote it was heavily defeated and the way was paved for Smuts to form a new government. The United Party was no more, and what was left were two hostile opposing political forces.

The dispute between Smuts and Hertzog unmasked bitter pro-British and anti-British sentiments that had had their origins in the previous century and the Boer War; sentiments that had penetrated deeply into the psyche. Political differences manifested themselves in many aspects of social life. Animosities between individuals with opposing political views were amplified; where there were disputes, attitudes hardened. While the outbreak of war had served to retard somewhat the progress of the dispute between Ellis and Laubscher, the newly charged political atmosphere again hardened Laubscher's attitude. The notion of a political adversary was grist to his emotions.

Towards the end of 1941 Cornelius Ellis' health had begun to deteriorate and he became increasingly aware of his own mortality. He decided that he was not prepared to die without ensuring that he, and his sons after him, would have a fair share of water from the Saffraan River. Laubscher remained equally determined that Ellis was not entitled to water, and neither of them was prepared to yield. It was inevitable that the matter would end up in court.

———◆———

Chapter Forty-five

Monday 9 March 1942

OLD CORNELIUS had slept restlessly and by four o'clock he could no longer stay in bed. He made coffee and went outside into the cool moist early morning air. He stood and sipped his coffee while he rehearsed what to say to Laubscher. He woke Cornelius at six and announced that he had decided that they should go and see Laubscher that morning in a final attempt to have the water issue resolved peaceably. Magreta, Ellis' wife, made breakfast while her husband and son sat silently at the kitchen table. They ate fried eggs and bread, and drank black coffee sweetened with brown government sugar. Cornelius harnessed their best two donkeys to the cart and shortly before seven on a clear late summer morning set off for Laubscher's farm. They rode without speaking and heard only the crunching sounds of the iron treads of the wheels on the gravel of the road, and the rhythmic clonking of thills in the harnesses. Cornelius glanced at his father. The old man's hat was set at an angle that showed resolve and urgency. It would be better not to try and engage him in conversation.

Laubscher was on his way to the toilet when he saw the donkey cart approaching. The sun was behind the cart and it was difficult to see who was on it. The toilet would have to wait. He was constipated anyway. He was not in a frame of mind to see Ellis. Cornelius jumped from the cart and held the donkeys still while his father alighted.

"Good morning, Gert," Ellis held out his hand.

Laubscher did not respond. He glared at them. "What do you people want here this early?"

"I need to speak to you Gert."

"If it is about the water, there is nothing to discuss. We have been over that enough times."

"Please, Gert, let us try to be reasonable."

"I have told you before that I am the reasonable one, Cornelius. You are asking what you cannot have. The book is closed. Amen. Finished. You are the unreasonable one." Laubscher poked his finger into Ellis' chest.

Cornelius looked at his father. The old man was crimson with rage. "You treat us like dogs, Gert. We do not enjoy that. You leave me no alternative."

"What are you getting at?"

"I shall have to go to law. You leave me no alternative."

"Go to law? So you think you have the law on your side! What a joke. Go to law, I'm sure you can afford it. You ride around like this, on a donkey cart and you want to challenge me by going to law! Go, and see where it will get you."

Laubscher had lost his temper and was shouting so that his wife came outside to see what the commotion was about. When she saw Ellis and his son she hurried inside.

Ellis was shaking. He nodded and moved his lips as if he was talking to himself. "Then that is how it will be Gert." He climbed onto the cart. Cornelius turned the cart around, and they left without a further word.

When they were out of earshot Old Cornelius turned to Cornelius. "I want to go and see van Yssen on the way back."

Douglas was surprised to see the Ellises. Maggie invited them inside in her usual cheerful manner.

"Thank you Missus van Yssen. I am sorry that we did not make an appointment, but we did not have time."

Cornelius sat down heavily at the dining room table and let out a huge sigh. He signalled with his hand that he wanted to write. Douglas waved his hand and shook his head. "Carry on Oom Cornelius, I'll understand."

Cornelius insisted on paper and pencil. "We have just been to see Laubscher. He treated us very badly. I want to take him to court."

Douglas raised his eyebrows. "It could cost a great deal."

"It no longer has anything do do with money. Laubscher has gone too far. If I have to spend every last penny I have, I will get what is rightfully mine. Let the two of us not quarrel about that. I need your help. Tell me who I must go and see. Will you accompany me?"

"Yes, I will help you. When I discussed it with my father some time ago he said we should go to Taute and Steyn."

"When can you go?"

"Whenever it suits you. I will ask my father to take us to town."

Tuesday 7 April 1942

At lunchtime on the Tuesday after Easter, van Yssen fetched Douglas and the Ellises and drove them to Oudtshoorn. An appointment had been made with Mr Steyn of the law firm, Taute and Steyn. They were shown into Steyn's office and an extra chair was brought in. "Mr Steyn will see you presently," a stern looking woman in a close fitting grey woollen skirt and hand knitted pink jersey announced.

Steyn was a tall man with a sallow complexion. To compensate for his baldness he had grown a white moustache that made him look as if he had drunk buttermilk. He had nervous hands and a slight stutter. He wore a pale brown striped suit and a white shirt with navy blue tie. He shook hands with Douglas and the Ellises and sat down, took a silver cigarette case from his desk drawer, offered cigarettes to his clients. Only Old Cornelius accepted a cigarette.

"Well what can I do for you?" Steyn asked as he blew out smoke.

"We have come to see you about water," Cornelius said.

"What water?"

"I think Mister van Yssen should explain." Ellis tapped Douglas on the shoulder so that Douglas could watch his mouth. "Please explain to Mr Steyn."

"Why is Douglas involved in this, Oom Cornelius?" Steyn asked.

"We asked him for advice. He has read the contract and says we have a right to water. Mister Lauscher will not give us water."

"Gert Laubscher?"

"Yes."

Steyn turned to Douglas and raised his eyebrows.

"Oom Cornelius has been trying to get his fair share of water from the Saffraan River, up there near Moeras River ever since he bought his farm in about 1911. The Saffraan River is a tributary of the Moeras River. First his neighbour Olivier refused to let him have water, and when Olivier sold his farm to Gert Laubscher, Laubscher refused to let Oom Cornelius have any water on the pretext of a notarial contract drawn up in 1906. Oom Cornelius asked me to peruse the contract, and I can find nothing in it that precludes Oom Cornelius from having his water. The Saffraan River flows through a part of Oom Cornelius' property and then through Gert Laubscher's property. That water was never divided between the two properties and certainly not divided according to the notarial contract. Oom Cornelius has been to see Laubscher several times and discussed the matter with him in the hope of coming to an amicable arrangement but Laubscher has treated his approaches with contempt. Oom Cornelius now feels that the matter should be resolved, if necessary, then by law."

"So what do you want me to do?" Steyn asked.

"We should start by writing to Laubscher to say that the water from the Saffraan River has not yet been divided between them, and that Oom Cornelius claims his reasonable portion. So that we don't back him into a corner I suggest we ask Laubscher if he is prepared to consider division of the water under supervision of impartial parties. Tell him that unless he agrees, Oom Cornelius would be forced to approach the Water Court."

"Is that not perhaps a bit extreme?"

"I don't understand," Douglas said.

Steyn took a piece of paper and wrote, "is that not too extreme?"

"Nee," Old Cornelius interjected, "not after the way he treated us."

"It is clear that you feel strongly about this, Oom Cornelius, but if we allow personal feuds to enter into this it will cloud things," Steyn said. "And Gert is a powerful man, with deep pockets."

"Never mind his pockets, Mister Steyn, all I seek is justice."

"The law and justice are separate things, Oom Cornelius. I think we should have some tea."

The secretary poured the tea and left, closing the door firmly behind her.

"You say you've examined the contract, Douglas?" Steyn asked.

"Yes I have been through it. You don't have to know the law to understand it. It is a simple agreement between various parties and all one has to do is use common sense. I have a suspicion that Gert Laubscher thoroughly understands the contract and that he is relying on his bluster and intimidation to deny Oom Cornelius his share of water. I am so sure of myself that I will stake all I have on this matter."

"That is all very well, Douglas, but on the strength of your opinion you are prepared to drag others into court. And the outcome is never certain, as you well know. You are gambling with other's people's money."

"We are not gambling, Mr Steyn," Douglas insisted.

Ellis made large nodding movements to show he agreed.

"Have you brought along a copy of the contract?" Steyn asked.

Cornelius took an envelope from his inside pocket and handed it to Steyn.

"Can you draw me a diagram to show me where the rivers run in relation to the various properties?" Steyn asked.

Douglas asked for a sheet of paper and a pencil. He first sketched the outlines of the properties and then with the help of the Ellises showed where the rivers were. He made a heavy line through the diagram and wrote on the side of the paper, '*bovenste bezitters*' and '*onderste bezitters*.' "The contract merely refers to those to groups of owners, which is of significance," Douglas said.

"Thank you," Steyn said. "Let me read the contract and form an idea of the facts of the case, and the legal implications, and I will advise you how to proceed. How can I get in touch with you, Oom Cornelius?"

"The best is to leave a message at van der Byl's shop. The exchange will know the number. He will get it to me. How long will this take, Mr Steyn?"

"Not long, a few days."

"Why don't we then just decide now that we will come and see you in a week's time, next Tuesday?" Cornelius looked at Douglas and wrote, "can we come back next Tuesday, at the same time?"

"Yes that would be fine?"

Steyn examined his appointment book. "We can meet next Tuesday."

Tuesday 14 April 1942

Van Yssen was unable to fetch Douglas and the Elisses, because of a business commitment, so they arranged to get a lift into town that morning with van der Byl.

They arrived at the offices of Taute and Steyn at a quarter past two and had to wait for Steyn to return from lunch. The secretary was friendlier than before. "Mr Steyn will be here presently," she said.

Steyn arrived just before half past two, showed them into his office, hung his hat on the hat stand in the corner and indicated to them to sit down. The notarial contract was on his desk. He put on his spectacles and picked up the contract. "I have read the contract. To my mind the matter is not quite as simple as Mr van Yssen has suggested." Old Cornelius Ellis' hand began to tremble. Douglas was not sure he understood, and handed his writing pad to

Steyn. Steyn wrote what he had said. Douglas smiled self assuredly. Steyn continued, "I agree that the contract deals with the division of water between two groups and does not say how the water is to be divided among the individuals in a group. However, we must remind ourselves that all the individuals in each group who were party to the agreement signed the agreement. When it comes to the Saffraan River the contract refers only to a 'bovenste bezitter,' in other words it uses the singular, and it seems to me that some might interpret this to mean that only Olivier, who was Gert Laubscher's predecessor in title, was meant to have use of the water. The Raubenheimer ladies, who were predecessors in title to Oom Cornelius, were signatories to the agreement. It could be argued that they understood, when they signed the contract, that they had no right to the water from the Saffraan River. In other words there was only meant to be one upper owner who had the right to use water from the Saffraan River."

"I understand your point Mr Steyn," Douglas responded.

"What do we do now?" Old Cornelius asked nervously.

"What about the Rider to the Contract?" Douglas asked.

Steyn frowned. "Yes, I have looked at that. What about it?"

"The way I see it," Douglas said, "is that the Rider shows us that '*bovenste bezitters*' found it necessary to make arrangements of individual rights among themselves. It is significant that they saw the need so soon after the signing of the Contract and must surely confirm that the Contract was between groups and allowed for subsequent individual agreements. "

"So what is your point?" Steyn asked.

"My point is that no such arrangement was made among the upper owners along the Saffraan River, and is still open to negotiation."

"Do you not think that the Raubenheimer ladies relinquished their rights by not making any claim to water?"

"No. They may not even have known that they had land that bordered on the Saffraan River. The Raubenheimer women did not sign the contract themselves. From what we can gather they were not even living on the farm when the Contract was signed. It was signed by someone who had their power of attorney. As you know, Mr Steyn, abandonment of rights, if claimed, must be clearly proved. Who in the present case can prove that? What is more, and this is very important, the Contract does not specifically allocate water to Olivier but merely obliges him to allow water to flow downstream for the use of the lower owners. If you do not support our argument you must please say so, for then we must turn elsewhere for help."

"Not so quick, Douglas. I am not saying that Oom Cornelius does not have a case. I must look at this thing as objectively as possible; otherwise I will not fulfil my responsibility towards my client. I need to be reasonably certain that we have a chance to succeed. I understand your reasoning. I am grateful for your contribution." Steyn fell silent. He put his elbows on his desk, interlocked his fingers and rested his chin on his thumbs. The clock on the wall ticked loudly. The secretary brought tea. Steyn offered Cornelius a cigarette, took one himself. "What do you want me to do?"

"Write to Laubscher, as Mr van Yssen suggested last time." Cornelius said. "I shall do that."

The Ellises and Douglas set off on foot for the van Yssens house to wait there until van Yssen could take them back to the farm. "I'm not convinced Steyn's heart is in our matter," Old Cornelius said. "And what is more, I can see that you are much smarter than Steyn, Douglas."

On April 28, 1942, Steyn wrote a letter to Laubscher saying that he had been instructed by his client Mr J C Ellis to say that water from a public stream the Saffraan River had not yet been divided among the upper owners. He went on to say that his client claimed his reasonable portion of the water and would like to know whether Laubscher would be prepared to consider division of said water under the supervision of impartial parties. He concluded by saying unless Laubscher agreed to this, Ellis would be forced to approach the Water Court.

Laubscher replied that he had handed the letter to his attorney Mr J F S Foster and that all future correspondence should be addressed to Mr Foster.

Friday 4 September 1942

Four months went by without a reply from Foster. Cornelius asked Douglas to visit Steyn when next he went to Oudtshoorn, and to impress on Steyn that they were not prepared to wait indefinitely.

On September 10, 1942, Steyn wrote a further letter to Foster saying that Foster's client had had ample time and opportunity to consider division of the water from the Saffraan River and that the time had arrived to call for a definite answer, failing which the client would have no alternative but to proceed with the Water Court application.

On Friday September 25, 1942, in the early afternoon, Garnett died. Paul, his son of three, found him where he lay heavily on the floor next to his bed, at a curious angle, in his cream coloured silk pyjamas with its pale blue collar, drenched in perspiration. Garnett's partner Lamprecht came with his clumsy ambitious hands and plunged a needle with adrenalin into his heart, to no avail. Sientjie the maid gathered Paul in her arms and ran with him to the kitchen. Mattie the cook fetched Aloise. While their father died, the innocent legs of the two small children dangled over the edge of the tall scrubbed kitchen table, held from harm, and consoled by the gardener, the cook and the maid. The servants wept with the powerful grief of the faithful.

On his bed Garnett was growing cold. Irene, pregnant with her third child, kissed him goodbye. Consummate finality. He who had loved her so was gone forever. She was alone in a sea of misery and anguish. Lamprecht stayed with Garnett's body. The practice would now be his. In one pocket of his waistcoat he fondled his fob watch, and in the other the ivory coloured fingers of his ambitious right hand caressed a small chamois bag of illicit diamonds. Garnett had suffered his last inglorious humiliation: of sharing the privacy of dying with such a man.

That night, as the heat of the day turned into dark clear cold, as the house creaked from the contractions of its roof, Irene lay alone in her bed with her new child inside her.

Douglas received the news of Garnett's death early that evening. While they were having supper a note was brought from van der Byl's store. He staggered under the weight of the news and slumped in his chair. He held his head in his hands and made huge bellowing sobs. His friend was dead.

Garnett's funeral was held two days later on Sunday afternoon. Van Yssen fetched Douglas and Maggie and Jane to attend the service. The Dutch Reformed Church was filled to utmost capacity. The *Oudtshoorn Courant* described Garnett as kind and genial and having a charitable disposition. There were more than two hundred cars in the funeral procession.

On the same day that Garnett died, Cornelius Ellis was outside his woodshed, sharpening an axe on a stone wheel, when he felt a sudden numbness of the left hand side of his face. The axe that he held in his left hand fell to the ground. He was confused. He felt dizzy and lost his balance. He fell heavily onto his face. Izak found him there and called his mother, who called Cornelius. They carried him into the house on an old door that stood in the woodshed, and transferred him to his bed. Old Cornelius was unconscious.

"Go to the shop and ring Dr Cloete," Mrs Ellis exclaimed.

Cloete came and examined Cornelius. "He's had a stroke. I'll prescribe something to thin his blood. Let him have as much rest as possible, and if you can manage feed him thin beef soup."

Tuesday 29 September 1942

It was not long before the news of Ellis' stroke reached Laubscher. As soon as he had had breakfast he telephoned Foster and hurried into town to see him. "They say Cornelius Ellis is critically ill. He may not live. I think we should write to Steyn as soon as possible, today if you can. Tell Steyn that I refuse to consider any division of the water."

"I will draft the letter while you wait Gert."

The letter was addressed to: Messrs Taute and Steyn, Solicitors, High Street Oudtshoorn.

Dear Sirs,

Re: C J Ellis vs. G J C Laubscher

Referring to your letter of the 10th instant re your client's claim for a division of Water of the Saffraan River, I am directed by Mr Laubscher to intimate that he refuses to consider any such subdivision. Mr Laubscher asserts that your client has no right to any water out of the Saffraan River in respect of his portion or portions of the farm Moeras River. Mr Ellis' predecessor in title also had no claim in respect of such water. Mr Ellis purchased his property in 1909, and took possession in or about May 1910.

I might mention that at the time when your client acquired the property he claimed a division of the water from Mr J S Olivier who was then owner of the properties now owned by Mr Laubscher, and that he was also denied the right to any water.

Yours faithfully,

(sgd) J F S Foster.

"I will take it to Steyn myself."

"It would be better if I send it, Gert."

"No, I will take it. I want to make sure that Steyn knows where I stand."

When the letter was ready Laubscher took the envelope and marched down High Street to the offices of Taute and Steyn. Steyn was at the Magistrate's Court. The secretary told him and would be back after twelve. Could he tell her what it was about? No it was a private matter. He still had to go to the bank and would come back after twelve.

When he had been to the bank, Laubscher again headed for Steyn's office. On the way he met Steyn coming out of the Magistrate's Court.

"I was at your office earlier," he said to Steyn.

"And to what do I owe the honour?"

"I have a letter for you, from Foster, that I want to hand to you myself."

"What is it about?"

"Cornelius Ellis has had a stroke. He is lying unconscious on his farm. They do not know whether he will survive. I want the whole matter of the water settled before he dies. I have told him in the letter that I will not consider any division of the water. I want him to know that, and I want him to accept that before he goes. You must go and see him."

"I thought you said he was unconscious?"

"Yes, but perhaps he will regain consciousness, perhaps you could persuade him…"

"But if he is seriously ill? What will his sons say?"

"It would be in his interest if this thing was settled before he dies." Laubscher held out his hand to say goodbye. He held Steyn's hand in both his hands and said with a pawky wink, almost as an afterthought, "I may have to change horses one day."

Thursday 1 October 1942

Steyn drove to Ellis' farm and arrived there at nine thirty in the morning. Cornelius had seen the approaching dust and was waiting at the front door.

"I am sorry to hear about your father, Cornelius. How is he?"

"He remains unconscious, since the twenty-fifth, almost six days. The doctor says it does not look good."

"May I see him?"

"Yes."

Cornelius showed Steyn inside. He called his mother and introduced her to Steyn. Steyn expressed his sympathies. Ellis lay on his back, in his modest bedroom. The sheets were neatly folded half way up his large chest. He looked as if he was sleeping. The left side of his face sagged. The air in the room was foul and smelt of urine and faeces and a rancid body. Steyn stood at the door and shook his head. He turned and retraced his steps to the entrance hall.

"Please sit Mr Steyn," Cornelius suggested. "There is coffee on the stove. My mother will bring it now."

"I am truly sorry to see your father like that. To think that such a strong man could now lie there like that."

"How did you hear about this?"

"News travels fast in these parts, Cornelius." Steyn folded his hands together piously, and assumed an attitude of great sympathy. "To be truthful Cornelius, Gert Laubscher told me, in the street, in town, just two days ago. He wants the matter settled before things get worse."

"That is good news, did he tell you that?"

"Yes, but it may not be news you want to hear."

"Is that why you have come to see us?"

"Well, that is not the only reason. I was concerned about your father."

"I thought you were acting for us, Mr Steyn. Now it appears as if Laubscher sent you."

'Oh, I am, I am, rest assured that I am. I mean I am acting for your father. And I must always act in the best interest of my client, Cornelius."

"In these difficult circumstances, what do you think is in our best interest?"

"Let go of this thing Cornelius. Don't drag your father's estate, I mean if the worst should come to happen, don't drag your father further into a legal morass. Let your father have peace."

"This thing has caused my father's illness. My father believes that he is right. If he dies we will take this matter further, Mr Steyn. My brothers and I are determined to carry on my father's work."

"Would that really be your father's wish?"

"Yes. Why do you doubt me?"

"I see an old man who is very ill Cornelius. Let us not make his life more difficult. Think about it. Let me know. I have the power to act as his agent. I could write to Laubscher and tell him that your father has withdrawn his claim."

"My father will never agree to that."

"I will not press you now for a reply, Cornelius. Think about it; discuss it with your family. But treat it with the urgency that it requires. Think about bringing peace to your father."

Mrs Ellis carried in a tray with coffee and a plate of small jam tarts. She was prepared for many visitors. Cornelius watched Steyn as he took his cigarette case from his jacket pocket and lit a cigarette. Cornelius fetched a small brass ashtray with figures of elephants engraved into it. Steyn knew Cornelius was observing him. He was unable to look up. He drank his coffee and although he had no appetite, forced down two jam tarts. He would eat to any brief.

"Well, I suppose you have much to attend to, Cornelius. I suppose I should be going. Please think about what I have suggested. I would like to say goodbye to your mother, if I may."

Cornelius watched as Steyn drove away from the house.

When he got back to his office Steyn immediately wrote as follows to Foster.

P O Box 104
Oudtshoorn.
1st October 1942

Mr J F S Foster,
P O Box 29
OUDTSHOORN

Dear Sir,
Re: C J Ellis vs. G Laubscher

We are in receipt of your letter of the 29th ultimo and note contents.

Under the circumstances our client has decided to withdraw his claim.

Yours faithfully,
TAUTE & STEYN.

On October 3 Cornelius Ellis regained consciousness briefly. Cornelius junior did not tell his father about Steyn's visit. On October 6, Cornelius died in the early hours of the morning while his wife sat asleep next to his bed and the flame of the candle that was nearly spent swayed weakly in the molten wax that lay in the bottom of the candlestick.

Cornelius' funeral was held on his farm. Steyn's conscience did not permit him to attend. The women in severe black, and the men in their best awkwardly fitting suits stood silently while the wind hissed in the pepper trees that bordered the family graveyard and pressed their clothes against them as they listened to the monotonous words of the clergyman. After Cornelius had been laid to rest, tea and coffee were served in the voorhuis. From the walls those who had gone before looked down calmly on the mourners from sombre sepia portraits.

Chapter Forty-six

The years 1942 – 1954

ALBERT VAN YSSEN DIED of heart failure in August of 1944 at the age of 69. He had asked to be buried on the farm. Only the van Yssens' closest friends attended the funeral. The service was held in the early afternoon in the church near Kleinmoerasrivier where Jane was christened. The weather was bitterly cold. The drawn faces of older mourners contemplated their own mortality and reflected how they had allowed life to treat them. Mrs Jacquard sat with Mrs van Yssen. Mrs de Lange played the piano and when the mourners sang, 'Nearer my God to Thee', Jane sobbed. Mrs Jacquard and Douglas had to support Mrs van Yssen at the graveside when she nearly fainted as her husband's coffin was lowered into the grave. A cold wind from the mountains whipped up dust from the heap of soil next to the grave and blew it into the eyes of the bystanders. They left Albert van Yssen lying beneath a mound of brown earth under the oak tree and had tea and coffee to comfort themselves next to the fire in the living room.

In 1945, when Jane started high school, she and Maggie moved to Oudtshoorn to stay with Mrs van Yssen. Maggie went back to work at Prince Vintcent to support the family. The farm was never prosperous and at best provided a way of life, or perhaps just a way of existence. Douglas remained on the farm and became increasingly reclusive. He read a great deal and neglected the farm as he came to rely more and more on Maggie's modest income. He decided that he did not want to have his father's car and encouraged his mother to sell it. Once a month he travelled into town by bicycle and spent a few days, usually over a weekend, with Maggie and Jane. When he was in town he often visited Irene Nel and spent many happy hours with her discussing history, literature, the classics, poetry. Maggie encouraged the visits to Irene because it gave Douglas the opportunity to have the stimulation he craved. He often thought of Frances and as a consequence became preoccupied with the genetic aspects of his deafness. He obtained a copy of a textbook that dealt with the specifics of his affliction. The book was written in French and the author was a professor of genetics at the University of Grenoble. He sat for months translating relevant passages with the aid of a French dictionary, and puzzling over the accompanying mathematical calculations. At one point he found what he thought was a possible error in a set of calculations and wrote to the author. The author replied to thank him for his interest and confirmed that there was indeed an error. The book was withdrawn from publication and the error rectified.

For a considerable period after Cornelius Ellis died, his three sons did not pursue their claim for water from the Saffraan River. Cornelius, the eldest, believed that the strain of the dispute had contributed to his father's death. Cornelius was burdened with guilt that he had hastened his father's demise by encouraging him to pursue the matter. At times the resolve that Cornelius had inherited from his father turned his thoughts towards resuming the fight, but fear that he and his brothers would have to oppose forces much larger than their resources would allow, acted as restraint. Izak, the middle brother, could not let the matter rest, and spoke about it from time to time. He visited Douglas on occasions, and after each visit came away more convinced that they should take Laubscher to court.

Whenever Izak broached the issue, Cornelius insisted that they had enough irrigable land along the banks of the Moeras River and although they sometimes practised dry-land farming at Elandskloof, when there was enough rain, there was no immediate need to irrigate there. As time passed all the land along the Moeras River was put under irrigation, and thoughts again turned to the water from the Saffraan River at Elandskloof. The quality of the soil at Elandskloof was the best the Ellises had, and if they could irrigate it their production would be increased considerably.

On Friday November 6, 1953, Cornelius wrote to Laubscher asking for an appointment to discuss the division of water. Laubscher had in the meantime become the Chairman of the Divisional Council at Oudtshoorn. His newfound self-importance nurtured his arrogance and hubris and made him less approachable than ever. When he received Cornelius' letter he immediately responded, and said curtly, that he would not under any circumstances give any further consideration to the matter, since it had been closed in 1942 at the time of their father's illness on instructions from their father to his attorney Mr H H Steyn. Laubscher added that Steyn in his capacity as Cornelius Ellis Senior's agent had written to his attorney, Mr J R S Foster to say that Cornelius had withdrawn his claim.

Saturday 14 November 1953

Cornelius collected his mail at van der Byls' shop that morning. A letter from Laubscher was among the items. Cornelius thought it would contain good news because of the prompt reply, and decided to open the letter when he could share its contents with his brothers. When they were together in the kitchen he opened it, full of expectations. His head began to shake and he became crimson with rage.

"What is the matter, Cornelius?" Izak asked.

"He says Pa withdrew his claim for water shortly before his death. He says he received a letter from Steyn."

"That is impossible! When Steyn came here Pa was unconscious" Izak said. "We should go and see van Yssen."

"I hope he's at home."

Douglas was at the living room table, reading. He looked about the room. The Persian rug was threadbare where a path had been worn across it; the bookshelves were dusty. Books and newspapers lay everywhere. Coffee cups were stuck to the table. The upholstery of the couch was worn through in places. Unwashed dinner plates were stacked on a chair. His eye caught the movements of the Ellises on the veranda. He went outside to welcome them.

"We have a problem," Cornelius blurted.

"Moring Izak," Douglas said.

"I wrote to Laubscher a week ago, and asked him for an appointment to discuss the water. This is his reply."

"Something is rotten," Douglas said.

"That's exactly my point," Cornelius replied.

"I meant to tell you, Cornelius, I heard in town a while ago that Steyn now acts for Laubscher," Douglas said.

Cornelius shook his head in disbelief. 'It make me so angry, that I will take that bastard to court, no matter what it takes.'

Douglas was looking at the letter. "I did not hear what you said?"

"I said I will take that bastard Laubscher to court no matter what it takes. Why would my father give away what was rightfully ours. When Steyn came to see him, after he had the stroke, he was unconscious; he did not even know that Steyn was there. I never told you, but mind you Laubscher also came to look at Pa, at that time, he said, to show sympathy. We must go and see an attorney."

"I will have to think about it."

"About helping?"

"No, of course I will help; about whom to see. You know how this matter has been eating away also at me. Give me a few days." Douglas again read Laubscher's letter. "I cannot believe that Steyn could have stooped to this. I would very much like to see a copy of the letter. Even if Steyn now acts for Laubscher, we could still ask to see the letter. I am going into town next weekend. I think I'll have a word with Hugo Pocock. He is a nice man. I'll explain to him what has happened and ask him whether he would be prepared to act on your behalf. I'll be back on the Monday afternoon." Douglas looked at the calendar on the wall. "Come and see me on Tuesday. Come early. In the meantime. don't say anything to anybody."

Saturday 21 November 1953

Douglas arrived at his mother's house early so that he could see Maggie before she went to work. She was in her room putting on her stockings. His mother was having a bath. He stood at the door and watched as Maggie clipped the ends of her suspenders onto the hems of her stockings. She had not put her pants on yet. He leant over to kiss her and ran his rough hand affectionately between her thighs and touched her. She stroked the back of his neck and smiled. 'Later, this afternoon, when your mother has her rest.'

"So, Douglas," his mother said when they were at the breakfast table. "You seem preoccupied."

"Not really."

"I know you too well, my son."

"It's the Ellises' water," Maggie said.

"Why don't you leave that alone, it's been so long," Mrs van Yssen asked,

"I can't. Principles don't know time. I'm going to see Hugo Pocock when I have taken Maggie to work."

Tuesday 24 November 1953

Cornelius and Izak Ellis arrived a little before eight in the morning. Douglas had made coffee and showed them to the dining room table.

"I went to see Hugo Pocock and had a long discussion with him. I explained the origins of the dispute, the letter of October 1, and all the rest. The good news is that he is prepared to handle the matter on your behalf. The bad news is that everybody is weary of going against Laubscher. I could see Pocock was nervous, and I am not quite sure that he grasped every point that I tried to make. But he is an honest decent man. To his credit he is cautious. He will not encourage you if he thinks your case is hopeless, and neither will I."

"Do you still believe we have a case?" Izak asked.

"Yes, I do. Pocock feels that we should get an advocate's opinion. I think that's a good idea. He'll make enquiries in Cape Town. If you are agreeable we should make plans to go and see Pocock as soon as possible, and inform Laubscher of our intention to proceed."

Cornelius banged his fist resoundingly on the table. "Then it is settled. When can we go and see Pocock?"

"You make the appointment, Cornelius. Telephone him; he is expecting your call. I will go anytime that suits you."

Wednesday 9 December 1953

A letter from Taute and Steyn was delivered by hand to Izak Ellis. The letter said that they had been consulted by Mr G Laubscher about water pumped on December 3, 1953 from a side stream of the Moeras River during Laubscher's turn to have the water. He, Ellis, was not entitled to the water since his father who was his predecessor in title had abandoned his rights in a letter of October 1, 1942.

Friday 11 December 1953

Douglas and the Ellis brothers met with Hugo Pocock at the offices of Pocock and Bailey in Church Street. They handed Pocock the letter that Taute and Steyn had written to Izak Ellis.

"Have you seen the letter of October 1, 1942 to which Steyn refers?" Pocock asked.

"We did not know there was such a letter," Cornelius replied.

"I wonder if there ever was such a letter," Izak remarked.

"Hold on, Izak, we'll come to that," Pocock responded. "As I said to Douglas when he came to see me, I think we should get an advocate's opinion.

I have made enquiries with our correspondents in Cape Town. There is a young advocate who is making a name for himself in riparian matters, Alwyn Burger. He qualified as a civil engineer before he studied law. I think he is the right man. I will invite him to come to Oudtshoorn. We should all be present and I would be glad if you too would be here at the time, Douglas. In the meantime I shall write to Taute and Steyn today and inform them that we do not accept Mr Laubscher's position and that unless a speedy resolution can be found, we will apply to the Water Court for a ruling.

"Of what significance is the letter of 1942?" Pocock asked Douglas.

"I have not seen it, and as they said earlier, neither have Cornelius and Izak. I would like to see it. Steyn never mentioned the letter to either of them. Cornelius and Izak are both convinced that no instruction was given to Steyn to write the letter. Their father was unconscious at the time the letter was written and was not capable of giving Steyn any instructions. Steyn must have done it off his own bat and one wonders what his motive was. You must agree that it is bloody odd that the only people who know about the letter are Laubscher and Steyn. At the time Steyn acted for Oom Cornelius and he now acts for Laubscher. Don't you think that's odd?"

Hugo Pocock drafted a reply to Taute and Steyn saying that his clients denied pumping water from a tributary of the Moeras River. They merely dammed up a trickle flowing in a ravine and pumped this. He went on to say that his clients as riparian owners of the Saffraan River intend claiming their rightful share of the normal stream of that river for primary and secondary purposes, and asked for a suitable date for discussion.

Friday 22 January 1954

Taute and Steyn finally responded to Pocock and Bailey's letter of December 11. They asserted that the water had already been apportioned. If Ellis were to dam up any of the ravines leading into the Saffraan River, legal proceedings would be instituted against him. By the time the letter reached Pocock and Bailey, Taute and Steyn learnt that a formal application to institute proceedings had been submitted to the Water Court.

Jane was in Oudtshoorn for her summer vacation. She had completed her Bachelor of Arts degree with majors in Roman Law and Latin and was busy doing her Bachelor of Laws degree. When her father arrived from the farm early on Saturday morning she had been waiting for him in the garden. She embraced Douglas. 'You must be excited now that it's really happening, Dad?'

He frowned.

"I mean the court case."

"Oh that, yes. The easy part is over. The difficult part lies ahead."

"What happens now?"

"Laubscher's people will enter a counterplea, and you can bet that they will claim prescription and that the Ellises or their predecessors abandoned their rights. Then there will be the customary requests for further particulars by both parties and things will drag on and on for a while. Both parties will want to know as much as possible about the intentions of the other side."

"Is Alwyn Burger a good advocate?"

"I think so. His argument is intriguing."

"Why do you say that? Come let us go inside. Ma wants to see you."

"He says if Laubscher claims prescription, the case will go the Ellises' way, because there was no adverse act upon which prescription can be based. You cannot just tell someone not to do a certain thing and then say that such an instruction is an adverse act."

"What is the relevance of an adverse act in this case?"

"As I am sure you know, Jane, for prescription to occur in our law there must be an 'adverse act.' Burger's argument is that there was no 'adverse act' in the Roman Legal sense on the part of Laubscher or his predecessors in title. Laubscher, and before him Olivier only received the water not used by the people above him. They never went onto the property above them and took water. Therefore to claim that the Ellises and their predecessors in title allowed their right to prescribe by not using the water is nonsense. And we don't know whether they used water or not. Furthermore Laubscher claims that the Ellises abandoned their rights to the water. The abandonment of rights is never implied and must be strongly proved. So you see we have a good case. And by the way, the adverse act has to be *nec vi, nec clam, nec precario*. The old Romans were pretty smart if you think about it. Just think about all the subtle implications of *nec vi, nec clam, nec precario* in this context."

Monday 1 November 1954

The hearing in the Water Court was the beginning of what was eventually to become known as the Ellis v. Laubscher case. The Court was presided over by Mr Justice C G Hall who was assisted by two assessors.

Douglas accompanied the Ellis brothers to court and sat close to them and their legal team. He positioned himself so that he could lip read what the witnesses, the judge and the advocates were saying.

Advocate Burger outlined the nature of the Application by C J Ellis and Others.

In his plea on behalf of the respondent, Advocate P Wessels Q.C. presented four defences. They were: that the predecessors in title of the applicants neglected to claim a portion of the water when they entered into the Notarial Agreement and by doing so abandoned their rights; that Cornelius Ellis senior abandoned his rights in terms of two letters written by his attorney and the attorney of the respondent in 1942; that the respondent and his predecessors in title obtained the water that the applicants were now claiming by prescription; that all the water from the Saffraan River was allocated in terms of the Notarial Deed of 1906 to the respondent's predecessor, J S Olivier.

Tuesday 2 November 1954

Douglas stayed with his mother and Maggie while the hearing was in progress. Jane had completed her end-of-the-year examinations and had started her summer vacation. It was clear to Mrs van Yssen that Douglas had become so involved in the case that his preoccupation had turned into an obsession. When they had supper that evening she asked him how things were progressing.

"Oh, the hearing was concluded today," he said.

"How does is look to you?" She asked.

"I have an uneasy feeling about the judge. He appears to have made up his mind. I think it was made up before he came here, on the basis of the written submissions. He's a difficult old chap, was very rude to Advocate Burger.

"It was clear to me from the first time that I read the old 1906 agreement that there was no specific allocation of water to Laubscher's predecessor, merely an obligation on him to let water go to the lower owners for eight days in each twenty one day cycle. Advocate Burger stressed the point again in his closing argument. Yet the judge, if I consider his cross examination of Laubscher – he even asked Laubscher whether he thought he had a turn of thirteen days – it seems to me that his view of the terms of the agreement is inconsistent with the facts. The evidence about the letter Steyn wrote is most damning and yet he seems to treat it quite casually. That evidence goes to the heart of Steyn's credibility."

"Is the case then not largely about the Notarial Contract?" Maggie asked.

"You've become so smart, Maggie, that it pleases me," Douglas said. "Interpretation of the Notarial Deed is crucial, but what lawyers do is to attack on as many fronts as possible, and to defend as widely as possible. So Laubscher's lawyer is saying that even if we are correct in the way we interpret the Contract, there is another good reason why the Ellises should not have water. Laubscher's team are saying that because the Ellises did not use the water from the Saffraan River for more than thirty years, their right to water has prescribed."

"Eat your food Douglas, it is getting cold," his mother said.

"The food is good, Ma." He patted Jane on her thigh. "And how is my girl?"

"I would like to come to the farm. Did you enjoy the proceedings?"

"From a theatrical point of view, yes. I followed most of what was said. It is amazing how treacherous people can be. The first witness for Laubscher, a Mr Mayer, could recall every word that Laubscher's predecessor Olivier said to him in 1910. What a memory! Then when Advocate Burger cross examined him he said he did not even know that the Ellises had land that straddles the Saffraan River. And then there was a matter of a letter that Steyn claims he wrote on behalf of old Cornelius Ellis. There was no copy of the letter in court and according to Foster, who acted for Laubscher at the time, the letter had been altered by hand. The typewritten word 'withdrawn' was replaced by the word 'abandon' presumably to give it stronger legal import. According to the evidence that was led, it was quite impossible for old Cornelius to have given Steyn any instructions at the time because Cornelius was unconscious and never regained consciousness."

Judgement was delivered on Tuesday December 7, 1954. Judge Hall ruled in favour of the Respondent, Laubscher, and awarded all costs to the Respondent. The Ellis brothers had lost their case, and had to pay costs that they could ill afford.

Wednesday 8 December 1954

The elder two Ellis brothers and Douglas met with Hugo Pocock at the offices of Pocock and Bailey. The atmosphere in Pocock's office was thick with resentment. Cornelius could not look anyone in the eye. Douglas felt sick. Pocock moved about uneasily in his brown padded chair, his body made the apologetic movements of someone who had never really believed in the merits of the case. Yet he had hoped against hope.

Douglas broke the uneasy silence. "I think it was a very poor judgement. Hall did not deal correctly with any of the points that Advocate Burger made. His interpretation of the Notarial Contract is erroneous. What he said about prescription is shallow. There's but one, little quoted case. He has completely missed my point about prescription."

"That might well be so, but we have lost the case and will have to pay for a lost case, and for rich Mr Laubscher's victory." Cornelius replied.

"We should never have lost the case," Douglas said.

Douglas held up his hand. "We should appeal. The judgement is really very poorly reasoned. Then there is Mr Burger's point about prescription. He did not grasp at all what was said about a negative servitude. It was beyond him. This whole thing is bullshit. It is a travesty."

"*Wat is 'n* travesty?" Izak asked.

"To put it bluntly, a shit representation of what is right," Douglas said.

"What happens if we appeal? If we win will we get our money back?" Izak asked.

"It is possible," Douglas said.

"Not for sure?"

"Nothing is ever sure in the law. Let's go over some of the points," Douglas suggested. "Take the way Hall dealt with the Rider. He reasons that the absence of a Rider in the case of the Saffraan River indicates acceptance by your predecessors in title, Izak, that Olivier had been given all the water. The mind boggles. In the case of the Moeras River there was a need for the Rider, precisely because the Notarial Contract did not divide the water from the Moeras River among the upper owners, *inter se*. Why the upper owners along the Saffraan River did not enter into an agreement among themselves, we shall never know – perhaps because they did not know that your predecessors had land there. The fact that they did not do so proves nothing. As Advocate Burger has pointed out, abandonment of a right has to be clearly proved and to argue that failure to enter into an agreement proves abandonment is sheer nonsense. A waiver is never presumed. It has to be proved. The respondent did not do that.

"Then there is the letter of October 1, 1942. Hall declined to deal with that. It sticks out like a dog's ball that Steyn and Laubscher connived – Hall ignores that. Why if Laubscher's case was so strong, was there a need to manufacture a letter like that? And remember that Steyn said he would consult the doctor and bring evidence to show that Oom Cornelius was *compos mentis* at the time before his death. He never did bring that evidence and once again Hall ignored it. He makes no mention of the uncontested evidence that Laubscher wanted to give the Ellises two days of water.

"Hall says that Wessels made no claim that Laubscher had acquired a right by prescription. That is a patent contradiction. On the second page of the judgement, Hall outlines the Respondent's plea. Please pass me your copy of the judgement Hugo. Yes, here in point 'c' 'that the Respondent and his predecessors in title acquired all the water that the Applicants now claim, by prescription.' On page fourteen of the judgement Hall says, here at the bottom of the page, 'the Respondent does not claim a right by prescription'. He cannot write a proper judgement…"

"I never knew a judge could make a mistake," Izak remarked.

Pocock smiled. "*Hulle is ook maar mense.* We all make mistakes. Mr van Yssen has said what had to be said."

Douglas had the bit between his teeth. "This is an unusual matter, namely the acquisition of a negative servitude by prescription. It is very complex legally. Unless a judge is capable of grasping Advocate Burger's point we will never win this case. That is the bad news. The good news is that a higher court is more likely to grasp the point. I think we should appeal."

Cornelius turned to Hugo Pocock. "Do you think we have a chance?"

"You should not ask me Cornelius, we should ask Mr Burger. It is a great disappointment to me that we lost. What Douglas says is correct. I think that the judge's interpretation of the Notarial Deed is incorrect. If a superior court were to agree on that, the case will turn on prescription. Of that I am sure. I am convinced that the advocate's view of prescription is correct. If we were to be given the chance I am sure he will prove that it is correct. At the same time I have a great responsibility towards you. I know how hard life is on a farm. I know that you don't have money to waste."

"It a matter of principle with us. We will discuss it and let you know," Cornelius said.

"It is a matter of principle, but we also need the water up there. We should appeal," Izak said.

"We have to speak to Martinus, Izak."

"Mr Pocock, we'll speak to Martinus. Let us have a few days; we'll come back to you. We appreciate all you have done for us."

Saturday 11 December 1954

Cornelius, Izak and Martinus arrived at Douglas' farm at eleven in the morning. Douglas had been bracing himself for the worst, and was relieved to find the Ellises in good spirits. They went to the dining room. Douglas had closed the shutters to keep the heat out.

It was clear that the Ellises had made up their minds. Cornelius was the first to speak. "What do you think we ought to do, Douglas?" Douglas passed him the writing pad.

When Cornelius started to write Douglas stopped him. "No, I understood what you said. That is there just in case we get into some tricky stuff. You want to know what I think? I have hardly slept at all since the judgement. The more I think about it the more dismayed I am at what Hall said. I have read it again and again. When I think of the attitude he adopted in court, how arrogant and rude he was, how courteously he treated Laubscher and abrupt he was towards us and Advocate Burger. He did not give the matter proper thought. That is the kindest thing I can say. Most important is: what do you think?"

"We think you should decide," Izak said.

Douglas threw his hands up. "Easy now, easy now, you can't do that to me. It is not my money."

"That's why we want you to decide. You're the only one who's impartial. The others will all benefit financially," Cornelius said.

"You're placing too much responsibility on me. I don't think that is fair."

"We trust your judgement. You are very clever." Izak replied. "Tell us what you think."

"What do you think?"

"We're playing games," Cornelius said.

"I think you should appeal."

"Then it will be so," Cornelius announced.

An appeal was noted on April 4, 1955. The appeal was heard in the Cape Provincial Division of the Supreme Court by three judges, Hall (who was no relation to the Judge C G Hall who presided over the Water Court at Oudtshoorn), van Winsen and van Wyk.

On January 5, 1956 the appeal was dismissed with costs. Douglas and the Ellis brothers were in the depths of despair.

After he had won his case in the Water Court, Laubscher strutted about the district and the streets of Oudtshoorn, larger than life, crowing. Whenever he could, he referred to the case. He boasted how he had enjoyed the drama and how he did not even have pay for all the entertainment. He preened himself in the Central Café, and regaled the willing, feeding their ears succulent morsels. How this one had said that, how his advocate had tripped up the witnesses for the other side. How Judge Hall had turned to him towards the end of the first hearing, to him, mind you, and asked him the questions that eventually settled the whole thing. What a stupid bunch the Ellises were, led by the nose by van Yssen who was far too damn smart for his own good. That they could have thought that they had a chance against a man like him. Bah! And they did not learn their lesson the first time round; they had to appeal to the Supreme Court in Cape Town and got another bloody nose, and had to pay again.

It was with incredulous mirth that Laubscher learnt that the Ellises had decided to take the ultimate step – to appeal again – this time to the highest court in the land, the Appeal Court in Bloemfontein. They must have lost their senses. If they thought the first two times were expensive, they had a thing coming in the Appeal Court.

Advocate Burger felt that a Queen's Council should handle the Appeal Court case, and in order to save costs, he unselfishly chose to play a lesser role. Burger decided to approach Advocate D P de Villiers, Q C. Burger believed passionately that his view of prescription was correct, and if his view could be presented to jurists with sufficient insight, the Ellises would triumph. In van Yssen, Burger had a wonderful ally. Van Yssen had grasped Burger's reasoning from the beginning, and he was able to convince the Ellises to proceed. De Villiers was a man of formidable intellect and when Burger outlined the facts of the case, and his view of prescription, de Villiers was immediately of the same mind as Burger.

Before the Appeal Court case began in earnest, Burger wanted to ensure that every possible contingency was covered and sought every possible reference source that could have a bearing on the legal aspects of the case. The Law Reports were searched; all cases in which precedents could be found were listed. Erskine's *Law of Scotland*, Angell's *Water Courses*, Farnham's *Water and Water Rights* were used as references. Sohm's *Institutes of Roman Law*, the *Corpus Juris Civilis*, and importantly, the medieval glossa of certain glossators on the *Corpus Juris*. Roman Dutch sources were scoured: Modderdam's *Romeinsch Recht*; Hunter's *Roman Law*; the works of the Roman Dutch authority Voet van Leeuwen, *Censura Forensis*.

Douglas translated previously untranslated Latin passages of Voet's work. He also translated relevant parts of commentaries by medieval glossators, and some of the work of Caepolla. He found that certain glossators in their glossa on the *Corpus Juris* argued that there was a possible basis for the acquisition of a negative servitude by means of a *praescriptio longi temporis*. Their reasoning was apparently founded in certain Roman remedies such as a specific interdict. Although the glossators, supported by Caepolla set a basis that would solve some of the difficulties attached to negative servitudes, it became clear that even in Roman-Dutch practice such a basis no longer embraced a practical possibility of the acquisition of a negative servitude by prescription. This was because of the essential connection between that basis and the Roman forms of process. Douglas spent countless hours doing translations. He also examined the translations of others. A case in point was Gane's translation of Voet. A phrase that Gane translated as 'has by giving notice in regard to the new work interfered with the work begun' read as follows in the original: *operi coepto intercesserit operas novi nunciatione facta.* Douglas felt that the translation was incorrect and needed explanation, because '*nunciatio operis novi*' had a specialised meaning which could not be conveyed by the words 'notice in regard to the new work.' In the old law '*nunciatio operis novi*' meant much more than merely 'giving notice in regard to new work.' Douglas found that Voet corroborated this view by setting out precisely in which circumstances the *nunciatio* could be applied to have the full power of an interdict as opposed to a mere warning by one party.

Douglas sent his translations and his commentary to Advocate Burger who in turn made them available to Advocate de Villiers who used Douglas' work as part of his written submission to the Appellate Division.

The case was heard in the Appellate Division of the Supreme Court in 1956. On the bench were: Centlivres, Chief Justice; Fagan, Judge of Appeal; de Beer, Judge of Appeal; de Villiers, Judge of Appeal; Beyers, Judge of Appeal.

Judgement was delivered on September 28, 1956. The case is reported in the *South African Law Reports*. It is of interest that several of the critical issues revealed by Douglas' research were pivotal to the Court's findings.

In his concluding paragraphs Judge Fagan said, 'I am also of the opinion that the mere assertion by one party that another party has not got certain rights, or that he forbids the other to exercise such rights, even though the other may also acquiesce therein, is not an adverse act whereon a claim of prescription can be based.'

'Also the respondent's second plea must therefore be rejected and the Judgement must be: The appeal succeeds with costs, both in this Court and the Provincial Court; the Judgement in the Water Court is set aside; and the matter is referred back to the Water Court for implementation.'

Centlivres, Chief Justice de Beer, Judge of Appeal and Beyers, Judge of Appeal, concurred in the judgement.

There was one dissenting view. Although de Villiers, Judge of Appeal, concurred that the plea of prescription, and the abandonment of rights by the appellants' predecessors in title were without foundation, he said he found it difficult to reject the respondent's plea based on the Notarial Deed of May 1906.

The Ellises had won their case with costs in the highest court of the land, presided over by a bench of unusual strength. The case, which became known as *Ellis and others* v. *Laubscher* became a landmark in South African law.

The extent of Douglas van Yssen's contribution to the ultimate success cannot be gauged precisely. Alwyn Burger, the young advocate who had handled the case on behalf of the Ellises in the Water Court, had virtually worked pro deo, so had Hugo Pocock the instructing attorney in Oudtshoorn. Alwyn Burger, after practising as a highly successful advocate, who specialised in riparian matters, became a judge in the Provincial Division of the Supreme Court in Cape Town. Judge Burger is now retired and lives in a small town in South Africa. He is regarded as a world authority on riparian law.

Judge Burger believes that Douglas van Yssen's contribution to the *Ellis v. Laubscher* case was invaluable. Douglas was able to grasp the intricate legal point on prescription that Burger had raised at the outset. Douglas' conviction that Burger was right persuaded him to encourage the Ellises to persevere against all odds.

A Settlement Agreement was drawn up between the Ellis brothers and Laubscher and was to be made an Order of Court at the sitting of the Water Court on May 29, 1957.

In recognition of the contribution that Douglas van Yssen had made to the ultimate success of the case, Advocate Burger wrote to him and invited him to attend the sitting of the Water Court on May 29. Douglas replied and thanked Advocate Burger for the invitation. He said that he regrettably had to decline and would not be able to attend because he could not afford a suitable bow tie for the occasion.

Chapter Forty-seven

Friday 21 October 1956

JUDGE ROSE and Mrs Rose had for some years slept in separate bedrooms. Punctually at seven in the morning the new maid gently knocked on the Judge's bedroom door, hesitated for a moment, and opened it. She carried in a silver tray with tea and water biscuits. A copy of the *Cape Times*, that she had ironed to ensure it had no displeasing wrinkles, lay neatly folded on one side of the tray. She drew the curtains aside to let early summer light into the room.

The Judge had been awake for a while and watched tortoise-like as she moved about. Not a bad figure. It was a pity that Hope and Gladys had to retire, and Doyle. They don't make servants like that any more. He wondered what his wife had got him for his birthday. "Thank you, Daisy," he said.

"Happy birthday, Sir. Is there anything else you need?"

"No thank you, I'll be fine."

He heaved the bedclothes to one side so that he could get himself upright and sit on the edge of the bed. He moved with difficulty. He had lost some weight recently. He yawned. He ran his hand over the white stubble on his face from which all colour had been leached. His mouth did not taste too good. He looked at his long slender feet. They were deathly white. His yellow bony toenails were too long. Would Frances telephone? It would be nice to hear her voice on his birthday. She no longer telephoned him on his birthday. It was nearly thirty years now that she had kept to herself. A barren spinster in Graaff Reinet. He looked at the back of his hand. The skin had become translucent and fragile, sprinkled with flowers of death, the veins a sluggish blue. He stood up stiffly and put on his red dressing gown in the same way he used to don his robes before entering his court. His carpet slippers stood ready. He sat down at the table on which the tea tray stood, and unfolded the newspaper.

He poured his tea with a trembling wrist. Confound old age, damnable curse it is. Good tea the new girl makes. She has a touch. He looked out of the window. It promised to be a fine day, if a bit windy, judging by the way the sash window rattled in the night. There was a knock at the door. "Come in," he called.

It was Mrs Rose, in her dressing gown. "Happy birthday, Jeremy. Here, I have got you a little thing or two." She handed him a small gift-wrapped package. "You've been in need of a new shaving brush." She handed him a larger parcel, "Your favourite cigars, and I thought a new tie to wear when you next go out. There you are!" She kissed him on his cheek. "I will run your bath presently. Daisy is making a scrumptious breakfast for the two of us."

"Thank you, dear, how thoughtful of you. Remember I am going to the club for lunch, so I won't eat too much now."

"It is your birthday dear, you must do exactly as you please. Except that I should remind you that James and Ethel are coming for dinner this evening."

"Yes, I do remember. Sit with me and have some tea. I wonder whether Frances will ring?"

"She probably will dear, she knows it is your eightieth birthday. I spoke to her earlier in the week."

"How is she?"

"As always. It is strange to think that she is fifty-two."

"Yes it is. I sometimes regret the way things have turned out. I sometimes regret what I said, but it had to be said. It is a pity that Frances took it so badly. Van Yssen was a loser. He did not deserve her. Married to some shop assistant woman because she became pregnant. Living, or should I say existing, on a little farm on the slopes of a mountain. I bumped into Foxie Hall, a little more than a year ago. I never mentioned it to you. He had some time earlier presided over a riparian case in Oudtshoorn, that citadel of riparian disputes. He spoke of a deaf man who sat with the instructing attorney and the advocate who acted for the applicants. They kept exchanging notes. The way he described the man it could have been van Yssen. I asked Foxie what he thought van Yssen was doing there, and he said he understood he was a friend of the applicants, and advising them. What a confounded joke. What would he know of the intricacies of riparian law!"

"He is a clever man Jeremy, there's no gainsaying that. You said so yourself; you often remarked on that. Don't you remember the holidays at the seaside; those conversations that you and Douglas had? How excited you were that Frances had such a companion?"

"Don't call him Douglas, it is too familiar."

"I sometimes still think fondly of him. He was so handsome and so athletic. I thought he was handsome and you thought he was very clever. How things have changed. Poor Frances."

"Well, I suppose I had better have my bath then, if you would oblige, Elizabeth."

At a quarter past twelve the Judge's chauffeur, Johnstone, announced to Daisy that it was time for him to take the Judge to the Civil Service Club. Daisy found Judge Rose dozing in a chair in his study, a *Law Report* open on his lap, his mouth at an odd angle, a small rivulet of thin saliva making its way along a fissure that ran from the corner of his mouth. She spoke to him. He did not respond. She thought he was dead. He snorted when she touched his arm, and sat up.

"Oh my goodness, I must have fallen asleep. What time is it? Am I late?"

"No, you are not late, Sir. Johnstone is here for you."

"Ah, good man. Tell him I will be with him presently. I need to go and see a man about a horse. Just give me a hand, to get up. And fetch my stick, if you will."

Daisy helped the Judge into the back of the car. There was a green, red and blue woollen tartan rug on the back seat of the Bentley. She pushed it aside and made sure the Judge's feet were in the car before she shut the door. Johnstone gave her a wink. He was a handsome rogue. She liked him, even though he was married.

Johnstone parked the car in a loading zone outside the Civil Service Club in Queen Victoria Street. He helped Judge Rose from the car, gathered his stick, and assisted him to the front door. The concierge took over from there. Judge Rose turned uncomfortably, "Remember to fetch me at three, Johnstone. I need to have a nap before this evening." The concierge offered his arm and the Judge took it. He shuffled towards the lift, drawing himself along with his bony shoulders, his head bent forward. They stood for a moment, waiting for the lift to arrive. The lift was in an open shaft. Its inside had dark wooden panels. Access was through an expanding and contracting sliding metal door. A revolving brass hand allowed the operator to drive the lift up and down. The Judge was put inside.

"Good afternoon Judge," the Malay operator, in navy blue serge uniform with bright red piping, said. "It looks as though the south-easter is coming up."

"Thank you Suleiman. Yes, we can expect wind."

They nearly overshot the first floor, and stopped so abruptly that the Judge felt light-headed for a moment. The maitre d' helped the Judge from the lift and assisted him to an easy chair where he would have his gin. There were already a few patrons at the club – newspaper people, glasses in hand, in animated conversation, and members of the legal fraternity.

His gin and tonic water arrived. He took a little sip to make sure that the proportions were right. First things first. He put his glass down and looked about. No contemporaries. They had all gone, somewhere. Wherever people go. He would soon find out. The gin was good. Kept him going all those years. He heard the lift arriving, and the clattering of its metal door. Some voices. Damn loud people were at clubs these days. They were people from the Bar. Advocate de Villiers, bright fellow he was, and Advocate Greyvenstein. They were in animated discussion, and clearly in a jolly mood.

The Judge had been invited to lunch by Basil Wainwright. He had retired as editor of the *Cape Times* some years earlier. The Judge looked at his watch. Wainwright was late. He wondered what de Villiers and his companion were talking about. He heard the sounds of motor traffic and car hooters in the distance. He had some gin and tried to hear what de Villiers was saying. More people had arrived and their sounds drowned de Villiers' voice. The lift opened. Two senior British naval officers emerged. Still no Wainwright. A waiter arrived and asked the Judge whether he would like to see a menu. He said he would rather wait and look at it at the table. At last Wainwright rushed in, hat in hand. "I'm so sorry Jeremy. I could not find a parking space. There's so much traffic these days. Oh, and a very happy birthday to you. I have brought you some cigars."

"Thank you, old boy. That's kind of you. Thank you for inviting me. Good chum you've been to me. Come and sit down, there's no need to hurry. Let's order you a drink. The usual?"

"Yes, that would be fine, thank you." Wainwright sat down.

"Tell me Basil, you know everybody and everything that goes on, who's that fellow with de Villiers, over there?"

"I don't know him. All I know is that de Villiers is celebrating."

"Celebrating? Celebrating what?"

"He won an appeal, in the Appeal Court, after the case was twice turned down: first in the Water Court and then here, in the Provincial Division, in January this year. The reason I know about it is because I happened to bump into Jack Brokensha, you must remember him, our former news editor, just the other day. He heard about it from that chap Blewett, who used to cover the courts. Blewett had heard about it in the Café Royal, you know how news travels. Well, anyway, what Brokensha told me was that was the second appeal that Foxie Hall has lost. And word is that he is smarting from it."

"Do you know where the Water Court matter was heard?"

"I am not sure, I think he said Oudtshoorn."

"That's odd, because Foxie told me a while ago, in fact just more than a year ago, that he had heard a case in Oudtshoorn." Judge Rose lent forward and lowered his voice. "He said a strange thing to me. I mentioned it to Elizabeth only this morning. He said there was a fellow in court, sitting with the applicants in the case, and their legal team. The fellow was deaf, and kept on swapping notes with the applicants. You must remember van Yssen?"

"Of course I do."

"I didn't have the courage to ask Foxie if he knew who the fellow was, but I wondered whether it could have been van Yssen. It nagged at me. I can't imagine what he was doing in court. He ended up on that little farm after the engagement was broken off. I never saw him again. He got some girl pregnant. I never told you about that. He turned out to be a real bounder."

Wainwright looked in de Villiers' direction. "He's a bright fellow, that."

"I'm no longer so sure that van Yssen was that bright."

"No, I mean David de Villiers." Wainwright looked up again. De Villiers nodded to him. Wainwright smiled. De Villiers excused himself from his companion and walked over to Wainwright. "Hello David, you know Judge Rose."

"Good afternoon Judge."

Rose nodded in acknowledgement. "Basil tells me you have reason to celebrate?"

De Villiers smiled his tall boyish bespectacled smile. His modesty became him.

"Pray tell us what it is all about," the Judge persisted.

"According to the grapevine you won an appeal, David," Wainwright prompted.

"I suppose one sometimes has a bit of luck."

"What was it about?" Rose asked.

"One of those tricky riparian matters. This one was more tricky than most."

"Basil says that it began in Oudtshoorn?"

"Yes, it did," de Villiers replied.

"Basil says the case was lost in the Water Court?"

"Yes, and the applicants appealed here in the Supreme Court, and lost that too. That's how it ended up in the Appellate Division."

"That sounds unusual," Rose remarked.

"It was an unusual case, Judge Rose, most unusual, to tell the truth."

"Tell me about it. It is my birthday today."

"Well, many happy returns. May you have many more."

"I'm not so sure that I will have many more. Why don't you ask your friend to join us for a drink and tell me about the case? I'm cut off from so much these days. And my eyes are not what they used to be. I would like to hear about the case."

De Villiers beckoned to Greyvenstein and introduced him. They sat down. A waiter took the drinks order.

"So you say it was unusual, eh?"

"Yes it was," de Villiers responded.

"How did it start?" Wainright asked.

"As these things always start. Two neighbours quarrelling about the division of water. On the one side were three brothers who were practically penniless. On the other side a wealthy arrogant farmer, Chairman of the Divisional Council.

"Sounds like a melodrama to me," Judge Rose sniggered.

"The brothers, and their father before them, had approached their neighbour several times with a request for an equitable division of water from a river that flowed first through their land and then through the neighbour's land, and each time the neighbour refused. So they took him to the Water Court. Judge Foxie Hall ruled against the applicants, and awarded costs against them. The three penniless brothers have a neighbour, a chap called van Yssen, an historian and Latin scholar. I met him. He's a strange chap. He is as deaf as a stone."

"What did he have to do with the case?" Judge Rose asked.

"I will come to that in a moment, Judge, because that is what makes the whole thing so unusual. First there was the original architect of the legal aspects of the case, Advocate Alwyn Burger. The respondent's counsel Advocate Wessels held out prescription as one of his defences. Burger realised that Wessels was mistaken. Burger was intelligent enough to understand why prescription was not possible under our law in the case concerned. Most of the credit must go to Alwyn Burger. He handled the case in the Water Court, and the subsequent appeal."

"Who is this chap Burger, to go up against a QC?"

"He is a young advocate who is making a name for himself in riparian law."

"What was the point he made?" Rose asked.

"The respondent in the original case relied on the prescription of a negative servitude. And, as I said, Burger's argument was that it is not possible under our law. And that was confirmed by the Appellate Division. For what it is worth, although the applicants appealed against Judge Hall's finding, the Provincial Division dismissed the appeal. To be fair, we had quite a lot of help from the van Yssen fellow. Greyvenstein and I were just talking about that now when I saw Mr Wainwright. Van Yssen is an interesting chap. He was quite obsessed with the case. He spent countless hours doing research for us, translating Voet that had not been translated before, finding errors in Gane's translations, translating commentaries by medieval glossators. He prepared an entire piece for me which formed part of my submission. He did absolutely extraordinary work. We would never have got to the Appeal Court without him. He was bright enough to grasp Burger's point right at the outset, and came to believe in it. As I mentioned he is a neighbour of the appellants and he encouraged them to continue with the case when all seemed lost. It is strange to think that there could be a person like that, stuck away in the mountains on a small farm. One wonders what could have become of such a man if he had not become deaf."

Judge Rose sat passively, his face white as a sheet.

"What did you say the chap's name was?" Wainwright asked.

"Douglas van Yssen."

The Judge's hand began to shake so that he had to put his glass down.

"What a story, David, my heartiest congratulations to you," Wainwright said.

"Without being too philosophical about it, without being too serious on your birthday, Judge, I have thought much about the outcome of the case. It seems to me that for a really great judgement to be formulated there has to be an extraordinary meeting of great minds, like the planets coming together for a special cosmic event. It is amazing how well this case illustrates that. Some people may think that when the planets come together it is a coincidence. It is not. You see, Burger grasped an essential point, van Yssen was intelligent enough to understand that, and then there was Judge Fagan. With great respect, Judge Hall could not understand Burger's argument – you only have to read Judge Hall's judgement to see how shallow his reasoning was, especially if you compare his judgement with Judge Fagan's judgement. Those who presided over the Divisional Court also did not grasp the point. But as soon as Judge Fagan heard the point I made, he immediately knew what Burger was driving at. That's what I mean by a meeting of the minds. It is such an event that creates new law."

Judge Rose's head was trembling and he looked fearfully at de Villiers through old rheumy eyes.

"I hope you enjoy your lunch Judge, and you Mr Wainwright." De Villiers and Greyvenstein got up and went to their table.

Judge Rose ate very little, and said even less. He had shrunk since Wainwright arrived. Wainwright and the concierge had to help him into his car. When he arrived home Johnstone and Daisy assisted him to his room, and helped him onto his bed. They took off his shoes and made him comfortable. Johnstone left to fetch Mrs Rose from Garlicks and Daisy stayed with the Judge. She offered him something to drink but he shook his head.

Johnstone told Mrs Rose that he feared the Judge was not well and took her directly home. She found him on his bed and asked him what the matter was.

"I need to sleep," he whispered hoarsely. "I will tell you later. Thank you for coming. Has Frances telephoned?"

"She will probably ring this evening, dear. How was your lunch?"

He just shook his head and looked away as though he had seen something frightening hidden inside himself.

◆

Chapter Forty-Eight

AFTER HER SEPARATION from her father, Frances never again went to Plettenberg Bay in the December holidays. When she did not go overseas to spend Christmas with her friends Florrie and Jeremy Borcherds, she mostly spent it with her uncle James Sterling. And so it was in 1956. She wrote to her mother to inform her of her plans and said that her mother would be welcome to visit her when in Klein Drakenstein.

Frances had become Vice Principal of Union High. The school closed on Friday December 7. The following morning Frances had a brief discussion with the Headmaster, and went to her classroom to tidy her desk. All that remained was to wait for the matric results.

On Sunday morning she had a bath, chose an attractive dress, groomed herself and went to the early church service. Afterwards she had a leisurely breakfast prepared by Hope, now a widow and employed by Frances. While she ate she listened to a recording of Beethoven's Fifth Symphony by the Boston Symphony Orchestra, conducted by Charles Munch. It was surely her most favourite piece of music. The opening three quick G's and the lingering E. Diddidy dum – 'Fate knocking at the door.' As always, the symphony was an expressive emotional journey; a journey that never failed to produce a catharsis. The focus of her consciousness shifted as she listened. Her thoughts and emotions drifted on top of the music. She thought of the reaction to the music of Helen Schlegel in Howards End, she thought of E M Forster and the Bloomsbury group. Forster knew Virginia Woolf and the others and Lytton Strachey whom her father disliked so much. She felt the resentful energy of the early part of the music.

The horns signalled hints of triumph. It was a sunny day. She looked through a large sash window at the summer green leaves of the trees in her orchard. Peaches and ripening apricots were visible. The irrigation furrows leading to the orchard were still damp. On the wooden floor her grey striped cat lay asleep in a rectangle of sunlight. His one foot twitched as he dreamt. She glanced at the material of her dress across her thighs, its pastel orange and blue reflections of the colours in the orchard and the sky and repeated in the Persian carpet. Hope wandered from tree to tree selecting fruit for her journey. Frances relished a fleshy piece of bacon and a small portion of fried banana that she had kept for last. The bold music inspired her. She was aware of sounds of individual instruments. The variations woven together by dual themes. "Yet a single motif permeates the entire work." Douglas was still the single motif that permeated her whole life.

The first movement was so charged with energy; grim conflict, and yet it offered hope. Someone once spoke of hope swirling through a relentless storm. She buttered a piece of toast and heaped marmalade onto it. She poured tea. Nice combination tea and marmalade. She was experiencing various forms of satisfactions made more intense as the tea heightened her awareness. Without warning the dynamics of the first movement began to change. The original key changed several times. Beethoven also started going deaf in his twenties, and like Douglas, had ringing in his ears.

She never knew what to make of the second movement; it was so unlike the first. Gentle but still with recurring hints of triumph. Beethoven too, was indecisive romantically. But he had resolve. She had loved Douglas despite his lack of resolve. "Mr Ramsay who got as far as 'Q'. 'Z' is only reached by one man in a generation." Douglas could have reached 'Z.' The tea was particularly fragrant. She visualized the road stretching before her. Must make sure the tyres are properly inflated.

The third movement returned a theme similar to the first. She had more tea and began to perspire. She was aware of the way her attention wandered and changed. How the music came and went. Her surging thoughts bestowed qualities on the music that the composer had never intended. She loved the last movement – in allegro – the entire orchestra; all the themes have a victorious air, mostly in major keys. Her most deferential emotions soared. She was not in mood to seek the spiritual today. She would indulge herself in uncluttered feelings and would not allow anything lofty to spoil it. Did the triumph express Beethoven's realization that the spirit will always triumph over the material, that his deafness was no handicap to his talent? She owed Anneke a letter.

When the music ended Frances sat for a while before she lifted the stylus from the record. The house was silent. She heard the back door open. Hope was no longer in the garden. Her fruit trees reminded her of *The Cherry Orchard* and she thought of her production of *The Three Sisters* for the amateur dramatic society. She had enjoyed directing the play, and taking the part of Olga the school teacher. She chuckled at the thought of how she had pressed some of the male teachers into taking the parts of the Russian soldiers and of how self conscious they had been on stage in their ill-fitting uniforms. But as time went on they grew into their parts and enjoyed themselves. It was an ambitious project and she had tried to show parallels between Chekhov's society and circumstances in Graaff Reinet. But alas, the response had been dull and the subtleties of the play fully not understood, except by a few. Her colleague, Miss Smithers, said it was excellent and that pleased her. She would try something else next year. A nice jolly Moliere farce with a bit of naughtiness.

Frances left Graaff Reinet at five o'clock the next morning. She enjoyed motoring and had purchased a new Morris Minor earlier in the year. As she had done on many occasions she arranged to stay over in Mossel Bay to be near the sea after the dry Karoo. From there her way would take her to Swellendam and then on to Worcester and Klein Drakenstein. She reached Aberdeen sooner than expected. She looked at her watch – less than an hour. Two hours later, just before eight o'clock, she reached Willowmore and decided to stop for breakfast at the hotel. She examined her road map while she waited for her meal to arrive. A strange desire to see Oudtshoorn took hold of her and she had no difficulty persuading herself that the journey to Mossel Bay via De Rust and Oudtshoorn would take no longer than via Uniondale and George. The road from Oudtshoorn to Mossel Bay would take her past Douglas' farm. She had been past there before, out of curiosity, and once she had seen him, or so she thought, with his back to her, standing outside his house with a child on his hip unaware of the passing car. Her eggs and bacon and toast arrived. There were quite a few people in the dining room; must be the school holidays. She could not remember whether she had closed the windows of her car. Never mind. Her food reminded her of the meals she and Douglas had on the train. She straightened her engagement ring and felt sad. What was going to be an unhurried breakfast was altered by her urgency to see Oudtshoorn.

A few miles beyond Ghwarriepoort she turned right and headed for De Rust. The road was not good and in dire need of grading and she had to take great care around the tighter bends. From De Rust the road was in better condition. At eleven thirty she reached Oudtshoorn. Suddenly she was anxious, fearful that she would encounter Anneke van Yssen, or Mrs Jacquard, or worse still, Douglas and Maggie. Fortunately neither Maggie nor Jane knew what she looked like. It was too early for her to be tempted to have lunch and she did not really feel like anything to drink. She stopped outside the Queen's Hotel, locked her car, and went to the ladies' cloakroom. She washed her hands and put cologne on her neck and her temples to cool herself, and combed her hair in the mirror. She studied herself. Why should she be anxious? She was almost disappointed now that she had not seen anyone she knew and in defiance decided to have tea on the veranda. It would only take about an hour and a half to Mossel Bay. She could swim in the sea in the late afternoon. Like they did at Plettenberg Bay. She should have seduced Douglas and got pregnant. She was lost in contemplation when a shadow came over her.

"You look so familiar." A large woman was standing beside her.

Frances looked up and smiled. "Do forgive me, but do I know you?"

"We met once, many years ago. And I shall never forget your face, Miss Rose. I am Mrs Leibner. I was introduced to you by Douglas van Yssen's mother, at the Waldorf Café."

"I have some recollection, although I must say it is faint."

"And what has brought you to town?"

"I am on my way to the Cape."

"Still in Graaff Reinet?"

Frances felt uncomfortable that the woman was so well informed and resented her intrusion. "Yes I am."

"Well, well, it was jolly interesting to meet you again. Shall I give your regards to anyone?"

"Oh, I am quite capable of sending my own regards, thank you." She turned her head and had some tea.

"Well then, I'll get going."

"Good day Mrs Leibner."

Mrs Leibner puffed herself up, straightened her feathers and strutted off on her muscular legs.

Unsettled by Mrs Leibner's intrusion, Frances was at first tempted to abandon her idea of going past Douglas' farm, but the notion that she might see Douglas had taken such a compulsive hold of her that she decided to have something light to eat and further consider what to do.

Mrs Leibner wasted no time heading home. Her husband was attending to a dental patient so she went into the passage and asked the exchange for Anneke van Yssen's number. The woman at the exchange rang repeatedly but there was no reply. She was so agitated, and so angry at the way Frances had dismissed her, that she stamped about her large kitchen huffing and slapping her hips. The servants knew to avoid her when she was like this and that irritated her more. What a wretched disgrace not to be asked to sit down. What an opportunity missed to hear it all from the horse's mouth. Dr Leibner had caught a glimpse of his wife's arrival and having attended to his patient found her taking her hat off in their bedroom. He could tell the state she was in and was first tempted to tease her but thought better of it.

"I found Frances Rose at the Queen's Hotel. I reintroduced myself since she did not remember me, and she was quite short with me."

"The girl Douglas was engaged to?"

"Yes, she still has the ring on her finger. What a disgrace!"

"He treated her badly. You should feel sorry for her."

"Not after the way she snubbed me. I shall tell Anneke. I tried to ring her."

"Rather don't, Antoinette."

But Mrs Leibner's raging frustration persisted.

Frances ordered sandwiches and fresh tea. She ate slowly. She was uncertain about going past Douglas' farm.

When Mrs Leibner rang again Mrs van Yssen answered. "Anneke, you won't believe what happened to me today!" Mrs Leibner was breathless. "I went past the Queen's Hotel earlier, and guess who was sitting on the veranda, cool as a cucumber, having a leisurely tea? You'll never guess!"

"Who?"

"Frances Rose, no less."

"It can't be, Antoinette. Here in Oudtshoorn? Are you sure?"

"How could I ever forget that face? I spoke to her. I addressed her as 'Miss Rose' and she responded. She said she only had a vague recollection of being introduced to me at the Waldorf that time."

"How strange. Did she say where she was going?"

"No. But she must be on her way to Cape Town."

"Douglas was here for the weekend. He is on his way to the farm now, on his bicycle. He left much later than usual because he first had to go to the bank."

By a quarter to one Frances had finished her sandwiches and prepared to leave. At the Mossel Bay signpost she turned towards Douglas' mountains. It was very hot so she left her window half way open, ready to close it against the dust of oncoming cars. There were no clouds over the mountains. She looked forward to swimming at Santos Beach. She thought of Anneke. How she loved her; how she would have loved her as a mother-in-law. She would have been a wonderfully kind grandmother. Now she is someone else's grandmother. It would be nice to meet Douglas' daughter. Anneke said she is smart like her father.

A lorry with farm labourers on the back approached, and she wound her window shut. She could hardly see anything while the dust cleared. She would have to be careful. The road became steeper as she approached the mountains. Trembling heat waves danced above the brown gravel of the road surface. The man on the bicycle ahead of her seemed to float and sway above a mirage. He was bent forward with effort. His hat was pushed down to prevent it from blowing off. She slowed so that she could more easily avoid him should there be more oncoming traffic. The back of his shirt was damp with perspiration. He had on khaki trousers and bicycle clips. As she passed him she glanced to her left. Their eyes met. A shock that made her extremities tingle went through her. It was Douglas, yet it was not. The man she remembered was much younger.

The car left him in a cloud of dust. He stopped, turned his back and held a handkerchief over his face until the dust cleared. When he could see the road again the car had vanished. Had it been an illusion? Was his mind going from the heat? After a while he saw the car going up the next incline. What could Frances be doing here? He involuntarily held up his hand and waved vigorously. The car kept going. He continued waving. In her rear view mirror she saw the man's figure holding his bicycle and his beckoning arm held high. The man who was waving was a stranger. It was not her Douglas. Douglas never had such big ears. Her Douglas standing in the dust at the side of the road holding a bicycle. She felt faint and gripped the steering wheel to steady herself. What would her father have said if he had seen Douglas now? It did not bear thinking. She could never tell her mother. It was better that she had not stopped. It would have destroyed the illusion that had become her reality. Yet she would have loved to look into those eyes. She would have loved to touch him again. She would have flung her arms around him and pressed her face into his damp shirt. Should she turn back? There may never be another opportunity. Would she want to die without touching him just once more? She was shaking. Soon she would pass his house. His empty house. She felt disembodied. A force was compelling her towards the mountain and directing her away from him. She could wait for him at his house. She could welcome him. She could have tea with him. But she might find Jane there, and what would she say to her? He might not like it if she waited for him at his house. But then he did wave to her, he beckoned. She felt uncomfortable having such intimate thoughts about the man on the bicycle. She was close to his house now. If another car passed she would wait for him, if not, she would continue. She needed a sign. She looked for the dust trails of approaching cars as she neared his house. The doors and the windows were closed. There was no life in the little house.

  She continued up into the mountain. When she reached the summit of the Robinson Pass, endless grey-green valleys lay below and in the distant haze she thought she was able to see the sea. It would be dangerous to turn the car around in the narrow pass. It became cooler as she started her descent. It was a relief to experience temperate air. She could not go back now. It would be contrived. The uniqueness of a chance meeting was lost. She passed Eight Bells. It was better this way. She was certain Mrs Leibner would tell Anneke that she had seen her.

It was nearly three when Frances reached Mossel Bay. She drove to the Grand Hotel and was welcomed by the owner, Mr Markowitz. A porter carried her things to her room. She always stayed in the same room. It had an uninterrupted view of the sea. Beyond the sea were the mountains she had crossed. She ordered tea, unpacked what she needed and lay down on the bed. The momentary encounter with Douglas had unsettled her profoundly and was compounded by the disorientation of travelling. Seeing him again closely after so many years had disturbed deeply buried memories. She felt alone and forsaken. She no longer looked forward to swimming in the sea. What had seemed like a simple pleasure now had no meaning. The tea had no flavour. The shortbread tasted like sawdust. The memories she had so carefully reconstructed over the years to make her happy were compromised. It was good not to have turned back. Being with him would have destroyed every fantasy. And what would she have had left? Nothing. She wept quietly and fell asleep.

When Frances woke it was nearly five o'clock. She pushed all thoughts aside. Mechanically she put her bathing costume, bath robe, swimming cap and towel into her beach bag and left for Santos Beach. The sun was still high and it was pleasantly warm. At the beach the red and blue and yellow primary colours of the pavilion set against the pale sands and the tranquil blue green sea soothed her. There were several families on the beach. Children played at the water's edge with new buckets and spades. Small boys had built a shallow dam and waited for the incoming tide to fill it. The bathing booths had a distinctive musty sea odour that brought back vivid recollections of childhood visits to the beach at St James. She changed into her bathing costume.

The sea was bracing. She enjoyed the salt water washing over her as she surrendered herself to the ocean. She allowed her body to surge and fall in glassy green swells. She tasted the sea and sniffed water to clear her nose. She floated on her back and looked up into the sky. She did not want to think about Douglas. She tried to remove the image of the man on the bicycle but the harder she tried, the more stubbornly the impression remained. The happiness and triumph that she had felt the day before, while she listened to her music were now replaced by dark regret. How could she have been so rash, so utterly impetuous, to decide to go past his farm? What terrible indiscretion. It was as if she had opened a Pandora's Box. Her soul felt disfigured. She felt a desperate need to reach her uncle's farm, to be among people who loved her. She resolved to leave Mossel Bay as early as possible the next morning and not to stay over in Swellendam but drive directly to Klein Drakenstein, even if it took her the whole day. Having made the decision she felt better, she had regained some direction. She again began to enjoy the water. The bright colours of the pavilion and the sparkling sunlight on the sea returned.

When Frances got back to the hotel the clerk at the reception desk handed her a message asking her to telephone Mr Sterling after eight o'clock. She had a leisurely bath and washed her hair, after which she dressed for dinner. She was quite hungry now.

Mr Markowitz welcomed her to the dining room, accompanied her to a table, and pulled a chair out for her. "I trust that you enjoyed the beach this afternoon, Miss Rose?"

"Oh, very much, thank you Mr Markowitz, after the Karoo. I am glad to have the opportunity to speak to you. I would like to leave very early in the morning as my travelling plans have changed. Do you think it would be possible for me to have a really early breakfast?"

"Anything is possible for you, Miss Rose, what time do you have in mind?"

"If I could eat at five?"

"I will arrange it. How is your esteemed father? He must be getting on now?"

"He is as to be expected. He turned eighty in October."

"That is a good innings. One's health is everything. I will go now and see to your breakfast arrangements. Please excuse me."

"Thank you very much Mr Markowitz. Oh, and I nearly forgot, I need to make a telephone call to my uncle at Klein Drakenstein after eight o'clock. Do you think that would be possible please?"

"With the greatest of pleasure. Come to my office when you are ready, I'll assist you."

"Hello, hello? Uncle James? This is Frances calling, how are you? Yes, I'm in Mossel Bay."

"How good to hear your voice my dearest niece. When will you be arriving?"

"I planned to stay over in Swellendam tomorrow but have decided to drive through."

"Isn't that too much in one day?"

"I dare say it is rather a jolly long way, but I am determined to do it. It is tarred road almost all the way if I take the coastal route."

"Your mother telephoned. I said I would get in touch with you. She is keen to see you. She mentioned coming over on Thursday. How will that suit you, dear girl?"

"That would be fine. I mentioned to Mr Markowitz just moments ago that my father turned eighty. I trust he is well?"

"I think that is what your mother wants to talk to you about. This telephone line is not very good, and it's a party line, so I cannot say much more. He evidently had a bit of a turn, but there's no need to be alarmed. What time will you be leaving?"

"I have arranged to have breakfast at five, and as soon after that as possible. I should get to you at about four, or thereabouts."

"Can't wait to see you, dearest girl. Lots of love."

"Can't wait to see you, thank you so much, James, give my love to all. See you tomorrow."

"See you tomorrow. Goodnight."

Frances thanked Mr Markowitz, asked him to add the cost of the call to her bill, and went to her room. She set her alarm clock for four o'clock, and prepared for bed. She had brought along a copy of *Tolstoy His Life and His Work* by Derrick Leon as holiday reading, and put it ready on the bedside table. Once she was settled in bed she opened the book. There was a picture of Tolstoy in 1851 from an early portrait. She scanned the contents page. She read an introductory quotation from the diary of Countess Tolstoy dated October 23, 1897: 'I have been reading Mendelssohn's Life, and have now started on the two volumes of Beethoven. But what is the use of biographies – how can one understand the spirit of the man from them? He creates with his spirit, and his art reflects the spiritual side of its creator, while the material side is usually wicked or insignificant.'

She put the open book across her chest and thought. Douglas was never wicked in any way nor was he insignificant – standing on the side of the road with his bicycle, in the dust. Perhaps what he did was right. She picked up the book. The introduction to Part 1 was a quotation from Tolstoy's *Recollections*: 'I think and even know, for I have experienced it specially in childhood, that the love of others is a natural state of the soul, or rather a natural relationship to people, and when that state exists, one does not notice it. It is noticed only when one does not love, but fears someone, or when one loves someone particularly...'

How strange that there should be a reference to Beethoven in the one quotation and now this. She tried to recall how her love for Douglas had developed. She could not remember how she had felt at the very beginning and conceded that it really must have been a natural state at first. So Tolstoy was right. She could recall details of how she became aware of her love, the expressions she loved, the humour and that wonderful mind – that must have been when she began to love him 'particularly.' But perhaps it was not quite as Tolstoy saw it. Each person has her own way of loving and being loved.

A desperate desire to see Douglas took hold of her. That was why she had gone via Oudtshoorn. Why could she not have stopped? She could go back tomorrow, what would a day matter? Standing at the side of the road in the dust. The book slipped from her hands. She closed it and put it onto the bedside table. She turned off the light. She felt the sand of the beach under her feet. It had been a long day. Her composure was returning. The part she had played all these years had transformed her. She was no longer sure whether the actress could leave the stage and return to her other life. She heard symphonic melodies and themes in the sea as she floated in clear green swells. Is he still standing there? Would he stand there forever? She could smell the sea.

In the early hours of the night she dreamed of herself travelling along the road to Douglas' farm. The sun was bright and the hot road was dusty. At first she was confused by what she saw. A grand piano stood at the side of the road, yet strangely it had no dust on it. Clouds of dust blew over it yet nothing settled on the piano. And then a man appeared, dressed in black. A bright white butterfly collar showed through his long hair as he stood with his back to her. He raised his right arm with the baton. The keys of the piano moved. Diddidy dum. The man leant forward, towards a small door marked 'Fate' on the side of the piano. He knocked – diddidy dum. Douglas turned to receive applause. Beethoven at the side of the road. Amidst the clapping of hands a bell began to ring. How silly of anyone to bring a bell to a symphony concert. The alarm persisted and she turned over to put it off. She dared not go to sleep again, and sat up.

Frances ate alone in the hollow early morning dining room. She wondered how Hope and her cat were getting on.

The waiter who had served breakfast carried her things to her car and washed the windscreen and back window. She gave him a tip, said goodbye, and left Mossel Bay. She looked at her watch; it was a quarter to six. Travelling in a westerly direction in the morning meant that the rising sun would be behind her. In her rear view mirror the eastern sky was already becoming brighter.

It was pleasant to travel on a tarred road. There was hardly any traffic. Swellendam was about four hours away. About one thing she never had a moment's doubt: Douglas' great intellect and his innate decency. Her father could never penetrate his own layers of pretence, pride and need for appearances and get to the things that really mattered. It was as though he feared that nothing of him would be left if he was just himself. With every mile she covered the day became brighter. The land wind that pushed the grasses on the side of the road towards the sea had dropped. There were small puffy white clouds in the pale blue sky.

She was pleased with her car. It was its first really long journey since she had acquired it. She looked with pride at the shining light green bonnet. She liked the feel of the steering wheel. She glanced at the speedometer – fifty five miles an hour. She slowed a little.

Frances reached Swellendam later than anticipated. She was nevertheless pleased with her progress. She parked in the shade of an oak tree outside the Imperial Hotel. She found a good table on the veranda and sat down in the delightful morning air. She ordered coffee. The town was becoming busier. Farmers and their families arrived to do shopping. Her watch said a quarter past ten. She might as well treat herself to a piece of cake. She lifted her hand to get the attention of her waiter. They only had fruit cake, he said, and she ordered some. The cake was a trifle dry but it had subtle flavours. For some reason the cake made her think of Anneke. She would like to visit her some day. Perhaps she should invite her to spend a few days in Graaff Reinet. Their enduring correspondence had meant much to Frances over the years. Douglas did not know about their letters. At Anneke's suggestion Frances' letters were addressed to a post office box so that they would not be delivered to the van Yssens' home.

In another four hours she would be in Somerset West, and then it was not too far to the farm. She looked to her left, at the towering Langeberg with all its mysterious shades of blue and green. Its folds and shadows still concealed her imaginary childhood creatures. She could never quite decide what they looked like but they were small and kind to children and she liked them. Perhaps they were fairies. In the upper reaches wet rock faces glistened in the sunlight. She would have loved to have a child. There were other suitors. But none could match Douglas. She thought of her friends in Graaff Reinet and the surrounding district; of the annual Spring Dance at Grootfontein. She loved the way the band played and how they danced till the early hours. She enjoyed the movements of her body. How good it was to feel the hard bodies of the men and their scent. Arthur Pringle danced so well. He was so light on his feet, and so gallant. She thought of the dinner parties she hosted. Hope is a great help. She understands every refinement of a good table. She was proud that her parties set the standard in Graaff Reinet. It was a privilege to be invited. She relished the interesting conversations and the jolly laughter at times and the smell of cigar smoke mixed with perfume.

The road from Swellendam was undulating. The wind now came from the south east and made driving more difficult. She listened to the rhythms of the sounds of the wind against the car and heard strands of Beethoven's Prometheus theme. Perhaps Beethoven first heard his theme in the wind. Eric Linklater once said that Grieg never composed any music but merely wrote down the sounds he heard in the pine trees. She could go and see Douglas on the way back in January. Why should she not do so? Be bold. The Leibner woman was bound to tell Anneke about their encounter.

Beyond Riviersonderend Frances entered the heart of the grain producing area. Harvesting had begun. Fields on either side of the road were a golden colour and presented timeless scenes. In places wheat was being cut and gathered by hand, tied into sheaves and stacked with the ears upright. Elsewhere sheaves were put onto waiting horse-drawn wagons to be taken away for threshing. The windows of her car were open and she imagined she could smell the wheat. The simplicity of the scene affected Frances. Her father could treat labourers with contempt but he was quite prepared to eat the bread produced by their efforts. Anneke once wrote that Douglas was growing wheat. Her car struggled up some of the long inclines and happily coasted down the other sides. She suddenly felt sad and tried to understand why. She felt as if she consisted of separate parts that refused to fit together. It was as if something essential had forsaken her. It was better that she had not stopped. She could not wait to get to Klein Drakenstein.

It was past three when she got to Somerset West. There were only about twenty four miles left. She felt hungry and thirsty but refused to stop now that she was so close to her uncle's farm. She hardly saw him as her uncle, more as a cousin, or an older brother. She could not decide whether to tell him about Douglas. He had liked Douglas. Her father never liked James and disliked him even more when Douglas also went farming. James had been the most understanding of her plight and most sympathetic. She needed someone to confide in, someone onto whom she could unload some of her burden. She could never tell her mother because the news would somehow get to her father. What a wretched mess.

She started preparing for her arrival. In the summer James sometimes slept in the afternoon. She walked past their sun filled window once and saw him lying next to Ethie with his arm over her, fast asleep. She envied their faithful happiness and their friendship.

The white gateposts of the farm appeared. Tall bluegum trees formed the avenue to the imposing farmhouse. She stopped below the steps that led to the front door. James Sterling appeared in the front entrance, pipe in his mouth. He held out his arms. She left the car door open, rushed up to him, embraced him passionately and burst into tears.

"Now, now, my dear, what is troubling you?"

Frances sobbed uncontrollably, "I'll tell you later."

"You're not ill, are you?"

"No, not at all."

Ethel had followed James and put her arm around Frances' waist. "Let's have something to drink and something to eat. The servants will get your things from the car. Come inside, it is cooler there."

It was a relief to be inside the farmhouse. Frances sat down on one of the Sanderson linen couches. She dried her eyes and blew her nose. "Could I please have some water, I am so thirsty."

Ethel brought Frances a glass of water. "Here you are my dear. I have warmed some soup and made sandwiches. When you are ready I shall ask one of the servants to bring it to the table," Ethel said.

"You are so kind, Ethie. I must be looking terrible," Frances sniffed. "I think I should visit the bathroom."

"You know the way," James looked at Ethel. "Perhaps you should see to Frances."

Frances composed herself as best she could and returned to the living room. "I'll get your soup," Ethel suggested. "We're having a roast this evening, to celebrate your arrival."

James smiled at Frances. "We are so pleased that you are here Frances. We hope you'll have a happy stay. At some time, closer to Christmas, if you like, we could go up to 'Seaspray.' The children and their children will be there. I have to see to a packing shed, if you'll excuse me for a while. May I suggest that you have a rest when you have eaten. Later on we could go for a walk. It gets dark very late now."

"That would be really nice."

Ethel sat with Frances while she ate. The warm soup and sandwiches seemed to soak into her and now that her long journey was over she realised how tired she was. Her hands and arms still trembled from gripping the steering wheel and her shoulders and upper arms were stiff. She felt quite miserable.

"I hope you're not sickening for something Frances?"

"No, I'm not. Hope sends her best regards."

"Thank you. I am so glad that you decided to use her services."

"She is wonderful. We do get in a servant, to do the tedious things, the scrubbing and cleaning. Hope cooks well, she grows vegetables and herbs. Her son will be spending his vacation with her. He is doing so well in his studies at the medical school. How times have changed: the son of a housekeeper becoming a doctor."

"How has your last term been?"

"Fair, but it is always the worst, preparations for the exams. I'm quite tired, and the journey has not made it easier."

"I don't know whether James said anything earlier but your mother has confirmed that she will be visiting on Thursday."

"Strange as it may sound, much as I wanted to see her, I now dread her visit."

"Oh Frances, how can you say that! She is most eager to see you."

"Ethie, may I take you into my strictest confidence – I shall also discuss things with James – for I have had a wretchedly awful experience." Frances could not contain her tears.

It was so unlike Frances to lose her composure. "Of course you can rely on me to treat whatever you have to say with the utmost discretion. Does your mother know?"

"No, no, no, nothing, and that's why I dread seeing her. She has good instincts. She'll know something is amiss. That's why I need to get as much as possible off my mind now. And at least I will have a few days in which to recover."

"Tell me what happened, better still, let's go to your room so you can lie down."

Frances had more soup, and another sandwich. "Gosh, I have such a headache."

"I'll get you some aspirin and hot tea."

Frances removed her shoes and made herself comfortable on her bed. Ethel drew the curtains, closed the bedroom door and sat down in an easy chair.

"What happened to me was most extraordinary, Ethie, and most unsettling. I was so happy and content when I left home. I was looking forward to seeing the sea and swimming at Mossel Bay. But as I got closer to Oudtshoorn the more obsessed I became with the idea of going there. It was as if something was driving me there. It was quite strange, to the extent that when the idea was first put upon me I even suspected my own motives; I was uneasy, as if I could not trust myself. Nevertheless, I arrived in Oudtshoorn, had tea at the hotel, and was recognised by a nosy woman who said she met me once when I was at a tearoom with Douglas and his mother. I should have seen that as an omen, as a warning to drive straight to George and from there to Mossel Bay, as I usually do. But no, I had by then formed an irresistible desire to drive past Douglas' farm, as I did years ago, in the hope of catching a glimpse of him. I did go past there on several occasions and once, many years ago, saw him standing with his back to me holding his child on his hip. He could not hear the passing car. That experience left me with a sadness that lasted for years. So I headed for the Robinson Pass, to go past his farm. On my way to the mountains, while going up a gradual incline I saw in front of me a man, going in the same direction, labouring on a bicycle and when I passed him I saw it was Douglas. He had pulled his hat down so that it would not blow off his head; his shirt was damp with perspiration. At first I did not see Douglas. I saw an older man. I shall always remember Douglas the way he was when we were engaged. Not as he is now. He must have recognised me, and seen my Graaff Reinet number plate, because when I looked in the rear view mirror moments later, there he was, standing and holding his bicycle in the dust of my car, waving frantically, as if pleading with me to stop.

"Ethie, you have no idea how I felt. How much I wanted to touch him once more, to look into those kind grey eyes. But I was too frightened to turn around. God, what an opportunity I missed. It would have been so spontaneous. Now the moment is lost forever. What a fool I am." Frances began to cry. "Forgive me Ethie, for burdening you with all my nonsense. How doltish can one be?"

Tears welled up in Ethel's eyes. Frances always had some vague unworldliness. Ethel's lips quivered as she tried to hold back her tears. Her voice broke. "I don't know what to say."

"I am so sorry to burden you with my nonsense, Ethie. I feel awful. There he was. It is my last image of him, one that will not leave me, of him standing at the side of that dusty road, holding his bicycle, and waving desperately. I felt so sad for him. My Douglas standing there. What have I done to deserve such pain and distress? So can you see why I dread seeing my mother? She gives me that special disapproving look of hers for still wearing his ring. She has encouraged other suitors, as you know. She will see through me. She'll know immediately that something is wrong. She will probe in her cunning way. And I will have few defences. But whatever it takes, I shall never tell her what I saw. I would not be able to suffer the humiliation. As time passed she has been less and less on my side and increasingly sympathetic to my father's point of view. It is a blessing that we are able to grow apart from our parents as we and they become older. It makes their final departure easier. My father would take such delight if he ever found out, if he ever knew of poor Douglas standing beside the road, covered in sweat and dust." Frances began sobbing again. "My father could never tolerate the flaws in others. As if he was perfect. And when I arrived here this afternoon and saw your magnificent old house, the poverty of Douglas' cottage was heart rending. I had so hoped to have a happy holiday here with the two of you and visiting 'Seaspray.' Now this."

"You have more strength than you credit yourself, Frances. We'll have to tell James. He knows how to deal with your mother in his disarming way. I am no match for her. As you know well, your father never liked me. I was never cultured enough for his liking. I have never said it before, not even to James, but your father is a snob and a cad. He has hollow feet." Having begun to release years of bottled up resentment Ethel could not stop herself. "And to think of that innocent boy that was hanged because of him." Ethel had crossed a threshold into forbidden territory. She began to shake uncontrollably. "What have I done!"

Frances was ashen. "What on earth do you mean?"

Ethel's nervous voice trembled as she spoke. "Everybody knows about it Frances. It was in the papers. Your mother knows, James knows, and above all your father knows. The casual way he dismissed the whole affair was an absolute disgrace. He showed not a single bit of remorse and he was always so critical of the criminals who stood before him who showed no remorse."

"I do not know anything about this. Is it possible?"

"I remember well when the dreadful truth came out, you were overseas.

Your mother was relieved at that and said you were never to know. She protected him." Ethel wept quietly. "I should never have told you, but I could not stop myself. I am so sorry to add to your grief." She glanced sideways at Frances.

"You say it was reported in the papers?"

"Yes, James made a cutting."

"Do you think I could see it please?"

"He put it into the front of his dictionary. I'll fetch it if you like?" Ethel went to James' study and returned with a yellowed newspaper cutting dated June 26, 1925. The headline read, 'Caledon boy posthumously pardoned.' An introduction followed. 'In what is possibly the first miscarriage of justice of its kind in the Union, Jan Kleynhans, who was hanged for the murder of his mother in 1922, has been pardoned after the confession and conviction of Simon Klaarman in the Cape Supreme Court. Examination of the records of Kleynhans' trial shows that forensic evidence was ignored …' The report went on to give an account of the evidence led in Kleynhans' trial.

Frances handed the cutting to Ethel. She was completely calm. The news had removed all doubt about the way she felt about her father. She no longer felt guilty about their separation. She no longer had to justify her actions. Such was her relief that she even felt happy for a moment. A missing piece of the puzzle had turned up in the most unexpected way.

Frances' poise frightened Ethel. "I should not have said what I said, Frances."

"No, you are wrong. You should have said what you said. I understand better than you realise why you could not conceal the truth any longer. It has been an unfair burden to you."

"Then you are not angry with me?"

"I am grateful to you, most grateful my dear Aunt Ethel that you have been so forthright. James would have been reluctant for fear of upsetting me, and going against my mother's wishes. I'm not suggesting that his loyalty is divided against me, no such thing. I am just grateful to you for your directness, Ethie. We'll deal with things, as we have to, on Thursday."

"I jolly well hope you won't let on that it was I who told you."

"I'll not say a thing about our conversation. I shall only tell James that I saw Douglas and that it has upset me."

"I am so relieved and at the same time I feel queer about letting such a large cat out of the bag, Francie. I think you should get some rest now, and go for walk later with James. He loves you so much."

Frances woke at half past six. She had a bath, dressed hurriedly and put on her sensible walking shoes. She found James and Ethel at their dining table.

"There you are Frances!" James said cheerfully. "I trust you slept well?"

"Ethie gave me aspirin for my headache and it gave me a dreamless sleep. My headache has gone and I feel refreshed."

James got up stiffly from his chair. "Let's get going Frances, I'd like to show you my more recently planted vineyards."

They went outside. The summer sun was still high. Frances could feel its warmth on her face. She thought for a moment of getting a hat but decided not to. "Let's go this way," James indicated. The farmyard was deserted except for a few stiff-legged chickens strutting about with brittle head movements. James led her past an orchard of fig trees and then through a large orchard of plum trees. He held a ripening yellow plum in his hand. "We're exporting these to Europe with great success. How the world has changed, Frances, from when I first came here. We're still not making much money but things have improved. There may even be a greater demand for wine grapes in the years to come. That's where I am taking you. You may remember that I managed to acquire really very good disease-free cabernet sauvignon vines from Stellenbosch. I don't think I have ever shown you what has become of them. I want you to see them. They give me so much pleasure. It is so rewarding to see how robust they are and how generously they have produced."

They made their way up a slope and stopping here and there to admire views of vineyards, orchards and sprawling farmlands lying in a dusty haze made thick by the declining sun. Several times Frances wanted to speak about Douglas but could not bring herself to. The emotion she had released to Ethel had emptied her. At times in the past she had felt guilty about they way she had distanced herself from her father and even felt sorry for him as he grew older. Now the confirmation of just how flawed he was redeemed her. She was at peace and felt reluctant to again disturb her own tranquillity. Yet having prepared herself to confide in James, she could not set aside the idea. Before she could stop herself she said, "I need to speak to you, James, about an intimate matter."

"Ah ha, and what could that be?" he laughed.

"Nothing frivolous, something rather sad and disturbing."

"Does your mother know?"

"No, and heaven forbid that she should. I fear that she will notice that I am not myself, so I need you to know. You handle her so well, I need your assistance. I saw Douglas."

James stopped and turned to Frances. "You saw Douglas?"

"Yes."

"You mean you visited him?"

"No I did not visit him." She paused to gather her thoughts. "As you know, I usually motor to George and then to Mossel Bay. But this time something possessed me to go via Oudtshoorn. Just to see the place again because of all the associations, I suppose, or some silly reason like that. Once I was there I became utterly obsessed with the idea of driving past his farm. I suppose that's really why I went via Oudtshoorn in the first place. On the way up to the Outeniqua Mountains I passed Douglas on his bicycle, presumably on his way to his farm. When I first saw a man on a bicycle I had no idea who it could be. I told Ethel the whole story. At first I did not realise who it was,

James, and when I did it was quite a shock. On a few occasions, and I have never admitted this, I did go past his farm in the hope of catching a glimpse of him, and once years ago I did catch a glimpse of him. But seeing him like this, his shirt soaked in perspiration, standing on the side of the road holding his bicycle, was an unbelievable shock. Then, when I had passed him I looked in the rear view mirror and saw him waving for me to stop, and I just carried on going. I had such a desire to be with him once more, but I could not bring myself to do so. I have been most distressed. I thought of what my father would say if he saw Douglas standing there in his shirt sleeves, his hat pulled down against the wind, his trousers tucked into bicycle clips. He would have had his 'I told you so' look, that special smug look with which he signals victory over flawed mortals. All these years I have believed in Douglas; I have believed, and still do that he is a brilliant man, and a good man. I am not saying that he is without fault. He did not treat me well but he must have had his reasons. I still love him as I did in the beginning. I should have stopped and flung my arms around him and kissed his face. Yet I drove on. What I had seen standing on the side of the road was an older man, not as handsome as I had made him, struggling on a little farm. His cottage is a modest affair, James, very modest. My shock was made worse by the fear that my father could just have been right about him after all and that my judgement was blinded by my romantic imagination. I feel so exposed, so vulnerable that I really dread seeing my mother. Being face to face with her while feeling that I may have lived a ridiculous fantasy, that I may have deceived myself with fanciful ideas, is going to be very difficult. You have always protected me and you know what it is like to be at the mercy of my father's cruelty." Frances' words were measured, without emotion.

"I know what you mean. I understand how you feel about your father. The way he behaved when your engagement ended was unforgivable. You know I have always understood your position Frances, and I shall continue to be on your side. I shall always defend your position. Your mother knows how close we are and she has at times tried to get me to alter my position. She is coming here with a purpose. I heard it in her voice. Between us we will be able to handle her as long as we use our wisdom. In the meantime I want you to have lots of rest and lots of gentle exercise."

"Thank you. I love you, James."

He kissed her on the side of her head. "Let's go and look at my vines."

Thursday 13 December 1956

Frances had a good night's rest and a generous breakfast with Ethel. James had gone to attend to the harvesting of plums in the early hours but promised to be back before ten. Mrs Rose was due to arrive at ten thirty. Frances groomed herself and put on an elegant floral dress. She wanted to present herself as well as possible. Ethel was just her usual self, humming as she went about the house with one of the servants. She had baked scones and opened a jar of her strawberry jam.

Frances fetched Tolstoy's biography and positioned herself on a couch in the living room so that she had a view of the road leading to the house. Her watch showed ten past ten. She heard James' voice in the kitchen. He hurried into the living room. "Jolly good crop this year. You have brought me luck Francie. Will be with you when I've been to see a man about a horse."

At twenty five minutes to eleven the Judge's Bentley slowly made its way along the avenue of bluegums. It stopped opposite the front entrance and Johnson assisted Mrs Rose from the car. Frances had decided that she would not go outside to meet her mother.

Mrs Rose reached the open front door and straightened her hat.

James was waiting for her. "How good to see you, Elizabeth."

"Hello James. How is Frances?"

"She's in the living room." He showed his sister inside.

Frances pretended to be absorbed in her book, knowing this would irritate her mother.

"Hello, Frances," her mother said sweetly.

Frances unhurriedly put her book to one side and got up. She kissed her mother on the cheek.

"Where shall I sit? My back is troubling me." Mrs Rose enquired.

"I think this will be the best chair Elizabeth."

"No, I'd rather sit over there so that I can see better."

Ethel arrived. "Good morning Elizabeth! I've made scones. I know you like them."

"Good morning Ethel. I am parched. If the tea is ready, we might as well have some."

"Shall we have it here or would you prefer it at the dining table?" Ethel asked.

"Well, I am settled now, here would be fine. How is the farm doing, James?"

"Fine Elizabeth. I was telling Frances what marvellous fruit we have this year, and the export prices are good. The grapes look promising."

"That is most fortunate. Jeremy always said farming is a risky business." Mrs Rose glanced at Frances.

"It's lovely to have Frances here, Elizabeth."

"She should be staying with us. Jeremy is not well." Mrs Rose waited for a response." Are you not going to enquire after your father, Frances?"

"Should I, Mother?"

"We are all getting older, Frances, and we do not want to leave things we ought to say unsaid."

"I do not have much to say, Mother."

Ethel wrung her hands. "I shall see to the tea."

James sought the comfort of his favourite chair. The atmosphere was charged.

"Are you not going to ask why your father is not well?"

"Is it not just his age, Mother?"

"He is eighty now and said he hoped you would ring him on his birthday, Frances. That day he went off to the club to have lunch with Basil Wainwright to celebrate, and instead of it being a happy occasion, he encountered the ghost of van Yssen."

Frances pursed her lips. Her mother had not made her usual introductory small talk or produced anything from her repertoire of pleasantries.

"What do you mean by that, Elizabeth?" James asked.

"Just that. Jeremy thought we were rid of him forever. After the way he destroyed Frances' relationship with her father. But no, it was not to be. He had to turn up one final time. Poor Jeremy. Johnstone drove him home from the club and Daisy had to telephone me at bridge to go and see to him. He was incoherent when I got to him and it took him two days to compose himself. I had to call the doctor."

"What was it that upset Jeremy?" James asked.

"What van Yssen did, that's what upset him!"

Frances sensed triumph in her mother's anger. She heard Beethoven's French horns announcing it. The approaching clinking tea cups played the Prometheus theme. "What did Douglas do, Mother?"

"Your father said he accomplished something special in a very complex legal matter that humbled some of the best legal minds in the world. He heard it straight from the horse's mouth – the advocate de Villiers who won the appeal – when he and Basil Wainwright were at the club. On his birthday of all days. The case that van Yssen helped to win involved obscure issues – Jeremy even confessed he did not grasp it all. A man who sits on a small farm outside Oudtshoorn reading Latin books! Advocate de Villiers said it will become a landmark case.

"Now, Frances, this is very difficult for me to say: your father wants you to know that he regrets what he said to you. He regrets hurting you those many years ago. He is afraid and he is troubled by what he has done, all the things he has done. He says that what he said that day, when he was so angry, was meant to illustrate how frustrated he was with the way Douglas treated you, not to hurt you by insulting the man you loved."

"Love, mother, not 'loved.' Isn't it bitterly ironical that it has taken this to bring about a change of heart? Don't you see that what Douglas accomplished is because of what Douglas always was, not because of what he has again become in Father's eyes? In the same way my father is what he has always been, and you know that, Mother. When I needed him most he drove me away because it is in his nature to behave as he does. As far as his ability as a jurist is concerned you know that he is not well regarded. You know, and have known for many years, that he cost an innocent man his life. Why did you try to conceal it from me? To protect him? My father has made his own legal history. He has a cruel streak in him. That will never change. My forgiveness will not change him, it will merely endorse what he has done to me and to others. I saw Douglas on Monday."

"Are you saying that to upset me?" Mrs Rose was shaking.

"No, I passed him on the road to Mossel Bay. He was on his bicycle, pedalling to his farm. His shirt was wet with sweat. He stopped because of the dust of my car and I saw him in the rear view mirror, waving to me and holding his bicycle. I carried on because I could not bear the thought of what my father would think if he saw Douglas like that. Your news has brought redemption Mother. I am free again. As far as my father is concerned, I cannot help him. History will judge him and against that judgement there is no appeal. I also realise now that Douglas saw through my father and must have known that he would never have been able to have an enduring relationship with him. That did not make things easier. I am not saying that Douglas is without fault and I am not making excuses for him, but there is no gainsaying that, unlike my father, he is authentic." Frances' voice was unnaturally clear.

There was a deathly silence in the living room. Mrs Rose began crying softly. She heaved as she sobbed. "Life used to be so jolly, so happy. Those summer holidays at the seaside with the lovely music. I was even a little bit in love with Douglas at times. I envied you Frances, and I was desperately sad when it all came to an end. But I had my husband to consider, for better or for worse. Can you not bring yourself to comfort your father in his last days, Frances?" Mrs Rose blew her nose in her handkerchief.

James looked at Frances. Ethel contemplated the patterns in the Persian carpet. The clock on the mantelpiece above the fireplace ticked loudly. Frances' head shook with refusal, as if she was replying to a question she had asked herself.

Mrs Rose eventually looked up and when she found enough courage she glanced at her daughter. Frances' calmness disconcerted her. "Your father is a broken man, Frances. I never thought I would hear myself saying such a thing, but it is true. He has shrunk, he hardly eats anything; his skin has become loose. He speaks about you, Frances. Please go and see him. He says Douglas has defeated him. Make peace for your own sake, not for his sake. Please. It is not easy for me to beg you."

"Do you know Mother, how much my father's approval meant to me? How much I admired him in my innocent years? I think you do know. He betrayed my trust for the sake of appearances and you want me to go and bless him? In the end each one of us is an island and where he is going he has to go on his own. He could have come to me at any time and made things right yet he chose not to. Now that he has to embark on his final journey, he needs to be comforted. If he knew he had another ten years to live he would not ask for forgiveness now; he would wait another nine years."

"You are cruel, Frances. You have a bit of your father in you."

"No, I am not cruel, Mother. I am gentle and I am kind. I have been hurt more than you could ever imagine. I have never thought one bad thing about Douglas for the way he abandoned me. I even imagine that I love his daughter and his wife. I have corresponded regularly with his mother over the years. I love her. I am afraid that I cannot do what you have asked, at least not right now. The best I can offer is to say that I shall consider what to do very thoroughly. And in the meantime I shall celebrate Douglas' achievement. I always knew he would do something great."

Mrs Rose summoned the stoicism that her breeding bestowed on her. "I'll have some of your tea now, Ethel," she said. "I would like to visit you again Frances, after all you are my daughter."

"I would welcome that, Mother."

They had their tea and scones. Mrs Rose gathered herself while the tea restored her spirits. She was scared to touch Frances when she said goodbye and kissed her lightly on her cheek. "Well, at least you have given me some hope, Frances. At least I am not leaving empty-handed."

Frances stood outside the front door with the Sterlings and watched as the Judge's Bentley lumbered down the road to the gate. James put his arm around Frances. "You handled that very bravely, Frances. I am proud of you, though I feel sorry for your mother. It could not have been easy for her."

Ethel cried a little. Frances tilted her head affectionately towards James, "You have no idea how much joy I am experiencing; how thrilled I am at Douglas' glorious achievement. I am proud of him. I knew he would do something special. He has vindicated himself and restored my faith. I was right about him. In fact, I am so happy and feel so complete I may even go and see my parents, for I no longer have any fear of my father."

◆

Chapter Forty-nine

DOUGLAS REMAINED standing at the side of the road. Frances would be quite far away by the time she reappeared, yet he stared in the hope of catching one more glimpse. She probably had not recognised him. What could she be doing here? He was disturbed at seeing her, too confused to return to an empty house. He turned his bicycle around. What if it was not Frances? The registration was unmistakably from Graaff-Reinet. And it was the start of the school holidays. How strange. Without thinking he mounted his bicycle and headed back to Oudtshoorn. Going downhill was less demanding and convinced him of the wisdom of returning. He would leave for the farm very early the next day. He should not have left so late, in the heat of the day.

When he reached his mother's house he found a note on the front door for Maggie to say that she was at Mrs Jacquard's house. He considered having a bath and putting on fresh clothes but instead went directly to Mrs Jacquard's house. He took off his bicycle clips and his hat and knocked loudly on the front door. A puzzled-looking Mrs Jacquard opened the door. "Douglas! Your mother said you had gone to the farm?"

"I have come back." He wiped his face with his handkerchief. He was still perspiring. Where his hat had been his forehead was white. Streaks of dust mixed with sweat showed on the sides of his face. His clothes and his boots were dusty.

"Do come inside." Mrs Jacquard looked him up and down.

"I won't sit down, thank you; I found a note and thought I should let my mother know that I have returned."

"She's in my studio."

Mrs van Yssen heard Douglas' voice. When Douglas and Mrs Jacquard entered the studio the two women glanced at one another. The way their eyes met told Douglas that they knew.

"It was very hot on the road. I should not have left so late. I'll leave early tomorrow morning." Douglas spoke mechanically while he tried to reason how they knew.

"Would you like something to drink?" his mother asked.

"Just some water please."

Mrs Jacquard went to fetch the water. His mother put her index finger over her lips and he nodded in agreement. Mrs Jacquard returned with a jug and a glass. Douglas drank two glasses of water and wiped his mouth with the back of his hand. "I'd better get going. I would like to have a bath before Maggie gets home. Thank you for the water Guillemette. Hope to see you soon, come and visit me. Stay for a few days. It's too busy in the shop this time of the year, so Maggie can't come. It's cooler up there than in this depression."

"I might consider that. I'll come and cook for you."

Mrs van Yssen touched Douglas' arm. "I'll walk home with you but I need to go to the toilet first."

When Douglas and Mrs Jacquard were alone she drew him aside. "Your mother is upset. Antoinette Leibner telephoned her to say that she saw Frances at the Queen's Hotel at lunch time. Your mother is not getting any younger. When you're in your seventies it is not easy in this heat. I will come and visit you and stay for a few days, before Christmas."

Douglas pushed his bicycle while he walked home with his mother.

She tapped his sleeve. "I need to speak to you before Maggie gets home. Fortunately we have some time. She won't leave the shop before six. Go and have your bath, I'll make you something to eat."

"I saw Frances. She passed me on my way to the farm. I don't know if she recognised me."

"Go and have your bath."

Mrs van Yssen was in the living room. "Douglas! Gosh, you look so much better. I made you a sandwich and some coffee. Come and sit down."

"Guillemette said Mrs Leibner saw Frances at the Queen's Hotel."

"Yes, she telephoned to tell me. You know how nosy she is."

"I waved when I thought it was she, but her car just kept on going."

"What would you have done if she had stopped?"

"I really don't know. It has been such a long time. Why would she, after all these years, suddenly decide to go past my farm?"

"It was not the first time, Douglas."

He frowned.

"Yes, she has gone past there before."

"How do you know that?"

"That is what I want to talk to you about. Frances and I have been corresponding ever since your engagement ended."

"And you never said anything? Does Maggie know?"

"No she does not. Only your father knew; he discovered a letter, and Guillemette knows. The letters came to your father's post box. I have kept them. I do not know what to do with the letters. I would not be able to bring myself to destroy them, not as long as I live. If I left them for posterity who knows what harm they may bring? I love Maggie and Jane. Maggie has been a wonderful wife and loving mother. She has been good for you. I have seen how much you enjoy one another, how compatible you are. When you come here for the weekends the lines of her face are softer in the morning, your movements are easier. It is a great blessing – to enjoy one another without guilt. It must be so pleasurable. Maggie gave you the kind of freedom no one else could have given you and I am grateful to her for that. Her natural ways had a healing effect on your father by removing his clinging doubt. It brought him great peace in his last years. Only she could have done that."

"Did you ever meet with Frances?"

"No. That would have destroyed our magic. It was as if we had an unspoken pact to conduct a relationship beyond the usual social trammels. We never met. I have felt for some time that I should tell you about the letters. Her presence here today is a sign that we should talk about it, Douglas. Much as I love Maggie I also love Frances. They are so different. Frances has very special qualities, Douglas. She believed in you from the beginning and even sacrificed her relationship with her father."

"How did that happen?"

"When it became clear that your engagement would not continue he said some awful things that hurt her very much. It is in the letters. She has not spoken to him since. Today was not the first time that she motored past your farm. When Jane was about six or seven she first went past there and saw you with Jane. You had your back to the road and did not know that she drove past. And there have been other times. Frances still believes that your destinies are linked. I don't know what to do about the letters. There is one in particular that I want you to read; not now. Just so that you know where the letters are, in case something happens to me, they are at Guillemette's house. She has locked them away. I will go there after supper and fetch the one I want you to read and I want you to take it with you when you leave tomorrow morning and read it when you get to the farm. Come to my room before you leave and I shall give it to you. There are some things I want to say before you read her letter. I have thought so much about your relationship with her; no doubt her letters have influenced me to imagine what could have been. Frances would have inspired you to bring out your full potential. She had the background. There would have been a constant challenge for you to excel yourself. I sometimes feel that you did not want to be challenged."

"When I knew that I had been cursed with such a cruel defect, I wanted to destroy everything. I had a mark on me. I could see it from the way her father looked at me. I was no longer what they had hoped for. It was even in her mother's eyes although she tried to hide it. What at first appeared perfect to them was blemished. All that mattered to them was what others might think."

"Frances was not like that, Douglas. You cannot blame her for her father's attitude. All she has ever wanted is for you to succeed. I have thought much about how things have turned out. Guillemette and I have had endless discussions."

"I too have thought for the last thirty years. I loved Frances for her refinement and her sincerity, for her style, for her insightful sensibilities. Whenever I think of her she does inspire me. In some ways Jane has taken her place. I am blessed to have Jane. What a mind she has. But we must remind ourselves that Jane is a product of her mother's love. Maggie's unconditional affection gave her the freedom to develop intuitively as well as intellectually."

"Read the letter, Douglas. I am glad for the opportunity to tell you about the letters. Perhaps Jane should read them one day. I must go and see to our supper now."

Because he wanted to leave early the next day, Douglas prepared for bed while Maggie had tea on the veranda. Mrs van Yssen went to Mrs Jacquard's house on the pretext of having left keys there.

Douglas closed the curtains of their room and began undressing. The dress Maggie had worn that day was on a hanger on the side of their cupboard. A pair of her well worn shoes stood shyly in the corner. She was so thrifty. She made do with so little that it made him sad. He loved her for that. She never asked for anything. He brushed his teeth over the hand basin in the corner of the room and got into bed. He recalled times on the sands at Plettenberg Bay. This was the time of the year when people went for seaside holidays. He and Maggie and Jane had been to Mossel Bay with Guillemette a few times and stayed in a modest rented house – so Jane could swim in the sea. Fragments of the events of the day came and went as sleep approached. He lifted the mosquito net to turn the bedside light off. The air inside the net was stifling. Up in the mountain there were no mosquitoes.

He woke when Maggie kissed him on his forehead. She had left her bedside light on so that he could see her lips. "I will make you a good breakfast tomorrow morning. I have set the alarm clock for four. I love you." She turned her light off and snuggled up next to him, her back against his front. He put his arm around her and cupped her breast in his hand. He loved doing that. He was wide awake now and felt the satisfying diminishing movements of her breathing as Maggie fell asleep. He thought of Frances and imagined that he was in bed with her, holding her breast. How would she have made love? Would she have abandoned herself or been restrained? She certainly seemed keen for them to explore one another. It was hard to tell what had inspired her. Was it spontaneous or a borrowed romantic notion? She may have been a wonderful lover. Her mother certainly had the makings of an enthusiastic woman, the way she looked at you, the way she moved her body. He felt the soft warmth of Maggie's body against him.

Maggie woke Douglas when the alarm clock sounded. She put on her dressing gown and went to the kitchen. He washed himself, dressed and fetched his bicycle from the garage. He made sure that the tyres were properly inflated and that his puncture repair kit was complete. Maggie warmed lamb chops from the night before, cooked several rashers of bacon and fried three eggs. She cut bread, put butter and marmalade ready and ground beans for his coffee.

She watched him as she sipped her coffee. He ate noisily. "I have invited Guillemette to spend a few days with me. She said she would cook for me," he said.

"That would be very nice for you. I like her food. Why did you come back?"

Douglas did not expect her to ask that. "Did I not mention it? I got away too late, much too late and the heat was unbearable. I also thought that I left the wages money on the mantelpiece. I could not find it in any of my pockets. When I got back here I realised that I had put it into my bag. I never do that; can't understand why."

She smiled. His eyes avoided hers. She knew him all too well. He must have had another reason or something else on his mind. He always had something on his mind.

Douglas washed the last crumbs down with coffee, kissed Maggie goodbye and went to his mother's room. She was awake. He put his hands under her shoulders and kissed her on the side of her face. When he withdrew she held onto his wrist with surprising strength and opened the drawer of her bedside table. She produced an envelope from under her bible and pressed it into his hand. He put the envelope into one of his buttoned shirt pockets. "Cheerio, Ma, I'll see you one of these days."

Maggie waited at the front gate in the cool morning air. He gave her another kiss and a hug and mounted his bicycle. In the east the sky was becoming lighter. He was conscious of the presence of the envelope in his pocket. It was not very thick.

As was usual, the early part of his journey was easy. The road became steeper closer to the farm. The morning was cool and his good night's rest had restored his strength. He wondered what Frances was doing. As had become his custom over the years, he stopped at the causeway across the Kandelaars River and made his way a few paces upstream to drink water from the river. He splashed his face and wet the top of his head. He looked at his watch. He was making good time and there was hardly any wind. He should be at the farm before nine. He was glad to be alone. He had become accustomed to living alone for weeks at a time. It had given him the opportunity to prepare for the court case. What a victory that was. He enjoyed encountering Laubscher at the bank. He played the humble fool and lifted his hat with exaggerated courtesy when he met Laubscher's scowl. That was fun! He chuckled to himself. The Ellises still owed him the cigarettes for the bet he had made that they would win the case. Ten thousand cigarettes is what they owed. It would be good to have Guillemette on the farm. She has aged well. Her sturdy walk and the sensuous way she carried herself still sometimes gave him ideas. He pressed his hand against the pocket containing Frances' letter.

He opened the gate to his farm and pushed his bicycle through. One of the labourers saw Douglas arriving and went to meet him.

"Is everything in order, Frans?" Douglas asked.

"Yes, Sir."

"I want to put my things away and have some tea and then we can plan what we are going to do this week."

"I thought Sir was sick when Sir did not come back yesterday."

"Thank you for your concern, but I am just fine."

Douglas unlocked the house and put his bag down in the living room. He lit his Primus stove and put a saucepan of water on for his tea. He carried his tea and a few ginger biscuits to the table on the veranda and settled himself in his favourite chair. While he waited for the tea to draw he took Frances' letter from his pocket written in her hand of twenty four years ago.

June 15, 1932.
Dearest Anneke,
Thank you for your lovely letter. I regret that it has taken so long to reply. I spent the entire winter holiday here in Graaff-Reinet.

It was rather lonely but I kept myself busy reading and going for long walks. We have had some very cold weather and there has been snow on the higher lying areas. The Putticks have been kind to me and I have had dinner with them several times. Their children are a pleasure. I also spent a few days on the farm of Charles Southey. His wife has been most hospitable, more so because I teach their son. They are sheep farmers and have the most magnificent farmstead. The Victorian house is built of sandstone, as are the outbuildings such as the shearing sheds.

The house is large and comfortable with a deep veranda that goes right around it. What is extraordinary is that they have central heating. How unusual for Africa! (Douglas would have quoted Plinius – 'ex Africa semper aliquid novi.') The house has a basement boiler room and the boiler uses anthracite as fuel. It is such luxury to have a house in the Karoo that is pleasantly warm throughout winter. At night they make a fire in the living room, more to have cheerful flames than to provide heat.

I understand your reluctance to write about Douglas for fear of upsetting me. But you need have no such fear. Any news of him is better than none. I think of my dearest Douglas many times each day. I long ago accepted that there was no hope. It was correct of you to inform me about his liaison, for the news I received last week, however disturbing, was easier to receive than it would have been if you had not been direct. My mother telephoned to say that my father heard from an attorney in Oudtshoorn, a Mr Luscombe, that Douglas has become married. The news was almost impossible to bear. I was numb. I had lessons to prepare that evening and was quite distraught. I felt as if I had left my body.

I became bereft of all thought. Although I tried my best to hide my grief I could think of nothing else for days. I moved about mindlessly and lost weight. All the time I tried to imagine what his wife is like. One night as I lay alone in my bed unable to sleep I had an unusual, almost mystical, experience (I was very tired).

I realised that I felt nothing but love for his wife. I want him to be happy because I love him so. My mother mentioned something about a scandal but I am sure that it is just my father's malicious way or an attempt to make me feel better. Please write to me about it and tell me all and do not try to spare my feelings. I am forever bound to Douglas and I know that we shall meet again even if it is only in the next life. Our relationship was truly unique. It was destiny for us to meet. It was so perfect that I felt at times as if our very souls touched. Such were the spiritual heights to which my love for Douglas soared, and when I re-live those moments, earthly things, even marriage, now seem trivial. The love I have always felt for him cannot be diminished by events in the temporal world.

Please tell me about his wife. Would she want children? Is she attractive? What did she do before they got married? Where is she from? What does her father do? Allow me to share his happiness. Oh Anneke, I do wish I could see him and embrace him, look into those kind eyes. When I remember those eyes I weep to think how cruel fate was to Douglas. I could see the change in him when he realised that his deafness was irreversible. He was angry and wanted to pull the pillars of the temple down on himself. He wanted to flee. He came to regard his earlier aspirations as enemies. He has so much talent. I sometimes think of the early years of our relationship: in what esteem he was held by his professors at university, how well he wore his learning, how my father never ceased to speak proudly about Douglas' abilities to our friends and his colleagues. I can see him now, standing tall and elegant in his tweed jacket and grey flannels at the lectern in Hiddingh Hall leading a debate against an opposing team. The smiling eyes and confident humour. He was like a god on the campus. Perhaps his wife will inspire him to produce something great. It would be good if marital fulfilment could arouse his abilities. I always hoped that he would produce a great historical work. He should be encouraged to do that. I shall always believe in him. I often think of Beethoven when I think of Douglas. Beethoven had so much to overcome and he did. I shall continue to pray for Douglas.

Please write soon, dearest.

Lots and lots of love,
Frances.

Douglas sat back in his chair and pressed the pages of Frances' letter against his chest. He closed his eyes. He remembered her the day she left Oudtshoorn after her sad visit. He thought of the times at Plettenberg Bay, of Garnett and her parents. He thought of the way he had loved her and the sounds he could hear then. Life had more possibilities then. He folded the letter and put it into its envelope. He sighed and had more tea.

Mrs Jacquard arrived three days later by taxi. Douglas helped her carry her things to the spare room. They put her baskets with wine, cheese, smoked sausages, spices, herbs and garlic into the pantry. Her easel and case with her paints and brushes were left in the living room. While Douglas went to see to a new fence the labourers were erecting, she made herself coffee and sat on the veranda. She looked up at the mountains and across the valleys below. The very middle of summer was approaching. The poplar trees along the river were lush. They were happily enjoying the damp earth in which they stood and the long hours of sunlight that gave them life. A breeze stirred their leaves. She thought how painting had changed her. She had become detached from the way she once was. Things were no longer finite. Whatever she observed now was a reflection of something more. It was as if what she saw were not things that existed objectively but expressions of a kind. Everything seemed alive. Her task was to find the essence of what she saw and to distort the obvious so others might see. She loved it here. It was much cooler. At least one could sleep at night. She thought of the meal they would have that evening. Douglas loved beef stews.

They ate in silence except for some appreciative grunts from Douglas to show how much he enjoyed the food. It pleased her. The meat was tender and saturated with flavours of carrots, beans, touches of garlic, smoked sausage and cloves, also a little sherry. Mrs Jacquard always brought along red Bordeaux wine obtained from a merchant in Cape Town. Douglas did not care much for wine but enjoyed it tonight. He was careful to have his best table manners, for Guillemette appreciated that. He had a second helping of stew and a few more boiled potatoes. His nose ran a little from the enjoyment of eating and he perspired slightly. For dessert they had slices of fresh peaches soaked in an orange liqueur.

    Douglas cleared the table and took the supper things to the kitchen. He made coffee and carried a tray with blue cheese and biscuits to the veranda.

    It was a mild windless evening. The branches and leaves of the almond trees near the house were startled shadows against a starry night sky. Mrs Jacquard decided to be content and made herself comfortable. Douglas placed a kerosene lamp on a table so that he could see her lips. He handed her coffee to her and patted his stomach. "That was a terrific meal, Guillemette, terrific. Thank you."

    She smiled and nodded. "Your coffee is good." She lit a fat Turkish tobacco cigarette.

    They sat without speaking. Mrs Jacquard listened to the night sounds. The frogs near the river were having a happy time. A cricket began to chirp. A dog barked. The sky was so thick with stars that it made her think of van Gogh. Since her arrival she had searched for indications that Douglas had read Frances' letter. There was none. She tapped him on his knee to get his attention. 'Your mother came to fetch one of Frances' letters on Monday evening. She was quite emotional.'

    "Yes, I know. She gave it to me."

    "Have you read it?'"

"Yes, I have."

"And?"

"It is quite sad."

"It is more than that. It is terribly sad. It is the saddest thing I have ever read."

"Yes, it is sad. It was written a long time ago."

"Time does not alter such things."

"Time alters our perspectives. I tried to think what I felt like when the letter was written and I could not, in all honesty. I was already completely deaf then. We are born with hope and expectations, Guillemette. When I lost my hearing part of me became empty. It is difficult to describe how I felt. At first I could remember what certain sounds were like but eventually I could not remember clearly. At the beginning it was quite frightening not to hear any sound. It was like being inside a glass bubble. I knew that there were sounds outside; inside there was nothing. I could not penetrate the glass. If something fell from a table, if Jane dropped a toy, I would wait for the clatter, but there was nothing. When it was dark and I could not see other people's lips they could not communicate with me. When Maggie and I were alone at night it was in complete silence because I did not know if anyone would hear our sounds. I have never heard my daughter's voice. At times I feel as if I have degenerated. And yet I am comfortable with the way I am now. I have created a world of my own and I enjoy that world. Irene Nel's son spoke to me recently, when I was at their house doing Latin translations for the court case, and told me about a new operation, called a fenestration operation, that could possibly restore my hearing. A friend of their family, a Dr Daniel Roux, pioneered such operations in the Union and offered to do mine free of charge as a gesture to Garnett. Irene's son urged me to have the operation. I told him I was comfortable the way I am. I no longer want the intrusion of sound. I do not want an intrusion of the past. I think Frances saw more in me than there really is. What I observe and touch, what I am able to reason about, is all there is for me. When Frances and I were courting, when I was so much in love with her, I accepted her abstract way, her notions of transcending the material world. I never really understood what she meant when she spoke of some of her intuitive experiences, as she does in her letter when she refers to an epiphany of some kind. When you are in love, as I was then, you accept many things, you make romantic compromises. In some ways Frances was too finely crafted for me, too delicate. It would have been a very demanding relationship because of the standards she and her family set. I have always been attracted to women, as you well know. Frances was beautiful, she probably still is, she was physically very attractive as I am sure you will remember. And she was quite adventurous. I was afraid of what our intimate contact might produce. Although she encouraged me to touch her in a certain way when we were at Plettenberg Bay, and I did, I felt miserable and guilty about it afterwards. My relationship with Frances would have been a refined and elevated affair. Not because of Frances but because of me. When I first saw Maggie standing behind the counter at Prince Vintcent, when I saw her body, I found her irresistible. It was primordial lust. I know that you speak openly about these matters and I shall be open with you. Maggie's total lack of inhibition, her generous spontaneity gave me something no other woman could ever have given me and our pleasure has become better as the years have gone by. I am comfortable with her. She asks for so little and takes such delight in giving herself to me. I would never have been able to abandon myself as I do with Maggie. With Frances there would always have been a reserve. It would always have remained a relationship of two minds. I know my mother still thinks 'of what might have been'. In the end Frances would have been disappointed in me."

Mrs Jacquard regarded him as he spoke. She did not know how to respond. She would have preferred to remain silent but what he was saying placed such weight on her. She moved about uneasily, knowing that she would have to find something to say. Perhaps he did not want a response. Perhaps she should not disturb the way he felt. He was completely sincere. She smiled wanly at him. "I don't think Frances would ever have been disappointed in you, Douglas."